Flood of Fire

Also by Amitav Ghosh

The Circle of Reason

The Shadow Lines

In an Antique Land

The Calcutta Chromosome

The Glass Palace

The Hungry Tide

Incendiary Circumstances

Sea of Poppies

River of Smoke

Flood of Fire

AMITAV GHOSH

Farrar, Straus and Giroux

NEW YORK

BEDFORD HILLS FREE LIBRARY

Farrar, Straus and Giroux
18 West 18th Street, New York 10011

Copyright © 2015 by Amitav Ghosh
All rights reserved
Printed in the United States of America
Originally published in 2015 by John Murray (Publishers), Great Britain
Published in the United States by Farrar, Straus and Giroux
First American edition, 2015

Maps drawn by Rodney Paull

Library of Congress Cataloging-in-Publication Data
Ghosh, Amitav, 1956–
Flood of fire : a novel / Amitav Ghosh. — First American edition.
    pages ; cm — (Ibis trilogy ; 3)
Previous titles in trilogy: Sea of poppies — River of smoke.
ISBN 978-0-374-17424-8 (hardcover) — ISBN 978-1-4299-4428-1 (ebook)
    1. Soldiers—Fiction.   2. Voyages and travels—Fiction.   3. Opium trade—
History—Fiction.   4. India—History—19th century—Fiction.   I. Title.

PR9499.3.G536 F58 2015
823.914—dc23

                                                                2015010118

Farrar, Straus and Giroux books may be purchased for educational, business, or
promotional use. For information on bulk purchases, please contact the Macmillan
Corporate and Premium Sales Department at 1-800-221-7945, extension 5442, or write to
specialmarkets@macmillan.com.

www.fsgbooks.com
www.twitter.com/fsgbooks • www.facebook.com/fsgbooks

1   3   5   7   9   10   8   6   4   2

All characters in this publication are fictitious and any
resemblance to real persons, living or dead,
is purely coincidental.

To Debbie
for our 25th

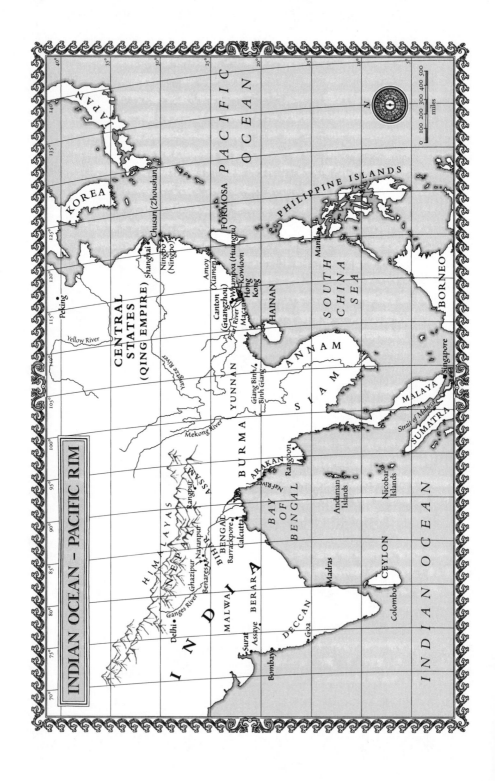

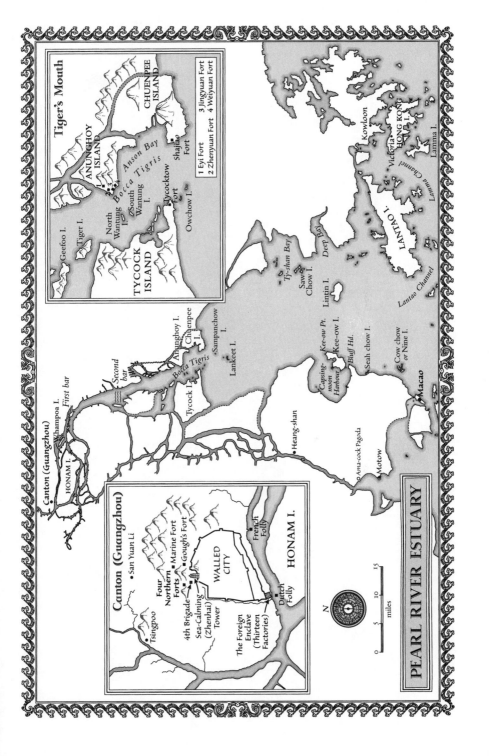

PEARL RIVER ESTUARY

Tiger's Mouth

ANUNGHOY ISLAND
CHUENPEE ISLAND
Anson Bay
Bocca Tigris
South Wantung I.
North Wantung I.
Geefoo I.
Tiger I.
TYCOCK ISLAND
Tycocktow Fort
Owchow I.
Shajiao Fort

1 Eyi Fort
2 Zhenyuan Fort
3 Jingyuan Fort
4 Weiyuan Fort

Canton (Guangzhou)
Whampoa I.
First bar
HONAM I.
Second bar
Anunghoy I.
Chuenpee I.
Bocca Tigris
Tycock I.
Sampanchow I.
Lankeet I.
Heang-shan
Ty-shan Bay
Saw Chow I.
Lintin I.
Deep Bay
Kowloon
Victoria
HONG KONG I.
Lamma I.
Lantao Channel
LANTAO I.
Lamma Channel
Kee-ow Pt.
Kee-ow I.
Bluff Hd.
Capsing-moon Harbour
Seah chow I.
Cow chow or Nine I.
Macao
Ama-cock Pagoda
Motow

Canton (Guangzhou)

San Yuan Li
Tsingpoo
Four Northern Forts
Marine Fort
Gough's Fort
4th Brigade
Sea-Calming (Zhenhai) Tower
WALLED CITY
French Folly
The Foreign Enclave (Thirteen Factories)
Dutch Folly
HONAM I.

N

0   5   10   15
miles

One

Havildar Kesri Singh was the kind of soldier who liked to take the lead, particularly on days like this one, when his battalion was marching through a territory that had already been subdued and the advance-guard's job was only to fly the paltan's colours and put on their best parade-faces for the benefit of the crowds that had gathered by the roadside.

The villagers who lined the way were simple people and Kesri didn't need to look into their eyes to know that they were staring at him in wide-eyed wonder. East India Company sepoys were an unusual sight in this remote part of Assam: to have a full paltan of the Bengal Native Infantry's 25th Regiment – the famous 'Pacheesi' – marching through the rice-fields was probably as great a tamasha as most of them would witness in a year, or even a decade.

Kesri had only to look ahead to see dozens of people flocking to the roadside: farmers, old women, cowherds, children. They were racing up to watch, as if fearful of missing the show: little did they know that the spectacle would continue for hours yet.

Right behind Kesri's horse, following on foot, was the so-called Russud Guard – the 'foraging party'. Behind them were the camp-followers – inaccurately named, since they actually marched ahead of the troops and far exceeded them in number, there being more than two thousand of them to a mere six hundred sepoys. Their caravan was like a moving city, a long train of ox-drawn bylees carrying people of all sorts – pandits and milk-women, shopkeepers and banjara grain-sellers, even a troupe of bazar-girls. Animals too there were aplenty – noisy flocks of sheep, goats and bullocks, and a couple of elephants as well, carrying the officers' baggage and the furniture for their mess, the tables and chairs tied on with their legs in the air, wriggling and shaking like upended beetles. There was even a travelling temple, trundling along atop a cart.

Only after all of this had passed would a rhythmic drumbeat make itself heard and a cloud of dust appear. The ground would reverberate, in time with the beat, as the first rank of sepoys came into view, ten abreast, at the head of a long, winding river of dark topees and flashing bayonets. The sight would send the villagers scurrying for cover; they would watch from the shelter of trees and bushes while the sepoys marched by, piped along by fifers and drummers.

Few were the tamashas that could compare with the spectacle of the Bengal Native Infantry on the march. Every member of the paltan was aware of this – dandia-wallahs, naach-girls, bangy-burdars, syces, mess-consummers, berry-wallahs, bhisties – but none more so than Havildar Kesri Singh, whose face served as the battalion's figurehead when he rode at the head of the column.

It was Kesri's belief that to put on a good show was a part of soldiering and it caused him no shame to admit that it was principally because of his looks that he was so often chosen to lead the march. He could hardly be held to blame if his years of campaigning had earned him a patchwork of scars to improve his appearance – it was not as if he had asked to be grazed by a sword in such a way as to add a pout to his lower lip; nor had he invited the cut that was etched upon the leather-dark skin of his cheek, like a finely drawn tattoo.

But it wasn't as if Kesri's was the most imposing face in the paltan. He could certainly look forbidding enough when he wanted to, with his scimitar-like moustaches and heavy brow, but there were others who far surpassed him in this regard. It was in his manner of wearing the regimental uniform that he yielded to none: the heft of his thighs was such that the black fabric of his trowsers hugged them like a second skin, outlining his musculature; his chest was wide enough that the 'wings' on his shoulders looked like weapons rather than ornaments; and there wasn't a man in the paltan on whom the scarlet coattee, with its bright yellow facings, showed to better advantage. As for the dark topee, tall as a beehive, he was not alone in thinking that it sat better on his head than on any other.

Kesri knew that it was a matter of some resentment among the battalion's other NCOs that he was picked to lead the column more often than any of his fellow sepoy-afsars. But their complaints caused him no undue concern: he was not a man to put much store by the opinions of his peers; they were dull stolid men for the most part, and it seemed only natural to him that they should be jealous of someone such as himself.

There was only one sepoy in the paltan whom Kesri held in high regard and he was Subedar Nirbhay Singh, the highest ranking Indian in the battalion. No matter that a subedar was outranked, on paper, by even the juniormost English subaltern – by virtue of the force of his personality, as well as his family connections, Subedar Nirbhay Singh's hold on the paltan was such that even Major Wilson, the battalion commander, hesitated to cross him.

In the eyes of the men Subedar Nirbhay Singh was not just their seniormost NCO but also their patriarch, for he was a scion of the Rajput family that had formed the paltan's core for three generations. His grandfather was the duffadar who had helped to raise the regiment when it was first formed, sixty years before: he had served as its first subedar and many of his descendants had held the post after him. The present subedar had himself inherited his rank from his older brother, who had retired a couple of years before – Subedar Bhyro Singh.

Theirs was a landowning family from the outskirts of the town of Ghazipur, near Benares. Since most of the battalion's sepoys hailed from the same area and were of the same caste, many were inevitably connected to the subedar's clan – indeed a number of them were the sons of men who had served under his father and grandfather.

Kesri was one of the few members of the paltan who lacked this advantage. The village of his birth, Nayanpur, was on the furthest periphery of the battalion's catchment area and his only connection to the subedar's family was through his youngest sister, Deeti, who was married to a nephew of his. Kesri had been instrumental in arranging this marriage, and the connection had played no small part in his rise to the rank of havildar.

Now, at the age of thirty-five, after nineteen years in the paltan, Kesri had a good ten or fifteen years of active service left and he fully expected to rise soon to the rank of jamadar, with Subedar Nirbhay Singh's support. And after that, he could see no reason why he should not, in time, become the battalion's subedar himself: he did not know of a single sepoy-afsar who was his equal, in intelligence, vigour and breadth of experience. It was only his rightful due.

*

In the course of the last several months Zachary Reid had met with so many reverses that he did not allow himself to believe that his ordeal was almost over until he saw the *Calcutta Gazette*'s report on the inquiry that had cleared his name.

5th June, 1839

. . . and this review of the week's notable events would not be complete without a mention of a recent Judicial Inquiry in which one Mr Zachary Reid, a twenty-one-year-old sailor from Baltimore, Maryland, was acquitted of all wrongdoing in the matter of the untoward incidents on the schooner *Ibis*, in the month of September last year.

Regular readers of the *Calcutta Gazette* need scarcely be reminded that the *Ibis* was bound for Mauritius, with two Convicts and a contingent of Coolies on board, when Disturbances broke out leading to the murder of the chief Sirdar of the immigrants, one Bhyro Singh, a former subedar of the Bengal Native Infantry who had numerous Commendations for bravery to his credit.

Subsequent to the murder, the *Ibis* was hit by a powerful Storm, at the end of which it was found that a gang of five men had also murdered the vessel's first mate, Mr John Crowle, and had thereafter effected an escape in a longboat. The ringleader was the Serang of the crew, a Mug from the Arakan, and his gang included the vessel's two convicts, one of whom was the former Raja of Raskhali, Neel Rattan Halder (the sensation that was caused in the city's Native Quarters last year, by the Raja's trial and conviction on charges of forgery, is no doubt still fresh in the memory of most of Calcutta's European residents).

In the aftermath of the storm the stricken *Ibis* was fortunate to be intercepted by the brigantine *Amboyna* which escorted her to Port Louis without any further loss of life. On the schooner's arrival the guards who had accompanied the Coolies proceeded to lodge a complaint against Mr Reid, accusing him of conspiring in the flight of the five badmashes, one of whom, a coolie from the district of Ghazipore, was the subedar's murderer. These charges being of the utmost gravity, it was decided that the matter would be referred to the authorities in Calcutta, with Mr Reid being sent back to India in Judicial Custody.

Unfortunately for Mr Reid, he has had to endure a wait of several months after reaching Bengal, largely because of the ill-health of the principal witness, Mr Chillingworth, the captain of the *Ibis*. Mr Chillingworth's inability to travel was, we are told, the principal reason for the repeated postponements of the Inquiry . . .

After one of those postponements, Zachary had thought seriously about calling it quits and making a getaway. To leave Calcutta would not have been difficult: he was not under physical confinement and he could easily have found a berth, as a crewman, on one of the ships in the port. Many of these vessels were shorthanded and he knew he would be taken on without too many questions being asked.

But Zachary had signed a bond, pledging to appear before the Committee of Inquiry, and to renege on that promise would have been to incriminate himself. Another, equally weighty consideration, was his hard-won mate's licence, which he had surrendered to the Harbourmaster's office in Calcutta. To abandon the licence would have meant forfeiting all that he had gained since leaving Baltimore, on the *Ibis* – gains that included a rise in rank from ship's carpenter to second mate. And were he indeed to return to

America to obtain new papers, it was perfectly possible that his old records would be dug up which would mean that he might once again have the word 'Black' stamped against his name, thereby forever barring his path to a berth as a ship's officer.

Zachary's was a nature in which ambition and resolve were leavened by a good measure of prudence: instead of recklessly yielding to his impatience, he had carried on as best he could, eking out a living by doing odd jobs in the Kidderpore shipyards; sleeping in a succession of flea-ridden flop-houses while he waited for the Inquiry to begin. A tireless self-improver, he had devoted his spare time to reading books on navigation and seamanship.

The Inquiry into the *Ibis* incident commenced with a well-attended Public Hearing in the Town Hall. Presiding over it was the esteemed jurist, Mr Justice Kendalbushe of the Supreme Court. The first witness to be called was none other than Mr Chillingworth. He provided extensive testimony in Mr Reid's favour, holding him blameless for the troubles of the voyage which he ascribed entirely to the late Mr Crowle, the first mate. This individual, he said, was of a notoriously fractious and unruly disposition and had badly mishandled the vessel's affairs, creating disaffection among the Coolies and the Crew.

Next to appear was Mr Doughty, formerly of the Bengal River Pilots Service. Mr Doughty bore eloquent witness to the sterling qualities of Mr Reid's character, declaring him to be exactly the kind of White youth most urgently needed in the East: honest and hard-working, cheerful in demeanour and modest in spirit.

Kind, crusty old Doughty! Through Zachary's long months of waiting in Calcutta, Mr Doughty was the only person he had been able to count on. Once every week, and sometimes twice, he had accompanied Zachary to the Harbourmaster's office, to make sure that the matter of the Inquiry was not filed away and forgotten.

The Committee was then presented with two affida-
vits, the first of which was from Mr Benjamin
Burnham, the owner of the *Ibis*. Mr Burnham is of
course well known to the readers of the *Gazette* as
one of the foremost merchants of this city and a
passionate advocate of Free Trade.

Before reading out the affidavit, Mr Justice
Kendalbushe observed that Mr Burnham was
currently away in China else he would certainly
have been present at the Inquiry. It appears that he
has been detained by the Crisis that was precipitated
earlier this year by the intemperate actions of the
newly appointed Governor of Canton, Commissioner
Lin. Since the Crisis has yet to be resolved it seems
likely that Mr Burnham will remain a while yet on
the shores of the Celestial Empire so that Captain
Charles Elliot, Her Majesty's Representative and
Plenipotentiary, may avail of his sage counsel.

Mr Burnham's affidavit was found to be an eloquent
attestation to Mr Reid's good character, describing
him as an honest worker, clean and virile in body,
wholesome in appearance and Christian in morals.
After the affidavit had been read out to the Committee
Mr Justice Kendalbushe was heard to remark that Mr
Burnham's testimony must necessarily carry great
weight with the Committee, since he has long been a
leader of the community and a pillar of the Church,
renowned as much for his philanthropy as for his
passionate advocacy of Free Trade. Nor did he neglect
to mention Mr Burnham's wife, Mrs Catherine
Burnham, who is renowned in her own right as one
of this city's leading hostesses as well as a prominent
supporter of a number of Improving Causes.

The second affidavit was from Mr Burnham's
gomusta, Baboo Nob Kissin Pander who was also on
board the *Ibis* at the time of the Incident, in the
capacity of Supercargo. He too is currently in China,
with Mr Burnham.

7

The Baboo's testimony was found to corroborate Mr Chillingworth's account of the Incident in every respect. Its phrasing however was most singular being filled with outlandish expressions of the sort that are so beloved of the Baboos of this city. In one of his flights of fancy Mr Burnham's gomusta proved himself to be a veritable chukker-batty, describing Mr Reid as the 'effulgent emissary' of a Gentoo deity . . .

Zachary remembered how his face had burned as Mr Kendalbushe was reading out that sentence. It was almost as if the ever enigmatic Baboo Nob Kissin were standing there himself, in his saffron robe, clutching his matronly bosom and wagging his enormous head.

In the time that Zachary had known him, the Baboo had undergone a startling change, becoming steadily more womanly, especially in relation to Zachary whom he seemed to regard much as a doting mother might look upon a favourite son. Bewildering though this was to Zachary he had reason to be grateful for it too, for the Baboo, despite his oddities, was a person of many resources and had come to his aid on several occasions.

Such being the testimonials accorded to the young seafarer, the reader may well imagine the eagerness with which Mr Reid's appearance was awaited. And when at last he was summoned to the stand he did not disappoint in any respect: he was found to be more a Grecian than a Gentoo deity, ivory-complexioned and dark-haired, clean-limbed and sturdily built. Subjected to lengthy questioning, he answered steadily and without hesitation, producing a most favourable impression on the Committee.

Many of the questions that were directed at Mr Reid concerned the fate of the five fugitives who had escaped from the *Ibis* on the night of the storm, in one of the vessel's longboats. When asked whether there was any possibility of their having survived, Mr Reid replied that there was not the slightest doubt in his mind that they had all perished. Moreover, he said, he had seen incontestable proof of their demise with his own eyes, in the form of their capsized boat, which was found far out to sea, with its bottom stove in.

These details were fully corroborated by Captain Chillingworth, who similarly affirmed that there was not the remotest possibility of any of the fugitives having survived. These tidings caused a considerable stir in the Native Section of the Hall, where a good number of the late Raja of Raskhali's relatives had foregathered, including his young son . . .

It was at this point in the proceedings that Zachary had understood why the courtroom was so crowded: many friends and relatives of the late Raja had flocked there, hoping, vainly, to hear something that might allow them to nurture the hope that he was still alive. But Zachary had no comfort to offer them: in his mind he was certain that the Raja and the other four fugitives had died during their attempted escape.

When questioned about the murder of Subedar Bhyro Singh Mr Reid confirmed that he had personally witnessed the killing, as had many others. It had occurred in the course of a flogging, when the subedar, on the Captain's orders, was administering sixty lashes to one of the coolies. Being a man of unusual strength the coolie had broken free of his bindings and had strangled the subedar with his own whip. It had happened in an instant, said Mr Reid, before hundreds of eyes; that was why Captain Chillingworth had been obliged to sentence him to death, by hanging. But ere the sentence could be carried out, a tempest had broken upon the *Ibis*.

Mr Reid's testimony on this matter caused another Commotion in the Native Section, for it appears that a good number of the subedar's kinsmen were also in attendance . . .

9

Bhyro Singh's relatives were so loud in their expressions of outrage that everyone, including Zachary, had glanced in their direction. They were about a dozen in number and from the look of them Zachary had guessed that many of them were former sepoys, like those who had travelled on the *Ibis* as the coolies' guards and supervisors.

Zachary had often wondered at the almost fanatical devotion that Bhyro Singh inspired in these men. They would have torn his killer limb from limb that day on the *Ibis*, if they hadn't been held back by the officers. It was clear from their faces now that they were still hungering for revenge.

At the conclusion of the Hearing the Committee retired to an antechamber. After a brief deliberation, Mr Justice Kendalbushe returned to announce that Mr Zachary Reid had been cleared of all wrongdoing. The verdict was greeted with applause by certain sections of the courtroom.

Later, when asked about his plans for the future, Mr Reid was heard to say that he intends soon to depart for the China coast . . .

And that should have been the end of it . . .

But just as he was about to go off to celebrate with Mr Doughty, Zachary was accosted by a clerk of the court who handed him a wad of bills for various expenses: the biggest was for his passage from Mauritius to India. Together the bills amounted to a sum of almost one hundred rupees.

'But I can't pay that!' cried Zachary. 'I don't even have five rupees in my pocket.'

'Well, I am sorry to inform you, sir,' said the clerk, in a tone that was anything but apologetic, 'that your mate's licence will not be restored until the bills are all cleared.'

So what should have been a celebration turned instead into a wake: ale had never tasted as bitter as it did to Zachary that night.

'What'm I going to do, Mr Doughty? Without my licence how am I to earn a hundred rupees? That's almost fifty silver dollars –

it'll take me more than a year to save that much from the jobs I've been doing here in Calcutta.'

Mr Doughty scratched his large, plum-like nose as he thought this over. After several sips of ale, he said: 'Now tell me, Reid – am I right to think that you were trained as a shipwright?'

'Yes, sir. I apprenticed at Gardiner's shipyard, in Baltimore. One of the world's best.'

'D'you think you're still up to snuff with your hammer and saw?'

'I certainly am.'

'Then I may know of some work for you.'

Zachary's ears perked up as Mr Doughty told him about the job: a shipwright was needed to refurbish a houseboat that had been awarded to Mr Burnham during the arbitration of the former Raja of Raskhali's estate. The vessel was now moored near Mr Burnham's Calcutta mansion. Having been long neglected the budgerow had fallen into a state of disrepair and was badly in need of refurbishment.

'Wait,' said Zachary, 'is that the houseboat on which we had dinner with the Raja last year?'

'Exactly,' said Mr Doughty. 'But the vessel's pretty much a dilly-wreck now. It'll take a lot of bunnowing to make her ship-shape again. Mrs Burnham bent my ear about it a couple of days ago. Said she was looking for a mystery.'

'A "mystery"?' said Zachary. 'What the devil do you mean, Mr Doughty?'

Mr Doughty chuckled. 'Still the greenest of griffins, aren't you, Reid? It's about time you learnt a bit of our Indian zubben. "Mystery" is the word we use here for carpenters, craftsmen and such like – men such as yourself. You think you're up for it? The tuncaw will be good of course – should be enough to clear your debts.'

A great wave of relief swept through Zachary. 'Why yes, Mr Doughty! Of course I am up for it: you can count on me!'

Zachary would willingly have started work the next morning, but it turned out that Mrs Burnham was preoccupied with the arrangements for a journey upcountry: her daughter had been advised to leave Calcutta for reasons of health, so she was taking her to a hill-station called Hazaribagh where her parents had an estate. Between this and her many social obligations and improving causes, Mrs Burnham was so busy that it took Mr Doughty several days to get a word in with her. He finally managed to catch up with her at a lecture that she had arranged for a recently arrived English doctor.

'Oh, it was frightful, m'boy,' said Mr Doughty, mopping his brow. 'A satchel-arsed sawbones jawing on and on about some ghastly epidemic. Never heard anything like it: made you want to dismast yourself. But at least I did get to speak to Mrs Burnham – she says she'll see you tomorrow, at her house. You think you can be there, at ten in the morning?'

'Yes of course I can! Thank you, Mr Doughty!'

*

For Shireen Modi, in Bombay, the day started like any other: later, this would seem to her the strangest thing of all – that the news had arrived without presaging or portent. All her life she had placed great store by omens and auguries – to the point where her husband, Bahram, had often scoffed and called her 'superstitious' – but try as she might she could remember no sign that might have been interpreted as a warning of what that morning was to bring.

Later that day Shireen's two daughters, Shernaz and Behroze, were to bring their children over for dinner as they did once every week. These weekly dinners were Shireen's principal diversion when her husband was away in China. Other than that there was little to enliven her days except for an occasional visit to the Fire Temple at the end of the street.

Shireen's apartment was on the top floor of the Mistrie family mansion which was on Apollo Street, one of Bombay's busiest thoroughfares. The house had long been presided over by her father, Seth Rustomjee Mistrie, the eminent shipbuilder. After his death the family firm had been taken over by her brothers, who lived on the floors below, with their wives and children. Shireen was the only daughter of the family to remain in the house after her marriage; her sisters had all moved to their husbands' homes, as was the custom.

The Mistrie mansion was a lively, bustling house with the voices of khidmatgars, bais, khansamas, ayahs and chowkidars ringing through the stairwells all day long. The quietest part of the building was the apartment that Seth Rustomjee had put aside for Shireen at the time of her betrothal to Bahram: he had insisted that the couple take up residence under his own roof after their wedding – Bahram was a penniless youth at the time and had no family connections in Bombay. Ever solicitous of his daughter, the Seth had wanted to make sure that she never suffered a day's discomfort after her marriage – and in this he had certainly succeeded, but at the cost of ensuring also that she and her husband became, in a way, dependants of the Mistrie family.

Bahram had often talked of moving out, but Shireen had always resisted, dreading the thought of managing a house on her own during her husband's long absences in China; and besides, while her parents were still alive, she had never wanted to be anywhere other than the house she had grown up in. It was only when it was too late, after her daughters had married and her parents had died, that she had begun to feel a little like an interloper. It wasn't that anyone was unkind to her; to the contrary they were almost excessively solicitous, as they might be with a guest. But it was clear to everyone – the servants most of all – that she was not a mistress of the Mistrie mansion in the same way that her brothers' wives were; when decisions had to be made about shared spaces, like the gardens or the roof, she was never consulted; her claims on the carriages were accorded a low priority or even overlooked; and when the khidmatgars quarrelled hers always seemed to get the worst of it.

There were times when Shireen felt herself to be drowning in the peculiar kind of loneliness that comes of living in a house where the servants far outnumber their employers. This was not the least of the reasons why she looked forward so eagerly to her weekly dinners with her daughters and grandchildren: she would spend days fussing over the food, going to great lengths to dig out old recipes, and making sure that the khansama tried them out in advance.

Today after several visits to the kitchen Shireen decided to add an extra item to the menu: *dar ni pori* – lentils, almonds and pistachios baked in pastry. Around mid-morning she dispatched a khidmatgar to the market to do some additional shopping. He was gone a long time and when he returned there was an odd look on his face. What's the matter? she asked and he responded evasively,

13

mumbling something about having seen her husband's purser, Vico, talking to her brothers, downstairs.

Shireen was taken aback. Vico was indispensable to Bahram: he had travelled to China with him, the year before, and had been with him ever since. If Vico was in Bombay then where was her husband? And why would Vico stop to talk to her brothers before coming to see her? Even if Vico had been sent ahead to Bombay on urgent business, Bahram would certainly have given him letters and presents to bring to her.

She frowned at the khidmatgar in puzzlement: he had been in her service for many years and knew Vico well. He wasn't likely to misrecognize him, she knew, but still, just to be sure she said: You are certain it was Vico? The man nodded, in a way that sent a tremor of apprehension through her. Brusquely she told him to go back downstairs.

Tell Vico to come up at once. I want to see him right now.

Glancing at her clothes she realized that she wasn't ready to receive visitors yet: she called for a maid and went quickly to her bedroom. On opening her almirah her eyes went directly to the sari she had worn on the day of Bahram's departure for China. With trembling hands she took it off the shelf and held it against her thin, angular frame. The sheen of the rich *gara* silk filled the room with a green glow, lighting up her long, pointed face, her large eyes and her greying temples.

She seated herself on the bed and recalled the day in September, the year before, when Bahram had left for Canton. She had been much troubled that morning by inauspicious signs – she had broken her red marriage bangle as she was dressing and Bahram's turban was found to have fallen to the floor during the night. These portents had worried her so much that she had begged him not to leave that day. But he had said that it was imperative for him to go – why exactly she could not recall.

Then the maid broke in – Bibiji? – and she recollected why she had come to the bedroom. She took out a sari and was draping it around herself when she caught the sound of raised voices in the courtyard below: there was nothing unusual in this but for some reason it worried her and she told the maid to go and see what was happening. After a few minutes the woman came back to report that she had seen a number of peons and runners leaving the house, with chitties in their hands.

Chitties? For whom? Why?

The maid didn't know of course, so Shireen asked if Vico had come upstairs yet.

No, Bibiji, said the maid. He is still downstairs, talking to your brothers. They are in one of the daftars. The door is locked.

Oh?

Somehow Shireen forced herself to sit still while the maid combed and tied her lustrous, waist-length hair. No sooner had she finished than voices made themselves heard at the front door. Shireen went hurrying out of the bedroom, expecting to see Vico, but when she stepped into the living room she was amazed to find instead her two sons-in-law. They looked breathless and confused: she could tell that they had come hurrying over from their daftars.

Seized by misgiving, she forgot all the usual niceties: What are you two doing here in the middle of the morning?

For once they did not stand on ceremony: taking hold of her hands they led her to a divan.

What is the matter? she protested. What are you doing?

Sasu-mai, they said, you must be strong. There is something we must tell you.

Already then she knew, in her heart. But she said nothing, giving herself a minute or two to savour a few last moments of doubt. Then she took a deep breath. Tell me, she said. I want to know. Is it about your father-in-law?

They looked away, which was all the confirmation she needed. Her mind went blank, and then, remembering what widows had to do, she struck her wrists together, almost mechanically, breaking her glass bangles. They fell away, leaving tiny pinpricks of blood on her skin; absently she remembered that it was Bahram who had purchased these bangles for her, in Canton, many years ago. But the memory brought no tears to her eyes; for the moment her mind was empty of emotion. She looked up and saw that Vico was now hovering at the door. Suddenly she desperately wanted to be rid of her sons-in-law.

Have you told Behroze and Shernaz? she asked them.

They shook their heads: We came straight here, Sasu-mai. We

didn't know what had happened – the chits from your brothers said only to come right away. After we came they said it would be best if we broke the news to you, so we came straight up here.

Shireen nodded: You've done what was needed. Vico will tell me the rest. As for you, it's better that you go home to your wives. It'll be even harder for them than it is for me. You'll have to be strong for them.

Ha-ji, Sasu-mai.

They left and Vico stepped in. A big-bellied man with protuberant eyes, he was dressed, as always, in European clothes – pale duck trowsers and jacket, a high-collared shirt and cravat. His hat was in his hands and he began to mumble something but Shireen stopped him. Raising a hand, she waved her maids away: Leave us, she said, I want to talk to him alone.

Alone, Bibiji?

Yes, what did I say? Alone.

They withdrew and she gestured to Vico to sit but he shook his head.

How did it happen, Vico? she said. Tell me everything.

It was an accident, Bibiji, said Vico. Sadly, it happened on the Seth's ship, which he loved so much. The *Anahita* was anchored near an island called Hong Kong, not far from Macau. We had just boarded that day, having come down from Canton. The rest of us went to bed early but Sethji stayed up. He must have been walking on the deck. It was dark and he probably tripped and fell overboard.

She was listening carefully, watching him as he spoke. She knew, from previous bereavements, that she was presently in the grip of a kind of detachment that would not last long: soon she would be overwhelmed by emotion and her mind would be clouded for days. Now, while she was still able to think clearly, she wanted to understand exactly what had happened.

He was walking on the *Anahita*?

Yes, Bibiji.

Shireen frowned; she had known the *Anahita* intimately since the day the vessel's keel was laid, in her father's shipyard: it was she who had named her, after the Zoroastrian angel of the waters, and it was she too who had overseen the craftsmen who had sculpted the figurehead and decorated the interior. If Sethji was walking, he must have been up on the quarter-deck, no?

Vico nodded. Yes, Bibiji. It must have been the quarter-deck. That's where he usually walked.

But if he fell from the quarter-deck, said Shireen, surely someone would have heard him? Wasn't there a lascar on watch? Were there no other ships nearby?

Yes, Bibiji, there were many ships nearby. But no one heard anything.

So where was he found?

On Hong Kong island, Bibiji. His body washed up on the beach.

Was there a ceremony? A funeral? What did you do?

Toying with his hat, Vico said: We held a funeral, Bibiji. Many other Parsis were in the area; one of them was a dastoor and he performed the last rites. Sethji's friend Mr Zadig Karabedian also happened to be around. He delivered the eulogy. We buried him in Hong Kong.

Why Hong Kong? said Shireen sharply. Isn't there a Parsi cemetery in Macau? Why didn't you bury him there?

Macau was impossible, Bibiji, said Vico. There was trouble on the mainland at the time. The British representative, Captain Elliot, had issued an order asking all British subjects to stay away from Macau. That was why the *Anahita* was anchored at Hong Kong Bay. When Seth Bahram died, we had no choice but to bury him in Hong Kong. You can ask Mr Karabedian – he is coming to Bombay soon and will come to see you.

Shireen could feel the grief beginning to well up inside her now. She sat down.

Where did you place the grave? she asked. Is it properly marked?

Yes, Bibiji. There aren't many people on Hong Kong island and the interior is very pretty. The grave is in a beautiful valley. The spot was found by Seth Bahram's new munshi.

Absently Shireen said: I didn't know my husband had hired a new munshi.

Yes, Bibiji. The old munshi died last year when we were on our way to Canton, so Seth Bahram hired a new secretary – a well-educated Bengali.

Did he come back to Bombay with you? said Shireen. Can you bring him to see me?

No, Bibiji; he didn't come back with us. He wanted to stay on in China and was offered a job in Canton, by an American merchant. So far as I know he's now living in Canton's foreign enclave.

*

June 10, 1839
Foreign enclave
Canton

My one regret in starting this journal is that I did not think of it earlier. If only I had embarked on it last year, when I first came to Canton with Seth Bahram! To have some notes to consult would have been helpful when I was trying to write about the events that led to the opium crisis in March this year.

Anyway, I have learnt my lesson and won't make that mistake again. Indeed so eager was I to start my journal-keeping that I pulled out my notebook as soon as I stepped on the junk that brought me from Macau to Canton. But it was a mistake: many people crowded around to see what I was doing, so I thought the better of it. I realized also that it would not be wise to write in English, as I had intended – better to do it in Bangla; it is less likely to be deciphered if the journal should fall into the wrong hands.

I am writing now in my new lodgings, in Canton's American Hong, which is where Mr Coolidge, my new employer, has taken an apartment. He does not live in the lavish style of Seth Bahram; his staff have been relegated to a servants' dormitory at the back of the Hong. But we manage well enough and even though the accommodation is rudimentary I must confess that I am overjoyed to be back in Canton's foreign enclave – that unique little outpost that we used to call Fanqui-town!

It is strange perhaps, to say this about a place where cries of *'Gwailo!'*, *'Haak-gwai!'* and *'Achha!'* are a constant reminder of one's alienness – but nonetheless, it is true that stepping ashore at Canton was like a homecoming

18

for me. Maybe it was only because I was so relieved to be gone from Hong Kong Bay, with its fleet of English merchant ships. Of late a forest of Union Jacks has sprouted there – and I must admit that a weight lifted from my shoulders when they disappeared from view: I can never be comfortable around the British flag. My breath seemed to flow more freely as the boat carried me deeper into China. Only when I stepped off the ferry, at the foreign enclave, did I feel that I was at last safe from Britannia's all-seeing eye and all-grasping hand.

Yesterday afternoon, I went to visit my old haunts in Fanqui-town. It was startling to see how much the atmosphere here has changed in the short time that I've been away. Of the foreigners, only the Americans remain, and the shuttered windows of the empty factories are a constant reminder that things are not as they were before the opium crisis.

The British Factory is particularly striking in its desolation. It is strange indeed to see this building, once the busiest and grandest establishment in Fanqui-town, all locked and shuttered, its verandas empty. Even the hands of the clock on the chapel tower have ceased to move. They are joined together at the twelve o'clock mark, as if in prayer.

Also empty are the two factories that were occupied by the Parsi seths of Bombay – the Chung-wa and the Fungtai. I lingered awhile near the Fungtai: how could I not, when it is so filled with memories? I had thought that by this time Seth Bahram's house would have been rented out to someone else – but no: the window of his daftar remains shuttered and a doorman stands guard at the Hong's entrance. At the cost of a couple of cash-coins I was allowed to slip in and wander around.

The rooms are much as they were when we left, except that a thin film of dust has collected on the floors and the furniture. It gave me an eerie feeling to hear my footsteps echoing through empty corridors – in my memories that house is always crowded with people, redolent of the smell of masalas, wafting up from the kitchen. Most of all it is filled with the spirit of Seth Bahram – I felt his absence very keenly and could not resist going up to the second floor, to look into the daftar where I had spent so many long hours with him, transcribing letters and taking dictation. Here too things are as they were at the time of our departure: the large rock the Seth had been gifted by his compradore is still in its place, as is his ornately carved desk. Even his armchair has not moved: it remains beside the window, as it was during the Seth's last weeks in Canton. In that darkened, shadow-filled room, it was almost as if he were there himself, half-reclining, smoking opium and staring at the Maidan – as though he were looking for phantoms, as Vico once said.

This thought gave me a strange turn and I went quickly downstairs, back into the sunlight. I thought I'd visit Compton's print-shop, and turned into Old China Street. Once a bustling thoroughfare, this too has a sleepy and forlorn look. It was only when I came to Thirteen Hong Street, where the foreign enclave meets the city, that things looked normal again. Here the crowds were just as thick as ever: torrents of people were pouring through, moving in both directions. In a minute I was swept along to the door of Compton's print-shop.

My knock was answered by Compton himself: he was dressed in a dun-coloured gown and looked just the same – his head topped by a round black cap and his queue clipped to the back of his neck, in a neat bun.

He greeted me in English with a wide smile: 'Ah Neel! How are you?'

I surprised him by responding in Cantonese, greeting him with his Chinese name: *Jou-ʋahn Liang ʋin-ʋaang! Nei hou ma?*

'Hai-aa!' he cried. 'What's this I'm hearing?'

I told him that I'd been making good progress with my Cantonese and begged him not to speak to me in English. He was delighted and swept me into his shop, with loud cries of *Hou leng! Hou leng!*

The print-shop too has changed in these last few months. The shelves, once filled with reams of paper and tubs of ink, are empty; the air, once pungent with the odour of grease and metal, is now scented with incense; the tables, once piled with dirty proofs, are clean.

I looked around in astonishment: *Mat-yeh aa?*

Compton shrugged resignedly and explained that his press has been idle ever since the British were expelled from Canton. There was little work in the city for an English-language printing press: no journals, bulletins or notices.

And anyway, said Compton, I'm busy with some other work now.

What work? I asked, and he explained that he has found employment with his old teacher, Zhong Lou-si, who I had met several times during the opium crisis ('Teacher Chang' was what I used to call him then, knowing no better). Apparently he is now a *mihn-ðaaih* – a 'big-face-man', meaning that he is very important: Commissioner Lin, the Yum-chai, has put him in charge of gathering information about foreigners, their countries, their trading activities &c. &c.

In order to do this Zhong Lou-si has created a bureau of translation, Compton said: he employs many men who are knowledgeable about languages and about places overseas. Compton was one of the first to be hired. His job is mainly to monitor the English journals that are published in this region – the *Canton Press*, the *Chinese Repository*, the *Singapore Journal* and so on. Zhong Lou-si's agents bring copies of these journals to him and he goes through them to look for articles that might be of interest to the Yum-chai or Zhong Lou-si.

The subject that Compton follows most closely is of course the *ðaaih-yin* – 'the big smoke' – and it happened that he was going through an article in the *Chinese Repository*, on opium production in India. It was lucky for him that I came by for he was having trouble making sense of it. Many of the words in the article were unfamiliar to him – 'arkati', 'maund', 'tola', 'seer', 'chittack', 'ryot', 'carcanna' and so on. Compton had not been able to find them in his English dictionary and was at his wit's end. Nor did he know of many of the places that were mentioned in the article – Chhapra, Patna, Ghazipur, Monghyr, Benares and so on. Calcutta was the one place he had heard of – it is known here as Galigada.

I spent a long time explaining everything and he thanked me profusely: *Mh-goi-saai, mh-goi-saai!* I told him that I was delighted to help; that it was but a small return for the many kindnesses that he and his family have shown me and for the long hours that I spent in his print-shop earlier in the year. It was wonderful to be back there again – Compton is perhaps the only person of my acquaintance who is as besotted with words as I am.

*

Before the start of the march, Kesri had been told that it would take the advance guard about five hours to get to the next camp-site. A scouting party had been sent ahead to choose a site on the shores of the Brahmaputra River. Kesri knew that by the time he arrived the camp's lines would already have been laid out, with sections demarcated for the officers' enclave, the sepoy lines, the latrines and the camp-bazar, for the followers.

Sure enough, around mid-morning, after five hours on the road, Kesri's horse began to flare its nostrils, as if at the scent of water. Then the road topped a ridge and the Brahmaputra appeared ahead, at the bottom of a gentle slope: it was so broad that its far bank was barely visible, a faint smudge of green. On the near shore, the water was fringed by a pale brown shelf of sand: it was there that the campsite's flags and markers had been planted.

A border of sand ran beside the river as far as the eye could see. Looking into the distance now, Kesri spotted a rapidly lengthening cloud of dust approaching the campsite from the other direction. At its head was a small troop of horsemen – their pennants showed them to be daak-sowars, or dispatch riders.

A long time had passed since the battalion's previous delivery of letters; almost a year had passed since Kesri had last heard from his family. He had been awaiting the daak more eagerly than most and was glad to think that he would be the first to get to it.

But it was not to be: within minutes of spotting the battalion's colours, one of the dispatch riders broke away to head directly towards the column. As the only mounted man in the advance guard, it was Kesri's job to intercept the sowar. He handed his pennant to the man behind him and cantered ahead.

Seeing Kesri approach, the rider slowed his mount and removed the scarf from his face. Kesri saw now that he was an acquaintance, a risaldar attached to campaign headquarters. He wasted no time in getting to the matter that was uppermost in his mind.

Is there any mail for the paltan?

Yes, we've brought three bags of daak; they'll be waiting for you at the campsite.

The risaldar swung a dispatch bag off his shoulder and handed it to Kesri.

But this is urgent – it has to get to your com'dant-sahib at once.

Kesri nodded and turned his horse around.

Major Wilson, the battalion commander, usually rode halfway down the column, with the other English officers. This meant that he was probably a good mile or two to the rear, if not more – for it often happened that towards the end of a day's march the officers took a break to do some riding or hunting; sometimes they just sat chatting in the shade of a tree, while their servants brewed tea and coffee. That way they could be sure that their tents would be ready for them when they rode into camp.

To find the officers would take a while, Kesri knew, for he would have to run the gauntlet of the entire caravan of camp-followers, riding against the flow. And no sooner had he turned his horse around than he ran into a platoon of scythe-bearing ghaskatas – to them would fall the task of providing fodder for the hundreds of animals that marched with the column. Behind them came those who would prepare the campsite: tent-pitching khalasis, flag-bearing thudni-wallahs, coolies with cooking kits, dandia-porters with poles slung over their shoulders; and of course, cleaners and sweepers, mehturs and bangy-burdars. Next was the battalion's laundry contingent, a large group of dhobis and dhobins, with a string of donkeys, laden with bundles of washing.

After leaving the dhobis behind Kesri slowed his pace a little as he drew abreast of the ox-carts that belonged to the bazar-girls. He had long been intimate with their matron, Gulabi, and he knew that she would be upset if he rode past without stopping for a word. But before he could rein in his horse a claw-like hand fastened on his boot.

Kesri! *Sunn!*

It was Pagla-baba, the paltan's mascot and mendicant: like others of his ilk, he had an uncanny knack for guessing what was on people's minds.

Ka bhaiyil? What is it, Pagla-baba?

Hamaar baat sun; listen to my words, Kesri – I predict that you will receive news of your relatives today.

Bhagwaan banwale rahas! cried Kesri gratefully. God bless you! Pagla-baba's prediction whetted Kesri's eagerness to be back at the camp and he forgot about Gulabi. Spurring his horse ahead, he trotted past the part of the caravan that was reserved for the camp-following gentry – the Brahmin pundits, the munshi, the bazar-chaudhuri with his account books, the Kayasth dubash, who interpreted for the officers, and the baniya-modi, who was the paltan's banker and money-monger, responsible for advancing loans to the sepoys and for arranging remittances to their families. These men were travelling in the same cart, chewing paan as they went.

It was the munshi who was in charge of letters: to him fell the task of distributing daak to the sepoys. As he was passing the cart, Kesri paused to tell the munshi that a delivery of post had arrived and he had reason to believe that he might at last have received a letter from his family.

Keep the chithi ready for me, munshiji, said Kesri. I'll meet you at the camp as soon as I can.

The throng on the road had thinned a little now and Kesri was able to canter past the bylees that were carrying the paltan's heavy weaponry – dismantled howitzers, mortars, field-pieces – and its squad of artillerymen, a detachment of golondauzes and gun-lascars. Next came the jail-party, with its contingent of captured Burmese soldiers, and then the mess-train, with its cartloads of supplies for the officers' kitchen – crates of tinned and bottled food, barrels of beer, demijohns of wine and hogsheads of whisky. This was closely followed by the hospital establishment, with its long line of canvas-covered hackeries, carrying the sick and wounded.

After leaving these behind, Kesri ran straight into swarming herds of livestock – goats, sheep and bullocks for the officers' table. The bheri-wallahs who tended the animals tried to clear a path for him, but with little success. Rather than sit idly in the saddle, waiting for the herds to pass, Kesri swerved off the path and rode into a stretch of overgrown wasteland.

This was fortunate for he soon spotted the battalion's dozen or so English officers: they had broken away from the column and were riding towards the sandy ridge that separated the river from the road.

They too saw him coming and reined in their horses. One of them, the battalion's adjutant, Captain Neville Mee, rode towards Kesri while the others waited in the shade of a tree.

'Is that a dispatch bag, havildar?'

'Yes, Mee-sah'b.'

'You can hand it to me, havildar. Thank you.'

Taking possession of the dispatch bag, the adjutant said: 'You'd better wait here, havildar – you may be needed again.'

Kesri watched from a distance as Captain Mee trotted off to deliver the bag to the commandant. Major Wilson opened it, took out some papers and then slapped Captain Mee on the back, as if to congratulate him. Within minutes the officers were all pumping the captain's hand, crying out: 'You're a lucky dog, Mee . . .'

The sight piqued Kesri's curiosity: had Captain Mee received a promotion perhaps? He had certainly waited for one long enough – almost ten years had passed since the last.

It so happened that Mr Mee was Kesri's own 'butcha' – his child – at least in the sense in which the word was used in the Bengal Native Infantry, which was to say that Kesri had been Mr Mee's first orderly when he joined the battalion as an eighteen-year-old ensign, fresh from the Company's military academy at Addiscombe, in England. Kesri was not much older than him but he had been recruited three years earlier and had seen enough combat to consider himself a veteran. From that time on Kesri had 'raised' Mr Mee, instructing him in the ways of the battalion, teaching him the tricks of Indian-style *kushti* wrestling, nursing him when he was ill, and cleaning him up after riotous nights of gambling and drinking at the officers' club.

Many sepoys did as much and more for their butchas yet their services were often forgotten when those officers rose in the ranks. But that was not the case with Kesri and Mr Mee: over the years their bond had grown closer and stronger.

Mr Mee was a tall, broad-shouldered man with a square-jawed, swarthy face and a receding hairline: his hearty manner belied an unusually sharp tongue and a quick temper. As a young officer his pugnacity had often got him into trouble, earning him a reputation as a regular 'Kaptán Marpeet' – 'Captain Brawler'. Nor had the passage of time smoothed his rough edges; from year to year his prickliness seemed only to grow more pronounced, his manner more abrasive.

Yet Captain Mee was in his way an excellent officer, fearless in battle and scrupulously fair in his dealings with the sepoys. Kesri in particular had good reason to be grateful to him: early in their association Captain Mee had discovered that Kesri secretly harboured the ambition of learning English and had encouraged and tutored him until Kesri surpassed every other member of the paltan in fluency, even the dubash. As a result Kesri and the captain had come to understand each other uncommonly well, developing a rapport that extended far beyond the battalion's business. When Mr Mee needed a girl for the night, he depended on Kesri to tell him which members of Gulabi's troupe were poxy and which were worth their daam; when he was short of money – which was often, because he was, by his own confession, always all aground, ever in need of the ready – it was Kesri he looked to for a loan, not the bankers of Palmer & Co. nor the baniya-modi.

It was not uncommon for officers to be in debt for many of them liked to gamble and drink. But Captain Mee's debts were larger than most: to Kesri alone he owed a hundred and fifty sicca rupees. In his place many other officers would have paid off their debts by dipping their hands into the regimental till, or by seeking a post in which there was money to be made – but Mr Mee was not that kind of man. Wild and intemperate though he might be, he was a man of unimpeachable integrity.

Even though Kesri and Captain Mee knew each other very well, they both understood that their relationship was undergirded by a scaffolding of lines that could not be crossed. Kesri would never of his own accord have ventured to ask the adjutant why his fellow officers had congratulated him. But as it happened, Captain Mee broached the subject himself as he rode up to dismiss Kesri.

'A word with you, havildar? It's something rather chup-chup, so you'll stow your clapper about it, won't you?'

'Yes, sir.'

'That dispatch you just brought? It was for me. I've been ordered to report to Fort William, in Calcutta. The high command's putting together an expeditionary force, for an overseas mission – I'd got wind of it and sent in my name. I'll be commanding a company of sepoy volunteers. They've asked me to bring an NCO of my choice which is why I'm telling you all this. The only man I can think of is you, havildar. What do you say? Do you think you might want to come along?'

Nothing could have been further from Kesri's mind that day than to volunteer for an overseas expedition: after eight months of garrison duty in a remote outpost on the border between Assam and Burma he was exhausted and looking forward to some rest. But out of curiosity he asked: 'To where will the force be going, sir?'

'Don't know yet,' said the adjutant. 'It's still in the planning stages, but I hear the prize money will be good.'

For a moment Kesri was tempted to sign on as a *balamteer*: 'Really, sir?'

'Ekdum!' said Mr Mee with a smile. 'I've outrun the constable long enough: this may be my last chance to pay off my debts. With battas and tentage I'll be earning four hundred and fifteen rupees! Between that and the prize money I should be able to square things with everyone, including you. So what do you say, havildar? You think you might want to cut a caper abroad?'

Suddenly Kesri came to a decision. 'No, sir, too tired now. Sorry.'

The captain pursed his lips in disappointment. 'That's too bad, havildar – I was counting on you. But think about it; there's time yet.'

*

Zachary was careful to make an early start for his appointment with Mrs Burnham.

Bethel, the Burnham residence, was in Garden Reach, a distant suburb of Calcutta where many of the city's wealthiest British merchants had built palatial homes. The area lay to the south of the dockyards of Kidderpore, on a stretch of shore that overlooked the Hooghly River.

The Burnham estate was one of the grandest in Garden Reach: the house was vast, surrounded by a compound that sprawled over two acres of riverfront. Zachary had been inside the mansion twice before, as a dinner guest. On both occasions, he had been ushered in through the front doorway, by a magnificently uniformed chobdar, and his name had been announced in ringing tones as he stepped into the Burnhams' glittering sheesh-mull.

But his fortunes had been on the rise at that time: he had just been appointed second mate of the *Ibis* and he had also been in possession of a trunkful of finery. Since then he had come a long way down in the world, and the change in his circumstances was made amply clear to him from the moment he presented himself at the estate's gate. He was taken around to a servants' entrance, where he was handed over to a couple of veiled maids who led him through a series of narrow corridors and staircases to Mrs Burnham's sewing room – a small sunlit parlour, with sewing boxes stacked on the tables and embroidery hanging on the walls.

Mrs Burnham was seated at one of the tables, dressed austerely in white calico, with a lace cap on her head. She had an embroidery frame in her hand, and did not look up from it when Zachary was shown to the door.

'Oh, is it the mystery? Send him in.'

Mrs Burnham was a tall, Junoesque woman, with reddish-brown hair and an air of placid indifference. At their previous meetings she had addressed hardly a word to Zachary which was just as well perhaps, for he had been so thoroughly cowed by her distant, languid manner that he might have found himself at a loss for an answer.

Now, without stirring from her seat or glancing at him, she said: 'Good morning, Mr . . . ?'

'Reid, ma'am. Good morning.'

Zachary took a step towards her, with his hand half-extended, but only to beat a hasty retreat when she failed to look up from her embroidery. He understood now why Mrs Burnham had elected to receive him in her sewing room rather than in one of the many reception rooms on the ground floor: she wanted to impress on him that his position in the house was that of a servant, not a guest, and that he was expected to behave accordingly.

'Mr Reid, I gather you are a trained mystery?'

'Yes, ma'am. I apprenticed at Gardiner's shipyard in Baltimore.'

Mrs Burnham's eye did not waver from her embroidery. 'Mr Doughty has no doubt explained the job to you. Do you feel that you will be able to refurbish the budgerow to our satisfaction?'

'Yes, ma'am. I'll certainly do my best.'

She raised her eyes now, and looked him over with a frown. 'You appear rather young to be an experienced mystery, Mr Reid. But Mr Doughty speaks highly of you and I am inclined to trust his word. He has also told me about your financial difficulties; he has led me to believe that you are deserving of our charity.'

'Mr Doughty is very kind, ma'am.'

Mrs Burnham carried on as if he had not spoken: 'My husband and I have always endeavoured to be sympathetic to the poor whites of this country. There are sadly too many such in India – they venture out from the Occident in the hope of making their fortunes but only to end up in difficulties. Mr Burnham feels that it is incumbent upon us to do what we can to prevent these unfortunate creatures from becoming a blight on the prestige of the ruling race. We have always made an effort to be generous to those who need it – I am inclined therefore to offer you the job.'

'Thank you, ma'am,' said Zachary. 'You will not regret it.'

Her frown deepened, as if to indicate that his thanks were premature.

'And may I ask, Mr Reid,' she said, 'where you intend to reside if I hire you for this job?'

This took Zachary by surprise and he began to stutter. 'Why, ma'am . . . I've been renting a room in Kidderpore—'

'I'm sorry,' she said sharply, cutting him off. 'That will not do. Those Kidderpore boarding houses are known to be dens of disease, iniquity and vice. I cannot allow it, in all conscience. Besides, the budgerow needs to be guarded at night and I have no chowkidar to spare.'

It occurred to Zachary now that she was hinting that he should live on the budgerow. He could hardly believe his luck: to be given a chance to escape the flea-bitten flop-houses he had been living in was as much as he could have hoped for.

'I'd be glad to move into the budgerow, ma'am,' he said, trying not to sound too eager. 'If you have no objection, that is.'

Now at last, she put her embroidery aside but only to subject him to a scrutiny that made his forehead pucker with perspiration.

'It must be clearly understood, Mr Reid,' she said, her voice growing sharper, 'that this is a reputable house where certain standards are upheld. While living on this estate you will be expected to comport yourself with the utmost propriety at all times. On no account will you be permitted any visitors, male or female. Is that understood?'

'Yes, ma'am. Clearly understood.'

Her frown deepened. 'This month I shall be away for a while,' she said, 'because I must take my daughter to my parents' country estate, at Hazaribagh. I trust there will be no laxity in my absence?'

'No, ma'am.'

'If there is, you may be sure that I shall learn of it. I know that you have been at sea and I confess that this is a cause of considerable concern to me. I am sure you are aware of the deplorable reputation that sailors have earned in the eyes of respectable people.'

'Yes, ma'am.'

'You should be warned, Mr Reid, that you shall be under observation at all times. Although the budgerow is moored at a good distance from this house, you should not imagine that the distance is enough to conceal unseemliness of any kind.'

'Yes, ma'am.'

Now falling silent, she transfixed him with a glare that was as sharp as the needle in her hand: it seemed to go right through his clothes and into his skin. 'Very well then,' she said, as he stood squirming in his shoes. 'Please start at your earliest convenience.'

*

Kesri's hopes of receiving a letter from home were so much buoyed by Pagla-baba's prediction that he spurred his horse into a full gallop as he rode to the camp.

He was only a few minutes away when he spotted his servant, Dhiru, running towards him.

Havildarji! Subedar Nirbhay Singh has asked you to go to his tent. At once.

Reining in his horse Kesri said: What does the subedar want? Do you know?

He's received a letter from his village, said Dhiru. I think it is bad news, havildarji. You'd better hurry.

Kesri gave him a nod and again nudged his horse into a gallop.

By the time Kesri entered the camp dozens of men were filing towards the subedar's tent. Most of them were close relatives of the subedar's, and Kesri could tell from their demeanour that there had been some kind of bereavement in the family. He was mildly flattered to be included in this gathering.

Dismounting near the tent, Kesri found himself face to face with the paltan's munshi.

What's happened, munshiji? What's going on?

Haven't you heard? said the munshi. The subedar's had very bad news from home. His brother, Bhyro Singhji, is dead.

Kesri started in shock: Bhyro Singh had always seemed to be destined to outlive his contemporaries.

Bhyro Singhji mar goel? He's dead? But how?

He was killed at sea, many months ago. He had taken a job on a ship, escorting girmitiya migrants. He was on his way to Mauritius when it happened. And there's some other news too – that's why the subedar has sent for you. You'd better go.

Kesri put a hand on the munshi's shoulder: Yes, munshiji, but first tell me – did a letter come for me in the daak?

The munshi shook his head: No, forgive me, havildarji, there was nothing for you.

Kesri bit his lip in disappointment. Are you sure? Nothing?

Nothing. You'd better go to the subedar now.

Kesri stepped into the tent to find the subedar seated on a mat: he was an imposing-looking man, with a broad, heavy face and a luxuriant, greying moustache.

Subedar-sah'b, said Kesri, you sent for me?

The subedar looked up at him with reddened eyes. Yes, havildar; there is bad news.

I heard about Bhyro Singhji, your brother. It is very sad—

The subedar cut him short. Yes but that's not all. The letter I

31

received had some other bad news too, concerning my nephew Hukam Singh, who is married to your sister.

Wohke kuchh bhael ba? Has something happened to him?

Hukam Singh mar goel. He too is dead.

This stunned Kesri. Dead? But how? What happened?

There is no explanation in the letter, said the subedar. But some relatives of mine are coming to Assam to meet me. They should reach our base at Rangpur soon – they will tell us everything. But what about you? Has your family sent any news of your sister?

No, subedar-sah'b. Nothing. I was hoping to get a letter in this daak, but the munshiji tells me there is nothing for me.

Kesri lowered his face. He could not believe that his family had not written to tell him that his sister Deeti had been widowed. The silence was bewildering: what could it possibly mean?

On the way to his tent Kesri stopped to vent his disappointment on Pagla-baba: Why did you say there was a letter for me? There was nothing – *kuchho nahin!*

Pagla-baba answered with a wide grin: I didn't say you would get a letter, havildarji. All I said was that you'd have news of your relatives. And you did, didn't you?

Two

Sunset was approaching by the time Zachary stepped on the budgerow, with his ditty bag slung over his shoulder. There was mud everywhere and the companion-ways were blocked by piles of dead leaves, fallen branches and discarded rigging. He almost tripped on a belaying pin as he went to hang his ditty bag on a spar; it was rolling about on the planks, mired in grease and dirt.

Less than a year had passed since Zachary had last set eyes on the budgerow but in that short time the condition of the houseboat had deteriorated so much that he was tempted to think that she had gone into mourning for her lost master, as abandoned dogs and horses are said to do: the colours of the hull had been bleached to dull shades of blue and grey and the Raskhali emblem – the stylized head of a tiger – had faded to a barely visible outline. Yet, even in this state of neglect it was evident that the budgerow was a fine, broad-beamed vessel that had been designed to suit the tastes of a wealthy man.

The first quick inspection proved reassuring: Zachary saw that his work would consist mainly of cleaning, retouching, polishing and making a few replacements. The budgerow's hull was fundamentally sound and no structural elements would require rebuilding. Many deck-planks needed to be replaced and the head-works and upper stem would have to be retouched and repointed. The intricately carved stem-cheeks had rotted and would need a thorough re-working. Many of the gammonings had come loose and would have to be overhauled; a few of the hawse-timbers, knightheads and bobstay pieces also required attention. But all in all the situation was not quite as bad as it appeared – with a little luck he'd be able to get the job done in six to eight months. And the best part of it, he reckoned, was that he would be able to manage most of the work on his own.

He decided to start by clearing the decks. Peeling off his shirt, he worked his way down the vessel's starboard side until he reached the door that led to the main reception room. When he turned the knob the door creaked open: the room smelled of damp and mildew; the chandelier was wrapped in a shroud of cobwebs and the furniture was blanketed in layers of dust.

This was where Zachary had first met the former Raja of Raskhali, Neel Rattan Halder. He remembered how surprised he had been to see that the host was quite young – a sickly-looking man with indolent eyes and a lethargic manner. Looking around the mouldy reception room now, Zachary was aware of a twinge of pity: who would have thought that day, when they were all sipping champagne in this room, that the Raja had but a few more weeks of liberty left and would soon end up feeding the sharks?

Stepping out of the reception room, Zachary set to work on the ladder that led to the open deck on top. Clearing the rungs one at a time, he slowly made his way into the fading sunlight and found himself looking at a fine view of the riverfront. The Burnham mansion was a few hundred yards downriver, on the same shore; on the far bank lay the tree-lined perimeter of Calcutta's Botanical Garden.

For Zachary the surroundings were steeped in memory, most of all of Paulette Lambert, the Burnhams' erstwhile ward: the Botanical Garden was where she had grown up and the Burnham mansion was where she had been living when Zachary first met her. Now, glancing at the twilit house, he was reminded of a dinner-party at which he and Paulette had been seated next to each other: he had never imagined then that she would soon run away, to board the *Ibis* in the garb of a coolie-woman; nor had he imagined that she would come into his cabin one night and that he would hold her in his arms. The recollection was vivid enough to send a pang of yearning through his body. Stepping quickly down the companion-ladder, he went back to the lower deck and began to open the doors of the cabins at random.

The last door was reluctant to yield and he had to force it with his shoulder. When it creaked open he found himself in a palatial stateroom, panelled with fine wood and fitted with brass sconces. This room appeared to have been spared the ravages that had consumed the other parts of the boat: the bed was still covered with sheets, curtained by a dusty mosquito net. Parting the netting, he threw himself backwards on the bed: it was so soft that he bounced a little and began to laugh.

The luxury! It was almost unimaginable after all he'd been through. The bed alone was bigger than his cabin on the *Ibis* – the very cabin in which he had held Paulette in his arms and briefly kissed her lips.

Through the last many months, in Mauritius and in Calcutta, Paulette had been Zachary's constant companion: whenever his plight had seemed insupportable he had conjured up her phantom, so that he could quarrel with her. 'You see, Miss Paulette, what you've put me through! Do you ever think about it, Miss Paulette? That I wouldn't be in the chokey now if it weren't for you?'

And then her tall slim frame would take shape in the shadows and she would step out of the corners of whatever hell-hole he happened to be in. Gawky, as always, half-tripping over her feet, she would come to sit beside him, just as she had during their last and fiercest argument on the *Ibis*: when she had pleaded with him not to prevent the escape that was to be attempted that night.

'You asked me to let the five of them get away, Miss Paulette and so I did – and you see where it got me?'

But sometimes the exchange would take a softer turn and the argument would end as it had that night, when he had thrown his arms around her and pressed his lips to hers. At times her presence would become so real, even in the cramped circumstances of a flop-house, that he would have to banish her from his mind for fear that the men around him would begin to snigger, as they always did when a man was heard to be working his pump.

But now, blissfully alone, for the first time in months, lying in this soft, yielding bed, there was no need to hold her off: his body seemed to be waking from a long sleep, tingling with an almost forgotten urgency of desire. A voluptuousness like he had not felt in an age took possession of him – it was all too easy to imagine that it was not his own hand but Paulette's that was snaking into his breeches.

Afterwards, as he was drifting off to sleep he thought, as often before, what a providential thing it was that the Creator, having cursed the race of Man with an unruly and headstrong organ, had also been merciful enough to give him a handy means of taming it.

He slept as soundly as he ever had and on waking in the morning he shared another brief but ecstatic encounter with Paulette before jumping out of bed, wonderfully refreshed. After making himself some tea and porridge he set to work, scouring the foredeck.

The boat had been so long neglected that it was slow going. Around noon a khidmatgar unexpectedly brought him a tray of leftovers from the Burnham bobachee-connuh and he carried it gratefully inside: there was rice, a large bowl of Country Captain, and relishes of all sorts, enough to last him through lunch and supper as well.

He ate his fill, and the drowsiness induced by the rich food prompted him to return to his cabin. It wasn't with any conscious intention of summoning Paulette that he lay down, but when she came to him, of her own accord, he could see no reason to push her away.

But afterwards, catching sight of the gluey stains on the bedsheets he was stricken with guilt. Pulling up his breeches, he went back to the foredeck and resumed scrubbing.

This part of the boat had no covering or shade and he was soon uncomfortably hot. Removing his shoes, socks and shirt made little difference: all his clothing was soon soaked in sweat; his breeches, already sticky, seemed to be plastered to his skin.

The river, muddy though it was, looked very appealing now. He cast an appraising glance at the Burnham mansion, wondering if anyone would see him if he stripped down to his underwear and jumped into the water.

The house was a long way away, with a wide expanse of lawn in between. It was siesta time and there was not a soul to be seen, in the house or on the lawn. He decided that the chance was worth taking: there were thick rushes along the shore – he was sure to be well hidden.

Tearing off his banyan and breeches he swung himself over the vessel's side, dressed in nothing but his knee-length drawers. The water was none too deep and refreshingly brisk: it took only a few minutes to cool off.

He was about to pull himself aboard again when he caught sight of the soiled belaying pin, lying on the budgerow's deck. It occurred to him that this was as good a time as any to give it the polishing it needed: it was within easy reach so he caught hold of it and dropped back into the river. A few steps towards the shore brought him into waist-deep water. He pulled up some rushes and began to scour the pin, his elbow pumping furiously in the water.

The pin was skittle-shaped, of about a handspan's length: the grease and mud had made it slippery, so he had to press it against his belly with one hand, while scrubbing it with the other.

After several minutes of hard rubbing the encrustation of dirt began to come off at last. The pin was almost clean when a child's voice broke in. 'You! You there!'

He was standing with his back to the lawn and was caught unawares. Spinning around, he found himself looking at a little blonde girl, dressed in a white pinafore: he guessed that she was the Burnhams' daughter.

Suddenly he realized that his chest was naked and that she was staring at it. Flushing in embarrassment, he retreated quickly into deeper water, stopping only when his body was submerged up to the neck. Then he turned to face her: 'Hello!'

'Hello.'

She looked at him gravely, cocking her head like a bird: 'You'd better get out of the water,' she said. 'Mama says the river's filthy and only horrid heathens and Gentoos bathe in it.'

'Does she?' he said, in panic. 'But then you mustn't tell her you saw me in the river!'

'Oh, but she knows already. She was watching you with her bring-'em-near, from her bedroom window. I saw her.'

Now another voice came echoing across the lawn: 'Annabel! Annabel! Oh, you badmash larkin, have you no shame?'

Zachary looked up to see the bonneted figure of Mrs Burnham streaming across the lawn in a torrent of lace and fluttering silk.

He retreated again, sinking even deeper into the water, allowing it to cover him almost to the chin.

'Oh Annabel! What a bandar you are running out into the hot sun. We'll be lucky if we're not roasted half to death!'

Mrs Burnham was running so hard that the bonnet had flown off her head: it would have fallen but for the pink ribbon that held it fast to her neck. Her ringlets were flying around her face and there were bright red spots on both her cheeks.

Chastened though he was, it did not escape Zachary that Mrs Burnham's appearance was in no small measure enhanced by her flushed cheeks and dishevelled hair. Nor was the Junoesque appeal of her generous bustline entirely lost on him.

'Oh Annabel!' With her eyes carefully averted from Zachary, Mrs Burnham clapped her bonnet over her daughter's face. 'This badmashee just will not do! Come away, dear. Jaldee!'

Zachary decided now that he had no option but to brazen it out. Adopting as airy a tone as he could muster, he said: 'Hello there, Mrs Burnham – terribly hot, isn't it? Thought I'd cool off with a quick bath.'

An outraged quiver went through Mrs Burnham's body, but she did not turn to look at him. Speaking over her shoulder, through clenched teeth, she said: 'Surely, Mr Reid, there is some provision for bathing inside the budgerow? And if there is not then some must be made – for we certainly cannot have you wallowing in the mud, like a sunstruck buffalo.'

'I'm very sorry, Mrs Burnham; I didn't think—'

She cut him off sharply. 'I must ask you to remember, Mr Reid, that ours is a Christian house and we do expect a certain modesty, in all things . . .'

Words seemed to fail her here, and she quickened her step, steering her daughter in front of her.

Zachary called out after her rapidly retreating back: 'I do apologize for my state of undress, Mrs Burnham. Won't happen again, I promise you.'

He received no answer, for Mrs Burnham and her daughter were already halfway to the house.

*

A fortnight went by without any mention of Bahram's finances. Through that time not a word was said to Shireen about the state of her husband's business affairs at the time of his death.

BEDFORD HILLS FREE LIBRARY

At first Shireen was too distraught to give this any thought. It was only after the initial shock of bereavement had passed that she began to wonder about the silence.

In a family like theirs, where matters of business weighed on every mind, there was something a little unnatural about the studied avoidance of this one topic, especially since it was well known to everyone that Bahram had travelled to China with the avowed intention of taking over the shipping division of Mistrie & Sons, a firm that had been in Shireen's family for generations.

Of Shireen's immediate relatives those who were best placed to be informed about Bahram's business affairs were her two brothers, who had jointly inherited the company upon their father's death, a couple of years before. Shireen could scarcely doubt that they knew something about the state of her husband's finances, yet neither of them showed any signs of broaching the subject, even though they visited her several times each day.

It was certainly no secret to Shireen that her husband and her brothers had been locked in a struggle over the company after her father's untimely death. The tussle was not unexpected: her brothers had never considered Bahram worthy of the Mistrie family and he in turn had heartily reciprocated their ill-will. Ever since the day of Shireen's wedding the tensions between her siblings and her husband had snapped and whirred around her, like ropes around a windlass. But through most of her married life Shireen had been privy only to the familial aspects of the conflict: where matters of business were concerned her father had enforced an uneasy peace. It was only after the patriarch's death that Shireen had herself become the pivot on which the family's tensions turned.

No one knew better than Shireen how betrayed and ill-used her husband had felt when her brothers had tried to pension him off so that they could dispose of the branch of the company that Bahram had himself built up – the hugely profitable shipping and export division. But to be a party to his own dispossession was not in keeping with Bahram's character: he had decided to acquire the export division for himself, and to that end he had invested in a massive consignment of goods for China, in the hope of raising the funds for an outright purchase. Not being a man for half-measures he had decided that his consignment would consist of the largest cargo of opium ever to be shipped from Bombay. To raise the money for it he had tapped every source of capital available to him – business partners, community leaders, relatives – and finding himself still short he had turned finally to Shireen, asking her to pawn her jewellery and mortgage the land she had inherited from her father, in Alibaug and Bandra.

Over the years Shireen had been at odds with Bahram over many things, most of all his apparent unconcern for their lack of a son. She had often pleaded with him to search for a cure, but he had never taken the matter seriously, which had caused her great pain and regret. But when it came to business she knew that his instincts were unerring – he had always proved his doubters wrong. She herself, being of a naturally pessimistic bent, had often been among those who expected his ventures to fail. But they never had – and in time she had grown to accept that in these matters it was best to trust her husband's judgement. So in the end she had yielded to his entreaties and allowed him to dispose of her inheritance as he thought best.

What had happened to that money? Why had nobody mentioned it to her? For a while she clung to the reassuring notion that her family was avoiding the subject because they did not want to raise it in company. It was true certainly that between her daughters, her sisters, her grandchildren and her own sizeable contingent of bais and khidmatgars, there was scarcely a moment when she was alone. Even her nights were not really her own, for there was always someone at hand to make sure that she took a liberal dose of laudanum before going to bed.

Shireen was not ungrateful for her family's support, yet, after a while, it became apparent to her that there was something odd about the nature of their sympathy. Her relatives' concern seemed to be focused entirely on herself – her departed husband seemed hardly to figure in their thoughts. When she made an attempt to reverse this, by announcing that she wanted to hold a lavish 'Farvandin roj' ceremony for Bahram, in the Fire Temple, no one paid her any mind. Instead, without consulting Shireen, the family organized a small service that was attended only by a few close relatives.

When she tried to question her daughters about this they fobbed her off by muttering about the expense. She knew then that something was being concealed from her and that she would have to take matters into her own hands. The next day she sent notes to her brothers asking them to visit her as soon as possible.

Next morning, punctilious as ever, they came up together, dressed for the day, in crisp angarkhas and neatly tied white turbans. After a few conventional words of greeting Shireen said: I'm glad you've come; I've been wanting to ask you about some things.

What things?

About my husband's business dealings. I know he had sunk a lot of money into this last trip to China. I was wondering what became of his investments.

There was a silence and Shireen saw that they were exchanging glances, as if to urge each other to go first. To make it easier for them to speak she broke in: You must tell me; I should know.

They fell on this opening with some relief.

The situation was very unfortunate, they said. Bahram-bhai had made some terrible mistakes; his love of risk had led to calamity; he had taken an enormous gamble and his wager had gone disastrously awry.

Shireen's fingers snaked through the folds of her white sari seeking the comfort of the sacred kasti threads that were girdled around her waist.

What happened? she said. Tell me about it.

After some hesitation they began to speak together: It was not entirely Bahram's fault, they said. He had been caught unawares by recent developments in China. Soon after he reached Canton a new viceroy had been appointed, a mandarin by the name of Commissioner Lin – by all accounts a power-crazed madman. He had detained all the foreign merchants and forced them to surrender the opium they had shipped to China that season. Then he had personally overseen the destruction of their cargoes – goods worth millions of Spanish dollars! Bahram was among the biggest losers; his entire cargo had been seized and destroyed – a consignment that he had bought mostly with borrowed money. As a result his debts to his creditors in Bombay were still unpaid; had he returned he would have had to default and declare bankruptcy – this wasn't surprising perhaps; he had always been a gambler and a speculator, just like his grandfather before him.

41

Shireen listened in a daze, with her hands clasped on her lap. When they had finished, she said: Is there really nothing left? Nothing?

They shook their heads: there was nothing. Bahram had left behind nothing but debts. Such were the circumstances that his flagship, the *Anahita*, had perforce been sold off at Hong Kong, to one Benjamin Burnham, an English businessman, for a price far below the vessel's value. Even the houses Bahram had built for his daughters would need to be sold. Fortunately she, Shireen, was provided for – she still had this apartment, in their family house; at least she would never have to worry about having a roof over her head. And her sons-in-law were both doing well; they had decided to put money into a fund that would provide her with a monthly allowance. She would have to economize of course, but still with a bit of care she would certainly be able to get by.

At this point an odd thing happened. A butterfly flitted through an open window, hovered over their heads for a bit, and then settled briefly on a framed portrait of Bahram. Shireen gasped and pulled off her veil: the portrait was one that Bahram had brought back from Canton many years before. It showed him in a dark blue choga, sitting with his knees slightly apart, his square face, with its neatly trimmed beard, looking startlingly handsome, a smile curling his lips.

Shireen had always believed that even the most trivial occurrences could be freighted with meaning; to her it seemed self-evident that when things happened in conjunction – even small things – the connections were never without significance. Now, even after the butterfly had flown away, she could not wrench her gaze from the portrait. Bahram seemed to be looking directly at her, as though he were trying to tell her something.

Shireen took a deep breath and turned to her brothers: Tell me; is there any chance at all that some part of my husband's investments may be recovered?

They glanced at each other and began to murmur in low, regretful voices, as if to apologize for quashing her hopes.

There was indeed a chance, they said, that some of the money might be recovered. Bahram was not the only foreign merchant to have his goods seized; many others, including several important

British businessmen, had surrendered their cargoes to Commissioner Lin. The authorities in London would not allow these confiscations to pass unchallenged: they were not like Indian rulers, who cared nothing for the interests of businessmen – they understood full well the importance of commerce. It was rumoured that they were already planning to send a military expedition to China, to demand reparations. If there was a war and the Chinese lost, as was likely, there was a good chance that some of Bahram's money would be returned.

But . . .

Yes? said Shireen.

But when the time arrived for the distribution of the recovered funds, there would be no one at hand to represent Bahram. There was sure to be a scramble for the funds and the other merchants would be there in person, present and ready to claim their share.

Shireen's mind cleared as she thought about this. But couldn't we send someone to represent us? she asked. What about Vico?

They shook their heads. Vico had already declined, they said. He was after all only Bahram's purser and had no standing either with the Canton Chamber of Commerce or the British government. The foreign merchants of Canton were a tight little circle, impossible for outsiders to penetrate. Bahram had himself been a member of that group, so they might well be sympathetic to his family's claims if approached by a blood relative – but unfortunately there was no one to play that part for Bahram.

Shireen knew exactly what was being implied – that things would have been different had she and Bahram had a son to represent their interests. She had so long tormented herself with this thought that she had no patience for it now. But what about me? she said, blurting out the first words that came to mind: What if I were to go myself?

They stared at her, aghast. You?

Yes.

You? Go to China? You've never even stepped out on the street by yourself!

Well, why shouldn't I go? Shireen retorted. After all, your wives and daughters go out in public, don't they? Don't you boast to your English friends about how 'advanced' our family is and how we don't keep purdah?

Shireenbai, what are you talking about? It's true that our wives don't keep strict purdah but we have a certain standing in society. We would never allow our sisters and daughters to wander around the world on their own. Just imagine the scandal. What would people say?

Is it scandalous for a widow to want to visit her husband's grave?

At that point, they seemed to decide that she needed to be humoured and their voices softened.

You should talk to your daughters, Shireen. They'll explain the matter to you better than we could.

*

August 11, 1839
Canton

Yesterday I ran into Compton while walking down Thirteen Hong Street. Ah Neel! he cried. Zhong Lou-si wants to see you!

I asked why and Compton explained that Zhong Lou-si had been very impressed by his work on the report on opium production in Bengal. On hearing of my part in it, he'd said that he wanted to *yam-chah* (drink tea) with me.

Of course I could not say no.

We agreed that I would come by Compton's print-shop the next day, at the start of the Hour of the Rabbit (five in the afternoon).

I arrived a few minutes before Zhong Lou-si's sedan chair came to the door. He looked older than I remembered, stooped and frail, with his wispy white beard clinging to his chin like a tuft of cobwebs. But his eyes were undimmed by age and they twinkled brightly at me.

So, Ah Neel! I hear you've been learning to speak Cantonese?

Haih Lou-si!

Zhong Lou-si is not Cantonese himself but he has been in Guangdong so long that he understands the dialect perfectly. He was very patient with my faltering efforts to speak the tongue. I did not acquit myself too badly I think, although I did occasionally have to seek help from Compton, in English.

It turned out that Zhong Lou-si had asked to meet with me for a special reason: he is composing a memorandum about British-ruled India – he used the word *Gangjiao*, which is the commonly used term for the Company's territories – and he wanted to ask me some questions.

Yat-ðihng, yat-ðihng, said I, at which Zhong Lou-si said that rumours had reached Canton that the English were planning to send an armed fleet to China. Did I have any knowledge of this?

I realized that the question was deceptively simple and had probably been phrased to conceal the full extent of the intelligence Zhong Lou-si had received on the subject. I knew that I would have to be careful in choosing my words.

Among foreigners, I said, it had long been rumoured that the British would soon be sending a military expedition to China.

Haih me? Really? Where had I heard this? From whom?

I explained that many men from my province Bengal – (*Ban-gala* is the term used here) – were employed as copyists and 'writers' by British merchants. There were some Bengali copyists even in the staff of Captain Elliot, the British Plenipotentiary, I told him. We often exchanged news amongst us, I said, and it was common knowledge that Elliot had written to the British Governor-General in Calcutta, in April this year, asking for an armed force to be assembled for an expedition to China. I told him that I had overheard Mr Coolidge and his friends talking about this recently, and they appeared to believe that the planning for the expedition had already begun, at British military headquarters in Calcutta. But nothing would be made public until authorization was received from London.

What did it mean, Zhong Lou-si asked, that the planning was being done in *Yinðu* – India. Would the troops be British or Indian?

45

If past experience was a guide, I told him, it was likely that the force would include both English and Indian troops: this was the pattern the British had followed in all their recent overseas wars, in Burma, Java and Malaya.

This did not come as a surprise to Zhong Lou-si. He told me that as long back as the reign of the Jiaqing Emperor, the British had brought shiploads of Indian sepoys – *xubo bing* he called them – to Macau. But Beijing had reacted strongly and the troops hadn't landed. That had happened thirty years ago. Ten years later, in the second year of the present Daoguang Emperor's reign, the British had come back with another contingent of Indian sepoys. This time they had briefly occupied Macau, before being forced to leave.

Then Zhong Lou-si said something that startled me: he said that at the time Chinese officials had concluded that the sepoys were slaves and the British did not trust them to fight; that was why they had left Macau without putting up much resistance.

But sepoys are not slaves! I protested. Like British soldiers, they are paid.

Are they paid the same wage as red-haired English troops?

No, I had to acknowledge. They are paid much less. About half.

Are they treated the same way? Do the Indian and British troops eat together and live together?

No, I said. They live apart and are treated differently.

And do the Indians rise to positions of command? Are there Indian officers?

No, I said. Positions of command are held only by the British.

A silence fell while Zhong Lou-si meditatively sipped his tea. Then he looked up at me and said: So the Indians fight for less pay, knowing that they will never advance to positions of command? Is this right?

None of this could be denied. *Jauh haih lo*, I said: what you are saying is right.

46

But why do they fight then?

I did not know how to answer: how does one explain something that one doesn't understand oneself? Something that no one understands? All I could say was: They fight because it's their job. Because that is how they earn money.

So they are from poor families then?

They are from farming families, I said. They come from certain places in the interior of the country. But they are not poor – many are from families of high rank and many of them own land.

This deepened Zhong Lou-si's puzzlement: Why do they risk their lives then, if not from necessity?

Look, I said, it is hard to explain, but it is because many of them are from clans – I could think of no word for 'caste' – that have always made their living by fighting. They give their loyalty to a leader and they fight for him. At one time their leaders were Indian kings, but some years ago it was the British who became the major power. Since then sepoys have been fighting for them just as they did for rajas and nawabs. For them there is no great difference.

But when they fight for the British, do they always do it sincerely, with their hearts in it?

Again I had to stop to think.

It is a hard question to answer, I said. The sepoys are good soldiers and they have helped the British conquer much of India. But at times they have also rebelled, especially when going abroad. I remember that about fifteen years ago there was a big mutiny, in Barrackpore, when a sepoy battalion was ordered to go to Burma. In general the sepoys from Bengal Presidency do not like to fight abroad. That is why the British often use sepoys from Madras for foreign campaigns.

Zhong Lou-si nodded thoughtfully, stroking his white beard. He thanked me for my help and said he hoped we would meet again soon.

*

Between Kesri and his sister Deeti there was a gap of eight years. Five other children had been born to their parents in between: two had survived and three had died. Yet, even though Kesri and Deeti were the furthest apart in age, they were more like each other than any of their other siblings.

One thing they shared was the colour of their eyes, which was a light shade of grey. For Deeti this had been something of a handicap, for there were many credulous people in their village who believed that light-eyed women were endowed with uncanny powers. The feature did not have the same consequences for Kesri as it did for Deeti – in a boy, light eyes were considered merely unusual, not a disturbing oddity – but it still created a bond between them and Kesri was always quick to jump to Deeti's defence when she was taunted by other children.

Another thing they had in common was that they both grew up believing that kismat was their enemy. For Deeti this was because her astrological chart showed her to have been born under the influence of an unlucky alignment of the heavens. Kesri had a different reason: it was because he happened to be his father's oldest son.

In most families to be the first-born son was considered a blessing – and if Kesri had been a different kind of person he too might have considered himself lucky to belong to a family that followed the custom of keeping the oldest boy at home, to tend the family's fields. But Kesri was not one to be content forever in a village like Nayanpur, always running behind a plough and shouting at the oxen. From his earliest childhood he had loved to listen to the tales of his uncles, his father, his gurujis, his grandfather and all the other men of the village who had gone a-soldiering when they were true *jawans* – fighters in the prime of their youth. He never had any ambition other than to do what they had done: go off to serve as a sepoy in one part or another of Hindustan or the Deccan.

Since theirs was a land-tilling family, all the boys were taught to fight from an early age. The times were such that bands of dacoits and armed men were always on the prowl: even to go out to the fields meant carrying shields and swords as well as ploughs and scythes; how could you farm your land if you could not defend it?

Kesri and his brothers had started to wrestle when they were very young. Not far from their village, there was a famous *akhara* – a gymnasium for the practice of various disciplines, of body and spirit. This one was attached to an ashram run by Naga sadhus, an order of ascetics who wore no clothing other than ash and were known as much for their valour in combat as for their practice of austerities. Distinctions of birth were a matter of indifference to Naga sadhus and it was, in any case, a hallowed tradition of akharas that differences of caste and sect were not recognized within their precincts: everyone who came there bathed, ate and wrestled together no matter what their circumstances in the world beyond.

This aspect of the akhara did not appeal to Kesri's father, who was a great stickler in matters of caste; Kesri on the other hand found it deeply congenial and did not in the least mind having to take a purificatory bath when he came home. He liked the camaraderie of the akhara as much as he enjoyed the physical challenges; being sturdy in build and active by temperament he particularly relished the rigorous regime of exercises. He enjoyed wielding weights like *naals* and *gadas* and unlike the other boys he never looked for excuses to get out of 'ploughing the wrestling ring', an exercise in which one boy sat on a wooden beam while another pulled him around the floor by means of a harness attached to his forehead.

But it was combat itself that Kesri most enjoyed: all his senses grew sharper when his wits and his body were under pressure; he was able to keep a cool head in situations where other boys tended to panic. Left to himself he would have spent most of his time learning manoeuvres like the dhobi's throw and the strangle pin; it irked him sometimes that the sadhus placed as much emphasis on the control of the breath, bowels and bodily emissions as they did on the mechanical skills of wrestling, but he accepted their demands as the necessary price of his training. Every morning he would dutifully study the serpent that crept out of his bottom, and whenever he found it to be dull in colour or less than properly 'coiled and ready to strike' he would report the matter to his trainers and change his diet according to their prescriptions.

With such a will did Kesri apply himself that by the time he was ten he was recognized to be one of the akhara's best wrestlers, by age and size. Soon his regimen of training was expanded to include the use of weapons – mainly the *lath*, a heavy cudgel-like staff, but also the *talwar*, or curved sword. Musketry he was introduced to at home, by his father, who would occasionally instruct all his sons in the handling of his matchlock.

In the use of weaponry, as in the wrestling ring, Kesri proved to be so adept that even before he turned fifteen – the age at which boys began to be recruited as jawans – he was one of the most feared fighters in the village. But in his father's eyes this was just another reason why he needed to remain at home: their land would be safer with him than with any of his brothers.

Kesri's younger brother was called Bhim. He did not lack for brawn, but he was a slow-witted youth, incapable of knowing his own mind. He did his father's bidding without question.

Their father, Ram Singh, had been a soldier himself and was a stubborn and quick-fisted man. To talk back to him was to invite a hiding with a lath. This did not deter Kesri from speaking his mind, and he received many a beating for his defiance. Eventually he came to realize that arguing with his father was a waste of time: Ram Singh was the kind of old soldier who digs in deeper in the face of opposition. Kesri understood that if he was ever to join an army he would have to go against his father and do it on his own. But how? No respectable recruiter would take him without his family's consent – without that they would have no surety for his conduct. Nor, without his family's help, would he be able to afford the equipment that a recruit was expected to bring, far less a horse. As for the other options – joining a band of fighting mendicants, for example, or some kind of gang – even tilling the land seemed preferable to those.

So Kesri had no choice but to hold his tongue when military men stopped by to ask Ram Singh about his boys. He would chew on his gall in silence while his father explained that he'd be glad to talk about the prospects of his second son, Bhim – but where it concerned his oldest boy there was nothing to talk about: his future had already been decided. Kesri would be staying at home to till the land.

To add to Kesri's misery, it was at about this time that offers of marriage began to pour in for the sister who was closest to him in age. It seemed that she too would soon be leaving home. It was as if new horizons of possibility were opening up for everyone but himself.

Since Deeti spent a good deal of time in the fields with Kesri she was the only person in the family who understood his state of mind. The other girls were kept indoors as much as possible, to protect their complexions, but Deeti's chances of a good marriage were slight in any case because of her ill-aligned stars, so it was decided that she needed to know how to work the land. She was no taller than Kesri's knee when he began to teach her how to handle a nukha – the eight-bladed instrument that was used to nick ripe poppy bulbs. They would walk along the rows of denuded flowers, each with a nukha in their hands, scoring the tumescent sacs to bleed them of their sap. When the heady odour of the oozing opium-gum made them drowsy they would sit together in the shade of a tree.

Even though Deeti was much younger than Kesri they were able to talk to each other as to no one else. Deeti's capacities of empathy and understanding were so far in advance of her age that there were times when Kesri would wonder whether she had indeed been gifted with powers beyond the ordinary. Sometimes, when he despaired of leaving Nayanpur, it was she – a tiny putli of a girl – who reassured him. She knew that he brooded about the horizons that were opening up before his brother and sister, and she often said to him: *Wu saare baat na socho.* Don't think of all that. Turn your mind to other things.

But to ignore what was happening was plainly impossible. Their home had never before attracted so many strangers; never had they experienced the excitement of being sought out and courted in this way. Often, at the end of the day's work, when they headed back to their mud-walled home, they would find their father talking to recruiters, in the shade of the mango tree out front; or they would learn that their mother was in the inner courtyard, deep in discussion with marital go-betweens.

Ram Singh was as well-informed about military matters as their mother was about the marriage market. He had spent many years in the army of the kingdom of Berar and was acquainted with a good number of the professional recruiters who roamed the villages of their region looking for promising young men. This stretch of the Gangetic plain had always provided the armies of northern India with the bulk of their soldiery. Since many of these jawans were from families like their own, they had relatives in at least a dozen armies. Ram Singh had tended to these connections carefully and long before anyone came to inquire about his sons, he knew exactly the kind of recruiter he wanted to talk to. He also knew which recruiters he would ignore – and it made no difference whether they were relatives or not.

One of the first recruiters to seek them out was an agent of the Darbhanga Raj, a zamindari with which they had a family connection. Being a relative he was given a polite hearing but no sooner was he gone than his offer was summarily dismissed.

The Darbhanga Raj is just a petty zamindari nowadays, said Ram Singh. It's not like it used to be in my father's time. They are vassals of the white sahibs; to work for them would be even worse than joining the English Company's army.

This was a matter on which Ram Singh had strong opinions. Their district had been seized by the East India Company a long time ago, but in the beginning the annexation had made little difference and things had gone on much as usual. But with the passage of time the Company had begun to interfere in matters that previous rulers had never meddled with – like crops and harvests for example. In recent years the Company's opium factory in Ghazipur had started to send out hundreds of agents – arkatis and sadar mattus – to press loans on farmers, so that they would plant poppies in the autumn. They said these loans were meant to cover the costs of the crop and they always promised that there would be handsome profits after the harvest. But when the time came the opium factory often changed its prices, depending on how good the crop had been that year. Since growers were not allowed to sell to anyone but the factory, they often ended up making a loss and getting deeper into debt. Ram Singh knew of several men who had been ruined in this way.

Of late the Company had even tried to interfere in the job market, taking steps to discourage men from joining any army but their own. For Ram Singh, as for many others, this was even more objectionable than meddling with their crops. That anyone should assert an exclusive claim to their service was an astonishing idea:

few things were as important to them as their right to work for whoever offered the best terms. It was not uncommon for brothers and cousins to take jobs in different armies: if they happened to meet in battle, it was assumed that each man would do his duty and fight loyally for his leader, having 'eaten his salt'. This was how things had been in Ram Singh's time and his father's before him; and so far as he was concerned it was yet another reason why he did not want his sons to join the Company's paltans.

Ram Singh was well-acquainted with the Company's army, having fought against it at the Battle of Assaye. The Berar forces had entered that battlefield in alliance with the army of Gwalior, and they had come painfully close to giving the British the greatest defeat they had ever suffered. Ram Singh never ceased to relive that battle, and he often said that the British victory was due solely to the cunning of their general, Arthur Wellesley, who had succeeded in sowing treachery in the opposing ranks, through bribery and deceit.

If there was one thing that Ram Singh was sure of it was that the East India Company's army was no place for any of his sons. In the English way of fighting, he liked to say, there was nothing to stir the blood, nothing heroic. No Company soldier ever stepped forward to offer single combat; none of their jawans sought glory by breaking from their ranks and taking the enemy unawares. Their way of fighting was like that of an army of ants, always lined up shoulder to shoulder, each man sheltering behind another, every soldier doing exactly the same thing at the same time, everyone making the same, drilled movements. There was something ant-like even about their appearance, with all of them in identical livery, no one daring to identify himself with his own insignia or his own unmistakable turban. As for the caravans that followed them, they were shabby and nondescript affairs, at least in comparison with the vast baggage-trains that accompanied the armies of Gwalior, Jaipur and Indore, with all their dancing girls and bazars.

What was the point of a soldiering life if it offered no pleasure or colour? Why would a man throw himself into a battle if he did not know that at the end of the fighting he would be able to take his ease amongst the camp-followers, seeking out his favourite girls, and being plied with rich food and heady drink? Better be a cowherd, pasturing livestock, than live like that. There was no honour in it, no izzat: it was contrary to the ways of their caste, and against the customs of Hindustan.

It dismayed Ram Singh that many Indian kingdoms and principalities had begun to imitate the English armies. But fortunately there still remained a few that were wedded to the old ways of war – Awadh, Jaipur, Jodhpur and Jhansi for instance. And then there was the Mughal army, which still remained a powerful draw: such was its centuries-old prestige that even now, when the old empire's territory was shrinking fast, a man who served in its legions could be sure of commanding the respect of his village.

For all these armies, the region around Nayanpur was a preferred recruiting ground so Ram Singh knew that his son Bhim would not lack for options. And sure enough other recruiters soon began to arrive at their door. Some were professional 'gatherers' of jawans – jamadars and dafadars – with links to several kingdoms and principalities. The jamadars were usually senior men and some were known to Ram Singh from his own soldiering days. When they came to visit, charpoys would be placed under the shade of the mango tree outside and hookahs, food and water would be sent for.

Often it was Kesri who was called on to serve the visitors and light their hookahs. No one minded if he loitered, listening to what was being said: since he wasn't available for recruitment, his presence made no difference. Bhim, on the other hand, was not allowed anywhere near the recruiters. That would have been as improper and unwise as for a girl to step out brazenly in front of a set of prospective in-laws.

Ram Singh would start by questioning the recruiters minutely about such matters as the salary that was being offered and how regularly it was paid; how booty was divided and what sorts of *battas* – or allowances – were provided. Was there a batta for clothing? Was there a marching-batta? Or a bonus for campaigns away from the home station? Who provided the food when in camp? How large was the camp-followers' bazar? What did it offer? Was accommodation provided in the home station?

Only if these queries were answered to his satisfaction would Bhim be produced before the recruiter. And just as their mother always found a way, when the time was right, to present her daughters to their best advantage before the families of prospective grooms, so would their father do the same for his son. When the moment came he would send Kesri to fetch his brother. The boy would arrive with a plough slung over his shoulders, dressed in nothing but a vest and langot, so that his impressive physique was bared for the recruiter to see. Then, Ram Singh would ask him to groom the jamadar's horse, which he would proceed to do with a will, thereby showing himself to be a well-brought-up, obedient boy who could follow orders respectfully.

The jamadars were not the only ones to come looking for able-bodied youths: some of the recruiters were serving jawans, back on leave. Bringing in recruits was a way of earning commissions, so rounding up a few young fellows was a good way to make a bit of money.

For Bhim and Kesri the younger soldiers were much more interesting than the grey-whiskered elders who usually came by. Some of the jawans were friends or acquaintances from nearby villages so there was no need to stand on ceremony with them; some even stayed the night and then the two brothers would lie awake till dawn, listening to their stories.

One day a cousin from a neighbouring village came to visit. Although not much older than Kesri he had already spent a couple of years in Delhi, in the service of the Mughal army. This was his first visit home and he could not, of course, be allowed to leave without spending the night: the boys took their charpoys out into the courtyard and were soon absorbed in their cousin's stories. He described Delhi's temples and mosques, forts and palaces. When he and his company went on marches, he said, their unit was far outnumbered by their camp-followers. The bazar that trailed them was like a small town, only much more colourful. One whole section of it was given to naach-girls – and they were the most beautiful women that anyone had ever seen, from Afghanistan and Nepal, Ethiopia and Turkmenistan. Boys like Bhim and Kesri, he said, could not conceive of the things these girls could do with their bodies – no more than they could imagine a banana being peeled with the tongue.

Of course it couldn't be left at that. The boys plied him with questions and after a little bit of nahi-nahi and other pretences of modesty, he told them all they wanted to know and more – how it felt to have the contours of your face stroked with a nipple, and what it was like to have your instrument enveloped by muscles that could squeeze, pluck, and even glide, like the fingers of a musician.

For Kesri this was dangerous territory, for one of the most important aspects of his regimen of training, as a wrestler, was the control of the inner workings of the body – especially its desires and their manifestations. To that end he regularly practised a variety of exercises, intended to prevent the loss, accidental or intentional, of his vital fluids. But that night his training proved unequal to the task: he woke suddenly to find that he had succumbed to a *swapnadosha* – a 'dream-mishap'.

As for his brother Bhim, he knew at once that this was exactly the brand of soldiering that would suit him best. With Kesri's encouragement he went to their father the next morning and told him that he wanted to go to Delhi with his cousin. Ram Singh willingly gave him his blessings and promised to make all the necessary arrangements.

Preparations for Bhim's departure started at once and involved the whole family. Clothes were made, bedding and blankets were prepared, and an array of equipment was assembled – flints, powder, musket-balls for his goolie-pouch, and an assortment of edged weapons, long and short.

While everyone's attention was focused on Bhim, Kesri was busy ploughing the poppy fields. Try as he might, he could not stop thinking of his brother's forthcoming journey to Delhi, mounted on a horse, with his weapons slung behind him and a fine new turban on his head. By contrast his own bare body, with a filthy langot knotted around the waist and flies settling on his pooling sweat, was a reminder of the lifetime that lay ahead of him, of trudging endlessly behind draught animals, jumping aside when they spurted dung in mid-stride, season after season, watching the crops come and go, counting it a luxury to snatch an hour's sleep in the shade of a tree in the afternoon, and at the end of the day, struggling to wash away the mud that had hardened into a second layer of skin between his toes. Meanwhile Bhim would be going from city to city, filling his bags with booty, eating rich meats and fowl and revelling in the embraces of beautiful women.

Abandoning the oxen in the middle of the field Kesri went to sit under a tree; tears trickled down his cheeks as he sat there, clutching his knees. That was how Deeti found him when she brought over his mid-day meal of rotis and achar: she understood without asking what the matter was; she stayed with him through the afternoon and helped him finish the ploughing.

At the end of the day, when they were walking home, she said: Don't worry, it will happen. You will leave too.

But when, Deeti? *Batavela*. Tell me – when?

*

For several days after his unfortunate encounter with Mrs Burnham and her daughter, Zachary lived in hourly fear of being evicted from his comfortable new lodgings on the budgerow. It seemed just a matter of time before a khidmatgar arrived with a letter to inform him that his employment had been terminated because of his lapse from decorum.

But as the days went by, with no dismissal, he decided that Mrs Burnham had perhaps decided to grant him another chance. Still, he knew he could not be complacent – occasional flashes of light in the mansion's windows suggested that he was still under observation – so he went to great lengths to observe all the proprieties in matters of dress and deportment. When working in exposed parts of the boat, he made sure that he was clothed from neck to toe, no matter how hot it was.

But other than this minor annoyance, Zachary was perfectly content to be living on the budgerow. His days were uneventful but not unrewarding: he got up early and worked steadily till sunset; when he needed help he called on the mansion's khidmatgars but mostly he was content to labour on his own. His quiet and frugal existence seemed to excite the pity of the household staff and they kept him supplied with leftovers – in fact he could not remember a time in his life when he had eaten so well and lived in such comfort.

Best of all were the nights. The bed was itself like an embrace, soft and yielding, and the solitude and quiet were an even greater luxury. Nourished by the fine food and peaceful surroundings his imagination grew so vigorously concupiscent that it took no effort to summon Paulette out of the shadows and into his bed – and the pleasures of his trysts with her were so intense that he often sampled them several times in one night.

One morning, while working on the foredeck, Zachary heard Annabel's voice, calling from the shore: 'Holloa there!'

He raised a finger to his cap. 'Hello, Miss Annabel.'

'I came to say goodbye – I'm leaving for Hazaribagh today.'

'Well, I wish you a safe and pleasant journey, Miss Annabel.'

'Thank you.'

She took a step closer. 'Tell me, Mr Mystery,' she said, 'you knew Paulette, didn't you?'

'So I did.'

'Do you think you may see her again soon?'

'I don't know,' he said. 'I hope so.'

'If you do, please tell her I said hello, won't you? I do miss her so.'

'So do I, Miss Annabel.'

She nodded. 'I'd better be off now. Mama doesn't like me to talk to you.'

'Why not?'

'She says it isn't decent for a girl to talk to mysteries.'

He laughed. 'Well, you'd better run then. Goodbye.'

'Goodbye.'

Annabel and Mrs Burnham left later that day and for a fortnight afterwards the Burnham mansion was silent and dark. Then suddenly the lights went on again and Zachary knew that Mrs Burnham had returned. A week later there was an explosion of activity around the house; khidmatgars, chokras, malis and ghaskatas went swarming over the grounds, stringing up lanterns and putting out chairs. One of the chokras told Zachary that a big burra-khana was to be held at the house to celebrate the Beebee's birthday.

In the evening a great number of gharries and buggies rolled up the driveway and the sound of voices and laughter wafted across the lawns until late into the night. Zachary sequestered himself in his stateroom and was careful to stay out of sight.

The next day, at suppertime, the khidmatgars brought over a lavish spread of leftovers as well as a few bottles of beer. Along with the food and drink they also delivered a small parcel. It was accompanied by an envelope that had Zachary's name written on it, in a steeply sloping scrawl.

This was the first communication Zachary had received since his last encounter with Mrs Burnham: he opened the envelope with deep trepidation, not knowing what to expect. To his surprise the tone of the note was not just pleasant but almost cordial:

August 30, 1839

Dear Mr Reid

I trust you have settled in comfortably and are making progress with the refurbishment. If you need anything I hope you will not hesitate to let the khidmatgars know.

Since Man does not live by bread alone you are no doubt in need of some improving Literature to relieve your solitude. I have thus taken the liberty of sending you two books. I hope you will find them of interest.

Yours &c.
C. Burnham

It was clear now that he had been granted a reprieve! With a groan of relief, Zachary deposited the note and parcel on the teapoy that stood beside his bed. Then he celebrated by opening a bottle of beer and proceeded to eat a hearty meal. Afterwards he went up to the deck above and summoned Paulette to sit beside him, under the stars. Her presence was so palpable that it made him long for the pleasures of his bed; he went hurrying back to his stateroom and tore off his clothes. Wasting no time, he parted the mosquito net and slipped between the sheets, pausing only to snatch up one of the stained and crusted doo-rags that lay strewn around the bed.

He was about to snuff out the candle when his eyes fell on the parcel that Mrs Burnham had sent him. Reaching over to the teapoy, he tore off the parcel's paper covering: inside were two books, of just the sort that he would have expected to receive from

Mrs Burnham. One was a biography of a long-dead missionary and the other was a collection of sermons, by a Reverend someone-or-the-other.

The books looked dull and Zachary was in no mood to read anyway: but just as he was about to put them away a little pamphlet tumbled out of one of them and fell on his chest. Picking it up, Zachary glanced at the cover. Printed on it, in bold, screaming letters, were the words:

ONANIA;
OR THE HEINOUS SIN
OF SELF-POLLUTION.

The title made him sit bolt upright: he wasn't quite sure what the words meant but their very sound was enough to cause alarm.

Opening the pamphlet at random he came to a paragraph that had been heavily underlined.

> Self-pollution is that unnatural practice by which
> Persons of either Sex, may defile their own Bodies,
> without the Assistance of others, whilst yielding to filthy
> Imaginations, they endeavour to imitate and procure to
> themselves that Sensation, which God has order'd to
> attend the carnal Commerce of the two Sexes, for the
> Continuance of our Species.

His eyes returned, as if hypnotized, to the words 'filthy Imaginations'. A chill of shame went through him and he quickly turned the page, but only to arrive at another underlined passage:

> . . . the Crime in itself is monstrous and unnatural; in
> its Practice filthy and odious to Extremity; its Guilt is
> crying, and its Consequences ruinous; It destroys
> conjugal Affection, perverts natural Inclination, and
> tends to extinguish the Hopes of Posterity.

He turned feverishly to another page:

> In Men as well as Boys, the very first Attempt of it has
> often occasion'd a Phymosis in some, and a
> Paraphymosis in others; I shall not explain these terms
> any further, let it suffice that they are Accidents which
> are very painful and troublesome, and may continue to
> be tormenting for some time, if not bring on Ulcers and
> other worse Symptoms. The frequent Use of this
> Pollution; likewise causes Stranguries, Priapisms and
> other disorders of the Penis and Testes but especially
> Gonorrhoeas, more difficult to be Cur'd than those
> contracted from Women . . .

Zachary's hands began to shake and the pamphlet dropped from his fingers. Reaching down, he pulled open his drawers and began to examine himself, looking for evidence of ulcers, stranguries and phymosises. What exactly they were he didn't know, but amongst the wiry hairs of his pubes and in the wrinkled folds of the sac below, there was no shortage of troubling manifestations – pimples, white-heads, creases, and swollen veins that he had never noticed before.

When had they appeared and what did they portend? He could not think and was grateful only that he could see no signs of incipient priapism. This was a disease he had often heard discussed among sailors: their name for it was 'fouling the fiddle-block', and he had heard it said that it could lead to terrible damage, sometimes even causing the head of the organ to erupt, like a boil or pustule. He could not imagine a more dreadful affliction.

And then a thought occurred to him that was even more frightful than the spectre of disease: what if the pamphlet's arrival was not an accident? What if Mrs Burnham had deliberately stuck it in the book, knowing that it would find its way into his hands?

No, that was impossible surely? It was beyond his imagining that she would even know of the existence of such a book, let alone possess a familiarity with the matters that were addressed in it. Surely a woman like her, a memsahib of tender sensibility, the most sheltered of Burra Beebees, would not allow her eyes to dwell on a booklet of this sort? And even if she had, surely – surely? – she would not have considered sending the pamphlet to a man whom she hardly knew at all?

For what could be the intent of such an act? What grounds could she have for imagining him to be an Onanist – indeed, of accusing him of it?

To know something so secret, so private, would mean that she had looked into his very soul. And to see so deep into the head and body of another person was to take possession of them, to achieve complete mastery; he might as well be her dredgy now for he would certainly never be able to look her in the eyes again.

And the worst part of it was that he would never find out whether she knew or not – a subject like this could never be mentioned between a mystery and his mistress.

A terrible dread swept over him now and all thought of his anticipated tryst with Paulette was erased from his mind. He was filled instead with a self-loathing so acute that he could not imagine that such filthy temptations would ever well up inside him again. And if they did he would fight them; he would prove that he was no Onanist: of that he was determined – his freedom, his mastery of his very soul, seemed to depend on it.

His eyes fell on the yellowing rags that lay around his bed and he shuddered. In light of what he knew now, they looked unspeakably vile, veritable founts of sin and contagion. He cast his hands around him until they fell on the rag he had brought into his bed, and he hurled it away with a shudder of loathing. Then he picked up the pamphlet and read it through one more time, from beginning to end.

Over the next few days Zachary wore the pages of *Onania* almost to shreds, reading the pamphlet over and again. The parts that made the most powerful impression on him were the passages on disease: every perusal deepened his apprehensions about the infections that were simmering inside his body.

Until this time he had been under the impression that the clap was the revenge of the pox-parlour and could not be caught without actually thrusting your cargo through a hatch, no matter whether fore or aft: that merely winching up your undertackle with your own maulers could produce the same result had never entered his mind.

On the *Ibis* he had seen the consequences of the clap on other sailors: he had listened to pox-ridden men screaming in pain as they tried to tap their kegs; he had viewed, with horror-struck curiosity, the fruit that blossomed on diseased beanpoles – the clumps of welts and boils, the dribbles of pus. He had also heard stories about how the treatment – with applications of mercury and even leeches – was just as painful as the disease. To spike one's cannon forever seemed better than to take that cure.

It had never occurred to him that his night-time trysts with Paulette might be leading in this direction. He had thought that his bullet-pouch was no different from his bladder or his bowels in that it needed an occasional emptying. He had even heard it said that coughing up your cocksnot every now and again was as much a necessity as blowing your nose. Certainly no one who had ever slept in a fo'c'sle could fail to notice the fusillades that shook every hammock from time to time. More than once had he been bumped in the nose because of an overly energetic bout of musketry in the hammock above. Just as he himself was sometimes shouted at, he'd learnt to shout: 'Will you stop polishing your pistol up there? Take your shot and be done with it.'

But he remembered now, with a sinking in his heart, that it was always the most trigger-happy gunmen who ended up with the clap. He himself had never been of that number – at least not until he fell under the sway of Paulette's phantom. Now, as he battled the temptation to sink into her arms again, the very sound of the letter 'P' became unbearable to him – as did words like 'gullet' and 'mullet' and everything that rhymed with 'Paulette'.

The worst part of it was that each day brought with it worrying signs of the one condition he thought he had been spared – priapism. It was a bitter irony that this disease had manifested itself only after he had forsworn its cause; no less was it an irony that the longer he abstained the more vigorously it asserted itself. On some nights it was as if his spuds were cooking in a kettle: to keep the lid on, with the pressure building up below, took a jaw-gritting effort, but he persisted, for to give in would be to capitulate, to acknowledge that he was indeed a congenital tug-mutton.

During the day he managed to keep the symptoms at bay by applying himself strenuously to his work. But even then, scarcely an hour passed during which his tackle did not stir in its stowage. The shape of a cloud would conjure up an image of a breast or a hip, and before he knew it his drawers would puff up like a spanker in a breeze. The sight of a boatwoman on the river, rowing a sampan or a paunchway, could bring on a situation in which he had to race off to find an apron to drape around his middle. One day, a glimpse of a goat, lazily grazing in the distance, evoked the curve of a woman's thigh – and before he knew it his hawser was trying to bore a hawse-hole through the flap of his breeches.

That night he wept to think that an animal – a goat! – had produced such an effect on him: how much lower was it possible to fall?

When the khidmatgars brought him trays he would stare morosely at them, wondering whether they too had ever visited the Onanian isles. He would examine their faces for signs of the symptoms listed in the pamphlet: pimples, inflammations, rapid blinking, dark patches around the eyes and an unnatural pallor. On none of them were the signs so prominently visible as they were on himself. They had probably married early, he guessed, and would thus never have needed to resort to the solitary vice.

But even these inoffensive reflections were fraught with danger. One thought would lead to another and visions of the khidmatgars' intimacies with their wives would flash through his head. The hairy hand that bore the tray would evoke the rounded shape of a breast; a calloused knuckle, on the fingers that gifted him a bowl of dumbpoke, would turn into a dark, swollen nipple – and all of a sudden his jib-boom would be a-taunt in his drawers and he would have to push his chair deeper under the table.

His condition being what it was, nothing was more terrifying to Zachary than the prospect of accidentally encountering Mrs Burnham. For this reason he spent all his time on the budgerow, hardly ever setting foot on shore. But one morning, in despair, he decided that confinement was making his condition worse and forced himself to go for a walk.

As he marched along the riverbank, his head felt lighter than it had in many days. The twitching in his groin also began to abate – but still, as a precaution, he kept his eyes rigidly fixed on the ground. But his confidence grew as he walked and he began to look around more freely. And to his surprise, many sights that would have hoisted his mizzen just the day before – the bulge of a breast under a sari; a woman's ankle, twinkling down the street – aroused not the faintest flutter.

As his assurance increased he let his eyes wander where they wished, allowing them to dwell, promiscuously, on voluptuous clouds and suggestively heaving trees. Finding no cause for concern he even ventured to pronounce the proscribed words: mullet, gullet and so on until he arrived finally at a full-throated 'Paulette!' – and still his foredeck remained perfectly ship-shape, with his tackle tightly snugged down.

He stopped and drew a breath that coursed euphorically through his body: it was as if he had been granted a reprieve, a cure! Turning around, he strolled joyfully back to the budgerow, and there, as if to confirm his exculpation, he found a visitor waiting.

It was Mr Doughty, bearing an invitation to the Harbourmaster's Ball, a fancy-dress ball intended to raise money for the Mariners' Mission in Calcutta: it was the custom to give away a few tickets to indigent but deserving young sailors.

Zachary understood that Mr Doughty had gone to some trouble to procure a ticket for him and thanked him profusely. 'But the trouble is, Mr Doughty, I don't have a costume.'

But Mr Doughty had thought of this too. 'Oh, don't you worry about that, my boy. I've got one for you – same thing I'll be wearing. Why don't you come over early and eat dinner with us that day? I'll get you all kitted out – won't cost a thing and you'll enjoy yourself, I promise.'

Three

Every year at the start of winter, around the time that the festival of Naga Panchami was celebrated, a mela was held at the akhara where Kesri went to train. Along with all the usual fairground attractions, a special raised ring was prepared and wrestlers came from far afield to test and prove themselves.

The mela lasted several days and attracted a great number of sepoys, jawans and other military men; thousands of them would converge on the shrine, along with hordes of naked Naga sadhus from distant points in the Indian subcontinent. The festival was considered particularly auspicious for new recruits so it was arranged that Kesri's brother, Bhim, would wait till it was over before leaving for Delhi with his cousin.

That year Kesri was in the open competition for the first time and much was expected of him. But his brother's imminent departure, and the prospect of his indefinite detainment in the village, had so demoralized Kesri that he lost quite early, dashing the hopes of his guruji. This added to his misery and the next day he was scarcely able to drag himself out of bed. For once his father took pity on him and let him off from going to the fields.

Since Bhim was soon to depart for Delhi, this became an occasion for the family to gather in the angaan in front of their dwelling. Their mother sent out snacks, sweetmeats and sharbat while everyone lounged on charpoys in the shade of the mango tree.

Around mid-morning, as they were savouring the treats, a horsecart was spotted in the distance, wheeling up the path that led to their straw-thatched home. Soon enough it became clear that the men in the carts were strangers. The food was swept away and the girls were sent inside. Ram Singh went to greet the visitors himself, with Kesri and Bhim on either side.

The first man to step out of the cart was of impressive, even intimidating appearance. His chest was as deep as a battle-drum and his hands were big enough to cover a brass thali. His upturned moustache glistened with wax, and his skin, which was the colour of ripening wheat, was burnished to a glow with mustard oil. Everything about his appearance and his manner – the taut mound of his belly, the heavy gold rings that dangled from his ears, the richly embroidered shawl around his shoulders – spoke of expensive tastes and voracious appetites. He gave his name as Bhyro Singh and said his village was near the town of Ghazipur, some sixty miles to the west.

This put Ram Singh on his guard. The people of the area around Ghazipur were known to have close links with the British because many of them were employed by the Company's opium factory. But Bhyro Singh did not look like a factory worker. Even though he was not in uniform, Ram Singh sensed that he belonged to the East India Company's army. Nor was he mistaken: the visitor soon explained that he was a havildar in the 1st battalion of the 25th Regiment of the Bengal Native Infantry – the famous 'Pacheesi'. The three men who were with him were sepoys from his own battalion; they were on their way to join their paltan and had decided to stop at the Naga sadhus' mela before proceeding to the regimental base at Barrackpore, near Calcutta. He had come, he said, to discuss a matter of some importance.

It turned out that Bhyro Singh was a recruiter who had heard of Kesri's prowess as a wrestler; he had come in the hope of persuading him to join the East India Company's army. When Ram Singh said that Kesri was not available for recruitment Bhyro Singh was taken aback; he was even more surprised when he learnt that his brother, Bhim, was soon to leave for Delhi to join the Mughal Badshah's army.

But why, Ram Singhji? Bhyro Singh protested. The boy is young and you are his father. You should explain to him that Delhi is not what it used to be; a soldier who wants to rise in the world needs to go to the East India Company's capital – Calcutta. There is no army in Hindustan that can match the terms offered by the British.

How so?

67

This prompted Bhyro Singh to launch into a detailed listing of the advantages of the Bengal Native Infantry: while the basic pay might not be higher than in other armies – just six rupees a month – what counted was that the money was always delivered in full and on time. Besides, there were regular increments, with rank: a naik received a basic pay of eight rupees, a havildar ten, a jamadar fifteen, and a subedar thirty. Best of all, the salary was always paid on schedule: never once, in all his years with the Company, had Bhyro Singh known it to be delayed.

Tell me, Ram Singhji, of which other army in Hindustan can it be said that their men are paid regularly? You know as well as I do that our rajas and nawabs purposely keep their soldiers' salaries in arrears so they won't desert. Such things are unheard of in the East India Company's army.

And the battas!

The Company's allowances were more generous, said Bhyro Singh, than those of any other army: they added up to almost as much again as the basic pay. There was a special batta for marching and another for campaign rations; still another for uniforms. As for booty taken in battle, the splitting of the spoils was always scrupulously fair. Why, after a major battle in Mysore, the English general had kept only half the loot for himself! The rest was divided fairly amongst the various ranks of officers and sepoys.

But that was still not the best of it, said the havildar. The Company Bahadur was the only employer in all of Hindustan that looked after its men even after they had left service. When they retired they were handed something called a 'pension' – a salary, of at least three rupees a month, that was paid to them for the rest of their lives. On top of that they could obtain land grants if they wanted. If wounded, they were provided with free medical care whenever it was needed.

Do you know of any employer in Hindustan that offers all this, Ram Singhji? Tell me, truthfully.

Ram Singh's eyes widened but he parried by asking: What about accommodation? In Delhi they give their soldiers quarters to live. Does the Company do the same?

Bhyro Singh acknowledged that this was not the case at his own regimental base: instead, every sepoy was given a hutting-allowance, to build his own shack.

But believe me, Ram Singhji, no one minds doing this because that way we can all live as we like, among our own kind.

Now, with the first seeds of doubt sprouting in his mind, Ram Singh began to voice other, more pressing objections to the Company's service.

Say what you like, Bhyro Singhji, he said. But these Angrez firangis are beef-eating Christians. For Rajputs it can only bring shame on our families if we work for them. Isn't it true that everyone who joins the Company's paltans must eat unclean and forbidden things? That he must live side by side with men of all sorts, including the lowest?

The havildar burst out laughing.

Ram Singhji, he said, you are completely mistaken: the English care more about the dharma of caste than any of our nawabs and rajas ever did. There is not a sepoy in our regiment who is not a Brahmin or a Rajput. And these are not impostors, trying to pass themselves off as twice-born: every sepoy's caste is carefully checked, as is his body. As you know, in the old days the armies of Hindustan were like jungles – men went into them to hide, so that they could change their origins. After a few years of fighting, ordinary julaha Muslims would pass themselves off as high-class Afghans, and half the men who called themselves Rajputs were just junglees and hill-people. Our badshahs and maharajahs put up with it because they were desperate for recruits. That is how it has been in Hindustan for hundreds of years: everything has become degenerate, people have forgotten the true dharma of caste and they do whatever they find convenient. But now at last things are being put right by the Angrezi Company. The sahibs are stricter about these matters than our rajas and nawabs ever were. They have brought learned men from their country to study our old books. These white pundits know more about our scriptures than we do ourselves. They are making everything pure again, just like it was in the days of the earliest sages and rishis. Under the sahibs' guidance every caste will once again become like an iron cage – no one will be allowed to move one finger's breadth, this way or that. Already the sahibs have done more to keep the lower castes in their places than our Hindu kings did over hundreds of years. In the gora paltan no one can join unless he is known to be of high caste, and no person of doubtful origin will last more than a couple of days. All our cooking we do ourselves or else we hire high-caste servants to do it for us. If we raise a question about any sepoy the officers will convene an inquiry at once. If there is anything doubtful about the man's caste-status he is sent straight back to his village. Why, even the girls supplied by the Company, for our 'red' bazars, are always from high castes.

Bhyro Singh paused to let his host absorb what he had said.

I tell you, Ram Singhji, he continued, the Company has more respect for the dharma of caste than we do ourselves. Why, just listen to this: some time ago the English officers made a new rule that a bell had to be rung in our camp after every few hours. Of course none of us wanted to do the extra work so we said that it was against our custom for high-caste men to ring bells. And what do you think? Immediately they hired special bell-ringers to do the job! Do you think our nawabs and rajas would care at all about such things? If we told them we couldn't ring bells they would have laughed and kicked us in the gaand.

Ram Singh was visibly impressed by these arguments but he continued to protest: But still, Bhyro Singhji, there's no izzat in working for firangi beef-eaters.

But Muslims are beef-eaters too, aren't they? Bhyro Singh countered. And that did not stop you from agreeing to send your son to the Mughal army in Delhi, did it? To serve the Mussalman badshahs was always a matter of honour for our fathers and grandfathers. With the Company there is even more reason for pride, since the British are purifying Hindustan. For thousands of years everything in this land has declined and degenerated; people have become so mixed that you cannot tell them apart. Under the British everyone is kept separate, each with their own kind – the whites are with the whites and we are left to ourselves. They are the true defenders of caste, Ram Singhji, and if you have any thought of your son's dharma you will send him to us.

But dharma is not just a matter of rules, Ram Singh objected. We are Rajputs and for us our worth, our *maryada*, lies in how we show our courage. No man can be a true warrior in the gora paltan – valour and skill count for nothing with them. Why, during the Battle of Assaye some of our best fighters went forward and challenged the enemy to send their bahadurs, for single combat. Do you know, not one man stepped out from the Company's ranks? There was not one man in their entire army who was brave enough to be a real bahadur! Even though most of their sepoys were Hindustanis, like us, they had lost both honour and courage, izzat and himmat, after joining the Company's army. Even we were ashamed for them.

A smile appeared on Bhyro Singh's face. But Ram Singhji, he said, in a silky voice: Tell me, who won at Assaye?

Unable to think of a retort, Ram Singh hung his head.

Bhyro Singh's smirk widened: The old ways of fighting may have been good for making heroes and bahadurs, Ram Singhji, but they didn't always win wars. And that's the thing with the English way of fighting – it does not depend on heroes. The Company's army is not made up of a great number of bahadurs: the whole army fights like a single brave warrior. That is why people speak of the 'Company Bahadur'. The entire army is like one man, one body, obeying a single head; every Company sepoy has to learn this by doing drills. Everyone has to obey the one above him, right to the very top. No one can ever refuse to follow orders or he will be shot. It is not like our Hindustani armies, made up of men whose main loyalty is to the sardar who pays them – and if that sardar takes a bribe they will all go off with him. Our Angrez officers understand this very well, and before every battle they send the baniyas to offer bribes to the sardars of the other armies. Almost always it happens that three or four of them accept, and then they either ride away or they stand aside during the fighting. Isn't it true that this is what happened at Assaye?

Yes, said Ram Singh. It cannot be denied. But that wasn't the only reason the Angrez army won. They had better cannon than us. Better bundooks too.

Exactly! said Bhyro Singh. Unlike our Hindustani rajas and nawabs, the Angrezes are always studying and making changes. Every year their cannon get better and better. They are always looking to make improvements in their weapons and they don't allow anything to get in the way of that.

Cutting himself short, Bhyro Singh jumped to his feet: Here, let me show you something.

He went to the horse-cart, which was tethered nearby, and came back with two swords, both sheathed in their scabbards. One of the swords was curved and the other straight; he placed them both on a charpoy, and seated himself beside them.

Look at this talwar! he said, drawing the curved sword from its sheath and laying its shining blade across his knees.

See how beautifully it is made? See how sharp the blade is?

He picked up a fallen mango leaf and held it to the sword's edge. The blade sliced right through the leaf, almost at the touch.

This is the weapon my father and grandfather carried, Bhyro Singh continued. It is the weapon I was first taught to use, and it is still the weapon of my love. Compared to it, the swords we are given by the English are nothing to look at.

Drawing the straight sword from its scabbard he laid it across his knees, beside the talwar. It was a dull grey in colour, with a sharply pointed tip and straight sides. There were no ornamental designs etched upon the blade and it showed no signs of having ever been touched by the hands of a craftsman.

These English swords are all alike, said Bhyro Singh. They make thousands and thousands of them, all exactly the same. Compared to our talwars, they are blunt, ugly things.

He thrust a leaf against the edge of the blade and succeeded only in bruising it.

But when it comes to fighting, said Bhyro Singh, it's a different matter. He rose to his feet and brandished the unsheathed talwar in front of him.

Look at this talwar, said Bhyro Singh. It is a weapon that cuts with its edge. To use it in battle a soldier must have plenty of space around him. Or else he will hurt his own men.

He motioned to the others to step back and made a slashing motion, so that the tip of the talwar drew crosswise arcs in the air, swinging from shoulder to waist on one side and then the other.

When I use this sword, said Bhyro Singh, none of my own men can be near me. We have to stand at least two swords' lengths away.

Laying aside the talwar, he now picked up the English sword and held it in front of him.

This weapon is also a sword, he said, but it works in a completely different way. It is meant not for cutting with the edge, but for impaling with the tip. That is what it is meant to do. With these weapons a column of men armed with swords and bayonets can advance shoulder to shoulder: they pose no danger to each other. Even if their numbers are much smaller, their column has more weight because it is more closely packed. When a line of our soldiers meets a line of men with talwars they will always break through. The fighters armed with talwars cannot turn us back, no matter how brave they are, or how highly skilled. If they try to form a mass they will hurt themselves more than us. Their talwars cannot be used in the same way as a straight sword or a bayonet – the curved blade does not allow that. To fight at all, they need space and that becomes their weakness, no matter what their numbers. That is why they always scatter in front of us.

The havildar handed his swords to his men, to be sheathed. Then he turned again to Ram Singh.

You see, Ram Singhji, he said, there are good reasons why there is no army in Hindustan that can withstand the forces of the Company Bahadur. Sometimes armies run away just at the sight of us. If you want your son to fight on the winning side, if you want him to come home alive, with money in his pouch, you will give him to me and I will turn him into a sepoy for the Company.

At this point Bhim intervened, saying to his father in a loud whisper that he had made up his mind: he wished to go nowhere but to Delhi.

That brought the argument to an end. Bhyro Singh gave a dismissive shrug, as if to say he had done what he could: All right, then I will take your leave now, Ram Singhji. I have said what I had to. If anything changes, I will be at the mela tomorrow.

With that he ushered his men to the horse-cart and they went on their way.

*

Shireen was returning from one of her daily visits to the Fire Temple when she was intercepted by a khidmatgar. A visitor had come to the house to offer his respects, he said; the gentleman was waiting for her in a receiving room on the ground floor, with her brother.

Kaun hai? said Shireen. Do you know his name?

73

The boy could tell her nothing except that the visitor was a *topeewala-sahib* – a hat-wearing white man.

Veiling herself with the end of her white sari, Shireen went to the door of her brother's baithak-khana. Seated inside, with her brother, was a tall man with a face like a wind-eroded cliff: his cheeks were scored by deep lines and his temples were marked by protruding, crag-like bones. He was clean-shaven, his complexion a weathered sunset pink. His jacket and trowsers were a funereal black and he was wearing a dark armband around his sleeve.

In complexion, as in clothing, the visitor looked very much a sahib, yet there was something about his deportment that did not seem entirely European. Nor was there anything Western about the gesture with which he greeted her – a salaam, performed with a cupped hand and a deep bow.

'Shireen, this is Mr Zadig Karabedian. I am sure his name will be familiar to you – he was a close friend of Bahram-bhai's. He has come to pay his respects.'

Shireen bowed her head without removing her veil. Bahram had often spoken to her about 'Zadig Bey'. She remembered that he had befriended him on a journey to England, some thirty years before. Zadig Bey had grown up in Egypt, Bahram had told her: he was an Armenian Christian, a clockmaker who travelled widely in connection with his trade.

Bibiji, said the visitor in fluent Hindustani; please forgive me for not coming earlier, but my visit to Bombay has been much delayed. Like you I have suffered a bereavement.

Oh?

He pointed to his armband: My wife of many years was carried away by a hectic fever a few months ago.

I'm very sorry to hear that, Zadig Bey. Where did it happen?

In Colombo. But I must count it my good fortune that I could at least be with her at the end. God did not grant you even that.

Behind the veil, Shireen's eyes suddenly filled with tears: No; He did not . . .

Bibiji, I cannot tell you how much I have been saddened by your husband's death. Bahram-bhai was my dearest friend.

At the sound of her late husband's name Shireen's eyes flew to her brother's expressionless face. Over the last few weeks Bahram's name had become almost taboo in the Mistrie mansion; people seemed to avoid mentioning him in order to spare themselves the ignominy of being reminded of his bankruptcy, and of the disgrace he had brought upon his family and relatives.

Shireen herself hardly ever spoke of Bahram now, except with her daughters, and even they talked about him as though he were someone else, a different man: it was as if his death, combined with the catastrophic failure that had preceded it, had become a kind of re-birth, begetting a man who was utterly unlike the person they had known: a man whose career had been doomed to failure from the start; whose every success was a portent of the disaster he would bring upon those he loved most.

The girls had always doted on their father but now they could no longer speak of him except in tones of shame and reproach – and nor could Shireen blame them, since Bahram's bankruptcy had robbed them not just of their expectations of inheritance, but also of a considerable part of the respect they had previously enjoyed in their husbands' families.

For Shireen herself Bahram's name had become an open wound, which she tried alternately to soothe, heal and hide – and to hear it uttered now, in tones of such unalloyed affection, was oddly painful.

My husband often spoke of you, she said quietly.

Bahram-bhai was the kindest, most generous of men, said Zadig. It's terrible that he went in this way.

Shireen glanced at her brother and saw that he was squirming in his seat. To listen to praise of Bahram was deeply distasteful to him, she knew, and she guessed that he would gladly have left the room if not for the impropriety of leaving her alone with a stranger. To spare him any further discomfort, she leant over and whispered in Gujarati, telling him that he could slip away if he liked – her maid was outside; he could send her in and tell her to leave the door open. It would be perfectly proper; she was veiled anyway – there was nothing to worry about.

He jumped to his feet immediately. All right, he said. I will leave you here for a few minutes.

The maid came in and seated herself beside the open door, with the curtain drawn. Then Shireen turned her veiled face towards Zadig Bey.

May I ask when you last saw my husband?

About two months before the accident. I left Canton soon after the crisis began. He was amongst those who remained behind.

But why did he stay behind? she said. Can you tell me exactly what happened?

Zaroor Bibiji.

Zadig went on to explain that in March that year the Chinese authorities had launched an all-out campaign to end the inflow of opium into China. The Emperor had sent a new governor to Canton by the name of Commissioner Lin; shortly after coming to Canton he had given the foreign merchants of the city an ultimatum, ordering them to surrender all the opium on their ships. When they refused he had posted soldiers and boats around the foreign enclave in Canton, cutting it off completely from the outside. The merchants had been given plenty of food and they weren't ill-treated, but the pressure was such that they had ultimately agreed to surrender their goods. After that Commissioner Lin had allowed all but the most important merchants to leave: Bahram was one of those who had been required to remain in Canton. He had stayed on with his entourage in his house, in Canton's foreign enclave.

As you may know, Bibiji, said Zadig, the foreign enclave in Canton has thirteen 'factories' – or Hongs as they are called over there. They are not really factories – they are more like big cara-vanserais. Each factory has a number of different apartments and lodgings, which are rented out to foreign merchants according to their means. Bahram always stayed in the same house, in the Fungtai Factory, with his staff. That was where I went to see him.

How was he?

Zadig paused to clear his throat, and when he spoke again it was in the awkward, hesitant tones of someone who is reluctant to convey bad news.

Bibiji, I don't know if I should tell you this, but Bahram-bhai was in a very downcast state of mind when I last saw him. He seemed quite ill to be truthful. I asked his munshi what the matter was, and he said Bahram-bhai rarely left his daftar: apparently he had taken to spending his days sitting by the window, in a chair, watching the Maidan outside.

Grief was welling up in Shireen now; she began to knead the hem of her sari with her fingers.

It is hard for me to believe all this, Zadig Bey. My husband was a man who could never sit still.

He was weighed down by his worries, Bibiji, and it's not surprising. He stood to lose a great deal of money and of course he was worried about his debts.

Zadig coughed into his fist.

I am sure you know, Bibiji, that nothing mattered to him more than his family. That was his religion – his second religion, I should say.

Shireen reached under her veil to wipe away her tears: Yes, I know that.

Zadig continued: That Bahram-bhai's health suffered is not surprising. He was already quite weak when I saw him, but still, I could not believe it when I heard that he had fallen from the deck of the *Anahita*. That is the last thing one would expect of a man who had so much experience of sailing. And the worst part of it is that if he had only lived a little longer he would have known that his losses would be recouped.

Shireen was suddenly alert: You mean there will be compensation for the losses?

Zadig nodded: the foreign merchants had set up a fund, he said, to put pressure on the British government to take action against the Chinese. The merchants had all contributed a dollar for every chest of opium confiscated by Commissioner Lin. A large sum of money had been collected and sent to Mr William Jardine, in London. Jardine was the biggest of the China traders and he had been making very good use of the money; he had paid off many Members of Parliament and a horde of newspapermen. Nothing like that had ever been seen before – merchants and seths using their money to buy up the government! So many speeches had been made, and so many articles had been published that now every Englishman was convinced that Commissioner Lin was a monster. It was rumoured that on Jardine's advice the British government was preparing to send an expeditionary force to China. The seizure of the opium was to be their reason for declaring war so it was quite certain that they would demand reparations.

Here Zadig leant forward in his seat: You must make sure, Bibiji, he said, that Bahram-bhai's claims are not overlooked when it is time for the money to be divided.

Stifling a sob, Shireen explained that this was exactly the problem: she had no one to represent her; her brothers and sons-in-law were busy with their own affairs and could not spare the time for a year-long journey to China.

There is no one to fill my husband's shoes, Zadig Bey – no son, no heir, and in a way he himself is to blame.

What do you mean, Bibiji?

Shireen was now so distraught, and Zadig's presence was so comforting, that without quite meaning to she began to talk about something that she had never before spoken of with anyone.

Zadig Bey, there is something you perhaps do not know: my husband had some sort of problem, something physical, that prevented him from begetting a son. We were told this by a sadhu who had cured many such cases; he offered to cure my husband too, but he just laughed it off. If he had taken the matter more seriously maybe things would have been different now.

Having listened intently to Shireen's words, Zadig fell into a ruminative silence. When he spoke again it was in English. 'Can I ask you a question, Bibiji?'

Shireen glanced at him in surprise and he made a gesture of warning, inclining his head in the direction of the maid. 'May I ask you something?'

'Yes,' she said. 'Please. Go on.'

'May I ask if Bibiji ever leaves the house?'

The question took Shireen by surprise. 'Why do you ask?'

'Let me put it like this: how might it be possible to speak to you in private, away from the hearing of your family and servants?'

She thought quickly. 'Thursday is the anniversary of the death of Mrs O'Brien, my English tutor. I will go to Nossa Senhora da Gloria Church to light a candle for her.'

'The Catholic church in Mazagon?'

'Yes.'

'What time?'

She could hear her brother's footsteps in the corridor now and she lowered her voice. 'Eleven o'clock, in the morning.'

He nodded and lowered his voice to a whisper: 'I will be there.'

*

Tears came into young Kesri's eyes as he watched Bhyro Singh's cart receding into the distance: it was as if his own hopes were being ground to dust under its wheels.

No one had listened to the havildar's words with greater attention than Kesri: the arguments about caste and religion had mattered little to him, but his observations on weaponry and tactics had made a profound impression, re-moulding Kesri's soldierly aspirations; no longer did he want merely to be a bearer of arms; it was the Company's army, the havildar's battalion, that he wanted to join. The attractions of the old ways of fighting had been scorched from his head: this new kind of war was much more attractive. This was what real soldiering was about: winning, adapting, out-thinking the enemy, and through it all, also making money.

That his brother Bhim had turned down such an opportunity seemed almost beyond belief to Kesri. Later, when they were out of earshot of their father, Kesri said to Bhim: *Batavo* – tell me, why didn't you go with Havildar Bhyro Singh? Was it because you're afraid of Babuji?

No, said Bhim, with a shake of his head. It's Bhyro Singh I'm afraid of. I would rather go with a demon than with that man.

But why do you say that? Can't you see how good the Company's terms are?

Bhim merely shrugged and shuffled his feet.

If only, said Kesri bitterly, if only I'd been in your place.

Why? said Bhim. What would you have done? Would you have gone with Bhyro Singh?

Kesri nodded, blinking back the tears that had boiled up in his eyes. If I were in your place, said Kesri, I would not have wasted one moment. I would be on that cart right now, with them . . .

If the desire to leave had been a dull ache before, it was now a fever raging in Kesri's belly. The heat of it curdled the rich food he had eaten that morning and he vomited in full view of his family.

In a way this was a blessing, for it gave him an excuse to keep to himself. He spent the rest of the day lying on his mat and went to sleep early. Next morning, when it came time to leave for the

Naga sadhus' mela he could not stomach the prospect of having to sit aside as Bhim received blessings for his journey to Delhi: pleading illness, Kesri stayed at home.

After the others had left, Kesri ferreted out his father's stock of opium and tucked a pinch of it in his cheek. He soon fell asleep, and although he woke briefly when the others returned, he did not stir from his mat. Night had already fallen so no one came to rouse him and he soon drifted off again.

When next he woke it was very late and his brother was whispering in his year: *Uthelu Kesri-bhaiya*, wake up – come outside!

Still groggy from the opium, Kesri held on to his brother's elbow and followed him through the sleeping house, to the charpoys under the mango tree.

Listen, Kesri-bhaiya, Bhim whispered. You have to hurry – Bhyro Singhji is waiting for you.

Ka kahrelba? Kesri rubbed his sleepy eyes with his knuckles. What are you talking about?

Yes, said Bhim. It's true. I spoke to Bhyro Singhji at the mela today: I told him that you wanted to join the Company's army but that Babuji does not wish it and wouldn't give his permission. He said that Babuji's wishes do not concern him at all. Babuji is not his relative, and he doesn't care about his views. Calcutta is too far for Babuji to do anything about it.

Kesri was suddenly wide awake: So what did you say?

I told him that if you left without Babuji's permission you would have no money or equipment, or even a horse. He said that this too would not matter – a horse is not necessary because they are travelling to Calcutta by boat. As for other necessities, he will give you a loan, to be paid back later.

And then?

He said that if you are sure in your mind that you want to go, then you should meet him and his men at the ghat by the river, at dawn. That is when their boat will be sailing. They will be waiting for you. *Der na hoi* – don't be late.

Is this true? cried Kesri. Are you sure?

Yes, Kesri-bhaiya. Dawn is not so far off. If you start walking you will be there in time to meet them.

Desperate though he was to leave, Kesri was reluctant to leave his brother to face their father's wrath alone. But Bhim reassured him, saying that he would be all right, their father wouldn't know of his part in arranging Kesri's departure so he would suffer no consequences. To the contrary he might even stand to benefit, because with Kesri gone he might well be asked to stay on at home, which would suit him nicely. In all likelihood Kesri would himself be forgiven once he started sending money home.

Kesri had never known his brother to think anything through so carefully. Was it you who came up with this plan? he said. Did you think of it yourself?

Bhim shook his head. Me? No. It was Deeti. It was all her doing. She told me to seek out Bhyro Singhji and she told me exactly what to say to him. She thought of everything. Even this.

He handed over a cloth bundle: It is a spare dhoti and some sattu. That is all you'll need. Now hurry!

*

September 2, 1839
Guangzhou

Yesterday I was again invited to Compton's print-shop, to meet with Zhong Lou-si.

It was a nice afternoon so we were able to sit outside, in the courtyard, under the cherry tree. For a while we spoke of inconsequential things, and then the conversation came around again, to the question of a British attack on China. Zhong Lou-si was a little more forthcoming today; he gave me to understand that he has been aware of the rumours for some time.

After a while he cleared his throat and spoke in a very gentle voice, as if to indicate that he was broaching a difficult and delicate subject.

Tell me, Ah Neel, he said. You are from Ban-gala are you not?

Haih, Lou-si.

We have heard, Ah Neel, he continued, that in Ban-gala there are many who are unhappy with British rule. It is said that the people there want to rise up in rebellion against the Yinglizi. Is this true?

It took me some time to compose my thoughts.

Lou-si, I said, there is no simple answer to your question. It is true that there are many in Bengal who are unhappy with foreign rule. But it is also true that many people have become rich by helping the British: they will go to great lengths to help them stay in power. And there are others who are happy to have them just because they have brought peace and security. Many people remember the turmoil of past times and they don't want to go back to that.

Folding his hands in his lap, Zhong Lou-si leant forward a little, so that his eyes bored into mine.

And what about you, Ah Neel? What do you feel about the Yinglizi?

I was caught off-guard.

What can I tell you? I said. My father was one of those who supported the East India Company and I grew up under British rule. But in the end my family lost everything. I had to leave home and seek my living abroad. So you could say, that for me and my family British rule has been a disaster of our own making.

Compton and Zhong Lou-si were listening intently and they exchanged glances when I finished. Then, as if by pre-arrangement, Compton began to speak.

Ah Neel, Zhong Lou-si wants me to convey to you that he is mindful of the help you have given us in the past and very much appreciates it. Earlier this year, during the crisis with the foreign merchants, you gave us a lot of useful information and advice. He thinks that there is more that we can learn from you – and as I've told you he is now in charge of a bureau of translation and information-gathering.

He paused, to let his words sink in, and then continued: Zhong Lou-si wants to know if you would like to work with us. In the months ahead we may need someone who has a knowledge of Indian languages. You would be paid, of course, but it would mean that you would have to live here in Guangzhou for some time. And while you are working with us, you would have to cut off your relations with India and with foreigners. What do you think of this?

To say that I was astounded would not express a tenth part of what I felt: I suddenly realized that I could not answer Compton without picking sides, which is alien to my nature. I have always prided myself on my detachment – doesn't Panini say that this is essential for the study of words, languages, grammar? This too was why I had liked Compton from the first, because I had recognized in him a kindred soul, someone who was interested in things – and words – merely because they existed. But I realized now that I was faced with a choice of committing my loyalties not just to a friend but to a vast plurality of people: an entire country, and one with which I have few connections.

Faced with this prospect my life seemed to flash past me. I remembered my English tutor, Mr Beasley, and how he had guided and encouraged my reading; I thought of the pleasure and excitement with which I had read Daniel Defoe and Jonathan Swift, and the long hours I'd spent committing passages of Shakespeare to memory. But I remembered also the night I was taken to Alipore Jail, and how I had tried to speak English with the British sarjeant who was on duty there: my words made no more difference to him than the chattering of crows. And why should I have imagined otherwise? It is madness to think that knowing a language and reading a few books can create allegiances between people. Thoughts, books, ideas, words – if anything, they make you more alone, because they destroy whatever instinctive loyalties you may once have possessed. And to whom, in any case, do I owe my loyalties? Certainly not to the zamindars of Bengal, none of whom raised a finger for me when I was carted off to jail. Nor to the caste of my birth, which now sees me as a pariah, fallen and defiled.

To my father then, whose profligacy ensured my ruin? Or perhaps to the British, who if they knew that I was still alive, would hunt me to the ends of the earth?

And as against this, what Compton and Zhong Lou-si were asking of me was to share the one thing that is truly my own: my knowledge of the world. For years I've filled my head with things that serve no useful purpose; few indeed are the places where the contents of my mind might be regarded as useful – but as luck would have it, this is one of them. Somehow, in the course of my life, I have acquired a great trove of information about things that might well be useful to Compton and Zhong Lou-si.

In the end it was this – not loyalty, nor belonging, nor friendship – that swung the balance: the thought that someone as useless as myself might actually be of *use*.

I was silent for so long that Compton said: *Ah Neel, neih jouh mh jouh aa?* Will you do it or not? Or do you need more time to think?

I put down my teacup and shook my head: No, Compton; there is nothing more to think about. I am glad to accept Zhong Lou-si's offer; I'd be glad to remain here in Guangzhou. There is nowhere else I need to be.

He smiled: *Dihm saai* – it's all settled then?

Jauh haih lo! I said. That's right – it's all settled.

*

The costume that Mr Doughty had chosen for the Harbourmaster's Ball was a simple one: a couple of loosely draped sheets, held in place by a few pins and brooches.

'A toga, my boy! Best thing the Romans ever came up with! Nautches would be a nightmare without 'em.'

The sheets and other accoutrements had been laid out in Mr Doughty's dressing room. Following his host's lead, Zachary stripped down to his drawers and banyan and then wrapped the sheets around his body.

'Now bunnow that corner into a little flap and lagow it with a pin – yes, just like that. Shahbash!'

It took a good hour of tucking and folding before the toga was properly bunnowed and lagowed. By the time they stepped into the baithak-khana for a pre-dinner brandy-pawnee, Zachary and Mr Doughty were identically dressed, in costumes that were held together with pins and brooches and finished off, a little incongruously, with socks, garters and polished shoes.

At dinner they were joined by Mrs Doughty, who was dressed as Helen of Troy, in a flowing white robe and tinsel tiara. She blushed modestly when Zachary complimented her on her costume. 'Oh, I shall be cast into the shade by the other Beebees,' she said. 'Why, I believe Mrs Burnham has decided to be Marie Antoinette!'

Here Mr Doughty flashed Zachary a wink: 'I gather her corset alone is worth a tola or two of pure gold!'

After dinner they went downstairs and stepped into the hackery-gharry that Mr Doughty had hired for the night. It took them down Chowringhee to the Town Hall, on Esplanade Row, where the ball was to be held.

The building was one of Calcutta's grandest, with massive columns and an imposing set of stairs in front. Music was already pouring out of the hall's four wide doorways when the gharry stopped to deposit its passengers at the foot of the steps. As they joined the flow of guests, Mr Doughty whispered in Zachary's ear, pointing out the notables: 'That's the Jangi Laat, General Sir Hugh Gough and that over there is Lord Jocelyn, dancing attendance on Miss Emily Eden, the Laat-Sahib's sister.'

The Town Hall's main assembly room had been cleared for the ball: gas-lamps blazed all around it and the ceiling was strung with bunting and coloured ribbons. One of the walls was lined with curtained alcoves where fatigued dancers could catch a little rest, on a chair or a chaise-longue. At the far end of the hall sat the band of a Highland regiment, costumed in kilts and sporrans.

On reaching the entrance, Mr Doughty came to a halt and gestured expansively at the whirling dancers, the glittering band, the lavish decorations and the brilliant lighting: 'Take a dekko, Reid: it's not often that you'll see such a chuckmuck sight!' And Zachary had to admit that the spectacle was indeed as splendid as any he had ever seen.

Scarcely had he had time to look around when Mrs Doughty took hold of his toga-draped elbow. 'Come along now – I'd like to introduce you to a couple of lassies and larkins.'

'Oh but Mrs Doughty,' Zachary protested. 'I was going to ask you for the first dance.'

Mrs Doughty dismissed his offer with a laugh. 'You can do your duty by us Beebees later. The missy-mems would never forgive us if we monopolized you from the start.'

It took only a few introductions for Zachary to discover that many of the missy-mems at the ball had read about him in the *Calcutta Gazette* and were keen to know more about his travels. He found partners aplenty, and between the punch, the music and the dancing, he was soon having a rollicking time.

But even so, when Mrs Burnham stepped into the hall, Zachary did not fail to notice her entrance: she was dressed in an unusual and eye-catching costume – a wide silk skirt, with a very narrow waist and tight bodice. Her lavishly powdered hair was piled high on her head, like a great white beehive.

Mrs Burnham was immediately swept off to the floor by Mr Justice Kendalbushe. After that Zachary caught only occasional glimpses of her within the whirling throng: although she gave no sign of having noticed his presence his eyes kept straying in her direction. Yet he would not have ventured to ask her for a dance if Mr Doughty had not suggested it: 'Have you put your name on Mrs Burnham's dance-card yet? Did I tell you that it's the tradition at the Harbourmaster's Ball for the young Tars like you to give the Burra Beebees a whirl? You'd better look to your duties, my fine young chuckeroo.'

It was not until midnight that an opportunity arose: during a pause in the music, finding himself elbow-to-elbow with Mrs Burnham, Zachary bowed: 'I wonder if you would care to dance, Mrs Burnham?'

She looked at him with a frown and for a moment he thought he was going to be rebuffed. But then she shrugged in her usual imperious way. 'Well I do not see why not: it is the Harbourmaster's Ball after all, so one mustn't be too particular.'

The band was playing a polonaise and they began to circle sedately to its rhythm. Although the tempo was slow, Zachary noticed that Mrs Burnham was not breathing easily; he soon became aware also of an odd, creaking sound, like that of bone scraping on bone. He had been at pains so far not to look at Mrs Burnham too

86

closely, but a quick glance showed him that her bustline was even more ample than usual: he realized then that her corset had been pulled so tight that it was now creaking under the strain.

Averting his eyes, he said quickly: 'It's very crowded, isn't it?'

'Ekdum! A dreadful squeeze,' she agreed. 'And so frightfully hot! I can scarcely breathe.'

The band switched to a waltz now, forcing them to quicken their pace. After a few minutes of energetic whirling Mrs Burnham's face became so florid as to cause Zachary some concern. He was about to suggest a break when she pulled her hands free and clasped her palms to her chest.

'Oh Mr Reid! I'm suffocating!'

'Shall I lead you to a chair, Mrs Burnham?'

'Would you please?'

Zachary looked to his right and to his left, and finding no chair on either side he turned on his heel to see if there was one behind him. Instead he spotted a curtained alcove, only a step away: a tug on the curtain revealed an unoccupied chaise-longue inside, illuminated by a cluster of candles.

'There's a couch in here, Mrs Burnham.'

'Oh thank heaven . . . !' She hurried over to the chaise-longue and eased herself into it. 'Please Mr Reid – would you be kind enough to draw the purdah? I wouldn't care to be seen in this condition.'

'Of course.'

Drawing the curtain across the entrance, Zachary turned to look at Mrs Burnham's face: there were scarlet patches on her cheeks and she was still labouring to catch her breath.

'Would you like me to fetch someone? Mrs Doughty perhaps?' said Zachary. 'Maybe she could help?'

'Oh no, Mr Reid!' cried Mrs Burnham. 'I fear there isn't time. What if I have a seizure while you're gone?'

'Is it as bad as that?' said Zachary, in alarm.

'Yes, there is not a moment to lose.' She patted the spot beside her, on the chaise-longue. 'Could you come here for a minute, Mr Reid?'

'Certainly.'

After he had seated himself she turned her back to him: 'I would be most grateful, Mr Reid, if you could undo the buttons at the top of my gown. You will see there the end of a leather fastening. All you need do is to pull on it.'

Zachary was quite nervous now, but he swallowed his apprehensions. 'I'll do my best.'

Fortunately the alcove was brightly lit, so he had no difficulty in locating the cunningly concealed buttons of her gown. When he had tweaked them out of their silken eyes, the cloth parted, just as she had said, to reveal something that looked like a leather shoestring. He gave it a tug and there was a loud creak, followed by a sudden easing in Mrs Burnham's constricted posture.

'Oh thank you, Mr Reid! You've saved me – I'm most grateful!'

Now, as Mrs Burnham's bosom began to rise and fall, in a steady rhythm, Zachary's eyes were drawn over her shoulder, to the jewelled pendant that lay at the centre of her chest. On its tip, suspended just above the bustline of her gown, was a sparkling diamond: it pointed towards the triangle of velvety darkness where began the valley that ran between her breasts. The dark little hollow seemed to grow when she exhaled: Zachary's gaze was drawn so powerfully towards it that he unconsciously edged a little closer.

Meanwhile Mrs Burnham had braced herself for an even deeper intake of breath: squaring her shoulders, she suddenly flung back her arms, in the manner of a bird spreading its wings. The motion carried her right hand towards Zachary so that the tips of her fingers brushed lightly across his lap.

The touch was no more than the skimming of a feather, but it drew a muted shriek from Mrs Burnham's throat: 'Oho!'

Quicker than Zachary could move, she whipped around, with her eyes wide open. He too looked down now, following her gaze. He saw to his horror that his toga had parted to reveal his drawers: the fabric had risen through the folds of the white sheets, and was now standing poised over them, like a tent hoisted upon a pole.

He snatched at the cloth, hurrying to cover himself, but it was already too late. Mrs Burnham had collapsed against the armrest of the chaise-longue, with her eyes shut and her hands clasped to her chest.

'Oh! Oh! Oh! . . . Never did I think . . . ! Not in a hundred years . . . ! Oh my eyes! . . . If I could but wipe them clean . . . !'

Zachary had turned a colour that was closer to mauve than red; such was his shame that he could think of nothing to say except: 'Oh please, Mrs Burnham, please – I'm so very sorry.'

'Sorry? Is that all you can say?'

Zachary's throat had gone dry; if he could have fainted from mortification he would gladly have done so – but his treacherous body offered him no such relief.

'Look, Mrs Burnham,' he mumbled, 'it's just that I've been rather ill of late.'

She made a hissing sound and he began to fumble for words: 'You got'a understand, it just happens sometimes. It's like having a pet that sometimes slips its leash.'

'Indeed?' said Mrs Burnham. 'Is that what it is, a pet?'

Zachary was now incoherent with shame. 'I'm sorry . . .' He stood up and reached for the curtain. 'That's all I can say, Mrs Burnham – I'm sorry. I think I'd better go now.'

He had thought that she would be glad to see the last of him but he was wrong. She stopped him with an emphatic gesture. 'Absolutely not! I will not hear of it! I cannot let you go back to the dance, Mr Reid, my conscience will not allow it! If a woman of my age can cause your . . . your pet . . . to misbehave like that then I dread to think of the antics that may be provoked by some fetching young missy-mem. And can you imagine, Mr Reid, what would happen if some tender little pootlie were to have an encounter with your . . . pet? Why, I shouldn't be surprised if she went completely poggle and ran screaming out of here! Just imagine the scandal if people found out that we had sheltered you on our grounds! Why, I should not be surprised if we were *ruined*!'

She paused to catch her breath. 'No, Mr Reid, I cannot allow it: it would be criminal to set you loose in that ballroom in your condition. You are right to say that you are ill – you are indeed in the grip of an illness, a disease. It is my good fortune that I am neither impressionable nor in the first blush of youth. I am fortunate also in having the blood of a long line of soldiers in my veins. My grandfather fought at Wandiwash, I'll have you know, Mr Reid, and my father was at Assaye. I am a strong woman and will not flinch from my duty. While you are under my supervision you can do no harm; it is my civic obligation to see to it that you are safely removed from these premises. I will take it upon myself to escort you back to the budgerow. At once.'

Zachary was now completely crushed. Hanging his head like a chastened schoolboy, he mumbled: 'All right – let's go then.'

Turning her back on Zachary, Mrs Burnham issued a stern command. 'Would you kindly do up the buttons, Mr Reid? Mine, I mean.'

'Yes, Mrs Burnham.'

'Thank you, I'm sure.' She kept her eyes carefully averted from him as she rose to her feet: 'Mr Reid, are you in a fit condition to step outside? Is your pet under sufficient restraint?'

'Yes, ma'am.'

'Come then. Let us put a good face on it and make our way back to the carriage.'

With her head held high, she thrust the curtain aside and surged into the crowd. Zachary trailed meekly behind, with downcast eyes, and followed her out of the hall and into the road beyond, where her buggy was waiting.

They got in and seated themselves, as far apart as the breadth of the coach would allow. The horses set off at a brisk trot and for a while they sat in silence, looking out of their respective windows. Then Mrs Burnham said, in a voice that was quiet but firm: 'You are aware, are you not, Mr Reid, that you have brought this illness upon yourself?'

'I do not take your meaning, ma'am,' he responded.

'Oh do you not?' Now suddenly she turned to him, eyes flashing. 'If you think your affliction is a secret you are mistaken, Mr Reid. The world has been alerted to this scourge by a few brave doctors, and you should know that one of them is here right now in Calcutta, attempting to combat the disease. I have attended his lectures and am perfectly well aware, as indeed you should be, that the unnatural excitability of your . . . pet . . . is a direct consequence of certain practices . . . beastly practices . . . you will forgive me if I cannot bring myself to name them. Suffice it to say that the name evokes a continent of darkness and degradation. To soil our lips with the word is unnecessary in any case for you are not, I think, a stranger to those shores, are you, Mr Reid?'

A rush of anger took hold of Zachary now and he said: 'I do not know how you dare make such an accusation. On what basis, madam? And on what evidence?'

'The evidence of my own eyes, Mr Reid!' she declared. 'Or rather, of my spyglass. I saw you that day – the day of your arrival, when an attack of morbid excitation caused you to tear off your clothes and fling yourself into the river. You had perhaps imagined that you were unobserved when you were giving release to your condition, though why I can't think, since you were in full public view.'

Thunderstruck, he protested: 'But I wasn't ... you are quite wrong, madam. I can assure you that I was not ... doing what you think.'

'What were you doing then?' she challenged him.

'I'd be happy to tell you, Mrs Burnham,' he said. 'I was merely polishing a pin.'

'Hah!' She gave a derisive little laugh. 'That's what you choose to call it, do you? But might you not just as well have said that you were flaying a ferret? Or banging the bishop, for that matter?'

'No, no,' he protested. 'You don't understand, it was a belaying pin.'

'Which you were no doubt buttering?' She laughed again. 'You must not think me a gudda or a griffin, Mr Reid, for I assure you I am neither. I am a good deal older than you and am not easily foozled. I can assure you that the meaning of "jailing the Jesuit" and "jerquing the jamandar" are not lost on me. Why, I have even heard of "soaping the sepoy" and "saluting the subedar". But it doesn't matter, you know: they all add up to the same thing. And it really will not do, Mr Reid, to conceal from yourself the true causes of your unfortunate condition. It is but a disease and the first step towards a cure is to accept that you are a sufferer and a victim.'

Now she reached out and gave his arm a sympathetic pat. 'You need help, Mr Reid,' she said, in a softer voice, 'and I am determined to provide it. I am aware that you are a stranger to this country, friendless and alone – but you should know that while I am here, you will not lack for a pillar to lean upon. I will not begrudge the loss of a small measure of my own modesty in order to rescue you from sin and disease. Mine will be but a trifling sacrifice, compared to those of the missionaries who daily run the risk of being thrown into cooking pots by brutes and savages. For many years my husband has exerted himself to save wayward girls from lives of sin. It is only right that I should do the same, for you. I shall consult a specialist and arrange to meet with you, in private, so I can pass on his advice about a course of treatment.'

They had now reached the compound of the Burnham mansion. The coach came to a stop where a path branched off from the driveway, leading in the direction of the budgerow's mooring.

Zachary jumped out, mumbled a hasty good night, and was hurrying away, when Mrs Burnham leant out of the window: 'And remember, Mr Reid – your hands are for prayer. You must be strong. Together we will conquer the continent of darkness that lurks within you – you need have no fear on that score!'

Four

Kesri's first voyage down the Ganga, to the military cantonment at Barrackpore, was a slow one, in a three-masted pulwar that stopped at every small river port on the way. But it was the most eventful journey of his young life, and for years afterwards he would be haunted by his memories of it.

It was on this journey that he made the acquaintance of his brother-in-law to be, Hukam Singh, Deeti's future husband. He was a nephew of Bhyro Singh's and even though he was about the same age as Kesri, he had already served a couple of years in the Pacheesi. He was put in charge of the recruits, of whom there were six altogether, including Kesri.

Hukam Singh was tall and well-built, and he liked to use his physical presence to bully and intimidate those of lesser bulk. But Kesri yielded nothing to him, in either size or strength, and was not as deferential as the other recruits. This did not sit well with Hukam Singh, for he had grown used to lording it over the recruits. He quickly understood that Kesri was unlikely to fear him in the same way the others did so he took another tack, trying to wear him down with insults and spite, ridiculing his dark complexion and constantly reminding him that he had left home without a daam in his purse and was travelling on borrowed money. Nor were his insults always uttered to Kesri's face: Kesri learnt from the others that out of his hearing Hukam Singh had cast doubt on his origins and parentage, and was putting it about that he had been thrown out by his own family.

Through the first week, Kesri bit his lip and shrugged off the provocations. But then one day, Hukam Singh took it a step further: he threw his soiled langot and vest on the deck and ordered Kesri to pick them up and wash them.

Kesri was left with no option but to take a stand: he shrugged and turned away, which enraged Hukam Singh. Didn't you hear me? Go on. Do it!

Or what? said Kesri.

Or I'll tell my uncle, Havildar Bhyro Singh.

Go ahead, said Kesri.

See if I don't . . .

Hukam Singh went storming off to look for his uncle and shortly afterwards all the recruits were summoned to the pulwar's foredeck. This was where Bhyro Singh spent his days, enjoying the breeze. He was lying on a charpoy, taking his ease with a hookah, as the boat wallowed slowly along. He crooked a finger at Kesri, motioning to him to squat on his heels in front of him. Then he went on smoking, in silence, until the discomfort in Kesri's knees had begun to turn into real pain.

E ham ka suna tani? said Bhyro Singh at last: So what is this I hear? I'm told that you're beginning to get big ideas about yourself?

Kesri said nothing and nor did Bhyro Singh expect an answer.

I should have known, said the havildar, that a boy who'll run away with strangers, disobeying his own father, will never be anything but a cunt and chootiya.

Then all of a sudden his hand flashed out and slammed into Kesri's cheek.

Bhyro Singh's weight and size far exceeded Kesri's, for he was, after all, still a stripling. The force of the blow turned his head sharply to the side and sent him sprawling on the deck. There was a ringing sound in his ears and his nose was choked with the smell of his own blood. He brushed his hand across his face and saw that it was streaked with blood. He understood now that Bhyro Singh had hit him not just with his hand but also with the mouthpiece of his hookah, which had ripped open his cheek. Nothing that he had encountered as a wrestler had prepared him for this.

Then he heard Bhyro Singh's voice again: It's time for you to learn that the first rule of soldiering is obedience.

Kesri was still sprawled on the deck. He raised his head and saw that Bhyro Singh was standing over him. Now, the havildar drew one leg back and slammed his foot into Kesri's buttocks, sending him skidding over the deck-planks. As Kesri rolled away, the havildar followed behind, hitching up his dhoti with his hands. He kicked him again, and then again, aiming the last blow so that the nail of his big toe dug right into the crack of Kesri's buttocks, tearing through the thin folds of his dhoti and langot.

Kesri brushed his eyes again and then slowly raised himself to a crouching position. He could see the other recruits cowering in the background, their terrified eyes flickering between himself and the havildar, who was standing above Kesri, with the bloody mouthpiece of his hookah in one hand. His other hand was inside his dhoti, scratching his crotch.

Kesri realized then that his beating had no actual cause as such, but was a kind of performance, meant not just for him, but for all the recruits; he understood also that Bhyro Singh wanted them all to know that inflicting pain and humiliation was, for him, a kind of animal pleasure.

Then Bhyro Singh flung the mouthpiece of his hookah at Kesri: Go and clean this – wash your filthy blood off it. *Yaad rakhika* – and remember, this is just your first dose of this medicine. If it doesn't cure you then there'll be a lot more.

The beating left Kesri bruised in body – but it did not escape anyone that in enduring it he had also earned a minor victory: for at the end of it Bhyro Singh had not, after all, ordered him to wash his nephew's underclothing. Nor for that matter had Hukam Singh plucked up the courage to remind his uncle of his original complaint. Kesri took this to mean that Bhyro Singh had no great regard for his nephew. He concluded also that Hukam Singh both feared the havildar and desperately wanted to emulate him; this was the noxious soil in which the young sepoy's swagger and spite were rooted.

After this incident Hukam Singh's attitude towards Kesri changed in subtle ways. His barbs became more guarded and he seemed to accept that Kesri would not put up with being treated as a servant. At times he even seemed to acknowledge that Kesri was probably the most soldierly of the recruits.

As the end of the journey approached, the recruits became increasingly interested in learning about the life that awaited them. One thing that particularly intrigued them was the matter of their future *wardi*, or uniform. It was a great disappointment to them that the sepoys in their contingent were all travelling in civilian clothes – not once did any of them so much as unpack their military clothing.

Shortly before the end of the journey Hukam Singh gave in to the recruits' entreaties and agreed to show them his uniform: but on no account, said he, would he dress up like a doll for their benefit. If they wanted a demonstration one of them would have to volunteer to be a tailor's dummy.

Despite their earlier enthusiasm, none of the recruits stood up. Kesri was the only one who was of the right size but the bad blood between Hukam Singh and himself made him wary of stepping forward.

In the end it was Hukam Singh who beckoned to Kesri and told him to remove his dhoti and jama. When Kesri had stripped down, Hukam Singh pointed to his string-tied loincloth and said that a langot like that would do for now, but it was not to be worn with a uniform. It was all right to wear it off duty, with a dhoti and a regulation tunic called an ungah, but when in uniform you had to wear a knee-length undergarment known as a jangiah; the English officers insisted on it. If there was an inspection and you were caught wearing a langot then you'd find yourself in trouble.

Why? said the recruits.

Who knows? It's just one of their whims.

Then Hukam Singh went to fetch his knapsack and the boys saw that an almost-spherical brass lota was strapped on top of it: Hukam Singh told them that by regulation this utensil had to be of a size to carry exactly one seer of water, and it had to be tied on with a string, so that it could be lowered into wells if necessary. The lota had to be on your knapsack at all times, even in battle; if it wasn't properly secured you could get into a lot of trouble. On the parade ground officers loved nothing more than to see a gleaming string of lotas, lined up straight and glinting in the sun. At equipment inspections lotas were the first thing to be examined and punishments were freely handed out if they weren't properly polished.

Over the next few minutes, with the boys looking on eagerly, an extraordinary array of objects emerged from Hukam Singh's knapsack, one by one: an iron *tawa* to make rotis; a six-foot by three-foot durree to sleep on; pipeclay to apply on leather belts and footwear; a chudder to wrap up in at night. The total weight of a fully-packed knapsack, said Hukam Singh, was half a maund, about fifty pounds; it took a long time to get used to it.

Then came a folded garment.

Patloons – these are worn over the jangiah.

The pantaloons puzzled the recruits. The garment looked like a pyjama but they could see no drawstrings. Nor could Kesri understand how he was to climb into something with such a narrow waist.

Hukam Singh showed him how to unbutton the garment's waist – but even then Kesri had some difficulty in wriggling into it. He had never worn anything that clung so tightly to the skin and when he looked down he could hardly recognize his own legs. They seemed much longer than they were in a dhoti – and stronger too, because of the way the fabric hugged his muscles.

The recruits were watching wide-eyed and one of them said: But what do you do if you have to make water? Do you take the whole thing off?

No.

Hukam Singh showed them how the front flap of the pantaloons could be lowered by undoing a couple of buttons.

Kesri could not see that this was of much help. Flexing his knees, he said: But I'm still not able to squat.

When you're wearing patloons, said Hukam Singh, you can't squat to piss.

The recruits goggled at him: You mean you pass water standing up?

Hukam Singh nodded. It's difficult at first, he said. But you get used to it in time.

Reaching into the knapsack again, Hukam Singh produced the next item: it was a sleeveless vest that was fastened with ties, not unlike those that Kesri normally wore with his dhotis. Then came a bright flash of colour: a scarlet coattee.

This was called a koortee, Hukam Singh explained; it was similar to the red coat of an English trooper, except that they called it a 'raggy'. He showed Kesri how to get into it, by reaching back and thrusting his arms through the sleeves.

The front of the koortee was fastened with leather laces and when these were drawn tight Kesri had difficulty in drawing breath. He looked down at the jacket and saw that the rows of horizontal stripes on its front had come to life and were stretched like plumage across his chest. Studded between them were shining, metal buttons.

Are these made of gold?

No, said Hukam Singh. They're made of brass, but they're still expensive. If you lose one they'll dock your pay for eight annas.

Eight annas! This was more than Kesri had ever paid for an article of clothing. But the price did not seem excessive – if the buttons had been made of real gold they could not have been brighter or more becoming.

At the throat of the koortee there was another set of laces, and before tightening these Hukam Singh took out a bead necklace. He put it on Kesri so that the brightest beads were framed by the koortee's stiff, gold-edged collar.

The beads too were paid for by the Company, Hukam Singh explained. The officers insisted that sepoys wore them. If lost, two weeks' wages would be deducted from your salary.

With the laces at the neck drawn taut, the collar was like a yoke. When a *kamar-bandh* was tightened around his waist, it was as if he had been trussed like a chicken. Kesri could barely turn his head, and his chin was pushed up in such a way that his throat hurt when he tried to talk.

How could a man fight all bundled up like this?

Hukam Singh showed him how to stand erect, with his head tilted back.

When you're in a koortee, you can't let your head droop, he said. Your eyes have to be up and your shoulders have to be straight.

As he squared his back, Kesri caught a glimpse of the upcurved yellow extensions on the shoulders of the koortee. They were like the tips of an eagle's wings, and it seemed to Kesri that his shoulder had never seemed so broad or so strong.

All through this Kesri's head had been covered, as usual, by a cotton bandhna. His hair was tied up under it, in a coil.

Now Hukam Singh reached up and whipped off the bandhna so that his hair fell down over his shoulders. You'll have to cut your hair shorter, he said. The officers won't let you tie it in a coil under the topee.

Then, reaching into another bag, he produced a two-foot-high cylinder covered with shiny black cloth.

When the topee was placed on his head, Kesri's chin sagged into the points of the collar, almost choking him. It weighed as much as a pile of bricks.

Hukam Singh laughed at the expression on Kesri's face. Removing the topee from Kesri's head, he showed the recruits what was inside: hidden under the outer wrappings of cloth was a brass frame.

It's heavy when you're marching, he said, but you'll be glad of it in a fight. It protects your head.

The recruits took it in turn to try the topee and afterwards they fell silent: its weight conveyed to them more graphically than anything they had yet heard, how different the future would be from the life they had known before.

*

As the anniversary of her English tutor's death drew closer, Shireen grew increasingly nervous about her planned meeting with Zadig Karabedian. Thinking back, she could not understand why she had so readily agreed to meet with him – and that too without having the least idea of what he wanted.

Never before had she contemplated seeing a virtual stranger without the knowledge of her family. She knew that if any of her relatives – even her daughters – came to know of the assignation there would be much untoward talk. But nor could she forget how warmly Bahram had spoken of his old friend, Zadig Bey. To have him arrive on her doorstep was like being presented with a messenger from Bahram himself: it was almost as if he were reaching out to her from his grave.

Nossa Senhora da Gloria was only a short distance from the Mistrie mansion but to walk there, even with an escort of maids and khidmatgars, might have excited comment so Shireen decided to ask her brothers for a buggy instead. When the morning came she was glad she'd done so, for the sky was heavy with threatening banks of cloud.

The first shower came pouring down as the carriage was pulling up to the churchyard gate. Fortunately the syces had come prepared and one of them escorted Shireen down the path with an umbrella.

Leaving him to wait under the portico, she bought a few candles and made her way to the church's doorway. It was dark inside: the tall windows were shuttered against the rain and the interior was lit only by a few flickering lamps.

Shireen's face was covered with one of the loosely knitted shawls that she used as veils when she left the family compound. Now, looking through the shawl's apertures, she spotted a tall figure sitting in a pew halfway between the entrance and the altar. She advanced slowly up the nave, holding her veil in place with her teeth, and on drawing level she checked her step for just as long as it took to ascertain that the man was indeed Zadig Bey. Then she made a gesture to let him know who she was, and motioned to him to move further back, to a dark corner that was screened by a pillar. He answered with a nod and she proceeded towards the altar.

The candles had begun to shake in her hands now; she tried to calm herself as she lit them and stuck them in place. Then she turned around and went slowly to the spot where Zadig's tall figure sat hidden among the shadows. Seating herself at a carefully judged distance, she whispered through her veil: 'Good morning, Mr Karabedian.'

'Good morning, Bibiji.'

The rain had begun to drum on the church's metal roof now: it struck Shireen that this was a lucky thing because they were less likely to be overheard.

'Please, Zadig Bey,' she whispered. 'I do not have much time. My brother's coach is waiting outside – you can imagine the scandal if I am found here, with you. Please tell me why you wanted to meet me.'

'Yes, Bibiji . . . of course.'

She could hear the uncertainty in his voice, and when he fell silent she prompted him again: 'Yes? What is it?'

'Please forgive me, Bibiji,' he mumbled. 'It is a very difficult thing to relate, a very personal thing, and it is especially hard . . .'

'Yes?'

'Because I do not know who I am speaking to.'

'What do you mean?' she said in surprise. 'I don't understand.'

'Well, Bibiji, I have seen pictures of you in Bahram-bhai's rooms in Canton – yet I do not think I would recognize you if I saw you on the street. And there are some things that are hard to speak of with someone whose eyes you have never seen.'

Shireen could feel her face growing flushed. As she fumbled with her shawl, she had a vivid recollection of another time when she had parted her veil to show her face to a stranger: it was on the day of her wedding. Sitting on the dais, she had been so overcome with shyness that she had been unable to raise her head: it was as if a great weight had suddenly descended on her. No matter how hard she tried, she could not make herself look into the eyes of the man with whom she was to share her life. In the end her mother had been forced to reach over and tilt her head back. Years later Shireen had herself done the same for both her daughters – yet now it was as if she were once again a girl, presenting her face to a man for the first time.

There was something unseemly about this train of associations and she forced herself to put them out of her mind. Parting her veil, she held Zadig's gaze for just long enough to see his eyes widening in surprise. She had already turned away when she heard him exclaim, in surprise: *Ya salaam!*

'What is the matter, Zadig Bey?'

'Forgive me – I'm sorry. I did not expect . . .'

'Yes?'

'That you would look so young . . .'

She stiffened. 'Oh?'

He coughed into his fist. 'The pictures I saw in Bahram-bhai's rooms – they do not do you justice.'

She gave him a startled glance and drew the shawl over her face again. 'Please, Zadig Bey.'

'I am sorry,' he said. 'That was not right – *maaf keejiye* – please forgive me.'

'It's not important. But please. You must be quick now. Tell me why we are here – why did you want to speak to me in private?'

'Yes of course.'

With great deliberation he folded his hands in his lap and cleared his throat. 'Bibiji, I do not know if what I am doing is right – what I have to say is not easy.'

'Go on.'

'Bibiji, you remember when you were talking to me the other day, about Bahram-bhai and how he had left no son to fill his shoes?'

'Yes, I do.'

'I felt that there was something you should know. That is why I asked to meet you here.'

'Go on.'

She heard him swallow and saw the Adam's apple bobbing in his thin, leathery neck.

'You see, Bibiji – what I wanted to tell you is that Bahram-bhai *did* have a son.'

The announcement made no immediate impression on her: the sound of the rain was so loud now that she thought she had misheard.

'I think I did not hear you properly, Zadig Bey.'

He shifted uncomfortably in his seat. 'Yes, Bibiji, what I say is true. Bahram-bhai was the father of a boy.'

Shireen shook her head and uttered the first words that came to her, in a rush. 'No, Zadig Bey, you do not understand. What you are saying is impossible. I can assure you of this because we once visited a man who knows of these things, a renowned Baba, and he explained that my husband would not be able to have a son without undergoing a long treatment . . .'

She ran out of breath and fell silent.

Zadig spoke again, very softly. 'Bibiji, forgive me, but I would not say it if I were not certain. Bahram-bhai's son is a young man now. He has had many difficulties over the years. That is one of the reasons why I thought you should know about this.'

'It's not true! I know it's not.'

Under the cover of her shawl, Shireen dug her fingers into her ears. They felt unclean, defiled, and she was filled with disgust at herself for having agreed to meet this man – this man who felt no qualms about uttering such obscenities in a place of God. She thought she might vomit if she continued to sit where she was, within touching distance of him. Struggling to her feet, she said, in as steady a voice as she could muster: 'I am sorry, sir. You are a liar – a foul, filthy liar. You should be ashamed of yourself, telling such lies about a man who believed you to be his friend.'

Zadig said nothing and sat frozen on the pew, with his head lowered. But as she was pushing past him, she heard him whisper: 'Bibiji, if you don't believe me, ask Vico. He knows everything. He will tell you about it.'

'Please,' she responded, 'we have nothing more to say to each other.'

It occurred to her that he might try to follow her outside, in which case he would be seen by the Mistrie coachmen and word would get back to her family.

'If you have any honour at all,' she said, 'you will not move from here until I am gone.'

'Yes, Bibiji.'

To her relief he stayed seated as she hurried down the nave and out of the door.

*

September 30, 1839
Honam

Only after I had accepted Zhong Lou-si's offer did I begin to worry about the practicalities: what would I do about lodgings? About food? Working for Mr Coolidge was very dull but the job did at least provide me with a place to sleep and eat. What was I to do now?

I decided to speak to Asha-didi, the proprietress of the only Achha eatery in Canton: she is the kind of woman who is known here as an 'Ah Je' – someone who can manage everything. Although she is from Calcutta's Chinese community, Asha-didi knows many people here since she is Cantonese by origin. Her husband, Baburao (I've tried to get into the habit of using their Chinese names but it's difficult since they usually speak Bangla with me), also has extensive connections among the boat-people of Canton: I thought for sure they'd know of rooms for rent. And I was not wrong: no sooner had I mentioned my problem than Asha-didi said that there was a spare room in her own place of residence – the house-boat that she and Baburao share with their children and grandchildren. It is moored on the other side of the Pearl

River, at Honam Island. Asha-didi warned me that the room was being used as a storage space and would need to be cleaned out. I told her that I didn't mind in the least.

But it turned out that the room was being used as a poultry coop as well as an attic. I was completely unprepared for the blizzard of feathers and chicken-shit that was set a-whirl by the opening of the door. When the storm subsided, I saw that the birds were roosting on stacks of oars, yulohs, battens, sprits, rudders, sweeps and coils of bamboo-rope. I thought to myself: How could anyone possibly live here? There isn't even a bed.

The look on my face made Asha-didi laugh. *Bhoi peyo na*, don't worry, she said in Bangla (I have yet to get over the wonder that seizes me when this thin, brisk woman, whose clothes and manner are indistinguishable from that of other Canton boatwomen, addresses me in Bangla, and that too in the dialect of Calcutta – it seems marvellous to me, even though I know very well that it should not be. After all, her family home in Calcutta was separated from mine by only a few streets).

Yet, in some ways Asha-didi is completely Cantonese: she doesn't like to waste words or time. Minutes after she had shown me the room, she was busy seeing to its cleaning and refurbishment. A poultry-keeper tied the chickens into bunches, by their feet, and carried them away like clusters of clucking coconuts. Then a half-dozen of her sons, grandsons and daughters-in-law got to work, scraping feathers and excrement off the deck, mopping the bulwarks and moving lumber and equipment. Soon, bits of furniture began to appear: chairs, stools and even a charpoy that had travelled all the way to Canton from Calcutta.

Only after the furniture had been arranged did Asha-didi open the door at the far end of the room. That was when I learnt that the bedroom had a little appendage. There's a little *baranda* here, said Asha-didi. Come and have a look!

The 'veranda' was heaped with rotting beams, spars and ropes. I stepped out gingerly, expecting another unwelcome surprise – geese maybe, or ducks. Instead, the panorama of the city burst upon me like a breaking wave.

It was a clear day, and I could see all the way to Wu Hill, the ridge that overlooks Guangzhou; I could even see the great five-storey edifice at the hill's peak: the Zhenhai Lou or Sea-Calming Tower. In the foreground, on the other side of the river, was the foreign enclave; the channel in between was crowded with vessels of many shapes and sizes: Swatow trading junks could be seen towering over rice-boats and ferries; and everywhere one looked there were circular coracles spinning from one bank to another (it is in these that I cross the river every day, for the price of a single cash-coin).

I could not have asked for more: to step out on that veranda is to have a perpetual tamasha unfolding before one's eyes!

At night, when darkness falls on the city, the river comes alive with lights. Many of Canton's famous 'flower-boats' float past my veranda, lanterns blazing, leaving behind sparkling wakes of music and laughter. Some of the flower-boats have open-sided terraces and pavilions, in which women can be seen entertaining their clients with songs and music. Watching them I can understand why it's said of Canton that 'young men come here to be ruined'.

The location too could not be better. The houseboat is moored by the shore of Honam Island, which is much quieter than the heavily built-up northern side, where the city of Guangzhou lies. The contrast between the two banks is startling: the north shore is densely settled, with as great a press of buildings as I have ever seen. On this side we have mainly woods and farmland, along with a few hamlets, monasteries and large estates. The surroundings are peaceful, yet Compton's print-shop is within easy reach.

The houseboat is itself a constant source of diversion. Asha-didi's sons sometimes come to chat with me, and often the talk turns to Calcutta. Most of them were very young when their family left Bengal to return to Guangdong but they've all preserved a few memories of the city. There's not one among them who doesn't remember a few words of Bangla and Hindustani and they all have a taste for masala. The little ones – Baburao and Asha-didi's grandchildren – also ask about Calcutta and Bengal. The strength of their ties to India is surprising – I think it must have something to do with the fact that their grandfather and grandmother are buried by the Hooghly River, in the Chinese cemetery at Budge-Budge. This creates a living bond with the soil, something that is hard to understand for those such as myself, whose forefathers' ashes have always been scattered on the Ganga.

Of Asha-didi's children the one who lived longest in Calcutta is their eldest daughter, who everybody calls Ah Maa. She is perhaps a year or two older than me and has never married. She is very thin and her face has more lines than is merited by her age. Much like the unmarried *aiburo* aunts of Bengal, she looks after the young children and takes on much of the responsibility for the running of the household. She is never idle for a moment, yet there is something a little melancholy about her. When I first arrived she was the only member of the family who seemed to resent my presence. She would never speak to me or even look at me; instead she would avert her face in the way that a Bengali woman might do with a stranger. This struck me as odd, because here in Canton women of the boat-people community do not keep purdah, or bind their feet, or observe any of the constraints that prevail among other Chinese. Nor indeed does she display any shyness in dealing with other strangers.

I had the feeling that the sight of me had re-opened some old wound. And just as it sometimes happens with an old scab, she seemed unable to ignore me. Sometimes she would bring me food from Asha-didi's kitchen-boat. She would hand it over without a word: I could tell that there was something about me that troubled her but I could not think what it might be.

But two days ago she began to speak to me in Bangla, haltingly, as though she were dredging pebbles out of the silt of memory. Her 'Calcutta name', she told me, was 'Mithu'. Then she told me her tale: as a young maiden in Calcutta she had come to know a Bengali boy, a neighbour. But both families had objected; her parents had tried to marry her off to a man from Calcutta's Chinese community, but she, being stubborn, had refused him.

And so the years had gone by until it was too late for her to marry.

*

The night before their journey's end, the recruits stayed up late. By this time they had developed strong bonds with each other. They were all of roughly the same age – in the mid-teens – and none of them had been away from their families before.

A couple of the boys were from remote inland villages and had seen even less of the world than Kesri. The most rustic of them all was a weedy fellow by the name of Seetul, and he was regarded as the clown of the group.

That night they talked about what lay ahead and what it would be like to be under the command of English officers. Seetul was the one who was most concerned about this. One of his relatives, he said, had recently visited a town where there were many Angrez. On his return he had told them a secret about the sahib-log – white-folk – something that could not on any account be repeated.

What is it?

Kasam kho! Promise you won't tell anyone?

After they had all sworn never to tell, Seetul told them what his relative had said: the sahib-log's womenfolk were fairies – they each had a pair of wings.

When the others scoffed he told them that his relative had seen proof of this with his own eyes. He had seen a sahib and memsahib going by in a carriage. Not only was she dressed in clothes that were as colourful as a fairy's wings, but when the carriage came close everyone saw, with their own eyes, that the sahib had put his hands on her shoulder, to prevent her from flying away. There could be no doubt that she was a fairy – a *pari*.

Kesri and the others laughed at Seetul's rustic gullibility – but the truth was that they too were apprehensive about encountering the sahib-log; they had also heard all kinds of stories about them, back in their villages.

But the next day, when they arrived at Barrackpore, the novelty of seeing the sahib-log paled before the utter strangeness of everything else. Even before the boat docked they spotted a building that was like nothing they had seen before – a palace overlooking the river, with peacocks on the roof, and a vast garden in front, filled with strange, colourful flowers.

Hukam Singh sneered at the awed expressions on their faces. The Barrackpore bungalow was only a weekend retreat for the Burra Laat – the English Governor-General: it was a mere hut, he said, compared to the Laat-Sahib's palace in Calcutta.

Once ashore the recruits didn't know which way to look – everything was a novelty. Marching past a high wall they heard sounds that made their blood run cold: the roars and snarls of tigers, lions and leopards. In their villages they had heard such sounds only from a distance. Here the animals seemed to be right next to them, ready to pounce. The only thing that prevented them from taking to their heels was that they didn't know which way to run.

Hukam Singh laughed at their panic-stricken faces and told them they were chootiya gadhas to be scared – these animals were just the Burra Laat's pets. They were kept in cages, on the other side of the wall.

Then they came to the cantonment and the sight took their breath away. Everywhere they looked there were shacks, tents and long, low structures made of wood; in between were large parade grounds, where thousands of soldiers were at drill. Sahib-log could be seen everywhere, drilling, marching and lounging about, in uniforms of astonishing colours. But the most remarkable thing about them – the thing that made the recruits' jaws drop – was that none of them had beards or moustaches. Their faces were completely smooth, their cheeks and lips as hairless as those of boys or women.

The recruits' journey ended at an empty tent where they were told to wait.

At some point Seetul slipped away. The others were busy talking about the sights they had seen that morning and no one noticed his absence: their first inkling of it came when there was a sudden outburst of shouts, yells and shrieks, somewhere nearby. They ran out to see what had happened – and there was Seetul, being dragged towards them by a sentry.

It turned out that Seetul's stomach was upset and he had felt an urgent need to relieve himself. Not knowing where to go, he had decided to do what he would have done in his village: with a lota-ful of water in hand, he had set off to find a secluded place. After some searching he had found a convenient gap in a dense wall of greenery. Keeping a careful watch for passers-by, he had pulled up his dhoti; lowering himself to his haunches, he had backed into the gap and let fly.

Unfortunately for Seetul the greenery happened to be the hedge of a colonel-sahib's garden. Worse still, his performance had intruded upon a ladies' picnic.

The burden of the blame fell on Hukam Singh, who had neglected to show them where the latrines were. He would later make Seetul pay dearly for his error, but now, on the sentry's orders, he took the recruits straight to the *pakhana*: this too was an astonishing sight and it made them wonder whether their bowels would ever move again.

There were a few long ditches, and over them, platforms with rows of holes. A number of men could be seen, squatting on the platforms, lined up next to each other, like crows on a rope. The stench was overpowering and the rhythmic plopping sound that rose from the ditch was a constant reminder of what might happen to a squatter who lost his balance.

Back in their villages the recruits were accustomed to going out to the fields and squatting in the open, with a breeze on their faces; moreover, even though they often went in twos or threes, for mutual protection, there was usually some greenery to afford each of them a little privacy.

It made them squirm to think of being lined up like that, next to one another – but within a day or two they got used to it and quickly absorbed the unspoken protocols of the latrines, whereby certain rows were always reserved for seniors at busy times of the morning: recruits were the last in precedence.

On their third day at the depot, Bhyro Singh appeared in person at the door of their hut. This was the first time the recruits had seen him in uniform. With his height extended by his helmet and his shoulders broadened by his epaulettes, he seemed twice his size.

They followed him to a building that looked like a daftar: he told them to wait on the veranda and went inside. When he came out again, he was furious to find the recruits sitting in the shade. He berated them for sitting without permission and swore that they'd get a beating if they ever did it again: a Company sepoy could never sit unless he was expressly told to.

They jumped to their feet, unnerved, and stood rigidly upright, shoulder to shoulder, not daring to move.

In a while, an English officer appeared with a big stick in his hands. This further unnerved the recruits because they thought they were going to be beaten as a punishment for sitting down. But it was only a measuring stick, with a notch on it. The officer went down the line with it, making sure that they all stood taller than the mark.

Kesri could not stop staring at the officer's smooth, beardless face. He had nurtured his own moustache so carefully, from the day when the first hairs appeared on his lip, that he found it hard to believe that any man would choose to shave off something so precious. But when it was his turn to be measured he saw that the officer's lack of hair was indeed a matter of choice rather than a curse of nature – there was a distinct stubble on his cheeks, so there could be no doubt that he regularly shaved his face.

After they had all been measured, the officer sat down at a desk, picked up a pen and began to write. Kesri, like most of the other recruits, knew how to read and write in the Nagari script, but only with a slow and deliberate hand. The speed at which the officer's pen flew over the paper was dazzling to his eyes.

The sheet of paper was then handed to Bhyro Singh who now led them to another daftar. Kesri happened to be at the head of the line, so when they got there he was the first to be picked out. Bhyro Singh beckoned to him to step forward and left the others to wait where they were. He then led Kesri to a room that smelled pungently of medicines. An English doctor was waiting inside with two memsahibs, dressed in white. As soon as Kesri had stepped in, Bhyro Singh shut the door, leaving him alone with the doctor and the two women.

The doctor now spoke to Kesri in Hindustani and told him to remove all his clothes – not just his jama but also his dhoti and langot.

At first Kesri thought he had mistaken the doctor's words. He could not imagine that it would enter anyone's mind to ask him to strip himself naked in front of strangers – of whom two were women! But the doctor then repeated what he had said, in a louder, more insistent voice, and one of the women spoke up too, loudly dhamkaoing Kesri and telling him to obey the doctor and take off his clothes.

Kesri had a sudden recollection of his father's warnings about the Company's army and how those who joined it would lose their dharma. He realized now that this was true and was assailed by a terrible onrush of remorse for not having heeded his father's words.

As these thoughts were flashing through his head, the doctor-sahib took a step towards him. It seemed to Kesri that the doctor was about to attack him and tear off his clothes. At that instant he made up his mind. He spun around, threw himself at the door, and flung it open. Racing past Bhyro Singh and the recruits, he sprinted towards the cantonment's bazar.

If he could lose himself in the crowd, he reckoned, he would be able to make his escape. And then whatever happened, would happen; if it came to that, he could always go back home.

He ran as he had never run before. He could hear Bhyro Singh's voice behind him but he knew that he was rapidly outpacing the havildar.

But just as he reached the bazar, who should appear in front of him but Hukam Singh, with two other sepoys? He saw them too late to slip past: they threw him to the ground and held him down.

Although the blood was pounding in Kesri's head he could hear Bhyro Singh's heavy tread.

Haramzada! Bahenchod!

Bhyro Singh was panting as he spat out the curses: Bastard, you think you can get away from me? Chootiya, haven't I loaned you money and fed you for a month? You cunt, you think I'm the kind of man you can steal from and get away . . . ?

Kesri felt the havildar's massive hand seizing the back of his neck. It pulled him to his feet and then lifted him off the ground. Then Bhyro Singh's other hand took hold of his dhoti and langot and tore them off.

A crowd had gathered now. Bhyro Singh hoisted up Kesri's writhing body and turned it from side to side, showing the onlookers his underparts.

Here, have a look – this is what the haramzada thought he would hide.

Then he flung Kesri to the dust and gave him a kick.

You're no better than a runaway dog, Bhyro Singh spat at him. Don't think you can cheat me like you did your father. You have no one to turn to now, and nowhere to go. This is your jail and I am your jailer – you had better get used to it.

The bitter truth of the havildar's words dawned on Kesri as he was covering himself with his retrieved clothes – with neither friends nor kin to come to his aid, he had become a kind of pariah as well as a prisoner. Only now did Kesri grasp that in choosing to run away from home, with Bhyro Singh, he had abandoned not just his family and his village, but also himself – or rather the person he had once been, with certain ideas about dignity, self-containment and morality.

For Kesri the significance of this incident was not diminished by the discovery that many recruits had suffered similar, and even worse, humiliations at the hands of NCOs. One of the lessons he took from it was that every soldier had two wars to fight: one against enemies on the outside and the other against adversaries on the inside. The first fight was fought with guns, swords and brawn; the second with cunning, patience and guile.

The next few months were a blur of beatings, dhamkaoings and sleeplessness as the recruits were drilled into shape. Along the way there were many moments when Kesri might have run away had he not been so vividly reminded that he had nowhere to go and no one to turn to. But then at last came a day when the first four Articles of War, on the subject of desertion, were read out to Kesri and his cohort of recruits, after which they were administered the oath of fidelity in front of the regimental colours. From then on, even though they were on probation for one month more, without any salary or battas, things became a little easier because the recruits were now considered full-fledged members of the Pacheesi.

It was in that month of continuing pennilessness, when the new sepoys had to subsist on an allowance of two annas per day, that Kesri discovered another, sweeter lesson in the memory of his humiliation by Bhyro Singh: he learnt that unexpected rewards were sometimes to be found amidst the rubble of defeat.

One day while walking past the cantonment's 'red' area – the 'Laal Bazar' – he heard a girl's voice calling to him: Listen, you there, listen!

The voice was coming from an upstairs window, in a tumbledown house that was known to be a *lal kotha* – a 'red house'. There was a window ajar, on the floor above. When he stepped up to the house, it opened a little wider, revealing the painted face of a young girl. She smiled and beckoned to him to come up.

He climbed up a narrow staircase and found her waiting at the top.

What's your name?

Kesri Singh. And yours?

Gulabi. You were the one, weren't you, who was trying to run from Havildar Bhyro Singh that day?

He flushed and retorted angrily: What's it to you?

Nothing.

She smiled and led him into a room where there was a charpoy in one corner.

Once inside he was overcome with panic; his many years of training in self-control was suddenly at war with his desires in a way that he had never experienced before. In his head there was an insistent voice of warning, telling him that to discard the disciplines of wrestling would come at a cost; some day he would pay a steep price for his pleasure.

But he was helpless; flattening his back against the door, he said: *Samajhni nu?* You understand, no? I have no money.

He was half-hoping that she would tell him to be gone, but instead she smiled and lay down on the charpoy. It doesn't matter, she said. You can pay some other time. You're not going anywhere and nor am I. We are both *fauj-ke-ghulam* – slaves of the army.

Her face was delicately shaped, with rounded curves that were echoed by her nose ring. In her mouth there was a hint of the redness of paan and it made her lips look so full that she seemed to be pouting.

Why are you just standing there? she said. Rising from the bed, she went up to him and unfastened the waist flap of his trowsers and pulled on the drawstrings of his jangiah.

Young as she was, she seemed to know his uniform as well as he did: he looked down at himself and saw that his body was bare exactly from the bottom of his belly to the middle of his thigh.

She seemed to think that this was all the unclothing that was necessary, and lay down again – but this only confused him further and he stood where he was, with his hands clapped over his groin.

A frown appeared on her face now, as if to indicate that she could not understand why he was still standing motionless by the door. She reached out, caught hold of his hand and pulled him towards her. He could take only small steps, because his trowsers were now snagged around his knees, and finally he just toppled over, collapsing on the bed.

She smiled bemusedly: it was as if she had never before encountered a man who did not know what to do, and was hard put to believe that such a species existed.

Her face grew serious as she helped him untangle his legs. *Pahli baar?* First time?

He was about to lie, but then he saw that she was not asking in a belittling way, but only because it had not occurred to her that a man, a sepoy, could be confused and uncertain in these matters.

She began to help him, guiding his hands into her gharara. But his fingers were soon lost in her skirts – he had never imagined that there could be so much cloth and so many folds in a single garment. In his dreams this part had always been easy.

And even when his hands at last found their way to her limbs, nothing was as he had expected: those parts that he had glimpsed when women were bathing, or relieving themselves in the fields, seemed completely different now that they were joined together in another human being.

At some time they both realized that they would never again be able to recapture the amazement and wonder of this moment – and even for her, who had already grown accustomed to being with men, his discovering hunger came as a surprise, so that she seemed to see her own body in a new light. At a certain moment she found, to her shock, that she was naked – she would tell him later that she had never been in such a state with a man before; it was something the other women would have despised her for had they known – but that day she was heedless of all restraint and this became a bond between them, for now they both knew a secret about one another.

For many weeks after that day Kesri could not stop thinking about Gulabi. He went to her so often that his credit with the house ran out. When Seetul and the other recruits laughed and said, *Piyaar me paagil ho gayilba?* Have you become mad with love? he did not deny it.

For a long time it was a torment to him that Gulabi was visited by other men. But eventually he grew used to it and it even gave him a grim kind of pleasure to know that her other clients were being cheated, because none of them would ever have from her what he had.

It was not till some years had passed that she told him why she had waved to him from the window on the day when they met.

You remember, Kesri, that time when you were stripped by Bhyro Singh? You were not the only one to be beaten that day.

Who else then?

After he had finished with you, he came to me – he took me into a room and after he had done what he came for, he slapped me and hit me.

But why?

She made an uncomprehending gesture. *Kya pata?* What do I know? But he's done it to some other girls too. It seems to give him pleasure.

Kesri thought about this for a bit and it made him shudder.

I swear, Gulabi, he said. The day that Bhyro Singh dies I'll give away a maund of sweets – that is if I don't kill him myself first.

She laughed: Don't forget to give me some of those sweets. I can't wait to taste them.

*

For several days Zachary neither saw nor heard from Mrs Burnham: so complete was the silence that it seemed as though she had forgotten about arranging a private meeting with him. But just as he was growing accustomed to the idea that the meeting would never happen, a khidmatgar arrived with a parcel. There was an envelope inside, sitting on top of a fat book.

October 10, 1839

Dear Mr Reid

I offer you my sincerest apologies for my prolonged silence. The news from China has been very disquieting of late and we have all been much preoccupied. But you must not imagine that I have allowed the affairs of the World to drive from my mind the Pledge I had made to you. Nothing could be further from the truth. You and your Sufferings are constantly on my mind: you could even say that I am haunted by them.

You will remember that I mentioned a doctor who has made a special study of your Affliction. His name is Dr Allgood and he has been sent here from England to attend to the lunatics in the Native and Europeans-Only Asylums (lunacy being, of course, a prime symptom of your Malady, in its more advanced stages). Not only is Dr Allgood one of the world's leading authorities on your Disease, he has dedicated his life to its eradication. It is because of his Crusade that the people of this city have come to be alerted to the spreading Epidemic.

It so happens that I had helped to arrange a few Lectures for Dr Allgood and am therefore well acquainted with him. Wanting to profit from his wisdom I had sought an Interview but this proved difficult to obtain for the Doctor is exceedingly busy with the conduct of his Researches. Yet, despite his many preoccupations, the doctor was kind enough to grant me some time yesterday and it is in order to communicate his Advice that I have now picked up my quill to write to you.

You will no doubt be interested to learn that your Condition is one of the principal areas of inquiry in modern medicine: it has come to be recognized as one of the chief causes of human debility. It is thought that the costs of the Disease, physical and economic, are of such magnitude that the Nation that first conquers it will thereby secure its position as the world's Dominant Power. You can imagine then the urgency with which a remedy is being sought – yet, despite the best efforts of a great number of Doctors and Men of Science, there has as yet been little Progress. Dr Allgood assures me that there is every reason to hope that a Cure – perhaps even a Vaccination – will soon be found, but alas, none has yet been discovered. This was of course, a great disappointment, for I had hoped that he would be able to prescribe some soothing Tonics, Drugs or Poultices to help in combating your Seizures – but it appears that at present the best hope of effecting a cure lies in educating Patients and making sure that they become fully cognizant of the terrible consequences of this Disease.

This being the prescribed mode of treatment, I shall endeavour to obtain books and other materials for you. Enclosed herewith you will find the first volume in your proposed course of Study. Bookmarks have been inserted in the chapters that particularly require your attention, and I urge you to commit these passages to memory. The Doctor says that it is most necessary in such courses of Study, that occasional Tests and Examinations be administered to make sure that the Patient has fully absorbed the prescribed lessons. To that end I will endeavour to arrange a private meeting to test you on your progress.

In concluding this missive, I urge you not to lose hope: while it is undoubtedly true that the road ahead is long and arduous, there is every reason to believe that with persever-ance, faith and resolve you will succeed in finding your way to a Cure. And you should know that you are not alone – I will do everything in my power to speed you on your Path.

Yours &c.
C. Burnham

p.s. In order to preserve the confidentiality of our Collaboration it may be best to destroy this note immediately.

The book that accompanied the note was called *Elements of Physiology* and it was by a professor of medicine at the University of Paris, one Anthelme Balthasar Richerand. It was a weighty tome, but fortunately the sections recommended for Zachary's scrutiny were quite short and had been clearly bookmarked.

The first of these chapters was a detailed study of the case of a fifteen-year-old shepherd boy in France who

> became addicted to onanism, and to such a degree, as to practise it seven or eight times in a day. Emission became at last so difficult that he would strive for an hour, and then discharge only a few drops of blood. At the age of six and twenty, his hand became insufficient, all he could do, was to keep the penis in a continual state of priapism. He then bethought himself of tickling the internal part of his urethra, by means of a bit of wood six inches long, and he would spend in that occupation, several hours, while tending his flock in the solitude of the mountains. By a continuance of this titillation for sixteen years, the canal of the urethra became hard, callous, and insensible . . .

Chills of dread and horror shot through Zachary as he read on to the study's sickening conclusion in which the unfortunate shepherd's much-abused organ had split into two longitudinal halves, like an over-grilled sausage. Despite the best efforts of the doctors at the hospital in Narbonne, the shepherd had died shortly afterwards.

Scarcely had Zachary recovered from the nightmares evoked by this passage than another parcel arrived, accompanied by another note.

October 14, 1839

Dear Mr Reid

I have just this minute returned from one of Dr Allgood's
Lectures on the Affliction to which you have fallen victim:
it was perhaps the most moving that I have yet heard. In
the conquest of this disease, says Dr Allgood, lies the difference between primitive and modern Man. All modern
philosophers are agreed upon this he said, and he quoted at
length from one Mr Kant who is said to be the most
Enlightened thinker of the Age. I felt it necessary to make
some jottings for your edification.

'The physical effects are absolutely disastrous,' says the
philosopher, 'but the consequences from the moral perspective are even more regrettable. One transgresses the limits
of nature, and the desire rages without end, for it never
finds any real satisfaction.'

Afterwards Dr Allgood was kind enough to lend me
another Book: Mr Sylvester Graham's *Lecture to Young
Men on Chastity.* You will find it enclosed herewith. We
are very fortunate that Dr Allgood has made this book
available to us. It has only very recently been published
in America and has already sold many thousands of
copies there. Dr Allgood assures me that if any remedy
for your Condition could be said to exist then this book
is it. I urge you to spend this day and the next in studying it and absorbing its lessons. Your first catechism
should, I think, be conducted while the book is still fresh
in your mind so I think we should meet the day after the
morrow.

As to the venue, I confess that I have been at something
of a loss to decide on one – for a Discussion of this nature
requires a degree of privacy that is hard to come by in a
house that is as plentifully supplied with servants as ours.
But at length I have hit upon a stratagem that will, I think,
admirably serve the purpose. I have put it about that some
of the shelves in my Sewing Room are broken and the

nokar-logue have been informed that the Mystery-sahib will be coming to the house to repair them.

Today being Tuesday, I suggest you come to the front door of the house at 11 in the morning on Thursday. One of my maids will show you to my Sewing Room. Of course you must not neglect to bring your tools with you, and nor must you forget to bring the books that Dr Allgood has so kindly lent us – hundreds are clamouring for them, so great is the concern about this Epidemic.

Yours &c.
C. Burnham

p.s.: I enclose with this letter a packet of biscuits made to a recipe by the author of the *Lecture on Chastity*. They are said to be a marvellous antidote for your Disease, and are widely used as such in America, where they are known as 'Graham Crackers'.

p.p.s.: needless to add, this note too should be destroyed as soon as it has been read.

Five

It didn't take long for Kesri to realize that the Pacheesi was a fiefdom for Bhyro Singh and his clan. Behind the battalion's external edifice of military rank there lay an unseen scaffolding of power, with its own hierarchy and loyalties. This was not just tolerated but even encouraged by the battalion's British officers, who relied on this fraternity to bring in new recruits and to pass on information about the men.

Not being a member of the clan, Kesri had to look elsewhere to learn about the Pacheesi's inner workings. The man he turned to was a gifted but unlikely source of advice: none other than Pagla-baba, the Naga ascetic who travelled everywhere with the battalion.

Pagla-baba was thin and very tall, with limbs that looked as if they were made from fire-blackened bamboo. His joints were huge and gnarled, and his skin was smeared from head to toe with ash, as was his matted hair, which he wore on his head in a thick turban of coils. When the battalion was on the move, he marched with his earthly possessions on his back, slung on a length of rope – they consisted of a rolled-up mat, a set of three sharp-edged discs and a standard-issue brass lota, no different from those that were strapped upon the knapsacks of the sepoys. At the insistence of the battalion's English officers he would sometimes wear a band of cloth around his waist, but when out of their sight he usually tucked it in so that it covered nothing. The ash was his clothing, he liked to say, and his genitals and pubes were daubed even more liberally with it than the rest of his body.

The English officers hated Pagla-baba and not just because he liked to bring the blush to their cheeks by flaunting his impressive manhood: they resented him for his hold on the soldiers and were flummoxed by his appeal. They never tired of pointing out to the sepoys that every paltan had its contingent of regimental pundits and maulvis to serve their religious needs; these functionaries were army employees, just like the Anglican chaplains who ministered to the officers, and the Catholic padres who tended to the battalion's drummers, fifers and musicians (most of whom were Christian Eurasians and had entered the ranks through orphanages and poorhouses).

To the officers it was baffling that with so many respectable men of religion to turn to, the sepoys should resort instead to a naked badmash who didn't even take the trouble to wear a langooty and went around with his artillery preceding him, as if to deliver a barrage.

What they didn't understand was that as far as most sepoys were concerned regimental pundits and maulvis were important only for formal observances; when it came to their private hopes and fears, sorrows and beliefs, they needed messengers of a different kind. Ascetics like Pagla-baba were not just men of religion but also soldiers, and had served in armies and warrior bands. They understood the lives of sepoys in a way that no pundit or maulana ever could: they provided practical advice as well as spiritual guidance. In the battlefield, sepoys had much more faith in the protection of the amulets they received from faqirs and sadhus than in the blessings of pundits and imams.

It was also a great help that the ascetics were unusually well-informed: their networks extended everywhere and they frequently had access to better intelligence than the army's spies. For all these reasons there was scarcely a battalion in Bengal that did not have an ascetic in its camp – and it didn't matter what religion they professed to follow or whether they called themselves gosains or sufis. This too was a great annoyance to the Angrez officers for they liked to have people neatly in their places, with the Gentoos and Musselmen in their own corners.

Kesri was fortunate in being drawn into Pagla-baba's inner circle through no effort of his own. It so happened that Pagla-baba had paid many visits to the annual mela that was held near Nayanpur. He had an astonishing memory for names and faces and he remembered having seen Kesri there, many years before. Because of that chance connection he took an interest in Kesri's welfare from the time he entered the paltan – and Kesri, for his part, felt an instinc- tive affinity for Pagla-baba, largely because he made fun of pundits and purohits and all their endless observances of rules and rituals.

It was Pagla-baba who told Kesri about a way to get ahead in the paltan without having to depend on Bhyro Singh and his clan: volunteering for overseas service. Officers always took special note of a sepoy who volunteered, he said, because balamteers who were willing to travel on ships were hard to find in the Bengal Native Infantry. Most of the sepoys of the Bengal army were from inland regions like Bihar and Awadh, and they didn't like to cross the sea: some felt that it compromised their caste standing; others objected to the additional expense as well as the inconvenience and danger. This was why overseas service was generally voluntary in the Bengal army: mandatory foreign deployments had led to disaffection in the past, so when troops were needed for missions abroad it was usually the Madras army that supplied them.

Yeh jaati-paati ki baat sab bakwaas haelba – all this talk of caste is bakwaas of course, said Pagla-baba, in his hoarse, crackling voice. When travel battas are offered, Bihari sepoys run like rabbits to sign up. The same if there's any talk of prize money. Afterwards, they'll pay for a little ceremony to remove the taint of crossing the black-water, and that'll be that. Any sepoy will volunteer when there's a glint of gold – but it's when you sign up without any money on offer that the Angrez officers will really take notice of you.

Kesri would have volunteered at once had that been a possibility, but it took a while before an opportunity arose. One day the CO-sahib announced that balamteers were being sought to reinforce a British garrison on the Bengal–Burma frontier. The garrison was on an island called Shahpuri, at the mouth of the Naf River, which marked the border between the East India Company's Bengal territories and the Burmese Province of Arakan. The island was a few hundred miles from Calcutta and the reinforcements were to be sent there by ship: this being just a spell of garrison duty, there were to be no special travel battas; nor was there any possibility of prize money or any other emoluments.

Kesri lost no time in putting his name on the list of volunteers – and since there were no financial incentives, he assumed that nobody else from his battalion would sign up as a balamteer. But when the full list was posted, it turned out that Hukam Singh had also volunteered, having been promised a temporary rank of naik, or corporal: worse still, Kesri was assigned to his very platoon.

When they arrived at the island there was not a man among them who did not regret having come. The encampment was a stockade on a sand-spit, hemmed in by jungle and marshland, river and sea. A sizeable Burmese force had already assembled on the far side of the Naf River, with obviously hostile intent.

Kesri did not have to wait long for his first taste of combat. One day, while out on patrol, his company was ambushed by a Burmese raiding party. The sepoys could only get off a single volley before their attackers closed on them: after that it was every man for himself, with the sepoys' bayonets pitted against the spears and cutlasses of the Burmese.

Kesri found himself facing an onrush from a man with a fearsomely tattooed face and a huge, flashing cutlass. He dropped to one knee, as he had so often done in drills, and took his bayonet back, in preparation for the thrust. His lunge, when he made it, was perfectly executed. The attacker was evidently unprepared for the length of the weapon and was caught in mid-stride. The bayonet went right through his ribs and into his heart.

This was the first time that Kesri had killed a man. His attacker's tattooed face was so close that he could see the light dimming in his eyes – but to his horror the head kept coming towards him, even after the eyes had gone blank. He gave his rifle a savage thrust, trying to extricate his bayonet from the dead man's ribs. But he succeeded only in shaking the corpse, so that the head whipped back and forth: a ribbon of drool curled out of the dead man's mouth and hit Kesri in the face. He realized now, in mounting panic, that his bayonet was trapped between the man's ribs.

From the edge of his vision Kesri glimpsed another man bearing down on him with an upraised cutlass. He tugged on the butt of his rifle again, but it wouldn't come free. The impaled corpse clung stubbornly to the bayonet, with the eyes wide open, staring into Kesri's face.

The other attacker was so close now that there was no time to lower the corpse to the ground and coax out the blade. Kesri had no choice but to use the dead man as a shield. When the attacker's cutlass began its descent, he torqued his body, as he had learnt to do in the wrestling pit, and levered the corpse up to absorb the blow.

The first stroke hit the corpse on the back, pushing the tattooed face against Kesri's and knocking him to the ground. The strike was blunted, but not entirely deflected. Kesri knew he had been hit, because he could see his blood spurting over the dead man's face.

Then the attacker came at him from the other side. Kesri had the full weight of the corpse on him now. Again he waited until the blade had begun its descent and then he heaved on the butt of his rifle, using the corpse to block the slashing cutlass.

Again the strike was only partially deflected. It hit him in the arm, glancing off an amulet that Pagla-baba had given him. At the same time it somehow also jerked loose his bayonet. Still covered by the corpse, Kesri pulled the blade free, taking care to keep it hidden from his attacker. He waited for the man to close in for the kill and only then did he make his thrust, shoving his bayonet through the gap between the corpse's arm and flank. This time he aimed for the stomach, and was lucky to hit home. The second attacker collapsed upon the first and the impact of his fall knocked the breath out of Kesri, who was now buried under both their bodies. His head began to spin and the last thing he was aware of was Hukam Singh's voice, shouting at him, telling him to get up.

Because of his wounds Kesri was quickly evacuated to India. During his time in hospital he promised himself that when it was his turn to put recruits through bayonet drill, he would teach them always to aim for the stomach: it was the softest part of a man's body and there was no danger of getting your bayonet trapped between any bones.

Kesri was still recuperating, in Barrackpore, when a letter arrived from his village: his brother Bhim had dictated it to a letter-writer.

In the intervening years Kesri had regularly sent money home, through sepoys who were going on leave. Through them he had also received news of his family: he knew that after his departure, Bhim had stayed back to look after their land.

Now Bhim was writing to say that it was time for Kesri to return to the village for a visit. Their father had forgiven everything and was eager to see him, for many reasons. One was that he was involved in some litigation over a piece of land and had been told that the magistrate, who was English, was more likely to rule in their favour if Kesri was seen in the courtroom, dressed in the uniform of a Company sepoy. Another reason was that they had received a splendid proposal of marriage for Kesri: it was from a family of rich landowning thakurs. The girl's brothers were also Company sepoys, so it was a perfect match in every way.

Bhim ended with the observation that he was himself eager to see the matter of Kesri's marriage settled so that he could start thinking of getting married himself.

Kesri was in no hurry to find a wife: he had thought that he would do what many sepoys did, and wait till he had left service. But he was also keen to be reconciled with his parents, so he took leave for four months and went home.

On reaching Nayanpur, he was astonished by the stir that was created by his arrival. It turned out that in his absence he had become a figure of some note in the village. The money he sent home had provided his family with new comforts and had also allowed them to hold pujas at the local temples. All of Nayanpur turned out for the *prayashchitta* ceremony that his family held, to remove the stain of his overseas travels. When he appeared in court with his father, the English magistrate took special note, and the ruling did indeed go in his favour.

As for Kesri's doubts about getting married, they were quickly swept aside by his family. The dowry that had been offered was so substantial that there would have been no question of saying no to the alliance, even if he had wanted to, which he didn't, since there were no grounds for objection: the bride was plump, fair and quite amiable; and she also got on well with his mother and sisters – especially Deeti, who doted on her. Kesri saw immediately that his family had chosen well, and he, for his part, was prepared to do his best to live up to all that was expected of him, as a husband. The wedding was a grand affair, attended by hundreds of people. His in-laws had wide connections, so all the zamindars of the district came, as well as the mukhiyas of the nearby villages.

With things going so well, Kesri briefly contemplated retiring from service and moving back home permanently. But a couple of months of playing the householder resolved his doubts. He found, to his surprise, that he missed the orderliness of his life with the Pacheesi; he missed the regularity of knowing exactly when he would eat and sleep and bathe; he missed the cheerful camaraderie; he missed his hut, where everything was within reach and in its place; he missed the straight, well-swept streets and lanes of the cantonment – the galis of the village he had grown up in now seemed to him chaotic and dirty.

After a few months of family life even the oppressive hierarchies of military rank seemed more bearable. At least you knew exactly where you stood with everyone around you – and coping with the petty tyrannies of naiks and havildars was no more difficult than dealing with his father. And compared with the complications of the marital bed, his transactions with Gulabi were vastly more satisfying.

But even if Kesri had been inclined to stay, he knew it wouldn't have been feasible. The family had grown accustomed to the money he sent home; and in different ways they had all come to relish the prestige of being closely related to a man who wore the uniform of a power that was increasingly feared and respected. What was more, by the time his leave drew to an end Kesri could tell that his family – all except Deeti – were tiring of having him at home. He understood that the gap left by his departure from home had been filled by the continuing flow of their lives; his return, although welcome at the start, had now begun to disrupt the new currents.

Strangely, all of this added to the poignancy of his departure: it was as if his family were lamenting not just the fact of his leaving but also their acceptance of its inevitability.

A few months later his family wrote to say that his wife was expecting a child. In due time there was another letter announcing the birth of a son: his father had named him Shankar Singh.

Kesri was then stationed upcountry, at Ranchi. He spent a week's salary on sweets and distributed them all over the cantonment.

*

Punctually on Thursday morning, Zachary walked across the lawn, holding in one hand a box of tools and in the other the two books Mrs Burnham had lent him, neatly wrapped in paper.

At the door of the mansion, Zachary was met by a veiled, sari-clad maid who led him through a maze of staircases and corridors to Mrs Burnham's sunlit sewing room.

Mrs Burnham was waiting inside, austerely dressed in white calico. She greeted Zachary off-handedly, without looking up from her embroidery. 'Oh, is it the Mystery-sahib? Let him in.'

When Zachary had stepped in she glanced up at the maid, who was still standing at the door. 'Challo! Jaw!' she said briskly, waving her away. 'Be off with you now.'

After the woman had gone, Mrs Burnham went to the door and fastened the bolt. 'Come, Mr Reid. We haven't much time so we must use it as best we can.'

In the centre of the room stood an exquisite sewing table, of Chinese make, with sinuous designs painted in gold upon a background of black lacquer. Two chairs had been placed to face each other across the table, on top of which lay a slim pamphlet.

Mrs Burnham gestured to Zachary to take the chair opposite hers. 'I trust you have brought your tools with you, Mr Reid?'

'Yes.'

Zachary lifted up his wooden toolbox and placed it on the table.

'Well then, I suggest you tap your hammer on the box from time to time. This will give the impression that you are at work and will serve to allay the suspicions of anyone who might be listening at the door. The natives are prying little bandars you know, and just as curious. Precautions are always in order.'

'Certainly, ma'am.' Zachary took out his hammer and began to tap lightly on the lid.

'I trust, Mr Reid, that you have read and absorbed Dr Richerand's chapter on the unfortunate shepherd lad?'

'Yes, ma'am.' Zachary fixed his attention on the toolbox, grateful for an excuse to keep his eyes lowered.

'May I ask what effect it had on you?'

Zachary swallowed. 'It was very disturbing, ma'am.'

She was quick to pounce on this. 'Aha! And is that because you feel yourself to be in danger of arriving at a similar plight?'

'Why no, ma'am,' said Zachary quickly. 'My condition is not, I assure you – nearly so serious as that of the shepherd.'

'Oh?' The exclamation was not devoid of some disappointment. 'And what of the *Lecture*, Mr Reid? Have you studied it with due attention?'

'Yes, ma'am.'

Here she reached into her reticule, took out a handkerchief, and proceeded to dab it on her cheeks. The gesture momentarily drew Zachary's eyes away from his toolbox to Mrs Burnham's neck, but he quickly wrenched them away and resumed his tapping.

'Well then, Mr Reid, could you kindly recount for me the ailments that are associated with your condition? I trust you have committed them to memory?'

'Yes, ma'am,' said Zachary. 'As I remember they include head-aches, melancholy, hypochondria, hysterics, feebleness, impaired vision, loss of sight, weakness of the lungs, nervous coughs, pulmo-nary consumption, epilepsy, loss of memory, insanity, apoplexy, disorders of the liver and kidney—'

She broke in with an aggrieved cry: 'Aha! I notice you have made no mention of various ailments of the bowels!'

'Why no, ma'am,' said Zachary quickly. 'I did not wish to be . . . indelicate.'

At this Mrs Burnham gave a laugh that forced Zachary to look up from the table again: he could not help but note that two bright spots of colour had now appeared on her cheeks.

'Oh Mr Reid!' she cried. 'If I were so feeble a creature as to be put to the blush by a mention of kabobs and dubbers I would scarcely have shouldered the burden of helping you to find a cure for your condition!'

But even as she was saying this, her words were contradicted by the expansion of the spots of colour on her cheeks. Now, as if to distract herself, she reached for an embroidery frame and picked up a needle.

'Please do not be concerned about sparing my ears,' she said, as her needle began to fly. 'Our missionary sisters have to endure far worse in order to rescue heathens from sin. If you have encountered any problems in your visits to the tottee-connah you may be frank in confessing it.'

Zachary dropped his eyes again to the toolbox. 'No, ma'am; I have not.'

'Oh?' This too was said on a note of slight disappointment. Again she paused to dab herself, a little lower this time, near the base of her throat. Once more Zachary's eyes wavered and rose from the toolbox to fasten upon Mrs Burnham's bosom; only with a great effort did he succeed in forcing them to return to the tabletop.

In the meantime Mrs Burnham had reached for the pamphlet that was lying on the table. Opening it, she pointed to a paragraph that had been marked with a pencil.

'Dr Allgood has lent me a recent essay of his,' she said. 'It concerns the treatment of mental disorders and lunacy brought on by this disease. Would you be good enough to read out the marked passage?'

Taking a deep breath, Zachary started to read: 'The onset of lunacy, brought on by Onanism, may yet be delayed by the judicious use of the following treatments: the application of leeches to the groin and rectal area; enemas with a very mild solution of carbolic acid. In some cases more advanced treatments may be necessary, such as the application of leeches to the scrotal sac and perineum; injections of small doses of calomel into the urethra with a catheter; cauterization of the sebaceous glands and the membraneous portion of the urethra; and surgical incisions to sever the organ's suspensory ligament—'

Here Zachary was cut short by a cry: 'Oh!'

His eyes flew up just as the embroidery ring was tumbling out of Mrs Burnham's hands; he saw that a drop of blood had welled up on the tip of her index finger. Mrs Burnham winced and fastened a fist upon the finger: 'Oh dear! I fear I've given myself quite a little prick.'

Zachary leant a little closer and his eyes travelled from her pricked fingertip to her throat, now flushed with colour. From there they dropped to her bosom, which was covered by a chaste confection of white netting: he saw that the lace had begun to flutter and heave, and he noticed also that with every exhalation, a tiny triangular shadow seemed to appear beneath, to point to the opening of the crevice that had been the cause of his last undoing.

Across the table Mrs Burnham was staring at her finger in dismay. 'My mother always said,' she muttered absent-mindedly, 'that one must be careful with a prick.'

Zachary's eyes were still fixed on the tiny, almost invisible triangle at the centre of her bosom – and the little shadow beneath the lace now assumed so seductive an aspect that he suddenly had to move his legs deeper, under the table.

The movement was fleeting but it did not escape Mrs Burnham's eye. Her gaze moved from her finger to his red face, taking in his oddly upright posture and the way his belly was pressed flat against the edge of the sewing table.

Suddenly she understood. A breathless cry broke from her lips: 'Dear heaven! I cannot credit it!'

Springing to her feet, Mrs Burnham directed a disbelieving gaze at Zachary's head, which was lowered in shame. 'Has it happened again, Mr Reid? Answer me!'

Zachary hung his head, speechless with mortification.

A look of pity came into her eyes and she gave his shoulder a sympathetic pat. 'You poor, unfortunate young man! You are perhaps yourself unaware of the extreme seriousness of your condition. But do not despair – I will not abandon you! We will persist, and you may yet avert the fate that awaits you.'

She walked slowly to the door, and after undoing the bolt, turned to look at him again. 'I must go now to tend to my pri . . . my wound. I will leave you here to collect yourself. You shall soon receive more materials from me, and when you have studied them we shall meet again. But for now, Mr Reid, may I request that you remain here until your seizure has subsided and you are presentable?

*

Over the next few days Shireen did everything she could to erase her meeting with Zadig from her memory. She mostly succeeded, but at times Zadig's words would rise to the surface of her consciousness like bubbles ascending from the sediment of a pond, catching her unawares: 'But it is true, Bibiji . . . Bahram did have a son . . . You can ask Vico . . .'

The words would stir her into a bustle of activity: snatching a duster from one of the maids, she would begin to clean the souvenirs that sat on her shelves, most of which had been brought back by Bahram from China: dolls with nodding heads, painted fans, intricately carved ivory balls and so on. Often she would end up facing the luminous square of glass that had Bahram's portrait on it – and sometimes within its familiar lines she would glimpse shapes that were not quite visible to her eyes. It was like looking at a cloud in which everyone but you can see a hidden shape.

Yet she could see no profit in pursuing the matter. What good could come of exhuming the lives of the dead? Anything she learnt about Bahram would only bring more disgrace upon herself and her daughters – and hadn't they been shamed enough already?

Then, unexpectedly one morning, a khidmatgar came to say that Vico was at the door and wanted to speak to her.

Vico? Her heart went cold and she sank into the nearest seat. What does Vico want?

The man looked at her in surprise: What do I know, Bibiji? Why would he tell me?

No, of course not. Send him in.

She took a deep breath and collected herself. When Vico entered the room she was able to welcome him with a smile. *Khem chho Vico?* she said in Gujarati. Is everything well?

He looked just the same, with his dark, heavy-set body clothed impeccably, in European style, in a pale, beige suit.

Khem chho Bibiji? he said with a lively twinkle in his large, protuberant eyes.

She was reassured by his wide smile and his affable demeanour. Come, Vico, sit down, she said, pointing to a settee.

He had always been reluctant to sit in her presence and he declined now with a shake of his head: No, Bibiji, it's not necessary. I just came to ask a question – it won't take long.

Yes?

Bibiji, I would like to organize a small gathering in memory of your late husband. Despite all that has happened, there are many people in Bombay who would like to pay their respects to Sethji.

Oh? Her eyes swept across the room and came to rest on Bahram's portrait. Where do you plan to do it?

In my village, Bassein – at my home. And of course we would like you to be there too – it wouldn't be the same without your presence.

And when do you want to do it?

Next week Bibiji.

Why so soon?

Bibiji, I would like to invite Sethji's friend, Mr Karabedian. He may be leaving for Colombo soon.

She started: Mr Karabedian! You are planning to invite him?

Vico's eyebrows rose. Yes of course, Bibiji. He was Sethji's closest friend.

Shireen turned her face away and was trying to think of something to say when a tearing sound ripped through the room. She looked down at her hands and saw that she had involuntarily torn a rent in the loose end of her sari.

Vico had noticed it too.

What is the matter, Bibiji? Did I say something to upset you?

With her agitation in plain view, it served no purpose to pretend. Listen, Vico, she said, in a shaky voice. I need to ask you something . . .

Her eyes flew to the portrait on the wall and she muttered under her breath: Heaven forgive me for what I am about to say.

Yes, Bibiji?

Vico, some rumours have come to my ears. About my husband.

Oh? Vico's voice was guarded now and a watchful look had come into his eyes.

Yes, Vico. It is rumoured that my husband had an illegitimate child, a son.

She watched him carefully as she spoke; he was twirling his hat in his hands, looking at the floor.

Of course there is no truth to it, is there, Vico?

He answered without hesitation. You're right, Bibiji. There is no truth to it.

Even though his voice was steady, she knew from the evasiveness of his gaze that he was hiding something. She understood also that if she did not insist now she would never find out. And at the thought of this her hesitation disappeared.

Vico, tell me the truth. I must know.

He continued to stare at the floor so she rose to her feet and went up to him.

Vico, she said, I know you are a religious man, a good Catholic.

I want you to take an oath, on the crucifix you wear around your neck. If it is the truth, then I want you to swear on the Cross that my husband did not have an illegitimate son.

Vico raised his hands to his crucifix and drew a deep breath. But he faltered as he was parting his lips to speak, and his hands dropped to his sides.

Bibiji, you should not ask this of me. I would like to spare you needless grief, but this I cannot do.

At this something came apart inside her. One of her hands flew out and without quite meaning to, knocked a framed picture of her late husband to the floor.

The crash brought a troop of servants into the room: Bibiji? Bibiji? What happened?

Shireen could not face them and was glad when Vico took charge, in his accustomed manner.

It was just an accident, he said to the servants, in a brisk, off-hand voice. Bibiji had a giddy spell. Bring me her smelling-salts – she'll be fine in a minute.

The fact that Shireen had slumped into a chaise-longue lent this some plausibility. After a few whiffs of her smelling-salts she was able to sit up again. Once the floor had been cleaned she waved the maids out of the room and told them to shut the door.

All right, Vico, she said. Now tell me: who was the boy's mother?

A Cantonese woman, her name was Chi-mei.

Was she a – a tawaif? Some kind of dancing-girl? A woman of the streets?

No, no, Bibiji, not at all. She was an ordinary person, a boat-woman. You could say a kind of dhobin – she used to wash clothes for foreigners. That was how Sethji came across her.

And how old is the boy? What's his name?

He is a young man now, in his mid-twenties: Sethji used to call him Freddie – short for Framjee. But he had a Chinese name too, and a nickname – Ah Fatt.

Where is he now? Where did he grow up? Tell me about him, Vico – now that I know about him, I need to hear more.

Bibiji, he was brought up by his mother, in Canton. Sethji was always generous with them. He bought her a big boat and she turned it into an eating place. She did quite well, I think, at least for a while. But she died some years ago.

And the boy, Freddie, did he work in the eatery?

Yes, he did when he was little. But Sethji wanted to give him a proper education so he hired tutors for him and made sure that he learnt English. But still, the boy didn't have an easy time of it. In Canton even ordinary boat-people are treated like outcastes and he wasn't even a boat-boy.

Shireen could not sit still any more. She went to a window and looked out towards the sea.

Vico, there is something you must do for me.

Yes, Bibiji?

I want to meet quietly with Mr Karabedian. The family must not know, not even my daughters. Can you arrange this?

Why not, Bibiji?

How will you do it?

After a moment's reflection, Vico said: Bibiji, let us do it this way. You inform your family that my wife has invited you to visit our house next week and that we will take you to Bassein in a private boat. They can't raise any objection to that, no?

No.

And the rest you can leave to me.

*

October 20, 1839
Honam

Quiet though it is, Honam Island is not without surprises. Nearby lies a Buddhist monastery which is said to be one of the largest in the province. It is called the Haizhuang or 'Ocean Banner' monastery – Vico used to talk about it; I'd heard from him that there were many Tibetan monks living there.

I started visiting the Ocean Banner Monastery soon after I moved to Honam. It is a vast honeycomb of a place, with monumental statues, ancient trees and gilded shrines. One could lose oneself there for days.

Sometimes I would come across groups of Tibetan monks. Recognizing me as an 'Achha' they'd smile and nod. I would have liked to speak with them, but there was no language in common. The monks speak very little Cantonese.

But one day, while I was wandering through the inner courtyards of the monastery, I made the acquaintance of an elderly lama. His face is like some ancient river-bed, cross-hatched by deeply scored grooves. Clinging to the cracks and wrinkles, like tenacious plants, are a few white hairs. That day he was sitting in the shade of a banyan tree and he called me over with a wave. As I approached, his lips parted in a smile, revealing a few pebble-like teeth. Then he joined his hands together and uttered a greeting – *Ka halba?*

Bhojpuri? In Canton? Spoken by a Tibetan lama?

At first I was literally bereft of speech.

The lama told me that he had spent many years visiting Buddhist holy places in Bihar, like Gaya and Sarnath. It was at Sarnath that he learnt Bhojpuri. He even has a Bhojpuri name: Taranathji.

I asked what other places he had seen and a flood of stories came pouring out.

Taranathji is almost eighty now, and he has travelled very widely. At the time of the Qing dynasty's Gurkha wars, he served as a translator for the Chinese commander, the Manchu General Fukanggan; he spent many years in the retinue of the last Panchen Lama, serving as his interpreter when the British sent a Naga sadhu, Purangir, as an emissary to Tibet. He has disputed theological matters with Russian Orthodox priests and has preached in the lamaseries of northern Mongolia. The mountains, deserts and plains that lie sprawled across this vast landmass are like rivers and seas to him: he has crossed them many times. He has travelled to Beijing, with the Panchen Lama; he was even present at one of his meetings with the Qianlong Emperor.

He said something that amazed me: was I aware, he asked, that the Qianlong Emperor, the greatest ruler of the Qing dynasty, had written a book about Hindustan?

I stared at him, astounded, and confessed that I had no knowledge of this.

Taranathji's eye twinkled. Yes, he said, such a book did indeed exist. In the latter years of his life the Qianlong Emperor had been much concerned with Yindu – or Enektek, as the Manchus called it. This was because the Qing had extended the borders of China into Tibet, up to the very frontiers of India, which had resulted in many new problems for them. Perhaps the most bothersome was that of Nepal and its Gurkha kings, who had harboured designs on Tibet. After repeated provocations, the Qianlong Emperor had sent an army into Nepal and the Gurkhas had been soundly beaten. At one stage the Gurkhas had even tried to get assistance from the British – unsuccessfully however, for the East India Company had demurred, for fear of jeopardizing its lucrative trade relations with China. The Gurkhas were thus vanquished, and became tributaries of China; in the years since they have served as Beijing's chief channel of information about Bengal and Hindustan.

Taranathji told me also that over the years the Gurkhas have given the Qing many warnings about the British and their ever increasing appetites. If China did not act quickly, they had told them, then the British would threaten them too one day; they had even proposed joint attacks on the East India Company's territories in Bengal, by a combined Gurkha and Qing expeditionary force. If only their warnings had been heeded in Beijing, if only the Emperors had acted decisively at that time, then China would have been in a different situation today. But the Gurkhas' warnings were ignored because the Qing did not entirely trust them; nor were they convinced that the Firingees the Nepalis spoke of were the same people as the Yinglizis who traded at Canton.

All of this was new to me. After a while I could no longer contain my amazement. I told Taranathji that he was a living treasure and that he should meet Zhong Lou-si.

Taranathji told me then that he knows Zhong Lou-si and has spoken at length with him and other highly placed officials, not just in Guangzhou but also in Beijing. They have questioned him about his travels and he has tried to share his knowledge of the world to the best of his ability. How much of it they have actually taken in he does not know.

It is not a lack of curiosity that hinders the mandarins, he says: their problem lies with their methods and procedures. They have an instinctive distrust of spoken reports; they place far greater reliance on written documents. When they hear something new, they are reluctant to give it credence unless they can reconcile it with everything they have learnt from older books. They are hindered not by credulity but by an excess of scepticism; they accept nothing that is not known for certain.

Since then I have paid Taranathji a few more visits. Every time I go I am amazed by his stories. When I took up residence in Baburao's houseboat, I had not imagined that there would be so much to learn, so close by.

*

The next parcel from the big house arrived sooner than Zachary had expected. He opened it with much trepidation, expecting to find a lengthy reproof of his conduct in the sewing room. But Mrs Burnham's note made no reference to that incident.

October 25, 1839

Dear Mr Reid

Enclosed herewith is another book – a Treatise by Dr Tissot, a very famous Practitioner of medicine: Dr Allgood describes him as the Newton of Onanism. This volume is, I gather, the most comprehensive and up-to-date study of your Condition that is presently available. I have spent two days reading it, and I must confess that it has made me quite ill. My sympathy for you grows ever more keen when I imagine you labouring in the grip of this frightful Malady.

I implore you to read the Book with the greatest care, and when you are done, I shall arrange a Meeting. Until then, I beg you to be mindful of the Author's warnings – let us hope that it is not too late already.

Yours &c.
C.B.

The letter so alarmed Zachary that his fingers began to shake as he tore apart the parcel's paper wrappings. Nor did the book's title – *Onanism, or a Treatise upon the Diseases Produced by Masturbation: or, the Dangerous Effects of Secret and Excessive Venery* – allay his fears. When he started to read, his apprehensions turned quickly into a horrified fascination and he could not stop turning the pages. Dr Tissot provided ample evidence to show that onanism was not only a disease in itself, but that it also served as a gateway for a great host of other ailments: paralysis, epilepsy, feeble-mindedness, impotence and various disorders of the kidneys, testes, bladder and bowels.

These warnings caused Zachary so much disquiet that he was hardly able to sleep or eat, that day or the next. When Mrs Burnham's next note arrived, he greeted it with relief.

October 30, 1839

Dear Mr Reid

I am sure you have read Dr Tissot's Treatise by now, and are impatient to discuss its contents. I too am keen to proceed with your Treatment, and I am pleased to report that an unforeseen circumstance has greatly augmented my ability to be of Assistance to you.

Yesterday, I again sought, and was granted, an interview with Dr Allgood. But it so happened that soon after I was admitted to his study he was called away, to inspect a seizure of the disease in a Native Victim. He was occupied with the young man for quite a while and in his absence I was able to examine a notebook that was lying on his desk

– it happened to be the journal in which the doctor records his interviews with your Fellow-sufferers. This has given me a much clearer idea of how the Treatment should proceed.

It was obvious from Dr Allgood's notes that an effective course of treatment must commence with Inquiries of a somewhat Delicate nature. Needless to add, such an interview will require an extraordinary degree of privacy, especially since your condition is such (as was evident at our last meeting) that untoward Occurrences cannot be ruled out.

This has created a Quandary for me, and I have had to rack my brains to think of a Venue for our Consultation. After weighing every possibility it has become apparent to me that the only safe location is the one that I am most loath to contemplate – my own Boudoir. But now that we have set out on this path I can see no other means of Proceeding, and being fortified by the example of such a martyr as Dr Allgood, I am willing to over-ride my reservations for the sake of our Medical Collaboration.

I need scarcely impress on you the attendant Risks, for I am sure that you are well aware that this house is filled, on most days, with an abundance of prying eyes and idle hands. But fortunately the Natives are as whimsical as they are inquisitive, and on certain days and nights they become so possessed by their heathenry that they completely vanish from view, running off to join in mummeries of one kind or another. One such pageant is to be held Friday week and I think it very likely that the house will be, if not empty, then certainly much less full.

But while this may reduce the Risks, it will not eliminate them, so it will be necessary to employ some other Precautions. My Boudoir faces the river and is on the first floor: it is situated at the corner of the house that is furthest from the budgerow. Below is a small doorway: this is a servants' entrance, and is used mainly by the muttra-nees who clean my Goozle-connuh (or Powder room). It would be advisable I think, for you to make use of this doorway to effect your entry. It is usually locked at night, but I will make sure that it is off its latch on that day.

When you open the door, you will see a flight of stairs – I will leave a candle there for you. The stairs will lead you to my Goozle-connuh, which directly adjoins my Boudoir.

By eleven at night the house will be quiet and the nokar-logue will have left: it will be best if you come then. And of course you must not forget to bring the Treatise, for Dr Allgood is most anxious to have it back.

Yours &c.
C.B.

*

Two years after his first foray overseas Kesri was back in Burma.

The campaign got off to a bad start. While the force was still being assembled, in Barrackpore, the troops learnt that they would have to bear many of the expenses of the march – they would even have to buy bullocks for the baggage-train with their own money. Nor would there be any extra battas to offset the cost.

This caused a great deal of discontent, especially in a regiment that had long been notorious for the laziness and incompetence of its English officers. Feelings ran so high that one morning the regiment refused to parade when ordered to do so.

On the following day the Jangi Laat (or 'War Lord' as the Commander-in-Chief was known) arrived suddenly in Barrackpore, with two British regiments and a detachment of cannon. The sepoys who had refused to fall in were called out and ordered to surrender their arms. When they hesitated to obey the War Lord ordered the artillery detachment to fire on them. Many sepoys were killed and the rest ran away or were taken prisoner. Eleven men were hanged and a large number were sentenced to hard labour or transportation to distant islands. The regiment was disbanded, its colours were destroyed and its numbers were struck from the Army List.

The violence of these measures silenced the rest of the force, but morale was low and sank even lower when they arrived in Burma. Their route led through dense forests and long stretches of marshland. The Burmese were experienced in jungle warfare and did not offer the set-piece battles at which the British excelled; nor was the terrain such that the British could fully exploit their advantage in artillery. Provisioning was extremely difficult for there was little cultivation along the route. Most of the villages had been abandoned, so it was impossible to procure food locally.

On top of all this, fevers and disorders of the stomach took a terrible toll. Such was the rate of attrition that the naik of Kesri's platoon was twice replaced, the second time by none other than Hukam Singh.

One day, Kesri's platoon was sent ahead of the column to reconnoitre a village. The settlement was just a cluster of huts, shaded by coconut palms – the very picture of tranquillity. But by the time the sepoys got there they were tired out, having been on the march for several hours. In any case, they had passed through many such villages before, without incident. They were not at their most vigilant, as a result of which they walked straight into a close-quarters ambush.

Hukam Singh was in the lead and he was the first to be cut down, with multiple wounds to his thigh and groin. Kesri happened to be with him at the time. He fought off the attackers until the platoon regrouped and drove the Burmese away.

Hukam Singh was still alive but was bleeding profusely. They tied up his wounds, made a litter, and took turns carrying him back. For much of the way Hukam Singh seemed to be in a delirium, alternately thanking Kesri for saving his life and apologizing for his past behaviour. At the end, when they handed Hukam Singh over to the battalion's medical orderlies, he caught hold of Kesri's hand and said: You saved me – my life is yours now. I cannot forget what you did for me.

Kesri didn't put much store by these words, thinking them to be a part of his delirium. But a few days later he received a summons from Bhyro Singh, who was now a jemadar. Bhyro Singh told Kesri that on the basis of a strong recommendation from Hukam Singh the battalion's CO had decided to promote him to the rank of naik.

Kesri was so elated that it was only at the end of the interview that he remembered to inquire about Hukam Singh's condition.

Hukam Singh kaisan baadan? How is Hukam Singh?

Bhyro Singh did not mince his words: Hukam Singh's soldiering days were over, he said. He would have to go back to his village to recover from his wounds.

Many months went by before Kesri saw Hukam Singh again. In the interim the Pacheesi saw a great deal of fighting, in the Arakan and in southern Burma. Kesri was himself wounded again, in an action near Rangoon. Fortunately for him the wound was a 'lucky' one in that it wasn't severe.

For it also got him a bonus that excited much envy among his friends – so much so that Seetul said: *Kesri, tu ne to hagte me bater maar diya!*, 'Kesri, you dropped a turd and killed a partridge!'

The bonus was that he was evacuated to Calcutta on a steam-powered vessel, the first ever seen in the East – the *Enterprize*.

After returning to Barrackpore Kesri went to see Hukam Singh at the cantonment hospital. He found him so changed that it was as though he had become a different man. He was walking now, but with a pronounced limp; he was also much thinner, and looked as if the flesh of his face had wasted away. But the changes in his speech and demeanour were even greater than the altera-tions in his appearance. A look of resigned melancholy had replaced the malice that had so often lurked in his eyes before. He seemed almost gentle, like a man who had found some kind of inner peace.

Over the next few years, the men of the Pacheesi were almost continuously in the field, fighting in Assam, Tripura and the Jungle-Mahals. Occasionally sepoys would go home on leave, and since many of them were related to Hukam Singh, Kesri would occa-sionally get news of him. He learnt that Hukam Singh had gone back to his village, near Ghazipur, and that Bhyro Singh had got him a good job at the opium factory.

Then one day, several years after the Burma campaign, Kesri was summoned by Bhyro Singh, who was now at the very top of the ladder of sepoy ranks – a subedar. His brother, Nirbhay Singh, now a jamadar, was also with him.

Was it true, they wanted to know, that Kesri had a younger sister who was still unmarried?

This was completely unexpected but Kesri gathered his wits together and said yes, it was true that his youngest sister, Deeti, was still unmarried.

They explained to him that they had received a letter from Hukam Singh: he and his brother Chandan had gone to the mela near Nayanpur, and had learnt about Deeti from the sadhus. Hukam Singh was keen to marry her and had asked Kesri to intercede with his parents.

But is Hukam Singh well enough to get married? said Kesri. He wasn't in good health when I last saw him.

Bhyro Singh nodded: Yes, Hukam Singh has recovered his health; his only problem is that he limps. He wants nothing more than to marry.

Seeing that Kesri was still unconvinced, Bhyro Singh added: What is to lose? I hear your sister's stars are not good, and she is already of an age when it will be hard for her to find a husband. Hukam Singh has a good job and several bighas of land. Isn't this a good offer?

The truth of this could not be denied: Kesri knew that his parents were worried about Deeti's marital prospects and he did not doubt that they would be overjoyed by the proposal. And nor would Hukam Singh, in his present state, make an objectionable husband: he was a changed man now; no longer was he the vicious bully he had been in the past.

Yet, something in Kesri jibbed at the thought of handing his beloved Deeti to a member of Bhyro Singh's family.

Bhyro Singh must have read his reluctance on his face, for he said: Listen, Naik Kesri Singh, there is another thing you should consider: this marriage would link your family to ours and it would make you one of us. And if you were one of us, we would see to it that you were quickly promoted to havildar. What do you say? Why don't we settle it right now? I am going home on leave soon, and I would like to see Hukam Singh settled and married while I am there.

Kesri realized then that this was not just an offer but also a threat. A promotion had been due to him for a while and he knew that the only reason he had not received it was because Bhyro Singh, as the battalion's subedar, had not supported it. If he turned down this offer now another promotion might never come his way.

He took a deep breath.

Hokhe di jaisan kahtani, he said. Let it be as you say; I will send a letter home.

Within a few months the marriage was arranged. Kesri was

unable to attend the wedding but he heard about it from Bhyro Singh, who told him that everything had gone exactly as it was meant to and the marriage had been duly consummated on the wedding night. Deeti had been found to be a virtuous woman, a virgin.

At the end of the year, he heard from his family that Deeti had given birth to a daughter, by the name of Kabutri.

The next year Kesri went on leave again, for the third time in his twelve years of service. He was now the father of two children, a boy and a girl. His daughter had been born after his last visit and he had yet to see her.

During his stay in Nayanpur, Deeti had come to visit, with her baby daughter. She had looked a little careworn and had stayed only a couple of nights, but as far as Kesri could tell she was content with her lot. Kesri had seen her once again, on his next spell of leave, four years later, and then too she had made no complaint. Before returning to her husband's home she had painted a picture of Kabutri and given it to Kesri. He still had it in his keeping.

It grieved Kesri now to think of his little sister as a widow already. He could not understand why his family had not written, or sent word of what had happened.

Six

November 4, 1839
Honam

Two days ago an urgent letter arrived from Zhong Lou-si, who is away in another county, touring with Commissioner Lin. The letter said that Compton and I were to leave immediately for Whampoa, to catch a passage-boat. We were to travel to Humen, which is the location of a customs house where every incoming ship has to obtain clearance to proceed to Canton.

Apparently a British-owned vessel, the *Royal Saxon*, had just come in from Java; the captain, an Englishman, had indicated that he wanted to take his ship, and his goods, to Canton. The captain had even indicated that he was willing to sign a bond, forswearing the opium trade, on penalty of his life. This was good news for us, because Captain Elliot has for the last several months prevented British merchants from coming to Canton because he did not want them to sign the bond. But here at last was a sign that British merchants might at last be willing to defy the Plenipotentiary himself – this was exactly what Commissioner Lin has been hoping for. One other English vessel had already broken Captain Elliot's embargo: if the *Royal Saxon* too was able to proceed to Canton then many others would surely follow – it would be a great victory for Commissioner Lin!

Our instructions were to serve as translators for the customs house officials who'd be dealing with the captain and crew: our job was to make sure that there were no misunderstandings. The sailors were mainly lascars, which was why it was necessary for me to be present. Since I'm classified as a *yi*, a foreigner, Zhong Lou-si had enclosed a special chop, to make sure that I encountered no official difficulties.

Humen overlooks the channel that Europeans call the Bogue or Bocca Tigris – the 'Tiger's Mouth'. It is about one hundred and eighty Chinese *li* from Guangzhou – about sixty English miles – and the journey, by boat, usually takes a day and a half.

We had no time to waste: the tide had just crested at Guangzhou and Compton said that the passage-boats would depart when the current turned. I went home to pack a few things, and we met again at Jackass Point, in the foreign enclave. From there a ferry took us to Whampoa where we caught a passage-boat for Humen.

These boats are long, caterpillar-like vessels, crowded with passengers, livestock, cargo and vendors. Our official chop was a big help and we were able to find a quiet corner in which to settle in for the night.

We reached Humen in the late afternoon, on the second day. The town is of modest size, but it adjoins the largest defensive field-works of the Pearl River. There is a fort there with a massive battery of guns; it serves as the channel's gatekeeper – foreigners call it the fort of Anunghoy. Behind the fort, the shore slopes steeply upwards, to form a crested ridge. At the top of this hill there is another fortified gun-emplacement with a powerful battery of cannon.

The harbour at Humen is dominated by the customs house: this is where we had been told to go. On arriving there we learnt that the *Royal Saxon* was already at anchor nearby: the ship's captain was under instructions to proceed to the customs house next morning, to sign the bond. But in the meantime, a squadron of British vessels, with Captain Elliot on board, had also sailed in from Hong Kong, no doubt with the intention of preventing the *Royal Saxon* from approaching Humen. Everyone was on edge, wondering what would happen the next day.

Compton had thought that we would stay either at the customs house in Humen or at a nearby yamen. But on inquiring we learnt that there was no room for us in either. We were told that we would have to make other arrangements. Although Compton was disappointed, I was relieved: I sensed that the customs house officials were suspicious of me despite my official credentials; I was none too keen to remain there.

We went into Humen, to look for an inn, but these too were filled to capacity: apparently a massive project is under way to strengthen the fortifications of the Tiger's Mouth, and large numbers of workers and overseers have flooded into the town.

Fortunately, Compton has relatives nearby, which is only natural since he is a native of that county. They live in a hamlet, on a neighbouring island called Shaitok (foreigners call it Chuenpee). We took a ferry over and met with a warm welcome from Compton's relatives.

In the late afternoon the boys of the house took us for a long walk. The island is lush and leafy, with two conical hills. But its prettiness is deceptive: like Humen, Chuenpee bristles with cannon. Right on the water, there is a massive gun-emplacement: it looks across the Tiger's Mouth towards Tycock, on the far side of the channel, where there is another large battery. On the summit of Chuenpee's tallest hill there is another fort, a small one. The hill commands a panoramic view of the surroundings. The landscape was breathtaking: it was as if a scroll-painting had appeared before my eyes. To the east the estuary broadens into a wide funnel, with Hong Kong on one side and Macau on the other; to the west, the Pearl River meanders through a verdant plain, heading off in the direction of Guangzhou. The water of the estuary is a brilliant, sparkling blue, broken here and there by forested islands. On the far shore there are jagged mountains, with misted peaks.

Compton had brought a telescope with him, and we took turns examining the ships below. The Chinese fleet was concentrated at Tycock, on the other side of the channel: it consisted of sixteen war-junks, with castellations, fore and aft. Matted sails hung from their masts, projecting obliquely upwards, like the wings of moths. They were bedecked with streaming pennants and banners, and their bows were decorated with large, painted eyes. They were certainly *faa faa hik hik* – extremely colourful in appearance – but in size they were small, no more than a hundred feet in length, about as much as the *Ibis* if not less. Even ordinary trading junks are larger; as for European vessels, even a sixth-rate British warship is far bigger and heavier.

Swarming between the war-junks were many small boats and a dozen or so rafts with black flags: these were 'fire-vessels' Compton said; they are used as incendiary weapons, to spread flames amongst enemy ships. Some of them also carry 'stink-bombs' – chemical devices that disperse noxious gases and fumes.

The British ships were a couple of miles to the east, where the estuary broadens. The squad was a small one, consisting of a couple of ships' boats and two warships. By British standards these were small vessels, and far from fearsome; one was, I think, a sloop-of-war and the other a small frigate. I guessed that according to the Royal Navy's scale of ratings, they were fourth- or fifth-rate warships.

Between the two squadrons, like a plump fish caught between two schools of predators, was the *Royal Saxon*, anchored beside an island. Scanning her decks with a spyglass, I spotted many turbaned heads – lascars! I began to wonder how I'd have felt in their position, caught between British and Chinese warships?

On the way back to the hamlet, Compton said he thought the British warships would *beih fung tauh* – avoid trouble. There are just two of them, what can they do against sixteen ships?

I thought it best to say nothing.

Next morning we went back to the customs house at Humen. The officials told us that we would not be needed after all: a chop had already been issued to the *Royal Saxon* and she would soon be coming through, on her way to Whampoa.

There was nothing for us to do, so we decided to go back to Chuenpee to pick up our things. As we were approaching the hamlet, we saw the boys of the house running towards the top of the hill. We began to run too and soon caught up with one of Compton's nephews. We went up the hill together and on reaching the top we saw that the *Royal Saxon* had hoisted sail and was heading towards the Chinese customs house at Humen. This had roused the two British warships to give chase: they were about half a mile behind her, with every mast and yard crowded with canvas.

All of this had happened very quickly, and the Chinese fleet was clearly taken unawares. The war-junks and even the smaller boats were still at their moorings; not a single vessel had budged.

The two British warships closed quickly on the *Royal Saxon*. First the frigate flashed warnings with her signal flags. Then, with a puff of smoke and a booming report, a single cannon-shot was fired across the *Royal Saxon*'s bows.

Compton, who was standing beside me, could not believe his eyes: Are they going to attack an English ship?

I told him that they weren't really attacking the *Royal Saxon* – they were warning her not to break the embargo by proceeding to Canton.

The *Royal Saxon* had taken heed and had already begun to change course. She now tacked steeply to starboard. Meanwhile, the Chinese ships had begun to move too; led by the largest of the junks, they brought their bows around and began to advance towards the British ships.

The two English warships slackened pace a little, but when it became clear that the junks were on course to intercept them, the sloop fell behind the frigate, to form a line of battle.

The war-junks were now bunched together, with the fire-boats and rafts swarming between them. As the warships drew abreast, one of the fire-boats was set alight and pushed towards the approaching frigate. Neither of the warships veered from their course – the fire-boat was moving too slowly to do them any harm. Holding steady, the English ships closed to a distance of less than a hundred feet. When the Chinese squadron was directly a-beam of them, the frigate flashed a signal, and the two warships unloosed their first broadside.

Puffs of smoke blossomed along the starboard beams of both warships. By the time the sound had crossed the water, the Chinese fleet was obscured from our sight by a dense white cloud. Moments later a noise of a different kind came across – a sickening sound of splintering and crackling, pierced by screams and shouts.

When the smoke cleared the stretch of water where the Chinese fleet had been was utterly transformed: it was as if a sheet of lightning had come down from the sky, to set the channel on fire. Dozens of masts had been shattered; some had been blasted into the water and some had crashed down on the junks' decks, killing and maiming the men below. A couple of junks were listing steeply, their bows rising as water flooded into their punctured hulls. Of the burning fire-boat nothing remained but a few, flaming pieces of wood. Around the wreckage, the water was churning with flailing limbs and bobbing heads.

I had to shut my eyes. When I opened them again I saw that the largest of the junks had begun to move again: apparently this was the only vessel in the Chinese fleet that was still capable of functioning. Although two of her masts were gone, she slowly turned her bows around and fired off a volley. It served no purpose: the two British warships were far away, turning sharply for their next run.

Compton told me the big junk was Admiral Guan's and handed me his telescope. Putting it to my eye, I caught a glimpse of an elderly man, trying desperately to rally his blood-spattered, reeling crew. Meanwhile the two British warships had completed their turn and were heading back to deliver their second broadside. As they drew abreast, the admiral turned to face them, looking directly into the cannon: it was an act of hopeless defiance.

Once again a curtain of smoke rose from the flanks of the two warships; once again the junks disappeared from view. This time, the sound of the fusillade was followed by a much greater noise, an explosion that sent great sheets of flame and debris shooting into the air. When the blast reached the hill the ground shook beneath our feet. It was clear that they had hit a magazine because a great tower of flame rose from the water.

When the smoke cleared we saw that one of the junks had burst open, like a shattered eggshell. The detonation hurled a mass of flying debris at the surrounding vessels, riddling them with gaping holes.

In the distance, the two British warships were sailing serenely back to their anchorage. They had suffered no damage other than a few minor burns caused by flaming debris.

Around us, many were weeping, including Compton's nephew.

It's the end, he sobbed, it's finished.

Compton put an arm around his shoulders. No, it's not finished, I heard him say. This is just the beginning.

*

Infidelity and unfaithfulness were unknown countries to Shireen. When she listened to relatives talking about the trespasses of others – for example a distant cousin who had been found in compromising circumstances with her sister's husband – she was often more puzzled than shocked. How did such situations come about? What were the words with which these liaisons were proposed? How were they concealed from the khidmatgars and maids and all the other naukar-log?

She was at a loss to understand why anybody would choose to involve themselves in such complicated manoeuvres. Wasn't it easier to go about things in a normal way? And more pleasant besides?

It astounded her now to think that her own husband had been leading another existence for some thirty years, a life of which she had not had the faintest suspicion. To think of a man who could successfully juggle these two utterly different realities was to conjure up a complete stranger. The most disturbing part of it was the way in which Bahram had reached out from his grave to pull her into this spirit-world, this strange dimension of existence where everything was deceit and trickery. What made it worse still was that she had been drawn into it of her own volition, by arranging to meet Zadig Bey again, alone – and not just to apologize, but mainly because she wanted to learn more about Bahram's son. What good would come of it she didn't know – but now that this window had opened she was powerless to turn away from it. To expunge her husband's child from her mind was no more possible than it would have been to forget her own daughters.

As the trip to Bassein approached she obsessed about all the little things that might go wrong. She knew that the coachmen who drove her to the docks that morning would be under orders to escort her aboard, to make sure that she was comfortably settled in. She knew that when they returned they would be questioned. What would they report to her brothers and their wives? What if they caught sight of Zadig Bey and concluded that the meeting had been pre-arranged?

On the way to the docks her apprehensions grew so acute that she broke a fingernail by nibbling on it too hard. But on arriving she realized that she need not have worried: Vico was nothing if not discreet; he knew exactly what to do and had anticipated every eventuality.

The boat was a fine, two-masted batelo, with a crew of six and a curtained cabin in the middle – an eminently respectable vessel. Zadig Bey was nowhere in sight and there was a chaperone present, notably genteel-looking. Her name was Rosa and her clothing, like her deportment, was reminiscent of a nun: she was wearing a severely cut black dress, with long sleeves and a high neck. Her only adornment was a gold cross.

Vico explained that Rosa was a cousin of his, the daughter of an aunt who had married a Goan; Rosa's husband had died the year before, leaving her a widow at the age of thirty.

Widowhood created an instantaneous bond between the two women. They linked arms with each other as Rosa talked about her childhood in Goa, and how she had married a master-cannoneer and moved with him to Macau, where he had died. Alone and childless, she had returned to India to return some of his effects to his family.

Zadig Bey did not make an appearance until the batelo had hoisted sail and pulled out into the bay. Nor was there anything awkward about the manner of his entry. Vico gave Shireen ample warning and she had plenty of time to cover her face with her sari.

Then the four of them sat together, drinking tea and nibbling on khakras. Zadig began to talk about watch-making and the atmosphere was so comfortable that Shireen began to feel silly for being in purdah – especially since Rosa, who was so much younger, was sitting beside her without a veil. She allowed her sari to slip off her face and thought no more of it.

Only when Shireen was completely at her ease did Vico and Rosa slip away, on a pretext, leaving her alone with Zadig. To Shireen's great relief Zadig carried on talking about timepieces so there were no difficult moments of silence. His tact and delicacy went straight to her heart and gave her the courage to say the words that she had prepared.

'Zadig Bey – I owe you an apology.'

'For what?'

'For what I said that day, at the church. I am very, very sorry that I did not believe you.'

'Please, Bibiji, think nothing of it. To tell you the truth, I was moved by your loyalty to your husband.'

'Even though it was undeserved?'

'Bibiji, this I can tell you – he loved you and his daughters very much. Everything he did was for you.'

Shireen could feel her eyes welling up now, and she didn't want to waste any time on tears. 'Tell me about the boy, Zadig Bey, my husband's son. What is he like?'

'Freddie? What can I tell you? Things have never been easy for Freddie. Bahram did what he could for him – but he could not give him the thing he most wanted.'

'What was that?'

Zadig smiled. 'You, Bibiji. Freddie wanted to meet you; he wanted to know you; he wanted to be accepted by you, to be taken into the family. You must understand that Freddie grew up in Canton's floating city, among the "boat-people", who are like outcastes in the eyes of many Chinese – and he wasn't even fully one of them. Yet he knew that his father was rich and had married into a prominent family. He desperately wanted to claim some part of this birthright. He begged Bahram-bhai to take him away from Canton and bring him to Bombay – but Bahram-bhai knew that Freddie would not be accepted, by your family, or by the Parsi community. He knew that it would only make things worse for him.'

There was a catch in Shireen's throat now, and she paused to clear it.

'I can't deny what you say, Zadig Bey: my husband was probably right. There would have been a terrible scandal and my brothers would not have allowed the boy to set foot in the house. Perhaps I too would have refused to meet him. But now that my husband is gone everything has changed. Now that I know about this boy, I will have no rest until I see him. Do you think he might still want to meet me?'

Zadig nodded vigorously. 'Of course, Bibiji. Bahram-bhai's death has left him orphaned and adrift. He has no one in the world now, except a half-sister. He needs you more than ever.'

'But how is it to be arranged, Zadig Bey?'

Zadig steepled his fingertips: 'Bibiji, I have learnt that Freddie is now in Singapore. If you were to travel to China you would have to stop there. To arrange a meeting would not be difficult.'

'You think you will be able to find him?'

'Yes, Bibiji. I am certain that I'll be able to trace him. If you make the journey you will surely meet him. It all depends on you.

*

In preparation for his night-time appointment with Mrs Burnham, Zachary spent many hours walking around the Bethel compound, scouting the grounds and plotting his route. There were several stands of trees between the budgerow and the far corner of the house so he knew that he would not lack for cover. The only foreseeable hazard was the gravel border that ran around the mansion: he would have to tread softly when he crossed it, in case the sound gave him away.

But in the event, these calculations were rendered superfluous by the weather: shortly before it came time for Zachary to leave the budgerow a storm broke over the city.

Zachary found a piece of tarpaulin and wrapped the *Treatise* in it. A few minutes before eleven he tucked the parcel under his arm, stuck a cap on his head and threw an old oilskin over his shoulders. Then he went gingerly down the gangplank, which was slippery with rain, and sprinted across the grounds. With the help of a few flashes of lightning he quickly found his way to a tree that faced Mrs Burnham's boudoir.

The house was in total darkness now, but he was able to detect a trickle of candlelight, spilling out from under Mrs Burnham's curtains. He looked around to make sure there was no one about, and then darted over to the house, crossing the gravel border with a flying leap. The servants' door flew open at the first try and he slipped quickly inside, sliding the bolt into place behind him.

A candle was waiting, as promised, on the first rung of the narrow staircase that lay ahead. His shoes were caked with mud, so he kicked them off, depositing them at the bottom of the stairs, along with his dripping cap and oilskin. Then he grabbed the candle and ran up the steps, to the landing above. A faint glow was visible in the distance, through a pair of interconnecting doors. He began to walk towards it, stepping carefully around the commodes, basins and racks of the goozle-connuh.

Ahead lay the boudoir, a large, comfortably furnished room illuminated by lamps that flickered gently in the draughts that were whipping through the house. At the centre of the room was a huge four-poster bed, swathed in a gauzy mosquito-net. On the far side of the bed were two armchairs: Mrs Burnham was seated in one of these and when Zachary appeared in the doorway she rose to her feet, holding her tall, Junoesque figure stiffly upright.

Until then, Zachary had allowed himself to imagine that the unusually intimate circumstances of their meeting might lead to a slight relaxation in Mrs Burnham's unbending demeanour. This hope was quickly dispelled: the avatar of the Beebee of Bethel that stood before him now was even more forbidding than her other incarnations – in her hands, which were clasped against her chest, she was holding a gleaming, blunt-nosed pistol. Her clothing too was of a warlike aspect: on her head was a velvet turban, and her body was fully encased, from the base of her throat to the tip of her toes, in a garment that shimmered like armour. Only at second glance did Zachary realize that it was a silken robe – a voluminous and heavily embroidered 'banyan' gown, held together, at the waist, by a tasselled cord.

Mrs Burnham wasted no time on pleasantries: she greeted Zachary by wagging her pistol, to signal to him to step inside. But when she saw that his eyes were locked apprehensively upon her weapon, she permitted herself a slight smile.

'I trust my little tamancha will not incommode you, Mr Reid,' she said in a tone of mild amusement. 'The hour of night being what it is I thought it prudent to make sure that it was you and not some unwanted intruder who had gained entry to my boudoir. Now that I am satisfied on that score I will disarm myself.'

Turning aside, she placed the pistol on a nearby teapoy – but although the weapon was indeed out of her hands, it did not escape Zachary's attention that it was still within easy reach; nor did he disregard the note of warning in her voice when she added, off-handedly: 'I am an excellent shot I might add – my father was a brigadier-general in the Bengal Native Infantry you know, and he liked to say that a memsahib's honour is only as good as her marksmanship.'

'Yes, ma'am.'

Zachary was glad now that he had taken the precaution of wrapping the *Treatise* in tarpaulin: he did not like to think of the reproof he might have earned had it been damaged or drenched. He stepped forward, extending the package towards her. 'Here is the book, madam – untouched by rain, I'm glad to say.'

'Thank you.'

She received the book with a nod and pointed to the armchair that faced her own, across a low table. 'Please, Mr Reid, do take that cursy.'

'Thank you.' Zachary was glad to see that there was a tray on the table, with a decanter and two glasses.

Following his gaze, Mrs Burnham said: 'I thought it might be advisable to have some brandy at hand, on a stormy night like this. Please pour some for yourself, Mr Reid – and for me too.'

Zachary filled a glass and was handing it to her when he noticed that she had now armed herself with a notebook and pencil.

'We are pressed for time,' she said by way of explanation, 'and in order to make good use of it I have taken the precaution of listing a few of the questions that I will need to ask. Shall we proceed?'

Zachary made a half-hearted effort to procrastinate: 'Well I don't know . . .'

'Of course you don't,' said Mrs Burnham tartly. 'How could you, since I have yet to put any questions to you? It is important for you to understand, Mr Reid, that the malignancy of your malady varies greatly with the time of its onset and other early experiences. It is thus of the utmost importance to ascertain the precise history of your experience of this illness. So we must start by determining when you fell prey to the disease. Do you remember how old you were when the symptoms first manifested themselves?'

Zachary flushed and dropped his eyes: 'You want to know when I . . . it . . . started?'

'Exactly. And it is important also to establish how you contracted the infection. Did the symptoms present themselves spontaneously? Or were they, so to speak, transmitted by contact with another victim?'

At this, a cry of indignation burst from Zachary's lips. 'Good God, madam! Surely you do not expect me to tell you that?'

Mrs Burnham's face hardened. 'Yes, I most certainly do, Mr Reid.'

'Well then you must prepare for a disappointment, madam,' Zachary retorted. 'It is none of your business and I'll be damned if I answer.'

Mrs Burnham was unmoved by this show of defiance. 'May I remind you, Mr Reid,' she said, in an implacably steely voice, 'that the question – and such answers as it may elicit – are likely to be far more distasteful to me than to you? Nor should you forget that it is through no fault of my own that I find myself in the unfortunate situation of having to make these inquiries. Indeed I cannot understand why you are now affecting these airs of modesty, considering that it was you who presented your . . . your symptoms . . . unbidden before my eyes. Not once but twice.'

'Those were accidents, madam,' said Zachary, 'and they do not give you the right to subject me to such an inquisition.'

'I assure you, Mr Reid,' said Mrs Burnham, the menace in her voice growing ever more pointed, 'that what I have asked of you is by no means as intimate as the disclosures that will be required of you by Dr Allgood should he learn of your condition.'

The colour drained from Zachary's face and his voice fell to a whisper. 'But surely,' he pleaded, 'surely you would not tell him?'

'Well that remains to be seen,' said Mrs Burnham briskly. 'But you should know, in any case, that if Dr Allgood were in my place you would be required to do much more than merely answer questions.'

'What do you mean?' said Zachary, shrinking fearfully into the armchair. 'What else could he want?'

'He would consider it necessary also to examine the . . . the site of your affliction.'

'What?' Zachary looked at her in appalled horror. 'Surely you do not mean . . . ?'

She nodded firmly. 'Yes, Mr Reid. Dr Allgood believes that examinations are imperative in such cases. I will not flinch from disclosing to you that his journals contain many detailed measurements and drawings of a certain element of the male anatomy.' She gave a little sniff and straightened her turban: 'You too would probably be required to sit for a portrait, if you know what I mean.'

'God damn my eyes!' gasped Zachary. 'Has the man no shame?'

'Oh come, Mr Reid,' she said. 'Surely you would not expect a doctor to treat a disease without examining its lesions, would you? And if you are gubbrowed by the thought of being sketched and measured for posterity, then you should know that these are by no means the most intrusive of the doctor's methods.'

A shiver went through Zachary: 'What else then?'

'When necessary the doctor also makes surgical incisions to prevent the recurrence of the seizures.'

'No!'

'Yes indeed,' she continued. 'In particularly recalcitrant cases, he even inserts a pin into the prepuce. He says that a great many lunatics have been cured by these devices.'

'Geekus crow!' Squirming in his seat, Zachary crossed his legs into a protective knot. 'Has the man no mercy?'

Mrs Burnham smiled grimly. 'You see, Mr Reid, you have good reason to be grateful that it is I and not Dr Allgood who is conducting this interview. It should be amply evident to you that your best course is to provide frank and honest answers to my questions.'

The peremptoriness of her manner fanned the winds of mutiny that were stirring inside Zachary. He jumped to his feet. 'No, madam!' he cried. 'This interrogation is utterly iniquitous and I will not submit to it. I bid you good night.'

He strode to the door and was about to open it when Mrs Burnham's voice forced him to halt, in mid-stride. 'You should know, Mr Reid,' she said, in sharp, ringing tones, 'that in the event of your refusing treatment I will be compelled to disclose to Dr Allgood all that I know of your condition. And I do not doubt that when he hears of the incident at the ball, he, in turn, will deem it necessary to inform the relevant authorities.'

Zachary spun around. 'You mean you'll go to the police?'

'So I shall, if necessary.'

'But that is utterly monstrous, madam!'

'To the contrary,' said Mrs Burnham, 'it is a great deal less monstrous than the manner in which my modesty was outraged, at the ball, and in my sewing room. Are you not forgetting, Mr Reid, that I am the victim in this? Would I not be failing in my duty towards my sex if I did not exert myself to make sure that no other woman suffers such outrages? Is it not a matter of public safety?'

Shifting his weight from one foot to another, Zachary drew his sleeve across his face, which was now beaded with sweat.

Mrs Burnham was quick to seize on his hesitation. 'It is wise of you to reconsider, Mr Reid,' she continued. 'If you give a moment's thought to the courses that are open to you I think you will perceive that your best option is to answer my questions. And it is all for your own good, is it not?'

Zachary's shoulders sagged, as though his chest had been suddenly emptied of air. Dragging his feet slowly across the rug, he returned to the armchair and poured himself some more brandy.

'So what else do you want to know, Mrs Burnham?'

*

Kesri was not in the lead on the day when the Pacheesi finally completed its march back to Rangpur, where its Assam base was located. He and his company were assigned to rearguard duty that day, which meant that they did not get on the road until the tents were struck and the magazine was loaded on to carts and mules – and even then they had to march slowly in order to keep pace with the hackery carts that were carrying the sick and the wounded. The carts stopped frequently to allow the physick-coolies to tend to their patients; and at each halt Kesri and his company had to mount guard to protect them from looters and dacoits.

Marches were usually so timed that they ended before the full heat of the day. But only the forward parts of the column benefited from this – the rearguard often had to be on the road at the very hottest time of day. Baked by the afternoon sun, the iron frames of the sepoys' armoured topees became so hot that it was as if they were carrying boiling cauldrons on their heads.

The march was even harder on Kesri than the others since he was the oldest among them – some of the younger men were less than half his age, and none of them had to carry so large a burden of old scars and wounds. Out of consideration for himself he ordered a long rest after the mid-day meal, so that they could wait out the heat. To get everyone moving again took longer than he had expected so that it was almost sunset before the hackery carts were back on the road. By the time the lights of the Rangpur camp came into view it was late at night and Kesri's koortee was soaked in sweat; a thick layer of dust had settled on the wet cloth, clinging to it like plaster.

A mile from the base, Pagla-baba materialized suddenly out of the darkness. Kesri! he cried, tugging at his arm. You have to hurry – the subedar wants you, right now!

Why?

I don't know, but you have to go to his tent ekdum jaldi. He's got many of the sadar-log with him – jamadars, havildars, naiks.

How many?

Nine or ten.

The number startled Kesri. It was very unusual for so many sepoy-afsars to assemble in one place, either in a cantonment or a camp: large meetings were expressly forbidden by the British officers, who believed such gatherings to be conducive to conspiracies and mutiny. A meeting could only be held with the approval of the adjutant; permission was very rarely granted, and then too, only for matters relating to family and caste. It was almost unheard of for such a meeting to be held so late at night.

Pagla-baba knew exactly what was going through Kesri's head.

The subedar has taken permission from the adjutant-sah'b, he said. It must be some kind of family business; only the subedar-sah'b's closest relatives have been asked to attend. They are meeting with some visitors who have come all the way from their village, near Ghazipur.

Do you know who the visitors are?

I know only one of them, said Pagla-baba. He's related to you – Hukam Singh's brother.

Chandan Singh?

Yes. Isn't he your sister Deeti's brother-in-law?

That's right. What's he doing here?

I don't know, Kesri – but you'd better hurry!

*

Mrs Burnham glanced at her notes: 'You will remember, Mr Reid, that I had asked if you could recall when the symptoms of the disease first appeared.'

Zachary drained his brandy and poured himself another: 'I was twelve or thirteen I guess.'

'And did the symptoms manifest themselves spontaneously? Or was the infection transmitted by another victim?'

Zachary swallowed a mouthful of brandy. 'My friend Tommy showed me.'

Mrs Burnham's pencil flew across the notebook. When it came to a stop she cleared her throat. 'And may I ask, Mr Reid, if you are a stranger to that . . . that act which Divine Providence has intended to be consecrated to the purposes of procreation?'

Zachary cleared his throat. 'If you're asking whether I've ever been with a woman, the answer is yes.'

'And how old were you, may I ask, when you were first intimate with a woman?'

He tossed off his brandy and poured more, for both of them. 'Maybe sixteen?'

'And who was she?'

'A ladybird, if you must know.'

'You mean . . . a woman of the streets?'

He gave a derisive snort. 'More like a woman of the house – a bawdy-house, that is.'

'And have you visited those often, Mr Reid?'

'Four or five times – I'm not sure.'

'I see.' She paused to take a deep breath. 'And are those the only women with whom you have . . . fornicated?'

'Yes.'

'Mr Reid.' She cleared her throat and took a sip of brandy. 'Mr Reid – it is really important that you be candid with me.'

He raised his eyebrows. 'I don't understand what you mean, Mrs Burnham. I have been as candid with you as it is possible to be.'

She frowned in reproof. 'Mr Reid – I know that is not true.'

He answered with an angry glare. 'How can you possibly say that? You don't know nothin about me.'

'Please, Mr Reid,' she persisted. 'I urge you to reflect and to be frank with me. Were I to ask if you had ever seduced and compromised a young, innocent girl, would you be able to deny it, in good conscience?'

'Yes, you're darn right I would,' Zachary shot back. 'I've never done nothin of that kind.'

'But I happen to know otherwise, Mr Reid. I know for a fact that you have ravished at least one unfortunate young woman.'

This incensed him. 'It is not a fact, Mrs Burnham, because it ain true! I never ravished no one.'

'But what if I were to inform you, Mr Reid, that it was from the victim herself that I learnt of this? And in this very room at that.'

'I tell you there is no victim!' Zachary cried. 'I don't know who you could be thinking of.'

Looking steadily into his eyes, Mrs Burnham said: 'Paulette Lambert. Can you deny that you have seduced and violated that sweet innocent girl?'

Zachary's mouth fell open and he stared at her in disbelief, temporarily bereft of words. 'That's impossible,' he spluttered at last. 'Paulette could not have said anything like that. It's not possible.'

'But she did. I heard it from her own lips. In this very room.'

'And what exactly did she say?'

'I will tell you, Mr Reid: it happened last year, when Paulette was living with us. I had summoned her here in order to inform her that Mr Justice Kendalbushe was desirous of suing for her hand, in marriage. I will not conceal from you that I was eager for her to accept. I had grown exceedingly fond of Paulette in the short time that she spent with us. I knew that if she accepted the judge's offer she would remain nearby, and the tender companionship that she and I had come to enjoy would be preserved and prolonged. But it was not to be: despite all my dumbcowings Paulette was adamant in her refusal – so much so that my suspicions were aroused. I asked if she had lost her heart to another. She did not deny it, so I asked if the chuckeroo in question was you – and again she did not deny it. My suspicions were further inflamed by this, so I asked if she had compromised herself with you. Again she did not deny it: to the contrary she confirmed to me that she was . . . with child!'

'Impossible,' protested Zachary. 'Mrs Burnham, I am not a stranger to the act of procreation, as I have said, and I can assure you that nothing like that transpired between Paulette and me.'

'I am sorry, Mr Reid,' she retorted, 'but I am sure you will admit that it is impossible to give any credence to the word of someone such as yourself, a chokra of acknowledged lewdness, who thinks nothing of "polishing the pin" in full view of the riverfront – a man so lacking in self-control as to be aroused, in a public place, by a woman who is old enough to be his aunt!'

'Oh come, Mrs Burnham,' he said weakly. 'Surely you are not that old?'

'If I were as old as your grandmother, I doubt that it would make any difference to a badmash as wayward as yourself!' Mrs Burnham's voice rose: 'Let me tell you, Mr Reid, that from the day Paulette ran away from this house I knew that you were to blame for her disappearance. I did not doubt for a minute that she had run off to give birth to your bastard child. The one person in whom I confided my fears was fully in agreement with me: Baboo Nob Kissin. Other than him I told no one, not even my own husband, because I did not wish to add to Paulette's burden of shame. But you may be sure that I did not intend for the matter to pass without retribution either. From the day you arrived here I have been determined to make you see the error of your ways, and to make restitution for what you have done to Paulette.'

Mrs Burnham's manner had grown increasingly heated as she was speaking and two bright spots of colour had appeared on her cheeks. The fraying of her composure had a strangely calming effect on Zachary, and when she fell silent he took a moment or two to think of how best to persuade her of the absolute groundlessness of her conjectures.

'You are certainly right about one thing, Mrs Burnham,' he said at length, in a level tone. 'It is true that I felt very powerfully drawn to Paulette, from the moment of our first meeting, on the *Ibis*, last year. But we were alone together only a couple of times and all our meetings ended badly, with quarrels and arguments. And yes, once there was a kiss, but that was all. I even asked her to marry me one time, but she wouldn't hear of it. As for being seduced or compromised by me, that would be laughable if it were not offensive. She was never in the least danger of that. If she was with child, it certainly wasn't because of me . . .'

Here, suddenly, a thought occurred to him that made the words wither on his lips.

He sat back and looked up at the ceiling, fingering his chin, as ideas and possibilities raced through his mind.

'What is it, Mr Reid?'

Lowering his gaze, he saw that she had put her notebook aside and was leaning forward in her chair, watching him with an expression of the most intense curiosity. This sent a thrill of satisfaction through him; it was as if there had been a sudden shift in the balance between them, as happens on a ship at the change of watch, when the powers of command are transferred from one officer to another.

'Oh it's nothing, Mrs Burnham,' he said, making a pretence of off-handedness. 'Just a thought that came into my mind.'

'What is it? Please tell me.'

He paused to savour the note of supplication in her voice. 'I don't know if I should, Mrs Burnham,' he said.

'But why not?'

'That's the thing, Mrs Burnham: this isn't about me and Paulette. It concerns you too and may cause you great distress.'

Mrs Burnham's eyes dropped. 'Mr Reid,' she said, in a dry, taut voice, 'tell me . . .' – it was she who now had to pause to mop her face – 'tell me, is it something to do with . . . with my husband?'

He nodded. 'Yes.'

She clasped her hands and pressed them to her chest. 'Mr Reid, you must speak. I need to know.'

Her tone was one of entreaty, all trace of her former imperious-ness having now disappeared. It seemed hardly possible that this was the same woman who a short while before had been issuing veiled threats, in a voice of steely command.

'Are you sure, Mrs Burnham?' said Zachary. 'There'll be no turning back, you know.'

'Yes. I'm sure.'

'Very well then.'

A peal of thunder sounded nearby and Zachary waited for the sound to rumble through the room.

'Mrs Burnham – I hope you will not regret hearing this, but here it is. One night, soon after she ran away from your house, Paulette arranged to meet with me. She told me that she did not want ever to return to Bethel and begged me to get her a passage to Mauritius, on the *Ibis*. I asked why she was so desperate to go, and she told me she wanted to escape from Calcutta, at all costs, because she was afraid of . . .'

'Mr Burnham?'

'Yes. So I asked her if anything unseemly had happened between herself and your husband and she answered by telling me a strange story.'

'Please go on. I am listening.'

'She said that while she was here Mr Burnham would often call her into his study, to give her scriptural lessons in private.'

'Go on, Mr Reid.'

'She said that as the lessons progressed Mr Burnham had asked her to do . . . certain things.'

'What things?'

'Well, I may as well say it: what he wanted was a larruping – I guess he likes the feel of a girl's hand on his rump. Don't understand it myself, but there're all sorts in this world.'

'Did she do it?'

Zachary nodded. 'She agreed because he had been kind to her and she did not wish to appear ungrateful. But one day she realized that what she was doing was very dangerous so she decided to run away.'

'Please be honest with me, Mr Reid – did she run away because she had been seduced? Violated?'

'It seems almost certain to me now that she was,' said Zachary, 'but she did not say so at the time. She said rather, that she had decided to escape before it came to that. I believed her story then, but now that I've heard your tale it seems clear to me that Paulette was hiding something – lying, not to put too fine a point on it.'

Mrs Burnham began to sob quietly into her hands, covering her face.

'But Mrs Burnham,' said Zachary quickly. 'No matter what happened between your husband and Paulette, this I can tell you: Paulette was not actually with child – what she expressed to you was only, perhaps, the worst of her fears.'

'How do you know?'

'Because we met again, months later, on the *Ibis*, and had she been with child, it would certainly have shown by that time. But there was no sign of anything like that. I hope you will find some consolation in that.'

'Consolation?' said Mrs Burnham, sobbing into her cupped hands. 'Oh Mr Reid, how can you speak to me of consolation . . . when you have just confirmed my worst fears and suspicions?'

The heaving of her shoulders had loosened the stays of her robe and a lapel had dropped, to provide a glimpse of the nightdress she was wearing underneath: Zachary saw that the thin, cotton cloth was straining against the swell of her bosom. Drawing his eyes guiltily away, he said: 'So you had some suspicion, then?'

She nodded. 'In the past, yes – I had often wondered whether there might be something untoward between my husband and the young girls we sometimes sheltered in our house. But I would never have thought it possible with Paulette, who seemed to me the purest spirit I had ever come across. That was why I *lavished* my affection on her. And now I don't know which betrayal is worse, hers or my husband's.'

Burying her head in her hands she began to weep. Slowly her statuesque figure seemed to crumple and her head fell almost to her knees.

Zachary rose from his chair and went to kneel beside her. 'Mrs Burnham,' he said quietly. 'You are not the only one who has been betrayed, you know. I too have been lied to and betrayed by Paulette. And I thought she was the love of my life.'

He couldn't tell whether she had heard him, so he put a hand on her shoulder. 'Mrs Burnham?'

At his touch she raised her face and narrowed her eyes. 'Why Mr Reid . . .' she whispered, her eyes straying to his head. 'Oh, look at you – your hair is still wet . . . from the rain, I suppose.'

She stretched out a hand and touched his dark hair, gingerly, with a knuckle. Then her fingers opened, entwining themselves in his curls, and suddenly she pulled his face towards her lips.

He responded with such eagerness that her armchair began to tilt slowly backwards and then fell over sideways, spilling them both on the floor and knocking the turban off her head. With his lips still locked on hers, Zachary began to tug at the lapels of her robe. In the process of sloughing it off they rolled over once, and then again. Then his fingers went to the neck of her nightdress and he pulled at the cloth. When he was unable to make any headway there, he lost patience and tore through the soft cotton to reveal her breasts.

Then it was her turn to claw at his shirt which came apart suddenly, with a tearing sound. He was trying at the same time to kick off his drawers and breeches and in the midst of their struggles they tumbled over each other again, bumping into something which fell over with a great crash of splintering wood and shattered glass.

Zachary looked up, startled, but she pulled his face down again. 'It's just the brandy, and the table,' she whispered in his ear. 'It doesn't matter. No one will hear it over the storm.'

Her torn nightdress had wound itself around their shoulders now, and his half-discarded drawers and breeches were wrapped around their ankles. When they tried to move they began to roll in the other direction and crashed into something else.

Zachary's lips were on her breasts and he didn't bother to look up. But he caught the sound of her voice, whispering: 'It's just my tamancha.'

Throwing her arms around him, she wrapped her legs around his hips, clinging to his body as though she were holding on to a branch in a storm. Then a moan broke from her parted lips and grew slowly into a prolonged, rising cry that ended with a steep arching of her body. Suddenly she went limp in Zachary's arms and he too stopped moving – now it was as if a fuse had been lit in the depths of his body, and a spark were going around and around, in a descending spiral, travelling down a wire to the bottom of a very deep mine-shaft. When the wire ran out there occurred a detonation that shook him to the core, creating a blast that rattled his bones and wrenched his muscles. When the explosion reached his head everything turned yellow, as if in the light of a flame, and then slowly, the glow faded away, to be replaced by darkness.

Afterwards, the sensation of returning to awareness was like none that Zachary had ever experienced before. It wasn't like rising upwards, from darkness towards light; rather it was like falling from a cloud. He had no conception of how much time had passed but he knew that he was still on the floor, his limbs entwined with Mrs Burnham's.

When he stirred and tried to disentangle himself, she whispered into his ear: 'No not yet: wait a little. Tomorrow we will wake to an eternity of guilt and remorse. Since we have only this one night together, we may as well deserve our punishment.'

Zachary pulled his head back in surprise. 'What do you mean, Mrs Burnham? Are you sayin there won't be another time?'

She brushed her lips tenderly against his face. 'Yes, m'dear – I'm sorry but it must be so. This is the last and only time. Don't you see? It is too dangerous – if even a whiff were to reach Mr Burnham, he would murder us both. It is too great a risk.'

'But why should any whiff reach him? We can be careful, can't we? There will be other nights when the house is empty, surely?'

She shook her head and gave him a melancholy smile. 'And to what end? Where can it lead? You're a penniless boy, and I'm a wife and mother, much older than you.'

'How old are you then?'

'Thirty-three. And you?'

'Twenty-one. Almost twenty-two.'

She kissed him on the forehead. 'You see,' she said. 'I'm old enough to be your aunt. You'll grow tired of me soon enough. Let us forget about the future and make the best of the hours that are left to us.'

*

The subedar's tent was at the head of the sepoy lines, facing the parade ground. The tents of the English officers lay on the other side: in one of them an immensely enlarged silhouette of Captain Mee's head could be seen, projected upon the canvas by a brightly glowing lamp.

The subedar's tent was also well illuminated, with candles and lamps. Assembled inside were some fifteen men. Of these a dozen were Kesri's fellow afsars – NCOs of the Pacheesi. They were all blood relatives of the subedar: unlike Kesri, who was in his soiled uniform, they were dressed in off-duty clothes, dhotis and ungahs.

As for the visitors, Kesri recognized only one: Chandan Singh, Deeti's brother-in-law – a scrawny youth with a slack mouth and darting eyes. Kesri had met him once before, at the cantonment in Barrackpore. He had come to take Hukam Singh back to their village, after his discharge from the army. On that occasion he had especially sought Kesri out to thank him for saving Hukam Singh's life.

It was on Kesri's lips now to say some customary words of con-dolence to Chandan Singh, in acknowledgement of his brother's death. But when Chandan Singh turned to look at him the words died on Kesri's lips – the youth's face was screwed into an angry scowl; his eyes were bloodshot and filled with rage.

Kesri realized now that something was very wrong. He noticed also that he was the only man standing – the subedar had not invited him to take a seat even though everyone else was sitting, including a couple of men who were junior to him in rank. It dawned on Kesri now that this was not just a deliberate insult: it was as if he had been summoned before a tribunal, a cross between a court martial and a caste panchayat, with the subedar presiding as the supreme judge.

Kesri stiffened, as if on parade, and turned to face Nirbhay Singh. Subedar sah'b, he said, you sent for me?

Yes, Havildar Kesri Singh, said the subedar. I sent for you. It is because we have received some very serious news today.

The subedar's voice was slow, measured and grave. Kesri recognized his tone, because he had watched him testify at several courts martial: his bearing was the same today as it had been on those occasions. His expression was one of unsmiling gravity; his words flowed at a slower pace than usual and were more clearly enunciated. The pitch was perfectly steady and when he wanted to emphasize something he did it not by raising his voice but by stroking his moustache.

Some time ago, said the subedar, looking directly into Kesri's eyes, I told you that I had received a letter with news of deaths in my family. I told you that my brother Bhyro Singh had passed away, as also my nephew Hukam Singh, with whom you had served in Burma, and who was married to your sister. Today we have learnt much more about their passing, from Chandan Singh and these others from his village. They have travelled for months to bring us the news. We have learnt that the matter was much more complicated than we had thought.

The subedar paused: And we have learnt also that you are implicated in it.

Me? cried Kesri. But how is that possible? I was here, with all of you. I did not even know of these things. How can I be implicated?

Through your sister.

Here a slight tremor entered the subedar's voice and he paused to stroke his moustache and collect himself. When he resumed, his voice was steady again.

It appears, havildar, that your sister had been having illicit relations with another man – a herdsman of low caste.

At this a collective sound, a groan of horror and revulsion, rose from the assembled men. Kesri stared at the subedar for a moment, in disbelief. Then he cried out: Impossible! I know my sister – I know she would not do anything like that.

Now Chandan Singh, who had been crouching tensely in a corner, lost control of himself and began to shout. If you knew that bitch, he screamed, then you would know that she is a *randi* – a whore! And a murderer too. She poisoned my mother . . . and my brother . . .

Chup rah! The subedar signalled to Chandan Singh to hold his tongue: It's not your place to speak here.

Then he turned to Kesri again.

What we have learnt today, havildar, is that your sister ran off with the herdsman immediately after Hukam Singh's death. It seems she had made preparations for her escape even before – she had sent her daughter into hiding. This is why there is a strong suspicion that she poisoned Hukam Singh; but we will let that pass since it cannot be proven. What is certain, in any case, is that the two of them had planned their escape with great care: their intention was to pose as girmitiyas and run off to the island of Mauritius, across the sea. But on the way they were recognized by my brother, Bhyro Singh – that was how he met his end. It was your sister's lover who killed him, with her help.

Kesri had never heard such an unlikely tale. *E na ho saké –* this cannot be true. He shook his head in disbelief: Subedar-sah'b, you know I have the greatest respect for you. But how can I believe all this? My sister has never been out of our zilla; how could she have planned to go across the sea? It is just not possible.

But that is what happened, said the subedar. An official inquiry was held in Calcutta many months ago. We were not aware of it because we were in the jungle. But the conclusions and judgements have been printed and published – in English and Hindustani.

He held up two pieces of paper.

Here are the judgements. We have all gone through them – there can be no doubt of what happened. Chandan Singh and the other men travelled to Calcutta so that they could attend the hearings and ensure that the killers were brought to justice. But God has already seen to one part of that: Bhyro Singh's murderer, your sister's lover, is dead. He drowned while trying to escape from the ship. But your sister is still alive, and while she lives, neither I nor my family can be at peace, for we cannot forget the shame and dishonour she has brought on us – and on you too, Kesri Singh, for you are her brother.

Kesri shook his head again. Subedar-sah'b, he said, there must be some mistake; it must be some other woman. I know my sister . . .

Aur ham tohra se achha se jaana taani! And I know her better than you!

Chandan Singh leapt up and took a couple of steps towards Kesri, shaking his fist. Your sister is a whore and a bitch, he shouted. She has lived next to my house these last seven years so I can tell you about her. Day after day she offered herself to me, in the fields. She would plead with me to take her, to give her another child. I would cry shame on her, reminding her that she was married to my brother – but what is shame to a whore? Finding no one else, she took up with that filthy ox-herder. We have seen that man leaving their house in the mornings – you ask anyone in our village. We have seen it with our own eyes . . .

Suddenly Kesri's feet began to move. Before he knew it, one of his hands was on Chandan Singh's throat. Drawing back his other hand he hit him across the face, throwing the weight of his body behind the blow. Chandan Singh went spinning past his companions to collapse against the canvas of the tent.

Kesri would have jumped on him but before he could make another move, four men flung themselves on him. Pinioning his arms, they wrestled him around to face the subedar again.

The subedar's composure was undisturbed.

Listen to me, Kesri Singh, he said, in his grave, steady voice. We of our family have done a lot for you. We accepted you into this paltan even though you were not one of us. Because of our generous natures we treated you fairly and encouraged you to feel at home here and helped you reach the rank that you now enjoy. We went still further and accepted your sister into our family, even though she had a dirty complexion and was past the age of marriage;

as for her dowry it was not fit for a pauper. All this we did for you, but you never showed any gratitude for it; nor did you give us any sign of appreciation. Behind our backs you scorned us, and made fun of us. We know that you think that this paltan cannot get on without you. None of this is a secret to us. We have put up with it all this time, because we are by nature generous and forgiving. Why, the other day it even came to my ears that after hearing of my brother's death you had distributed sweets in the camp-bazar, to the randis and naach-walis! But still I said nothing, knowing that your punishment would come from the heavens. And so it has – for what has happened now cannot be overlooked. It is a stain on our family's honour – and your face too is blackened by it. The only way you can redeem your honour, Kesri Singh, is by delivering your sister to us so that she can be made to answer for what she has done. Until that day no one in this paltan – not the afsars and nor the jawans – will eat with you or accept water from you, or even exchange words with you. From now on you have no place in this paltan – if you choose to remain here it will be as a ghost. I will explain all this to the English officers in the morning; as you know, in matters of family and caste, they always respect our decisions. I will tell them that as far as we are concerned you are now a pariah, an outcast. In our eyes you are no better than a stray dog; you are worse than filth. For you to remain in this tent for another moment is intolerable: it is an insult to our biraderi. You will never set foot in any of our tents ever again. That is all I have to say to you.

The subedar hawked up a gob of phlegm and spat it on the ground.

Abh hamra aankhi se dur ho ja! Now get out of my sight, Kesri Singh! I never want to set eyes on you again.

Seven

The walk from the subedar's tent to his own was one of the longest of Kesri's life. Despite the lateness of the hour many men were still up, whispering outside their tents. Kesri passed a few sepoys from his own company and not one of them uttered a greeting or even looked him in the face: it was evident that they knew that he had been declared an outcaste. Everyone drew back, so that an empty space seemed to open around Kesri, following him down the path. It was as if he had become a moving source of defilement.

Kesri could feel their eyes burning into his back; he could hear their voices too, sniggering and whispering. He wished that one of them would say something to his face: he would have liked nothing better than to pick a fight – but he knew there was no hope of that. None of them would offer him that satisfaction; they feared him too much to take him on alone.

When his tent came within sight, Kesri saw that a pack of dogs had gathered around it. They were fighting over a heap of bones and offal that someone had emptied there, in his absence. Knowing that he was being watched, he skirted around the dogs without slackening his step – he was determined not to give them the satisfaction of gloating over his downfall.

Stepping inside his tent, he saw that his belongings were lying scattered about on the ground. His servant had disappeared: it seemed that the chootiya had seized the opportunity to run away with some of his utensils.

Kesri lit a candle and began to gather his things together. As he was picking through the pile he came upon a small picture, painted in bright colours on a scrap of cloth. It was a drawing of a little girl, done in bold, flat lines. He recognized it immediately:

it was Deeti's handiwork; the child was her daughter, Kabutri. Deeti had given it to him at their last meeting in Nayanpur, when Kesri was on leave at home.

Kesri sat down on the edge of his charpoy and stared at the picture, with his elbows on his knees.

What had become of Kabutri? And of Deeti?

The tale of her eloping with a lover and boarding a ship for Mareech seemed like nonsense to him, hardly worth a thought. But some of the story's details were certainly believable: that Hukam Singh had died for instance – his health had been declining for a long time so his death could hardly be counted as a surprise. Nor was it hard to believe that Deeti would try to extricate herself from the clutches of her husband's family once he was gone.

Clearly something had happened to her, and even though Kesri had no way of knowing what it was, he sensed that it was the cause of his family's long silence: clearly the matter was too delicate to be disclosed to the paid scribblers who usually wrote their letters for them. To learn the truth he would have to wait till he went home – which would not be for a long time yet.

Kesri fell on his charpoy and lay still, listening to the familiar sounds of the camp: the bells of the watch; the drunken laughter of men returning from the camp-bazar; the horses, whinnying in their enclosure. Somewhere a young sepoy was singing a song about going home to his village.

The paltan had been his home and family for nineteen years, yet it was clear to him now that he had never truly belonged to it. He understood that his dream of rising to the rank of subedar had never stood any chance of being realized. The present subedar and his kinsmen would never have allowed it – in their eyes he had always been an interloper and they would have found some pretext for evicting him. And the worst part of it was that none of this was truly new: he had known it all along, in his heart, but had failed to recognize and act on it.

This realization brought on a wave of disgust, directed as much at himself as towards the men he had considered his comrades-in-arms. He remembered that Gulabi had often tried to warn him about his enemies but he had never paid attention. Now she too would have to sever her connections with him: if not, she would lose her place in the camp-bazar – the subedar would make sure of that.

For Gulabi's sake, as much as for his own, Kesri understood that he would have to leave the battalion. Once a sentence of ostracism had been passed it was impossible for a man to continue in his old paltan. Kesri had seen it happen before so he knew the subedar had it in his power to make it impossible for him to discharge his duties: if he were to turn up at the parade ground tomorrow, his orders would not be obeyed.

There was no doubt of it – he would have to leave. But where was he to go? To transfer to another unit at this point in his career would be very difficult; and to retire now would mean sacrificing the pension that he would be entitled to if he remained in the army a few more years. But what was he to do in the interim?

The cruellest part was that this had happened at a time when he was too tired to think clearly. He stretched himself out on his charpoy and dozed off. When he woke next it was to find Pagla-baba sitting beside him.

Arré Kesri, why are you sleeping? Haven't you heard? Mee-sah'b is leaving for Calcutta tomorrow.

Kesri sat up with a start. What are you saying, Pagla-baba?

Didn't Mee-sah'b ask you something the other day?

Suddenly Kesri remembered the adjutant's offer.

Are you saying I should volunteer for the expedition?

Yes, Kesri, what else?

Kesri jumped to his feet and lifted the canvas flap of his tent. It was well past midnight now, but across the parade ground, in the adjutant's tent, a lamp was still burning.

Go, Kesri – go now.

Kesri caught hold of Pagla-baba's hand. I'll go, he said, but listen – tell Gulabi to come to me tonight. I want to see her – one last time.

Theek hai.

A moment later, Pagla-baba slipped away, as softly as he had come. Kesri stepped out of his tent, stiffened his shoulders and began to walk towards the officers' lines.

Had the adjutant been anyone other than Captain Mee, the

thought of intruding upon him at this hour of the night would not have occurred to Kesri. But his bond with Captain Mee was different from the usual relationship between sepoy and officer: looking at the lamp in the adjutant's tent he had the distinct feeling that Captain Mee was expecting him.

'Sir? Mee-sah'b?'

'Yes? Who is it?' The flaps at the tent's entrance parted and Captain Mee's face appeared between them.

'Oh it's you, havildar. Come in.'

Stepping inside, Kesri saw that Captain Mee was preparing for his departure. An overfilled trunk stood beside his cot and a heap of papers lay piled on his desk.

'I'm leaving early tomorrow,' said Captain Mee curtly, 'for Calcutta.'

'I know, sir,' said Kesri. 'That is why I have come.'

'Yes, havildar. Go on.'

'I also want to go, sir. With you.'

'Really?'

'Yes, sir. I want to go as balamteer.'

Captain Mee's face broke into a wide smile. He stepped up to Kesri with his hand outstretched: 'That's the barber, havildar! Knew you'd come up trumps. Don't know why you've changed your mind, but I'm fizzing glad you have!'

Kesri was not taken in, either by the captain's jocular tone, or by his profession of ignorance. As with any good adjutant, very little happened in the battalion without the captain knowing of it: scuffles and quarrels; thefts and arguments – nothing evaded his attention. Having himself served as Mee-sahib's first and most trusted informer, it was no secret to Kesri that the captain had sources in every company and platoon. News of the meeting in the subedar's tent would have reached him within minutes of its conclusion and he would have grasped immediately what it meant for Kesri. Sentences of ostracism had been passed before in the paltan, not just among the sepoys but also among the officers: when they did it to one of their own they'd say that he had been 'sent to Coventry'; among them too it amounted to a sentence of expulsion.

Kesri understood that it was not out of ignorance but tact that the captain had made no reference to his plight. He was deeply touched: 'Thank you, Kaptán-sah'b.'

Captain Mee brushed this aside. 'Well it's settled then,' he said. 'I don't think the CO will object, but still, I'd better get you to sign the papers right now so that he can see them first thing in the morning.'

Through the rest of the interview Mr Mee's demeanour remained crisply matter-of-fact. But at the end, when all the paperwork had been completed, his manner changed: he stepped out from behind his field-desk and placed a hand on Kesri's shoulder.

'I'm glad you're coming along, havildar,' he said in an unusually sombre voice. 'I was hoping you would. I doubt there's another pair of men in the battalion who know each other as well as you and I.'

The directness of Captain Mee's words took Kesri aback. He would not have expressed himself in this way, but it struck him now that the adjutant was right. It was a fact that after having spent almost two decades in the paltan, none of his fellow sepoys had uttered a word of sympathy to him; the only man who had put a friendly hand on his shoulder was not someone of his own caste and colour but rather an Angrez on whom he had no claim whatever. The thought caused an unaccustomed prickling in Kesri's eyes and he realized, to his shock, that he was near tears.

Fortunately, the interview was almost at an end.

'All right then, havildar,' said Captain Mee. 'Please report to the officers' mess after choti-hazri tomorrow.'

Ji aj'ten-sahib. Kesri snapped off a salute and stepped outside.

It was very late now and the campground was empty. Back in his tent Kesri packed a few of his things before lying down. For a while he listened for footsteps thinking that Gulabi might come, although in his heart he knew she wouldn't. He could not find it in himself to blame her for staying away; if she were found out the subedar was sure to visit some dire punishment on her: to risk her livelihood, and that of her girls, would be foolhardy.

But even though he understood her situation, the thought that he would never see her again filled him with sadness. No one knew his injuries as well as she did. Her touch was so deft that she could make the sensitive edges of old scars pulsate with feeling; her fingers worked such magic that it was as if old wounds had been miraculously transformed into organs of pleasure. Now it was as if all his scars were weeping for her touch.

He remembered the very first time he had lain with Gulabi, as a raw recruit, and he recalled how a voice in his head had warned that he would pay for his pleasure one day. Now that the day had come, he resolved that he would go back to practising the disciplines of celibacy that he had abandoned on joining the Pacheesi: to return to the wrestler's state of *brahmacharya* would be his penance for the years he had wasted as a sepoy.

Kesri thought of his years with the Pacheesi – the battles and skirmishes, and the pride he had taken in the paltan – and a bitter, ashen taste filled his mouth. He remembered that it was Deeti who had conspired to get him into the battalion, and he wondered if it had been written in their shared kismat that she would also be the cause of his leaving it. Yet he felt no rancour towards her. He had only himself to blame, he knew, not just for having cherished a vain hope, but also for sacrificing Deeti to his own ambitions and sending her into the family of Subedar Bhyro Singh, knowing full well what those people were made of.

If Deeti had willed this retribution on him, he would not have blamed her.

*

For Zachary, the consequences of his night with Mrs Burnham were even worse than she had predicted: not only did he have to deal with a heavy burden of guilt and remorse, he also had to cope with the bone-chilling fear of her husband's vengeance. Everywhere he looked, he saw reminders of Mr Burnham's power. What would the Burra Sahib do if he got a whiff of his wife's infidelity? The thought sent shivers through Zachary and he cursed himself for having taken such a senseless risk, merely for a single night's gratification.

Yet, strangely, contrition was not enough to expunge the night from Zachary's memory. Even as his head was aching with apprehension other parts of his body would stir and tingle as they exhumed, from their own storehouses of memory, recollections of the explosive pleasures that he had experienced. Then his self-reproach would turn to regret and he would curse himself for not having made the night last longer; involuntarily he would find himself yearning to relive that night, just one more time.

But that was impossible of course. Hadn't she said, with absolute finality, 'this is the last and only time'? He often repeated those words to himself, for they offered a kind of comfort when his burden of guilt and fear weighed most heavily on him. But there were times also when the sound of the words would change, even as they echoed through his head, and he would wonder whether they had been said with as much conviction as he had imagined. Sometimes one thought would lead to another and he would begin to dream of receiving another message from the boudoir, heralding another assignation and another sprint across the garden.

But that message, at once dreaded and hoped-for, never came. Week after week went by, and not only was there no note or chitty, he did not even properly set eyes on Mrs Burnham – all he saw of her was a shadow on the purdahs of her buggy, as it rattled down the driveway, ferrying her to some levée, lecture or burra-khana.

Her silence, as it lengthened, grew increasingly frightening. He could imagine that having repented of her adultery, she might now seek to absolve herself of all guilt by making up a story about him; back in Baltimore he had heard tales of great ladies who had seduced their slaves and then accused them of unspeakable things.

And then one night he was seized by a paroxysm of shivers as a thought flashed through his mind. Could it be that she was avoiding him because their night together had resulted in a pregnancy?

This possibility ripped apart the last shreds of his peace of mind. He had been working on the budgerow's stem-cheeks that day but now he put down his tools and began to brood, trying to think of some way in which he might contrive to meet Mrs Burnham, in private. It occurred to him that he might be able to break into her boudoir by picking the lock on the door that led to the servants' staircase. But he could not summon the courage to go ahead with it – his fevered mind kept returning to her pistol, conjuring up reasons why she might elect to shoot him.

One day, as he was agonizing over what to do next, Mr Doughty dropped by. It turned out that he had come to invite Zachary to a tiffin the following week.

In his present state of mind Zachary had no inclination to go to a nuncheon at the Doughties': but so disordered were his emotions that he could not summon the wit to make a convincing excuse. 'Oh thank you, Mr Doughty,' he stammered, 'but I don't think I have the proper rig . . .'

Mr Doughty gave a hearty laugh. 'Well then, my dear young chuckeroo, you can always tog yourself up in a toga again. I'm sure Mrs Burnham would be most diverted – she had a grand old cackle about it the last time. Said you looked like the rummest Rum-johnny she'd ever seen.'

At the mention of Mrs Burnham's name, Zachary's mind began to race. He scratched his chin and said, with an off-handed air: 'Oh? So, Mrs Burnham will be there too?'

'Yes – and a few other mems, missies and larkins as well. But we're a little short of launders and chuckeroos which is why Mrs Doughty sent me over to puckrow you.'

'I'll be there,' said Zachary. 'Thank you, Mr Doughty.'

'Good. And if you're looking to tog yourself out on the cheap you couldn't do better than to visit the auction houses on Sunday. They often sell off the estates of the recently deceased – you'll get all you need for a copper or two.'

Zachary decided to heed Mr Doughty's advice, and when Sunday came he reached under his mattress and pulled out his purse. The coins in it were miserably few: counting them out one by one, it seemed to Zachary that all his other travails would have been bearable if only he had not been so damned poor.

His eyes strayed to the gilded sconces that lined the interior of the budgerow and it occurred to him that it would be easy to sell a couple of them in the market: nobody would notice. He rose to his feet and went to take a closer look. Prying them off would be simple enough, just a matter of extracting a few nails.

He fetched an awl and was about to dig into the wood when a sudden qualm made him withdraw his hand. Behind that gilded sconce he could see a tunnel that led to some mysterious unknown – thievery – and he could not bring himself to go in. He put aside the awl and stuffed his meagre few coins into the pocket of his breeches.

A long walk brought Zachary to the centre of Calcutta from where he asked his way to the doors of one of the auction houses on Russell Street. At the cost of almost emptying his pocket, he was able to acquire a suit that had belonged to a recently deceased apothecary by the name of Quinn.

Not till the morning of the Doughties' tiffin did it occur to him that the suit had a strange smell – of mildew and sweat mingled with the odour of something medicinal – but of course it was too late to do anything about it. He put it on, hoping that no one would notice – in vain, for the khidmatgar who opened the door for him, at the Doughties' residence, recognized the suit immediately and gave a shriek, as if he'd seen a ghost: *Quinn-sahib? Arré dekho – Quinn-sah'b ka bhoot aa giya!*

The noise brought Mr Doughty to the door and he too uttered a cry of surprise: 'Good God, Reid! Those aren't old Quinn's togs you're wearing, are you? He had only one suit, you know, and his shop was around the corner so we saw him in it every day. Mrs Doughty and every other memsahib in the city bought their laudanum from him.'

Zachary spluttered in protest: 'Well, it was you, Mr Doughty, who said to go to the auctions. How was I to know?'

'Oh well, never mind. You can hardly take it off now. Come into the bettuck-connuh and put your bottom to anchor.'

Zachary had taken only a few steps into the receiving room when he caught sight of Mrs Burnham. She was on the far side, seated on a settee, wearing an airy gown of pink tulle, with trimmings the colour of rich red wine; her face, with its tumbling halo of curls, was framed by the rim of a heart-shaped bonnet. The feather on the bonnet's crown was swaying gently under the punkah that was swinging overhead, stirring the sultry air.

Although Zachary was well within Mrs Burnham's field of vision she seemed to be oblivious to his presence: she was chatting to two severe-looking memsahibs with her usual air of languid indifference.

Almost at once Zachary's eyes dropped to her midriff. Seven weeks had passed since that night and it was conceivable that if it had led to the outcome that he most feared – a pregnancy – some sign of it would already be visible. He saw nothing to confirm his fears – but he could not wrench his gaze away. And then his eyes played a cruel trick on him: they stripped away the frothing pink fabric of her dress to reveal what lay beneath. He beheld once again the slope of her belly, curving steeply down towards a forest of soft, downy curls. He remembered the ease with which he had slipped through that silken canopy and how the warmth of his welcome had led him to plunge deeper and deeper until he reached what seemed to be an unattainable extremity; he remembered how joyfully he had been received in that haven and how this had created the illusion that he had been accepted into an empire where he had never thought he would belong; and as that fantasy faded, and his nose caught, once again, the musty smell of his threadbare suit, he wondered how it was possible that the most secret parts of himself could have been given so warm a welcome by someone who would not grant the least gesture of recognition to his clothed body.

The injustice of it kindled a spark of defiance in him, propelling him to move towards the settee. It was only natural, he told himself, that he should make his salaams to her – it was no secret, after all, that he was an employee of her husband's, almost a retainer: and had she not danced with him in public, at the ball?

Mrs Burnham was still gossiping airily with her companions and showed no signs of having noticed his presence. As he approached the settee, he caught the fluting sound of her voice: 'Oh I assure you, my dear Augusta, the trouble in China is due solely to Commissioner Lin – he's a monster, Mr Burnham says, an absolute dragon . . . !'

She seemed to be intent on her story and took not the slightest notice of Zachary until he was directly in front of her, bowing. Then she gave a little start and glanced up. ''Pon my civvy! Oh it's you . . . Mr . . . Mr . . . ? Never mind . . .'

She inclined her head slightly, to give Zachary a perfunctory nod: the gesture was not so much a greeting as a sign of dismissal. Then, turning her shoulder on him, she resumed her conversation.

The snub stunned Zachary: he turned on his heels quickly, to hide his flaming cheeks, and shambled off in the other direction.

As he was making his retreat he heard her say, in a piercing whisper: 'I'm sorry I didn't introduce him, Augusta dear, but I can't for the life of me remember his name. Anyway it doesn't signify – he's a nobody, just one of Mr Burnham's mysteries.'

'A mystery, is he? From the smell of him, I'd have taken him for a druggerman.'

'Whatever made the Doughties think of asking him?'

'Really, I must have a word with them – they'll be inviting the malis and moochies next.'

It was all that Zachary could do not to clap his hands over his ears: if a whip had landed on his back it could not have had a harsher sting.

To remain in that room another minute was more than he could bear. Giving Mr Doughty the slip he headed straight for the door. But as he was picking up his hat he threw a glance over his shoulder – and at exactly that moment Mrs Burnham's eyes happened to look in his direction.

Their eyes met for only an instant but it was enough for her gaze to lodge in his head like an anchor-fluke.

*

For several weeks after Shireen's visit to Bassein there was no word from Zadig Bey: knowing that he was due to leave for Colombo soon, she began to wonder whether she would see him again before his departure.

As the days went by this question assumed an urgency that confused Shireen: it seemed shameful to her that her mind should dwell so much on this subject. She tried to persuade herself that it was only because of his connection with Bahram that Zadig figured so often in her thoughts; sometimes she told herself that his entry into her life was a sign; that Bahram himself had sent his friend to her, to open a window at the darkest hour of her life, to let a breath of air into the hushed gloom of her existence.

Had she been able to think of a way to contact Zadig directly, Shireen might have done so. But her only means of reaching him was through Vico, and she fought shy of raising the subject with him.

A month went by and when there was still no word from Zadig, Shireen assumed that he had already left. So her surprise was all the greater when Vico came by to say that Zadig Bey had asked to meet with her, to take his leave.

Through Vico it was arranged that they would again meet at the Catholic church at Mazagon. When the day came Shireen set off early and arrived several minutes before the appointed hour. To her surprise Zadig was already there, sitting in the same place where they'd sat before.

He rose as she approached and bowed formally: 'Good morning, Bibiji.'

'Good morning, Zadig Bey.'

She seated herself beside him, on the pew, and slipped off her veil. 'So you are leaving Bombay are you, Zadig Bey?'

'Yes, Bibiji,' he said, a little awkwardly. 'Christmas is coming so I must go to Colombo to be with my children and grandchildren. But before leaving I wanted to give you some news.'

'Yes, Zadig Bey – what is it?'

'I have been told in confidence,' said Zadig Bey, 'that the decision to send an expeditionary force to China has been taken in London, by Lord Palmerston, the Foreign Secretary. It is from India that the expedition will be launched: half the troops will be sepoys, and much of the money and support will also come from here. Apparently the preparations are already under way, in Calcutta, in secret. The planning started some months ago, but only when everything is ready will it be announced to the public.'

'How do you know this?' said Shireen.

'Bibiji, I'm sure you know that William Jardine, the big China trader, is the principal partner of Seth Jamsetjee Jejeebhoy, the Parsi merchant?'

'Yes, of course I am aware of that.'

'Well, William Jardine has been helping Lord Palmerston with the planning of the expedition. I have just learnt that he has written to Seth Jamsetjee, asking for the support of the merchants of Bombay. He has made it clear that one of the expedition's principal goals is to extract compensation for the opium that was confiscated by Commissioner Lin – those who provide help will naturally be paid first.'

'Oh?' said Shireen. 'So you think compensation will be paid after all?'

'I am sure of it,' said Zadig. 'And as Bahram's friend, I must tell you, Bibiji, that it is very important that your interests do not go unrepresented in the months ahead. Since you cannot send anyone to China you must go yourself. That is what Bahram-bhai would have wanted, I am sure of it.'

Shireen sighed. 'Zadig Bey, you must understand that for a woman and a widow it is very difficult to make such a journey.'

'Bibiji! European women travel in ships all the time. You are educated, you speak English, you are the daughter of Seth Rustamjee Mistrie who built some of the finest ships to sail the ocean. Why should it be difficult for you to go?'

'And if I did go to China, where would I stay?'

'I have friends in Macau. I will write to them to find a place for you to rent.'

Shireen shook her head. 'But there are many other practical problems, Zadig Bey. How will I finance such a journey? How will I buy a passage? All I have is some jewellery that I'd hidden away – Bahram left nothing but debts, you know.'

Zadig wagged a finger to signal his disagreement. 'That is not true, Bibiji – Bahram-bhai was very generous to his friends and he left behind many things. With me for instance.'

'What do you mean? What has he left with you?'

'Over the years he gave me many presents and did me many favours. In the flow of life, these things too are like loans. Since you are his widow, it is only right that I should discharge those debts by paying for your passage.'

A startled blush rose to Shireen's cheeks. 'Zadig Bey, that was not what I meant. I couldn't possibly accept money from you.'

'Why not?' said Zadig insistently. 'It would be merely a repayment of my debts to Bahram-bhai. Not even that – it would be an investment, rather. When you reclaim Bahram-bhai's dues, you can pay me back. With ten per cent interest if you like.'

Shireen shook her head. 'That's all very well, Zadig Bey – but what will I tell my family? They will want to know where the money came from.'

'Tell them the truth. Tell them you had some jewellery hidden away and you've decided to sell it. That's all they need to know.'

Shireen began to fidget with the hem of her sari. 'Zadig Bey –

you don't understand. Money is only one small part of the problem. I also have to consider my family's name and reputation. There's sure to be a huge scandal if people hear that I'm thinking of going to China – a widow, travelling alone! The Parsi Panchayat may even expel me from the community. And I have to think of my daughters too. They'll worry about my safety.'

Zadig scratched his chin pensively. 'Bibiji – I too have been thinking about these matters and a solution has occurred to me. As you know, Vico's cousin Rosa has spent some time in Macau. While she was there she worked in the Misericordía, which is a Catholic charity that runs hospitals and orphanages. The sisters have asked her to return and she is keen to do so but cannot afford the fare. She will gladly travel with you if her passage can be arranged and paid for. I have spoken to her about this. Your family cannot object to your going if you have a companion with you, can they?'

Instead of calming Shireen, this cast her into despair. 'A passage for Rosa!' She struck her forehead with her hand. 'But Zadig Bey, how could I possibly make all these arrangements? It's too difficult – I can't do it on my own.'

Zadig Bey brushed the back of her hand with his fingertips, very lightly. 'Please, Bibiji, do not upset yourself. Try to think of it calmly. Vico will help with the arrangements, and so will I. As it happens I myself am due to travel to China next year. I will arrange matters so that I can sail on the same ship as you and Rosa. Your ship is sure to stop in Colombo – I will join you there. Vico will let me know so that I can book my passage accordingly.'

'You!' The blood rushed to Shireen's face with such force that it was as if her cheeks had been scalded. 'But Zadig Bey . . . what would people say if they found out that we were travelling together? You know how people gossip.'

'There's no reason why they should find out,' said Zadig. 'And if they do, we can tell them that it was just coincidence that we were on the same ship.' He paused to stroke his chin. 'For myself, I confess it would be a pleasure to make this journey with you—'

Cutting himself short, he coughed into his fist. When he resumed it was as if he were correcting himself for having been too forward: 'What I meant is that it would be a pleasure to be of service to you on the journey. I would particularly like to arrange a meeting between you and Freddie, in Singapore.'

Shireen clapped her hands to her cheeks. 'Please stop, Zadig Bey, please stop!' she cried. 'I can't make a decision like this at the snap of a finger.' She rose to her feet, pulling the veil over her head. 'I need more time.'

Zadig rose too. 'Bibiji,' he said quietly, as she was lowering her veil, 'please do not worry about the details. The difficulties are all in your head. Once you make up your mind everything else will fall in place.'

Even though Zadig Bey had completely won her trust, Shireen still could not bring herself to take the leap.

'Let me think about it, Zadig Bey. When I am ready, I will let you know, through Vico. But for now, let us say goodbye.'

*

November 18, 1839
Honam

The disaster at Humen has galvanized Commissioner Lin and his circle of officials – but no one would know it from the look of the city. In Canton and beyond, everyday life continues unchanged – and this, says Compton, is exactly what the authorities want: that people go about their business as usual. The battle has been underplayed even in official dispatches: Beijing has been informed that it was a minor clash, in which the British also suffered significant casualties. Compton says that it is in order to avoid panic that the battle is being treated as a minor event – but I wonder if it isn't also meant to save face and avert the Emperor's wrath?

Underneath the surface though, the battle has opened many eyes. Compton for one, has been deeply shaken by what we saw that day at Humen. Since then an aspect of him that is usually concealed by his habitually cheerful demeanour has come to the fore: a tendency to fret and worry. He makes no apology for this propensity of his: when teased about it, he quotes a line from Mencius, something to the effect of: 'It is by worrying about adversity that people survive; complacency brings catastrophe.'

Nowadays Compton's fretfulness bubbles over quite often. In the past his attitude towards translation was fairly matter-of-fact. But now it is as if language itself had become a battleground, with words serving as weapons. He sometimes explodes with indignation while reading British translations of official Chinese documents: Look, Ah Neel, look! Look how they have changed the meaning of what was said!

He disputes everything, even the way the English use the word 'China'. There is no similar term in Chinese he says; the English have borrowed it from Sanskrit and Pali. The Chinese use a different expression, which is mistakenly represented in English as 'Middle Kingdom'. He says that it is better translated as 'the Central States' – I suppose it is the equivalent of our Indian *Madhyadesha*.

What makes Compton angriest is when the Chinese character *yi* is translated as 'barbarian'. He says that this character has always been used to refer to people who are not from the Central States: what it means, in other words, is 'foreigner'. Apparently this was not disputed until recently – Americans and Englishmen were quite content to translate *yi* as 'foreigner'. But of late some of their translators have begun to insist that *yi* means 'barbarian'. It has repeatedly been pointed out to them that the word has been applied to many revered and famous people in China – even to the present ruling dynasty – but the English translators contend that they know better. Some of these translators are notorious opium-smugglers: they are clearly twisting the Chinese language in order to make trouble. Since Captain Elliot and his superiors know no Chinese, they accept whatever the translators tell them. They have come to believe that the word *yi* is indeed intended as an insult. Now they have turned this into a major grievance.

This drives Compton to despair: How can they pretend

to know, Ah Neel? How can they claim to know that the picture they see when they say '*barbarian*', is the same that we see when we say '*yi*'?

Mat dou gaa – it's all a pack of lies!

Thinking about this I realized that I too would protest if Sanskrit or Bangla words like *yavana* or *joban* were translated as 'barbarian'. I think Compton is right when he says that the reason the English use this word is because it is *they* who think of *us* as 'barbarians'. They want war, so they are looking for excuses and even a word will do.

But the Humen battle has had some good consequences even for Compton. For instance Commissioner Lin has begun to pay even greater attention to matters like translation and intelligence. As a consequence Zhong Lou-si's position has been greatly strengthened in official circles. This is a matter of much pride for Compton; he feels that his mentor has at last been given his due.

According to Compton, the subject of Zhong Lou-si's studies – overseas matters – has generally been regarded as unimportant and even disreputable in official circles. And the fact that he does not hesitate to seek out sailors, shipowners, merchants, emigrants and the like is considered unseemly by many of his peers: those are classes of men that Chinese officialdom has traditionally regarded as untrustworthy.

For all these reasons Zhong Lou-si's work was long overlooked. Compton says that he was able to continue with it only because he succeeded in gaining the ear of a former governor of Guangdong Province who was interested in learning about foreign traders and their countries. He gave Zhong Lou-si a job in a prestigious new academy of learning in Guangzhou and it was there that Compton entered his orbit.

Compton is not from the kind of family that generally produces scholars and officials: he is the son of a shipchandler and was raised on the Pearl River, in close proximity to foreign sailors and businessmen: it was they who taught him English; it was from them too that he learnt about the world overseas; they also gave him his English name.

But Compton isn't the only one who has learnt about the world in this way: along the banks of the Pearl River there must be hundreds of thousands of people who make their living from trade and are in close contact with foreigners. Millions of them also have relatives who have settled overseas; they too are privy to reports about what is going on in other countries. But knowledge such as theirs rarely filters through to the scholars and bureaucrats who are at the helm of this country's affairs. Nor are ordinary Chinese at all eager to be noticed by officialdom: what business is it of theirs, what the mandarins make of the world? Compton says that for centuries people in Guangdong have taken comfort in the thought that *saang gou wohng dai yuhn* – 'the mountains are high and the Emperor is far away'. What is the sense of stirring a pot that is sure to scorch you if it spills over?

I suppose this is much how things were in Bengal and Hindustan at the time of the European conquests, and even before. The great scholars and functionaries took little interest in the world beyond until suddenly one day it rose up and devoured them.

*

Zachary's only consolation for the snub that he had been dealt at the Doughties' tiffin was his memory of the glance that Mrs Burnham had directed at him as he was leaving – if not for that fleeting look, he would have begun to believe that the tendernesses of his night in the boudoir were indeed imaginary; that he really was a 'nobody, just a mystery'.

It was that memory too that made him suddenly alert when a khidmatgar came to the budgerow a few days later, bearing a tray of pale yellow sweets.

But what were they for?

A few questions were enough to establish that they had been sent to mark an important festival, in honour of which the mansion's staff had been given a special holiday, by the Burra Beebee herself.

The tray could not be refused of course, so Zachary accepted it and took it inside. Placing it on the dining table he stared at the sweets, which were covered in a layer of silver foil.

What did the gift mean? Was there a message encoded in it? The khidmatgar had not said explicitly that Mrs Burnham had sent it – but Zachary knew that nothing happened in that house without her being aware of it.

He went to his bed, lay down, and closed his eyes so that they would not stray towards the boudoir – on no account, none at all, could he allow his thoughts to wander in that direction. To relive the torments of the last few weeks was unthinkable; he knew he would not be able to endure it.

He lay on his back and tried to shut his ears to the sounds of the mansion's staff as they poured out of the compound.

Soon the grounds would be all but deserted . . .

The thought had no sooner occurred to him than he tried to erase it from his mind. When this proved impossible he decided that it would be best to leave the budgerow and go into town. Pocketing his last few coins, he walked all the way to Kidderpore where he stopped at a sailors' doasta-den, near the docks, and spent an anna on a dish of karibat and a glass of thin grog. Trying to draw out the hours, he struck up conversations with strangers, buying them watery drinks until his pockets were empty. He would have stayed till dawn, but, as luck would have it, the grog-shop shut its doors early, because of the festival, and he found himself back at the budgerow shortly before midnight.

The mansion was in darkness now and the staff seemed to have disappeared except for a couple of chowkidars, who were drowsing by the gate. Zachary was about to walk up the budgerow's gang-plank when his eye was caught by a glimmer of light, somewhere in the distance. He looked again but saw nothing this time. It struck him that an intruder might have stolen into the Burnham compound and it seemed imperative that he go to investigate. Before he knew it his feet were taking him towards the house; he promised himself that he was only going to take a quick look, to make sure that all was well.

The route that he had staked out was still fresh in his memory; with practised stealth he slipped through the shadows and crept up to the tree that faced the boudoir: a thin trickle of light was spilling out from the edges of the curtained window.

He saw no sign of an intruder but it struck him now that having come this far he might as well make sure that the servants' door, at the side of the house, was properly secured.

Tiptoeing over the gravel border he put a hand on the knob: the door swung open at the first touch. There was a candle inside, placed exactly where it had been the last time. He latched the door and picked up the candle.

It was too late to stop now. Stealing softly up the stairs, he paused to breathe the perfumed air of the powder room before stepping towards the luxuriant, golden glow that was spilling out of the boudoir.

She was standing on the far side of the bed, dressed in a simple white nightgown; her hair was untied, falling over her shoulders in chestnut curls; her arms were clasped across her breasts.

They stared at each other, and then, under her breath, she said: 'Mr Reid . . . good evening.'

'Good evening, Mrs Burnham,' he said, and added quickly, 'I just wanted to make sure that everything was all right.'

'That was very thoughtful of you.'

She stepped around the bed and came towards him. 'Your shirt's torn, Mr Reid.'

He looked down and saw that the tip of her finger had vanished into a rent in his shirt. A moment later he felt a fingernail brushing lightly against his skin – and then, all of a sudden, their bodies collided and they tumbled into the luxurious embrace of the bed's satin sheets and feathery pillows.

Soon it was as if his night-time imaginings had sprung to life, becoming almost too real to be true: so intense was the pleasure that he almost forgot the fears that had tormented him these last many weeks. But those apprehensions would not be quelled; they broke upon him without warning, so that suddenly he heard her voice in his ear, exclaiming in dismay: 'Oh but what's this? Why have you stopped? You have not spent yourself already, have you?'

'No,' said Zachary hoarsely. 'I cannot go on, I must not – it is too dangerous, the risks are too great. After the last time I was haunted by the fear that you were with child.'

She pulled his head down and kissed him. 'You should not have worried,' she whispered in his ear. 'It was perfectly safe.'

'How do you know?'

'Because of my monthlies.'

'Oh thank heaven!' A great wave of relief swept through him.

'And providentially, we are safe now too. You may spend when and where you will.'

'No.' He grinned and shook his head. 'Not till you do.'

After that it was a while before either of them had the breath to say another word – and it was only when she snuggled up to him afterwards, to whisper endearments into his ear, that he recalled the pain he had suffered these last many weeks.

'You say all these fine things as we lie here now, Mrs Burnham,' he said abruptly. 'And yet that day, at the Doughties', you pretended not to know me – he's just a mystery, you said, a nobody.'

Her head flew off the pillow and she cried out in protest: 'Oh, you are too cruel, Mr Reid! Will you throw that in my face? You cannot have any conception of how hard it was for me to say what I did. Could you not see that I was terrified that I would betray myself – as I would certainly have done if I had acknowledged you? Augusta Swinhoe, who was sitting beside me, is the most notorious Shoe-goose of this city – nothing escapes her lynx-like eye. It was she who undid poor Amelia Middleton: a stray glance, at the dinner table, between memsahib and khidmatgar, and Augusta knew at once what was afoot. Within a fortnight poor Amelia was disowned by her husband and packed off to England. I'm told she ended her days in a Blackpool bawdy-house.'

A chill crept through Zachary. 'So that is all we shall ever be then? Beebee and khidmatgar? Memsahib and mystery?'

'Oh no, my dear,' she said with a smile. 'We shall make a sahib of you soon enough. But the price of it is that no one can ever know, or we should both be ruined.'

He turned his head on the pillow, so he could look directly at her. 'So do you want to be rid of me then?'

Her gaze did not falter. 'Oh my dear, I think we both know, don't we, that neither of us is strong enough to be rid of the other? You have turned me into a weak, wayward gudda of a woman, Mr

Reid. The one thought that consoles me is that I am at least assisting you in overcoming your affliction.'

'But then why not cure me forever? Why not run away with me?'

She laughed. 'Oh Mr Reid! Now it is you who is being the gudda. Surely you can see that it would not suit me at all to be a mystery's mistress, living in some dank hovel? And if I were on your hands all day long, you too would quickly tire of me. In a week or two you would run off with some larkin of your own age and then what would become of me? I would end up as a buy-'em-dear, trawling for grapeshot on Grope-chute Lane.'

She ran her fingertips over his face. 'No, my dear – soon enough a day will come when we will have to forsake each other forever. When it does we will meet one last time, for a night of delirious delight, and then we shall say goodbye and go our separate ways.'

'You promise?'

'Yes of course.'

Now, once again, they entwined their arms around each other and by the time they unclasped them it was almost dawn.

She climbed out of bed as he was pulling on his breeches; after he had slipped on his shirt she took hold of his hand and pressed something into it. He opened his palm to find himself looking at three large gold coins.

'B'jilliber!' His fingers flew open, scattering the coins over the damp, crumpled sheets. 'I can't take these from you.'

'Why not?' She picked the coins off the bed and circled around him. Putting her arms around his waist, she pressed her stomach to his back. 'If you are to be a sahib you must have some proper clothes, mustn't you?'

'Yes, but this isn't how I should get them.'

'Like this then?' She slipped a hand into the pocket of his breeches and let her fingers roam as the coins trickled out, one by one.

'No – stop!' He tried to dig her hand out, but she had anchored her fingers in the fork of his legs and would not let go.

'It's just a loan,' she whispered, flicking her tongue over his ear. 'You'll pay me back one day, when you're a rich sahib.'

'Shall I be a rich sahib?'

'Yes of course you shall. Between the two of us we will contrive to make it so. You shall be the richest and most mysterious sahib there ever was.'

Her hand was now so busy in his pocket that he forgot about the coins. Turning around he picked her up in his arms and carried her to the bed.

'No!' she cried. 'You must go now. There isn't time.'

'You're right,' he said. 'There isn't.'

But several minutes passed before he left and it was not till he was back on the budgerow that a metallic jingling reminded him that the coins were still in his pocket. Two of the guineas he put aside but the third he took into town the next day and ordered himself some fine new clothes.

Eight

The journey from Rangpur to Calcutta took Kesri and Captain Mee almost a fortnight, most of which was spent on a hired Brahmaputra river-boat.

For Kesri the journey was a time of recuperation. The boatmen did all the work, so he had plenty of leisure. The food was exceptionally good, being produced by a cook who fully lived up to the vaunted culinary reputation of Brahmaputra boatmen: he worked wonders with the freshly netted fish they bought on the way.

Captain Mee had brought along the normal officers' travelling rations of salted meats, biscuit and so on, and these were usually prepared for him by his own servant. But he soon tired of the sameness of the fare, and having long had a liking for karibat, he hinted to Kesri that he would not be averse to an occasional plateful. Had any other officers been on board it would have been difficult for the captain to share Kesri's food – but this was a fine opportunity to flout the rules of his caste and he did so not only in the matter of food but also drink: in the evenings, when the boat was moored and the crew had retired below deck, he and Kesri would share the occasional bottle of beer from his rations.

'Only because we're in mufti, havildar – mind you, not a word to anyone!'

'No, sir!'

Never once, in their conversations, did the subject of Kesri's shunning by the paltan arise; yet Kesri sometimes sensed that the captain was trying to express sympathy for his plight, although without speaking of it directly.

One evening they talked about London, where Captain Mee had grown up but which he had visited only once after moving to India. While reminiscing he made a disclosure that astonished

Kesri: he revealed that his father, now dead, had been a shopkeeper – 'a banyan', he said, with a slightly embarrassed laugh.

Kesri understood immediately why he had never spoken of this before: the English officers, no less than the sepoys, were very particular about the castes of the men they admitted to their ranks. Most of the officers were from professional, landed or military backgrounds and it was through their family connections, Kesri knew, that they secured the recommendations and letters patent that enabled them to obtain their commissions. How a shop-keeper's son had managed to do this Kesri could not imagine, but the disclosure helped him make sense of some things that had always puzzled him about his former butcha.

He remembered one evening, many years before, when Mee-sahib had got very drunk at the officers' mess. He was then an eighteen-year-old ensign and Kesri was his orderly; he had been summoned to the mess to take his butcha back to his rooms. On the way, Mee-sahib had drunkenly blurted out a garbled story about how he had wanted to join some club in Calcutta: all the other ensigns and second lieutenants had been admitted; he alone had been blackballed. That was when Kesri had understood that there was something about his butcha – perhaps to do with his parentage or caste – that set him apart from the other officers.

For Kesri his butcha's rejection by the club was like a personal affront: he never spoke of the matter to anyone, and whenever there was any talk about Mr Mee among the men, he always made a point of mentioning that he was 'a man of good family' – *khandaani aadmi* – knowing that such things mattered as much in the sepoys' estimation of their officers as they did in their judgements of each other.

It happened that the paltan was then stationed at Ranchi, along with a number of other battalions. The picturesque little town was then listed as a 'family station' and many British civil and military officers had their wives and children living with them. As a result there were many parties, hunts and burra-khanas; as for dances there were so many as to wear out the regimental bands.

Mr Mee had plunged into the social whirl with all the energy of a healthy and gregarious young ensign. Kesri knew of his butcha's doings because word of the officers' antics would always trickle back to the sepoy lines, either through the soldiers who were on guard duty at the regimental clubs and messes, or by way of the cooks, stewards and punkah-wallahs who worked in the officers' residences. Sometimes the news would even cause trouble among the sepoys: some were so closely bonded with their butchas that a quarrel between two lieutenants could spark angry exchanges between their orderlies.

So it happened that Kesri found himself being singled out for some good-humoured teasing on account of Mr Mee.

Arré Kesri, do you know what your fellow's been up to now?

He's quite the loocher, always got his eyes on a girl.

Wu sawdhan na rahi to dikkat hoé – if he's not careful, there'll be trouble.

Through hints like these Kesri was given to understand that Mr Mee was involved in a flirtation with the most sought-after missy-memsahib in the station: she was striking to look at, tall, full-busted with reddish-brown hair; she was also the daughter of a brigadier-general who belonged to one of the highest of twice-born military families.

This entanglement of Mr Mee's put Kesri in a strange situation for it so happened that he was himself acquainted with this missy-mem. As a recruit he had once accompanied a hunting party organized by her father, the brigadier-general: he had ended up being assigned to the missy-mem, as a gun-loader. She was a fine shot and that day she had outdone herself, bagging a dozen ducks. For some reason she had chosen to give Kesri the credit, claiming that he had brought her luck. After that, whenever the paltan was in a family station, she would insist on having him as her gun-loader when she went hunting.

During duck-hunts, Kesri would sit behind her, in the blind, and they would talk. Having been reared by Muslim ayahs the missy-mem could speak fluent Hindustani when she wanted to: she would often ask questions about Kesri's village, his family and how he had found his way into the Pacheesi. She was the only person to whom he had ever told the story of how Deeti had helped him escape from Nayanpur.

It was she too who was responsible for connecting Kesri with Mr Mee. Soon after Mr Mee joined the battalion, she had asked

Kesri whether he would like to be the new ensign's orderly. When he said yes, she had told him that she would put in a word for him with Mr Mee.

Kesri had been grateful to her but it had not occurred to him that there might be anything between her and Mr Mee other than the usual casual acquaintanceship that existed between subalterns and the children of senior officers. But in Ranchi, when the rumours began to circulate, he realized that the matter had taken a troubling turn. He knew that his butcha stood little chance of gaining this missy-mem's hand: Mr Mee had no money and was in no position to get married – having given him several loans already, Kesri was well aware of this. The missy-mem, on the other hand, had many suitors, some of whom were extremely eligible. Kesri did not doubt that when it came to marriage her family would compel her to do whatever was best for her future.

When he overheard others gossiping about Mr Mee and the missy-mem, Kesri would scoff, saying that it was just a friendship, of a kind that was common among sahibs and mems; it meant nothing. But this became harder and harder to maintain: after parties and balls Kesri would hear that the missy had given more dances to Mr Mee than to anyone else, even turning down some high-ranked officers. Then one day a steward whispered in Kesri's ear that while serving soup at dinner the night before, he had seen Mee-sahib and the general's larki holding hands under the table.

One day Mr Mee fell ill with a fever and had to absent himself from the social whirl. At the end of the week a summons arrived from the general's house, for Kesri, to accompany his guests and family on a hunt – and as always he was assigned to serve as the missy-mem's gun-loader. That day the group was a large one and she was constantly surrounded by people. Only for a few minutes were they alone, and she immediately began to ask Kesri about Mr Mee: How was he? Was he being properly looked after? Then she handed over a thick pink envelope and whispered: Kesri Singh, can you please give him this, *mehrbani kar ke?*

Kesri had no choice but to accept: he left the envelope on Mr Mee's bedside teapoy, without a word of explanation. They never spoke of it, but one day the sweeper who cleaned Mr Mee's rooms came to him and said that there was some hair lying on Mr Mee's desk: he wanted to know if he should throw it away. Kesri went to take a look and saw a lock of reddish-brown hair, tied up neatly with a ribbon, lying on top of the envelope.

Kesri knew at a glance that nothing good would come of this. Risking a berating, he picked up the letter, and the enclosed lock of hair, and handed them to Mr Mee, telling him that it was dangerous to leave such things lying around and that people were already talking. Predictably Mr Mee flew into a rage and shouted at him, calling him a blackguard and telling him to mind his own bloody business and keep his maulers off his things.

Kesri understood then that his butcha was possessed, *majnoon*, mad with love, and he wished that it had happened for Mr Mee in the same way that it had for himself, with Gulabi – that he too had chosen a woman he could have had. This way he knew there would only be trouble.

It wasn't long before things came to a head. That year the officers and their ladies had taken up a strange new kind of entertainment, apparently in imitation of a fashion in their homeland. They would ride into the jungle with baskets of food and drink; then they would spread out sheets and blankets and sit down to eat – right there, in the open. This was a great annoyance to the orderlies because they would be taken along to chase away snakes and keep a lookout for tigers and elephants. It seemed senseless to them that anyone should wish to eat in places where they might them-selves be eaten by wild beasts – but orders were orders and they went along and did as they were told.

The worst job of all was to look after the horses, for they were like bait for leopards and were in a constant state of agitation. That day Kesri was attending to a horse when he caught sight of Mr Mee and the missy-mem wandering into the jungle. They were gone long enough that her parents began to worry and asked for a search party to be formed. Since Kesri knew which way they'd gone, he slipped away and went ahead of the others, shouting: *Mee-sah'b! Mee-sah'b!*

In a while he heard an answer and saw Mr Mee and the missy-mem coming towards him. They looked flushed and dishevelled and Kesri thought at first that this was only because they'd lost their way and had been stumbling about. But then he noticed that there was a new glow on the missy's face; he saw also that Mr Mee's collar was disarranged. He knew then that something had happened between them. Trying to banish all expression from his face, he whispered a warning to Mr Mee to straighten his collar.

By the time the couple returned to their party, they had had time to compose themselves and were able to persuade the others that they had merely lost their way. The rest of the day passed without incident – but Kesri knew that the matter wouldn't end there. He was not surprised to learn, a day or two later, that the missy and her mother had left for Calcutta.

Although the girl was never mentioned between Mr Mee and himself, Kesri knew that his butcha had been hard hit by her departure. The bichhanadar who made his bed would often find her letters under his pillow, and Kesri would sometimes find Mr Mee sitting alone in his room, with his head slumped disconsolately on his desk.

Kesri was glad when the battalion received orders to move back to Barrackpore; he thought the change of scene would be good for Mr Mee. But on arriving at the depot they learnt that the jarnail-sahib's daughter was soon to be married, to a rich English merchant in Calcutta.

On the day of the wedding, the officers' quarters were deserted because they were all at the ceremony. Only Mr Mee stayed behind; it was rumoured that he had not been invited.

The next morning Kesri saw that the bichhanadar had put Mr Mee's pillow in the sun; he touched it and found that it was soaked through.

The cantonment in Barrackpore was large enough that it had a 'Lock Hospital', maintained by the army, to ensure that the bazar-girls who were provided for white soldiers and officers were free of disease. Kesri knew that in the past Mr Mee had occasionally visited the 'Europeans Only' military brothel in the cantonment's Red Bazar. That night he found an opportunity to mention to him that he had heard that a nice young girl had just arrived there. In the past Mr Mee had been grateful for tips like these, but this time he shouted at Kesri and told him to mind his own fucking business.

Kesri understood that Mr Mee was seething inside, not just because he had lost the missy-mem but also because he had been humiliated in the eyes of his fellow officers. Knowing how hot-headed his butcha was, Kesri feared that an explosion was inevitable – and it wasn't long before it happened. One night a steward ran over to tell Kesri that Mr Mee had been involved in a drunken quarrel in the officers' mess: he had overheard another officer gossiping about him, in the worst kind of language, and had challenged him to a duel.

Kesri was fully in sympathy with his butcha on this: to be called 'bastard' and 'swine' in a joking way was one thing; but every soldier knew that words like *haramzada* and *soowar-ka-baccha*, when used in earnest, had to be answered in blood – only a coward would fail to defend his izzat. This way at least there would be a resolution of some kind – and whatever happened, it was better than shedding solitary tears for an unattainable woman.

The one thing Kesri regretted was that the duel was to be fought with pistols: had swords been the chosen weapon he would have had no doubt that his butcha would win. Not that Mr Mee was a bad shot – but with guns luck always played a large part, especially if the gunman was overwrought, as Mr Mee would probably be.

Sure enough, Mr Mee was in a state of wild-eyed agitation when he returned to his room. Anticipating this, Kesri had already made preparations. He handed him a glass and told him to drink the contents: he would sleep well and his hand would be steady when he woke up.

'What's in it?' said Mr Mee.

'Sharbat – with afeem.'

Nothing was said between them about the duel and nor was it necessary. After Mr Mee had drunk the sharbat, Kesri fetched his pistols and wrapped them in a velvet cloth. He took them to his hut and spent several hours cleaning and oiling them. Then, as was the custom before a battle, he took the pistols to the regimental temple, laid them at the foot of the deity and had them blessed by the purohit. In the morning, after handing over the guns, he dipped the tip of his little finger in a pot of vermilion and placed a *tika* high up on his butcha's temple. Mr Mee did not object, although he made sure that the tika was well hidden by his hair.

When the time came, and Mr Mee's seconds arrived to take him to the field, Kesri was glad to see that his butcha was perfectly calm, even cheerful. It was Kesri who was fearful now, much more so than he would have been had he himself been stepping into the field. His hands trembled as he went to join the throng of spectators who had gathered at a discreet distance.

Duelling between officers was not uncommon, even though the high command disapproved of the practice. Kesri had watched duels before, but this time, when the signal to fire was called out, he closed his eyes. Only when the men around him began to pound him on his back did he know that his butcha had won – and in the best possible way, not by killing his opponent but by felling him with a flesh wound.

The duel had a palliative effect on Mr Mee, restoring his sense of honour and draining him of some of his rage and grief. But he was to feel the repercussions of that episode for years afterwards: it meant that promotions were always slow to come his way, despite his qualities as an officer.

Mr Mee's entanglement with the general's daughter was also to have a lasting effect on his personal life: Kesri did not doubt that it was the principal reason why his butcha had never married. Kesri had thought that once the general-sahib's daughter was safely out of reach Mr Mee would begin to run after some other missy or memsahib. But nothing like that came to pass. When on the march, Mr Mee would sometimes patronize Gulabi's girls; while in a cantonment he would occasionally visit its military brothel when he was in need of a little chivarleying, as he put it. But he showed no signs of wanting to find himself a wife, which was not unusual in itself, since many of the British officers put off marriage till they were in their forties – but Kesri knew that Mr Mee's was no ordinary bachelorhood: he was still haunted by the lost missy. Kesri knew this because he was with Mr Mee once when he suffered a chest wound in a skirmish: later, when the medical orderlies were trying to get his jacket off, a small package had fallen out of the inner pocket. Kesri knew at a glance that it contained the missy's letter: evidently Mr Mee had taken it into battle, wearing it next to his heart.

Since then a lingering bitterness had slowly crept into Captain Mee's life. The light-hearted exuberance of his youth had been replaced by resignation and resentment. The one thing that seemed to sustain him now was his bond with the sepoys.

It saddened Kesri to think how different his butcha's life and career might have been if not for that unfortunate entanglement. But none of this was ever spoken of between them, not even during the long journey from Rangpur to Calcutta when they talked more as friends than as officer and sepoy. Of course Captain Mee did not neglect to ask after Kesri's wife and children – and had the captain been married Kesri would have done the same. But that was different: the family of a married man was safe ground – this other thing was not.

On the last day of the journey, Captain Mee said: 'So, havildar, what will you do when we return from this expedition? Do you think you'll put in for your pension and go back to your family?'

'Yes, sir.'

Then Captain Mee made a disclosure that was not entirely unexpected. 'Well, havildar, I wouldn't be surprised if I put my papers in myself,' he said. 'I don't know that the Pacheesi has been any better for me than it's been for you.'

*

After his second tryst with Mrs Burnham, Zachary's burden of contrition became far less oppressive: it wasn't that guilt ceased to weigh on him – it was just that his eagerness to return to the boudoir made him less mindful of it.

But the next visit did not come about as soon as he would have liked: there was a long, almost unendurable, wait before he heard from Mrs Burnham again. A full fortnight passed before the next message arrived, hidden inside a weighty tome of sermons: it consisted of a single cryptic marking, on a scrap of paper – *12th*. The reference was clearly to a date, one that happened to be two days away.

In preparation for the assignation, Zachary made a careful study of the routines of the chowkidars and durwans who guarded the compound; he learnt to listen for their footsteps and tracked the glow of their lanterns. When the night of the 12th came he evaded the gatekeepers with ease: this part wasn't difficult, he told Mrs

Burnham; he had figured out how to navigate the grounds without the watchmen being any the wiser.

His certainty on this score buttressed Mrs Burnham's confidence and they began to meet more often. Instead of exchanging messages, they would settle on a date at the time of parting. No longer did they care whether the servants were away or not; it was always in the small hours of the night that Zachary stole over to the mansion anyway, and at that time the grounds were usually deserted. As his familiarity with the grounds increased, he learnt to make good use of every scrap of cover, including the wintry mists that often rolled in from the river, at night.

In no way did the increased frequency of their meetings diminish Zachary's appetite for them: each assignation was a fresh adventure; every visit seemed to conjure up a new woman – a being so unlike the Mrs Burnham of the past that he would not have imagined that she existed if their connection had not taken this unforeseen turn. Yet he knew also that there was nothing accidental about what had happened between them: it had come about because his body had sensed something that was beyond the grasp of his conscious mind – that hidden within the Beebee of Bethel's steely shell there existed another, quite fantastical and capricious creature; a woman who was endlessly inventive, not just with her body but also with her words.

One night he got caught in a shower of rain and arrived at the top of the staircase completely drenched. Mrs Burnham was waiting for him in the goozle-connuh. 'Oh look at you, my dear, dripping pawnee everywhere. Stand still while I take off your jammas and jungiah.'

After stripping him of his clothing, she made him sit on the rim of the bathtub and knelt between his parted thighs. Pulling up her chemise, she draped the hem over his legs and pressed herself against his belly. Murmuring gently, she began to dry his head and shoulders with a towel, clasping him ever closer as she reached around to rub his back. Suddenly she looked down at the unlaced throat of her chemise and gave a little cry: 'Oh look! I see a helmet! A brave little havildar has climbed up my chest and is raising his head above the nullah, to take a dekko! Oh, but look! He is drenched, even under his topee!'

She delighted in tantalizing him with unfamiliar words and puzzling expressions, yet, no matter how intimate their bodily explorations, no matter how much they indulged their appetite for each other, there remained certain matters of decorum on which she would not yield: even when the organ that she had nicknamed the 'bawhawder sepoy' was entrenched within her, its master and commander remained Mr Reid, the mystery, and she was never anything but Mrs Burnham, the Beebee of Bethel.

Once, when 'her shoke was coming on' as she liked to say, he felt the onset of her tremors and cried out, to urge her on: 'Oh spend, Cathy, spend! Don't stint yourself!'

No sooner had the syllables left his mouth than she froze, her shoke forgotten.

'What? What was that you called me?'

'Cathy.'

'No, my dear, no!' she cried, twitching her hips in such a way as to abruptly unbivouack the sepoy.

'I am, and I must remain, Mrs Burnham to you – and you must ever remain Mr Reid to me. If we permit ourselves to lapse into "Zachs" and "Cathies" in private then you may be sure that our tongues will ambush us one day when we are in company. In just such a way was poor Julia Fairlie found to be loochering with her groom – for who has ever known a syce to call his memsahib "Julie" as the wretched ooloo was heard to do one day as he was helping her into the saddle? And so was it revealed that much of their riding and saddling was done without horses and in no time at all poor Julia was packed off to Doolally – and all because she'd allowed that halalcore of a syce to be too free with two syllables. No, dear, no, it just will not hoga. "Mrs Burnham" and "Mr Reid" we are, and so we must remain.'

If Zachary bowed to her in this matter it wasn't only because he accepted her reasoning: it was also because there was something startlingly sensuous about hearing her moan after the passing of a shoke: 'Oh Mr Reid, Mr Reid! You have made a jellybee of your poor Mrs Burnham!'

The invocation of her married name was a reminder that theirs were stolen, adulterous pleasures, which meant that inhibition was meaningless and restraint absurd: so deadly was the seriousness of their crime that it could only be effaced by frivolity – as when she would cry, with a playful tug: 'It's my turn now, to bajow your ganta.'

She deployed these strings of words with the skill of an expert angler, teasing, mocking and egging him on to further advances in the art of the puckrow.

'Oh Mr Reid, I do not doubt that it is a joy to be a launder of your age, with a lathee always ready to be lagowed – and a dumb-poke is certainly a fine thing, not to be scorned. But you know, my dear mystery, a plain old-fashioned stew can always be improved by an occasional chutney.'

'You've lost me, Mrs Burnham,' he mumbled.

'Oh? Have you never heard of chartering then?'

'You mean like chartering a boat?'

'No, you silly green griffin!' She laughed. 'In India, chartering is what you do with this' – here she reached between his lips and pinched the tip of his tongue – 'your jib.'

Thus began a new set of explorations, in which he was soon revealed to be a complete novice, blundering about with all the aptitude of a luckerbaug. 'Oh no, my dear, no! You are not chewing on a chichky, and nor are you angling for a cockup! Making a chutney dear, is not a blood-sport.'

Her caprices made him long to please her and the mixture of severity and tenderness with which she treated him was far more arousing to him than words of love would have been. On the night when his experiments in chartering finally succeeded in bringing on her shoke, his heart swelled with pride to hear her say: 'It is a wonder to me, my dear, how quickly you have mastered the mystery of the gamahuche!'

Her teasing enchanted him, and if he was bewildered by her refusal to take him seriously, he was also captivated by it. He took it for granted that she possessed boundless experience in the amorous arts, and considered it fitting that he should be treated as a neophyte. Yet there was a certain innocence about her too, and sometimes, when she was exploring his body, she would betray an ingenuousness that startled him.

One night when she was toying with the 'sleeping bawhawder' and exclaiming over its docile charms, he grew impatient: 'Oh come now, Mrs Burnham! You are a married woman and have given birth to a child. Surely this is not the first time you've handled a co—'

Her hand was on his mouth before he could say the word.

'No dear, no,' she said, 'we will have none of those vulgarisms here. A woman may be bawdy with a woman, and a man with men, but never the one with the other.'

'But why not?' he demanded. 'Why should we not use the words that others use? Why shouldn't we speak of things by their accustomed names, as all people do?'

Her riposte was swift and unerring: 'That is exactly why, my dear Mr Reid. Because all people do it, and we are not "all people". We are you and I; no one is like us, and nor are we like them. Why should we borrow words from others when we can use our own?'

'But that is unfair, Mrs Burnham,' he protested. 'I never was no word-pecker – How'm I to keep pace with you?'

'Oh fiddlesticks!' she said, illustrating the exclamation with a flick of her fingers. 'And you a sailor! You should be ashamed to admit to a lack of words!'

'Very well then, Mrs Burnham,' he said, 'I will put my question in ship-language. You are a married woman and have had your mate's licence for many years. Surely you are not ignorant of the lay of a man's mast and hatches?'

'Oh please, Mr Reid!' she cried with a laugh. 'Do you imagine that respectable married people would be so wanton as to remove all their clothes and let their hands roam as do you and I? If so, you are much mistaken. I can assure you that for most wives and husbands, coupling is merely a matter of dropping the chitty in the dawk: it is done with a quick hoisting of nightgowns, and that too only when all the batties have been extinguished.'

'But surely when you were first married . . . ?'

'No, Mr Reid, you are mistaken again,' she said with a sigh. 'Mine was not that kind of marriage: my union with Mr Burnham came about for many purposes, but pleasure was not among them. I was but eighteen and he was fifteen years my senior: he wanted respectability and an entrée into circles that had been closed to him. My father was a brigadier-general in the Bengal Native

Infantry, as I've told you, and it was in his power to open many doors. My dear papa, like many soldiers, was not provident in his ways and was always in debt. He and Mama had pinned their hopes on a brilliant marriage for me – and although a match with Mr Burnham was not quite that, he was a coming man, as they say, and already a Nabob. He offered my parents a very generous settlement.'

There was a confiding note in her voice that Zachary had not heard before; it was as if he were at last being admitted into a recess that was still deeper and more intimate than those he had already explored. Eager for more, he said: 'Was there no feeling between you and Mr Burnham then? No attachment at all?'

She gave him one of her teasing smiles and tickled him under the chin, as though he were a child. 'Really, Mr Reid, what *are* we to do with you?' she said. 'Don't you know that a memsahib cannot allow mere feelings to get in the way of her career? Sentiments are for dhobis and dashies, not for women like us: that is what my mother taught me and it is what I shall teach my daughter. And it is not untrue, you know. One cannot live on love after all, and nor is mine an unhappy existence. Mr Burnham asks nothing of me except that I move in the right circles and run his house as a pucka Beebee should. Beyond that he leaves me to my own devices – so why should I do any less for him?'

'So did you know all along then,' Zachary persisted, 'about what he was getting up to, with girls like Paulette?'

'No!' she said sharply. 'I had my suspicions, but I did not inquire too closely, and if you want to know why I will tell you.'

'Why?'

'Because I too have not been the best of wives to him.'

He turned on his side and looked into her face with puzzled, questioning eyes: 'What do you mean?'

'Well, I'll tell you if you must know,' she said. 'It goes back to the night of our wedding. When Mr Burnham came to my bed, I was seized by such dread that I fell into a dead faint. Nor was that the only time: I would fall into a swoon whenever he tried to embrace me. It happened so often that it was decided that I needed medical attention. I was taken to see the best English doctor in the city and he told me that I was suffering from a condition of frigidity brought on by hysteria and other nervous disorders. It took years of treatment before I was able to conceive – and suffice it to say that since that time Mr Burnham has come to accept that I am in some respects an invalid, and he has been, in his own way, kind about it. And I, for my part, have long assumed that he had his outlets, as men do – but I had never imagined that it was of the kind that Paulette described to you.'

'So what did you think . . . ?'

But her mood had already changed, and she cut him short, with a playful tightening of her fist. 'You are an inquisitive little mystery today, aren't you, Mr Reid? I confess I would rather answer to your sepoy than to you.'

The rebuff stung him: it was as if she had slammed a door on his face. He pulled himself abruptly free of her hands and reached for his breeches: 'Well, you need answer to neither of us, Mrs Burnham – it is time for us to go, so we will bid you good night.'

On his way out, when she tried to push some money into his pocket, as she usually did, he brushed her hand brusquely aside. 'No, madam,' he said. 'You insult me if you think that I would rather be paid in silver coin than a few honest words.'

Without waiting for an answer he ran down the stairs.

*

For several weeks, Shireen thought of little else but the journey that Zadig had proposed. Her desire to go was so strong that this was in itself a reason for doubting her motives. Was it in order to escape the house that she wanted to go? Was it out of a vulgar curiosity about her husband's son? Or was it because of a desire to see Zadig again?

These queries milled about in her head, generating other doubts. Would her family's objections be quite as insurmountable as she imagined? Or were the difficulties indeed primarily in her own mind, as Zadig Bey had said?

The only way to find out was to try.

One day in early December Vico came by. While talking to him Shireen suddenly came to a decision.

Vico, she said. I've made up my mind. I'm going to travel to China.

Really, Bibiji?

Vico made no attempt to disguise his scepticism: And what will your brothers say to that?

The question made her bristle. Look, Vico, she said, I am not a child. How can my brothers stop me from going if that's what I want to do? There is nothing scandalous about a widow going to visit her husband's grave. Besides, when I explain to them about recovering Bahram's funds, they will understand – they may not approve, but they are people who understand the value of money.

And your daughters?

They will worry about my safety of course, said Shireen. But if I tell them that I'll be travelling with a companion they'll be reassured. It is true, isn't it, that Rosa would like to go too?

Yes, Bibiji, but you would have to pay for her passage and her expenses. It will not be cheap.

I've thought of that, Vico. Wait.

Shireen went to her room, and returned with a jewellery box.

Vico, look – these are some pieces that I'd kept for myself. Do you think they would cover the costs of the journey?

Reaching into the box, Vico weighed a few of Shireen's necklaces in the palm of his hand.

These will fetch a lot of money, Bibiji, he said. Certainly enough for your passage, and Rosa's too. But think about it – do you really want to risk it all on this journey?

Yes, Vico, because it will be well worth it, if things turn out right.

Shireen sensed that Vico was still unconvinced, so she dropped the subject: Anyway, don't talk about this yet, Vico. Let me work it out first.

Yes of course, Bibiji. It's a big decision.

Shireen slept very little that night: all she could think about was how best to present her plan to her family.

It was clear to her that she would need her brothers' consent, at the very least, if she was to travel to China: such was their position in Bombay's social and commercial world that no reputable shipowner would grant her a passage if it came to be known that her brothers were against it. The only alternative was to steal off in secret and that was a path that she could not contemplate: if she was to go at all she would have to do it openly, but in such a way as to silence Bombay's busybodies and bak-bak-walas. This would be no easy thing, she knew, for a great gale of disquiet was sure to sweep through the purdah-ed interiors of the city's mansions when it was learnt that the Mistries' widowed daughter was planning to travel to China, on her own.

After much thought Shireen decided that a scandal of some kind was probably inevitable – but if her family presented a united front it would be of no great consequence; they would be able to weather it. The matter might even be cast in an advantageous light, to show the world that the Mistries, who had been pioneers in industry, were in advance of their peers in other respects as well.

But how was she to bring around her daughters and brothers? How was she to get her way without causing a rupture in the family?

Shireen could see so many obstacles ahead that she took to reminding herself of one of her late father's maxims: to scuttle a boat you don't have to rip out the whole bottom; you just need to remove a few planks, one by one.

The most important planks in this boat, she decided, were her daughters. If only she could enlist their support then it would be much easier to persuade her brothers. Yet she knew also that no one would be harder to convince than her two girls; they would oppose her partly out of concern for her safety, and partly because they had developed a great dread of scandal after their father's bankruptcy.

Shireen was still wondering how to broach the subject when kismat presented her with an unforeseen opportunity. One night when her daughters and their husbands had come over for dinner the conversation veered of its own accord to China. One of her sons-in-law happened to mention that Bombay's leading shipowners had held a secret meeting. It turned out then that her other son-in-law knew exactly what was afoot: Bombay's wealthiest businessmen were vying with each other to provide support for the British expedition to China. Lakhs of rupees had been pledged, at very advantageous terms, and many shipowners had offered their best vessels to the colonial government to use as troop-transports. It was understood of course that those who were most supportive of the British effort would be the first to be compensated when reparations for the confiscated opium were extracted from the Chinese goverment.

Although Shireen added nothing to the conversation, she made sure that her daughters stopped fussing with their children and listened to what the men were saying. Later, when she was alone with the two girls, she said: Did you hear what your husbands were talking about at dinner?

The girls nodded desultorily: Wasn't it something about getting compensation, in China?

Yes, said Shireen. Vico tells me that if compensation is paid, our share of it could be as much as two lakh Spanish dollars.

The figure made them start, and Shireen waited a couple of minutes to let it soak in. Then she added: But Vico says that we aren't likely to receive anything at all unless . . .

Unless?

Shireen took a deep breath and blurted it out: Unless I go to China myself!

The girls gasped. You? Why you?

Kain ke, said Shireen, because a lot of the money that went into your father's last shipment of opium was mine, it came from my inheritance. But if I'm to prove this to the authorities I'll have to go there myself. Vico says that Captain Elliot knew your father; he says that if I go there and petition him directly he will be sympathetic – and your father's friends from the Canton Chamber of Commerce will support me too.

But why do you have to be there in person? Won't the money be paid to us anyway?

No, said Shireen. We can't count on that.

She explained that the money she had given Bahram was considered joint property, and was therefore regarded as a part of his estate. In the normal course of things the estate would be the last to be compensated. But if Shireen were to be personally present when reparations were paid, then Bahram's friends in the Chamber of Commerce would make sure that she was treated like any other investor; she might even be the first to be compensated.

The girls chewed their lips as they thought this over. A good few minutes passed before they started to voice other objections.

But to go there and back could take a year or more, couldn't it?

Ne ahenu bhav su? What about the cost?

Shireen went to her wardrobe and unlocked the iron safe in which she kept her jewellery.

Look, she said to the girls, I still have some of my *sun-nu* – the gold ornaments I received at my wedding. I had kept them for the two of you – but it would be much better, wouldn't it, if I sold them now and spent the money on the journey? That way they'll bring back ten times as much.

The girls exchanged glances and chewed their knuckles.

But what will people say . . . ?

A woman of your age . . . a widow . . . travelling alone?

Shireen heard them out quietly, lowering her eyes. When they had finished she said: It's not just the money, you know: I would also like to visit your father's grave before I die. If we tell people that, who could possibly object?

Having planted the thought, she left it to germinate, making no further mention of the matter that evening.

A few days later Vico came by to say that he had received a letter from Zadig Bey: he had now completed his arrangements for travelling to China – he would be sailing on a ship called the *Hind*, which was owned by Mr Benjamin Burnham.

Mr Burnham? said Shireen. Isn't he the one who bought our ship, the *Anahita*?

Exactly, Bibiji, said Vico. Mr Burnham was also your husband's colleague on the Select Committee in Canton. Zadig Bey is sure that Mr Burnham would provide a fine cabin for you, on very advantageous terms, if he knew of the circumstances. Zadig Bey will arrange everything – all he needs is a word from you.

Having already told Vico that she had decided to go, Shireen could not back down now. All right, Vico, she said. You can write to Zadig Bey. I met the Burnhams once when they were visiting Bombay – I think they will remember me. Please tell Zadig Bey to go ahead with the arrangements. Somehow or the other I will get my family to agree.

Once they had been uttered, these brave words deepened her resolve: she knew that there was still a long way to go, but the obstacles seemed a little less insurmountable now than they had before. What was more, the mere fact of having a purpose to work towards energized her as nothing had done in many years. The very textures and colours of the world around her seemed to change and things that had been of little concern to her before – like business, finance and politics – suddenly seemed to be of absorbing interest.

It was as if a gale had parted the purdahs that curtained her world, blowing away many decades' worth of dust and cobwebs.

*

December 16, 1839
Honam

This morning, when I arrived at the print-shop Compton greeted me with a broad smile: *Naah Ah Neel!* Listen – you're coming to a meeting with the Yum-chai!

At first I thought it was a joke. *Gaai choi,* I said. You're giving me a pile of 'mustard cabbage'.

He laughed: *Leih jaan* – seriously: you're going to see Commissioner Lin today. *Faai ði laa* – come on! Hurry!

It turned out that I owed this opportunity to the *Sunða,* a British vessel that recently foundered off the coast of Hainan. There were fifteen survivors, including a boy. Most of them are British subjects and on Commissioner Lin's orders they have been treated very well. An official escort transported them from Hainan to Guangzhou and since their arrival here they have been accommodated in the American Factory. They are soon to begin their journey back to England.

Commissioner Lin had asked to meet with the survivors a couple of days ago. Accordingly a meeting was arranged, at a temple within the precincts of the walled city. I was given permission to attend at Zhong Lou-si's special request!

If anyone had said to me when I woke up this morning that I would soon be stepping into the walled city I would not have believed him: foreigners are almost never allowed in and I had long despaired of getting past the gates. Nor for that matter had I ever been in the Commissioner's presence – I had only ever set eyes on him from afar. The prospect of a close darshan made my head spin.

Compton and I went together to the south-western gate of the walled city where we found a sizeable company already assembled. Among the foreigners there were a dozen or so survivors from the *Sunda* and also several American merchants, including Mr Delano and Mr Coolidge. Among the Chinese there were a half-dozen mandarins and also a few Co-Hong merchants.

For me the most interesting members of the assembly were Commissioner Lin's personal translators: I had heard a great deal about them from Compton, but had never met them, because they live and work within the walled city.

The most distinguished of the translators is Yuan Dehui: a quiet, affable man, he has studied at the Anglo-Chinese College at Malacca and has spent several years in England. He now occupies a senior post in Beijing and is in Guangzhou at the Commissioner's express request. Then there is Lieaou Ah See, a studious-looking man whose 'English' name is William Botelho: he is one of the first Chinese to be educated in America and has attended schools in Connecticut and Philadelphia. Another member of the group is a youth barely out of his teens, Liang Jinde, the son of an early Protestant convert. Lastly there is Ya Meng, the son of a Chinese father and a Bengali mother: stooped and elderly, he has spent many years at the Mission College in Serampore, near Calcutta.

Ya Meng still speaks a little Bangla and there is much that I would have liked to ask him. But barely had we exchanged a few pleasantries before gongs and drums began to sound, to signal the opening of the city gates. They swung apart to reveal a broad, straight avenue, lined with soldiers: a series of arches, spaced at regular intervals, rose over the thoroughfare. The houses on either side were of two or three storeys, with green-tiled roofs and upturned eaves: their windows were filled with the faces of curious onlookers.

Much to my disappointment the walk was a short one, allowing barely a glimpse of the walled city: the temple where the meeting was to be held was just three hundred yards from the gate. The entrance to the complex was blocked off by soldiers, but a large and noisy crowd could be seen behind the ranks, jostling for a glimpse of the foreigners.

The venue of the meeting was at the rear of the temple complex. After crossing several courtyards we found ourselves in a large hall that looked like a library, being packed with books and scrolls. At the far end was a raised alcove where chairs had been placed for the Commissioner and a couple of other top officials.

The Commissioner's arrival was heralded by gongs. Everyone in the hall knelt when he entered – all but the foreign merchants who bowed but did not kneel. The Commissioner is stocky in build and was dressed rather plainly in comparison with the members of his entourage. He is of middle age, vigorous in his movements, with a brisk, unceremonious manner. His voice is pleasant and his face good-humoured, with bright, sharp eyes and a wispy beard.

Excited as I was, I have to admit that my darshan of the Commissioner was strangely anti-climactic. I'd heard so much about him that I'd imagined that he would be somehow out of the ordinary. But of all the mandarins present he was perhaps the least exceptional, at least in appearance. Where other high officials go to great lengths to create an impression of splendour and pomp, he seems to exert himself in the other direction: this perhaps is the most extraordinary thing about him. His manner is almost grandfatherly – he even patted the English boy on his head and talked to him for several minutes.

Unfortunately the rest of the proceedings offered little of interest. It appears that Commissioner Lin had sought the meeting because he wanted to persuade the Englishmen of the justice of his cause. To this end he had brought along several books and pamphlets on the subject of opium and the harm it is doing to China (some of these had been brought to his attention by none other than Compton and myself). On the Commissioner's instructions a passage was read out from a European treatise on international law to show that the banning of the opium trade was perfectly compatible with universally recognized legal principles.

The Englishmen listened politely but seemed puzzled that the Commissioner should appeal to them: after all it is not as if they are the kind of men who have their hands on the helm of Empire.

Compton too thought that the meeting was nothing but a waste of time.

Later, when we were back in the print-shop, Compton said that the Yum-chai's chief failing is that he places too much faith in reason. He thinks that if only ordinary Englishmen could grasp the reasoning behind his policy there would be no dispute. In his heart he doesn't believe that any sensible group of men would want to go to war for something like opium. This is why he wanted to meet these survivors: he now thinks that his best hopes lie in reaching out to ordinary Englishmen. He has lost faith in Captain Elliot and other British officials, he thinks they are corrupt, self-seeking officials who are deceiving the people they are meant to serve.

I suspect he believes that ordinary Englishmen, like the survivors of the wreck of the *Sunda*, can petition their government, as people do in China. He doesn't understand that it isn't the same in England; these men cannot petition their government or do anything to affect official policy.

I suppose everyone finds the despotisms of other peoples hard to comprehend.

*

Only after his abrupt departure from Mrs Burnham's boudoir did Zachary realize that they had not settled on a date for their next meeting. He cursed himself, not only for leaving so precipitously, but also because he could not understand why the thought of being banished from her boudoir should fill him with panic. He knew, after all, that this connection – whatever it was – would have to end soon. Yet he was powerless to silence the part of him that kept crying out: 'Not yet, not yet!'

Fortunately he did not have long to wait: within a few days a message arrived, hidden inside another weighty tome.

When he next appeared at the door of Mrs Burnham's goozle-connuh it was clear from the ardour of her greeting that she was in an apologetic mood.

'My dear, dear Mr Reid,' she said, wrapping her arms around him. 'I am so glad you came – I thought you might not.'

'Why?'

'Because I think I may have mis-spoken when I saw you last. I've always been a dreadful buck-buck-wallee you know. My tongue has a way of running away with me – a flying jib, Mr Doughty calls it – and you must make allowance for it. Am I forgiven? Tell me, am I?'

He smiled. 'Yes, my dear Beebee – you are.'

'Thank you!' She pressed her hips against his and gave a cry of delight. 'Oh, and better still, I see that our sepoy too is full of forgiveness – and I warrant that he shall rise to even greater heights of bawhawdery when he sees the present I have bought him.'

She helped Zachary peel off his clothes and led him to the bed, which was covered with towels. When he was lying on his back, with his head propped up against a bank of pillows, she turned to her bedside table and picked up a small bowl. Placing it on his chest, she said: 'Careful now, Mr Reid – you mustn't move or there'll be a dreadful spill.'

Zachary saw that the bowl was half-filled with perfumed oil, amber in colour. Submerged in the oil was something that looked like a child's stocking, except that it was made not of cloth but of a transparent material, and was fitted with a ribbon of red silk at the open end. The ribbon had been artfully arranged to hang over the lip of the bowl so that it hung free of the oil.

Now, pinching the ribbon between her fingertips, Mrs Burnham lifted the sock out of the bowl and held it up so that the oil dripped off the tapered end in a thin trickle, pooling between the ridges of Zachary's abdomen.

'Do you know what this is, Mr Reid?'

His eyes widened. 'Is it . . . ? Could it be . . . ? A French letter?'

She boxed his ear playfully. 'Oh you are too coarse, Mr Reid! Let us call it a capote – a topcoat for our brave sepoy, so that he shall never again have to suffer the ignominy of shooting his goolies into the air.'

She stooped to give Zachary a long, slow kiss. 'I know how hard it has been for you, my dear, to so often deny yourself a proper spending. Your sacrifice has weighed heavily on me, and you cannot imagine how glad I am that you will not have to do it again.'

Zachary was touched, as much by the tenderness in her voice as by her gesture. 'That is thoughtful of you, Mrs Burnham. Was the capote hard to get?'

'Exceedingly, because I had to be so very discreet. Suffice it to say that on Free School Street there lives an Armenian midwife who is now considerably the richer.'

'It was expensive then?'

'Capotes are only a shilling apiece in England but here they cost twice as much – a whole rupee for one. And I got a few dozen of them so that they will last us awhile yet. Have you ever used one before?'

He shook his head. 'Mere mysteries cannot afford such luxuries, Mrs Burnham,' he said. 'I've heard of them of course, but I'd never seen one till now.'

'Nor have I any experience of them,' she said, 'but I will do my best to fit it correctly – you can help by lying on your back and holding your sepoy at attention.'

Crawling across the bed, she climbed over his leg and positioned herself between his thighs.

'I am told that capotes are made from lambs' intestines,' she said, as she dipped her fingers into the bowl. 'Is it not diverting, Mr Reid, to think that the animal that fills our bellies with mutton-gosht at dinner can also offer us this other service at night?'

She held up the length of intestine and slowly pried its lips apart, dribbling a thin trickle of oil down his stomach and groin. Then followed a few minutes of fumbling as she tried to slip the sock into place.

'It is a slippery business, Mr Reid, and our sepoy is making it no easier with all his twitching and quivering. Can he not be made to understand that this is no time to practise a bayonet drill?'

Her face had sunk deep between his legs now, and he could see only her brow. A frown appeared on it as she concentrated on the ribbon: 'Oh I have made a mess of it and must use my teeth to undo the knot. Hold still, Mr Reid, do not move!'

He was aware of the nipping of her teeth and the puffing of her breath: it blew on him like a warm breeze gusting against a flagpole. Throwing his head back he groaned: 'Oh Mrs Burnham, please be done, or I shall be fetched and finished.'

'On no account! Hold your fire!'

He felt the flight of her fingertips again, and then she gave a little squeal of delight: 'Oh Mr Reid! I wish you could see the pretty little bow I have tied for you! I am tempted to fetch you a looking-glass so that you may admire it.'

'No! Please – enough!'

'Well, I assure you, my dear mystery, there is not a bonnet in the world that sports a better-tied ribbon: the bow sits upon your goolie-pouch like a wreath below a mast! The Queen herself has never had a finer flag hoisted in her honour.'

He was now at the end of his ratline: removing the bowl from his belly, he took hold of her arms and pulled her upon him. 'And you, Mrs Burnham, have earned yourself a royal gun-salute!'

She laughed and kissed him on the tip of his nose: 'You see, Mr Reid – you are not as poor in invention as you would have us believe.'

Afterwards, when the ribbon, now sodden, had been undone and the freshly filled intestine was back in the bowl, he said: 'You are so expert in these arts, Mrs Burnham – I cannot but wonder how often you have done this before.'

She raised her head from the pillow and frowned at him. 'But never!' she cried. 'I have never done this before, Mr Reid.'

'But there have been others before me, have there not, Mrs Burnham? Lovers with whom you've deceived your husband?'

She shook her head vigorously. 'No; never! I swear to you, Mr Reid, before you entered this boudoir, I had never been unfaithful, never foozled my husband. I was, in my own way, a virtuous wife.'

'But you have told me yourself, Mrs Burnham, that you hardly ever share a bed with him. And I have seen for myself how ardent you are. Surely you have had your . . . wants?'

She smiled and raised her eyebrows. 'What have "wants" to do with husbands and faithfulness, my dear?' she said. 'A mem has no want that cannot be satisfied by a long bath, in which she is waited on by maids and cushy girls – or even another memsahib. You may take my word for it, Mr Reid, mems are never happier than when the sahibs are away – which is just as well since they are always gone anyway, on their endless campaigns and voyages.'

Zachary's mouth fell open, in disbelief. 'You cannot mean it! Do you mean that your cushy girls give you shokes in your bath? Does Mr Burnham know?'

'Well it is certainly no secret, my dear: intimate massages, by a nurse, was the cure that was prescribed for my hysteria, by the doctor. It is the standard remedy for the disease, you know, so I have always had to employ a maid or two to administer it. Mr Burnham is well aware of that and he does not disapprove – how could he, when a doctor has prescribed it? It may even be a source of satisfaction to him that he does not have to concern himself about my fidelity. And indeed, until a certain mystery entered my life I had never felt the slightest inclination to stray with any man – and it is amazing to me now, my dear, to think that when you first arrived here, I saw you as a rival, rather than a lover.'

'You've lost me, Mrs Burnham – a rival for what?'

She smiled impishly and scratched him on the chin. 'Well, my dear, you should know that the reason I was so peevish with you, when you first came here, was that I held you responsible for confounding my plans for Paulette. If not for you, I thought, she would have taken my advice and married Mr Kendalbushe, after which she and I would have been able to share many a happy goozle. I blamed you for dashing my hopes and was utterly resolved to punish you for your loochering; but such is kismet that it is you who are here now, and one day, when you leave me and run off with Paulette, I do not know who I shall be more jealous of – you or her.'

This strange notion cast Zachary's head into a whirl: as so often with Mrs Burnham, he had the sense that he was floundering in waters that were far deeper and more turbulent than any he had ever been in before. Yet, strangely, instead of cutting him adrift it made him want her all the more.

She was perfectly well aware of this and gave a little laugh. 'Ah, I see that our sepoy has heard the reveille and is ready to present arms again – although it is but a few minutes since he retired from the fray.'

He smiled grudgingly: 'One thing I'll say for you, Mrs Burnham – you sure know how to rattle a fellow's rigging.'

Nine

Although Kesri had spent a fair amount of time in Calcutta over the course of his career he had never before been quartered inside the walls of Fort William, the citadel that kept watch upon the city across the treeless expanse of the Maidan. Sepoys were rarely billeted within the fort, which was garrisoned mainly by white soldiers. Indian troops were usually quartered in the Sepoy Lines, an area that was separated from the fort by a wide stretch of empty ground.

On his previous postings to Calcutta, Kesri too had stayed in the Sepoy Lines, where the conditions were similar to those of other bases and cantonments, with the sepoys being responsible for their own food and housing – the army provided neither barracks nor messes. Rank-and-file jawans either built their own huts or pooled their money to rent them, and their food was prepared by shared servants. Havildars and other senior NCOs usually hired individual hutments and were looked after by their personal attendants.

But Calcutta's sepoy encampment was special in one important respect: it was far bigger than most others. The bazar that was attached to it was a vast, permanent establishment, a town in itself – its offerings were so varied that a young jawan could spend months there without wishing to venture out.

Left to himself, Kesri would have liked to return to the bazar at the Sepoy Lines, but it was out of the question this time, for he was under strict orders not to step out of Fort William. The formation of the expeditionary force was still a secret because no formal orders had yet been received from London: to keep word from leaking out, it had been decided that the volunteers would be confined to the precincts of the fort.

Kesri had grumbled when he was first told that he could not leave Fort William. But once installed in his new lodgings he found the confinement less irksome than he had expected. His quarters were in a barracks, which was itself a new experience, and being among the first to move in, he was able to commandeer one of the best rooms for himself. It occupied a corner of the building and had big windows on two sides; it was also on the third floor which added to the novelty, for Kesri had never before lived so high off the ground or enjoyed such a good view of his surroundings.

On the other hand it was burdensome to be constantly on duty. In most bases and cantonments there was a comfortable division between the sepoys' military duties and their living arrangements: at the end of the day, when they returned to their living quarters, they would change into dhotis and vests. At Fort William, by contrast, sepoys had to be in uniform all through the day, just like every English swaddy, and this took some getting used to. But still, these arrangements were not without their advantages: it was good to be spared the trouble and expense of dealing with a servant and managing a household.

The barracks that had been allotted to the Bengal Volunteers were in a secluded corner of the fort. Only a small part of the building had been set aside for them since their unit was to be a 'battalion' only in name. Even at full strength their numbers would be less than half that of a regular paltan: it would consist of two companies, each of about a hundred men.

That the unit would be a small one was welcome news to Kesri: he had expected to have jemadars, and perhaps even a subedar, sitting on top of him, poking their noses into everything. He was delighted to find that he was to be the highest ranking NCO in B Company. Equally pleasing was the discovery that the commander of the battalion, one Major Bolton, was a kind of supernumerary officer who was likely to be appointed to the staff of the expedition's commanding officer. This meant that the battalion's two companies would effectively function as independent units, which was exactly as Kesri would have wished it to be, since it meant that he and Captain Mee would be left largely to themselves in dealing with their men. There was of course the minor matter of some half-dozen subalterns to consider, but Kesri did not doubt that Captain Mee would be able to keep these young English officers from making nuisances of themselves.

It turned out that Captain Mee's counterpart, the commander of A Company, was not a particularly energetic or forceful officer. The advantages of this became obvious when it came time to pick out the junior NCOs: with Captain Mee's help, Kesri was able to get exactly the men he wanted as his naiks and lance-naiks.

When the first groups of rank-and-file sepoys began to trickle in, they too exceeded Kesri's expectations. He knew from experience that soldiers who were allowed to 'volunteer' for overseas service were often rejects of one sort or another – misfits, shirkers, layabouts and drunks – men that any unit would be glad to get rid of. But these balamteers were not quite as bad as Kesri had feared: many of them were ambitious young jawans who wanted to see the world and get ahead, just as he once had himself, many years before.

Still, there was no getting around the fact that the volunteers were young and inexperienced soldiers, drawn from regiments of uneven standard. Kesri knew that it would be no easy task to mould this rag-tag bunch into a coherent fighting unit.

But once drills began in earnest, Kesri discovered that there were some advantages to working with a motley crowd of balamteers: since these men were not related to each other, as in a regular sepoy battalion, there were no meddlesome cousins and uncles to be taken into account. They could be harassed, ghabraoed and punished at will, without having to answer to their relatives. It was exhilarating to taste the power that came with this – it was as if Kesri had become a zamindar and a subedar all at once.

In the past Kesri had often been awed by the iron discipline of European regiments. He had wondered what it was that enabled their NCOs to mould their men into machines. He understood now that the first step in building units of that kind was to strip the men of their links to the world beyond. In the regular Bengal Native Infantry it was impossible to do this; the ties between the men and their communities were just too strong.

It was a help also that here they were all living in unfamiliar conditions. None of the sepoys had ever been quartered in barracks before, and Kesri was much struck by the difference. He himself was now sharing a room with four naiks, and within a week he felt he knew them better than he had ever known his subordinates. They were from different places – Awadh, Mithila, Bhojpur and the mountains – and of different castes as well: Brahmin, Rajput, Aheer, Kurmi and a few others. At the start some of them grumbled about eating together, but Kesri was quick to dhamkao the complaints out of them. Didn't they know that they would have to travel on transport ships? Didn't they understand that on ships it was impossible to carry on as if they were back in a village? And so on. It wasn't long before they forgot about their complaints and this had a salutary effect also on the jawans, who became much more amenable to messing together when they saw that the NCOs were doing it too.

For a while things went better than Kesri had expected but he knew it wouldn't last – and indeed it didn't. Soon enough, the enforced isolation began to take a toll. The men were unused to being cooped up in a place where they had no access to the varied amenities of a camp-followers' bazar. Living with strangers, in barracks' rooms, and being constantly in uniform made them uneasy as well.

Matters took a turn for the worse when the second lot of balamteers was sent in, to make up the company's numbers. Almost to a man they were 'undesirables', who had been induced to volunteer because their parent units wanted to be rid of them – either because they were physically unfit or because they were incorrigible troublemakers.

Soon nerves began to fray and since there were no cousins and uncles around to intervene before quarrels got out of hand, petty disagreements frequently escalated into fights. On two successive weeks a man was stabbed to death, which meant that the company lost a total of nine men altogether, because the killers' accomplices had to be dismissed as well.

As the weeks went by Kesri began to see more and more signs of faltering morale: dishevelled uniforms, disorderly drills and many instances of mute, mulish insubordination of the kind that could not be remedied with ordinary punishments. To keep the men in hand became a constant struggle: for the first time in his career

Kesri began to regret that flogging had been abolished in the Bengal Native Infantry.

At length Kesri hit upon the idea of setting up a wrestling pit. This was a common feature in the sepoy lines of military depots and cantonments, many of which organized regular tournaments, within and between battalions. Kesri had himself continued to wrestle throughout his military career; for a few years he had even reigned as the champion of the Pacheesi. He knew that the sport helped to strengthen bonds within units and his youthful memories of the akhara told him that it was especially likely to do so in a situation where the participants were strangers to each other. He did not expect that Captain Mee would object – he was one of the few British officers who himself entered the pit from time to time – and he was right. The captain declared the project to be a whizzing idea and obtained the necessary permissions within a week.

To dig a more or less satisfactory pit took only a day or two, and then Kesri himself took on the role of guru for the first volunteers. The effect was exactly as he had hoped: the men joined in enthusiastically, glad of the distraction, and there was a sudden rise in spirits. Soon the whole company was seized by a wrestling mustee and every platoon began to field teams to compete against the others.

Despite these heartening signs, one basic problem remained unchanged, which was that the volunteers still had no idea where they were going. This gave rise to all kinds of unsettling rumours: they would have to fight savages who ate human flesh; they were to be sent into a waterless desert; and so on. To combat the speculation Kesri began to talk to the NCOs about what seemed to him like possible destinations: Lanka, Java, Singapore, Bencoolen and Prince of Wales Island in Malaya. Sepoys had campaigned in all of these theatres and Kesri had heard innumerable stories about them from his seniors. But when Maha-Chin – China – cropped up he derided the suggestion: who had ever heard of sepoys going to China? That country lay far afield of the ring of territories where sepoys had been deployed in the past. The very name Maha-Chin suggested a realm that was unfathomably remote: what little he knew of it came from wandering pirs and sadhus who spoke of crossing snow-clad mountains and freezing deserts. The idea of a seaborne campaign being launched against such a land seemed utterly absurd.

*

December was Calcutta's social season, and thanks to the Doughties Zachary received a fair number of invitations to Christmas celebrations, and even more for the arrival of the New Year – 1840. Mrs Burnham was also present at some of these events and when they happened to come face to face they would exchange perfunctory greetings, barely acknowledging one another.

But her presence always kept Zachary on his toes: he knew that she would be watching him covertly and that there would be a detailed post-mortem later, in which he would be taken to task if he had lapsed in any way from the best standards of sahib-dom in clothes, manners or deportment. Sometimes, rarely, she would offer a few words of praise and he would lap them up eagerly. Every word of approbation made him hungry for more; nor did it diminish his appetite that he could never be sure whether she was teasing or in earnest.

On New Year's Day their paths crossed briefly at a tiffin and that night, in the boudoir, Mrs Burnham said with a laugh: 'Oh Mr Reid! You're becoming quite the sahib, aren't you? Soon you're going to be so perfectly pucka you'll turn into a brick. That cravat! The fob!'

'And the suit?' he said eagerly. 'What did you think of it?'

Somewhat to his chagrin, this made her giggle. 'Oh my dear, dear mystery,' she said, cradling his face in her palms, 'there is not a suit in the world to match the one you were born with. And now that I have it in my hands, I'd like to slip into it myself . . .'

As a prominent hostess Mrs Burnham herself entertained regularly at home, but it was made clear to Zachary that he could not expect to be invited and would do well to stay out of sight. When forewarned he would usually go into town or make other arrangements. But sometimes he would get busy with his work and forget: thus it came about one day that he was laying down some deck-planks when he noticed a long line of gharries and buggies rolling up the driveway. Only then did he remember that Mrs Burnham was holding a levée that afternoon.

It happened that he was working in a part of the budgerow that was hidden from the house so he decided that there was no need to retreat to the interior of the vessel as he sometimes did when Mrs Burnham was entertaining. He stayed where he was, doubled up on his knees, hammer in hand.

He was hard at work, with his back to the vessel's prow, when he heard a voice behind him: 'Hello there!'

Leaping to his feet, he turned around to find himself facing a flaxen-haired girl, of about seventeen or eighteen.

'Don't you remember me, Mr Reid?' she said, with a shy smile. 'I'm Jenny Mandeville: we danced at the Harbourmaster's Ball – a quadrille, I think. You said to call you Zachary.'

'Oh yes, of course.' He glanced down at his soiled work-clothes – scuffed breeches and a sweat-soaked shirt – and made a gesture of embarrassment. 'I'm sorry; I'm not dressed for company.'

She gave a tinkling laugh: 'Oh I don't mind in the least! What you're doing looks *most* diverting. Can I try?'

'Why yes, of course. Here.'

She gave a little cry as he handed her the hammer. 'Ooh! It's heavy!'

'Not really,' he said. 'Not if you hold it right. Here – let me show you.'

He took hold of her palm and closed her fingers around the hammer's wooden handle.

Their hands were still joined when another voice cut in: 'Ah! There you are, Jenny! The mystery of the missing missy-mem is solved at last!'

They looked towards the foredeck and found a glowering Mrs Burnham standing there, with her fists resting on her hips; despite her dread of sunlight, she was, for once, devoid of either a hat or a parasol.

The girl snatched her hand guiltily away. 'Oh Mrs Burnham!' she cried. 'I was just looking . . .'

'Yes, dear,' said Mrs Burnham tartly, 'I can see what you were looking at. But it's time for you to be off now – your parents are already in their carriage.'

Without a word to Zachary, both women hurried off, leaving him standing foolishly in the gangway, hammer in hand.

It had been arranged between Zachary and Mrs Burnham that he would come to the boudoir that night – she liked to have him visit on nights when she had been entertaining – but he was so upset by the brusqueness of her manner that he decided not to go. He went to bed early and was sleeping soundly, sheltered by his mosquito net, when the door of his stateroom flew suddenly open. He woke with a start to find Mrs Burnham standing in the doorway, lamp in hand: her expression was like none he had ever seen before – her face was contorted with anger and her eyes were ablaze.

'You blackguard!' she hissed at him. 'You vile chute-looter of a luckerbaug! How dare you? How dare you?'

Leaping out of bed, Zachary pushed the door shut. In the light of the lamp he saw that she had not changed after her levée and was still wearing the same dress he'd seen her in earlier.

'You filthy cheating ganderoo . . . !'

'Mrs Burnham – calm down.' Taking the lamp from her hands he led her towards the bed. 'And please! Lower your voice.'

'Oh how dare you?' she cried. 'First you flirt with that slammerkin of a girl, and then you keep me waiting? How dare you?'

He had never before seen her in such a fury: he kept his own voice down so as not to further incense her. 'I wasn't flirting with her,' he said. 'It was she who came looking for me.'

'You're lying!' she said. 'You've been seeing her behind my back. I know you have!'

'That's not true, Mrs Burnham,' he said. 'This is the first time I've spoken to her since the Harbourmaster's Ball.'

'Then why's she always asking about you? Why is it always Zachary this, Zachary that, whenever I see her?'

'I have no idea,' said Zachary. 'Don't know nothin bout that.'

This seemed to calm her a little, so Zachary took hold of her elbow and led her to the bed. Parting the mosquito net he said: 'You'd better get in, Mrs Burnham, or you'll be eaten alive.'

She shrugged his hand off but allowed herself to be ushered inside the net. Blowing out the lamp, he climbed in beside her, to discover that her rage had now turned into a flood of tears.

'Why didn't you come?' she said, between sobs. 'I waited and waited.'

'Mrs Burnham,' he said quietly, 'I don't know if this has occurred to you, but I'm not just a mystery, you know: I'm also a human being, and it hurts when you treat me like a stray dog, as you did this afternoon.'

'What the devil do you mean?' she retorted. 'Do you expect me to shower choomers on you in public? You know perfectly well I can't be familiar with you in front of people.'

'Lookit, Mrs Burnham,' said Zachary patiently, 'I understand that you're a memsahib and I'm a mystery and we have to act a certain way to keep up appearances. But do you always have to be so rude to me in company? Why, there's not a servant in the house you treat so badly. Even the way you look at me – it's like I was a chigger or something.'

Her hands flew to her face and she shook her head convulsively from side to side. 'Oh what a fool you are, Mr Reid!' she said, swallowing her sobs. 'You're no mystery – what you are is an absolute and complete gudda.'

'And how do you figure that?'

'Oh Mr Reid,' she said, 'do you not understand? The reason I cannot bear to look at you in company is that I am gubbrowed half to death.'

'Why?'

'I am stricken with terror that my face will give away the gollmaul that wells up in me at the very sight of you!'

Zachary reached for her hand, in the dark, and found that it was shaking. 'But it isn't only in public that you're hard on me, you know,' he said. 'Even when we're alone, you have no praise for anyone but "our little sepoy" as you call him.'

She wrenched her hand defiantly from his grasp: 'Look – if you want miss-ish sighs and swoonings and protestations of love, you would do well, Mr Reid, to seek out the Jenny Mandevilles of this world. You certainly won't get them from me. I have long outgrown such girlish fancies.'

'But you too were a girl once, Mrs Burnham – were you never in love then?'

Hearing a sharp intake of breath, Zachary steeled himself for a rebuff. But when she spoke again it was in a tremulous whisper: 'Yes, I was in love once.'

'Tell me about it.'

'It was a long time ago and I was no older than that silly minx, Jenny. He was a subaltern in my father's regiment, fresh from England – only a year older than me. He was a little wild, as ensigns should be, and very handsome, in a dark-haired way. Almost from the moment I set eyes on him, I was lost – completely, utterly in love, as only a girl of seventeen can be. Your little Miss Mandeville has yet to feel a tenth part of the passion that agitated me then.'

'And he?'

'He too. We were both besotted.'

'Why did you not marry him then?'

'It was impossible. My parents would not have allowed it – he was utterly unsuitable in their eyes. His father was a greengrocer in Fulham, and it was said that his mother was a Levantine Jew. The rumour was that he had got his officer's commission through blackmail: his mother had been the mistress of a member of the Board of the East India Company and she had forced her lover to use his influence. And it wasn't as if he could have afforded a wife anyway. He was never one to play cards for craven-stakes – he had not a groat to his name.'

'So what became of him?'

'I cannot tell you – I have neither seen nor heard from him since the day we were torn apart, seventeen years ago.' Her voice began to tremble again and she paused until she had regained control of it. 'That year my father's regiment was quartered in Ranchi, which is a town in the hills. It was winter, and the station was very gay, with many parties, picnics and tumashers. One day we were at a picnic, in a forest – there are lovely woodlands in those hills – and we slipped away for a walk. We got a little lost, the two of us, and I did not object when he put his arm around me; nor did I resist when he put his lips on mine. Indeed I would not have resisted if he had done more than that – we were burning for each other.'

'But he did not?'

'No. We heard his orderly's voice, shouting for us: we hurried back and told my parents that we'd lost our way. But there must have been something in my expression to arouse my mother's suspicions for when we got back to our bungalow she went to speak to my father. The next day I was whisked off to Calcutta to avert a scandal: my mother was terrified that people would think that I had been compromised so she decided to marry me off as quickly as possible. In those days Mr Burnham was dancing attendance on my father in the hope of securing a contract to provide supplies for a military expedition. One day I was told that Mr Burnham had offered for my hand. My mother said I could not hope for a better match.'

'And the ensign? What became of him?'

'He is still with his regiment, I expect. No doubt married, with a paltan of children swarming around his feet.'

'Do you still think of him?'

'Oh don't! . . . It is too cruel.' She turned her face away but he could tell that she was trying to stem a fresh flow of tears.

Never before had Mrs Burnham evinced so much emotion in front of Zachary: it was clear to him that the emotions the lieutenant had stirred in her were of a singular intensity, surpassing by far anything that she had ever felt for him. Certainly she had never shown signs of such passion with him; indeed he hadn't thought her capable of it. A burst of vexation flashed through him and somewhere inside his chest a cinder of jealousy began to glow: who was this man, this lieutenant, whose memory could reach out to her through such a long tunnel of time, making her seem a stranger to him while she was in his own bed?

'I'll ask no more questions,' he said, 'but only if you answer one more.'

Having said this, he stumbled, for his query was strangely difficult to put into words. At last, lamely, he said: 'Tell me: the ensign – was he . . . ? Am I . . . ? Are we . . . at all alike?'

At this she gave him a wan smile. 'Oh no, my dear dear. You are as unlike each other as two men could possibly be – toolsmith and warrior, Eros and Mars.'

Zachary winced: who exactly she was referring to he did not know but he had the impression that the comparison was not, in any case, flattering to him. It was as if she had said, in so many words, that she would never love him, or anyone else, as much as she had loved her lost lieutenant; that he would be forever the captain of her heart.

*

Slowly, with much help from Rosa and Vico, Shireen was able to convince Shernaz and Behroze that there was no great danger in her travelling to China and that the voyage would be in their common interest. The next step was to carry the fight to her brothers and for this part of the campaign Shireen enlisted the help of her daughters. They arranged to meet with their uncles, hoping to test the waters on her behalf.

The meeting did not go well. The girls came back in tears, to report that their uncles had berated them for falling in with Shireen's plan: if she went to China a terrible scandal was sure to ensue, they had said, and the whole family's reputation would be endangered. The seths had accused their two nieces of being unfeeling, shameless and undutiful, to their mother and to their relatives.

All kinds of unfamiliar emotions surged up in Shireen as she listened to Shernaz and Behroze. Usually anger had an enervating effect on her, making her weary and listless, but in this instance she was roused to a fury. After the girls had left, she found that she could not sit still: as if girding for battle, she changed into a fresh sadra vest and a plain white sari. Then she marched downstairs and stormed into her brothers' shared daftar, disregarding the protests of their shroffs and munshis. Standing in front of them, with her hands on her hips, she demanded to know if they really thought that it was in their power to keep her from visiting her husband's grave?

Shireen's brothers were younger than her and as children they had always been a little scared of her. The passage of time, and the reverses that Shireen had suffered over the years, had diluted their childhood fear of her but a trace of it surfaced again now. Other than a few evasive mumbles they could offer no answers to her questions.

Seizing upon their confusion, Shireen declared that the matter was not in their hands anyway; it was up to her to make up her mind, and she had already done so – neither they nor their wives, nor even her own daughters could prevail on her to give up her plan. It only remained for them to choose what kind of scandal they wanted to deal with. Did they want a public rift within the family? Or would they prefer to stand beside her, as their father and mother would surely have wanted them to? Did they not see that it was to their benefit to tell the world that their sister was doing what any grieving and dutiful widow would want to do? Didn't they understand that if the family presented a united front to the world then the prestige of the Mistrie name would swing the balance and everyone would surely come around?

They started to fidget now and Shireen sensed that they were wavering. Planting herself in a chair she looked them directly in the eyes.

So tell me then, she demanded. How shall we go about this? What shall we tell people?

Instead of answering her questions they made a feeble attempt to reason with her.

Hong Kong was a long way away, they said. Getting there would entail a voyage of many weeks and she, with her uncertain health, would find it difficult to be at sea for such a length of time.

Shireen laughed. She was just as hardy as either of them, she said – and as proof of this she reminded them that her 'sea legs' had always been better than theirs. As children, when they went on sailing trips with their parents, she was the only one among the siblings who had never suffered from sea-sickness; the two of them had scarcely been able to step on deck without heaving up their insides.

Their faces reddened and they quickly changed tack. What about the costs? they said. The journey would be expensive – where was the money to come from?

This aspect of the plan had so occupied Shireen's thoughts that she knew the numbers by heart: reaching for a quill she jotted down some figures on a sheet of paper and pushed it across the table.

Leh, she said. There – have a look.

Frowns appeared on the seths' faces as they went through the numbers. Their disapproval was focused on one particular figure, which they underlined and thrust back at her.

The price of the passage had been greatly underestimated, they told her. The voyage would cost much more than she had allowed for.

This was exactly the opening Shireen had been waiting for.

I have been offered a special price, she announced triumphantly, by Mr Benjamin Burnham, who was my husband's colleague on the Select Committee at Canton. He will provide me with a fine cabin on one of his ships, the *Hind*, which will be arriving soon in Bombay. The *Hind* will sail at the end of March, going from here to Colombo and then Calcutta, where she will pick up some troops for the eastern expedition.

She paused: So you see – it will be a very safe and economical way to travel.

Her brothers looked at each other and shrugged. Their expressions were such that Shireen knew that she had carried the day even before they said: *tho pachi theek che*, all right then; do what you want.

*

January 14, 1840
Honam

I have been very, very fortunate in chancing upon my lodgings in Baburao's houseboat. I'll warrant that nobody in Canton has a better view of this vast city than I do. A fortnight ago the residents of the American Factory put on a fireworks display in the foreign enclave, to celebrate the arrival of the year 1840, of the Christian era. I watched it from my terrace and it was as if the show had been put on expressly for my benefit; where others saw only the display in the sky, I saw it replicated also in the water, on the surface of the Pearl River and White Swan Lake.

Later, Zhong Lou-si interrogated me at length about calendars and was very curious to know which are in use in India and why. Often, when he questions me I am reminded of the tutors of my childhood, the learned pundits who schooled me in *Nyaya*, logic, and Sanskrit grammar. Like them Zhong Lou-si has an inexhaustible fund of patience, a tenacious memory and an unerring eye for inconsistencies and contradictions. With him too I have to be very careful in choosing my words – he examines everything I say and if I were to make extravagant claims I know I would be quickly taken to task.

In Lou-si's demeanour too there is something that reminds me of my old punditjis: like them he sometimes lapses into woolly distractedness and sometimes bristles with irascibility. Yet there is one great difference: unlike the pundits of my childhood, Zhong Lou-si has no taste for abstractions or philosophical speculation. He is interested only in 'useful knowledge' – *chih hsueh* – which includes a great variety of things, mainly pertaining to the world beyond. In months past he would sit with me for hours, asking questions about one subject after another: were the people who Tibetans and Gurkhas call 'borgis' the same as the 'Marathas'? What was the date of the Battle of Assaye by the Chinese calendar? Was Sir Arthur Wellesley the same man as the Duke of Wellington? I am sure Zhong Lou-si knows the answers to many of these questions – he asks them either for confirmation or to check my own reliability. He treats every statement critically; to him the provenance of what is said is just as important as its content: how did I know that the British expedition to Burma had come close to defeat in 1825? Was it just hearsay? What were my sources?

But since the disastrous naval battle at Humen there has been a marked change in the direction of his inquiries. He no longer seems to be so interested in history and geography: his questions now are mainly about military and naval matters.

One day he questioned me at length about paddle-wheel steamers. I told him that I well remembered the day, fourteen years ago, when a steamer called *Enterprize* had steamed up to Calcutta, having come all the way from London: this was the first steamer ever to be seen in the Indian Ocean and she had won a prize of twenty thousand pounds for her feat. Being young at that time I had expected that the *Enterprize* would be a huge, towering vessel: I was astonished to find that she was a small, ungainly-looking craft. But when the *Enterprize* began to move my disappointment had turned to wonder:

without a breath of wind stirring, she had gone up and down the Calcutta waterfront, manoeuvring dexterously between throngs of boats and ships.

I told Zhong Lou-si that the arrival of the *Enterprize* had set off a great race amongst the shipowners of Calcutta. Within a few years the New Howrah Dockyards had built the *Forbes*, a teak paddle-wheeler fitted with two sixty-horsepower engines. This had inspired my own father to enter the race: he had invested five thousand rupees in a company launched by the city's most eminent Bengali entrepreneur, Dwarkanath Tagore: it was called the Calcutta Steam Tug Association, and it was soon in possession of two steamers. I told Zhong Lou-si that steamers and steam-tugs are a familiar sight on the Hooghly now; people have grown accustomed to seeing them on the river, churning purposefully through the water and exhaling long trails of smoke, soot and cinders.

Zhong Lou-si remarked that if steamers had been built in Calcutta then surely it should be possible to build one in Guangzhou as well, *me aa*?

Gang hai Lou-si! Yes, of course.

I told him that I did not see why not: it all depended on the engine. The engines for the Calcutta steamers had come from England, as I remember, but I have heard that a Parsi shipbuilder has built similar engines in Bombay. If it could be done in Bombay then there is no reason why it should not be possible in Guangzhou.

From the drift of these questions I realized that there was a plan afoot to bring steamers to China. Later Compton told me that a steamer had already visited Canton some years before – he confided also that a local shipyard is now experimenting with a prototype.

From this, and from some other tasks that we'd been set, it became clear to me that the lessons of the disastrous naval engagement at Humen have not been lost on Commissioner Lin and his entourage: they have realized that China's war-junks are antiquated and are making every effort to acquire some modern sailing vessels of the Western type.

A while ago Zhong Lou-si had asked us to look out for notices of sale for Western-built ships. As luck would have it, I soon came upon one. It was in one of the journals that Lou-si's agents procure for us – the *Canton Press*.

The notice was for a ship called the *Cambridge*; she had been put up for sale by her owner, an Englishman by the name of Captain Douglas. The notice said that she was a merchantman of 1,080 tons, built by Fawcett's of Liverpool, armed with thirty-six guns – perfect in every way from Lou-si's point of view. But would Mr Douglas sell to a Chinese buyer? Would Captain Elliot allow him to make such a sale?

I doubted it, but still, I showed the notice to Compton who gave a triumphant shout – *Dak jo!* – and went racing off to Zhong Lou-si. I heard nothing more about it until today, when Compton made a triumphant announcement: Ah Neel! We have got that ship – the *Cambridge*!

This is how it happened: apparently the owner of the *Cambridge*, Captain Douglas, is well-known to the officials of Guangdong Province – he is a notorious trouble-maker and has for months been disrupting the traffic on the Pearl River, sailing up and down the estuary, firing at will on fishermen and trading junks. The local authorities had even put a price on his head, of a thousand silver dollars.

These being the circumstances, Zhong Lou-si had guessed that Captain Douglas would not willingly sell the *Cambridge* to a Chinese buyer. To get around this problem he had enlisted the help of a wealthy Co-Hong merchant. He in turn had persuaded his American partner, Mr Delano, to buy the ship. Mr Delano's bid had been accepted and the *Cambridge* had been duly handed over to him. After waiting a few days Mr Delano had sold the ship to his Chinese partner, who had then presented her to Commissioner Lin, as a gift! The *Cambridge* is now in the possession of the Chinese authorities who are planning to equip her with a new set of guns.

The deftly handled acquisition has been hailed as a triumph for Zhong Lou-si, said Compton, and my small part in it had not gone unrecognized either. Zhong Lou-si had sent a fine bottle of mao-tai to thank me for having brought the notice to his attention.

It is heartening – and rather surprising! – to see a high official, and an elderly one at that, being so nimble in his thinking and so far-sighted.

*

Zachary was hard at work on the budgerow one morning when he heard a khidmatgar's voice: '*Mistri–sah'b! Chitthi!*'

The man had brought over an envelope that Zachary knew, at a glance, was from Mrs Burnham.

January 30, 1840

Dear Mr Reid

I need to see you immediately. Please come to my sewing room at once. I've told the nokar-logue that I need your advice on some new pelmets so be sure to bring your tape-measure.

C.B.

Within minutes Zachary was at the sewing room door. 'Madam? Mrs Burnham?'

He heard her voice on the other side of the door, speaking to a maid, as unruffled as ever: 'Oh, is it the mystery? Let him in. Chullo!'

The maid opened the door and hurried away. Zachary stepped in to find Mrs Burnham sitting at her sewing table, looking perfectly composed, with her embroidery in her hands.

But the moment the door closed she dropped the frame.

'Oh Mr Reid!' she cried, jumping to her feet: 'Everything has been turned on its ears!'

'What do you mean, Mrs Burnham?'

'He is here, Mr Reid! My husband – Mr Burnham! He has returned from China with two ships – the *Ibis* and another vessel that he has recently acquired, the *Anahita*. They are anchored at the Narrows, which is some twenty miles away. He has sent a chitty with a sowar – he will be here this evening.'

Zachary stared at her, aghast: 'Were you expecting him?'

'No! I had no conception!' She pressed a fluttering hand to her throat. 'Oh Mr Reid – and that's the least of it.'

'What else then?'

'You will not credit it – my husband has decided that we must move to China!'

'To China!' said Zachary. 'But why?'

'He says that a new free port is soon to be created on the China coast. A decision to that effect has already been taken in London. He says that great new opportunities will open up and he must be there to make the best of them.'

'And your daughter?'

'She is to remain with her grandparents for the time being.'

Zachary's head was spinning now. 'So what does this mean for you and me? Will we not be able to meet after this?'

'Absolutely not!' she cried. 'We can never again meet as we used to. You must not allow that thought to so much as cross your mind. Mr Burnham is fiendishly clever and it is not in your power, or mine, to deceive him while he is here.'

'So this is it? The end?'

'Well, Mr Reid, we knew, didn't we, that it would have to end one day? Apparently that day has come and we must accept it.'

A lump rose to Zachary's throat.

'But you promised, Mrs Burnham, that when the time came we would end it properly.'

'Well it is impossible now, don't you see? He will be here this evening.'

She put a hand on his arm. 'Look, Mr Reid – it is as hard for me as it is for you. No – truth to tell, it is much harder for me. I have only my old life to go back to – levées, church, improving causes, and laudanum to put me to sleep at night. But you are young, you have your life ahead. You will go on to find happiness, with Paulette or someone else.'

'Paulette be damned!' snapped Zachary.

Over the last few months, as his intimacy with Mrs Burnham had deepened, so had Zachary's feelings towards Paulette grown increasingly rancorous: what was most vexing to him was that she should put it about that he had seduced her, whereas the truth was that his behaviour towards her had never been anything other than honourable. Why, he had even proposed marriage once, only to be rudely rebuffed! If such were the wages of righteousness then he could scarcely be blamed for having turned to adultery.

'I don't give a fig for Paulette!'

'No! Do not say that! Paulette may have made mistakes but she is a good girl – I am convinced of it. She would make a good wife for you.'

Zachary had to fight back an urge to stamp his feet, like a petulant child.

'I don't want to marry her! I don't want to marry anyone.'

A look of concern came over Mrs Burnham's face. 'Oh but Mr Reid, of course you must marry, and soon at that, or else your old ailment may again claim you. If any good has come of our connection, it is surely that that chapter is closed, is it not? Now that you have cured yourself you must not, on any account, allow yourself to relapse. All the most enlightened men are agreed on this subject – better the bordello than the indulgence of selfish, solitary pleasures.'

'Surely, Mrs Burnham,' said Zachary, 'you are not urging me to resort to knocking-shops and bawdykens?'

'By no means,' said Mrs Burnham. 'What I am urging you to do is to conquer the primitive who lurks inside you. We are in an age of progress and in order to belong to it you must destroy everything that is backward in yourself. And I am convinced that if you set your mind to it you will not find it difficult. With hard work, prayer, regular exercise, a soothing diet and cold baths you can surely vanquish the affliction. You must become a man of the times, Mr Reid – you must change yourself. If you succeed the whole world will be at your feet! It is what I expect of you; it is what you deserve.'

'It's all very well for you to say so, Mrs Burnham,' said Zachary. 'But what I really deserve is for you to make good on the promise you had made to me – about how our connection would end.'

'Now, now, Mr Reid.' Her tone had changed now; there was a note of command in it that he had not heard in a while. 'You're not a child; you mustn't make a tumasher of it.'

With a wave of a handkerchief she ushered him towards the door. 'You must be off before the harry-maids come back.'

For a moment Zachary stood his ground, in mulish defiance, so she leant closer and whispered into his ear: 'Remember, Mr Reid – if my husband should have the faintest suspicion he will destroy us both. So please, you must get ahold of yourself.'

Slowly Zachary's feet began to move. On reaching the door he turned to her again: 'Goodbye, Mrs Burnham.'

She was dabbing her eyes with a handkerchief.

'Goodbye, Mr Reid.'

He opened the door and stepped out.

*

It wasn't till the end of January that Kesri learnt where the Bengal Volunteers were going. It was Captain Mee who told him: 'Havildar, I have some important news. The Burra Laat, Lord Auckland, and the Jangi Laat, General Sir Hugh Gough, have received formal instructions from London. Our orders are to proceed to southern China.'

This stunned Kesri. China had seemed to him so unlikely a destination that he had discounted all the rumours. But when Captain Mee asked if he wanted to reconsider his decision to volunteer he answered without hesitation. 'No, Mee-sahib. I've given my word and I will go. But about others I don't know.'

'You think we'll lose a lot of men?'

'Let's see, sir,' said Kesri. 'Some we are better without.'

Kesri mustered the company the next day and Captain Mee made the announcement in his usual businesslike way, speaking through an interpreter. He ended by telling the sepoys that if they wanted to change their minds they had three days to do so. Later, when it was Kesri's turn to speak to the company, he elaborated on this a little, explaining that anyone who wanted to withdraw from the unit would have to return the travel battas and other emoluments they had received for volunteering. This too would have to be done within three days; after that no withdrawals would be permitted: anyone who developed second thoughts would be treated as a malingerer.

Kesri knew that the prospect of having to return battas and emoluments would be a deterrent to most of the Volunteers. He did not expect many withdrawals – but in this he was wrong. Nine men, almost a tenth of the company, came to see him and asked to be sent back to their units. He released them immediately and had them removed under escort, so that they would have no further contact with the company: better to be rid of them now than to have them lingering and spreading their poison.

After the third day had passed, Kesri reminded the company that the time for withdrawals was over. From then on he kept the men under even closer watch. Mutiny or disaffection was not what he was afraid of – in the enclosed circumstances of Fort William signs of recalcitrance would be easy to detect and quell. What worried him more was another possibility: desertion. Now that the eastern expedition was public knowledge, the men were free to apply for permission to leave the fort for short periods. Kesri knew that in the company's present state of morale, a few desertions were inevitable. He resigned himself to dealing with them as and when they occured.

But the disclosure of the expedition's destination did have one fortunate consequence: Kesri was free at last to visit the paltani-bazars and Sepoy Lines, to make a start on something that he had had to postpone all this while: the business of putting together the company's contingent of camp-followers – a body that would exceed the fighting men in number when all the necessary dhobis, darzies, cobblers, bhistis, bhandari-walas, porters and baggage handlers had been recruited. On top of that there were the auxil-iaries and daftardars to be considered, which would consist of another sizeable contingent, including medical attendants, clerks, interpreters, accountants, gun-lascars, golondauzes, fifers, drummers and the like.

Recruiting the camp-followers was a tedious business but it was not without its rewards. The followers were usually provided by sirdars, ghat-serangs and other labour contractors, many of whom made handsome profits from the army's contracts and were willing to pay good dastoories in order to secure them. The officers gener-ally left this matter to the senior NCOs and clerical staff who were often able to collect quite substantial sums from the contractors.

This was an accepted perquisite and Kesri knew that he could count on it to bring in a tidy little sum.

There were no such benefits attached to the choice of auxiliaries, who were all employees of the military establishment. But in this matter too Kesri was able, with Captain Mee's support, to pick and choose his men. He was particularly careful when it came to choosing the drummers and fifers, who were provided by the army's Boy Establishment. These youngsters, some of whom were as young as ten or eleven, were mainly Eurasians. Some were the illegitimate sons of British soldiers and came from orphanages; some were descended from the legendary 'topaz' corps – the Goan and Portuguese artillerymen who had served the British during their early conquests in India.

Although the 'banjee-boys', as they were known, were relatively few in number, Kesri knew that they played a disproportionate role in keeping up morale. They often became mascots for their units, and the sepoys sometimes grew so attached to them that they treated them like their own sons.

Kesri insisted on auditioning the boys himself, calling on them to step out of line, one by one, when they mustered for inspection. During one audition a boy accidentally dropped his fife; he was eleven or twelve but tall for his age, with amber eyes, brown hair and a snub nose. He carried on bravely, but at the end of the performance his lower lip began to quiver. Kesri understood that he was afraid that he would not be picked so he beckoned to him to step forward.

Naam kya hai tera? What's your name?

Dicky Miller, havildar-sah'b.

Do you know where the expedition is going?

Ji, sir. China.

And you're not scared?

The boy's amber eyes suddenly brightened. No, sir! he replied, puffing out his chest: *Main to koi bhi cheez se nahin darta!* I'm not scared of anything!

His eagerness drew a laugh from Kesri and he made sure that the boy was included in the company's contingent of fifers and drummers. And when the fifers made their first appearance at the parade ground he knew he had made a good choice: with his bright eyes and jaunty step young Dicky Miller was just the kind of lad who was likely to keep up the unit's spirits.

*

After his abrupt dismissal from Mrs Burnham's sewing room, Zachary walked back to the budgerow with his head a-whirl, hardly aware of what he was doing. He had known all along, of course, that his visits to the boudoir would end one day but he had thought that he would at least be granted the night of leave-taking that he had been promised.

The truth was that despite all of Mrs Burnham's repeated warnings he had always believed that their liaison would somehow continue, in secret: he had never allowed for the possibility that he might one day be tossed overboard like a worn-out jack-block. But along with anger, bitterness, grief and jealousy, he was aware also of a powerful sense of gratitude towards Mrs Burnham for all that she had given him, money being the least of it; nor was his admiration of her in any way diminished by his sudden jettisoning.

This too served to deepen his confusion, making him wonder about the nature of their connection: what exactly was it that had come into being between them? It was not love, surely, for that word had never been used by either of them; nor was it only lust, for her voice, her words and the things she talked about were at least as bewitching to him as her body. She had opened a window into a world of wealth and luxury where the finest and most voluptuous pleasures were those that were stolen – and it was that very act of thievery, as when he was in her bed, that made them so delectable, so intoxicating. It was as though she had placed his feet on the threshold of this world: all that remained was for him to make his way in – and he was determined to do it, if only to prove to her that he was capable of it.

But how?

Defeated by the question, he went off to a bowsing-ken in Kidderpore and did not return till late at night.

On waking the next day he realized that it behooved him to go to the big house to pay his respects to the Burra Sahib. But he kept putting it off, unsure of whether he would be able to maintain a normal demeanour, fearing that he would betray himself with some chance word or gesture.

But as the hours went by it became ever clearer that it was by staying away that he was most likely to draw suspicion to himself. So in the late afternoon he screwed up his courage and walked over to the mansion to ask for Mr Burnham.

A khidmatgar led him to a withdrawing room, where the Burra Sahib was conferring with an important-looking gent. As Zachary stood waiting, hat in hand, the force of the tycoon's presence began to work on him like a spell: Mr Burnham's commanding stature, his wide, masterful chest, his shining beard, and even the swell of his belly helped to create an aura such that to gain his good opinion seemed a prize worth striving for.

Nor, somewhat to his own surprise, was Zachary beset by pangs of guilt or jealousy as he had feared he might be. To the contrary he was aware of a peculiar kind of sympathy, a sense of kinship even, born of the knowledge that neither he nor Mr Burnham would ever be able to lay full claim to his wife's heart, which had forever been lost to her first love.

When at last Mr Burnham turned to him, Zachary shook his hand with unfeigned warmth.

'I'm very glad to see you, sir.'

'I'm glad to see you too, Reid. Are you finished with the budgerow yet?'

'Not quite, sir, but I will be very soon.'

'Good! I'm glad to hear it. Let me know when you're ready and I'll come by to take a look.'

With that Mr Burnham turned on his heel and disappeared into his daftar.

This exchange, brief though it was, was hugely energizing for Zachary; he began to work harder than ever before, polishing, hammering, carving, holystoning. Sometimes, when he stopped to rest, his mind would wander, and then it would seem to him that the last few months had passed in a kind of delirium in which nothing had been real except the feverish voluptuousness of his nights with Mrs Burnham: whether he was with her or not, her voice had always been in his head; even when he was in his own unkempt bed, he had felt himself to be cradled in her satiny sheets.

Had his memories of those nights been a matter of the mind alone then he would have been able to deal with them without too much difficulty. But his body too had acquired a great trove of memories, and having grown accustomed to the fleshly pleasures of the boudoir, it often cried out insistently for release. But in this matter he was unyielding. Mrs Burnham's words on the subject were loud in his ears and following her advice he began to eat judiciously, subsisting on crackers and bland, unspiced foods. He started to exercise vigorously, with dumb-bells and weights, and after rousing his body to a great heat he would shock it with a long, cold bath. At night, when the fear of lapsing became especially powerful, he would tie his hands to the bedstead, to prevent them from straying, as recommended by Dr Tissot. One evening he even attended a prayer meeting in the city, and for the first time in his life he understood what the preacher was talking about when he spoke of Man's fallen nature, and the devil that lurked in every heart; he too was among the worshippers who left the meeting armed with a precious trove of fear and dread.

And sure enough, just as Mrs Burnham had predicted, his mounting anxieties began to work a slow but steady change in him; he started to see why it was more important to hoard than to waste, he understood why accumulating was more important than spending, and slowly he came to be filled with a great disgust for the life he had led before – a life of profligacy and poverty, in which he had wasted his mind and body in pointless pursuits, squandering his essences, bodily and spiritual, in fanciful imaginings. He longed to leave that life behind him but was again confounded by that hateful query: how?

One day he saw the Burnham carriage rolling by, with both master and mistress seated within, and was seized by a yearning to prove to both of them that he was not 'just a mystery'; that he too was fit to be a Burra Sahib with a mansion, a carriage and ships to his name.

But how?

He could think of no answer. After many hours of fruitlessly racking his brain he went off to Kidderpore and bought himself a bottle of rum.

Ten

Now that they knew where they were going, the balamteers talked of little else but China. And the more they spoke of it the faster the rumours flew: it was as if the very name – Maha-Chin – were enough to stir up elemental fears in them. They knew nothing about China of course, except that the people there were different in every way, not least in appearance – they looked like Gurkhas, some said, and this too was cause for disquiet. The sepoys were well aware of the Gurkhas' fearsome reputation as fighters; many of them had relatives who had fought in the East India Company's wars against the Gurkha empire some twenty-two years before. One of the naiks in B Company was the son of a sepoy who had died at the Battle of Nalapani, where the Gurkhas had inflicted a severe defeat on the British. Like all professional soldiers, the sepoys had long memories: they knew that a few decades earlier the Gurkhas, for all their martial prowess, had been thoroughly defeated and subjugated by the army of Maha-Chin ka Faghfoor – the Emperor of China.

All of this created misgivings and these were compounded by speculation and rumours: some sepoys put it about that the Chinese had supernatural powers and were masters of the occult; others said that they possessed secret weapons and were ingenious in spreading confusion among their enemies.

Kesri was not impervious to these rumours: he had personally experienced many strange things on the battlefield and did not doubt that unknown forces could intervene in times of war. Why else did soldiers offer prayers before fighting? Why else did they carry protective amulets and have their weapons blessed? To speak of 'luck' and 'chance', as the British officers did, was merely an evasion to Kesri: what were those things but names for the interventions of kismat? And if the Angrezes really believed that supernatural and divine forces played no part in war, then why did they go to their churches to pray on the eve of a battle? Why did they allow their orderlies to take their weapons to the temple to be blessed?

But of course these thoughts could not be voiced to anyone, least of all the naiks and lance-naiks: instead Kesri told them stories about his wartime experiences in Burma, where the people were also akin to the Chinese and the Gurkhas. It was true, he said, that they were fierce and skilful warriors, and that they used all kinds of arts and ruses to confuse their enemies. But in the end the Burmese, who had in the past vanquished the armies of the Emperor of China, had themselves been defeated: there was no reason to be awed by Chinese soldiers, said Kesri; like everyone else they could be beaten.

By this time Kesri's personal authority over the men was strong enough for his words to have a steadying effect: through the wrestling pit he had built close personal connections with many of the sepoys, and they had come to trust him. Besides, it was reassuring to them to know that they were serving under a havildar who had campaigned overseas before. As the days went by their performance on the parade ground improved to the point of wresting a few grudging words of approbation out of Captain Mee: 'The men seem to be shaping up at last havildar. Good work.'

In late February Captain Mee held a briefing for Kesri and the other NCOs. With the aid of a large map and two interpreters, he explained that their company had been assigned to the *Hind*, a civilian transport ship that would take them first to Singapore, and from there to southern China. Depending on the weather, the initial leg of the journey would take fifteen to twenty days; the next might take a little less, but sailing times could not be predicted with any certainty. They could expect to leave after the retreat of the northerly monsoon, and before the onset of the summer rains – probably in March or April, which meant that their departure was now only a few weeks away.

The length of the voyage came as a surprise even to Kesri. None of his previous sea-journeys had lasted more than a week – it was daunting to think of spending a month or more at sea. It was not that he was concerned about the discomforts of the voyage: what worried him was the question of how to keep up the men's morale so that they would be in a condition to fight when they reached their destination. Very few of them had ever sailed before and they all harboured that dread of the *kalapani* – the black water – that was prevalent in their home regions.

Kesri knew that Captain Mee's briefing would stir the men's misgivings and he was not wrong. One day a medical orderly came to tell him that one of the company's sepoys had suffered a serious bayonet wound. When Kesri went to the infirmary to inquire, the man claimed that he had hurt himself accidentally. But Kesri knew at a glance that he was lying – the wound was in the fleshiest part of the thigh, where it would do the least harm. He guessed that the man had done it to himself, in the hope of getting out of the army with an unblemished record of service, so that he could keep all his battas and perhaps get a pension as well.

Captain Mee agreed with Kesri that they would have to make an example of this man if they were to prevent an outbreak of self-inflicted wounds: a court martial was quickly convened and the man was given a seven-year sentence of transportation and hard labour, to be served on Prince of Wales Island.

*

Baboo Nob Kissin's gaze was usually wary and vigilant, like that of a ruminant watching out for hungry predators. But Zachary's presence often had a transformative effect on him, and now, as he pushed open the door of his stateroom, the Baboo's eyes grew moist in anticipation of beholding the object of his devotion.

A year and several months had passed since Baboo Nob Kissin had last laid eyes on Zachary. Through most of that time he had been in China with Mr Burnham and had returned to Calcutta with him, on the *Anahita*. Had circumstances permitted he would have come at once to visit Zachary – but Mr Burnham had decided otherwise. On the very day of their return he had dispatched Baboo Nob Kissin to Patna and Ghazipur, to make inquiries about that season's poppy crop. Now, having completed his mission, Baboo Nob Kissin had come hurrying to the budgerow, in the spirit of an eager pilgrim – and as the door of the stateroom swung slowly open, he saw to his shock that Zachary was lying sprawled across the bed, clothed in nothing but his drawers, with his fingers still fastened on the neck of an almost empty bottle of rum.

In other circumstances the odour of sweat and liquor would have aroused Baboo Nob Kissin's utmost revulsion, but this being Zachary he took the signs of drunkenness to be intimations of something unknown and unexpected, some perplexing mystery that would lead him towards illumination. Tiptoeing inside, the Baboo slowed his steps so that he could take full advantage of this rare opportunity for an unguarded darshan: as he contemplated the snoring, sweating figure his heart swelled up with the almost uncontainable emotion that Zachary sometimes inspired in his breast, transporting him back to the moment of his epiphany, when he had stepped on the *Ibis* for the first time.

That day walking aft, towards the officers' cabins, Baboo Nob Kissin had heard the piping of a flute, the instrument of the divine flautist of Vrindavan, god of love as well as war. The sound of the flute had aroused a sudden stirring in his vitals. After an initial moment of alarm he had realized that the rumbling was not intestinal – it had been caused by the awakening of his late Gurumayee, Ma Taramony, who had transmigrated into his own body after shedding her earthly form. The stirring was an intimation that she was coming to life and beginning to grow, deep inside him, like an embryo inside an egg, and he had known that the process would end only when the occupation of his body was complete and his own outward form was ready to be discarded, like a broken shell. He had fallen to his knees at the door of Zachary's cabin; and just then it had flown open to reveal the flute-player himself – a sturdily built young man dressed in a shirt and breeches, with a dusting of freckles and a head of dark, curly hair.

It was a comely vision, not unworthy of a messenger of the beautiful Banka-bihari of Vrindavan: only in one respect was it disappointing and this was in the colour of his skin, which was of an ivory tint and utterly different from the blue-black hue of the Dark Lord. But the Butter-Thieving Imp was nothing if not playful and Baboo Nob Kissin had always known that when the Sign came its carrier would be wrapped in many disguises in order to test his powers of perception. The truth, he knew, would be hidden in some unexpected place – and sure enough, he had found it while examining the *Ibis*'s crew list: there, recorded against the name 'Zachary Reid', was the word 'black' under the column of 'race'.

Baboo Nob Kissin had needed no other confirmation; it was exactly as he had known it would be: the outward appearance of the messenger was but a disguise for his inner being, an aspect of the flux and transformation of the material world, of Samsara. Tearing the page from the log-book he had hugged the secret to himself: it had become his bond with Zachary, the relic that marked the beginning of his own transformation.

From that day on the barrier that separated Baboo Nob Kissin's spiritual and material lives had begun to dissolve. Till then he had always been careful to separate the sphere of his inward striving from the domain of his profane existence as a cunning and ruthless practitioner of the worldly arts who prided himself on promoting the interests of his employer, Mr Benjamin Burnham. The transformation initiated by Zachary's arrival had swept away the embankment that separated the two rivers of Baboo Nob Kissin's being; like a tide surging over a bund, the love and compassion of his inner life had flooded into the channel of his gomusta-dom and the two streams had gradually merged into one vast, surging flow of love and compassion.

None of this would have happened, Baboo Nob Kissin knew, but for Zachary's advent into his life: this was the emissary's singular gift; that he possessed the power of animating mighty emotions in the hearts of all who came into his orbit – love and desire, rage and envy, compassion and generosity. Yet – and this too was a sign of who he was – the youthful emissary was utterly unaware of the effect he had on those around him.

The trance was not broken even when Zachary opened his eyes, and snapped irritably, 'Hey Baboo, I didn't hear you knock. What're you gawpin at like that?'

'Like what?' said the gomusta.

'Like a pig lookin at a turd.'

Baboo Nob Kissin was not unused to being sharply addressed by the vessel of his devotion; indeed he expected and even craved these outbursts, thinking of them as reminders of the obstacles that lay strewn upon the path he had embarked upon. But for the sake of appearances, he made a pretence of huffiness, puffing up his chest in indignation until it filled out his capacious alkhalla robe: 'Arré! But who is staring? Just only looking and keep-quieting. Why I should stare? Mind also has eyes no? Earthly forms are not necessary for those who can perceive hidden meanings.'

As with many of the gomusta's utterances, the import of this pronouncement was lost on Zachary. 'Just wish I'd known you were coming, Baboo,' he grumbled. 'Shouldn'a jumped me like that – knocked me flat aback.'

'How to inform? Too much busy no? After returning back from China with Burnham-sahib, I was issued orders to go to Ghazipur to inspect opium harvest. As soon as I could make my escapade I came to catch hold of you.'

'So how was your voyage to China then?'

'Nothing to grumble, all in all. And I also have a good news for you.'

Zachary sat up and pulled on his shirt. 'What is it?'

'I paid call on Miss Paulette.'

This brought Zachary quickly to his feet. 'What? What was that you said?'

'Miss Paulette,' said the gomusta, beaming; 'I met her on island called Hong Kong. She has obtained employment as assistant to an English botanist. They have made nurseries on the island, where they are putting all junglee trees and flowers.'

Zachary turned away from Baboo Nob Kissin and sank on to the bed again. It was a long time since he had thought of Paulette; he recalled now with a twinge of nostalgia his nightly quarrels with her and how she would step out of the shadows to come to him – but then he remembered also that this Paulette was merely a phantom, born of his own imaginings, and that the real Paulette had subjected him to a deception that he would not have discovered but for Mrs Burnham.

He rose to his feet, scowling, and turned to Baboo Nob Kissin. 'Did Paulette ask about me?'

'Most certainly. A copy of *Calcutta Gazette* had fallen on her hands and she had read the report about you. She was cognizant that all charges were cleared off your head and you were planning to proceed to China. She made copious inquiries about when you would come. She is getting heartburns all the time waiting, waiting. I told that most probably you will sign up on a ship and go. After all you are sailor, no?'

Zachary's response was instantaneous. 'No, Baboo. I'm sick of that shit – sailing, risking your life every day, never having any money in your pocket. I don't want to be one of the deserving poor any more.' He sighed: 'I want to be rich, Baboo; I want to have silk sheets and soft pillows and fine food; I want to live in a place like that.' He pointed in the direction of the Burnham mansion. 'I want to own ships and not work on them. That's what I want, Baboo; I want to live in Mr Burnham's world.'

Zachary's incantatory repetition of the word 'want' sent a shaft of illumination through Baboo Nob Kissin: he remembered that Ma Taramony had always said that the present era – Kaliyuga, the age of apocalypse – was but a time of wanting, an epoch of unbounded craving in which humankind would be ruled by the demons of greed and desire. It would end only when Lord Vishnu descended to the earth in his avatar as the destroyer, Kalki, to bring into being a new cycle of time, Satya Yuga, the age of truth. Ma Taramony had often said that in order to hasten the coming of the Kalki a great host of beings would appear on earth, to quicken the march of greed and desire.

And it struck Baboo Nob Kissin suddenly that perhaps Zachary was the incarnate realization of Ma Taramony's prediction. Everything fell into place now and he understood that it was his duty to assist Zachary in his mission of unshackling the demon of greed that lurks in every human heart.

As to how it could be done Baboo Nob Kissin knew exactly the right means: a substance that had a magical power to turn human frailty into gold.

'Opium is the solution,' he said to Zachary. 'That is how people can be made to want: opium can stroke all desires. That is what you must do: you must learn to buy and sell opium, like Mr Burnham. You are most apt for the part.'

Zachary grimaced uncertainly. 'I don't know about that, Baboo. I've never had a head for business – don't know if I'd be any good at it.'

Baboo Nob Kissin clasped his hands together, in an attitude of prayer. 'Do not worry, Master Zikri – if you channelize energies and indulge in due diligence, you will excel in this trade. You will even surpass Mr Burnham! For thirty years I have done gomusta-giri – all the know-hows are in my pocket. I will intimate every-thing to you. If you burn the candle and by-heart all my teachings then you will quickly achieve success. Must exert to win, no?'

'But where do I begin, Baboo? How do I start?'

Baboo Nob Kissin scratched his chin. 'How much money you have got?'

'Let's see.' Reaching under his mattress Zachary pulled out the pouch that contained the money that Mrs Burnham had given him over the last few months. Some of it had gone to the Harbourmaster's office, for the settling of his debts, but a good deal still remained: when he untied the string and upended it over his bed, the coins tumbled out in a stream of silver.

'By Jove!' cried Baboo Nob Kissin, goggling at the glinting pile of metal. 'Must be at least one thousand rupees. How you got so much?'

'Oh, I've been doing a few odd jobs,' said Zachary quickly. 'And I've been careful to save too.'

'Good. This is enough to start – and gains will come quickly.'

'So what do I do next?'

'We will start tomorrow only. You must meet me at Strand, with money-purse, at 5 p.m. Kindly do not be late – I will be punctually expectorating.'

*

February 18, 1840
Honam

Yesterday was the day of the Lantern Festival. During the preceding fortnight, after the start of the festivities of the Chinese New Year, the city had become a vast fairground. Everybody stopped working and many people left to visit their villages. In the evenings the streets would erupt with merry-making; the sky would light up with fireworks and the waterways would fill with brightly lit boats.

The days went by in a whirl of revelry with the words *Gong Hai Fatt Choy!* ringing in one's ears wherever one went. Sometimes I celebrated with Compton and his family, sometimes with Asha-didi, Baburao and their children and grandchildren, on the houseboat. Every day Mithu would bring me auspicious delicacies from the kitchen: long, long noodles, never to be snipped for fear of cutting short one's life; golden tangerines with leaves attached; fried rolls, to invoke ingots of gold. By the end of it, I confess, I was quite worn out: it was a relief to set off as usual today, for a quiet day's work.

But it proved to be anything but that. Around mid-morning, Compton and I received an urgent summons from Zhong Lou-si. We were both asked to present ourselves immediately at the Consoo House.

I guessed that the summons had something to do with the ongoing saga of the *Cambridge*, which both Compton and I had been following with keen interest. The vessel has been becalmed for a while because of a paucity of crewmen – a very unexpected thing, since Guangdong is a province of sailors after all. There's even a saying here: 'seven sons to fishing and three to the plough'. Yet a long search produced fewer than a dozen men who were both willing and able to sail an English-style vessel.

It isn't that Guangdong lacks for men with experience of working on Western ships. But most of them are reluctant to reveal that they have travelled abroad for it is considered a crime to do so without informing the authorities. This fear is particularly vivid in the community of boat-people, who have often been mistreated by the authorities in the past. Since most of the sailors in the province are from this community this was a major hurdle – very few came forward when the authorities went looking for volunteers. Things reached a point where it seemed that the *Cambridge* might never hoist sail.

Compton had been hinting for a while that Zhong Lou-si has been contemplating some unusual measures. Today in the Consoo I discovered what they were.

The Consoo – or 'Council House' – is situated behind

the foreign factories, on Thirteen Hong Street, cater-corner to the entrance of Old China Street. It is surrounded by a forbidding grey wall and looks much like a mandarin's yamen. Inside there are several large halls and pavilions, all topped with graceful, upswept roofs.

We were led through the compound's pathways to a pavilion deep in the interior of the complex. It was a chilly day and the windows were closed but we could see the outlines of a number of men through the moisture-frosted glass: they were seated as if for a meeting.

Stepping in through a side door we went to join a group of secretaries and attendants, who were standing huddled against a wall, chatting in low voices *lo-lo-si-si*. In the middle of the room, seated in stately armchairs, were a half-dozen officials, formally dressed, in panelled gowns, with their buttons and other insignia prominently displayed. As the seniormost member of the council, Zhong Lou-si was seated at the centre of the group.

The proceedings started with the banging of a gong. This in turn set off a relay of chimes that receded slowly into the hidden recesses of the building. A silence descended, through which many feet could be heard, shuffling along a corridor. Then a group of five manacled men appeared, escorted by a squad of tall, armour-clad Manchu troopers.

The prisoners were dark-skinned and dishevelled; hushed whispers of *haak-gwai!* and *gwai-lo!* greeted their entry. Even I was startled by their wild and wasted appearance. They looked as if they had been dragged out of a dungeon: neither their hair nor their beards had been trimmed in a long time and their eyes were sunken, their cheeks hollow. Their clothing, which seemed to have been especially provided for the occasion, was akin to the usual costume of Cantonese boatmen – loose tunics and pyjamas – but I knew at a glance that they were lascars. They had tied rags and scraps of cloth around their heads and waists, like the cummerbunds and bandhnas that lascars like to wear.

The guards positioned the prisoners to face the officials, and Compton and I went to stand beside them. A couple of questions revealed that the prisoners' preferred language was Hindustani, so it was decided that I would translate their words into English and Compton would then relay them to the officials, in formal Chinese.

Zhong Lou-si asked the first question: Can you ask these men why they were imprisoned?

When I put the question to the prisoners, it became clear that they had already appointed a spokesman to speak on their behalf: he was not particularly imposing in appearance, being slight in build and only of middling height. But there was an alertness in his eyes and a confidence in his bearing that set him apart from the others. His face was wreathed in a curly beard and his sharp eyes were sheltered by a brow that would have stretched across his forehead in a single, bushy line had it not been divided by a couple of deep scars.

He took a step forward, bringing himself closer to me. I saw then that he was even younger than I had thought: his copper-coloured face was completely unlined, and his beard was but the first growth of early youth, still uncoarsened by the edge of a razor.

With every eye on him, the youth made a gesture that took the whole assembly by surprise. He placed his right hand on his heart, closed his eyes, and said, on a note of almost theatrical defiance: *Bismillah ar-Rahman ar-Rahiim . . . !*

What is he doing? Compton whispered to me.

I answered: He is saying a Muslim prayer.

Only when the invocation had been completed did the youth begin to address the astonished audience. I translated as he spoke: 'You asked how we came to be in prison. It happened right here in Guangzhou, a year ago. We were then in the employment of one Mr James Innes, a British merchant and shipowner. We had been working on one of his ships, as lascars, for some months before that time.'

The youth's Hindustani was fluent, but I noticed that it bore the traces of a Bengali accent.

'One day, while our ship was anchored at Whampoa, Innes-sahib ordered us to load some chests into two of the ships' boats. He told us that we were to row these boats to his factory, in Canton, the next day. We were not told what was in those chests, but we guessed that it was opium. We said no, we would not go, but Mr Innes threatened us and forced us to follow his orders. The next day, we loaded the chests into two of the ships' boats and rowed them to the foreign enclave. When we arrived at Mr Innes's house there was a raid by customs officials: they opened the chests and found that they contained opium. We were immediately arrested and taken before a magistrate. Then we were sentenced to prison.'

He raised his voice: 'We had committed no crime and broken no law – the whole thing was the doing of Mr Innes. Yet it is we who have been made to suffer. Nothing could be more unjust!'

After I had translated this for Compton, I turned towards the young lascar and saw that he was looking directly at me: he had narrowed his eyes as though he were trying to peer into a darkened room. Then suddenly the expression on his face changed and I had the disconcerting feeling that I had been recognized.

I looked away, startled, my mind racing. After a moment I glanced at the lascar again, and now recognition dawned on me too, all of a sudden: I realized that the youth was none other than my fellow fugitive, Jodu, from whom I had parted at Great Nicobar Island, following on our joint escape from the *Ibis*.

I could not have imagined that two pairs of eyes looking into each other could create such an extraordinary impact: it was as if a bolt of lightning had gone through me.

We both turned quickly away, fully aware that we were being watched by many people. Meanwhile, Compton had begun to translate the council's response: I heard him out and turned to face Jodu.

Listen, this is what I've been asked to tell you. The council is willing to make you an offer: the Province of Guangdong has recently acquired a ship, built in the European fashion. Experienced seamen, familiar with the functioning of such vessels, are needed for the crew. If you agree to serve on this vessel, for one year, then your sentences will be commuted and you will be set free at the end of that period. Is that acceptable to all of you?

Jodu gave me a nod and stepped away to confer with the others. He returned a few minutes later.

Tell the mandarins, he said to me, that what they are offering will involve much danger and hard work. We will agree to it only if we are paid proper wages, equivalent to what we would have earned if we were working on a ship at sea – the equivalent of ten sicca rupees a month, which is equal to two Spanish dollars.

It seemed to me that he was in no position to make demands so I said to him in an undertone: Are you sure you want me to say this?

Jodu answered with an emphatic nod, so I translated his words faithfully. I did not think anything would come of it: knowing the ways of Chinese officials I fully expected that Jodu and his friends would meet with a summary refusal.

For a while it seemed that my fears were well-founded – but then, after a heated discussion, Zhong Lou-si made an intervention that took the matter in a different direction.

He told me what to say and I explained it to Jodu: The Chinese officers are willing to give you what you asked for, but they have certain conditions. They will pay your salaries as a lump sum at the end of your period of service. In the interim you will be provided with rations and supplies and you will also be given a small allowance for expenses. At the end of your service, if your work has been satisfactory, you will be paid a bonus equivalent to a month's wages. Moreover, if your vessel succeeds in sinking any enemy ships you will be rewarded with a prize equivalent to two months' wages; and if you capture an enemy ship then you will be given a share of the spoils. But it must be clearly understood that you will all bear collective responsibility for your conduct: in the event of an attempt to desert, or of treachery of any kind, the agreement will be annulled; your wages will be forfeit and you will stand trial for treason, the penalty for which is death. If you accept all of this then agreements will be drawn up to that effect.

The lascars had been listening carefully and they needed only a few minutes to make up their minds.

Tell them, Jodu said to me, that we have conditions of our own. Tell them we are all Muslims so our provisions must be halal and they must be provided by tradesmen of the local Hui community, as is done in our prison, for Muslim prisoners. If we are near Guangzhou then on the last Friday of every month, we must be allowed to visit the Huaisheng mosque, in the city. Tell them that we know from experience that in China people are often suspicious of foreigners so we will expect them to provide adequate protection for us in order that we may have peace of mind and serve to the best of our ability.

Here Jodu paused for a moment.

And tell them, he resumed, that if they agree to all of this then they need not fear for our loyalty. We are men of our word and we would never be disloyal to the hand that provides our salt.

Once this had been translated, Zhong Lou-si and the other officials rose to their feet and withdrew to another room to deliberate in private. I had hoped that Jodu and I would have a little time to talk but no sooner had the officials left than the lascars were led back into the interior of the building.

My rapport with Jodu had not escaped Compton. He asked if I knew him and I said we had once sailed on the same ship. I also said that I would like to speak with him if possible.

265

Compton did not think this unreasonable; he asked me to find out if Jodu and the lascars are honest and reliable men. He has promised to arrange for him to visit me, in my lodgings.

I came back to the houseboat with my head in a whirl: when Jodu's eyes met mine, in the Consoo House, it was as if our lives had changed. A strange and powerful thing is recognition!

*

For several successive nights, Shireen woke with a jolt, in the small hours, her nerves fluttering, her heart racing. It seemed incredible that all the obstacles that had loomed so large in her mind had disappeared; that she was now free to go to China – she, Shireen, mother of Behroze and Shernaz, a grandmother who had lived in the same house all her life and had never travelled beyond Surat! She had never quite believed that the wall she was pushing against would give way, and now that it had, she felt that she was toppling over.

At this critical time, when her confidence was beginning to falter, it was Rosa who steadied her by shifting her attention to practical things – like bowlas and baggage. She asked Shireen how many trunks she had and whether they would suffice for all her things.

Shireen remembered that she had put some of Bahram's old sea-trunks and bowlas in a storage loft. She had them brought down and found, to her dismay, that they were in a bad way: the trunks' wooden frames had been shredded by termites and their leather coverings had been eaten by mildew. But there were two that were not past salvaging – and to Shireen that seemed good enough: she could not imagine that she would need more.

But Rosa laughed when she heard this: No, Bibiji, you'll need at least three more trunks and a couple of bedding rolls as well. We should go to China Bazar and order them straight away.

So Shireen asked for a carriage and they went across town to visit the leather-workers' shops in the China Bazar. After their orders had been placed Rosa sprang another surprise: since they had a buggy for the morning, she said, they might as well visit Mr da Gama, the tailor, at his premises near the Esplanade.

Shireen had planned to buy a few white shawls and saris for the journey, but it had never entered her mind to visit Mr da Gama, who specialized in making coats and pelisses, mainly for Europeans.

Why Mr da Gama? Shireen asked, at which Rosa proceeded to explain that winters were sometimes bitterly cold on the south China coast. Shireen would need not just shawls and scarves but also pelisses, surtouts, hats, dresses . . .

Dresses! Shireen clamped a hand over her mouth. After hearing of Bahram's death she had adhered strictly to the rules of widowhood, which prescribed, among other things, that only white saris could be worn: to wear a dress would mean breaking with an ages-old custom.

Shaken by tremors of disquiet, Shireen said: You don't think I'm going to wear dresses, do you, Rosa?

Why not, Bibiji? said Rosa, with her bright, mischievous smile. At sea dresses are easier to manage than saris.

But what will people think? What will the family say?

They won't be there, Bibiji.

Shireen wondered how to explain that the thought of herself, costumed in a gown, seemed not just scandalous but also absurd.

I can't, Rosa! I'd think everyone was laughing at me.

Rosa smiled and patted Shireen's hand.

No one will laugh at you, Bibiji, she said. You're tall and thin – a dress will suit you very well.

Really?

In trying to envision herself in a dress, Shireen realised that the journey ahead would entail much more than just a change of location: in order to arrive at her destination she would have to become a different person.

In the following weeks, as a procession of darzees, mochis, rafoogars and milliners filed through her apartment, Shireen began to catch glimpses of this new incarnation of herself.

The sight made her avert her eyes from the looking-glass. Apart from Rosa she allowed no one into the room where she was being measured and fitted; she hid her new wardrobe even from her daughters, locking her almirah whenever they or their children came to visit.

The deception was so successful that she succeeded in concealing her wardrobe until her departure was just a week away. But one morning Shernaz and Behroze came over with their children, to help with the packing, and one of their little girls somehow managed to find the key to the almirah in which Shireen had hidden her new clothes.

A shriek rang through the apartment and suddenly it was as if Aladdin's cave had appeared in Shireen's bedroom: everyone ran to the almirah and stood staring in disbelief at the hats, shoes and pelisses that were stored within.

After that Shireen could not refuse to show her daughters and granddaughters how she looked in her new clothes. Yielding to their entreaties, she changed into a complete ensemble of memsahib clothing – dress, pelisse and hat – and paraded defiantly through her bedroom, challenging them to laugh.

But instead their eyes widened with a wonder that was not untinged with envy.

'Oh Mamá!' cried Shernaz, who had never addressed Shireen in that way before.

'What do you mean, Mamá?' said Shireen. 'Since when have you called me that?'

Shernaz looked startled: 'Did I call you that?'

'Yes.'

'Well then it's because you don't look like our Mumma any more.'

'What do I look like then?'

'I don't know. You look different – younger.'

Then Shernaz burst into tears, taking everyone by surprise. After that no one else could stay dry-eyed either.

For the last two days before the *Hind*'s departure, Shernaz and Behroze moved into Shireen's apartment with their children. This was meant to make things easier for Shireen, but of course it did nothing of the kind; still, she welcomed the extra work because it kept her occupied.

On the evening before Shireen's embarkation, her brothers organized a special jashan at home to seek blessings for her voyage and to wish her godspeed. Shireen was a little nervous about the event, but it went off very well. Every prominent Parsi family in the city sent a representative, including the Readymonies and Dadiseths; even Mrs Jejeebhoy dropped by for a few minutes. Better still, the jashan was attended by several members of the Parsi Panchayat – this was a great relief to Shireen for she had not quite rid herself of the fear that the community's highest body might declare her an outcast. This way it was almost as if they had given their imprimatur to her voyage.

Next morning Shireen arrived at the dock, with her daughters and their families, to find that a large crowd had already assembled there. Many of Rosa's relatives had also come to see her off and Vico had hired a band, to play rousing tunes.

The captain of the *Hind* had been alerted to Shireen's arrival and was waiting for her with a bouquet in his hands. A tall sunburned man with muttonchop whiskers, he led her personally to her stateroom, which was in the roundhouse, on the starboard side. It was actually a suite of cabins, a small one to sleep in, and another slightly larger one, with both a sitting and a dining area. Attached was a pantry with a bunk for Rosa.

'I hope it's to your satisfaction, madam?'

Shireen could not have hoped for anything better. 'It's wonderful!' she said.

After the captain had left, Shireen's daughters and grandchildren helped her settle in. In a very short while the cabins were arranged to the satisfaction of everyone except Shireen herself – she could not rid herself of the feeling that something was missing. She remembered just before it came time for all visitors to go ashore. Plunging into a trunk she brought out a *toran* – an embroidered fringe of the kind that hung around the doorways of all Parsi homes.

Shernaz, Behroze and their children helped her drape the toran around the entrance hatch. When it was properly affixed, they crowded into the gangway to look at it.

Ekdum gher javu che, said Shernaz with a sigh. It's just like home now, isn't it?

Yes, said Shireen. So it is.

*

Zachary's initiation into the opium trade began on Calcutta's Strand Road, which adjoined the busiest section of the Hooghly River.

Pointing to six sailing vessels that were anchored nearby, Baboo Nob Kissin explained that the opium fleet had just arrived from Bihar, with the year's first consignment from the East India Company's opium factories in Patna and Ghazipur. This year's crop had exceeded all previous records; despite the troubles in China, production had continued to increase at a tremendous pace in the Company's territories.

'Opium is pouring into the market like monsoon flood,' declared Baboo Nob Kissin.

They watched for a while as the drug was unloaded. Each of the cargo ships had a small flotilla of sampans, paunchways and lighters attached, like sucklings to a teat. Under the scrutiny of armed overseers and burkandazes, teams of coolies were transferring the chests of opium from the ships to the brick-red godowns that lined the riverbank.

Each chest held two maunds – roughly one hundred and sixty pounds – of opium, said Baboo Nob Kissin; the cost to the Company, for each chest, was between one hundred and thirty and one hundred and fifty rupees. Of this the farmer received perhaps a third if he was lucky: there were so many middlemen – sudder mahtoes, gayn mahtoes, pykars, gomustas – to be paid off that he often ended up earning less than he had spent on his poppy crop. The Company on the other hand would earn eight to ten times the cost-price of each chest when they were sold off at auction – somewhere between one thousand and fifteen hundred rupees, or five hundred to seven hundred Spanish dollars.

Then the chests would travel eastwards, to China and elsewhere, but even before they went under the auctioneer's hammer, they would pass through another market, an informal one – and it was at this very unusual bazar that Zachary's initiation into the trade was to begin.

Plunging into a side-street, Baboo Nob Kissin led Zachary to Tank Square, which was within hailing distance of the Strand. This was the heart of official Calcutta: at the centre of the square lay a rectangular 'tank' of fresh water; overlooking it was the East India Company's headquarters, a great pile of a building, honeycombed with columns and arches and crowned with elaborate tiaras of wrought iron.

On the other side of the tank lay the Opium Exchange: a large but unremarkable building with the reassuring look of a reputable bank. This was where the East India Company's opium auctions were conducted, said Baboo Nob Kissin: the next one would be held there tomorrow morning – but for now the building was empty, and its heavy wooden doors were locked and under guard.

The bazar that they were heading for was in a dank, dirty little gali behind the Opium Exchange. Mud and dung squelched under their feet as they walked towards it, pushing past ambling cows and loitering vendors. The marketplace consisted of a small cluster of lamplit stalls: turbaned men sat on the cloth-covered counters with ledgers lying open on their crossed legs.

To Zachary's surprise there were no goods on display: he was at a loss to understand what exactly was being bought and sold – and it didn't help much when Baboo Nob Kissin explained that this was not a bazar for opium as such; rather it was a place in which people traded in something unseen and unknown: the prices that opium would fetch in the future, near or distant. In this bazar there were only two commodities and both were pieces of paper – chitties or letters. One kind was called *tazi-chitty* or 'fresh letter'; the other kind was *mandi-chitty* – 'bazar letter'. Buyers who thought that the price of opium would go up at the next auction would buy tazi-chitties; those who thought it would go down would buy mandi-chitties. But similar chitties could be written to cover any period of time – a month, a year or five years. Every day, said Baboo Nob Kissin, lakhs, crores, millions of rupees passed through this bazar – there was more wealth here than in any market in Asia.

'See! In every nook and corner there are beehive activities!'

The riches evoked by Baboo Nob Kissin's words cast a new light on the bazar: Zachary's pulse quickened at the thought that fortunes could be made and lost in this dirty little alley. Through the odour of dust and dung he recalled the perfumed scents of Mrs Burnham's boudoir. So this was the mud in which such luxuries were rooted? The idea was strangely arousing.

'You see the men who are sitting there?' said Baboo Nob Kissin, pointing at the stalls. 'They are shroffs – brokers. From all over India they have come. Many are from far-away places – Baroda,

Jodhpur, Mathura, Jhunjhunu. All are lakhaires. Some are million-aires and some are even crore-patters. So much money they have, they can buy twenty ships like *Ibis*.'

Zachary looked at the shroffs with renewed interest: their clothing seemed to be of the simplest cotton and there was nothing of any expense on their persons, apart from a sprinkling of gold jewellery – mainly studs in the ears, and neck-chains. Elsewhere in the city these men would scarcely have attracted a second glance. But here, enthroned upon their counters, with their solemn, unsmiling faces, they exuded a gnomic aura of authority.

Soon it became clear that Baboo Nob Kissin was intimately familiar with the sellers and their procedures. Zachary watched carefully as he went up to one of the counters to greet the proprietor.

Now began a curious charade: without saying a word aloud, both men began to make rapid gestures with their hands and fingers. All of a sudden, the Baboo thrust his hands under the shawl that lay draped over the broker's lap. The shawl began to bounce and writhe as their hidden fingers twined with each other, twisting and turning in a secret dance. Gradually these motions built to a climax and a shudder of understanding passed through both of them; then their hands fell inert under the shawl and they exchanged a quiet smile.

Hardly a word had been said all this while, but when Baboo Nob Kissin stepped away the broker bent quickly over his ledger and began to make rapid notations with a pencil.

It was through hand-language, Baboo Nob Kissin explained, that most transactions were done in this market; that way others did not know what was being purchased and at what price.

To Zachary's surprise it turned out that Baboo Nob Kissin had placed his money in tazi-chitties: the cost of a chest of the best Benares opium had fallen to nine hundred rupees at the last auction and the general feeling in the marketplace was that it would fall still further because of the troubles in China. Baboo Nob Kissin, on the other hand, was sure that there would be a modest rebound in the price.

Zachary took alarm when he realized that his savings had been wagered on an outside chance. 'But Baboo,' he protested, 'you just told me the market was flooded with opium. Doesn't that mean the price will go down?'

Baboo Nob Kissin put a finger to his lips. 'Never mind, dear – it is just an eyewash. No need for you to take up tensions. Just only trust me.'

That night Zachary experienced spasms of anticipation that were no less intense than those that had seized him before his assignations with Mrs Burnham. It was as if the money that she had given him had suddenly taken on a new life: her coins were out there in the world, forging their own destiny, making secret assignations, colliding with others of their kind – seducing, buying, spending, breeding, multiplying.

The next day Zachary and Baboo Nob Kissin arrived early at the Opium Exchange, but only to find bailiffs at the door, holding back a large and noisy group of men. Baboo Nob Kissin had nothing but contempt for this crowd – 'Just only riff-raffs!' These men were but messengers and runners, he said, waiting to relay the outcome of the auction to speculators across the country. He led Zachary through the throng, to the entrance, where he was recognized by the stern-looking bailiffs who were standing guard. They waved him through to the building's capacious lobby and he hurried in with Zachary following at his heels.

The auction room was on the second floor, Baboo Nob Kissin explained, and only ticket-holders were allowed to enter. This was a highly privileged group: a ticket to Calcutta's opium auctions was the most valuable asset that any trader could acquire, anywhere in the world, and businessmen from many countries competed fiercely for them.

Although Baboo Nob Kissin was not a ticket-holder himself he was permitted, as Mr Burnham's gomusta, to observe the auction from a small gallery above the room: this was where he led Zachary.

The gallery was like a box in a theatre: it projected over the auction room and was fenced off by brass rails. Leaning over the rails, Zachary saw that the room was merely a large hall with several rows of chairs laid out in neat rows, facing in the direction of an auctioneer's lectern. A ceremonial armchair stood beside the lectern: this was the seat of the director who presided over the proceedings. On the wall behind hung an enormous velvet curtain imprinted with the seal of the East India Company.

Mr Burnham's commanding figure was prominently visible in

the auction room: he was seated in the front row, dressed in a suit of sombre colour, with his glossy beard flowing down his chest. In the rows behind were some of the city's most prominent personalities, among them several scions of Bengal's grandest families – Tagores, Mullicks and Dutts. There were also Parsis from Bombay, and Marwaris and Jains from the distant villages and market-towns of Rajputana and Gujarat. As for the rest, they were as variegated a gathering as the crew of a transoceanic ship: Greeks, Turks, Armenians, Persians, Jews, Pathans, Bohras, Khojas and Memons. Looking down from above it seemed to Zachary that he had never seen such a profusion of headgear: turbans and astrakhans, calpacs and a varied assortment of prayer caps – Muslim and Jewish, embroidered and lacy, colourful and plain.

A hush fell when the director and the auctioneer walked solemnly up the aisle and took their places at the head of the room. The proceedings began after a brief prayer for the health of Queen Victoria: the auctioneer held up a board with a number and immediately hands shot up, signalling in an unintelligible semaphore.

The opium would be sold in lots of five chests each, Baboo Nob Kissin explained; the bidders would purchase them sight unseen – a chest of the East India Company's opium was as sound as any currency note, and no inspections were permitted or expected. Bidders were required to cover only ten per cent of their purchase; they were allowed a full thirty days to make good on the rest.

As the auction proceeded the bidders' enthusiasm began to build. Even though Zachary couldn't quite follow what was going on, he soon found himself caught up in the excitement. There was something wild about the way the men were bidding, jumping up and down, waving their hands and shouting: it reminded him of a mêlée in a tavern – even the smell was similar, a rancid brew of sweat, fear and ambition.

The fiercest of the bidders was none other than Mr Burnham himself: every few minutes he would jump up, shouting, waving, holding up fingers. The sight excited Zachary's envy as well as his awe. He would have given anything to be down there himself, bidding like Mr Burnham, snatching away the lots he most desired from under the noses of his competitors.

This was one of the most thrilling spectacles Zachary had ever witnessed. That he was merely a spectator, watching from the gallery, made him seethe: he swore to himself that he too would be a ticket-holder one day; this was where he belonged; there was nothing he wanted more than to be amongst the players, lavishing his unspent energies upon the pursuit of wealth.

By the time the last lot of opium was sold Zachary was drenched in sweat: when he looked at his watch, he could not believe that the auction had lasted only forty-five minutes. He felt drained; no less spent than he was after a bout of love-making. Only in bed with Mrs Burnham had he felt such a fierce onrush of passion. It was as if his hoarded essence had at last found the true object of its desire.

Down below many of the bidders had gathered around Mr Burnham and were thumping him on the back.

With a beaming smile Baboo Nob Kissin explained that Mr Burnham had ended up as the day's biggest buyer, acquiring three thousand chests of opium at a price of thirty lakh rupees, equal to almost one and a half million Spanish dollars. He had single-handedly pushed up the price, against all expectations, to one thousand rupees per chest. This meant that Zachary had earned a great bonanza. The bets Baboo Nob Kissin had placed for him had paid off handsomely – his savings were now worth double what they were the day before.

Zachary gasped: 'I'll be dad-boggled! When can I have the money?'

This amused Baboo Nob Kissin: with an indulgent smile he explained to Zachary that his money was gone; it had been spent in buying the wherewithal with which to launch his new career – twenty chests of raw opium, of which he now owned ten per cent. He had thirty days to cover the rest.

'But how, Baboo?' cried Zachary, aghast. 'Where am I going to find so much money in thirty days?'

'Do not worry, dear,' said Baboo Nob Kissin, 'I have already looked ahead – arrangements will be made. What you must do now is to go to Singapore and China, to sell your cargo.'

'But Baboo,' said Zachary. 'You've spent all my money. How'm I going to buy a passage?'

'For that too I have made bandobast,' said Baboo Nob Kissin.

'I have already oiled the boss – he will do the needful. You will travel without pocketing any expenses.'

He would not explain any further, but on the way out, as they were making their way through the crowded lobby a voice cried out: 'Reid! Hold on there!'

It was Mr Burnham himself. Zachary saw that many heads had turned to look in his direction, no doubt wondering who this young newcomer was to be singled out for special attention by the victor of the day.

Despite himself, Zachary was flattered and a blush rose to his face. 'I'm glad to see you, sir!' he said, energetically pumping Mr Burnham's hand.

'I'm glad to see you too, Reid. Especially here. Is it true that you've decided to try your hand at trading?'

'Yes, sir,' said Zachary.

'Good man, good man!' said Mr Burnham, patting him on the back. 'We need more Free-Traders, especially young, energetic white men like yourself. I'll visit the budgerow soon – I have a proposition that I think will interest you.'

'I'll look forward to hearing about it, sir.'

With a nod and a smile Mr Burnham walked away, leaving Zachary transfixed, almost unable to believe his luck.

*

It was not till late February that some of the expedition's British soldiers began to arrive in Fort William: one battalion of the 26th, known as the Cameronian, and another battalion from Her Majesty's 49th Regiment. Together with the two companies of Bengal Volunteers, the total strength of the force assembled in Calcutta now came to a little over a thousand men. To Kesri this seemed a paltry number with which to launch an invasion of a country like China. He was glad to be told by Captain Mee that the force was to be strengthened by a battalion from the 18th Royal Irish Regiment, which was now stationed in Ceylon, as well as a small detachment of Royal Marines. But the single largest contingent was to be contributed by the 37th Madras Native Infantry Regiment – more than a thousand sepoys and a sizeable number of sappers, miners and engineers. In total the force would consist of about four thousand men.

The Cameronians were the first to arrive, after a long march from Patna. They had campaigned around the subcontinent, over a period of several years, and it soon became evident that their years in India had hardened them against Indians: they never missed an opportunity to hurl abuse at sepoys. Particularly offensive was a colour-sarjeant by the name of Orr, who would unloose torrents of galees for no good reason: 'cowardly kaffirs', 'filthy niggers', 'black bastards' and so on. Kesri had to confront him several times and on a couple of occasions they almost came to blows.

Fortunately the Cameronians were billeted at a fair distance from B Company so it wasn't hard to stay out of their way; Kesri dreaded to think of what might have happened if they had moved into the empty building that adjoined the Bengal Volunteers' barracks.

Luckily for the sepoys the neighbouring building was assigned to the 49th who were a rowdy but easy-going lot. To live next to them was an interesting novelty for the sepoys: even though they often campaigned with British units they were rarely billeted in adjoining quarters.

With their loud mouths and swaggering ways the men of the 49th quickly transformed what had previously been a quiet corner of the fort. Every evening they would be off drinking, privates and NCOs alike, each in their own canteens. They would remain in them until the firing of the night gun, which was the signal for the closing of all the canteens on the fort's precincts. Nor was that the end of their revelries, for they, like many other British soldiers, were ingenious in finding ways to procure illicit liquor. The sweepers and bhisties who serviced their barracks made fortunes by smuggling liquor to them, in all kinds of containers – tubes of hollowed-out bamboo and bladders of goatskin that they would conceal under their dhotis. At all times of the night, cries would break out: 'Where's that fuckin beasty? I swear I'll beat the beast out'a him if I don't get my grog soon!'

The men of B Company watched these antics with bemused curiosity. Among sepoys it had long been said that alcohol was the white soldier's secret weapon: it was what made him such a fearsome fighter. It was widely believed that this was the reason why British units were almost always chosen to lead charges in the battlefield – because the stiff doses of liquor that they were given beforehand made them almost suicidally reckless.

Amongst sepoys too it was common to take intoxicants before a battle: this was something that soldiers had always done in Hindustan. But the sepoy's preferences were for hashish, ganja, bhang and a form of opium known as maajun: these drugs acted on the nerves to create a sense of calm and to make the body insensible to the exertion and fatigue of battle. Alcohol was different: it served as a fuel for the faculties of aggression and it was common knowledge that it was precisely in order to nurture this 'fighting spirit' that British commanders paid so much attention to providing liquor to their men.

A wise old subedar had once said to Kesri: It's alcohol that gives the sahibs their strength; that's why they drink it from morning to night – if ever they stop they will become weak and go into decline. And if a day comes when they start taking ganja, like we do, then you can be sure that their empire will be finished.

Kesri began to see the sense of it now. He was by no means averse to sharaab himself – he was especially partial to gin although he liked beer and rum well enough. But European-style liquor of any kind was difficult for sepoys to acquire because they were not allowed to enter the canteens that served white soldiers. Except on certain occasions when they were issued special 'wet-battas' of grog, the sepoys had to get their supplies from Native Liquor Shops, which often sold foul-tasting rotgut. A better, though more expensive, alternative was to buy liquor from British soldiers – they all received a daily ration of two drams, which they were sometimes willing to exchange for money. Another option was to pay them to procure liquor from their canteens, and with the arrival of the 49th Kesri found a friend who was more than willing to oblige. He was a burly, weather-beaten sarjeant called Jack Maggs: it turned out that he had once been a fairground pugilist and within a few days of arriving he insisted on leaping into the wrestling pit with Kesri. There followed a hard-fought bout and it was only because Sarjeant Maggs was unfamiliar with the rules of Indian wrestling that Kesri managed to prevail. But the sarjeant took his defeat in good part and he and Kesri soon began to share the odd glass of gin.

At a certain point it fell to Kesri to be of assistance to Sarjeant Maggs in a little matter of a girl in the Laal Bazar who was charging him a good deal more than the approved army rate. Kesri managed to resolve the situation by telling the girl that he would send a police-peon to take her to the Lock Hospital to be checked for venereal disease: the threat was enough to subdue her.

After that the sarjeant became quite forthcoming and it was from him that Kesri learnt that the expedition's British soldiers were being trained in the use of a new weapon – a percussion-fired musket. Sarjeant Maggs could not stop singing the gun's praises; he said that it was a huge improvement on their old flintlocks.

Kesri was very attached to his own flintlock, an 'India-pattern' Brown Bess, almost six feet long without its bayonet. With the new cylindrical bullets, the musket had a maximum range of about two hundred yards although it was accurate only up to half that distance. But at one hundred yards or less, fired in mass, with volleys of three shots every forty-three seconds, the Brown Bess was lethal. Its long thick barrel, when topped with a bayonet, also made it handy in skirmishes and close combat, which was one reason why Kesri was so attached to it.

Yet, despite all the care that he had lavished on his beloved bandook, Kesri would dearly have loved to get his hands on one of the new percussion-fired muskets, but Sarjeant Maggs told him that there was no immediate chance of that, for they were still being tried out.

Kesri assumed that it was only a matter of time before the sepoys too were trained in the handling of the new guns. But after a few weeks, when there was still no sign of any moves in that direction, he decided to dispense with discretion: he confronted Captain Mee, asking if he knew about the new guns and whether they were to be issued to the sepoys or not.

Captain Mee was evasive at first, but after some prodding it became apparent that he too was indignant about the matter: he had been pressing to have the gun issued to the Bengal Volunteers, he said, but had been told that too few of them had been sent out from England. Besides, the new muskets had been introduced very recently and were still on trial, which was why the high command had decided that they would be issued only to British regiments.

'It's always the same story, isn't it, havildar?' said the captain, in a tone of embittered resignation. 'They send us to fight with old equipment and then they complain that sepoys don't match up to white troops.'

One day, with Sarjeant Maggs's help, Kesri was able to observe a training session with practice ammunition, in the Instruction Shed. He noticed that when the new musket was fired there was no puff of smoke, like those that always preceded a shot from a flintlock like his own. Later, when he examined the gun more closely he found an even more important difference – the new guns did not have powder pans like the old Brown Besses. The significance of this was immediately evident to him: unlike the flintlocks, which were difficult to fire in wet or damp conditions, the new percussion guns were all-weather weapons.

That night he asked Captain Mee: 'Sir, there is much rain in China, sir?'

Captain Mee knew exactly what he was getting at. 'Let's hope we get to fight when it's dry, havildar – there's not much else we can do about it.'

Kesri was careful not to mention the new musket to his own men, knowing that their morale would be further eroded if they learnt that they were to be sent overseas with inferior weapons. But it was impossible to conceal something like that indefinitely. The sepoys found out soon enough – and the effect on morale was just as Kesri had feared.

Eleven

Zachary's brief encounter with Mr Burnham, at the opium auction, made him impatient to be done with all his commitments in Calcutta. His debts to the Harbourmaster's office he had already paid off and his mate's licence had been duly restored to him. The work on the budgerow was also close to completion: he had finished with the deck-planks and other parts that needed replacing; the vessel's head-works and upper stem had been thoroughly overhauled; the cabins had been cleaned and repolished; all that remained now was the carving of the stem-cheeks and some final finishing touches.

A few days of hard work brought the refurbishment to a close. Once it was done Zachary wasted no time in sending a chit to the Burra Sahib, to tell him that his vessel was ready to be inspected.

Mr Burnham came over the next morning and spent a good hour looking over the budgerow. At the end of it he thumped Zachary on the back – 'Good job, Reid! Well done!' – bringing a flush of pride to his face.

Zachary was eager now to hear about the proposition that Mr Burnham had mentioned at the auction, but he had to contain his impatience for a while yet: the Burra Sahib seemed to be in no hurry to get to it. Seating himself in a large armchair, Mr Burnham ran a hand over his lustrous beard.

'It gladdened my heart, Reid,' said Mr Burnham pensively, 'to hear that the spirit of enterprise has stirred in you. A new age is dawning, you know – the age of Free Trade – and it's men like you and I, self-made Free-Traders, who will be its heroes. If ever there's been an exciting time for a venturesome white youth to seek his destiny in the East, then this is it. You are aware, I hope, that a military expedition is soon to be sent to China?'

'Yes, sir.'

'Good. In my view it is but a matter of months before the largest market in the world is forced open by the troops that are now being assembled in this city. When that happens China's Manchu tyrants, who are the last obstacles to the universal rule of freedom, will also be swept aside. After their fall we shall see the birth of an epoch when God's design will be manifest for all to see. Those who have been predestined to flourish will come into their own and to them will be awarded custody of the world's riches. You are singularly fortunate to have been presented with what might well be the greatest commercial opportunity of this century: now if ever is the time to discover whether you too are among the elect.'

'Indeed, sir?' said Zachary in some puzzlement. 'I'm not sure I understand.'

'I am speaking, Reid, of the China expedition . . .'

This venture, Mr Burnham proceeded to explain, was itself an opportunity of unmatched dimensions. Not only would vast profits be created when the markets of China were opened to the world, but the expedition would also establish a new pattern of war-making, in which men of business would be involved in the entirety of the enterprise, from the drafting of strategy to dealing with Parliament, informing the public, and providing logistical support. This conflict would be nothing like the wasteful and destructive campaigns of the past; here all the hard-earned lessons of commerce would be applied to the full and the emphasis throughout would be on minimizing losses for Great Britain, of money as well as life.

To a degree unheard of before, said Mr Burnham, the expedition would rely on private enterprise for support, and this itself would open up innumerable avenues for profit, in matters ranging from the chartering of vessels to the procurement of supplies for the troops. Moreover, as the expedition advanced northwards along China's eastern coast it would provide access to many hitherto unexploited markets. Under the protection of the Royal Navy's warships, British merchant vessels would be able to sell their goods offshore, near heavily populated areas where the demand for opium was sure to be huge, because of the recent disruptions in the supply of the drug. Every chest would fetch a fortune.

'Make no mistake, Reid: although this expedition is trifling in size, it will create a revolution. Mark my words: it will change the map of this continent!'

So great would be this change, Mr Burnham predicted, that the very locus of commerce would shift eastwards. One of the expedition's chief aims was to force the Chinese to cede an island off the China coast: a new port, embodying all the ideals of Free Trade, would be created there. His old friend and colleague, Mr Hugh Hamilton Lindsay, the former president of the Canton Chamber of Commerce, had been advocating such a course for many years, especially in relation to one perfectly placed island, Hong Kong. Thanks to the influence of Mr Jardine, it appeared that the government had at last decided to heed Mr Hamilton's sage advice. Come what may, a new port would be created in China, one that would be safe from the oppressions of that empire's Manchu despots. No longer would tyrants be able to stamp the label of 'smuggler' upon honest opium traders like Mr Burnham: from this new bastion of freedom, the products of Man and the word of God would alike be directed, with redoubled energy, towards the largest, most populous nation on earth.

There could be little doubt, Mr Burnham continued, that the new port would soon waylay much of the trade that now went to Canton. This was why several tycoons, including Mr Lancelot Dent and Mr James Matheson, were already manoeuvring to be the first out of the gate when the island was seized. This indeed was why he himself had decided to move his own operations eastwards, to the China coast.

'Blessed indeed are those, Reid, whom God chooses to be present at such moments in history! Think of Columbus, Cortez and Clive! Is there any greater or more satisfying endeavour for a young man than to expand his own fortunes while extending God's dominion?'

'No, sir!'

But not to everyone did it fall, said Mr Burnham, to recognize these emerging avenues of opportunity. Many timid and cautious men were sure to be scared off by the uncertainties of war – these creatures of habit were predestined to fall by the wayside while the bold and the chosen claimed the prize.

As for himself, said Mr Burnham, he did not doubt for a moment that a new empire of commerce was opening up, for all who had the foresight and courage to seize the day. Such was his conviction that he intended to send the *Ibis* to China immediately, with a large cargo of opium; the schooner would be skippered by Captain Chillingworth and Baboo Nob Kissin would be the supercargo. He would himself proceed to China later in the year, after all his affairs had been settled in India; his ship, the *Anahita*, would also be carrying opium, in addition to a large consignment of other goods.

But that was not all; Mr Burnham explained that he had lent a vessel to the expeditionary force – the *Hind*. She was now at Bombay collecting a load of Malwa opium and a few passengers. On returning to Calcutta, she would take on a contingent of troops and equipment; then she would sail with the rest of the expedition's fleet, under the command of Mr Doughty.

Only now did Mr Burnham come to his proposition.

'What I need,' said Mr Burnham, 'is a good, sound man to sail on the *Hind* as her supercargo. To him will fall the task of safe-guarding my consignment of Malwa opium. Should he be offered attractive prices at ports along the way, he will be free to use his own judgement to make sales. He will be comfortably accommodated, and he will have the right, as do all supercargoes, to carry a certain quantity of goods to trade on his own account. In addition to whatever profits he may make – and they may be considerable – he will also be paid a salary. And last, but not least, if he acquits himself well on this venture, he will be assured of my support in the advancement of his career.'

Mr Burnham paused now to stroke his glossy beard before focusing the full intensity of his gaze on Zachary. 'Well, Reid,' he said, 'it is no secret that you have long enjoyed my good opinion. In you I can see certain aspects of myself as I was when I first came out East. The other day when I saw you at the opium auction it seemed to me that you may now be on the brink of discovering your true vocation. Baboo Nob Kissin, as you know, holds you in the highest regard. He believes that you are the perfect man for the job I have described; he is, no doubt, a dreadful old heathen, but he is also a shrewd judge of men. He tells me that you need to cover the purchase price on twenty chests of opium.'

'Yes, sir.'

'Well, Reid, I am willing to loan you the money, as an advance on your salary.' He paused again, as if to give Zachary a moment to collect himself. 'It only remains now for you to tell me, Reid: are you ready?'

Zachary had been listening to Mr Burnham's words just as closely as he had once hung upon the utterances of his wife: the effect they had on him too was, in a strange way, not dissimilar. A shiver of anticipation passed through him now as he straightened his back and placed his hand over his heart.

'I am indeed ready, Mr Burnham,' he said. 'God willing, you will not find me wanting.'

*

With the day of departure rapidly approaching, the balamteers' performance continued to improve: a joint exercise with the 49th exceeded everyone's expectations and a series of inspections, including one by a staff officer, went off with only a few minor hitches. Nor, fortunately, were there any desertions, as Kesri had feared.

All of this seemed to augur well, but Kesri knew that the real test was fast approaching – the day of Holi.

This festival was by tradition celebrated with great gusto in the Bengal Native Infantry. Kesri knew that the men of B Company would want to go to the Sepoy Lines on that day, to make merry. Bhang would flow liberally, everybody would be doused in colour, guns would be fired into the air, dancing boys would put on frenzied performances and the bazar-girls would be under siege. It would be a wild mêlée of a mela, and Kesri guessed that if anybody had it on their minds to desert this was when they would do it. He voiced his concerns to Captain Mee and they decided between them that to prevent the men from participating would only create trouble; it would be best to let them go in small groups, each accompanied by an NCO. Moreover, they would be under orders to report back by sunset and there would be a head-count in front of the barracks. As a further precaution, Captain Mee decided also to notify the fort's intelligence officers.

In the past Kesri himself had always celebrated Holi enthusiastically but this year revelry was the last thing on his mind. When the day came he went to the Sepoy Lines with the men and did his best to keep an eye on them, quaffing hardly a tumbler of bhang. But to keep track of everyone was impossible: the festivities were too exuberant and there were too many people milling about. In the evening, when the ghanti was rung for roll-call, the head-count was found to be short by six men. Further inquiries revealed that four of the missing sepoys were merely incapacitated by bhang and ganja; this meant that only two men were missing. Captain Mee sent a report to the intelligence bureau and within minutes runners were dispatched to the city's roadheads and crossing points.

Kesri doubted that the two deserters would have the wiles to effect a getaway; they were both young, not quite twenty yet. Sure enough they were apprehended while trying to board a ferry.

Kesri spoke with Captain Mee and they agreed that the deserters would be court-martialled and that the maximum penalty – death – would be sought, as a deterrent to others. But they agreed also that it was important to find out why they had deserted, and whether they had been aided by others in the battalion. To that end Captain Mee arranged for Kesri to interrogate the two boys.

Kesri questioned the prisoners separately and received more or less the same answers from both. Their complaints were not un-familiar: the most important of them concerned their pay. It was now common knowledge that the expedition's Indian troops would be paid less than their British counterparts, and this had become a matter of great resentment for many sepoys – Kesri himself was none too pleased about it.

It had long been a grievance with sepoys that they were paid less than white soldiers. Few were persuaded by the military estab-lishment's argument that British troopers needed better pay because they were serving in a foreign country. Now the disingenuousness of this line of reasoning stood exposed: China was foreign to sepoy and swaddy alike; why then should the expedition's white soldiers earn more than them? But other than grumble there was nothing the sepoys could do: to make a bigger issue of it was to invite a court martial.

Another item that figured large in the deserters' list of grievances was the matter of inferior weaponry: they had taken the army's refusal to upgrade their guns as a slight on their izzat as fighting men. This in turn had bred other suspicions: they had heard that their transport vessels, like their weapons, would be of inferior quality, more likely to go down in bad weather. They had also heard that in the event of a shortage of rations their provisions would be commandeered for white soldiers – they would be made to eat potatoes and other loathsome things; or else they would be left to die of starvation and disease.

This set of grievances was not new to Kesri. But the deserters also mentioned certain rumours that took him completely by surprise: they told him that dire omens and auguries were circulating in the battalion; an astrologer was said to have predicted disaster for the expedition; a purohit had declared that the Bengal Volunteers were cursed.

It worried Kesri that nobody had told him about these rumours: this was itself a sign that they had had a powerful impact on the men.

Had someone like Pagla-baba been attached to B Company Kesri would have been kept informed of everything that was being said amongst the sepoys. Moreover, Pagla-baba would have known exactly how to counter the omens; he would have found some alternative interpretation to reassure the men. That was why regular sepoy battalions were always accompanied by a mendicant – they were indispensable in situations like these.

But of course, the Bengal Volunteers were not a regular sepoy battalion: they were a motley group, assembled for a single expedition. As a unit they would not be together long enough for a pir or sadhu to find a place in their midst.

On the other matter – of instigators, abettors and conspirators – Kesri could get nothing out of the boys. They would not tell him whether they had been encouraged to desert by other members of the company; nor would they reveal the names of other men who had talked about deserting. Even severe beatings wrung no answers from them – and their very silence suggested that this kind of talk was rife in the battalion.

One of the deserters was from a village not far from Nayanpur: he was actually distantly related to Kesri by marriage. At the end of his interrogation, after a long, hard beating, the boy evoked that relationship, falling on the floor and clutching Kesri's feet with his bloodied hands, begging for mercy.

It occurred to Kesri that had he been in the boy's place he too might well have chosen to desert. But he knew also that he would not have set about it in such a stupid, thoughtless way – and this gave his anger a perverse edge as he kicked the boy's hands aside.

Darpok aur murakh ke ka raham? he said. What mercy do cowards and fools deserve? Whatever happens to you, you should know that you have brought it on yourself.

As expected, the boys received sentences of execution by firing squad. Captain Mee decided that the firing squad would be provided by their own company and it fell to Kesri to pick the men. He made a few inquiries and chose exactly those men who were known to be friends or associates of the boys. He also elected to command the firing squad in person: it was distasteful but it had to be done.

*

March 18, 1840
Honam

Until Jodu appeared at my door I had no conception of how powerfully I would be affected by our reunion. It was not as if he and I had ever been friends, after all, and nor did we share any other connections or commonalities – of family, religion or even age, since Jodu must be a good nine or ten years younger than I. It was our flight from the *Ibis* that brought us together, but even as fugitives we'd spent very little time in each other's company: no more than the few days during which we'd foraged for survival on the island of Great Nicobar, where our boat had washed up after our escape from the *Ibis*. After that we had gone our separate ways, with Ah Fatt and I heading towards Singapore, while Jodu, Kalua and Serang Ali had caught a boat to Mergui, on the Tenasserim coast.

Yet when Jodu stepped into my lodgings something dissolved within both of us and we wept as if we were brothers, reunited after a long parting. The shared secret of our escape from the *Ibis* has become a link between who we were then and who we are now; between past and present. It is a bond more powerful even than ties of family and friendship.

I had guessed that Jodu would be ravenously hungry and had arranged for Asha-didi to send over plenty of food – rice, beans, bitter melon, fish curry. Mithu had also made some luchis.

Everything was halal; I had made sure of that – and Jodu was grateful for it . . .

Seating himself cross-legged on the floor, Jodu began to shovel food into his mouth with his fingers, eating as though he were fuelling a furnace. But from time to time he would stop to catch his breath, and I took advantage of these pauses to ask how he'd found his way to Canton.

Jodu told me that on reaching Mergui, Serang Ali had decided that it was time for them to split up: his advice to Jodu and Kalua was that they travel eastwards. So Kalua had signed up as a lascar, on an opium ship that was heading towards the East Indies, and Jodu had joined the crew of a British brig – the shipmaster was none other than James Innes, whose intrigues would cause trouble for so many people, not least Seth Bahram!

I asked where Serang Ali was now, and Jodu said he didn't know; at the time of their parting he had talked of going to a port called Giang Binh, on the frontier of China.

Of course, he too wanted to know what I had been doing since we last met, so I told him how Ah Fatt had run into his father, Seth Bahram, in Singapore, and how he had given me a job, as his munshi. Jodu was amazed to hear that I was in Canton with Seth Bahram through the months of the opium crisis – it is strange to think that our paths might have crossed in the foreign enclave last year, on the day when Jodu was taken to prison.

It didn't take Jodu long to eat his fill – a starved tiger could not have been quicker to devour its food. But afterwards he showed no signs of torpor or sluggishness: to the contrary he seemed more awake and alert than ever, almost pulsating with energy. I hesitated to ask him about his time in prison, but the words came pouring out of him anyway.

The jail where he was imprisoned is in the Nanhae district of Guangdong. To my surprise, Jodu said that the conditions there were far better than those they had experienced before, when they were incarcerated in a cage, in a mandarin's yamen. They were put on display in their cage, he said, like animals. People would come to look at them and prod them with sticks, shouting all the while: *haak gwai! Gwai-lo!*

It was hell, he said, *jahannum, narak.*

Things got better after they were sentenced and sent off to the Nanhae prison. There at least they were not on show and the food was better too. In the yamen all they were ever given was rice and salt and rice-water. In the prison they were allowed a few scraps of vegetables as well. One day they were even given a bit of meat but Jodu suspected that it was pork and didn't take it. The jailers asked why and the lascars told them that it was against their religion. That was when they learnt, to their amazement, that they were not the only Muslims in the prison, as they had thought. There were many others of their faith there – most of them Chinese! Some were from the community known as 'Hui', which is well-represented in this region. But there were Muslims from other places too, in and around China – Turks and Uzbegs, Malays and Arabs. These prisoners welcomed the lascars into their midst as if they were brothers. There are so many of them there that special arrangements have been made for them, by the authorities. They are allowed to cook their food separately. No one makes trouble for the Muslims because they are known to stand by each other.

Soon Jodu's words began to flow with an almost uncontainable intensity: he started to pace the room as he talked, turning from time to time to fix his eyes on me.

I tell you, Neel-da, he said, only in Nanhae did I see what great good fortune it is to be born a Muslim. Wherever you go you find brothers, even in Chinese prisons! And wherever there are Muslims there is always a bond between us.

Go on, I said, tell me more . . .

I think now that it was kismat that sent me to that
prison, said Jodu, and I'll tell you why. One of our fellow
prisoners, a Muslim, was a man of some influence.
Sometimes, on 'Id and other special days, he would bribe
the prison officials and they'd allow imams from the local
mosques to visit us. I don't know if you are aware of this,
but in Guangzhou there is a very famous mosque and
maqbara – the tomb of Shaikh Abu Waqqas, an uncle of
the Prophet, peace and blessings be upon him.

Here Jodu stopped to point to a tower in the distance:
its tip was just visible above the city walls.

Do you see that minar there? he said. It belongs to the
Huaisheng mosque, built by Shaikh Abu Waqqas himself.
People say it is one of the oldest mosques in the world.
Pilgrims come from far and away to visit the mosque and
the maqbara, from places as distant as Cairo and Medina.
Sometimes the imam of the Huaisheng mosque would
come to the prison to lead our prayers. One day, during
Ramazan, he brought a foreign pilgrim along to see us.
The pilgrim was a shaikh from somewhere near Aden, in
the Hadramaut. He was a small man, very simple in
appearance; his name was Shaikh Musa al-Kindi, and we
learnt later that he was a merchant who had travelled
everywhere – all around Arabia, Africa, Persia and
Hindustan; he had visited Bombay, Madras and Delhi,
and had lived for two years in Kolkata. But I knew none
of this then so you can imagine how astonished I was
when he spoke to me in Bangla and told me that he knew
me, and that it was because of me that he had come to
visit the prison! I was amazed; I said: That's impossible;
I've never met you, never seen you, never heard of you.
The shaikh told me then that he had seen me in his
dreams; he had had a vision of a young lascar from
Bengal, who was a Muslim in name but had yet to understand the truths of the Holy Book. This angered me and I
cried: What do you mean? Why are you insulting me?
And he smiled and asked if it wasn't true, what he had

said? This made me still angrier and I told him he knew nothing about me and had no right to speak to me like that. He smiled and told me that I would soon understand the meaning of his words.

A few days later I got into an argument with one of the prison guards. He accused me of stealing something and came to hit me. I side-stepped and the guard fell down and hurt himself. He accused me of attacking him and the matter became quite serious: I was removed to the part of the prison where condemned men are kept. The guards told me that I too would be executed and I believed them – I had no reason not to.

Here Jodu stopped pacing and put his hand on my neck.

Neel-da, he said, do you know how they execute people here? They tie them to a chair and strangle them. I saw twenty or thirty men being strangled in that way. I thought that I too would be killed like that. You can imagine my state of mind; how afraid I was. But then a strange thing happened. It was the day after Bakri-Id. One of the guards was a Muslim: he took me aside and told me that he had paid a visit to the Abu Waqqas maqbara the day before; Shaikh Musa had given him a gift for me – a tabeez that he had removed from his own arm.

Here Jodu pulled back the sleeve of his tunic to show me the amulet: it is made of brass and is fastened just above the elbow of his right arm.

I tied it on, Jodu continued, and when I went to sleep that night I had a dream in which I saw myself on the Yoom al-Qiamah – the Day of Judgement – trying to answer for myself. Suddenly I realized that the fear that had taken hold of me was not of death itself, but of what would happen afterwards, when I would have to face the moment of judgement. And then, as I lay trembling on my mat, for the first time in my life I felt the true fear of God. I understood that even though I had gone through the motions of being a Muslim, my heart had forever been filled with filth; my whole life had been steeped in shame and wrong-doing. I had been brought up in a house of sin; a house in which my own mother was the kept woman of an unbeliever, Mr Lambert; a house in which his daughter, Paulette, and I were allowed to run around like wild creatures, with no thought of religion, or even of hiding our shame from each other.

Through all this Jodu's tone was of testimony; it was as if he had temporarily stepped outside his skin and were watching himself from afar.

In a way I was like an animal, he said. My heart was ruled by lust and I thought of nothing but fornication, and of seducing women – this is how I had brought my fate upon myself, during the voyage of the *Ibis*. All of this became clear to me, and once I had understood it, my fear of death evaporated – no, you could say I longed for death, because I felt that whatever punishment was given to me would be well-deserved.

Now Jodu's voice fell to a lower pitch.

It was then, he said, that I submitted to the teachings of the Prophet and became a true Muslim. I was ready to die – I had no more fear of it. But strangely, a few days after my conversion – for that was what it was – I was removed from the cell of the condemned men and sent back to join my lascar crewmates.

Here Jodu paused to draw a deep breath; his voice was calmer now: it was as if a fever had flowed out of him with his torrent of words. I sensed that behind the disclosures there lay a need not only to confide but also to persuade: it was important to Jodu to convey to me the significance of his transformation, the full extent of which could only be apparent to those who had known him before.

You mentioned Paulette, I said quietly. Do you know that she too is in these parts?

The blood ebbed from Jodu's face as he turned to look at me: Putli? he said. Here? What do you mean?

I told him that Paulette was at Hong Kong, with an

English plant-collector – a friend of her father's who had more or less adopted her as his daughter.

Jodu was pleased to hear about her good fortune. I'm glad for her, he said. It wasn't her fault that she was brought up as a *kaafir* . . .

This made me smile. I said: I'm a kaafir too, you know.

Jodu laughed: Yes, I know you were born a kaafir – but you don't have to remain one forever.

I could only laugh.

Kaafir I am, I said, and kaafir I will remain. But let me ask you this. The Chinese are kaafirs too, and as you know they may soon be at war with England. That is why they are outfitting this ship they want you to work on, the *Cambridge*. If you accept you may find yourself fighting for the Chinese kaafirs. Could you bring yourself to do this, my friend, with a whole heart?

Jodu's smile grew wider. But why not? he said. Both sides are kaafirs: one worships idols and animals, just as you Hindus do, and the other worships flags and machines. Of the two I would far prefer to fight for the Chinese.

Really? I said. Why?

It turned out that this was something that Jodu and his fellow Muslims had talked about at length in the prison at Nanhae. The prisoners from Muslim lands – Johore, Aceh and Java – had told the others about how the Europeans had taken control of their countries and how they wanted to grab still more.

The Chinese are the only ones who can resist the firinghees, said Jodu. The shaikh has told us that in a conflict between the Chinese and the Europeans it is the duty of Muslims to take the side of the Chinese.

The smouldering intensity in Jodu's eyes removed whatever doubts I may have had of his sincerity. I told him that the Chinese were unsure of his loyalties; they thought it possible that he and his friends might go over to the British.

He laughed and said they need have no concern on this score. If they wanted he and the other lascars would be glad to to swear an oath at the maqbara of Shaikh Abu Waqqas.

*

Two days before the *Ibis* was to weigh anchor for China, Baboo Nob Kissin came to the budgerow to deliver Zachary's twenty chests of opium. As he was about to leave he said: 'Master Zikri, when I reach Hong Kong, it is possible that Miss Lambert will once again make inquiries regarding your good self. Maybe you would like to file off a missive for her? It is better that way since you are in her soft corner – you can yourself furnish all necessary details about your movements. I will facilitate safe delivery.'

This alarmed Zachary, making him wonder what Paulette's expectations were in regard to himself: did she believe that they were as good as betrothed? If so, would it not be best to correct this misunderstanding?

'All right, Baboo,' said Zachary grimly. 'I'll give you a letter for Miss Lambert.'

'Tomorrow morning I will come to get.'

Zachary started the letter after supper, thinking it would take only a few minutes. But after two hours and many sheets of paper he was still unable to find the right words to express his outrage at the insinuations that Paulette had made to Mrs Burnham, in regard to himself. Exhausted by the struggle, he went to bed and on waking the next morning he decided that it would be best to write briefly without going into too much detail.

April 16, 1840
Calcutta

Dear Miss Lambert

I hope this letter finds you in the best of health. I am writing because our common acquaintance, Baboo Nob Kissin Pander, in relating the circumstances of his Meeting with you in China, has mentioned certain matters that suggest that a Misconception may be afoot in regard to our standing in relation to each other.

I am sure you will remember that shortly after your

Flight from Mr Burnham's home you appealed to me to obtain a Passage to the Mauritius islands for Yourself. You will recall also that I advised you against this Course and instead made an Offer of Matrimony, which you rejected.

Although I did not feel so at the time, on thinking of this Matter I have realized that I owe you a great debt of Gratitude for refusing my sincere but rash offer of Matrimony. It is perfectly clear to me that we are in no wise well-suited to each other, and that I should consider myself fortunate that your Refusal spared me the Necessity of embarking on a course of the most reckless Folly. In truth we are but acquaintances whose paths have crossed by Hazard and neither of us is justified in entertaining any Expectations of the other.

I felt it necessary to offer you this Explanation since I too am soon to depart for China and it is not unlikely that our paths will cross on those shores. Should we meet again, I trust it will be merely as Acquaintances.

Until then I have the honor to remain

Your faithful servant

Zachary Reid, Esq.

As he was signing his name Zachary heard the crunch of wheels, somewhere nearby. Looking out of a window, he saw that Baboo Nob Kissin had arrived in a hackery-garee.

'Master Zikri!' shouted the gomusta. 'I have brought a gift.'

Zachary stepped out on deck to take a look. 'What's the gift?'

'A servant!' said Baboo Nob Kissin, beaming. 'He will look after your good self during voyage. You must at once bag this golden opportunity.'

Inclining his head towards the hackery-garee, Baboo Nob Kissin clapped his hands. 'There – look!'

Turning to the carriage now, Zachary saw, to his astonishment, that a boy had climbed out of it and was looking expectantly in his direction. He was dressed in pyjamas, slippers and a long white tunic, bound at the waist by a cummerbund – the usual garb of a khidmatgar – but the lad could not have been more than ten years old. He was too young for a turban even, and had only a narrow bandhna around his forehead, to hold back his long black hair.

'Hell and scissors, Baboo!' Zachary cried in outrage. 'How's he going to be my servant? He's just a gilpy of a boy. It's I who'll be feeding him and swabbing his ass.'

'Arré baba, he may be young,' said Baboo Nob Kissin, in a soothing tone, 'but he is attentive and diligent. Clean and healthy also – tongue is clear so motions must be regular. Eating-sheating also not too much. Whatever you ask he will do – make bed, give bath, press foot. You can just sit back and enjoy. He will adjust very well on you; he will be topping khidmatgar.'

'God dammit, Baboo! I don't need a topping kid-mutt-whatever.'

The expression on Baboo Nob Kissin's face now changed to one of earnest entreaty as he explained the boy's predicament: 'Father has expired and prospects are dim in Calcutta. Mother is very poor. If he remains here then child-lifters may catch hold of him. That is why he wants to go to Macau – his father's co-brother is working there. He is my friend so that is why I must provide assistance.'

Something about this didn't seem right to Zachary. 'But I don't understand, Baboo,' he said. 'If the boy's uncle is your friend then why isn't he shipping out with you, on the *Ibis*?'

'Mr Chillingworth may not permit, no?' said the gomusta. 'That is why I am requesting you only. It will not be much trouble for you, Master Zikri. After you get to China you can wash your hands with him and dispose him off to uncle. He will happily work as khidmatgar for you – salary also is not necessary. He is extremely helpful, suitable for all donkey-works. Talkative in English also.'

Still unpersuaded, Zachary continued to protest. 'But listen, Baboo – where's he going to blow the grampus? There won't be room for him to bunk down in my cabin.'

'No problem,' said the gomusta. 'You can put in your bedding. No formalities.'

'Fuckin'ell!' Zachary spluttered. 'I'm not going to take no nipper into my bed!'

Baboo Nob Kissin carried on undeterred. 'Arré baba, he is a little fellow, no? He can lie on the floor even, no problem. If he makes a mischief you can shoe-beat. Just think of it as commission, for me, because of help I have given to you.'

This was an argument that could not be gainsaid. 'Well, if you put it like that . . .'

Zachary beckoned to the boy and was somewhat encouraged when he came skipping up the gangplank as though he had been doing it all his life: at least he was nimble on his feet, not a clumsy landlubber. He was a lively-looking fellow too, with a sharp, expressive face. Despite himself, Zachary liked the cut of his jib.

'What's your name?'

'Raj Rattan, sir,' he said in a clear voice. 'But everyone calls me Raju.'

'You sure you want to go all the way to China?'

'Yes, sir!' cried the boy, his eagerness plainly visible in his shining eyes. 'Please, sir.'

'Oh all right then!' said Zachary. 'I'll give it a try and see if it works out between us. Go git your things.'

The boy ran to the gharry and jumped in, leaving the door ajar. Zachary saw now that there was a woman inside: her head was hooded by her sari and he could not see her face.

'Who's that?' he said to Baboo Nob Kissin.

'Boy's mother only. Has come for leave-taking purposes.'

For a minute or two the woman clutched the boy to her chest; from the angle of her head, it was clear that she was weeping. Then the boy whispered in her ear and she let go of him; he jumped out and came running back to the budgerow, with a small bundle slung over his shoulder. On reaching the top of the gangplank, he turned to look back at the carriage, where a glimmer of his mother's sari could still be seen, in the crack of a window.

'All will be well,' Baboo Nob Kissin said to Zachary. 'Do not worry. He is a good boy.'

'I sure hope so,' Zachary growled, 'or I'll bring him to his bearings soon enough.'

In the midst of all this, Zachary had forgotten about his letter to Paulette. It was Baboo Nob Kissin who reminded him: 'And the letter for Miss Lambert? Better to give now since I will weigh anchors early tomorrow.'

'Here it is,' said Zachary, handing it over. 'Please give it to Miss Lambert with my compliments.'

'Do not fear, dear sir; it will arrive with blessings-message.'

'And have a good voyage, Baboo.'

'You too, Master Zikri – the *Hind* will come to Calcutta soon. It will not be long before we are reunited in China.'

'I guess. Goodbye, Baboo.'

After the carriage had rolled away, Zachary turned to the boy and raised an eyebrow: 'What the hell am I going to do with you, kid-mutt?'

With a cheerful smile the boy said: 'Don't worry, sir. There will be no problem.'

Surprised by his fluency Zachary said: 'Say, kid-mutt – where'd you learn English?'

The boy answered without hesitation: 'My father was a khidmatgar in an English house, sir; they taught us.'

'Did a good job too. You'd better take your things inside.'

Now again the boy surprised Zachary, because he seemed to know exactly where to go.

'Hey, kid-mutt – you ever been on this boat before?'

'Why no, sir,' said Raju quickly. 'Never. But I have been on other budgerows.'

Zachary was glad to hear this. 'Good. So you'll be able to look after yourself then?'

'Yes I will, sir. Please don't worry about me. I will manage.'

The boy was as good as his word. Zachary saw no more of him till the next morning, when he went up to the budgerow's upper deck to watch the *Ibis* setting off for China, with a steam-tug towing her downriver.

Raju was already there and they both waved as the *Ibis* sailed by.

Afterwards Zachary noticed that Raju had a paper kite in his hands.

'Hey, where'd you find that, kid-mutt?'

'It was in my cabin, sir,' said the boy. 'Someone had hidden it under the bunk.'

*

Within a day of leaving Bombay, the *Hind* ran into heavy swells. Many of the passengers were prostrated by sea-sickness but Shireen was an exception. On Rosa's advice she chewed on a piece of fresh ginger and experienced no discomfort. The next day, heeding Rosa again, she changed into 'English' clothes. In practical terms the difference was not as great as she had been led to expect – but yes, she had to admit that her plain-cut black dress was indeed a little easier to manage than her sari had been. She was able to take several turns around the deck and the air was so exhilarating that she was loath to go back inside. After that, whenever the sun was up and the ship was not pitching too wildly she would step outside to pace the deck. She loved the feel of the wind in her hair and the touch of spindrift on her face.

The coast of northern Ceylon appeared off the *Hind*'s port bow after five days at sea. No sooner had the island been sighted than a strange fear took hold of Shireen: she began to wonder whether Zadig Bey would indeed join the ship as he had promised. There were no grounds for this concern – Vico had assured her that Zadig Bey was a man of his word – but somehow Shireen persuaded herself that something would go wrong and he wouldn't appear.

When Colombo was sighted she hurried up to the quarter-deck, hoping to get a glimpse of the city. But a disappointment was in store: it turned out that Colombo, for all its fame as a port, did not have a proper harbour; ships had to anchor at a roadstead, well out to sea. That was where they were provisioned and unloaded, by flotillas of bumboats, bandar-craft and lighters.

All that Shireen could see of the city was a distant smudge, and this too fuelled her anxiety. She stayed on deck, scanning the waters, examining every bandar-boat that approached the ship – and it was not till she spotted Zadig Bey, sitting in the prow of a lighter, that her fears were finally set at rest.

Now Shireen became anxious about what people would think if they knew that her rendezvous with Zadig had been pre-arranged. She retreated quickly to her stateroom and did not emerge again until later in the day. When she ran into Zadig she feigned surprise, and to her great relief he responded in kind: 'Is that you, Bibiji? How amazing! What a coincidence!'

Later, when they were taking a turn around the maindeck, she thanked him for humouring her but he shrugged her words off with a laugh. 'I assure you, Bibiji – I was not pretending. My surprise was real.'

'But why?' she said. 'You knew I would be on this ship, didn't you?'

'Well frankly, I wasn't sure you would go through with it, Bibiji,' said Zadig. 'And besides I didn't expect to find you looking so much at home here – walking around without a veil, dressed like a memsahib and smiling at everyone.'

She blushed and quickly changed the subject, asking him if he had received any more news from China.

'Yes, Bibiji,' said Zadig with a smile. 'I had written to a friend of mine in Macau, asking him to find a place for you to rent. I received a letter from him a few days ago: you will be glad to know that he has found a nice house for you, in the centre of town.'

'Really? And who is this friend?'

'His name is Robin Chinnery, Bibiji.'

'Does he live in Macau?'

'He used to, but of late he has been helping some botanist friends with their nursery, at Hong Kong.'

After that, when the *Hind* set sail again, Shireen and Zadig began to take their walks together, on deck. One day Zadig said: 'Do you know, Bibiji, this is how your late husband and I became friends? We used to walk together on the deck of a ship, the *Cuffnells*. Bahram-bhai loved to promenade on deck.'

Shireen had no inkling of this. It seemed unfair to her that Zadig should know so much about her husband and her family when she knew next to nothing about him.

'Tell me about Colombo, Zadig Bey,' she said. 'Are your children there too?'

Zadig fell in step beside her, with his hands clasped behind his back. 'Yes, Bibiji, my son and daughter live in Colombo too. They are both married, with children of their own – they are all I have by way of family.'

A few more steps brought them to the starboard deck-rails where they stopped to look towards the horizon. Then Zadig cleared his throat awkwardly: 'Actually, Bibiji . . . what I said is not true. In Egypt, where I was born, I have another family . . . and other children.'

For a moment Shireen thought she had misheard. 'Another family? I don't understand. Do you mean you had been married before?'

'Yes, Bibiji – but it's not so simple.'

'Then?'

'Bibiji – what happened is this. I was married off very young, to my cousin. The marriage was arranged within the family, mainly for reasons of business. It did not work out very well, although my wife and I had two sons and a daughter. I was always travelling, because of my work – and it happened that while passing through Colombo once I met Hilda. She was a widow, a Catholic. I began to spend more time in Colombo, and then my son was born.'

Shireen gasped, and her hand flew to her mouth. 'So this woman in Colombo – she was not your wife . . . ?'

'She was my common-law wife, Bibiji. But in time it was she who became the woman to whom I felt I was really married.'

'And your real wife? What became of her? Was she . . . abandoned?'

'No, Bibiji!' Zadig protested. 'It wasn't like that. In Cairo we lived in the midst of many relatives, in the family compound – just as you do in Bombay. My wife was not alone – and I settled most of my property on her, and on our children. She was well looked after.'

Shireen's ears were beginning to burn. 'So you left your wife, your children to go and live with . . . ?'

She could not bring herself to say the word 'mistress'.

'Bibiji, the children I had with Hilda were mine too – and the fact that they were not recognized as such, by law, meant that they needed me more. There was no family in Colombo to look after them. Surely I could not have left them to their fate?'

Shireen felt her gorge rise, and had to lean against the bulwark.

'What's the matter, Bibiji? Are you all right?'

Turning her back on him, Shireen rushed off to her stateroom. Fortunately Rosa wasn't there: Shireen threw herself on the bed and closed her eyes.

Over the next few days Shireen could not bring herself to step out on deck again. Her mind kept returning to the plight of Zadig Bey's wife: an abandoned woman who had been forced to bring up her children by herself, while her lawfully married husband went off to live with another woman, in another country. She tried to think of what her own life would have been like, if she had had to live out her years in the Mistrie mansion as an abandoned wife.

Her family would have been sympathetic of course, but she knew she'd have been crushed by the shame alone.

She realized now that this fate might well have befallen her as well: Bahram too must have contemplated abandoning his family in order to live with his Chinese mistress and his illegitimate son. He and Zadig had surely discussed the matter and he must have been tempted to follow his friend's example.

The thought sickened Shireen, making her feel that she never wanted to have anything to do with Zadig Bey: the man was a libertine, a rake, a *luccha*.

When she finally resumed her walks on deck she made sure that Rosa was always with her. If they happened to come across Zadig Bey, she would acknowledge his greetings with a polite nod, without saying a word in return.

The coldness of her demeanour surprised Rosa, who said: Bibiji, are you not speaking to Mr Karabedian? Why?

It's not proper, said Shireen curtly. Word may get back to Bombay.

Rosa gave her a shrewd look but did not dispute what she had said.

It was not till the *Hind* was approaching Calcutta that Shireen again found herself alone with Zadig Bey, by chance one day. Crossing the deck, he came straight over to her.

'Bibiji, I'm sorry if I offended you that day. I should not have spoken as I did.'

She bit her lip, to keep it from quivering. Suddenly the question that had been circling in her head these last many days burst out of her mouth.

'Zadig Bey, tell me: did my husband ever think of doing what you did? Did he think of leaving me and my daughters and going off to live with his . . . with his mistress?'

Zadig answered with an emphatic shake of his head. 'No, Bibiji! That is one thing I can assure you of. You and your daughters were too important to him. He would never have done what I did – he was a different man.'

Although this did much to set Shireen's mind at rest it did not entirely assuage her misgivings about Zadig. She continued to avoid him until the *Hind* arrived in Calcutta.

But once the ship had anchored it became harder to stay out of his way. They were both shown around Calcutta by members of their own communities and it turned out that there was a great deal of to-ing and fro-ing between the Parsi and Armenian families of the city. What was more, they all lived in the same area and the Parsi agiary on Ezra Street, where Shireen daily went to pray, was just around the corner from the Armenian Church on Old China Street. Since Zadig was often there it was hard to avoid him. When they met it was easier to behave in a normal way than to be unnaturally stiff and distant.

Soon enough, they were again pacing the *Hind*'s quarter-deck together.

*

Four days after the *Hind* dropped anchor in Calcutta, Captain Mee took Kesri and a team of camp-followers on board, to make preparations for the company's embarkation.

Down in the steerage-deck two large compartments and a few cabins had been set aside for the Bengal Volunteers. One of the cumras was assigned to the sepoys and the other to the camp-followers. Both cabins were cavernous, spanning most of the length and width of the ship; yet, even when empty, they appeared cluttered and congested, partly because the ceiling was so low that a man could not stand up straight without knocking his head. Moreover the compartments were divided up by long lines of upright beams, from which hammocks were suspended in double rows, one above the other.

Kesri disliked hammocks and was quick to commandeer a cabin for himself. Not only was it equipped with a bunk, it even had a small window. The stench of bilgewater was already strong in the steerage deck and Kesri knew from experience that the smell would get far worse when the *Hind* was at sea and her insides were all churned up. A breath of fresh air would seem like the rarest of luxuries then.

The Volunteers' last morning was spent mostly in the garrison's hospital: regulations called for every sepoy to clear a medical examination before boarding a transport ship. Afterwards, B Company mustered on a parade ground and Captain Mee made a brief speech, through interpreters. He told the sepoys that they were embarking on a historic mission and would gain great honour. In

China they would have many opportunities to cover themselves with glory, he said, and the trophies they brought back would be treasured forever in their homes.

The talk of history and glory made little impression on the sepoys. They listened impassively, their faces even stiffer than usual. Only when the captain announced that he had arranged for money to be distributed, as advances on salary payments, did the sepoys liven up. Accountants from the company's daftar were in attendance and the men quickly formed lines at their desks; also in attendance were shroffs who could arrange for remittances to be sent to Bihar, through hawala networks. As always the sepoys sent most of their money home, keeping only a little for themselves. This, in the end, was what mattered to them most, neither history nor glory, but the sustenance of their families, back in their villages.

Later in the day there was a dangal, a wrestling tournament that Kesri had organized in the hope that it would take the sepoys' minds off their impending departure. He himself played the part of referee, and even though the event went by without incident, Kesri could tell that the participants' hearts were not in it: the bouts were like practice sessions and there was little cheering.

Afterwards the company's pundit, who was also travelling to China with them, performed a puja followed by a recitation of the Hanuman Chaalisa.

Kesri had hoped that the familiar ceremonies would help the men get past the untoward happenings of the last few weeks – desertions, executions, omens and the like. But instead the rituals seemed to deepen their sense of foreboding: even from the way they prayed, Kesri could tell that their minds were filled with misgiving.

Later that evening the company's daftar sent over a half-dozen munshis to transcribe the sepoys' last letters home.

The munshis set up their desks in front of the barracks and the men gathered around in small groups, to dictate their letters. Kesri took the first turn and being well aware that the men were listening to him he was careful to strike an optimistic note. Addressing his letter to his brother Bhim, he said:

Tomorrow we will leave for Maha-Chin and we will soon return, with abundant prize money and also bonuses for overseas service. The Honourable Company Bahadur has made ample provision for us and we will be well looked after so you must not concern yourselves about me. When I return I would like to buy more land with my prize money to add to our family's holdings. I hope the poppy harvest on our lands was good this year. Have you been able to pay off the loans that the Company's arkatis gave? For the rest of the year, until it is time to plant poppies again, you should grow rice, mustard and vegetables on my fields. Please tell my children and their mother that I will soon be back, with many gifts.

Although the men listened attentively, few of them echoed Kesri's optimism. When it was their turn to dictate letters most of them struck a note of resignation.

Tomorrow our paltan will leave for Maha-Chin to fight for the Honourable Company Bahadur. We do not know when we will return. Tell Babuji and Ammaji not to worry. My health is good, although last month I was in hospital with a fever. If I die do not grieve – I will go wearing a warrior's garb, sword in hand. In my absence it will fall to you to look after my children and their mother. If there is any delay in obtaining my pension then you should send someone to petition the district officers in Patna. In addition there will be arrears of salary and prize money. Do not fail to recover everything. It should be enough to provide for my children till they are grown.

And:

We are going to a place that is very far. We know nothing about it. If I do not return I want to make sure that my field with the mango tree goes to my brother Fateh Singh. It saddens me that I have not fulfilled all my obligations to my family. For that reason alone will I regret my death. Other than that it is the duty of every Rajput to give up his life for the honour of his caste. I am ready for what may come.

306

The mood of the men gave Kesri much to worry about for the next day. He knew that an embarkation was a performance in its own right and the army's Burra Sahibs would be watching closely. It was vital for the sepoys to get off to a good start by acquitting themselves well – and in their present state of mind he doubted that they would.

But when the time came, B Company did him proud by putting on a flawless display. With drums beating, and fifes trilling the notes of 'Troop', they marched out of the fort's western gate in double column. On reaching the designated staging ground they wheeled into line and presented arms in perfect order, after which the Articles of War were read out to them by Major Bolton. Then, squad by squad, they fell out and were ferried to the *Hind* in lighters. After the last sepoy had boarded, the lighters began to transfer the company's allotment of howitzers, mortars and field-pieces.

The camp-followers had embarked earlier and by the time the sepoys came aboard everything was in order to receive them. But despite all the planning and preparation, there was still a great deal of confusion. Very few of the sepoys had been on an ocean-going ship before and some of them became disoriented when they stepped below deck. As tempers rose the camp-followers bore the brunt of it, as always: many had to put up with cuffs and kicks.

After ignoring the gol-maal for a while Kesri brought things to order by unloosing a bellow that shook the timbers: *Khabardar!* He made the men stand to attention, beside their hammocks, and proceeded to give them a dhamkaoing that made their breath run short. He ended with dire warnings about what lay ahead: sea-sickness, flooding, objects caroming around in bad weather, and so on. His most urgent strictures, however, concerned a hazard of a different kind – the lascars. These were the greatest budmashes on earth, he told the sepoys. To a man, lascars were thieves, drunkards, lechers and brawlers, with skulls as thick cannonshells. They were the sepoys' natural enemies and would steal from them at the least opportunity: they had to be watched at every moment, especially when they were hanging from the ropes like bandars.

Chastened, the men began to settle down, and when it came time to weigh anchor Kesri did not have the heart to confine them below deck. He gave them permission to go above to take a last look at the city.

Leading the way was Kesri himself: he stepped on the maindeck just as the *Hind* began to move. Almost simultaneously a battery in Fort William started to fire a salute of minute-guns.

Zachary too was up on deck: as the shots rang out, the planks under his feet seem to tremble in response. He remembered the last time he had set sail from this city, on the *Ibis*, with a shipload of coolies and overseers. It amazed him to think that only twenty months had passed since that day – for the difference between that departure and this one seemed almost as great as the gap between the man he had been then and who he was now.

From the other end of the maindeck, Kesri drank in the sights of the receding city – the temples, the houses, the trees – as if he were seeing them for the last time.

As the city slipped past a strange, cold feeling crept through him and he realized, with a shock, that deep in his heart he too had come to believe that he would never see his homeland again.

Twelve

The *Hind* had advanced only a few miles downriver when Raju came running down in search of Zachary, who was in one of the cargo holds, taking inventory of Mr Burnham's consignment of Malwa opium.

'Mr Reid sir!' cried the boy. 'You'd better come up.'

'Come where, kid-mutt?'

'To the cabin, sir.'

The cabin that Zachary had been assigned was in the poop-deck, and, exactly as Mr Burnham had promised, it was of comfortable size. This was providential since the *Hind*'s holds were filled to capacity with the Bengal Volunteers' armaments, equipment and baggage. Storage space was now so short that Zachary had been forced to stow five chests of opium in his own cabin. That was where he had left Raju, with instructions to see to it that the five chests were properly stacked and covered with tarpaulin.

'Did you finish with the chests, kid-mutt?'

'No, sir. I couldn't.'

There was a note of fright in his voice which made Zachary look at him more closely. 'What's happened, kid-mutt?' he said, softening his tone. 'What's going on?'

'You'd better come and see, sir.'

'All right then.'

With Raju at his heels Zachary made his way up through the innards of the ship, past the crowded, noisome chaos of the steerage deck, up to the maindeck and past the dining salon. On reaching the gangway that led to his cabin he beheld a startling sight: all his baggage, including the five chests of opium, had been shoved out.

More in surprise than indignation, Zachary turned to Raju: 'What happened here, kid-mutt? Who did this?'

Raju made no answer but gestured mutely ahead, in the direction of the cabin. 'I tried to stop them, sir . . .'

Stepping up to the cabin Zachary saw, to his astonishment, that two young lieutenants were lounging in the bunks, in full uniform, devoid only of their shakoes, with their swords strapped to their sides and their booted feet thrust against the bulkheads.

The casual brutality of this usurpation astonished Zachary and he was unable to keep his voice down: 'What the hell're you doing in my cabin?'

'Your cabin?'

One of the lieutenants swung his boots off the bunk and came right up to Zachary. He was a thin, pimply youth but what he lacked in bulk he more than made up for in swagger and sneer.

'You are mistaken, sir,' said the lieutenant, thrusting his nose to within a few inches of Zachary's. 'This is not your cabin. It has been reassigned.'

'On whose authority?'

Now suddenly another voice cut in: 'On my authority, sir.'

Turning on his heel Zachary found himself facing another officer.

'I am Captain Mee of the Bengal Volunteers; I am in command of the soldiers on this ship. It is on my authority that this cabin has been reassigned.'

The captain was a man of imposing build and stature: even without his gold-braided shako he towered above Zachary by at least a full head. His broad, deep chest had a yellow sash slung diagonally across it, running from his right epaulette to his waist. There was a bend in his nose that gave him a look of natural disdain; his jaw was massive and there was something about its cut that indicated a fiery temper: it was almost bristling now as he returned Zachary's gaze with hard, unsmiling eyes.

'You had no right to reassign my cabin, sir,' Zachary protested. 'Only the captain of this vessel has that authority.'

'You are mistaken, sir,' said Captain Mee. 'This vessel is currently a military transport. Army personnel have priority in all matters.'

'Sir, this cabin was allotted to me by the shipowner himself,' said Zachary, trying to sound reasonable. 'I am his representative and the supercargo of this vessel.'

'Oh is that what you are?' The captain lowered his eyes to the chests of opium, all of which bore the markings of the Ghazipur opium factory. He drew his foot back and kicked one of the chests: 'Why, sir, I could have sworn that you were a common opium-pedlar.'

The captain's curled lip, and the glint of contempt in his eye, made Zachary's face burn. Controlling his voice with some difficulty, he said: 'I am carrying a cargo, sir, that is legal by the laws of this land. I have every right to take it where I wish.'

'And I, sir,' retorted the captain, 'have every right to tell you that I do not care for drug-pedlars.'

'Then your quarrel, sir,' said Zachary sharply, 'is not with me but with the Honourable East India Company, whose uniform you wear – for as you can see, the seal of the Company's factory is clearly stamped upon these chests.'

At this the captain's scowl deepened and his hands moved towards the hilt of his sword. 'Don't you get gingery with me, sir,' he growled. 'You are insulting my uniform and I will not stand for it.'

'What I said, sir, is no more than the truth,' said Zachary.

'Well here is another truth for you then,' said Captain Mee. 'You would do well to get yourself and your cargo out of my sight right now. And let me assure you, sir, that if it should come to my ears that you've been peddling your merchandise to my sepoys, I shall personally see to it that your cargo is thrown overboard. You may consider that fair warning.'

A rush of blood flooded into Zachary's head now and he forgot about the captain's sword. Bunching his fists he took a step in his direction – 'Why you . . .' – but only to find that someone had taken hold of his elbow and was pulling him back.

'Reid! Haul your wind!'

It was Mr Doughty who had appeared at his side: 'Let's not make a goll-maul here, Reid. These military fellows will have their way, one way or another. We'll make other arrangements, don't worry. There's a nice little cumra down in the steerage deck that will be ekdum theek for you. Come on now, let's be off to freshen hawse.'

After a moment's hesitation, Zachary allowed himself to be led away, but under protest: 'This is all wrong, Mr Doughty. I was assured that I'd have that cabin . . . !'

Glancing back, Zachary saw that the three officers were observing his retreat with expressions of amused contempt. Their voices followed him as he was led away:

'. . . lucky little cockquean, to get off without copping a porridge-popper . . .'

'. . . another minute and he'd have been jawed in the fiszog . . .'

'. . . if anyone ever needed a fist in the frontispiece it's that little sprig of myrtle . . .'

Zachary could do nothing but grind his teeth.

*

Once the *Hind* was on the open sea, cruising towards Singapore, Shireen became increasingly preoccupied with the prospect of meeting her husband's unacknowledged son.

'Tell me about Freddie, Zadig Bey. You must know him as well as anyone. What was he like as a child?'

Zadig's hand rose to stroke his chin. As a boy, he said, Freddie had been good-natured, trusting, a little bewildered; left to himself he would probably have been content to be apprenticed to a boatman or fisherman, as was the custom with the children of Canton's boat-people. But Bahram would not hear of this. He had nurtured many ambitions for his son: he had wanted him to grow up so that he would be able to hold his own among gentlemen of all sorts – European, Chinese and Hindustani. He had wanted him to be able to quote poetry and he had also wanted him to excel in gentlemanly sports like fencing, boxing and riding. He had hired tutors to teach him English, Classical Chinese, and many other things – no easy matter that, since there were strict rules in China about who could learn what and from whom. But with the help of his compradore Bahram was able to ensure that the boy got an education, although Freddie himself had shown little inclination for it.

Bahram had certainly meant well, said Zadig, but he hadn't made life any easier for the boy. Freddie's peers knew of course that his father was an 'Achha' – which was what Hindustanis were called in Canton – and they knew also that he was a rich merchant, of the 'White Hat' variety (which was what they called Parsis). This made it hard enough for Freddie to fit in, and the fact that he received lessons from tutors, and was often given expensive presents, made it harder still. At times he had felt very lonely and had even spoken of escaping to India. He had dreamt of meeting his half-sisters and stepmother, and had longed to live in Bombay, with his rich step-family; having grown up on a kitchen-boat in Canton's floating city, the idea of a mansion, with servants and coachmen, was no doubt impossibly attractive.

But on this matter Bahram had been inflexible: indulgent though he was of Freddie he made it clear that he would not, on any account, take him to India. Bahram had been convinced that if the boy's existence were made public a terrible scandal would ensue; that he would be destroyed, as a father, a husband and a businessman.

So Freddie had had no option but to fit in as best he could in Canton, which meant that he had drifted into the company of others like himself – the half-Chinese children of sailors, merchants and other foreigners. At a certain age Freddie had moved out of his mother's kitchen-boat and gone off to live somewhere else: he would visit Chi-mei occasionally but when she asked what sort of work he was doing he would give evasive answers. This had led her to believe that Freddie had fallen in with one of the many criminal gangs and brotherhoods of the Canton waterfront.

At their last meeting Chi-mei had confided to Zadig that she feared for the life of her son.

Shortly afterwards Freddie had disappeared. On a subsequent visit to Canton, Zadig had learnt that Chi-mei had been murdered at about the time of Freddie's disappearance, in the course of what appeared to be a burglary. Bahram was back in Bombay then, and Zadig had written to let him know that Chi-mei had died and Freddie was untraceable.

After that, for a long time, there was no news at all of Freddie. Both Bahram and Zadig had begun to fear that he was dead – but then he had re-surfaced again, in Singapore.

Bahram was on his way to Canton then, for what would prove to be his last visit. It so happened that Zadig was in Singapore too, en route to the same destination. They had met up and Bahram had offered Zadig a berth on his ship.

Zadig was on the *Anahita* one day when Vico went ashore to buy clothes at a weekly market on the outskirts of Singapore – and there, unexpectedly, Vico had run into Freddie. He was with a friend, a Bengali – this was none other than Anil Kumar Munshi, the man who would later become Bahram's secretary.

Bahram had been overjoyed to be reunited with his son. He had invited Freddie to move to the *Anahita*, with his friend, and they had spent several happy days together on the ship. Freddie had seemed a changed man, mellower and more forgiving of his father. But about himself he was still reticent: when asked where he had been these last few years all he would say was that he had been travelling around the East Indies.

When the *Anahita*'s repairs were completed and it came time for Bahram to leave Singapore, he had asked Freddie to accompany him to Canton. But Freddie had declined, saying that he wanted instead to go to Malacca where his half-sister lived.

'Was that the last time my husband saw him?'

'Yes, Bibiji. It was the last time I saw him too – more than a year and a half ago.'

'After all this time do you think you'll be able to find him in Singapore?'

'Yes, Bibiji. If he's there I should be able to trace him.'

*

In lieu of his cabin Zachary was allotted a cubicle in the steerage-deck: formerly a sail-maker's closet it was sandwiched between the fo'c'sle, where the lascars were berthed, and the large cumra that was occupied by the camp-followers. The cubicle had no window and was so cramped that there was barely space for the single hammock that was strung up in it. At first glance it seemed impossible that it could accommodate a man and boy as well as five crates of opium. But in the end, by tightening the ropes of the hammock until it was almost flat against the ceiling, Zachary was able to fit everything in. His chests and sea-trunk he stacked underneath the hammock so that they became a makeshift bunk for Raju to curl up on.

The boy made no complaint and even seemed to enjoy sleeping on the chests: he would lie there for hours, with an ear pinned to the bulkhead that separated the cubicle from the adjoining cumra.

This bulkhead was no more than a thin partition, made of a few badly fitted planks of wood. When the ship tossed or heaved, cracks would open up between the planks, providing glimpses of the adjacent cumra; sometimes the planks would rise, so that gaps opened up in the partition. Peeping through the openings, Raju saw that a squad of fifers and drummers, many of them of about his own age, had been berthed right next to the cubicle.

The banjee-boys were a high-spirited lot; to Raju even their quarrels were interesting, not least because of the way they spoke. That swear words like 'bahenchod' and 'motherfucker'; 'bugger' and 'chootiya' could be used so easily and so often, was a revelation to Raju; nor could he have imagined that a simple syllable like *ya*, could be used in so many ways and with such eloquence.

Sometimes, when the ship heaved, the partition between the cubicle and the cumra would rise clean off the deck-planks, allowing small objects to slip through. One evening, when he was alone in the cubby, Raju looked down to find that a gleaming silver-coloured pipe had appeared on his side of the divide. It had lodged itself under Zachary's sea-trunk, in a position where it was in danger of being crushed.

Raju hurried to rescue the instrument and no sooner had he done so than a commotion broke out on the other side of the bulwark. Putting his ear to a crack in the wood, Raju realized that someone was searching frantically for the fife that he was now holding in his own hands.

How to let the boy know that his fife was safe? An idea came to Raju: he had taken music lessons and was not unfamiliar with instruments like flutes and recorders. Putting the fife to his lips he played a few notes.

The effect was exactly as he had hoped. There was a silence followed by a whispered question: Is that a fife?

Yes, said Raju. It rolled over here.

Another pause and then an entreaty: Can you meet me outside?

Raju stepped out into the narrow gangway that ran past the cubicle. Shortly afterwards a snub-nosed, brown-haired boy came running towards him.

The gangway was lit by a single, flickering lamp. In the dim light Raju saw that the fifer was not much taller than himself, although he looked much more grown-up because of his uniform, with its braided epaulettes.

The fifer received his pipe gratefully and stuck out his hand: *Tera naam kya hai yaar?* What's your name?

Raju. *Aur tera?*

Dicky.

Gesturing in the direction of the camp-followers' compartment, the fifer added: I have to practise now but we can talk tomorrow.

The next day the boys talked briefly on the maindeck. Later, they continued their conversation below deck, whispering through cracks in the partition.

Raju was amazed to learn that the banjee-boys actually marched into battle with the sepoys. Theirs was a vital job, Dicky told him; the drummers provided the rhythm for the march, and the fifers piped the signals for the manoeuvres. Without them the sepoys would not know when to wheel from column to line; nor would they be able to form an echelon for an attack. The pitch of the fifers' instruments was so high that they could be heard over the din of battle.

Still more amazing was the discovery that Dicky had actually been in battles himself. Dicky did not make too much of it: 'We were fighting some Pindarees. Bloody buggers would always turn and run after the first volley. Junglee bastards, ya – all beard and no balls.'

After that, when he was alone in the cubby, Raju would often talk to Dicky, whispering through cracks in the bulwark, and soon enough he was speaking exactly like his new-found friend.

Dicky's stories mesmerized Raju: the lives of the fifers and drummers seemed impossibly glamorous; it was hard for him to believe that boys of his own age could have such exciting careers. His own existence seemed embarrasingly commonplace by comparison and he was surprised when Dicky displayed a keen interest in the dullest details of his past: had Raju studied in a school? Did he have a mother? A father? Did they eat in a mess or did his mother cook for them? Where had he learnt English?

Sometimes Raju would drop his guard and reveal a little more than he had intended – as, for example, when he borrowed Dicky's fife and played a tune on it.

'Where'd you learn to play like that, ya?'

'Took music lessons, no? On the recorder.'

Dicky goggled at him. 'Arré ya! What kind of khidmatgar you are, taking music lessons and all?'

Raju had to think quickly to retrieve the situation; he did so by inventing a story about how he had once been employed by a bandmaster.

The next day one of the fifers fell ill and Dicky suggested to the fife-major that Raju be allowed to take his place for a few days. The fife-major was a short, hirsute man with a scowl permanently affixed to his face: behind his back the boys called him Bobbery-Bob, because of the exclamations and obscenities that constantly flowed off his tongue.

Raju was allowed to audition and was dismayed to learn afterwards that Bobbery-Bob had said that he'd played like he was 'shitting the squitters'. But Dicky laughed into his crestfallen face and said that this was actually a rare accolade: 'What it means, bugger, is that your notes flowed really smoothly. You're almost one of us now, ya!'

*

Kesri, no less than the younger sepoys, was awed by the sight that greeted them when the *Hind* sailed into Singapore's outer harbour. Six warships were riding at anchor there, one of them a majestic triple-decked man-o'-war.

The transport and supply vessels were moored at a slight distance from the warships. There were no fewer than twelve of them, their decks aswarm with red-coated soldiers and sepoys. The *Hind* dropped anchor right next to the troopship that was carrying their brother unit – the other company of Bengal Volunteers. The sepoys gathered on deck to exchange shouted greetings.

Looking around the harbour, Kesri saw that the Royal Irish Regiment had already arrived, as had the 49th and the left wing of the Cameronians. Only the 37th Madras Regiment was still to come.

Later that day Captain Mee summoned Kesri to the quarter-deck for his daily report on the conditions below. Their business was quickly dispatched and afterwards the captain identified the warships for Kesri, rattling off their names one by one: that over there was the eighteen-gun *Cruiser*, and there was the ten-gun

317

Algerine riding beside two twenty-eight-gun frigates, *Conway* and *Alligator*. And towering over them all was the man-o'-war, *Wellesley*: she was a ship-of-the-line, said Captain Mee, armed with no fewer than seventy-four guns.

The *Wellesley* was the tallest sailing vessel that Kesri had ever set eyes on. He assumed that she was, if not the most powerful vessel in the Royal Navy, then certainly of their number. But Captain Mee explained that by the standards of the Royal Navy the *Wellesley* was but a vessel of medium size, rated as a warship of the third class. Much the same could be said of the fleet itself, the captain added – although large for Asian waters, it was small by the standards of the Royal Navy, which frequently assembled armadas of fifty warships or more.

Kesri was both chastened and reassured to learn of this. He understood from the captain's tone that from the British perspective this expedition was a relatively minor venture and that they were completely confident of achieving their objectives. This was just as well, as far as Kesri was concerned. Heroics were of no interest to him – he had wounds enough to show for his years in service, and all that concerned him now was getting himself and his men safely back to their villages.

Later in the day Captain Mee and his subalterns went off in a longboat, to attend a meeting on the *Wellesley*. When they returned, several hours later, Captain Mee summoned Kesri to his stateroom for a briefing.

There had been some major changes in the expedition's chain of command, the captain told him. Admiral Frederick Maitland, who was to have commanded the expedition, had taken ill and another officer had been given his post – Rear-Admiral George Elliot, who, as it happened, was the cousin of the British Plenipotentiary in China, Captain Charles Elliot.

Rear-Admiral Elliot was on his way from Cape Town and would join the expedition later; until then Commodore Sir Gordon Bremer would be in command and Colonel Burrell would be in charge of operational details. The colonel had already taken some important decisions regarding the force's stay in Singapore. One of them was that the soldiers and sepoys would remain on their ships, through the duration of the stay.

Kesri was disappointed to hear this, for he had been hoping to spend a few days on dry land. 'Why so, sir?'

'Singapore is a small colony, havildar, not yet twenty years old,' said Captain Mee. 'To set up a camp large enough to hold all of us would be difficult because the island's forests are very dense. And there are tigers too – a couple of men were killed just this week, on the edge of town.'

'So how long will we be here, sir?'

'There's no telling,' said the captain. 'A third or more of the force is still to arrive. I'd say it'll take another couple of weeks, at the very least.'

'Will there be liberty, sir? Shore leave?'

The captain shot him a glance. 'It wouldn't be much use to you, havildar,' he said with a wry smile. 'If you're thinking of bawdy-baskets, you can put that out of your mind. Women are as scarce as diamonds in Singapore – the knocking-shops are full of travesties so you'd probably end up with a molly-dan. And if back-gammoning isn't to your taste, then the only other diversion is chasing the yinyan.'

'So what will the men do here, sir, for two weeks?'

The captain laughed. 'Drills, havildar, drills! Boat drills, attack drills, bayonet drills, rocket drills. Don't worry – there'll be plenty to do.'

*

When Shireen learnt the name of the tall seventy-four-gun frigate in the harbour she gave a cry of recognition: 'The *Wellesley*! Why, I know that ship – she was built in Bombay, by our friends the Wadias. I was there for the launching. They named her in honour of Sir Arthur Wellesley.'

'The Duke of Wellington?'

'Yes,' said Shireen. 'I saw him once, you know. It was just after he'd won the Battle of Assaye. He was being fêted in Bombay and the Wadias threw a big burra-khana for him at Tarala, their mansion in Mazagon, and we were invited. They allowed the girls and women to watch from a jharoka upstairs. Sir Arthur was the sternest-looking man I've ever seen.'

Zadig burst into laughter. 'Bibiji, for a woman who has spent much of her life in purdah, you've certainly seen a lot!'

Shireen laughed too, but more out of nervousness than amusement. Zadig understood exactly what was on her mind. 'You're worrying about Freddie, aren't you, Bibiji?'

Shireen bit her lip and nodded. 'Yes I am, Zadig Bey – I can't stop thinking about him.'

'Would you like to come along when I go to look for him, tomorrow?'

The question threw Shireen into a panic. The prospect of meeting her late husband's son in an unfamiliar place, without preparation, was deeply unsettling. 'No, Zadig Bey,' she said, 'it can't happen like that. You must give me time, and warning, so that I can be ready.'

'All right, Bibiji. As you say.'

When it came time for Zadig to go ashore the next morning Shireen was on deck to see him off. Through the rest of the morning she and Rosa took it in turns to keep watch for his return.

Around noon, there was an excited knock on the door of Shireen's stateroom.

Bibiji! said Rosa, sticking her head in. Zadig Bey is back – he's waiting for you on the quarter-deck.

Shireen went hurrying out and found Zadig sitting on a bench, under the awning that had been rigged up to cover the quarter-deck. He rose to his feet with a smile.

'Bibiji – good news! I found Freddie!'

'Where, Zadig Bey? Tell me everything.'

'Finding him was easy, Bibiji. It was he who spotted me as I was walking along Boat Quay. He came hurrying up to greet me, which was lucky, for if I had seen him in a crowd I wouldn't have recognized him.'

'Why is that?'

'He is completely changed, Bibiji, in many different ways – even his way of speaking English is different now. His looks have changed too: he is very thin and has grown a beard. To be honest, he does not look well.'

'Why do you say that?'

Clearing his throat, Zadig said: 'There is something I haven't told you, Bibiji.'

'Yes? Go on.'

'Bibiji, you should know that Freddie is an opium-smoker. This is not unusual in itself, for many people in China smoke occasionally. But Freddie is one of those who has had problems with it. I thought he had given up, but I think he has started again. This has been a difficult time for him, no doubt – Bahram-bhai's death, especially, has been very hard on him.'

Only now did it occur to Shireen that her husband's death, which had so powerfully affected her own life, might have had similar repercussions for his son.

'Do you suppose he misses his father?'

'Yes, Bibiji. Even though things were never easy between them, Bahram-bhai was like a great rock that Freddie could both rage against and shelter behind. Now that his father is gone, and his mother too, he is truly alone. It has come as a great blow to him, especially because he was not there at the end, for either of them. In his heart, you know, he is very Chinese, and it weighs on him that he was not able to put his father's soul to rest. He seems, in a way' – Zadig tipped his head back and looked up at the sky as though he were searching for a word – 'haunted.'

'Haunted?' A shiver ran through Shireen. 'By whom? I don't understand, Zadig Bey. Please explain.'

'I don't know how to tell you this, Bibiji, but what Freddie said is that he sometimes hears Bahram-bhai's voice and feels his presence. In fact he said that this was the reason he moved from Malacca to Singapore. He said he knew I would be coming – he's been waiting for me.'

'Had you written to him?'

'No, Bibiji – I don't know how he learnt that I was coming. It's very strange – we can ask him about it tomorrow, when he comes to visit.'

'Is he coming tomorrow?' cried Shireen. 'So soon?'

'Yes, Bibiji,' said Zadig, on a note of finality. 'He will be here tomorrow morning; of course you need not meet him, if you don't wish to.'

Shireen passed a restless night and in the morning, when she saw Zadig on the quarter-deck, she was unable to conceal her misgivings: 'Zadig Bey, I don't know if it's well-advised for me to meet Freddie. What good can possibly come of it? I am beginning to feel that I made a mistake. I should not have set out to look for the boy just to indulge my curiosity.'

Zadig shook his head. 'No, Bibiji. That is not why you have sought him out – it's because only you can give this boy peace of mind. Only you can give him a sense of having a place in his father's world. Very few women would have the courage to do what you are about to do, Bibiji. You must not flinch now.'

Shireen's hands rose to her fluttering heart. 'Oh but I'm afraid, Zadig Bey!'

'Bibiji, you don't have to go through with it if you don't want to,' said Zadig. 'Why don't you wait and see? I will say nothing to him until you give me a sign.'

So it was arranged between them that Shireen would watch from a distance while Zadig welcomed Freddie on board.

When Freddie's lighter pulled up Zadig went down to the main-deck while Shireen hid herself in a corner above, on the quarter-deck. From the shelter of the balustrade she kept watch, veiled by a shawl, as Freddie stepped off the side-ladder and boarded the *Hind*.

He was trim in figure and of medium height, dressed in shabby European clothes: a fraying linen suit and a wide-brimmed hat. The sun was at such an angle that Shireen could not get a good look at his face, which was shaded by the hat. But then, as Zadig was leading him across the deck, they happened to run into Zachary, with whom Zadig had become acquainted in the course of the voyage. He stopped now to make introductions: 'Mr Reid, this is my godson – Mr Freddie Lee.'

'I am glad to meet you, Mr Lee,' Shireen heard Zachary say as he stuck out his hand.

'And I too, Mr Reid,' Freddie responded. Looking a little flustered he took off his hat and held it to his chest; only now was Shireen able to get a proper look at his face.

He was skeletally thin, with sunken cheeks, hollow eyes and an unclipped beard – but none of this surprised Shireen. What startled her was that the cast of his countenance seemed completely Chinese, so much so that at first it seemed impossible that he could be Bahram's son.

But then, as she looked on from above, Shireen slowly began to revise her first impression: the more she looked at Freddie's face the more she saw echoes of Bahram's – in his dark, heavy eyebrows, his full lips, and most of all, in his fine nose, with its hint of a curve. Then Freddie happened to smile – 'You have never been in Singapore, eh Mr Reid? I would be glad to show you around, lah!' – and for an instant it was as though she were looking at a long-ago version of Bahram himself. It amazed her now that she could have doubted for a minute that the boy was her husband's son.

When Zadig's eyes flickered in her direction she gave him a nod and went hurrying down to the passengers' salon.

To her relief the salon was empty. She seated herself on a settee, facing the door, and removed the veil from her face.

Freddie entered the salon ahead of Zadig and, to Shireen's astonishment, when their eyes met he gave her a smile and a nod, as if to say that he recognized her and knew who she was.

'Freddie,' said Zadig. 'I want to introduce you to someone—'

Freddie cut him short. 'There is no need, lah. I know who she is.'

Summoning a smile, Shireen patted the space beside her, on the settee.

'Please . . . won't you sit down?'

When he'd sat down, hat in hand, she pronounced his name experimentally – 'Freddie' – and extended her hand towards him. If he had put out his hand too she would perhaps have shaken it, but he didn't, so her hand strayed towards his face and her fingertips skimmed over his eyebrows, touching his nose and chin – and suddenly it was as if Bahram had come alive and was sitting beside her. Her eyes flooded over and she pulled Freddie towards her so that his forehead sank on to her shoulder: she could tell that he too was sobbing now, just as she was.

When she looked at him again, his eyes were red and there was a kind of wildness in them: it was as if the curtains of adulthood had parted to give her a glimpse of a deep well of suffering that went back to his boyhood.

'I've been waiting for you, lah,' he said, almost on a note of accusation. 'I was thinking when you would come, eh?'

'But how could you know that I would come?'

He smiled. 'Because my father tells me, ne? He always say you will come, before month of Hungry Ghosts.'

Here, seeing that Shireen had gone pale, Zadig signalled to Freddie to say no more. But Shireen would not let him stop. 'Go on. Please. What else does your father say?'

A few minutes passed before Freddie spoke again. 'He say that I must go with you. I must burn offerings for him and Mother, at his grave in Hong Kong.'

*

Zachary's first impressions of Singapore were disappointing: from a distance the settlement had the appearance of a clearing in the jungle. Nor did it improve greatly on closer inspection: Boat Quay, where he had disembarked from the lighter that had brought him over from the *Hind*, was a muddy mess, and he had to scramble across a teetering bamboo jetty to get to the shore.

Yet, even though the port looked more like a fishing-village than a town, there was nothing sleepy about it. Stepping off the jetty, he was swept along by a crowd to an open crossroads that went by the name of Commercial Square. It was lined with saloons, shipchandling establishments, shops, brokerages, barbershops and the like.

Spotting a sign with 'tiffin' on it, Zachary went in and ordered some tea and mutton patties. While waiting to be served he picked up a copy of a paper that had been left behind by another customer. The paper was called the *Singapore Chronicle* and Zachary's eyes went straight to a column that began: 'In some quarters of this town, the retail price of a chest of the best Bengal opium has risen to 850 Spanish dollars.'

Zachary sat back, stunned. He had been led to expect that his chests would fetch seven hundred dollars each if he was lucky: this was a windfall!

Wolfing down his patties and draining his tea, he stepped outside, into the sunshine, and looked at the square with new eyes. How was it possible that a ramshackle place like this could pay such steep prices? It defied belief.

A touch on his elbow woke him from his reverie.

'Good day, Mr Reid!'

Turning with a start, Zachary found himself face to face with the man he had met yesterday on the deck of the *Hind* – he could not immediately remember his name. He was dressed as he had been the day before, in a light linen suit.

'Freddie Lee,' said the man, extending his hand.

'Hello, Mr Lee!' said Zachary, giving his hand a shake. 'Nice surprise to run into you here.'

'Why surprise?' said Freddie gruffly. 'Singapore is a small place, ne? You have seen the town?'

'No,' said Zachary. 'This is my first time ashore.'

'Come – I show you around,' said Freddie. 'Small place; will not take long.'

Some instinct stirred within Zachary, making him hesitate. But then Freddie added: 'Don't worry, lah – you and I, soon we will be shipmates.'

'Really? You'll be travelling on the *Hind*?'

'Yes. My godfather, Mr Karabedian, he invite me share his cabin. I will go with all of you to China, lah.'

Reassured, Zachary said: 'All right then, Mr Lee. I don't mind taking a look around.'

Falling into step beside his guide, Zachary followed him down one street and then another, taking in the sights as they were pointed out to him: this building here was the London Hotel, recently established by Monsieur Gaston Dutronquoy; that over there was the portico of St Andrew's Church; and there in the distance was the governor's mansion.

'Look around you, Mr Reid,' said Freddie. 'Look at this town, lah, Singapore, and all fine new buildings. Look at ships in the harbour. You know why they come? Because this is "free port" – they pay no duties or taxes. So where does the city get money?'

'You tell me, Mr Lee.'

'Opium of course – is a monopoly of British government. Opium pays for everything – hotel, church, governor's mansion, all are built on opium.'

In a while the streets became narrower and dustier and Zachary had the sense that they had left the European part of the city behind. Then they came to a road that was little more than a dirt path, winding up a hillside; it was rutted with cart tracks and lined on both sides with shacks and huts. There were plenty of people around, but they were all Indian or Chinese, and none too reputable by the looks of them.

A twinge of apprehension shot through Zachary now, slowing

his steps. 'Thank you, Mr Lee – but it's getting late. I think I'd better get back to my ship.'

Instead of answering Freddie nodded, as if to signal to someone behind them. Glancing over his shoulder, Zachary saw that they were being followed by two burly men. They too had slowed down.

It dawned on Zachary now that he had allowed himself to be led into some kind of trap. He came to an abrupt halt. 'Look, Mr Lee,' he said, 'I don't know what your game is, but you should know that I've got nothing of value on me.'

Freddie smiled. 'Why you insulting me, eh? Don't want your money, Mr Reid.'

'What do you want then?'

'Want you visit my friend, lah.' He pointed to a door that was only a few yards away.

'Why?'

'My friend want to meet you, that's all,' said Freddie laconically.

They had reached the door now; Freddie held it open and ushered Zachary in. 'Please, Mr Reid – step in.'

The room that Zachary stepped into was so dimly lit that he was momentarily unsighted. As he stood on the threshold, blinking his eyes, he became aware of a strong, cloying smell – the sweet, oily odour of opium smoke. When his eyes grew accustomed to the murky light he saw that he was in a large, cave-like chamber, with several couches arranged along the walls. The windows were shuttered and what little light there was came from gaps between the tiles on the roof.

In one corner a pot of raw opium was bubbling upon a ring of glowing coal. Two boys were tending the stove, one stirring and the other fanning the flames. When Zachary and Freddie stepped inside, one of the boys came over to remove their shoes. The floor was made of beaten earth; it felt cool beneath Zachary's bare feet.

'Come na, Mr Reid.' Freddie ushered him towards the far end of the room, where two waist-high couches were arranged around an octagonal, marble-topped table.

Stretching himself out on one of the couches, Freddie gestured to Zachary to recline on the other. 'Please be comfortable, Mr Reid.'

Zachary seated himself on the edge of the couch, in a stiffly upright posture.

'Tea, eh Mr Reid?'

A boy appeared, with a tray, but Zachary was now so ill at ease that he ignored it.

Freddie reached over, picked up a cup and handed it to him: 'Please, Mr Reid, is just tea, lah. You must allow me to welcome you properly. Two years back did not think we would meet again like this.'

It took a moment for this to sink in and when it did Zachary almost dropped his teacup. 'What the hell do you mean, "two years ago"?'

'Mr Reid, still you do not know who I am?'

The light was so dim that Zachary heard rather than saw him smile.

'I don't know what you're getting at, Mr Lee,' he said quietly. 'As far as I know we met yesterday, on the deck of the *Hind.*'

'No, no, Mr Reid. On another ship we met, long ago, lah. Maybe will help you remember, eh, if I call you "Malum Zikri"?'

Zachary sat bolt upright and strained to look through the dimness. 'I don't know what in hell you're talkin about, Mr Lee.'

'If you would try you would remember Malum Zikri.' Freddie laughed. 'It was on *Ibis*, ne? Remember Mr Crowle, lah? First mate's cabin? Remember his knife? He try do something – maybe stab you, maybe worse? But something happens – you remember? Someone comes in, ne?'

Suddenly, with the vividness of a nightmare, the memories came flooding back to Zachary: he was back on the *Ibis*, in the first mate's cabin, trying to steady himself against the pitching bulkheads. Mr Crowle was looming above him, holding a page torn from the crew manifest: 'Lookit, Reid, don't give a damn, I don't, if ye're a m'latter or not . . . y'are what y'are and it don't make no difference to me . . . we could be a team the two of us . . . all ye'd have to do is cross the cuddy from time to time . . .' Then the flash of a knife-blade, and a snarl: 'I tell yer, Mannikin, ye're not nigger enough to leave Jack Crowle hangin a-cock-bill . . .'

'Remember, eh, Malum Zikri?'

Freddie rose to light a lamp and held it to his face. 'See now who I am, lah?'

It was not so much his face as the manner of his movement –

quick, economical, precise – that confirmed to Zachary that Freddie was indeed the convict from the *Ibis*. Exactly so had he appeared in the hatchway that night, armed with a marlinspike, intent on settling his own scores with Mr Crowle. And no sooner was that done, than he had vanished, like a shadow – Zachary's last glimpse of him was on the *Ibis*'s longboat, with the other four fugitives, pulling away as the storm howled around them.

Zachary dug his knuckles into his eyes, in an effort to erase these images, trying all the while to hold on to everything he knew to be true: which was that the fugitives had died soon after his last glimpse of them. It was impossible for a craft like the longboat to survive a storm of such violence, he was sure of that – and besides, had he not seen proof of their drowning? The boat itself, upended, with its bottom stove in?

It struck him that the fumes from the boiling opium might have disordered his mind: everything around him seemed uncanny, hallucinatory, alien. He extended a hand towards his host, as if to make sure that he was real and not a shadow.

The figure on the couch did not flinch. 'Yes, Mr Reid. Is me – not a ghost.'

Zachary turned away and leant back against the headrest. What did this escaped quoddie want with him? Why had he revealed his identity unasked? Surely he knew that Zachary would have to report him to the authorities? And if he did know that then there was no way, surely, that he would allow Zachary to leave that den alive? He was a practised killer after all.

Zachary's eyes strayed towards the door. He saw nothing reassuring there: the two men who had followed them were standing guard in front of it.

Freddie seemed to guess what was going through his mind.

'Look, Mr Reid – you must not think to leave this place just now, eh? Need time to think, or bad mistake you may make. Supposing now you will go to police and say, "Lookee here, have found prisoner who escaped from *Ibis*" – what you think happen next, eh? How you will prove it? There is nothing to tie me to *Ibis*, lah. Cannot prove anything – and even if can, what will happen then, eh? I tell them it was you helped us escape. I will tell that you yourself killed Crowle. Because he try do something to you, lah.'

Zachary shrugged. 'No one would believe you – it's your word against a sahib's.'

Freddie smiled, narrowing his eyes. 'Maybe, eh, I will even tell that Malum Zikri is not so much white as he looks. What then, eh? Maybe that will make big trouble for you among the sahibs?'

This knocked the wind out of Zachary. Knitting his fingers together, he tried to calm himself. 'Just tell me, Mr Lee – what is it that you want from me? Why have you brought me here?'

'Said already, ne? Friend wants to meet. Talk with you. Maybe do little business, eh?'

'Where is your friend then?'

'Not far.' Freddie signalled to one of the boys, who went running to a door on the other side of the room. A moment later it opened to reveal the figure of a man dressed in a Chinese gown and cap.

The face was thin and weathered, the eyes hidden inside crevices of skin that had been burned and narrowed by the sun; the mouth was framed by a wispy, drooping moustache and the teeth were stained blood-red by betel.

'Chin-chin, Malum Zikri!'

This time Zachary made no mistake. 'Serang Ali? Is it you?'

'Yes, Malum Zikri. Is me, Serang Ali.'

'By the ever living, jumping Moses!' said Zachary. 'I should'a known . . . I guess the five of you have stuck together, haven't you, after getting away from the *Ibis*?'

'No, Malum Zikri,' said the serang. 'Not together – that way too easy to find, no?'

'So where are the other three then?'

Seating himself next to Freddie, Serang Ali smiled: 'Malum Zikri meet allo. In good time.'

Now, as he peered into the serang's unreadable eyes, an eerie feeling went through Zachary: it was as if he were looking at something that was as implacable and elusive as destiny itself. He remembered that it was Serang Ali who had first planted in his head the ambition of becoming a malum and a sahib; he remembered also the last words he had said to him, shortly before escaping from the *Ibis*: 'Malum Zikri too muchi smart bugger, no?' Even then the words had worried Zachary, because he had suspected that the serang was taunting him. His every sense was on guard now, as he said: 'What do you want with me, Serang Ali?'

'Just wanchi ask one-two question.'

'About what?'

'How Malum Zikri come to Singapore-lah?'

'I think you already know the answer to that,' said Zachary warily. 'I've come on the *Hind*, as her supercargo.'

'Your ship carry soldier also?'

'Yes – a company of sepoys.'

'How many?'

Zachary narrowed his eyes. 'Why do you want to know, Serang Ali?'

'Hab rich friend China-side, wanchi know.'

Suddenly Zachary understood: 'Oh so that's the game, is it? You're spying?'

Serang Ali had been chewing paan all this while and he paused now to empty a mouthful of spit into a brass spittoon.

'Why Malum Zikri talkee so-fashion? We blongi friend, no? Just wanchi little help.' Serang Ali leant forward. 'See – Malum Zikri have too muchi chest opium, no? He answer my question; he get very good price. One thousand dollar.' He paused to let this sink in. 'Good, no-good, ah?'

'You mean one thousand dollars per chest?'

'Yes,' said Serang Ali. 'One thousand. In silver.'

Zachary began to chew his lip; the offer was almost too good to be true. At this price after ten chests everything else would be profit.

'So what do you want of me then, Serang Ali?'

'Nothing, Malum Zikri,' said Serang Ali. 'Just wanchi ask one-two question. Come, we shake on it.'

Serang Ali stuck out his hand but Zachary ignored it.

'No, Serang Ali. Nothing's settled yet, and it's not gon'a be until I've sold you ten chests of opium at the price you've promised: a thousand silver dollars per chest. If we're going to do any talking, it'll be after that.'

Serang Ali's eyes lit up. Clapping Zachary on the back, he said: 'Good! Malum Zikri still too muchi smart bugger! So-fashion only must do busy-ness. Money down, allo straight.'

*

May 30, 1840
Honam

This morning I arrived at the print-shop to find Zhong Lou-si seated inside. This had never happened before so I knew something unusual was going on.

Zhong Lou-si and Compton were leafing through a stack of papers. Their faces were sombre, yet incredulous; they looked as though they had received news that they could not quite believe.

Mat liu aa? I said to Compton and he shook his head despondently. *Maa maa fu fu Ah Neel* – things are not so good.

What's happened?

Ah Neel, we have received word from Singapore, he said. A British fleet has arrived there, from Calcutta. There are six warships including one that is very big, armed with seventy-four guns. There are also two steamers and twenty transport ships, carrying soldiers and stores. Many of the soldiers are Indians, some from Bang-gala and some from Man-da-la-sa, in the southern part of Yindu. The transport ships all belong to Indian merchants.

How do you know? I asked, and Compton explained that Zhong Lou-si had sent an agent to Singapore, to keep an eye on what was going on. This man is apparently a master-mariner and was once a pirate; he is said to be very well-informed.

And where were the ships heading? I asked, and Compton told me then that their destination is China. As proof of this he showed me a copy of the *Singapore Chronicle* that had been forwarded to Zhong Lou-si by his agent: it was clearly stated in the paper that the fleet would soon be proceeding to southern China. From there the expedition would sail northwards, to some point from which it could exert pressure directly on Beijing.

Apparently all of this is now public knowledge in Singapore.

The news has come as a great shock to both Compton and Zhong Lou-si. Despite all the warnings, in their hearts I think neither of them believed that the British would actually attack China. Commissioner Lin himself has been known to say that he does not think that it will come to war; he has believed all along that British opium merchants were just rogue traders who had no governmental support. I suspect he finds it impossible to conceive that any country would send an army across the seas to force another country to buy opium.

I asked if they knew how many soldiers had reached Singapore. They said that by their agent's reckoning there were about three thousand, of whom about half are Indian. Zhong Lou-si has taken some reassurance from the size of the force; he thinks the British would have brought more troops if they really intended to wage war. He cannot believe that they would attempt to attack a country as large and as populous as China with such a small army. He thinks the British want only to make a show of force, as they have done twice before – in 1816 and 1823 – when they sent sepoys to Macau.

Surely, said Zhong Lou-si, if they were planning to make war they would send mostly English troops?

He finds it hard to imagine that they would depend on sepoys for something so serious – in similar circumstances the Chinese would never use *yi* troops.

I pointed out, as I have before, that the British have always relied heavily on Indian sepoys in their Asian campaigns – they did so in the Arakan, in Burma, in the Persian Gulf and so on. I told them also that the number of troops signified nothing: the main thrust of the attack would come from their warships, not their infantry. They would be relying on their navy to overwhelm the Chinese fleet.

Zhong Lou-si conceded that on the water it would be hard for the Chinese forces to resist the English fleet. But he added that at some point the English would also have to fight on land. There they would find themselves at a huge disadvantage in numbers. They would be taught a lesson if they made such a great mistake as to launch a ground assault.

But it appears that the British troops are preparing to do exactly that. According to the agent's reports from Singapore, the soldiers have been conducting many drills, on land as well as water. One of their weapons has made a great impression on the townsmen because it bears a resemblance to the fireworks that light up the sky on Chinese New Year. The agent has learnt from an informer that the weapon is called a 'Congreve rocket' (these two words were written in English, on the margins of the letter, no doubt by the informer).

Zhong Lou-si asked if I knew anything about this weapon and I said no. He then asked if I could find out about it.

At first I was dumbfounded: where on earth was I going to find out about rockets?

But then I had an idea: I remembered hearing that there was a large library in the British Factory in Canton, with books on all manner of subjects.

The factory's residents are all gone of course, but the building is still looked after by its Chinese servants, many of whom are employees of the merchants of the Co-Hong guild. It struck me that if prodded by Zhong Lou-si they might be able to arrange for Compton and myself to visit the library.

I put the idea to Zhong Lou-si and he was much taken with it: within a few hours we received word that the requisite arrangements had been made.

Shortly after sunset Compton and I went to the British Factory and were led through its deserted interior to the shuttered library, which is on the building's highest floor.

The library is much larger than I had thought, with comfortable leather armchairs, large desks, and rows and rows of glass-fronted bookcases. There were so many books that we were dismayed; we thought it would take us days to go through each of the shelves.

Fortunately there was a catalogue, lying on a desk.

With its help I quickly located a treatise called *The Field Officer's Guide to Artillery*: sure enough it contained a section on the Congreve rocket.

Turning to it, I discovered to my amazement that this rocket is actually a refinement of a weapon that was invented in India. Of course the Chinese have had rockets for centuries, but apparently they've only ever used them as fireworks, not for military purposes: rockets were first used as military weapons by Sultan Haider Ali of Mysore and his son Tipu, some forty years ago, during their wars with the East India Company. It was in south India, in the fortress of Bangalore, that rockets were adapted to carry explosives. Haider Ali used them to spread terror and confusion and caused the present Duke of Wellington some notable setbacks. Although the Mysore sultans were eventually defeated the British recognized the value of their innovation and sent a number of captured rockets to the Royal Arsenal in Woolwich, where one Mr William Congreve (a descendant of the playwright no doubt) then refined and improved the weapon. Since that time the British have used Congreve rockets in the Napoleonic wars and in the war of 1812. Now evidently they are planning to use them in China.

Compton and I lingered for hours in the library. We found several other 'useful' books – one on fortifications for example, and another on navigation – but to our disappointment there was nothing on steamships or boiler engines.

On our way out, I helped myself to a few books of my choice. It has been a long time since I last read a novel, romance or play: I scooped them off the shelves and stuffed them into my bag – *Pamela*, *Love in Excess*, *Robinson Crusoe*, *The Vicar of Wakefield*, *Tristram Shandy*, a translation of Voltaire's *Zadig*, and a half-dozen more.

As we were about to leave my eyes fell on a book that stood out among the library's sober tomes because of its brightly embossed spine: *The Butterfly's Ball and the Grasshopper's Feast* by William Roscoe.

334

It was the very edition that I'd bought for Raju in Calcutta when I started teaching him English, years ago; it cost a guinea as I recall, even though it was the cheaper, American edition. I could not resist it – I pulled it off the shelf and dropped it in the bag.

When I returned to my lodgings, the first book I took out of the bag was *The Butterfly's Ball and the Grasshopper's Feast*. I have read it to Raju so many times that I know it almost by heart. As I ran my eyes over the familiar illustrations, Raju's voice filled my ears, lisping over the words:

Come take up your Hats, and away let us haste
To the Butterfly's Ball . . .

I could feel my son's weight on my lap and I could hear myself, correcting his pronunciation: 'No, Raju – this is how you say it . . .'

The memories were so vivid that the book dropped from my hand and my eyes filled with tears.

To brood uselessly serves no purpose – that is why I do not dwell on the past; that is why I try not to think too much of Raju and Malati. But *The Butterfly's Ball* took me unawares and pierced my defences. It was as if an embankment had been swept away and I were floundering in a flood, trying not to drown in my grief.

*

The eastern expedition's fleet grew steadily larger as the days lengthened into weeks. The vessels from Madras trickled in slowly, bringing not only sepoys from the 37th Regiment but also two companies of sappers and miners and a substantial corps of engineers. But there were other ships still to come from Madras, notably the *Golconda*, which was carrying the regiment's commanding officer, as well as the equipment, supplies and personnel for its headquarters establishment. The tardiness of these vessels kept the expedition at anchor in Singapore even as the men grew increasingly impatient to move on.

The month of May was almost over when Captain Mee summoned Kesri to his stateroom to tell him that the *Golconda* and another ship, *Thetis*, had been indefinitely delayed and would join the expedition later, off the China coast. There being no further reason for the fleet to tarry in Singapore, Commodore Bremer had ordered most of the fleet's vessels to depart the next morning. They would proceed directly from Singapore to the mouth of the Pearl River.

'How many days from here, sir?'

'Ten to fifteen, I would say.'

The next morning, the departing ships were led out of the harbour by the *Wellesley*. The man-o'-war put on a splendid display, with crewmen standing erect on the cross-trees and stirrups, silhouetted against the billowing sails. The frigates followed in two rows, booming forward with their bows to the breeze, and then came the steamers, with the water frothing under their paddle-wheels. The troop-transports were the next to make sail, in groups of two and three.

On the *Hind*, the banjee-boys were up on the maindeck; they played a rousing tune as the ship's sails filled with wind. Looking on from above, Zadig, Shireen and Freddie were charmed by the diminutive eleven- and twelve-year-olds, in their white uniforms. As for Raju, he did not know which way to turn – towards the band, or the *Wellesley*, or the steamers, or the azure waters ahead. The first thing he would tell his father, he decided, was that there was no grander sight on earth than that of a fleet setting sail.

Thirteen

The last leg of the *Hind*'s eastwards voyage was markedly different from the first. From Calcutta to Singapore, the expedition's vessels had sailed largely on their own, occasionally sighting each other or drawing alongside, but each travelling at their preferred pace. After leaving Singapore they sailed together, cruising in convoy, with the lofty skysails of the *Wellesley* leading the way.

The *Hind* was in the thick of the fleet, far to the rear of the flagship. The waters around her were crowded with sails, trikat and gavi, kilmi and sabar: it was as if the sea had become the sky, a blue firmament dotted with scattered clouds, all scudding in the same direction. Between the white shoals rose stacks of smoke, dark as thunderheads, spouting from the funnels of the expedition's three steamers as they zigzagged through the convoy, delivering messages, rounding up stragglers, and lending a hand where needed.

The superb seamanship and perfect trim of the Royal Navy's warships put the merchantmen on their mettle: 'all ship-shape and Bristol fashion' became the maxim of the day and skippers began to drive their crews like never before. Every now and then races would break out, with one ship or another attempting to overhaul the vessel ahead. Even the passengers got into the spirit of it, urging the sailors on and cheering loudly when their vessel took the shine out of another.

Until the second week of the voyage the weather was exceptionally fine but then came a change. The wind picked up strength and soon the *Hind* was being battered by powerful gusts from the south-west. The skies remained clear however, so the crew kept to their routines and the passengers continued to take the air on deck, as usual.

Among the daily on-board rituals there was one that always

attracted a large crowd of spectators: the slaughtering of poultry for the officers' table.

The *Hind*'s chicken coop was at the foot of the mainmast. Every day, around noon, when the captain and first mate were 'shooting the sun', the cook who officiated as the ship's butcher would come up to the maindeck, brandishing a shiny, sharp-pointed knife. He was a big, burly man with a flair for showmanship: after beheading a bird or two he would stroll nonchalantly back to the galley with the frantically twitching carcasses clutched in one fist.

That day, despite the blustery conditions, the cook appeared as usual, just after the noon-time bell. Raju happened to be on deck at the time and he was among those who went to the coop to watch.

The knife flashed twice as two chickens lost their heads. Then the cook bestowed a toothy grin on the spectators and sauntered off as usual, holding the headless birds in his right hand and the knife in the left.

The stairwell that led to the galley was slick with spume. No sooner had the cook stepped into it than the *Hind* gave a mighty lurch, knocking him off his feet. He fell heavily, face forward. Then came a piercing cry, after which he somehow struggled to his knees and turned around.

Raju was watching from the head of the stairwell: he saw now that the headless chickens were still clenched in the cook's right fist, but his other hand was empty – the knife had disappeared. Then he saw where it had gone: the hilt was protruding from the man's chest.

Slowly, disbelievingly, the cook lowered his gaze to his trunk. As if in a trance, he let go of the chickens. Fastening both hands on the hilt of the knife he wrenched out the blade in a single motion. With the dripping knife still in his hands he stared in astonishment at the blood that was now spouting, so improbably, from his body. Then his eyes rose to look directly at Raju, and he murmured, in a strangled, choking voice: *Bachao mujhe!* Save me!

The last syllable was still on his lips when he fell forward on his face.

For a long moment Raju could neither breathe nor move: he stood frozen to the spot, unable to tear his eyes from the macabre scene – the lifeless body, the bloody knife and the headless chickens

338

that were now whirling around the stairwell. Then suddenly his knees buckled and the deck came flying up towards him.

At the last minute his fall was broken by a pair of hands. 'It's all right, kid-mutt; it's all right.'

Zachary picked him up, threw him over his shoulder and carried him down to the cubicle.

After the shock had worn off, Raju gave Dicky a detailed account of what had happened. To his surprise, the fifer was unimpressed: with a matter-of-fact directness he said that he had seen many men die, and boys too, in even more horrible ways: 'Why, ya, in my first battle a bloody Pindaree shot the fifer next to me. Blew the bugger's head right off; found his ear in my collar.'

*

Through the night the wind grew stronger and at daybreak the sky was dark with thunderheads. The fleet had scattered now, with no more than one or two sets of sail visible on the horizon. From time to time a steamer would appear, struggling to make headway, wallowing along in the trough of a swell or hoisted aloft by a wave.

The howling continued unabated through the early hours but at the end of the morning there was still no rain, so the sepoys were served their hazree on deck, as usual. The rain held off while they ate and they returned to their cumra without incident.

Zachary was on the quarter-deck with Mr Doughty when the camp-followers came straggling up for their meal. Noticing a flash of lightning, in the distance, he remarked to Mr Doughty that it looked as though the storm was about to break: it might be best to clear the deck and send the men below.

Unfortunately for Zachary, his well-intended words were overheard by Captain Mee. 'Talk of singing psalms to the taffrail!' said the captain, in a tone of mocking disdain. 'This is more cheek than I've heard in many a long year: a cheap-jack Yankee opium-pedlar teaching an English sea-captain his business! Who's in charge of this ship, Mr Doughty, you or this little madge-cove?'

The subalterns burst into guffaws and Zachary went red in the face: muttering an excuse to Mr Doughty, he went down to the maindeck.

Scarcely had Zachary stepped away when the storm broke. The pelting rain set off a panicky rush among the camp-followers:

dozens of men and boys began to jostle with each other in their hurry to get to the hatches. As they were milling about, whipped by wind and rain, a bolt of lightning came forking through the clouds. It struck the *Hind*'s mainmast about halfway up its length, snapping it in two. The top half broke off cleanly and was carried away by the gale, crow's-nest, purwans, yardarms and all. But the purwans of the mainsail – the largest and heaviest of the cross-beams – remained attached to the stump, although only for a few more seconds. Then, with a thunderous creaking the two spars began to split away from the remains of the mast.

The camp-followers were still pushing and shoving when the purwans came crashing down, on either side of the mast. On the dawa side the purwan dropped heavily on the deck, killing a gun-lascar and severely injuring another before toppling over the bulwark and vanishing from view. The other half of the beam caused even more damage: fouled by a webbing of ropes it began to thrash about, its ten-yard length lashing the deck like a flail, battering the panicked camp-followers.

Zachary too was knocked down in the mêlée, but he regained his footing quickly and immediately spotted the problem. Crossing the deck with a couple of strides, he used the remnants of the rigging to haul himself atop the stump. It was a habit of his to carry a jack-knife in his pocket: flicking it open, he hacked at the tangled ropes until the runaway beam broke free and was blown clear of the ship.

On descending from the stump, Zachary's first thought was for Raju. He found him prostrate in the starboard scuppers, with the breath knocked out of him but otherwise unhurt.

'You all right, kid-mutt?'

'Yes, sir.'

'Good lad.'

Around them was a scene of utter confusion, the dead and wounded lying sprawled about on deck, the wind howling, boys screaming, men trampling each other to get to the hatches.

On the quarter-deck Captain Mee and the subalterns were strug-gling to keep their footing, their uniforms drenched. At the sight of them Zachary's temper boiled over. Cupping a hand around his mouth he shouted at Captain Mee: 'Sir! You can't say you weren't warned.'

The captain's eyes narrowed as they flickered briefly in his direction. But then he looked away, pretending he hadn't heard.

*

The storm blew over in a few hours but the toll that it exacted from the *Hind*, in the few minutes after the lightning strike, was very steep: dozens wounded and five dead – the fatalities were two gun-lascars, an assistant apothecary, a 'native dresser' and an artificer. Their bodies were consigned to the sea at sunset that very day.

The banjee-boys were among the worst hit. Of the fifers, Dicky was one of the few to escape injury; many were badly hurt in the mêlée around the hatches. One boy fell from the companion-ladder and broke his hip; another was so badly trampled that his legs were broken in several places.

Even the company's pundit was not spared: the runaway purwan hit him square in the ribcage, breaking several bones. There were so many casualties that the *Hind*'s infirmary could not hold them all; the litters of the injured spilt out into the gangways and cuddies of the quarter-deck.

The sepoys escaped unscathed, having been safely ensconced in their cumra when the storm broke; it was the camp-followers and lascars who bore the brunt of it – and steep though the toll was they all knew that it would have been worse still if not for Zachary's quickness and presence of mind. Gratitude was lavished on him in such measure that it even spilt over to Raju. To be the cynosure of the banjee-boys' attention was a new experience for him and it turned his head a little. Bragging on his master's behalf he launched into a long tale about Zachary's exploits on the *Ibis*.

The banjee-boys were suitably impressed. 'Is it true, ya?' said Dicky. 'Bugger was really involved in a mutiny is it?'

'What you think? There was even a court hearing about "the *Ibis* incident". It was in the papers and all.'

*

June 23, 1840
Guangzhou

Today I learnt from Compton that a fleet of British warships has appeared at the mouth of the Pearl River. Their coming has been so long heralded that we'd almost begun to think that they would never arrive. And now that they have, what next?

Actually the ships arrived a few days ago. The reason I didn't know was that I have been ill for the last ten days. At times I was so unwell I thought I might not recover. It is something to do with the heat, I suspect; the weather has been very oppressive these last few weeks.

It was Mithu who looked after me. Every day she brought me food – scalding hot soups and a rice gruel, not unlike our *panta-bhaat*. Knowing how much we Bengalis love butter and ghee, she even fetched me some from the Tibetan monastery! This was fortunate in more ways than one: because of her visit, Taranathji found out that I was sick and came to see me, bringing with him a lama who is adept in Tibetan medicine. He read my pulse and said that my condition was quite serious. He prescribed all kinds of foul-smelling tonics and teas – I have no idea what they were, but they worked wonders. Mithu brought them to me, at the prescribed times: I really don't know what I would have done without her.

A couple of days ago, when I began to recover, Mithu told me that 'something big' was happening in the foreign enclave: a 'mandarin-tent' had been set up in the Maidan, she said, and hundreds of men were flocking to it.

Today, on the way to Compton's shop, I stopped by to look: the tent is a large pavilion-like edifice, bedecked with official banners and pennants. Inside, a half-dozen blue-button officials were presiding over what appeared to be a trial of strength – a large iron weight had to be hoisted aloft. The young men who had gathered in the Maidan were led in one by one, to try their luck. Those who succeeded were led to another part of the tent, to have their names entered in a register.

These youths were dressed as if for exercise; some were carrying staves, and some were wearing strips of cloth around their foreheads, painted with Chinese characters. Even though it was a hot day some were exercising as they waited, squaring off against one another, with bare hands or staves, bouncing lightly on their heels as they ducked, parried and feinted.

It was Compton who told me what was going on: Commissioner Lin has sent out an order for local militias to be raised across the province. The notices have brought thousands of young men flocking to recruiting centres like this one. Some belong to clubs and societies that practise the arts of traditional fighting; some are *chau fei* – young thugs looking to make a little money.

And what was behind all this? I asked. That was when Compton told me about the arrival of the British fleet. Apparently dozens of ships are now anchored around the mouth of the Pearl River, in the stretch of coast between Hong Kong and Macau. They have transported thousands of soldiers, both English and Indian. The troops have been seen landing at some of the islands of the Pearl River estuary – Lintin, Capsingmoon, Hong Kong and so on. This has caused panic in that part of the province, but here in Canton the news is still not widely known – the authorities are none too keen to spread it about.

In Commissioner Lin's circle there is great alarm. That is why they have started to take extraordinary measures. They know that their war-junks will not be able to oppose the British on water so they are preparing to fight them on land. But this will be no easy matter; Compton says the forces at the Commissioner's disposal are not large – only a few thousand.

I was astonished to hear this: I'd have thought that in a country as populous as China, every province would have a huge army at its disposal. But apparently this is not the case; most of the empire's troops are spread out along the western frontiers which are very far from Guangdong.

I suspect, in any case, that the Commissioner does not repose great faith in his military commanders. That perhaps is why he has decided to arm ordinary people instead: apparently spears, swords and other weapons are being distributed across the province. In addition thousands of boatmen are being recruited to serve as 'water-braves'; I'm told that a week or two ago they succeeded in setting fire to several British ships that were anchored below Humen.

The Commissioner has a great belief in ordinary folk. He is convinced that it is they who will rise up and repel the British.

It strikes me that great mandarin though he is, Commissioner Lin is also, in a way, a kind of Jacobin.

Compton says a proclamation has been drawn up, offering rewards for enemy ships, officers and soldiers. For a top British officer the reward will be five thousand silver dollars if taken alive; one-third if dead; five hundred dollars less for officers of every lower rank, on a declining scale – the full sum to be paid only if they are taken alive; a third if not. For English and Parsi merchants, one hundred dollars if taken alive; one-fifth if dead. For 'black aliens' – sepoys and lascars, in other words – the reward is half that of white soldiers and sailors.

I didn't know whether to be sad or angry at that.

And what about me? I asked. Should I expect that people will come hunting for me in order to claim the bounty?

Compton said that I had no cause for worry, since I am neither a lascar nor a sepoy – and in any case I am generally thought to be from the Nanyang, not Yindu.

But what about Jodu and the other lascars on the *Cambridge*? I asked. Would they be safe?

Compton assured me that measures have been taken to ensure their safety. At Zhong Lou-si's insistence the provincial authorities have provided a special guard to protect them.

*

The day after the storm, from sunrise onwards, Zachary worked with the *Hind*'s carpenters, helping to rig up a jury mast. The job took many hours, under a burning hot sun. At mid-day, when Zachary returned to the cubicle to change his dripping shirt, he found Raju waiting.

'Sir, Havildar Kesri Singh told me to give you a message.'

Zachary raised an eyebrow: 'You mean the Indian sarjeant?'

'Yes, sir. He wants to meet with you, in private. He'll come here tonight at eight thirty, when the bell for the first watch is rung. He asked me not to tell anyone but you, sir. He doesn't want others to know.'

'What's he want with me?'

'It's something about the *Ibis*, sir.'

'The *Ibis*?' A puzzled frown appeared on Zachary's forehead. 'What's the *Ibis* got to do with him?'

'I don't know, sir,' said Raju. 'Yesterday I was telling the banjee-boys about you and the *Ibis*; he must have overheard.'

This mystified Zachary all the more: he'd had no inkling that Raju was aware of his role in the *Ibis* incident; the subject had never come up between them and nor would he have thought that the boy would have any interest in it.

'Where'd you hear about the *Ibis*, kid-mutt?'

'From you, sir,' Raju blurted out. 'In court.'

As soon as the words were spoken Raju knew he had made a terrible mistake; quite possibly he had betrayed his own identity, and perhaps his father's too. Stricken with guilt, he made a desperate attempt to retrieve the situation.

'I mean, sir . . . I heard Baboo Nob Kissin talking about it.'

Zachary's frown deepened. 'Why would Baboo talk to you about the *Ibis*? What the hell's the *Ibis* got to do with you?'

Raju was now too distraught to speak: he stared wordlessly at Zachary, lips quivering.

His response puzzled Zachary; he could not understand why the boy was so upset. 'What's the matter, kid-mutt?' he said in a softer voice. 'There's no cause to be all cabobbled. I don't mean you no harm. You understand that, don't you?'

The kindness of his tone only deepened Raju's confusion. In their short time together, Zachary had so completely won his trust that he would have been glad to tell him the truth – that his father had been on the *Ibis* too; that he was on his way to join him now, in Macau. But Baboo Nob Kissin had admonished him not to speak of these things, on any account: there was no telling what Zachary might do if he discovered who Raju was and that his father was still alive; quite possibly he would think it his duty to report the matter to the authorities.

Zachary had only to look at the boy's red, choking face to know that he was harbouring some kind of secret. In a quiet undertone, he said: 'What is it, kid-mutt? Is there something you want to tell me?'

Raju shook his head forcefully, pressing his lips together.

The ineptitude of his dissembling made Zachary smile. 'You know, kid-mutt,' he said quietly, 'there's a lot about you that don't add up: the way you speak English, your dainty ways. You can say what you like but I just don't believe you were always a servant.'

Raju made no answer but stared back at him, tongue-tied.

Seating himself on his sea-trunk, Zachary looked into Raju's eyes. 'Tell me, kid-mutt,' he said, 'did we ever meet before that day when Baboo Nob Kissin brought you to see me? Should I have recognized you when you came to the budgerow with him?'

Mutely shaking his head, Raju mouthed the words: 'No, sir.'

Zachary knew he would get nothing more out of the boy. With a rueful smile he said: 'Who *are* you, kid-mutt? I wish I knew.'

Now suddenly tears began to trickle out of the corners of Raju's eyes; he swallowed as if to choke back a sob.

The sight jolted Zachary. 'Hey there, kid-mutt! There's no call to cry and such. I'm not hollerin at you or anything . . .'

A twinge of remorse prompted Zachary to place a hand on Raju's shoulder. The weight of it made Raju stumble towards him, and without quite meaning to, Zachary caught him in his arms and hugged him to his chest.

The gesture demolished Raju's defences and his tears began to flow as if a dam had collapsed.

Since the day of his father's arrest, two and a half years before, Raju had not once given free rein to his emotions; not wanting to add to his mother's burdens, he had held everything in. Now it was as though all the tumult of the last two years was rising to his eyes and pouring out, on to Zachary's shoulder.

Zachary felt the warm wetness on his skin, and it brought on a moment of panic: never before had he hugged a child to his chest in this way; never had he had to comfort a small, helplessly sobbing creature like this one. It was instinct rather than reflection that told him what to do: a hand rose, as if of itself, and stroked the boy's head, awkwardly at first and then with increasing assurance.

'It's all right, kid-mutt,' Zachary mumbled. 'Whatever it is that's botherin you, you don't have to worry about it. I'll be around if you need me. I'll take care of you.'

The words shocked him, even as he was saying them. Never before had he told anyone that he would take care of them; nor had anyone ever uttered those words to him, except his mother. It was as if he were hugging an old version of himself; someone who was irretrievably lost to him now; a child whose absence he could not help mourning.

*

The ship's bell had no sooner tolled than Kesri stepped out of his cabin, dressed not in his uniform but in a plain white ungah and dhoti. He reached Zachary's cubicle just as the eighth peal was fading away. The door opened as soon as he knocked and Kesri found himself face to face with Zachary, who was in his breeches and a striped sailor's banyan.

The cubicle was lit by a single lamp: in its light Kesri saw that a few chests had been arranged at one end, to make a seat. Facing it, at the other end of the narrow space, was a sea-trunk.

'Come in, Sarjeant.'

Gesturing to Kesri to take the sea-trunk, Zachary seated himself on the chests.

For a minute or two they studied each other and then Kesri said: 'Good evening, Reid-sah'b.'

'Good evening.'

Kesri cleared his throat, trying to think of a suitable preamble; failing to find one, he came abruptly to the point: 'Reid-sah'b, is it true you were on *Ibis*?'

'Yes,' said Zachary. 'I was the second mate, on the voyage to Mauritius.'

'There was one Subedar Bhyro Singh, with you, no?'

'Yes, there was.'

'What happened to Subedar Bhyro Singh?'

In a few words Zachary explained that Subedar Bhyro Singh had had a run-in with a coolie and had insisted that the man be flogged. The coolie was a big fellow, very powerfully built. After a dozen lashes he had broken free of his bindings and turned the whip upon his tormentor, breaking his neck with the lash. All of this had happened in a matter of seconds; later it had come to be learnt that the trouble between the two men had begun with an assault on the coolie's wife, by the subedar.

'The woman,' said Kesri quickly, 'the coolie's wife – what was her name?'

Zachary had to scratch his head several times before the name came to him. 'It was something like "Ditty" as I remember.'

Kesri had been holding his breath and it leaked out of him now, in a long, deep sigh. His chin sank into his chest as he absorbed what Zachary had said.

So it was all true then? Deeti had indeed run away with another man: his little sister, who had never travelled even so far as Patna had set off to escape to an island across the black water.

As all of this was sinking in, Kesri slowly raised his head. Zachary saw now that the pupils of the havildar's eyes were grey and somehow familiar. A strange, uncanny charge shot through him and a moment later, when Kesri said, 'That woman – she is my sister, Deeti,' Zachary knew it to be the shock of recognition.

'Yes of course,' he said. 'I see the resemblance.'

'Where is Deeti now?' said Kesri hoarsely. 'Do you know?'

'I'm sure she's in Mauritius,' said Zachary. 'I heard she was allotted to a Frenchman – a farmer whose land is in the south-west of the country.'

A kind of incredulity took hold of Kesri now and he shook his head, in wonderment. Who would have imagined that this boyish-looking sahib would be able to give him news of Deeti? Who would have thought that they had been separated all this while by a few yards of timber?

'Was Deeti all right?' said Kesri gruffly. 'Her health was good?'

'Yes,' said Zachary. 'As far as I know, she was in good health.'

There was much more that Kesri would have liked to ask but he could hear someone calling for him, down the gangway.

'I must go now.'

Rising from his seat, Kesri said: 'Reid-sah'b, we will not speak of this to anyone else, no?'

'Of course not.'

With his hand on the door Kesri stopped and turned to face Zachary again.

'Reid-sah'b,' he said, 'I'm sorry how Captain Mee talks to you. He is a good man, good officer . . .' Unable to find the words he wanted, Kesri began again. 'Mee-sah'b – I have known him a long time. I was his orderly seventeen years ago – he is a good man, but sad, in his heart . . .'

Zachary made no answer, so Kesri said, simply: 'I am sorry.'

'It's all right, havildar,' said Zachary. 'It's not your fault.'

Kesri raised his hand to his forehead. 'My salaams, Reid-sah'b. If you ever need anything, please tell me.'

'Thank you, havildar.'

Just as Kesri was stepping out, Zachary remembered something: 'Oh wait, havildar. There's one other thing.'

'Yes?'

'Your sister. There's something you should know.'

'Yes?'

'When we reached Mauritius she was pregnant. The child must be more than a year old now.'

*

The next day, a plume of smoke was spotted on the northward horizon: the *Queen*, a steamer, was out searching for distressed vessels. A Congreve rocket was fired from the maindeck of the *Hind* and soon afterwards the steamer pulled alongside, to the accompaniment of rousing cheers.

Before taking the *Hind* under tow, the steamer's captain came over to freshen hawse with Mr Doughty. They spent a good while together, exchanging news over glasses of Bristol-milk, and later, when the *Hind* was under tow, ploughing steady northwards, Mr Doughty gave Zachary an account of what he had learnt while he was coguing the nose with his fellow skipper.

The British fleet had arrived off the China coast five days earlier, and Captain Elliot had rendezvoused with Commodore Bremer near the Ladrone Islands. After extensive deliberations the Plenipotentiary and the commodore had agreed on a strategy that required the expeditionary force to be split into two wings. The first wing, consisting of a small squad of warships and transports, would remain in the south, to enforce a blockade on the Pearl River, while the other, much larger wing, would proceed northwards, with the objective of seizing a strategically placed island called Chusan, which sat astride the sea routes to some of the most important ports of the Chinese heartland – Hangchow, Ningbo and Shanghai. In order that the powers in Beijing should know exactly why these actions had been undertaken, the expedition's leaders would attempt to hand over a letter from Lord Palmerston to the Emperor, listing Britain's demands and grievances.

Once Chusan had been seized, the eastern seaboard of China would be at the mercy of the expeditionary force. With the island as its operating base, the British fleet would roam the length of the coast, threatening important ports, drawing up maps and charts, and making sure that the Manchu overlords of Peking were not left in any doubt of their vulnerability. Chusan was so close to the capital that the mandarins would not be able to conceal the news of its seizure from the Emperor: he would soon realize that he had no choice but to accede to Britain's demands for the re-opening of trade and the restitution of past losses.

Since the resumption of the opium trade was one of the main objectives of the expedition, the fleet would be accompanied by a number of merchant vessels, many of them opium-carriers. The navy would ensure that British merchants were free to approach the major ports to dispose of their cargoes as they pleased.

For Free-Traders there was much to celebrate in this strategy which was closely modelled on the plans drawn up by William Jardine. They stood to make fortunes by selling opium in markets that had previously been beyond their reach. The accrual of demand in the Chinese heartland was thought to be like that of the Yellow River before a flood: prices were expected to shoot to unheard-of heights.

'We're arriving in the nick of time, Reid,' said Mr Doughty. 'The fleet will be sailing north in two days and I'm sure Mr Chillingworth will be keen to go along. Mr Burnham's cargo of opium will have to be transferred from the *Hind* to the *Ibis* as soon as we drop anchor.'

*

The next day the *Hind*'s passengers woke to find themselves in a stretch of water that seemed not quite of this earth. The colour of the sea had turned from deep blue to iridiscent turquoise, and hundreds of craggy islets had appeared, rising out of the depths like dragon's teeth. Many of these outcrops of rock were ashen in colour, with flinty ridges; most were edged by sheer cliffs to which clung stunted trees of fantastically gnarled shapes. Every now and then, from the lee of one of these islands, an improbable-looking vessel would appear – sometimes a high-sterned fishing boat, sometimes a junk with matted sails, or a galleon-like lorcha that seemed to belong to another age.

The strangeness of the surroundings created a kind of stupor on the storm-shocked *Hind*: only when a cry rang out to announce the sighting of the mainland – *kinara agil hai!* – was the spell broken. The lookout's shout set off a race to the maindeck; even some of the wounded, barely able to stand on their own feet, went hobbling forward to catch their first glimpse of the land of Mahachin.

At first the coast was only a distant smudge on the horizon, but when its contours began to take shape, maps and telescopes were fetched so that the salient features could be identified. Standing by the binnacle Mr Doughty raised a fingertip and turned it in a north-easterly direction. 'That over there is the island of Hong Kong!'

On the starboard side of the quarter-deck, Shireen's knuckles whitened on the gunwale as she leant forward, straining to look ahead.

'Here.' Jogging Shireen's elbow, Freddie held out a spyglass: 'Here, with this you will see better, lah. Hong Kong is that one – tallest and biggest of those islands, over there.'

The distant peaks were wreathed in cloud but the slopes below were treeless, strangely barren. The island seemed to be sparsely inhabited; the only dwellings to be seen were a few clusters of houses on the shore.

A lump rose to Shireen's throat as she stared at the windswept massif: so this was where Bahram had found his resting-place? This was where his journey had ended – this forbidding eyrie of an island, so far from his native Gujarat? The weather-battered desolation of the place created an aching melancholy in her: she tried and failed to envision Bahram's grave, lying amidst those slopes.

She turned to Zadig Bey, who was standing beside her. 'Do you think we'll be able to visit my husband's grave today?'

Zadig scratched his chin. 'I don't know if it'll be possible today, Bibiji,' he said. 'I must first find my friend Robin Chinnery, to make sure that arrangements have been made for your accommodation in Macau. But we will go to Hong Kong as soon as possible, I promise.'

*

'And you see that promontory, abeam of the larboard bow?' boomed Mr Doughty, pointing in a north-westerly direction. 'Somewhere there lies Macau!'

Down on the maindeck, Raju raised a hand to shade his eyes as he peered ahead: Macau was where his journey would end; this was where he would be reunited with his father!

Excitement and anticipation bubbled up in him until they could no longer be contained. 'Look!' he said to Dicky. 'That's where I am going – Macau! That's where my uncle is!'

Dicky pulled a face. 'Lucky bastard, ya!' he said enviously. 'How is it that you civvy buggers have all these bloody uncles, and aunts, and fathers, and mothers?'

The fifer spat overboard, into the foam-flecked sea. 'We Lower Orphanage fellows, we don't have even one bloody relative.'

Although Dicky's tone was jocular there was an edge to it that made Raju wilt: the pleasure with which he had been looking forward to leaving the ship now gave way to a guilty unease for having so joyfully welcomed the prospect of abandoning his friend. Turning away in confusion, Raju went down to the cubicle and began to gather his meagre belongings together. He was stuffing them into his ditty-bag when Zachary came in.

'So this is it I guess, eh kid-mutt? You and I will soon be going our own ways?'

'Yes, sir.' Raju shyly held out his hand. 'Thank you for bringing me with you, sir. If not for you I wouldn't be here.'

Zachary smiled as he shook the boy's hand. 'You're a good lad, kid-mutt,' he said. 'I hope things work out well for you.'

A minute later, the ship's bell began to ring, announcing the sighting of the fleet.

They went racing back to the deck to find that a mass of Union

Jacks had appeared on the waters ahead, at the western edge of the Pearl River estuary.

The grandeur of the landscape made the fleet look even more impressive than at Singapore: its masts, flags and pennants were so thickly bunched together that it was as if a great fortress had arisen out of the water.

Twenty warships were at anchor there, including three seventy-four-gun men-o'-war, *Wellesley*, *Melville* and *Blenheim*; two forty-four-gun frigates, *Druid* and *Blonde*, and no fewer than four steamers. Clustered around them were twenty-six transport and supply vessels with names like *Futty Salaam*, *Hooghly*, *Rahmany*, *Sulimany*, *Rustomjee Cowasjee* and *Nazareth Shah*. And everywhere in the channel, circling ravenously around the ships of the fleet, were bumboats – hundreds of them, bedecked with a vast array of wares: vegetables, meat, fruit, souvenirs.

Guarding the fleet's southern flank was a twenty-eight-gun frigate, *Alligator*. No sooner had the *Hind* drawn level with the frigate than her towropes were tossed off: in her present state she was in no condition to wend her way through those crowded waters to join her sister vessel, the *Ibis*, which was a good distance away.

Even before the *Hind* had anchored, cutters, lighters and bumboats were converging on her from every direction.

*

The *Hind*'s cargo of opium was large enough that it took a good few hours to offload it into a longboat. By the time Zachary stepped into the boat, to escort the cargo to the *Ibis*, it was well past noon.

The air was as heavy as a hot compress: the torpid stillness of the afternoon had created a steamy haze so that the towering masts of the anchored frigates shimmered like trees in a fog.

Zachary was sitting in the stern of the longboat, facing forward: rounding the prow of a sloop-o'-war he caught sight of a large daub of orange, sitting perched in the bows of a fast-moving gig.

In a few minutes the splash of colour resolved itself into a familiar shape and form.

'Baboo Nob Kissin?'

'Master Zikri!' cried the gomusta. 'Is it you?'

The gomusta, overjoyed, made an attempt to rise to his feet, almost overturning the gig. Sinking quickly back to the bench, he cried: 'Master Zikri, you will live a hundred years! For you only I was going to look – it is a very urgent matter!'

'What is it, Baboo?'

'Captain Chillingworth is laid down with severe indispositions: one day stool is like porridge next day like curds. Tongue has also become black and furry, like bandicoot's tail. He has been evacuated to Manila. In his absence I am glad to intimate an auspicious news: in lieu of himself Mr Chillingworth has appointed you captain of *Ibis!*'

'Me? Captain?' Zachary narrowed his eyes. 'Are you ironizing, Baboo?'

'*Hai, hai!*' Shaking his head solemnly, Baboo Nob Kissin bit his tongue. 'I would never treat such a matter with levitation. Look – I can prove to you that I am not laughing in my sleeve.' Baboo Nob Kissin drew out a sealed letter and handed it over: 'Here is authorization-chitty, issued by Mr Chillingworth. It is most fortunate that you have arrived today. You must join duty now only. Departure has been preponed – we must set sail tomorrow.'

As Zachary was examining the letter, Baboo Nob Kissin lowered his voice and leant a little closer. 'One secret I will impart: all this was my idea – I only told Captain Chillingworth that you are suitable for captain's job. Now see how nicely everything has worked out? You will be able to sell your own opium and Mr Burnham's also. Soon you will be making money, fist over wrist!'

Amazed by yet another unexpected upturn in his fortunes, Zachary was still staring at the letter. 'Holy gollation, Baboo! I don't know what to say.'

The gomusta's attention had already turned to another matter: 'And what about the boy, Raju? I hope he did not create botherations?'

'No, not at all. He's waiting on the *Hind* – he's got his things packed and is all ready to go off to his uncle.'

At this a scowl appeared on the Baboo's face. 'Regarding that matter unfortunately a problem has risen up. Raju's uncle has absconded from Macau – he has gone upcountry and is not reachable. Never mind. I will explain everything to Raju.'

'I left him on the *Hind* – you'll find him there.'

As the boats were pulling apart, a thought struck Zachary

and he turned around, cupping his hands around his mouth: 'Baboo, what about the letter I sent with you? For Miss Paulette Lambert?'

'She has received it, Master Zikri!' the gomusta shouted back. 'Not to worry – it has been delivered into her hands!'

*

Shortly after the *Hind*'s arrival Captain Mee and the subalterns left for the *Wellesley*, to meet with Colonel Burrell and Commodore Bremer. Kesri was not sorry to see the officers go: their departure left him free at last to give his attention to those who needed it most – the sepoys and camp-followers.

The events of the last few days – the lightning strike, the dismasting, the deaths and injuries – had reduced many of the boys and men to a state where they seemed unable to absorb, or even notice, what was happening around them. Nor did their numbness dissipate on arrival: many of them began to drift about the decks in a kind of trance, staring at the unfamiliar surroundings and listening bemusedly to the clamour that was rising from the circling bumboats.

They needed to be taken in hand, Kesri knew, but before he could do anything about it a team of surgeons and medical attendants arrived, to oversee the evacuation of the wounded. In the confusion of the moment Kesri forgot to order the men to go below. This was an unfortunate omission; later he would curse himself for having allowed the men to witness the evacuation.

Very few of the evacuees were in a condition to use the usual facilities for debarkation. Neither the side-ladders nor even the swing-lift would serve for the seriously injured so a special crane was set up to winch them down to the waiting boats in a hanging litter.

The agonized screams of the injured fifers, as they were transferred from their pallets to the litter, were harrowing enough to listen to; worse by far was what happened when it came time for the injured punditji to be moved. He was carried out of the infirmary in an immobile condition, lying prone on a pallet. When his litter was hoisted off the deck, he sat suddenly erect, like a puppet jerked up by the tug of a string. Raking the maindeck with wild, bloodshot eyes, he uttered a bone-chilling shriek, calling out the name of the god of death, Yamaraj.

By the time his litter reached the boat the punditji was dead.

*

Soon after the *Hind* dropped anchor Zadig hired a sampan and went off to look for Robin Chinnery. He was gone for what seemed to Shireen an inordinately long time. But just as she was beginning to worry, he returned, full of good cheer.

Everything was settled, he told Shireen; the house that Robin had found for Shireen, in Macau, was ready and waiting.

Shireen gave a sigh of relief. 'That is very good news, Zadig Bey. I hope you thanked Robin for me? I was beginning to think that something had gone wrong.'

Zadig was quick to apologize: it had taken him a long time to locate the *Redruth*, he said, and he had found Robin in a great state – it turned out that he was preparing to sail northwards, with the British fleet.

'But why?' said Shireen in surprise. 'Has he joined the navy?'

This drew a great guffaw from Zadig. 'No, Bibiji, Robin is the least martial of men. He is actually going along as an artist. He tells me that it is quite the thing nowadays for armies to be accompanied by painters so that their exploits and victories can be recorded for posterity. A colonel has invited him and it is too good an opportunity to be refused. Robin will set sail tomorrow.'

'What a pity,' said Shireen in disappointment. 'I would have liked to meet him.'

'He would have liked to meet you too, Bibiji. In Canton, during the opium crisis, he was often at Bahram-bhai's house. He wanted to offer his condolences but unfortunately there's no time today. He sends his salaams and says he will come to see you on his return. So will his friend, Paulette.'

'She was there too?'

'Yes, Bibiji – and she too will come to see you some day. She was at Hong Kong you know, when Bahram's body was found.'

'Oh?' said Shireen. 'I didn't know that. What an odd coincidence.'

'No, Bibiji, not really. Paulette spends a lot of time on the island.'

Zadig turned to point in the direction of Hong Kong. 'Do you see that tall mountain over there? That is where Paulette's guardian, Mr Penrose, has set up a nursery, for his collection of plants. Since Mr Penrose is rather infirm, it is Paulette who takes care of it: she goes there every day.'

'On her own?'

'Yes, Bibiji, she often goes on her own. She dresses up in breeches and a jacket and no one gives her any trouble. She was up there that day when Bahram died. The nursery has a very good view of the bay and the shore: Paulette noticed a great commotion and came hurrying down to the beach below the nursery. And there she found Vico, the munshi and some lascars from the *Anahita* gathered around Bahram's body.'

Shireen fell silent, resting her eyes on the looming island. 'I would like to talk to her, Zadig Bey.'

'I'm sure an opportunity will arise soon enough, Bibiji. She too is keen to meet you.'

*

Down in the shadows of the dimly lit cubicle, Raju listened numbly as Baboo Nob Kissin gave him the news: his father was no longer in Macau; he had gone off to Canton to take a job; he could not be contacted because the Pearl River was under blockade; even to try to send a message was fraught with risk, since it might bring down suspicion on his head – nonetheless, attempts would be made . . .

After listening for a while Raju broke in: *Apni chithi likhechhilen na?* You had written a letter to him, hadn't you? You had told him I was coming?

Yes, of course I had, said Baboo Nob Kissin. But my letter must not have reached him. He must have left Macau before it arrived. He was gone by the time I reached the coast; I have not been able to reach him since.

The explanation was lost on Raju, who turned on Baboo Nob Kissin as though he were personally to blame: But why? Why did he leave? Why didn't he wait?

Because he didn't know, said Baboo Nob Kissin. It's not his fault – how could he have imagined that you would set out in search of him? Had he known he would certainly have waited. We just have to send him word, somehow, and I am sure he will come for you.

But what am I to do till then? cried Raju in dismay. Where will I stay? With whom?

The boy's increasingly fraught tone alarmed Baboo Nob Kissin.

Listen, Raju, he said. Tomorrow I will be leaving to go north on the *Ibis* – Mr Reid will be the captain. You can come with us as a ship's boy if you want.

No! cried Raju, his eyes glistening. I don't want to move to another ship! I have friends on the *Hind* – why should I leave them? Isn't it enough that my father isn't here? Do you want me to lose my friends too?

Pierced by the note of accusation in his voice, Baboo Nob Kissin could only appeal to the heavens – *Hé Gobindo; hé Gopal!* Under his breath he cursed himself for having brought this calamity upon his own head: had he not sought out the boy and his mother, in Calcutta, he wouldn't have had this problem on his hands.

As so often in his life, the decision had been made for Baboo Nob Kissin by Ma Taramony, his guiding spirit. Having long regarded Neel with a maternal eye, she had decided that it was imperative for Baboo Nob Kissin to visit his wife, on his return from China to Calcutta: it was his duty, she had told him, to tell the unfortunate woman that her husband was still alive and would return some day, to take her and Raju away from Calcutta.

Although Baboo Nob Kissin had had his reservations, he had obeyed Ma Taramony's instructions in the belief that the matter would end there. Not for a moment had it occurred to him that he was in danger of being set upon by a wilful and headstrong boy who, on hearing the news, would proceed to beg, cajole and demand that he, Baboo Nob Kissin, a mere messenger, assist him in his quest to seek out his father.

Baboo Nob Kissin had protested to the best of his ability but his resistance had been hindered by an unfortunate quirk of his character: a besetting fear of children. Although more than a match for wily seths and ruthless zamindars, the gomusta was incapable of resisting the importunities of a child – not because of the softness of his heart but out of a deep dread of the terrible power of their powerlessness. When the look in their wide, expressive eyes turned to anger or disappointment, they seemed to him to be gifted with the ability to inflict all kinds of injuries. There was little he would not do to escape their maledictions – and somehow Raju had seemed to be aware of this and had turned it to his advantage, besieging him with pleas, entreaties, cajoleries and veiled threats.

Nor had the boy's mother done anything to restrain her son; to the contrary, she had added her own pleas to her son's: There is nothing for Raju in Calcutta; she had said. He has grown restless and I can no longer manage him. He will go to the bad if he remains here; it is best for him to fulfil his heart's desire and go off to search for his father.

So Baboo Nob Kissin had agreed to foist the boy on Zachary, fully trusting all the while that Neel was still in Macau and would be able to take charge of his son.

And now this . . .

Look, Raju, said Baboo Nob Kissin. I warned you at the outset that it would be difficult. It was you who were adamant that you wanted to come, no matter what. Now, you must be patient: I will arrange something, I promise, but you must wait.

At this, a look of exactly the kind that Baboo Nob Kissin most dreaded – wide, wounded and filled with disappointment – entered the boy's eye: Wait? How long?

Flustered, the gomusta rose to his feet: I don't know – and anyway I have to go now, to see Mr Doughty. While I am gone you should think about what you want to do.

Baboo Nob Kissin disappeared, leaving Raju huddled in a corner.

Through misted eyes the boy saw again the scene of his father's arrest, at their family home, in Calcutta, two years before. They had been flying kites together, on a terrace, when their steward came up to say that the Chief Constable had arrived, with a squad of armed men. Raju remembered how his father had told him to wait on the terrace; he would be back in ten minutes. So Raju had stayed there, waiting, even after his father was taken away, in a carriage.

He was aware now of a cold, empty sense of abandonment – a feeling very similar to what he had felt then, except that he was two years older now and no longer trusted in promises. He knew that he could not wait for Baboo Nob Kissin or anyone else to decide his fate: until such time as he was reunited with his father he would have to take his destiny into his own hands. But to know this only made things worse – for he had not the faintest inkling of where to go next or what to do.

Then came a familiar knocking, on the planks of wood that separated the cubicle from the camp-followers' cumra. It was followed by Dicky's voice: 'Arré Raju? You're still here, is it?'

'Yes.'

'What-happen? I thought you were leaving for that place – Makoo or something.'

'No can't, ya. Uncle has gone off somewhere.'

'So what you will do now?'

'Don't know, ya.'

There was a silence and then Dicky said: 'Arré you know something? You can always join our squad, no? We need more fifers, ya; I heard the fife-major talking about it only today.'

*

Daylight was fading when the officers returned from their meeting on the *Wellesley*. The subalterns came bounding up the *Hind*'s side-ladder, talking excitedly, with an exuberant young cornet leading the way.

'Just our luck to be left out of the action . . . !'

'Oh how I should have liked to bag my first slantie . . .'

Captain Mee came up last, but his voice was the loudest of all: 'And you can be sure that those bloody bog-trotters will never leave off blarneying about their little adventures up north . . .'

Listening to them Kesri understood that the Bengal Volunteers had been spared an immediate deployment. This was welcome news: after everything they had been through lately the unit was in no condition to face another voyage, even less to go into action. He could only hope that they would soon be sent ashore, to a camp on dry land.

Later that evening, when he was summoned to Captain Mee's cabin for a briefing, Kesri learnt that he had guessed correctly: most of the expedition's troops would be proceeding northwards the next day, to be deployed at Chusan. But B Company was to remain where it was – on the *Hind*, in the general proximity of Hong Kong. Along with a detachment of Royal Marines they were to provide protection for the merchant fleet and for all British subjects in the area.

'It's a pity we're going to miss the action,' said Captain Mee. 'But the high command has decided that we need time to recover from our voyage.'

'Some extra time will be good, Kaptán-sah'b,' said Kesri quietly.

Captain Mee shot him a quizzical glance. 'Why, havildar? What's on your mind?'

For Kesri the most worrying thing was the shortfall in camp-followers: without a full contingent of gun-lascars he knew it would be difficult to make good use of their mortars and howitzers.

'We have lost too many followers, Kaptán-sah'b. Gun-lascars especially – more are needed.'

'Well I don't know that there's anything to be done about that,' said Captain Mee. 'We aren't likely to find any gun-lascars here.'

'Sir, maybe we can recruit some sailors instead?'

'At a pinch perhaps,' said the captain. 'If you see any likely fellows let me know.'

'Yes, sir,' said Kesri. 'And when will we move ashore, sir? Do you know?'

Captain Mee's answer came as a disappointment.

'We're to remain on the *Hind* for the time being, havildar. It's up to Captain Smith of the *Volage* to decide – he's been placed in overall charge of the southern sector.'

Unrolling a chart, Captain Mee pointed to their location. Kesri saw that the Pearl River estuary was shaped like an inverted funnel, with the stem pointing north. The island of Hong Kong and the promontory of Macau were at opposite ends of the funnel's rim, forty miles apart. The *Hind* was currently positioned closer to Macau, but Captain Mee told him that they would soon be moving to Hong Kong Bay, where most of the British merchant fleet was at anchor.

Slowly the captain's fingertip moved up the chart, through clusters of islands to the point where the bowl of the funnel met the stem.

'This here is the Bocca Tigris, havildar,' said the captain. 'Some call it the Bogue.'

Kesri had heard of this place from lascars: they spoke of it as Sher-ki-mooh – 'the Tiger's Mouth'.

'It's a heavily fortified position,' said Captain Mee. 'If there's any fighting in this sector, that's where it'll be.'

*

Bahram's grave was at the far edge of a bowl-like valley, encircled by steep ridges. They rented horses and a guide at a village called Sheng Wan, where they'd got off the boat that had brought them over to Hong Kong. The guide explained to Freddie that the grave was in an area known as Wang nai Cheong or 'Happy Valley'. They made their way there by following a coastal pathway to the eastern side of the bay. Then they turned left to climb over a ridge before descending into the valley.

The valley floor was carpeted with rice paddies, some of which were fed by a bamboo aqueduct. On one side of the valley was a nearly vertical rock-face, of weathered granite. Perched on top of this was a gigantic boulder, elliptical in shape. At the foot of the boulder lay a great heap of red paper flags and joss sticks. The guide told Freddie that the rock was known as 'the Harlot's Stone', and was visited by women who wanted to bear children.

Bahram's grave was at the other end of the valley: it was a modest stone structure, without any embellishments. The inscription on the gravestone had only the words: Bahramjee Nusserwanjee Moddie.

'We decided not to add anything else,' said Zadig apologetically. 'We were not sure what the family would want.'

Shireen nodded. 'Yes, it was for the best. We will add some verses from the Avesta when it's possible.'

Shireen began to murmur the Srosh-Baj prayer while Freddie laid out some offerings that he had brought with him, of fruit and flowers. He had said hardly a word all day and it was not until they were on their way back to Sheng Wan that he spoke.

'Don't be angry, ne, Bibiji,' he said. 'But I will not go with you to Macau.'

'But where will you go then?' said Shireen in surprise.

'I will stay here, in Sheng Wan village – there are rooms to rent, ne? Guide has told me so.'

'But why?'

Freddie's voice fell to a whisper. 'He is here, my father. I can feel him. He wants me to stay.'

Fourteen

With the arrival of the British force, rumours began to circulate that the Chinese authorities were offering bounties for the capture or killing of aliens. There were reports also of clashes between foreigners and villagers at various places around the mouth of the Pearl River.

The island of Hong Kong, however, remained an exception: it was one place where foreigners could wander more or less freely, without fear of annoyance or molestation. Strangers had been visiting the island for many generations and over time the villagers had grown accustomed to having them in their midst; many had even learnt to profit from their presence, as for example the elder of Sheng Wan village who had rented Fitcher Penrose the plot of land for his nursery, on the slopes of the island's highest mountain.

It was not for its convenience that Fitcher had chosen the site: the path that led to it started at a secluded beach and wound steeply upwards, doubling back and forth across a number of spurs and nullahs. The ascent was so taxing that Fitcher, whose ageing bones were often racked by attacks of rheumatism, was sometimes unable to undertake the climb for weeks at a time.

But in some ways the height was also an advantage: Fitcher had noticed early on that the lower reaches of the island were marshy and infested with mosquitoes, while the higher slopes were relatively free of insects. In addition, the soil was richer up there and water was plentiful too because of a stream that came gurgling down from the elevated spine of the island. Being nestled inside a hollow the site was also sheltered from storms.

The magnificent views offered by the location, of Hong Kong Bay and of Kowloon, on the mainland, were of no moment to Fitcher, who was chronically short-sighted. But to Paulette they mattered a great deal: the vistas that opened up on the walk to the nursery were so enchanting that she even relished the steep climb.

To the islanders the mountain was known as Taiping Shan – 'Peaceful Mountain' – and so far as Paulette was concerned the name could not have been better chosen: the slope was a serenely tranquil setting and in all the time she had spent there she had never had the least cause to fear for her own safety. While at the nursery she always felt perfectly secure, not least because the two gardeners who had been hired to work there were a friendly, middle-aged couple from Sheng Wan: so reassuring was their presence that Paulette never felt the need to carry any weapons.

But after the arrival of the British fleet there was a change in the atmosphere: when rumours of attacks on foreigners began to circulate, Fitcher insisted that she carry pistols with her. She decided to indulge him, knowing that it would set his mind at rest – but still, she never imagined that there would come a day when she might actually have reason to be glad that she was armed. But so it did.

It happened at the end of a day's work, when Paulette was heading back from the nursery. On reaching the beach where the *Redruth*'s longboat was to meet her, she found an odd-looking stranger sitting on the sand, with his arms wrapped around his knees.

It was rare for that beach to attract visitors and the few who came were usually local fishermen. But this man appeared to be a foreigner: he was dressed in trowsers, a shabby jacket and a hat.

In the meantime he too had spotted her and risen to his feet. She saw now that even though he was dressed in European clothes he was not a white man, as she had thought – the cast of his countenance was distinctly Chinese. He was no longer young, yet not quite in middle age, with sunken cheeks and eyes, and a wispy beard. There was something unkempt and a little disturbing about his appearance; Paulette was concerned enough that she opened the flap of her satchel, so that her pistols would be in easy reach.

Then a look entered the man's eye that sent a jolt through her, reminding her of another encounter at that beach, the year before. Then too she had been recognized by someone who had sparked not the faintest glimmer of recognition in her own eyes.

'Miss Paulette?'

Raising his hat, the man bowed, in such a manner that the greeting was at once both European and Chinese.

'Forgive me,' said Paulette. 'Do I know you?'

'My name is Ephraim Lee,' he said gravely, holding his hat over his chest. 'People call me Freddie. But maybe you remember me by another name, lah? Ah Fatt – from the *Ibis*.'

Ciel! Paulette's hand flew to her mouth, which had fallen open in amazement. 'But how did you recognize me?'

He smiled. 'The *Ibis* – it has tied us all together in strange ways, ne?'

She had only set eyes on him from afar before, and the thing she remembered about his appearance was a vague sense of menace, exuded not just by his angular, unsmiling face, but also by the sinuous vigour of his musculature. But she could see none of that menace now, either in his face or in the way he carried himself – rather it was he who seemed to be menaced, hunted.

'What brings you here, Mr Lee?'

'For a long time I have been looking for this place, eh, Miss Paulette.'

'Oh? You had been here before perhaps?'

He shook his head. 'No. But I had seen it, ne?' He said it as though it were self-evident.

'How? When?'

'In dreams. When I saw it today, I recognized – I knew, this was where the body of Mr Bahram Moddie was found. You were there that day, ne? Mr Karabedian, my godfather, he tell me so.'

Suddenly Paulette remembered that this man was the natural son of Mr Moddie: Neel had mentioned this the morning the body was found.

'I am sorry for your loss, Mr Lee.'

He acknowledged this by tipping his hat. As he was making the gesture Paulette noticed that there was a distinct tremor in his hand. He too seemed to be aware of it, for he put his hands together, as if to steady them. Then he inclined his head towards a shaded spot, under an overhang of rock. 'Miss Paulette – maybe we can sit there for a few minutes? Maybe you can tell me what you saw that day, eh? When my father's body was found?'

She could see no reason to object: 'Yes, I will tell you what I remember.'

They seated themselves on a patch of wild grass and she told him how she had come down to the beach that day, to find a group of men, Indians, kneeling around a bare-bodied corpse. To her surprise, one of them had come towards her, with a look of recognition in his eye.

'Neel?'

'Yes, Neel – but he told me not to use that name.'

He nodded and fell silent. After a while, in a voice that was taut with apprehension, he said: 'Miss Paulette, one thing I would like to ask you. That morning, lah, did you see a ladder, hanging from my father's ship?'

With a start Paulette realized that she had omitted this important detail – the dangling rope-ladder that had drawn her eye to the *Anahita* that morning. The sight had puzzled her: why would a ladder be left dangling above the water? Who could have used it and for what?

'Yes, there was a ladder,' she said. 'I saw it hanging from the stern of Mr Moddie's ship. How did you know?'

'I see it too sometimes,' he said. 'In my dreams, lah.'

Turning towards her he asked, in a shaky voice: 'Miss Paulette, will you mind if I smoke, eh?'

'No.' She thought he would take out a wad of tobacco – but instead he reached into his jacket and pulled out a long pipe and a small brass box.

All at once everything fell into place: the quivers, the twitching, the gauntness of his face. She understood that he was an addict, and withdrew slightly. Yet her gaze was drawn back towards him with a new curiosity.

In the last few weeks, ever since she received Zachary's letter, Paulette had given a great deal of thought to opium and its curative properties. The letter had come as a terrible shock: it wasn't only that she had been wounded by it; she had also been forced to ask herself whether her fondest hopes and beliefs were nothing but delusions and pipe-dreams. She had remembered how, on reaching Mauritius, she had gone to the Botanical Gardens at Pamplemousses, to wait for Zachary; she remembered her joy when she found the garden abandoned and overgrown – this, it had seemed to her, was an Eden after her own heart, where she would happily await her Adam. She had decided that theirs would be a romance to surpass even that of Paul and Virginie, whose fate had so often moved her to tears – for their love would be freely and willingly consummated. Here, in this garden, she would joyfully take Zachary into her arms and they would be wedded under the stars, in body and in soul, on an island of their own imagining, far from the imprisoning imperatives of the world, their fates decided only by their own volition, their bodies joined together by that ecstatic, vital urgency that was the true and pure essence of life itself.

She had wandered through the abandoned house of the Garden's former curator until she came to a room that she knew would be the perfect setting for their first night together. On the floor she had made a nest, not a bed – because in Eden, surely, there were no beds? – and she had strewn flowers over the sheets and hung garlands of boys-love on the windows. She remembered how she had wept that night and the next, and the next, when Zachary had not come; and yet those nights had not been lost either, because she had reimagined them many times in her mind's eye – when she pictured herself seeing Zachary again, it was always on an island, with both of them in shirts and breeches, running hungrily towards each other.

There was a time when she had joyfully embraced these memories – but after receiving Zachary's letter, with its unexplained repudiation; after trying and failing to understand what could have caused his change of heart, she had come to be filled with shame, and also a loathing of her own foolishness and naïveté, a feeling so intense that she had longed to find some escape. She watched in fascination now as Freddie roasted a tiny droplet of opium and inhaled the smoke. She saw that its effect was almost immediate: his twitch disappeared and his hands seemed steadier. He closed his eyes and took a few deep breaths before he spoke again.

'Miss Paulette, why a ladder, lah? What was it for?'

'I don't know,' she said. 'I too have wondered what it was for.'

He smiled dreamily. 'When *Anahita* comes back maybe then we find out, ne?'

'Is the *Anahita* coming back?'

'Yes,' he said. 'Is coming – I have seen it in dreams.'

They sat for a while in companionable silence: for the first time since she had received Zachary's letter Paulette felt at peace. She sensed in Freddie a void far deeper than that which the letter had created in her, and it conjured up a powerful sense of kinship, overlaying the bond that already existed between them, the bond of the *Ibis*.

Had there been time she might have asked for a taste of his opium pipe – but just then she spotted the *Redruth*'s longboat, coming to fetch her from the island.

*

A week after the fleet's departure for the north, Kesri learnt that Captain Smith, the CO of the southern sector, had decided that it was time for the Bengal sepoys to leave the *Hind*: they were to set up camp on an island called Saw Chow.

Kesri received the news with whole-hearted relief – after so many months on the *Hind* nothing could be more welcome than the prospect of a move to dry land. But his jubilation ebbed when he went to the island for an exploratory visit, with Captain Mee.

Saw Chow was not far from Hong Kong: it lay halfway up the Pearl River estuary, in a cove that was known as Tangku Bay to foreigners. To the south lay the crag of Lintin island; to the north was the promontory of Tangku, where a detachment of Chinese soldiers could be seen going through their drills. Saw Chow itself was a desolate, windswept little island: there were no trees on its three shallow hills, and scarcely any vegetation either. A less hospitable place was hard to imagine, but orders were orders so they had no choice but to make the best of it.

They picked a site in a hollow between two hills and marked out the lines for the sepoys' and officers' tents. The next day a team of khalasis, thudni-wallahs, dandia-porters and tent-pitchers went over to set up the camp. A few days later the whole unit moved over to the island, sepoys, camp-followers and all, with their baggage, equipment and armaments.

Once installed in the camp, their lives settled quickly into a routine of drills and inspections in the early morning: the rest of the day was spent in waiting out the heat as best they could, under the scant cover of their canvas tents.

Every few days the officers would escape to Macau or Hong Kong Bay, but for the sepoys and camp-followers there was no such relief: for them the island was a prison-camp, a place of grinding monotony and discomfort. Other than occasional visits from bumboats there were no diversions.

One day, trying to think of ways to relieve the tedium, Kesri came up with the idea of digging a wrestling pit. Captain Mee readily gave his approval and Kesri went to work immediately: with the help of a few sepoys and camp-followers he dug a pit in a spot that looked across the sparkling blue waters of the estuary. It took a few days to properly prepare the soil, by mixing it with turmeric, oil and ghee; when the pit was ready Kesri inaugurated it himself, with a prayer to Hanumanji.

Once again, the pit had just the effect that Kesri had hoped for, channelling energies, creating camaraderie, and giving the men something to look forward to every day. If anything the impact here was even greater than at Calcutta, for Kesri made sure that the camp-followers were allowed to participate, sweepers, dhobis, barbers and all. Some of the sepoys were put out by this but Kesri silenced them by citing the inviolable ethic of the akhara, in which worldly rank had no place and all men were considered equal. As for the objection that the camp-followers would not be able to match the sepoys in strength, this too was quickly disproved: several of the gun-lascars, golondauzes and bhishtis were large, brawny men, more than able to hold their own in the pit.

Soon word of the pit spread beyond the island and one day a few Royal Marines came across and asked to participate. But it turned out that they were interested in the Angrezi kind of pugilism – mainly boxing, a form of combat that was abhorrent to Kesri, who saw it as no better than mere *marpeet* or brawling. Kesri told the marines that if they wanted to enter this pit they would have to abide by its rules. They took this in good spirit and became welcome additions to the widening circle of wrestlers.

One day, on returning from a visit to Hong Kong Bay, Captain Mee announced that a young Parsi merchant had just arrived from Manila, on his own ship: amongst his crew there was a lascar who was said to be a trained wrestler. The young Parsi was a great lover of sport and was keen to see how his lascar fared in the pit.

It so happened that the festival of Nag Panchami was just a few days away. This being an occasion of great significance for wrestlers Kesri had planned a tournament to mark the day: only the more accomplished wrestlers were to participate in this special dangal. He told Captain Mee that the lascar was welcome to try his luck.

The dangal was well under way when a cutter, rowed by a dozen oarsmen, drew up. A square-jawed, broad-shouldered young man got out and went to shake hands with Captain Mee – he was dressed in Western clothes and to Kesri's eye he looked every inch an Angrez. But when Captain Mee brought him over Kesri understood that he was the Parsi shipowner whose lascar had been invited to join the dangal: his name was Dinyar Ferdoonjee.

After exchanging a few words with Kesri, the young merchant gestured in the direction of his cutter: the wrestler, he said, was one of the oarsmen on his boat. There was no need to point the man out: even while seated he towered over the other rowers. When he started to rise it was as though his body were slowly unfolding, like a ladder with multiple sections. Once he was fully upright his shoulders were seen to be almost as broad as the boat; as for the oar, it looked like a piece of kindling in his hands. Unlike most lascars, he was dressed not in jama-pyjamas but in grey trowsers and a white shirt, which contrasted vividly with his dark skin. His head was of a piece with his frame, square, broad and massive – but as if to compensate for his intimidating dimensions, the expression on his face was one of extreme forbearance and gentleness. In his gait too there was a shambling quality which led Kesri to think that he might be slow of movement, and that his size and weight might be used against him in the pit.

But after he had stripped down to his wrestling drawers the lascar's demeanour underwent an abrupt change. Kesri watched him carefully as he was loosening up by slapping his arms and chest: his performance of these *dand-thonk* exercises was impressively fluid and supple. When he stepped into the ring, his stance was as fine as any that Kesri had seen: perfectly balanced, with his head poised over his leading leg, the chin in exact alignment with his knee.

The lascar's first opponent was a muscular young sepoy, one of Kesri's best students. The sepoy had recently mastered a move called *sakhi* and he tried it just as the bout was beginning, lunging for the lascar's right arm while trying to throw him over by hooking his knee with his foot.

But the lascar countered effortlessly, blocking the foot and pivoting smoothly into the attack, with a hold that Kesri recognized as a perfectly executed *dhak*. Within seconds the sepoy was pinned and the bout was over.

The next to enter the ring was a powerfully built marine: his best move was a throw called the *kalajangh* which was intended to flip the opponent over, by sliding under his chest and grabbing hold of his thigh. It was a common move and Kesri guessed that the lascar would know a *pech* with which to counter it. This proved to be exactly the case. The marine found himself grappling with thin air when he made his lunge; a moment later he was down on his belly, vainly trying to prevent himself from being rolled over.

The curious thing was that the lascar seemed to take little pleasure in his victories: instead of making a winning pehlwan's customary gestures of triumph he hung his head, as if in embarrassment. This encouraged a couple of others to try their luck; but they fared no better than those who had gone before them: the lascar pinned them both, displaying in the process a mastery of complicated moves like the *bhakuri* and *bagal dabba*.

At this point Kesri could feel the eyes of his men turning to him, as if to see whether he would salvage their honour by entering the pit himself. He could not disappoint them – besides, he was curious to see how he would fare against the lascar. Murmuring a prayer to Hanumanji he stepped into the pit.

For a couple of minutes Kesri and the lascar circled experimentally, feinting, each trying to trick the other into a hasty move. Then Kesri went on the attack, with a *multani*, spinning around on his back foot and trying to come at the lascar from the rear. Instead it was the lascar who ended up behind him, forcing him into a defensive crouch.

In the past Kesri had sometimes turned this position to his advantage by using the *dhobi pât* – a move in which the opponent was hauled over the shoulder, in the manner of a dhobi beating clothes. But it turned out that the lascar knew the counter-move for this too. All of a sudden Kesri was sprawled on his back, struggling to keep his shoulders off the ground.

Sensing that the pin was near, the lascar stuck his shoulder into Kesri's chest as he prepared to bring his full weight to bear. Their faces were now less than a foot apart, and suddenly their eyes met and locked. Now, just as the lascar was about to make the final thrust, an extraordinary thing happened: he was jolted into easing his grip – it was as if he had looked into Kesri's eyes and seen something that he could not quite believe. All at once the fight went out of him and the relentless pressure that he had been exerting lessened. Kesri seized his chance and flipped him over: a second later he had the pin.

The reversal of fortune was so inexplicable that it left Kesri feeling strangely grateful to the lascar: he would not have liked to lose in front of his own men and was glad to have been spared that fate. But he knew also that the lascar was the better wrestler and later, when they were out of the ring he asked: What happened? *Kya hua?*

Even though he had asked in Hindustani, the lascar answered in Kesri's own mother tongue: *Hamaar saans ruk goel* – I just lost my breath.

Taken by surprise, Kesri said: *tu bhojpuri kahā se sikhala?* Where did you learn Bhojpuri? Where are you from?

The lascar told him that he had been brought up in Ghazipur, in a Christian orphanage; his name came from the surnames of two priests: Maddow Colver.

Ghazipur? said Kesri: for him that town was indelibly linked to his sister Deeti. Do you mean the town with the opium factory?

Yes, that very one.

Kesri fell silent, seized by a strange sense of affinity with the man: that they were both wrestlers, that their paths had crossed on Nag Panchami, that they both had associations with Ghazipur – all of this seemed to imply that their fates were somehow intertwined.

All of a sudden a thought came to Kesri and he said to the lascar: *Sunn* – listen, my unit needs some strong men to haul our heavy guns. Would you be willing to join us? Just for the time that we are here? The pay will be good.

The man took his time in answering, looking towards the sea and scratching his head before turning back to Kesri.

Yes, he said at last, with a slow, thoughtful nod; if you can arrange it and if my present employer agrees, I will join you.

*

Zachary's return to the *Ibis* was like a homecoming.

This was the vessel on which he had shipped out from Baltimore, as a novice seaman, a ship's carpenter. Now, three years later, here he was boarding her again, as the skipper! The change was so great as to suggest the intervention of some other-wordly power: as a sailor Zachary knew that certain ships possess their own minds, even souls – and he did not doubt that the *Ibis* had conspired in making his transformation possible.

Nor was he surprised when the *Ibis* seemed to recognize him, bobbing her bowsprit up and down, as if in welcome. Yet, amongst the crew there was not a single face that was familiar to him. The lascars who had sailed with him on his earlier voyages were all gone; the new crew had been recruited in Singapore and consisted mainly of Malays and Manila-men. The mates too were strangers to Zachary: one was a tall, taciturn Finn and the other a dour Dutchman from Batavia. There wasn't much they could say to each other, beyond what was required for the running of the schooner. But this was soon discovered to be a blessing; lacking the words to run afoul of each other, they got on very well.

Zachary's instructions were to sail north in convoy with a couple of other opium-carrying vessels, a bark and a brigantine. Both belonged to Free-Traders, the older of whom was a Scotsman by the name of Philip Fraser. Youthful, soft-spoken and always fastidiously clothed, Mr Fraser looked more like a doctor than a sea-captain. It turned out that he had indeed studied medicine at Edinburgh before coming east to join his uncle, who was a well-established figure in the China trade. Being the most experienced of the three skippers he became, by tacit agreement, the leader of their little convoy. It was Mr Fraser who led their Sunday prayers and it was he too who taught them the special code that China coast opium-sellers had started to use, to dupe the mandarins in case their account books were seized by customs officials.

For the first two days the three ships sailed in the wake of the expeditionary fleet as it headed northwards. On the fourth day, at a pre-arranged signal from Mr Fraser, they broke away and turned eastwards. Heading towards the port of Foochow, they hove to just over the horizon; here, said Mr Fraser, they could safely wait for buyers without fear of official harassment – Chinese mandarin-junks rarely ventured so far out to sea. Pirates were a greater concern, but Mr Fraser was confident that they too would steer clear of these waters for fear of the British fleet. Still, for the sake of prudence it was decided that they would mount careful watch through the night, with their guns at the ready.

In the evening the three captains assembled on Mr Fraser's brigantine, for dinner, each bringing with him a few chests of opium. It was agreed that if boats approached, it would be left to Mr Fraser to decide whether they belonged to bona fide buyers; if so, he would negotiate prices on behalf of all three of them. The other two skippers were to remain on their vessels with their guns primed and ready, in case of trouble.

But in the event, no shooting was called for – the transactions of the night were remarkably quick and easy. Around midnight lights were seen approaching from a north-westerly direction. They were the lanterns of a 'fast crab', a kind of boat much favoured by dealers on the mainland. Mr Fraser's linkister hailed the boat and an agreement was quickly reached. The entire operation, including the transfer of three dozen chests of opium, was over in less than an hour.

Later, when Zachary went to collect his share of the proceeds, he discovered that the chests had fetched more than any of them had dared hope: fourteen hundred Spanish dollars each. Giddy with exultation, he realized that he was now in possession of a fortune large enough to buy a ship like the *Ibis*. 'Who bought the chests?' he said, and Mr Fraser explained that the buyer was an agent for one of the leading wholesalers of opium on the China coast – a man known to fanquis as Lynchong or Lenny Chan.

'He's quite a character,' said Mr Fraser, with a laugh, 'is our Lenny Chan. To look at him you'd think he was a grand mandarin, full of conceit and frippery. But he speaks English like an Englishman, and a Londoner at that.'

Lenny Chan's story was as singular as you could wish, said Mr

Fraser. As a boy, in Canton, he'd worked as a servant for one Mr Kerr, an English flower-hunter. After a few years Mr Kerr had sent him to London, as the caretaker of a collection of plants. Lenny had stayed on at Kew, spending many years there before coming back to Canton to start his own nursery. Branching out into the 'black mud' business, he had succeeded in building up one of the largest retail networks in southern China.

But things had changed for Lenny the year before, after Commissioner Lin came to Canton: he had had to flee the city because of the Yum-chae's crackdown on opium – his premises had been raided and a huge reward had been offered for his head. But Lenny, ever resourceful, had managed to slip away to the outer islands, to rebuild his network offshore.

After the proceeds had been divided Mr Fraser sent for a bottle of brandy and the three skippers talked for a while. Mainly it was Mr Fraser who spoke, in his quiet, reasoned way. What he had to say was so compelling, so persuasive, that Zachary listened spellbound.

To blame the British for the opium trade was completely misguided, said Mr Fraser. The demand came from Chinese buyers and if the British did not meet it then others would. It was futile to try to hinder the flow of a substance for which there was so great a hunger. Individuals and nations could no more control this commodity than they could hold back the ocean's tides: it was like a natural phenomenon – a flood. Its flow was governed by abstract laws like those that Mr Newton had applied to the movements of the planets. These laws ensured that supply would match demand as surely as water always seeks its own level.

It was misguided, even sinful, said Mr Fraser, of the Chinese government to cite the public good in opposing the free flow of opium. The truth was that the best – indeed the only – way that the public good could be arrived at was to allow all men to pursue their own interests as dictated by their judgement. This was why God had endowed Man with the faculty of reason: only when men were free to justly calculate their own advancement did the public good – or, for that matter, material advancement, or social harmony – come about. Indeed, the only true virtue was rational self-love, and when this was allowed to flourish freely it resulted, of itself, in a condition vastly more just and beneficial than anything that any government could accomplish.

If there was any country on earth, said Mr Fraser, that stood in breach of these doctrines it was China, with its subservience to authority and its minute control of everyday matters. Only with the destruction of their present institutions, only with the abandonment of their ways and customs, could the people of this benighted realm hope to achieve harmony and happiness. This indeed was the historic destiny of Free-Traders like themselves; opium was but another article of trade, and by ensuring its free flow they were promoting the future good of China.

Some day, following the example of men like themselves, said Mr Fraser, the Chinese too would take to Free Trade: being an industrious people, they were sure to prosper. Of all the lessons the West could teach them, this was the most important. And inasmuch as traders like themselves were helping the Chinese to learn this lesson, they were their friends, not their enemies. From this it followed that the more vigorous and persistent they were in selling opium the more praiseworthy their conduct, the more benevolent their friendship.

'It is all for their own good after all: China has no better friends than us!'

Zachary raised his glass. 'Well said, Mr Fraser! Let us drink to that!'

*

The house that Robin Chinnery had rented for Shireen was on a hill, in the centre of Macau. It was one of a row of 'shop-houses', flanking a sloping lane – Rua Ignacio Baptista.

The house reminded Shireen of the old Parsi homes of Navsari, in Gujarat: it was long and narrow, with a tiled roof and a small open courtyard at the back. Although sparsely furnished the rooms were cosy enough and it did not take long for Shireen and Rosa to settle in.

As it happened, this was a part of town that Rosa knew well: the São Lorenço Church, where she worshipped, was nearby, as was the Misericordía, where she worked during the day. Also very close was the part of town where soldiers and funçionarios from Goa were quartered, with their families. Rosa was well known to

376

the community, and her friends and acquaintances extended a warm welcome to Shireen as well. Much sooner than she would have thought possible, Shireen felt herself to be perfectly at home in Macau.

Often, at teatime, Zadig would come by; he was lodging with an Armenian merchant, a few streets away. He and Shireen would sometimes go for walks together, strolling through the town's winding lanes to the Praya Grande – a sweeping bayside corniche, lined with luxurious villas.

As they walked, Zadig Bey would fill her in on all the latest news.

The north-bound British fleet had called at the ports of Amoy and Ningpo on their way to Chusan. At every stop they had tried to hand over Lord Palmerston's letter to the Emperor, outlining Britain's demands and grievances, but the task had proved impossibly difficult: no one would accept it. The British emissaries had been repeatedly rebuffed by the mandarins of the ports they had visited; on a couple of occasions hostilities had broken out.

At Chusan the fleet had entered the harbour to find a small fleet of war-junks at anchor there. The Plenipotentiaries had tried to persuade the local defence forces to surrender without a fight, but to no avail. The Chinese commanders had declared that they would resist, come what may, so the British warships had lined up for battle and opened fire. In exactly nine minutes they had destroyed the Chinese fleet and all the defences along the island's shore. The troops of the expeditionary force had landed without any further opposition and the next day they had seized the island's capital, the city of Ting-hae. The Union Jack had been raised above the city and a British colonel had been given command of the island's civil administration.

Everything had gone exactly as Commodore Bremer and Captain Elliot had planned.

*

Around the middle of July 1840, no doubt because of the pressure of events, Neel's journal entries became a series of hasty jottings, written mainly in Bangla but sometimes in English as well.

It was around this time that officials in Guangzhou received

377

news of the seizure of Chusan and the fall of Ting-hae. It was then too that the city's officials learnt that a large number of British merchant vessels had accompanied the expeditionary fleet and were actively engaged in selling opium, up and down the coast.

These developments came as bitter blows to Commissioner Lin who had, even until then, nurtured the hope that a negotiated settlement, leading to a resumption of trade, would be worked out. But now, seeing that hostilities had already been launched by the British, he became convinced that the only way the opium trade could be brought to a halt was by wholly evicting the invaders from China. To that end notices were distributed along the coast offering rewards for the capture of enemy aliens. Not all foreigners fell under this head: Portuguese, Americans and some others were exempted. The notices were targeted solely at British subjects, which included Parsi merchants as well as Indian soldiers and sepoys.

Macau was the one place on the mainland where there was still a substantial British presence: it was there, if anywhere, that the notices were expected to produce results. And soon enough a courier came hurrying to Guangzhou to report that an Englishman had been captured in Macau, along with two Indian servants: they had been spirited into the mainland and were now in the custody of provincial officials.

The courier was sent back post haste: the captives were to be treated with the utmost consideration, wrote Commissioner Lin, and they were to be brought immediately to Guangzhou.

Over the next few days Guangzhou was swept by rumours: it was said that the captured Englishman was a personage of great consequence, possibly Commodore Bremer himself. This created much excitement, for the commodore had by this time achieved an almost mythic stature, being credited with all manner of demonic attributes: he was said to be fantastically tall, with burning eyes, an enormous mane of red hair and so on.

Much to everyone's disappointment the Englishman, on arrival, proved to be a short, slight young man, much given to striking extravagant poses, sometimes knitting his legs together as though in need of a chamber-pot, and sometimes rolling his eyes at the heavens, like a farmer yearning for rain. On questioning it turned out that his name was George Stanton, and that he was a twenty-three-year-old Christian evangelical who had interrupted his studies at Cambridge in order to save souls. Since there was no ordained clergyman in Macau he had claimed the preacher's pulpit for himself and had proceeded to deliver a series of sermons to the remnants of the city's English community.

Being a man of strict habits it was Mr Stanton's daily practice to bathe in the sea at sunrise, usually in the company of some other young men in whom he had tried to inculcate certain improving practices. It turned out that it was his diligence in this regard that had led to his capture: one morning Mr Stanton and his servants had arrived at Macau's Cacilhas beach to find it deserted. Mr Stanton had proceeded with his swim, as usual – and this was when a group of agents from the mainland had effected his capture, whisking him away in his still-wet breeches and banyan, along with his two servants.

It fell to Neel to question the two servants, whose names had been recorded by the captors as Chan-li and Chi-tu: it turned out that they were actually Chinnaswamy and Chhotu Mian, from the Madras and Bengal presidencies respectively. They were both in their late teens and had previously been employed as lascars, of the rank of kussab. They had entered Mr Stanton's service in Singapore where they had been stranded after a dispute with their former serang.

While corroborating Mr Stanton's account in a general sense the two lascars were emphatic in dissociating themselves from him, describing him as the worst, most foolish master that could be imagined, a complete ullu and paagal. He had made them rise before dawn every day to walk with him to the beach, all the while exhorting them to take cold baths themselves – this was the only sure method, he had assured them, of foiling the constant temptations of a horrible, debilitating disease.

It had taken them a long time to figure out what he was talking about and when they did, they had realized that he was completely insane. They had resolved to leave his service as soon as possible, but no opportunity for escape had arisen, and now here they were, captives in Guangzhou!

Bas! said Chhotu Mian with bitter relish. At least Stanton-sahib will get his punishment too. Without his bath he will be helpless, no? His hands will have no mercy on him.

But the lascars' satisfaction was misplaced: on Commissioner Lin's orders Mr Stanton was provided with excellent accommodation, in Canton's Consoo House. He was also given a Bible, writing materials and every facility that he desired.

As for Chinnaswamy and Chhotu Mian, on Neel's recommendation they were sent off to join Jodu, on the *Cambridge*.

After it had been determined that Mr Stanton was a person of no consequence there was no particular reason to detain him in Guangzhou. He would have been set free if the matter had not taken another turn: the Portuguese Governor of Macau sent a letter – evidently written under pressure from British officials – demanding Mr Stanton's immediate release, on the grounds that he had been illegally captured on Portuguese territory (of the lascars and their fate, Neel noticed, there was no mention).

The letter infuriated Commissioner Lin. This was not the first time he had been forced to remind the governor that Macau was not foreign territory but a sovereign part of China, on which the Portuguese had been allowed to settle as a special favour: he now decided that the time was ripe for an assertion of this principle. To that end a large squadron of war-junks was sent to Macau, through the inner channels of the Pearl River delta, in order to evade the British blockade. In addition a force of some five thousand troops was also sent down, to take up positions along the massive barrier wall that marked Macau's northern boundary.

All this happened very quickly, amidst an atmosphere of rising tension and uncertainty in Guangdong. Neel had a hazy idea that something significant was afoot but had no inkling of what it was. Then, on the morning of 14 August, Compton told him that Zhong Lou-si was proceeding towards Macau in person and had decided to include Neel in his entourage. Since Macau had a large number of people from Xiao Xiyang – Goa – it was thought that his services as a translator might be required.

Zhong Lou-si and his entourage left Guangzhou that afternoon. Their boat made its way southwards through the inland channels of the delta and brought them to their destination the next day. They landed slightly above the barrier that separated Macau from the rest of the mainland.

The barrier consisted of a heavily fortified wall that arced over the narrow but rugged isthmus that joined the mainland to Macau. On the mainland side the isthmus rose steeply, to a peak that commanded a panoramic view of the Portuguese settlement: from there the curved, tapering peninsula could be seen vanishing into the water like the tail of a gargantuan crocodile.

The area was familiar to Neel: during earlier visits to Macau he had often strolled up to the barrier. On a couple of occasions he had even walked through the gateway, advancing a good distance into the Province of Guangdong: in those days the customs house at the gate was but a sleepy little outpost; the guards would allow sightseers to go through in exchange for a few cash-coins.

Now, approaching the wall from the mainland side, Neel saw that the barrier's fortifications had been greatly strengthened: a large battery of cannon had been placed along the embrasures and a huge military encampment had appeared on the slope above, with rows of tents ranged behind fluttering banners.

Although Neel asked no questions it was evident to him that a military action was imminent.

*

When Kesri heard that a steamer had taken a group of officers – Captain Mee among them – to Macau for a reconnaissance mission, he guessed that a fight was in the offing. This was confirmed when the *Enterprize* came paddling back to Saw Chow: within a few minutes Kesri received a summons from Captain Mee.

'The men must be ready to embark early tomorrow morning,' the captain told Kesri. 'A transport vessel will come for us soon after dawn – the *Nazareth Shah*.'

At Macau the officers had seen much evidence of warlike preparations by the Chinese, said Captain Mee. They had deployed a large force just above the barrier; in addition a fleet of war-junks had appeared in the inner harbour. There was every sign that the Portuguese colony was shortly to be attacked, an eventuality that Captain Smith, the CO of the southern theatre, was determined to prevent. Accordingly he had decided to launch a pre-emptive action to disperse the Chinese forces. The ground attack was to be led by a detachment of one hundred and ten Royal Marines, supported by ninety armed seamen from the frigate *Druid*. The Bengal sepoys would accompany the assault force to provide support if needed. They would embark the next day with only a small detachment of essential camp-followers – gun-lascars, bhistis and a medical team; the sepoys' baggage was to be packed as per Light Marching Orders.

Kesri lost no time in summoning the company's naiks and lance-naiks: they had practised so many embarkation drills that everyone knew what had to be done.

Next morning reveille was sounded early but the *Enterprize* was late in arriving so the sepoys had to endure a long wait under the hot sun. But once the embarkation started it went off without mishap: towed by the *Enterprize*, the sepoys' transport ship drew close to the tip of the Macau promontory in the late afternoon. Several British vessels were already assembled there: two eighteen-gun corvettes, *Hyacinth* and *Larne*, a cutter, *Louisa*, a few longboats and the forty-four-gun frigate *Druid*.

Together the British vessels rounded the tip of the promontory and anchored in the Inner Harbour, on the western side of the city, facing the Praya Grande. Ranged opposite them, to the north, where the peninsula joined the mainland, were a dozen or more war-junks and a flotilla of smaller craft. It was evident to Kesri that these ungainly-looking vessels would be no match for modern warships, yet the very strangeness of their appearance, with castellations perched on the prow and stern, bred a certain disquiet, as did the inexplicable bursts of activity that broke out on their decks from time to time, accompanied by gongs, bells, clouds of smoke and massed voices, shouting in chorus. These peculiar outbursts put the sepoys' nerves on edge.

In the distance, on the ramparts of the Macau barrier, there was a large battery of cannons and ginjalls – tripod-mounted swivel guns, six to fourteen feet long. Beyond the barrier lay a steep slope on which hundreds of pennants and banners were fluttering in the breeze: Kesri reckoned that a few thousand men were bivouacked up there. After nightfall cooking-fires began to glow all over the slope, creating a curious, glimmering effect, like that of fireflies lighting up a tree. It was clear also, from the traceries of light that kept zigzagging across the campsite, that fresh orders were circulating constantly in the hands of runners with torches.

On the Chinese ships too there were signs that preparations were continuing through the night: the water's soft lapping was pierced every now and again by shouted commands and the sound of gongs.

When daylight broke it was seen that the war-junks had moved closer to the shore. They were anchored in a protective cluster around the projecting walls of the barrier. The battery on the battlements had also been augmented overnight and there were now some two dozen guns ranged along the parapet.

Through the morning Captain Mee and the other senior officers surveyed the defences, steaming back and forth, abreast of the shore, on the *Enterprize*. It was noon when the signal for the commencement of the attack was hoisted.

The operation began with the *Louisa*, the *Enterprize* and the two eighteen-gun corvettes converging on the barrier and taking up positions facing the Chinese vessels. The *Enterprize* went in so close to shore as to actually thrust her nose into the mud. Then, upon the hoisting of another signal, the warships opened fire from a range of six to eight hundred yards.

As the roar of cannon-fire rolled across the harbour flocks of waterbirds took wing, darkening the sky. Within minutes, the Chinese gunners were returning fire, even as cannonballs slammed into the battlements around them. For a while they kept up a spirited but erratic fusillade, with most of their shots sailing over their targets. Then, as the corvettes' thirty-two-pounders found their range, they began to fall silent, one by one, amidst explosions of shattered masonry and dismembered limbs.

Under cover of the bombardment the *Druid*'s marines and small-arms' men had already boarded a couple of longboats. Now, a signal went up on the frigate's foremast summoning the *Enterprize*. With a frantic churning of her paddle-wheels the steamer reversed out of the mud and turned her bows around. Pulling up to the *Druid*, she took the longboats in tow and went steaming past the barrier to the spot that had been chosen for the landing – a beach on the mainland part of the shoreline, from where the Chinese position could be attacked from the rear.

For a while the landing force disappeared from view, vanishing behind an outcrop in the shoreline. When Kesri next spotted the red-coated soldiers they were coming over the top of a spur, in double column, with the marines on the outer flank. Their position was exposed to the heights above as well as to battery on the barrier. Coming over the ridge they ran into heavy matchlock- and cannon-fire. Then detachments of Chinese troops began to advance on them from two sides.

Suddenly the British attack came to a halt. *Druid*'s small-arms' men had a field-piece with them but before they could assemble it the landing-party was ordered to fall back on the beach.

Even as the retreat was under way, another flag was hoisted on the *Druid*. Captain Mee took a look and turned to Kesri: 'The signal's up. We're to move forward to support the marines.'

Kesri snapped off a salute: Ji, Kaptán-sah'b.

The sepoys and their contingent of supporters were already on deck. The barrels of the howitzers and mortars, each of which weighed several hundred pounds, had been lowered into a cutter earlier; now the rest of the unit followed.

The camp-followers went first, led by the bhistis, their shoulders bowed by the weight of their water-filled mussucks; then came the medical attendants with rolled-up litters, and after them the gun-lascars, bearing the disassembled parts of a howitzer and its gun-carriage. Maddow, the newly recruited gun-lascar, was carrying a pair of hundred-pound wheels as if they were toys, one on each shoulder.

When the sepoys' turn came, Kesri positioned himself at the head of the side-ladder so that he could observe the men as they filed past: they were unblooded troops after all, going into action as a unit for the first time. As such Kesri would not have been surprised to detect signs of nervousness or distraction on their faces – but he saw saw none of those fleeting, uneasy movements of the eyes that were always a sure indication of skittishness. None of the sepoys so much as glanced at him as they stepped down the ladder: to a man their eyes were fixed on the knapsack ahead. It pleased Kesri to see them moving smoothly, like spokes in a wheel, with their minds not on themselves but on the unit: it meant that the hard work of the last many months had paid off, that their trust in him was so complete that they knew, even without looking, that he was there, his presence as certain and dependable as the hand-rail that was guiding them down the ladder and into the longboat waiting below.

The boat's tow lines had already been attached to the *Enterprize*: the craft surged ahead as soon as Captain Mee and the subalterns had boarded. The sound of the steamer's paddle-wheel drowned out the rattle of gunfire in the distance; the crossing seemed to take only a few minutes and then they were racing ashore to join the marines at their beachhead.

As the sepoys formed ranks bhistis came running through, pouring water into their brass lotas. In the column beside them, the marines were urinating where they stood, in preparation for the advance. Knowing that there would be no time to relieve themselves once the attack began, the sepoys followed suit.

Captain Mee took command now, ordering the columns to advance, with the marines on the right flank. They ran up the slope at a steady trot and as they came over the top of the elevation, the order to fire rang out. This time the sepoys and marines were able to throw up a thick curtain of fire, even as bullets were whistling over their own heads.

With volley following on volley, the charcoal in the gunpowder created a great cloud of black smoke, reducing visibility to a yard or two. Coughing, spluttering, the sepoys were half-blinded by the acrid smoke and half-deafened by the massed roar of the muskets. But there was no check in their stride: the habits ingrained by their training – hundreds of hours of daily drills – took over and kept them moving mechanically forward.

Kesri was in 'coverer' position, in line with the first row of sepoys. After the start of the battle his attention shifted quickly from the opposing lines to his own men. Many a time had he spoken to the sepoys about the surprises of the battlefield – the unpredictability of the terrain, the din, the smoke – yet he knew all too well that the reality always came as a shock, even to the best-prepared men.

Above the booms of the cannon and the steady rattle of musket-fire he caught the sound of a bullet hitting a bayonet, an eerie, vibrating tintinnabulation. Looking into the smoke, his eyes sought out the ghostly outline of the sepoy whose weapon had been struck: he was holding his musket at arm's length, gaping at the Brown Bess as though it had come alive in his hands and were about to skewer him. With a couple of steps Kesri crossed to his side and showed him how to kill the sound, by placing a flat palm upon the metal. Next minute, right behind him, there was the abrupt, metallic pinging of a musket-ball, ricocheting off the brass caging of a sepoy's topee. The man who had been hit would be deafened by the sound, Kesri knew: the noise would reverberate inside his skull as though his eardrums were being pounded by a mallet. Sure enough, the sepoy – a boy of seventeen – had fallen to his knees, with his hands clasped over his ears, shaking his head in pain. Leaping to his side, Kesri pulled the boy to his feet, thrust his fallen musket into his hands, and pushed him ahead.

Meanwhile the gun-lascars had finished assembling their gun-carriages; the howitzers opened fire together with the marines' field-piece. From the squat barrels of the howitzers came dull thudding sounds as they lobbed shells into the fortifications; from the field-piece came deep-throated roars as it hurled grapeshot and canister directly into the ranks of the opposing infantry.

Seeing the Chinese line waver, Captain Mee, who was in the lead, raised his sword to signal a charge. A great howl – *Har, har Mahadev!* – burst from the sepoys' throats as they rushed forward. When they emerged from the curtain of smoke, bayonets at the ready, the Chinese line swayed and began to turn; all of a sudden the opposing troops scattered, melting away into the forested hillside.

Now it was all Kesri could do to bring the men to heel: they were in the grip of that euphoria that seizes soldiers after a battle is won, a thing as elemental as the blood-lust of an animal after a hunt. This was when they were at their most dangerous, their discipline at its shakiest: Kesri ran after them, brandishing his sword and shouting dreadful threats as he dhamkaoed and ghabraoed them back into formation – yet in his heart, he was glad that their initiation into combat had happened in this way, in a minor skirmish rather than a pitched battle. As he watched them, sulkily falling back into line, a great pride filled Kesri's heart: he realized that he would never know a love as deep as that which bound him to this unit, which was largely his own creation, the culmination of his life's work.

*

Neel was watching from the crest of a nearby hill, along with Zhong Lou-si and his entourage: for him, as for them, the engagement had, through most of its duration, confirmed certain long held beliefs about the relative strengths and weaknesses of the Chinese and British forces. One of these was that British superiority at sea would be offset by Chinese strength on land; that the defenders' overwhelming advantage in numbers would allow them to repel a ground invasion.

No one in Zhong Lou-si's entourage was surprised by the damage inflicted by the British broadsides; they were well aware by now of the lethal firepower of steamers, frigates and other Western warships. The defenders too had been warned beforehand and had made preparations to wait out a bombardment. It was the ground assault that would be the real test, they knew, and when it was launched they had taken satisfaction in the minuscule size of the first landing-party – a total of fewer than three hundred men! They were jubilant when the marines and small-arms' men were forced into retreat by the thousands of Chinese troops that poured out to oppose them. At that moment Compton and his colleagues had felt that their beliefs had been vindicated and the battle had been won.

It was for this reason that the subsequent rout was doubly shocking, to Neel and Compton alike. Thousands of men put to flight by a force of fewer than three hundred! Not only did it defy belief, it challenged every reassuring assumption about the wider conflict, not least those that related to the effectiveness of Indian troops.

Although nobody mentioned the sepoys to Neel, he overheard Compton saying to someone: If the black-alien soldiers had not arrived the battle would have ended differently.

Neel took a perverse satisfaction in Compton's words for he had tried often, always unavailingly, to alter his friend's low opinion of the fighting qualities of Indian troops. Committed though Neel was to the Chinese cause, he was aware now of a keen sense of pride in his compatriots' performance that day. The matter of who the sepoys were serving was temporarily forgotten; he knew that he would have been ashamed if they had failed to give a good account of themselves.

In other ways too the day was a revelation to Neel. He had never witnessed a battle before and was profoundly affected by what he saw. Thinking about it later he understood that a battle was a distillation of time: many years of preparation and decades of innovation and change were squeezed into a clash of very short duration. And when it was over the impact radiated backwards and forwards through time, determining the future and even, in a sense, changing the past, or at least the general understanding of it. It astonished him that he had not recognized before the terrible power that was contained within these wrinkles in time – a power that could mould the lives of those who came afterwards for generation after generation. He remembered how, when reading of long-ago battles like Panipat and Plassey, he had thought of them as immeasurably distant from his own life, a matter of quaint uniforms and old-fashioned weaponry. Only now did it occur to him that it was on battlefields such as those that his own place in the world had been decided. He understood then why Shias commemorate the Battle of Kerbala every year: it was an acknowledgement that just as the earth splits apart at certain moments, to create monumental upheavals that forever change the terrain, so too do time and history.

How was it possible that a small number of men, in the span of a few hours or minutes, could decide the fate of millions of people yet unborn? How was it possible that the outcome of those brief moments could determine who would rule whom, who would be rich or poor, master or servant, for generations to come?

Nothing could be a greater injustice, yet such had been the reality ever since human beings first walked the earth.

Fifteen

On Zadig Bey's advice Shireen stayed indoors during the fighting. But Macau was so small that it was impossible to hide from the terrifying sound of cannon-fire: as she paced her darkened rooms Shireen was visited by all manner of dreadful imaginings. It was not till the late afternoon, when Zadig Bey came running to her house, that she learnt that the Chinese troops had been dispersed.

'Are you sure, Zadig Bey?'

'Yes, Bibiji, take my word for it, from now on Commissioner Lin will leave Macau alone. We will be perfectly safe here.'

Shireen was inclined to think that Zadig was being too optimistic but his prediction was vindicated soon enough. Within a day or two it was confirmed that all Chinese troops had been withdrawn from the vicinity of Macau. From then on both Macau and Hong Kong became, in effect, protectorates of the British expeditionary force. Foreigners no longer had anything to fear in either place.

The changed circumstances prompted many foreigners to move to Macau, among them the Parsi shipowner, Dinyar Ferdoonjee. Having made a fortune selling opium in the Philippines and Moluccas, he rented a large house that looked out on the bayside promenade of Praya Grande – the Villa Nova.

It so happened that Dinyar Ferdoonjee was a relative of Shireen's. When he heard that she was living in rented lodgings he went to see her and begged her to move in with him.

Bahram-bhai had helped him get started in business, Dinyar said to Shireen; he owed it to his memory to look after her. Besides, she would be doing him a favour; he had staffed the villa with cooks and stewards from his ship, the *Mor*, but being only in his mid-twenties, he was unaccustomed to running a household; he would be most grateful if Shireen could take charge.

Attractive as the offer was, Shireen was reluctant to accept, mainly because she thought Rosa would have trouble finding accommodation for herself. But Rosa told her not to worry; she had a standing invitation to move in with a Goan family of her acquaintance.

After that there was no reason not to accept. Within a week Shireen was comfortably settled in Dinyar's villa. Nor did she regret it: her new living quarters consisted of an entire wing of the villa; and it was pleasant also to be running a household again. Moreover the Villa Nova was in a splendid location, with a fine view of the Inner Harbour and the promenade, as it curved past the entrance to the Governor's palace. Its frontage consisted of a long, shaded veranda: sitting there of an evening, in a rocking chair, Shireen could see the whole town go by on the Praya Grande. Most days Zadig Bey would stroll past too and more often than not she would step outside to join him on his walk.

Dinyar proved to be an unusually congenial and thoughtful host: Shireen had wondered whether he might look askance on her wearing European clothes and going about without a duenna. But it turned out that Dinyar was exceptionally liberal in his views; not only did he applaud her choice of clothing he also declared her to be a pioneer: 'You'll see, Shireen-auntie, one day all our Bombay girls will want to dress like you.'

At the same time Dinyar was a proud Parsi, observant in his religious practices and fond of the old customs. He was delighted when Shireen made lacy torans and draped them around the doorways of the Villa Nova.

Shireen was by no means the only person to benefit from Dinyar's hospitality: he entertained frequently and prided himself on his table – in this, he liked to say, he was merely emulating Bahram, whose generosity and love of good living was a byword on the China coast. Thus, by living with Dinyar, Shireen was able to glimpse an aspect of her husband's life that she herself had never known.

As the weeks went by other Parsi merchants began to trickle into Macau and the Villa Nova quickly became the community's meeting place: on holidays the seths would assemble for prayers in the salon; afterwards they would exchange news of Bombay over meals of *dhansak*, steamed fish, stewed trotters and baked dishes of creamy shredded chicken: *marghi na mai vahala*.

But in the end the conversation would always veer around to the questions that most concerned them all: Would the British be able to extract reparations from the Chinese for the opium they had seized? Would the money be adequate? Would their losses be made good?

Shireen was the only person present who did not fret over these questions: rarely had she felt as content as she was at the Villa Nova.

*

In a few short weeks Zachary became so expert in selling opium to offshore buyers that he started seeking out new markets on his own, in remote coves and bays. Almost always his buyers were smugglers from the mainland, members of cartels affiliated with certain gangs and brotherhoods. Once Zachary had familiarized himself with their signals and emblems he had no difficulty in identifying reliable buyers. Nor did language present any difficulty: the negotiations were usually conducted in pidgin, with which Zachary was already familiar through his dealings with Serang Ali. He was well able to bargain on his own behalf.

As it happened many of Zachary's sales were to a single cartel: the network headed by the tycoon Lenny Chan. But Zachary's dealings were always with Mr Chan's underlings; knowing their boss to be an elusive man, Zachary assumed that he was unlikely to meet him on this voyage.

But he was wrong. One sultry August night, off the coast of Fujian, the *Ibis* was approached by a small, sleek-looking junk; unlike most such vessels, the junk had a canvas lateen sail; at the rear of the maindeck was a large 'house', with lanterns bobbing in front of it.

As usual, the negotiations were conducted by a linkister who came over to the *Ibis* for that purpose. Afterwards, when a deal had been reached, there was a shout from the junk, in Chinese.

Then the linkister turned to Zachary, with a bow: 'Mr Chan, he wanchi talkee Mr Reid.'

'Haiyah!' said Zachary in surprise. 'Is true maski? Mr Chan blongi here, on boat?'

The linkister bowed again. 'Mr Chan wanchi Mr Reid come aboard. Can, no can, lah?'

'Can, can!' said Zachary eagerly.

The *Ibis*'s longboat was already loaded and ready to go, with dozens of opium chests stacked inside: usually it was Baboo Nob Kissin who handled the transfer of the cargo, but this time it was Zachary who went.

As the boat approached the junk, an unexpected greeting reverberated out of the darkness: 'How're you going on there, Mr Reid?'

The voice was English in its intonation, yet the man who came forward to greet Zachary when he stepped on the junk's maindeck looked nothing like an Englishman: he had the appearance rather of a prosperous mandarin. His tall, corpulent form was covered by a robe of grey silk; on his head was a plain black cap; his queue was coiled in a bun and pinned to the back of his head. His face had the sagging, pendulous curves of an overfilled satchel, yet there was nothing soft about it: his nose was like a hawk's beak and his heavy-lidded eyes had a predatory glint. His hand too, Zachary noted as he shook it, was unexpectedly hard and calloused, talon-like in its grip.

'Welcome aboard, Mr Reid. I'm Lenny Chan.'

'I'm very glad to meet you, sir.'

'Likewise, Mr Reid, likewise.' Putting a hand on Zachary's shoulder he guided him aft. 'I hope you'll take some tea with me, Mr Reid?'

'Certainly.'

A gust of perfumed air rushed out at them as a sailor held open the door of the junk's 'house': Zachary found himself looking into a brightly lit, sumptuously appointed cabin, furnished with richly carved tables, couches and teapoys.

Seeing that his host had slipped off his shoes, Zachary bent down to follow suit. But Mr Chan stopped him as he was unlacing his boots: 'Wait!' He clapped his hands and a moment later a young woman stepped in. She was dressed in an ankle-length robe of shimmering scarlet silk; without looking Zachary in the eye, she sank to her knees, head lowered, and undid his laces. After removing his boots, she disappeared again into the interior of the vessel.

'Come, Mr Reid.'

Mr Chan led Zachary to a large, square armchair and poured him a cup of tea.

'We've done a lot of business together, haven't we, Mr Reid?' said Mr Chan, seating himself opposite Zachary.

'So we have, Mr Chan. I think I've sold more than half my cargo to your people.'

Mr Chan's head was cocked to one side, and his eyes seemed almost shut – but Zachary knew that he was being minutely studied.

'I hope,' said Mr Chan, 'that some of the goods you sold were your own?'

'Only ten chests I'm afraid,' said Zachary.

'Well that's not to be laughed at, is it?' said Mr Chan. 'I'll wager you're much richer than you were.'

'That I certainly am.'

'Though not quite so rich as Mr Burnham perhaps?'

'No.'

'But I'm sure you will be soon enough.' Mr Chan smiled thinly: 'People say you're quite the coming man, Mr Reid.'

'Do they?' Zachary was becoming a little unnerved now.

'Yes. I hope we will go on doing business with each other, Mr Reid.'

'I hope so too, Mr Chan.'

'Good, good,' said Mr Chan meditatively. 'But enough about business – you are my guest today and I would like to invite you to share a pipe. It is the custom, you know – men who have smoked together can trust one another.'

Taken aback, Zachary did not respond immediately.

His hesitation did not pass unnoticed: 'You do not smoke opium, Mr Reid?'

'I smoked once,' said Zachary. 'A long time ago.'

'Was it not to your taste?'

'No,' said Zachary. 'Not really.'

'But if I may say so,' said Mr Chan, 'perhaps the circumstances were not right? May I ask if you were sitting or lying down when you smoked?'

'Sitting.'

'There you are,' said Mr Chan, 'that's no way to smoke. Chasing the dragon is an art, you know – it must be done properly.'

Rising from his chair, Mr Chan went to a nearby shelf, picked out an implement, and brought it to Zachary. It was an ornate pipe, with a stem as long as a man's forearm. It was made of a silvery alloy, like pewter, but the mouthpiece was of old, yellowed ivory, as was the octagonal bulb at the other end of the pipe.

'This is my best pipe, Mr Reid. It is known as the "Yellow Dragon". People have offered me thousands of taels for it. You will see why if you try it.'

A shiver passed through Zachary as he ran his fingers along the long metal stem. 'All right,' he said. 'I'll try it, this one time.'

'Good – a man should sample the goods he sells.' Mr Chan smiled. 'But if you do wish to try it, Mr Reid, you must do it properly – and it is not possible to smoke properly in a jacket and trowsers. Better you change into Chinese robes.'

He clapped his hands and the girl appeared again; after exchanging a few words with Mr Chan she ushered Zachary through a door, into a room that looked like a large wardrobe. Handing him a dove-grey gown, she bowed herself out.

While he was changing Zachary heard the sound of furniture being moved. He stepped out of the wardrobe to find that the cabin's lights had been dimmed and two couches had been positioned next to each other, in one corner. Between the couches was a marble-topped table, on which lay an array of objects: a box with a lacquered top, a pair of needles with hooked ends, a couple of saucers, and of course, the 'yellow dragon', which was almost as long as the table itself. The girl was on her knees beside the table, holding a small lamp.

Mr Chan gestured to Zachary to take one of the couches. 'Please lie down, Mr Reid, make yourself comfortable.'

After Zachary had stretched himself out, Mr Chan lifted the lacquered box off the table. Handing it to Zachary he said: 'Look – this is freshly cooked opium, we call it chandu. It is made by boiling raw opium, such as you have in your chests.'

Inside the box lay a small, dark brown nugget. 'Smell it, Mr Reid.'

The odour was sweet and smoky, quite different from the smell of raw opium gum.

Taking the box from Zachary, Mr Chan handed it to the girl,

who was now kneeling between the two couches, with the lamp in front of her. She picked a needle off the table, dipped it into the opium and gave it an expert twirl: it came away with a tiny pellet of the gum, no larger than a pea. This little piece she now stuck into the lamp's flame; when it began to sizzle and blister she handed it to Mr Chan. Resting the mouthpiece of the 'yellow dragon' on his chest, he twirled and tapped the scorched opium on the implement's ivory cup. This process was repeated twice, without the mouthpiece yet being put to use.

Then Mr Chan said: 'We're almost ready now, Mr Reid. When I roast the opium again it will catch fire. The smoke will last for one or two seconds. You must be prepared – you must blow out your breath, emptying your chest so you can draw in all the smoke. When the opium begins to burn I will put it on the dragon's eye' – he pointed to the tiny hole in the pipe's octagonal cup – 'and you must draw hard.'

Handing the pipe to Zachary, he plunged the pellet of opium into the flame again. Suddenly it caught fire, and he cried out: 'Ready?'

'Yes.'

Zachary had already emptied the air from his chest: when the flaming pellet was placed on the 'dragon's eye' he inhaled deeply, filling his lungs with the smoke. Its consistency was almost that of a liquid, dense, oily and intensely perfumed; it poured into his body like a flood, coursing through his veins and swamping his head.

'You see, Mr Reid? The power that moves the world is inside you now. Lie back. Let it run through you.'

As he leant back against the cushions Zachary suddenly became aware of his pulse – except that it wasn't beating only in his wrist or his neck. It was as if his whole body were pulsating; the drumming of his heart was so powerful that he could feel his blood surging into his capillaries. The sensation was so strong that he looked down at his forearm and saw that his skin had changed colour. It was flushed and red, as if every pore had been awoken and irradiated.

He looked up at the ceiling and suddenly it was as if his eyes had become more sensitive, his gaze more powerful. He could see minute cracks in the wood; his hearing too seemed to have become more acute and the lapping of water was loud in his ears. He closed his eyes, luxuriating in the feeling of weightlessness, allowing the smoke to carry him away, as if on a tide.

Now it was Mr Chan's turn with the pipe. After he had finished, he laid it on the table and leant back against a bolster. 'Do you know why I have a yen for the smoke, Mr Reid? It is because I am a gardener by profession. I love flowers – and this smoke is the essence of the kingdom of flowers.'

His voice drifted away.

In a while Zachary became aware that Mr Chan had left the cabin and that he was alone with the girl. Now, for the first time, she raised her head and looked directly at him, with a slight smile on her lips. Zachary stared, unable to tear his eyes from her face: there was something familiar about her – he couldn't figure out what it was so he stretched out his arm and ran his fingertips over her face. Suddenly the answer came to him: she bore an uncanny resemblance to Mrs Burnham. Even the touch of her hands, as they roamed over his body and under his robe, was like hers; even more so was the feel of her limbs against his own.

When he clasped her in his arms the likeness seemed to grow more and more pronounced, making him hungrier and hungrier; it was as if he were making love to Mrs Burnham herself – so much so that at the end he even mumbled her name aloud. But no sooner had it left his lips than he was stricken with guilt; he turned away, mortified, alarming the girl, who seemed to think that it was a rebuke of some kind.

'No, no,' he said, to reassure her. 'It's not you; it's me.'

He could tell, though, that she hadn't understood. At a loss to explain, he took hold of her hand and gave himself a mock slap, as a punishment. The blow was very light, yet his skin, still irradiated by the smoke, began to tingle; his whole face was aglow. The feeling was pleasurable yet strange – precisely because the pleasure came from the sensation of being punished, of expiating a burden of guilt.

He did it again, a little harder, and it felt even better. Now she seemed to understand what he wanted and began to slap him playfully, not just on his face but also on his naked back and buttocks – and the pleasure was so intense that he knew that if he did not stop he would be compelled to start all over again, with another pipe.

The thought sobered him so he gave her a smile and said: 'I must go now – it's time for me to leave.'

When she fetched him his clothes he reached into the pocket of his trowsers and took out a handful of coins. But she would not take them; she shook her head and bowed herself out.

As he was putting on his jacket a door opened and Mr Chan stepped in: suddenly an uneasy thought entered Zachary's mind: was it possible that he had been watching all this while?

But he could see no hint of it in Mr Chan's manner which was once again brisk and businesslike. 'Well, Mr Reid,' he said, 'I trust you enjoyed the visit. I hope it will be the beginning of a long partnership.'

'Thank you, sir,' Zachary mumbled. 'I hope so too.'

'Oh I am sure we will deal very well together,' said Mr Chan, pumping Zachary's hand. 'I have been doing business with Mr Burnham for a long time, and I must say you remind me very much of him. The two of you are very much alike.'

'Thank you, Mr Chan. It is kind of you to say so.'

*

For Zhong Lou-si and his circle the Battle of the Barrier was a defeat on many counts. Even though they had watched the fighting with their own eyes they were unable to persuade Commissioner Lin of the truth of what they had seen. An army commander got to the Commissioner first and convinced him that the battle had resulted in a great victory for their side – that the British had been put to flight, with many casualties. The prefect of the district that bordered Macau corroborated these misleading reports, as did some other officials. Those who tried to tell the Commissioner the truth, like Zhong Lou-si, were vastly outnumbered and outranked.

The result was that the Commissioner accepted the military commanders' fictitious version of the Macau battle and his dispatches to the Emperor reflected these falsehoods.

If Lin Zexu can be deceived like this, said Compton despairingly, then what chance is there that the truth will ever reach the Forbidden City?

But soon enough it became clear that the Emperor could not be shielded from the realities of what was happening along the coast.

The Macau battle was still fresh in memory when it was learnt in Guangzhou that a squadron of British ships had sailed right up to the mouth of the Bai River, very close to Beijing. With the capital under immediate threat, the governor of that province, a very senior mandarin by the name of Qishan, had agreed to receive the letter that Captain Elliot had been trying to deliver to the Emperor for the last several weeks.

And the contents of this letter were even more shocking than anyone had previously imagined: along with many other demands the British had asked for a sum of six million Spanish dollars in compensation for the opium that Commissioner Lin had confiscated the year before. In addition they had demanded that an island be ceded to them, as a trading base.

The strangest part of it was that the British accepted no blame for their crimes: they made no acknowledgement of their smuggling, their repeated provocations, or their refusal to abide by Chinese laws on Chinese soil. Instead they placed the blame entirely on Commissioner Lin, accusing him of criminal conduct and unlawful seizures. It was as if the firepower of their ships had given them the right to dictate that night was day.

Such was the pressure on the Commissioner that he composed a long letter to the Emperor, trying to account for his errors and failures. While acknowledging that he had made some mistakes, he pointed out that he had followed the Emperor's express instructions in all his actions. He also placed much blame on the merchants of Guangzhou, who, he said, had colluded and conspired with the British at every step.

What the Emperor thought of this letter was not yet known, but rumour had it that he was not persuaded by the Commissioner's arguments. It was even being said that the Emperor had agreed to hand the Commissioner to the British, to face whatever punishment they saw fit.

For Zhong Lou-si and his circle these tidings were like tremors in the earth: it was impossible thereafter to ignore the indications of a coming upheaval in the firmaments of their authority. Every day there were fresh shocks and aftershocks, in the form of reports and rumours, to remind them that the ground was shifting under their feet.

From Compton's reports it became clear to Neel that a struggle had broken out in the official circles of Guangzhou, with many different factions competing for power. It was evident also that those who were getting the worst of it were the men of heterodox views, like Zhong Lou-si. The traditionalists were in the ascendant now, and as their stars rose a miasma of suspicion came to settle upon those who had advocated or practised the study of foreign affairs, such as Zhong Lou-si and his circle.

Nor was it only officials who were affected by the recent developments. Common people too were beginning to feel the effects of the British blockade of the Pearl River. Rumours of the attacks on Ting-hae, Macau and other cities had started to spread, creating much disquiet. In Guangdong all those who had connections with foreigners – and there were many such in the province – were increasingly coming under suspicion. Everywhere there was talk of *han-chien*, *faan gwat jai* and *chieng-shang*, traitors, rebels, spies and treacherous merchants who colluded with the British.

For Baburao and his family the problem was especially acute: it was now common knowledge that Indian *haak-gwai* soldiers and sailors were rampaging up and down the coast in tandem with the English *faan-gwai*. Baburao's connections with Bengal were well known on the waterfront; it was well known also that Asha-didi's kitchen-boat catered mainly to Achhas, men from Yindu. This led to so much unpleasantness that she was left with no option but to shut down the eatery.

Then, on a cool autumn evening, two months after the battle at Macau, there was a knock on Neel's door. It was Compton, looking utterly distraught.

I have some bad news, Ah Neel . . .

Commissioner Lin had been removed from his post, Compton announced, and that too in a deeply insulting manner. The Emperor had sent a letter to the Commissioner's deputy addressing him as Lin Zexu's successor.

In this ignominious way had that great man, Commissioner Lin, been deposed: no forewarning, no notification – just a letter to a junior to indicate that he had been replaced! This was the Commissioner's reward for his faithful and honourable service to the Emperor!

Neel had never seen Compton so much cast down.

Official confirmation came a few days later: Lin Zexu had been recalled to Beijing in disgrace. He was to be replaced by Qishan who had been appointed Governor-General of the two southern provinces of Guangdong and Guangxi.

The news created a furore in Guangdong where the former Commissioner remained immensely popular. People poured out to express their sympathy for him: wherever he went he was besieged by crowds; people would surround his palanquin and thrust gifts at him – shoes, umbrellas, robes, incense-burners and the like.

Lin Zexu's fall from grace was a defeat also for Zhong Lou-si, and thus, by extension, for Compton too. They both knew that under the new dispensation Zhong Lou-si's influence would be greatly reduced: effectively it would mean the undoing of all the work of the last two years.

Neel happened to be present in Compton's shop one afternoon when Zhong Lou-si came by for an unannounced visit. It seemed to Neel that Zhong Lou-si had aged many years in the last two months; he was leaning heavily on a stick, his expression resigned and careworn. They parted on a melancholy note.

Neel never saw Zhong Lou-si again.

The next day Compton went to Lin Zexu's residence to pay his respects before his departure. On arriving there he learnt that the former Commissioner would not be leaving after all. The Emperor had sent instructions for him to remain in Canton. He was to assist the new Governor-General, Qishan, in conducting an inquiry into his own conduct.

It was as if Lin Zexu had become the equivalent of an ancestral tablet, to be taken out and put away according to the needs of the moment.

Now, as Guangzhou waited for the arrival of the Governor-General, the disquiet that had gripped the city was deepened by a sense of drift and uncertainty.

One evening, on his way back to Baburao's houseboat, from

Compton's shop, Neel was surrounded by a gang of urchins as he stepped off the ferry. The boys began to shout curses and obscenities.

... *Yun gwai, faan uk-kei laan hai!*
... *laahn gwai, diu neih louh mei!*
... *jihn hai, haahng lan toi!*

It was not unusual for taunts like these to be directed at foreigners – or, for that matter, Chinese people from other provinces, or even neighbours from the next village – but there was a note of rage in the boys' voices that Neel had not heard before. The strange thing was that they had identified him not as a 'black alien' but rather as a 'traitor': what would have happened if they had realized that he was a *haak-gwai*? It was better not to know. What was clear in any case was that Neel could not go back to Baburao's houseboat: to lead the boys there might create problems for the family. Neel decided instead to head for the Ocean Banner Monastery which was just a few hundred yards away.

The urchins' shouts grew louder and louder as Neel walked towards the monastery. As he was stepping through the gates a rock hit him in the back – but fortunately the gang did not follow him inside.

Taranathji was his usual warm, welcoming self. He nodded gloomily on hearing Neel's story. The mood in Guangzhou was turning very ugly, he said. It wasn't just foreigners who were being targeted; Chinese people from other provinces were also being set upon by the local citizenry. Such was the situation that the monastery's Tibetan monks no longer stepped outside.

Taranathji told Neel that he was welcome to remain in the monastery and Neel gratefully accepted the offer. A message was sent to Baburao and he appeared at the monastery shortly afterwards with a bagful of Neel's belongings.

Baburao was not surprised to hear that Neel had been set upon. He had heard similar tales from friends and relatives; boat-people too were being stigmatized as traitors and spies. The provincial authorities had been heaping blame on their community for their failure to sink British warships. They had thought that boatman 'water-braves' would be able to destroy the foreign ships with their special powers; they were enraged that this had not come about.

Kintu amra ki korbo? said Baburao in Bangla. What can we do?

Landsmen may believe that we have miraculous powers but we don't – we are just ordinary folk.

The next morning Neel sent a message to Compton to let him know that he had taken refuge in the monastery. Compton came over to visit and advised Neel to stay where he was until some more permanent arrangement could be made.

A few days later Compton came to see Neel again. He had spoken to Zhong Lou-si, he said, and they had agreed that it would be best for Neel to move to the *Cambridge*, which was still anchored at Whampoa. He would be safe there since the *Cambridge* was under the special protection of the provincial authorities; and no doubt the crew would be glad of his services as a translator.

*

Zachary sold his last lot of opium in early December, off the coast of Manchuria. With the *Ibis*'s holds now empty he lost no time in turning the schooner around to head back to the south.

Two days from Hong Kong Bay the lookout spotted Philip Fraser's brigantine heading towards them. The two vessels hove to abreast of each other and Zachary went over for a meal.

Mr Fraser had much news to pass on: the British fleet had returned to the Pearl River estuary to await the opening of negotiations with Qishan, the new viceroy of Guangdong. One of the Plenipotentiaries, Admiral George Elliot, had fallen ill; he had resigned his command to Commodore Bremer. Captain Elliot was now the sole Plenipotentiary, which was a matter of no little chagrin to many in the expeditionary force. Among his fellow officers Captain Elliot had gained a reputation for being too soft on the Chinese; the prevalent feeling was that nothing would come of his strategy of talk-talk-talk; the military men were convinced that the Chinese were only using this time to build up their defences. Many officers took the view that Peking would make no concessions until it was given a bloody nose and they ridiculed the Plenipotentiary for his illusions. Many regarded him as a vacillating fool and did not hesitate to say so. Derisive nicknames abounded – Plenipot, Plenny-potty, Plenny-pissy-potty and so on.

In the meantime, the British fleet had been augmented by several more warships including a revolutionary new vessel: the *Nemesis*, an ironclad steamer, the first of her kind to venture into the Indian

Ocean. Mr Fraser had been given a tour of this marvellous vessel and he could not stop talking about her. The *Nemesis* was made almost entirely of metal; there was so much iron on her that a special device had to be fitted on her compass to correct the magnetic deflection. Her two massive paddle-wheels were powered by engines of one hundred and twenty horsepower which daily devoured eleven tons of coal. Yet the draught of this mighty vessel was so shallow that she could operate in waters of no more than five feet! This was because she had two keels that could be raised and lowered. Her armaments too were such as to induce awe: she carried two thirty-two-pound pivot guns, capable of shooting shell or canister, five brass six-pounders, and ten iron swivels; in addition there was a tube on the bridge between her paddle-wheels, for the launching of Congreve rockets.

It was thought by many, said Mr Fraser, that the *Nemesis* would forever change the nature of naval warfare: she was expected to serve as a secret weapon, striking terror into the Chinese.

Along with all the other news, there was a snippet that was of particular interest to Zachary: Mr and Mrs Burnham had come to the China coast on their ship, the *Anahita*. Mr Fraser had met them at Hong Kong Bay and they had both been very pleased to hear of Zachary's successes as a Free Trader.

The news prompted Zachary to crowd the *Ibis*'s masts with sail, sending the schooner skimming across the waves.

*

Chusan, and the progress of the campaign in the north, were subjects of much discussion in the sepoys' tents in Saw Chow. News was sparse in the early weeks but it was generally understood that the fighting had been light and Chusan had been taken with very few casualties.

But as August turned into September ominous rumours began to circulate, of outbreaks of sickness and disease. Kesri heard that sick and dying soldiers were being transported back from Chusan to the southern sector. The word was that they were being sent to Macau, to be accommodated either in the Misericordía or in a mansion that had been turned into a hospital.

One day news arrived that a contingent of sick sepoys from their brother unit – the other company of the Bengal Volunteers battalion – had been sent back from Chusan and were now languishing in the Misericordía. Kesri went to Captain Mee to ask if the reports were true; not only did the captain confirm them, he also gave Kesri permission to take a group of NCOs to Macau, to visit the sick sepoys.

Since their arrival in China the sepoys had not once set foot in Macau. Although this visit was anything but a pleasure trip, they were glad to have an opportunity to see the town. Nor were they disappointed: Macau made a tremendous impression on all of them, most of all on Kesri. Their group happened to land near the temple of A-Ma, the goddess of the sea, and Kesri could not resist going in to have a look. He was amazed by the number of things that looked familiar – the incense, the idols, the sacred trees, the carved figures that guarded the gates. Kesri had known of course that many Chinese were Buddhists but not till then did he have any sense of the similarities between their dharma and his own.

Afterwards, walking to the Misericordía, the sepoys got lost in the town's winding lanes. But at every turn there was someone to ask directions from, not just in English but also Hindustani – there were Goans everywhere, running shops, patrolling the streets, guarding doors. A squad of Goan sepoys even showed them their barracks and gave them gifts of fruit.

The Misericordía was a sombre, grey building. The compound was very crowded and no one paid them any attention. Fortunately Kesri spotted Rosa, who recognized him from the *Hind*: she led the way to a small, dark room at one side of the building – this was the ward in which the sick sepoys were housed.

On inquiring about the conditions in Chusan, Kesri learnt that the initial seizure of the island had indeed been relatively uncomplicated, as he had thought – it was in the aftermath of the fighting that things had taken a hellish turn. Epidemics of fevers and other diseases had broken out; hundreds of sepoys and soldiers had been struck down by chronic, uncontrollable dysentery. In the field-hospital mattresses were packed so close together that the attendants couldn't get through without stepping on sick and dying men.

The basic problem lay in the high command's ignorance of the island, said the sick sepoys. Their campsites had been chosen without due regard for the terrain: the fact that the low-lying areas of

Chusan were dotted with swamps and marshes had not been taken properly into account. As a result the troops had been exposed to noxious vapours and deadly miasmas. Often their tents would be flooded by rising waters. One detachment of sepoys had set up camp on a hill, but only to be beset by foul odours; the smells were so persistent that they had decided to dig down, in the hope of finding a solution to the mystery. Within a few inches of the surface they had hit upon skulls, skeletons and rotting bones: it turned out that the 'hill' was a burial mound. The officers had decided that the mound was a source of contagion and had ordered that it be blown up. The explosion had resulted in a crater of coffins and skeletons.

On Chusan, said the sepoys, fresh water was so difficult to find that they had sometimes had to drink from the ditches that irrigated the rice-fields. Provisions, most of which had been procured in Calcutta, were scanty or rotten, infested with weevils and fungus: it was evident to the sepoys that someone had earned huge profits by providing substandard supplies. Yet so dire were the shortages that the commissariat had been forced to keep on buying, at vastly inflated prices, from the merchant vessels that had accompanied the occupying force on its northwards journey.

And then there was the heat, which even the sepoys had found hard to cope with: for the white soldiers it had been almost beyond endurance. On top of that, the occupiers had also had to cope with the unrelenting hostility of the island's inhabitants. Because of the bounties offered by the Chinese authorities the soldiers had not been able to relax for a minute, for fear of being murdered or kidnapped. A few who had let down their guard had paid a steep price, among them a captain of the Madras Artillery who had been set upon by a mob and whisked away to the mainland: his Indian servant had died in the fracas.

Before arriving at Chusan the British high command had told the troops that they would be welcomed by the islanders; the Manchus were so widely hated, they had said, that the soldiers of the expeditionary force were sure to be greeted as liberators.

In Chusan it had become clear that these were delusions.

It was in listening to stories like these that Kesri realized how very fortunate B Company had been in being stationed in the south. Although life on Saw Chow Island was none too pleasant, their provisions were certainly adequate, with plenty of supplies being brought in by the bumboat fleet. Although they too had suffered from sickness and disease, their field-hospital had not been strained beyond capacity. All in all, there could be no denying that they had been relatively lucky in their lot.

In late October, the remaining battalions of the 37th Madras Regiment began to trickle in from India. They too were quartered on Saw Chow Island and they told harrowing tales of their voyage. In order to save money the military establishment of Madras Presidency had hired leaky old tubs as transport vessels. The ships were barely seaworthy, not fit to weather even a mild storm – and as luck would have it, they had run into a monstrous typhoon in the South China Sea; all four vessels in the convoy had been badly damaged and blown afield. One had spent several days under siege by pirates; if a British steamer had not come to their rescue there was no telling what might have happened. Another ship had vanished during the typhoon. The name of this vessel was *Golconda*: she was the 'headquarters ship' of the 37th Madras and was carrying the regimental daftar, three hundred sepoys, and most of the officers too, including the CO. The worst was feared.

A few days later Captain Mee confirmed to Kesri that the *Golconda* had capsized and all on board had perished. He confirmed also that the ship was not seaworthy and should never have been hired as a transport vessel. It was common knowledge that many palms had been greased and that some officers had been paid off – possibly even one of those who had gone down with the vessel. There would very likely be an official inquiry.

'It's those money-grubbing civilians who're to blame,' said Captain Mee, through clenched teeth. 'If there's one thing I can't stand it's these merchants who make money off soldiers' lives. The bastards are worse than grave-robbers!'

That night, lying in his cot, Kesri thought of the two boys who had tried to desert in Calcutta and how they had revealed, under questioning, that they were afraid that their provisions would be rotten and their ships unseaworthy – all of which he had dismissed as lies and rumours. He remembered also how he had commanded the firing squad that executed them and how they had died, falling forward on their blindfolded faces.

Now the dead boys began to appear in his dreams, calling him a fool for parroting the words of the Angrez officers, taunting him as a *nakli gora* – a white-faker.

Through this time Kesri continued to visit the Misericordía at regular fortnightly intervals, to deliver sattu and other provisions to the sick sepoys. Often he would make the journey to Macau with Captain Mee; while the captain went off to call on friends and acquaintances, Kesri would lead a line of porters through the now familiar lanes of Macau.

These visits did much to sustain the sick sepoys, many of whom were starved of news, desperate to know when they might go home. Kesri would tell them what he had heard: that the Plenipotentiaries were still up north, trying to get the mandarins to recognize their claims.

What he did not say was that the end was nowhere in sight.

With every visit there was a steady increase in the number of sick sepoys until the Misericordía could take no more patients: those who arrived afterwards were sent on to Manila.

And still they kept coming: in early November Kesri heard that of the two and a half thousand soldiers who had seized Chusan two months before, only eight hundred were still on their feet.

It was not till the middle of the month that there was finally a bit of good news to bring to the Misericordía.

Most of the expeditionary force's troops were returning to the south! The British had pledged to return Chusan to the Chinese in return for some other island, to be used as a base. Until that time a small British garrison would remain on Chusan, as a surety.

The rest of the troops were already on their way back to the south; they would enter the Pearl River estuary in a few days.

*

On arriving at Hong Kong Bay Zachary discovered that Mr and Mrs Burnham had gone to Macau on the *Anahita*. He wasted no time in boarding a Macau ferry-boat.

It was late in the afternoon by the time Zachary stepped on the *Anahita*: he was surprised to find the maindeck empty except for a couple of lascars, dozing in the shade of a staysail. It occurred to him to wonder whether Mrs Burnham was on board; it was not unlikely, he knew, and his heartbeat quickened.

Looking astern he saw that a canvas awning had been rigged over the *Anahita*'s quarter-deck, to shield it from the sun. He guessed that this amenity was intended mainly to accommodate Mrs Burnham's dread of direct sunlight, and the thought that she might be up there now flashed guiltily through his mind. He tried to disregard it: nothing good could come, he admonished himself, of letting his mind stray in that direction. Yet, when his feet began to move towards the quarter-deck, he made no effort to stop them either. What could be more natural, he asked himself, than that he, a skipper himself, should go up to the quarter-deck? It was what any ship's officer would do.

He climbed the companion-ladder slowly, and when his head drew level with the deck, he looked carefully from side to side. Seeing no sign of Mrs Burnham or anyone else, he breathed a deep sigh – whether of relief or disappointment, he himself did not know. Stepping up to the deck he saw that there was a carved, circular bench at the foot of the mizzenmast. That was where he would wait, he decided.

But as he was crossing the deck a door flew suddenly open. Turning on his heel, Zachary beheld a veiled figure, encased in an armature of clothing.

'Mr Reid!'

'Mrs Burnham?'

Even though it was a chilly day Mrs Burnham had spared no effort to protect herself from the sun: from neck to toe she was enveloped in white calico, trimmed with lace; her arms were covered with elbow-length cotton gloves and her head and face were sheltered by a circular hat, from the brim of which hung a visor-like veil of white netting. In one of her hands was a parasol, made of fine white linen, with a trimming of lace.

Now, as Zachary stood transfixed to the deck, her hat, with its visor of netting, began to swivel, turning from one direction to the other. Then, with a flick of her wrist, Mrs Burnham flipped her veil back upon the brim of her hat.

'It seems that we are alone for the moment, Mr Reid. My husband has gone to the *Wellesley* to call on Captain Elliot.'

Zachary could not think of what to say, how to respond. What was the most natural way for a man in his position to greet his employer's wife? Unable to think of an answer he moved towards the starboard bulwark, where he steadied himself by taking hold of the gunwale. Even when he heard the rustling of cloth behind him he did not look around but kept his gaze fixed ahead, on the *Wellesley*, a quarter-mile away. His senses were now at such a pitch that he could follow Mrs Burnham's movements without looking: he knew that she had stationed herself beside him, but at a distance that seemed to be precisely calibrated to suggest to an onlooker that they were but two casual acquaintances, standing at the bulwark to take in the view.

'I am very glad, Mr Reid,' she said, 'that we have been granted this opportunity to meet on our own.'

Suddenly a wave of thwarted desire surged over Zachary and he found himself saying, not without some bitterness: 'You surprise me, Mrs Burnham. When we parted last I had the clear impression that you wanted to be rid of me.'

From under the cover of her slowly spinning parasol Mrs Burnham shot him an imploring glance. 'Oh please, Mr Reid; you know very well the circumstances. If I seemed unkind it was only because it was so very difficult to forsake our . . . our intimacy. Anyway the past doesn't matter now: I have something of the greatest importance to say – and I don't know if there will ever be another opportunity. Mr Burnham will be back all too soon, so there is very little time.'

Startled by the intensity of her tone, Zachary said: 'What is it, Mrs Burnham? Tell me.'

'It is about Paulette: I know you have written to her, to sever your connection. She has told me about your chitty.'

'What did she say?'

'She did not say much but I could tell that she was deeply, deeply wounded.'

'Well I am sorry about that, Mrs Burnham,' said Zachary. 'I tried to be polite but the truth is that I too was deeply hurt by the things she had said about me.'

'But that's just the cheez!' Mrs Burnham caught her breath with a muted sob. 'Paulette didn't mean what I thought she had! It was all a terrible misunderstanding on my part.'

'I don't understand, Mrs Burnham.' Zachary's voice fell to a whisper. 'Do you mean that she never implied that she was "with child"?'

'Not intentionally. No.'

'But what of her relations with your husband? They were not entirely innocent surely?'

'Well Mr Reid, I do believe they were, at least on Paulette's part. I am sure her stories of the beatings were true; I am sure also that she did it without knowing what she was doing – and when she realized what it signified, she fled our house immediately, before things could go any further.'

Over the last many months Zachary had come to be convinced that Paulette had wilfully and maliciously deceived both himself and Mrs Burnham; that his suspicions might be unfounded was hard to accept. 'How do you know all this?' he demanded. 'Did you ask her about it?'

'No,' said Mrs Burnham. 'I did not ask her directly. But one day when my husband and I were in Macau we ran into her unexpectedly. I watched the two of them closely and you can take my word for it that she behaved in a way that entirely gave the lie to the conjectures that you and I had nurtured. She was completely natural and unafraid – it was my husband who seemed sheepish and apprehensive. I am convinced now that she told you the truth about what had passed between them – it was only that and nothing more.'

Still unconvinced, Zachary persisted: 'I don't see how you can be so sure.'

'But I am indeed sure, Mr Reid,' she said. 'I realize now that I had let my imagination run away with me. I was at a loss to understand why Paulette had fled our house and the only explanation I could think of was that you had seduced and impregnated her. When you came to ask for that job, this suspicion weighed heavily upon me; I thought that if I had you within my grasp, I could make you repent of your loocherism and cure you of it forever. But then something changed; against my own will I found myself drawn to you and was powerless to resist. That was why, perhaps, I was willing to believe the worst of Paulette – yet she was utterly without blame. The fault was entirely mine.'

Now, at last Zachary began to give ground. 'The fault was as much mine as yours, Mrs Burnham,' he said grudgingly. 'What you have owned of yourself is true for both of us. I too was prepared to believe the worst of Paulette – perhaps because it seemed to lessen our own guilt.'

'Yes, we are both guilty—'

She cut herself short as a skiff appeared in the distance, pulling away from the *Wellesley* and heading towards the *Anahita*.

'Oh there is my husband's boat!' said Mrs Burnham breathlessly. 'He will be here in a matter of minutes and after that I must go into town, to make a few calls. We have very little time left, so please, Mr Reid, you must listen, jaldee.'

'Yes, Mrs Burnham?'

'We – or rather I – have done Paulette a terrible injustice, Mr Reid. I would have liked to make amends myself, but I dare not, for fear of revealing too much, about us – you and I.'

'So Paulette doesn't know about us?'

'No, of course not,' said Mrs Burnham. 'I told her nothing for fear that it might put an end to the possibility of a future for you and her.'

Zachary's eyebrows rose: 'What do you mean by "future", Mrs Burnham?'

'I mean your happiness, Mr Reid.' Mrs Burnham raised a hand to brush away a tear. 'You were destined to be together, you and Paulette – I can see that now. And so you might have been, if not for me.'

She looked him in the face, eyes glistening. 'I am a vile, selfish, weak creature, Mr Reid. I succumbed to temptation with you and have been the cause of much unhappiness for yourself and for Paulette, for whom I have nothing but affection. I know all too well what it is to have one's love destroyed and I am tormented by the thought that I may myself have been the cause of it, for the two of you. You cannot let me go to my grave with that weighing upon my soul. I will have no peace until I know that you have been reunited with her.'

'But there is nothing to be done, Mrs Burnham,' protested Zachary. 'Paulette still has my letter – I cannot take it back.'

'Yes you can, Mr Reid. You can apologize to her; you can explain that you had been deceived by salacious gossip. You can beg forgiveness. You must do it for my sake if not for your own – if ever I meant anything to you, you must do it for me.'

Such was the urgency in her voice that Zachary could not refuse. 'But Mrs Burnham, how am I to meet with her? I doubt that she would receive me.'

'Oh do not worry about that, Mr Reid; I have already thought of a way to bring the two of you together.'

Mrs Burnham's voice grew increasingly hurried now, seeing that the skiff had pulled abreast of the *Anahita*.

'You will have an opportunity very soon. On New Year's Day, we are holding a sunset levée on the *Anahita*. Mr Burnham wants to receive and entertain some of the expedition's officers. There will be some ladies too, and I have invited Paulette as well. She has accepted – perhaps because she does not know that you are here. You must come – you can speak to her then.'

With that Mrs Burnham turned around and made her way down to the maindeck, with her parasol on her shoulder. Zachary followed a few steps behind her. As the minutes went by her posture grew steadily more erect and by the time Mr Burnham stepped on deck she was once again her usual, languid self. Watching the couple together, as they exchanged a brisk kiss and a few quiet words, Zachary was seized with admiration, not just for her but also for her husband, who was the picture of calm mastery.

'May I take the skiff now, dear?' said Mrs Burnham. 'I thought I would go to Macau to make a few calls.'

'Yes of course, dear,' said Mr Burnham. 'And if I may, I will charge you with an errand.'

'Certainly,' said Mrs Burnham. 'What is it?'

'You will perhaps remember Mrs Moddie, who we had once met in Bombay? I think I mentioned to you, didn't I, that she would be travelling to Macau on the *Hind*? Her late husband was my colleague on the Select Committee – a most remarkable man. Indeed, this expeditionary force might not be here today if not for Mr Moddie; at a crucial meeting of the committee, it was Mr Moddie who helped carry the day by standing fast in the defence of freedom.'

'Yes, I remember, dear,' said Mrs Burnham. 'You told me about it.'

'Well, I gather Mrs Moddie is now at the Villa Nova, her nephew's house on the Praya Grande. I was thinking that we should invite her to our New Year's levée.'

'Yes of course we must, dear,' said Mrs Burnham. 'I'll be sure to call on her.'

'Thank you, my dear,' said Mr Burnham, bending down to kiss his wife on the cheek.

*

Only after the skiff had departed did Mr Burnham turn to Zachary. 'Come, Reid,' he said, leading the way to the quarter-deck. 'I'm sure you have a lot to tell me.'

'Yes, sir.'

For the next half-hour they paced the deck together as Zachary talked about his voyages, on the *Hind* and the *Ibis*, and his sales of opium, in Singapore and along the China coast. Mr Burnham listened carefully but said very little, only nodding from time to time to indicate his approval. Only when Zachary mentioned Lenny Chan did he break his silence.

'Mr Chan's a very useful man to know, Reid; very useful indeed!'

Mr Burnham's approbation became even more animated when Zachary showed him the accounts and explained that he had netted a profit of close to a million dollars on this one voyage: from these figures alone it was evident that despite the best efforts of the Chinese government, the hunger for opium was only growing stronger and stronger, especially among the young.

'Shahbash, Reid! Splendid!' cried Mr Burnham. 'The rise in prices is proof of the power of the marketplace; a demonstration of the folly of those who would try to thwart the workings of nature's divinely ordained laws. To confound the tyrants is to do the Lord's work – a day will surely come when young Free-Traders such as yourself will be regarded as Apostles of Liberty.'

'Thank you, sir,' said Zachary gratefully. 'It was a pleasure to be of service. If there is anything else I can do I hope you will let me know.'

At this Mr Burnham's expression turned pensive and he seemed to experience a rare moment of uncertainty. 'Well, Reid,' he said at last, 'although you've done very well so far you're still young. I am not sure you are ready for other challenges.'

'Oh but please, sir,' said Zachary earnestly, 'I do hope you will give me a chance to prove myself!'

Mr Burnham turned aside, as though to weigh conflicting considerations. Then, coming to a decision, he put an arm around Zachary's shoulder and led him across the deck.

'Your hunger for self-improvement is most impressive, Reid. But you do understand, don't you, that certain matters must be kept in the strictest confidence?'

'Oh yes indeed, sir. I shall not breathe a word.'

'Well then, Reid, look ahead of you.'

Leading Zachary to the bulwark, Mr Burnham raised a hand to point to the *Wellesley* and the *Druid*, which were anchored a short distance away.

'Assembled in these waters are thousands of soldiers and sailors from many parts of the British Empire. Every one of them must be fed, several times a day, according to their tastes and prejudices. Of all those men the hardest to feed are sepoys, especially Bengal sepoys, because they adhere to a great variety of dietary rules. They will eat nothing but their familiar provisions: grains, lentils, dried vegetables, spices and the like. Fortunately these foods are cheap and easily available in their own country – but overseas they are often difficult to find. This sometimes results in a situation that is very well suited to the operation of the first law of commerce.'

'I'm not sure I understand, sir.'

'To buy cheap and sell dear,' said Mr Burnham, 'is the first law of commerce, is it not?'

'Oh I see, sir!' said Zachary. 'What you mean is that those foods are cheap in India but dear over here?'

'Exactly! And if someone happens to possess a ship that is loaded with such provisions – and I will not conceal from you that the *Anahita* is one such – the opportunity for profit is boundless. But in order to dispose of cargoes like these the co-operation of one or two officers is almost always necessary. And that is the trouble – to obtain the co-operation of military men is not always easy, for many of them harbour a perverse suspicion of commerce. Indeed it could be said that as a class they are no less benighted than the Celestials in their hostility to the God-given laws of the market.'

'Really, sir?'

'Yes – regrettably it is all too true. But fortunately there are always a few who understand that God would not have endowed Man with a love of profit if it were not for his own good. If assured a share of the gains, they are often very helpful. Many are able to exert great influence on the purchasing officers of their commissariats.'

'But how are such men to be found, sir?'

'Through careful observation and hard work, Reid. The most important task is to collect information: one must try to find out which officers are living above their means and need money to pay off their creditors. On an expedition like this one you can be sure that there are many such – they volunteer precisely in the hope of gaining enough prize money to satisfy their creditors.'

Mr Burnham began to drum his fingertips on the deck-rail.

'I do not mind telling you, Reid, that I have my eye on an officer who may be just the man we need. I met him on the *Wellesley* a few days ago and was able to observe him at cards. He is exactly the kind of headstrong, free-spending fellow who is likely to be mired in debt. But I suspect he is hot-tempered too so he may not be easy to approach. It is sure to be a challenge.'

Mr Burnham paused to turn a speculative eye on Zachary. 'I am of a mind, Reid, to let you handle him. Do you think you are up for it?'

Answering on impulse Zachary said: 'Why of course, sir! You can count on me.'

'Good,' said Mr Burnham. 'I will leave him to you then. He will be attending our New Year's levée – his name is Captain Neville Mee.'

That Mr Burnham would name the one officer with whom he had almost come to blows was the last thing that Zachary had expected: an exclamation of alarm rose to his lips but he was able to bite it back.

Fortunately Mr Burnham did not seem to have noticed his discomfiture. 'Do you happen to know Captain Mee?'

'A little,' said Zachary hesitantly. 'He was on the *Hind* too.'

'Oh yes, of course,' said Mr Burnham. 'I'd forgotten about that. It's certainly propitious that you are already acquainted with him. Do you think you might be able to obtain his co-operation?'

To bribe Captain Mee would be no easy thing, Zachary knew, but now that he had committed himself he would have to go through with it or risk losing Mr Burnham's good opinion. 'I shall certainly try, sir. I'll do my best.'

*

Outside the gates of Dinyar Ferdoonjee's villa was a bench, facing the Praya Grande: often, when Captain Mee was invited to a tiffin or luncheon at the villa, Kesri would wait there so that they could return to Saw Chow Island together.

Kesri was sitting on that bench, waiting for Captain Mee to emerge from the villa after a late luncheon, when he noticed a memsahib walking briskly in his direction, her skirts swinging like the casing of a bell. She was wearing a wide hat with a netted veil hanging from the brim; on her shoulder rested a white parasol trimmed with lace.

When it became clear that the memsahib was heading for the villa, Kesri rose respectfully to his feet and held the gate open. He thought she would sweep past, with at best a nod for him. But instead she came to a halt and cocked her head, at such an angle that Kesri found himself looking directly into the visor of netting that covered her face. Then, to Kesri's astonishment, a low, throaty voice emerged from the shelter of the veil, addressing him by name, in Hindustani: *Kesri Singh? Mujhe pehchana nahi?* Don't you recognize me?

He shook his head dumbly, squinting into her veil: not till then did she realize that her face was hidden from his eyes. With a flick of her wrist, she threw back the netting.

Abh? Do you recognize me now?

After scanning her face once, twice and yet again, Kesri mumbled, in a hoarse, disbelieving voice: Cathy-mem? *Aap hai kya?* Is it you?

She laughed and continued, in Hindustani: *Hā* Kesri Singh! It's me.

Kesri saw now, hidden within the contours of her visage, the chrysalis of the girl he had known some twenty years before, when he had served as her gun-bearer. He recalled the directness and spontaneity that had made such an impression on him then and it seemed to him of a piece with the way she had stopped to talk to him now. Yet, even though her face had filled out, he noticed also that it was suffused with a kind of melancholy.

Maaf karna – forgive me, Cathy-mem, he said, for not recognizing you. But you look different somehow.

She laughed. *Aap bhi* – you too have changed, Kesri Singh, except for your eyes. That was why I recognized you, even though so much time has passed.

It must be twenty years or more, said Kesri.

That is true. I am 'Mrs Burnham' now – and you, I see, are a havildar?

Yes, Cathy-mem. And how is your father, the Jarnail-sahib?

He is well. My mother too. They have returned to England and my daughter has gone with them.

Only one daughter?

Yes, said Mrs Burnham, I have only the one daughter. And you, Kesri Singh? How many children do you have?

Four, said Kesri. Two boys and two girls. They are at home in my village, with my wife and family.

And your sister, Kesri Singh? The one you used to talk about? What was her name?

The question jolted Kesri: it was as if Deeti had reached out to him again, from the distant past. There was something so uncanny about it that he exclaimed in astonishment: *Kamaal hai!* Amazing that you remembered my sister! Her name is Deeti.

Yes, of course, she said with a smile. And you, Kesri Singh – what brings you here, to China?

The expedition, Cathy-mem. I decided to balamteer.

She dropped her eyes now, and he understood that there was something else on her mind. When she looked up again her voice was quieter and more tentative.

And what about everyone else in the Pacheesi? she said. The officers? How are they?

Kesri knew from her tone that the question was deceptive in its vagueness; he understood also that her inquiry concerned one officer in particular – and who could that be but Mr Mee? After all, he, Kesri, was perhaps the only person who was aware of what had passed between herself and Mr Mee all those years before.

At the thought of this an intuition of danger stirred within

Kesri: no good could come to Captain Mee surely, from lapsing again into the madness, the *junoon*, that had possessed him at that time? Cathy-mem was no longer a girl; she was married now, and no doubt her husband was rich and powerful, fully capable of destroying an officer of the rank of Mr Mee.

On a note of warning, Kesri said, in a low, flat voice: Mr Mee is here with us, Cathy-mem; he is the commander of my company.

Oh!

Kesri saw that the colour had suddenly drained from her face. He added quickly: Mee-sahib is inside this house, Cathy-mem – he has gone there for tiffin.

Yahā hai? He is here?

Mrs Burnham froze and Kesri had the impression that she was about to turn on her heel and walk away. But just then a voice called out: 'Mrs Burnham, is that you?'

It was Shireen. 'How very nice to see you, Mrs Burnham!' She came hurrying down to greet the visitor. 'Do come in!'

'Oh hello, Mrs Moddie.'

As they were shaking hands Shireen noticed that Mrs Burnham's fingers were trembling slightly; glancing at her face she saw that she had turned very pale.

'What's the matter, Mrs Burnham? Are you not well?'

The parasol dropped suddenly from Mrs Burnham's grasp. She swayed, clasping a hand to her chest. Fearing that she would fall, Shireen took hold of her elbow and helped her towards the veranda.

'But Mrs Burnham! What in heavens is the matter?'

'Just a spell of dizziness,' said Mrs Burnham faintly, pressing a hand to her temple. 'I'm sorry to be such a gudda. It's nothing really.'

'Oh but you must sit down!'

Shireen helped her up to the veranda and showed her to a chair. 'Would you like a drink of water, Mrs Burnham?'

Mrs Burnham nodded and was about to say something when the voices of Dinyar and his friends came echoing down the vestibule. A moment later the front door flew open and Dinyar stepped out. Behind him came Captain Mee and a couple of other officers.

Captain Mee raised a hand to the bill of his shako: 'Goodbye, Mrs Moddie – thank you for the delicious karibat.'

'Goodbye, Captain Mee.'

418

Shireen noticed that the captain's eyes had wandered to her visitor. She turned to Mrs Burnham, thinking that she would introduce her to Captain Mee – but only to find that Mrs Burnham was sitting with her face averted and her veil lowered: it was clear from her posture that she did not wish to be introduced.

Shireen waved the men off and then went to sit beside Mrs Burnham. Before she could speak, Mrs Burnham whispered: 'Forgive me, Mrs Moddie, if I seemed rude – but I'm feeling too poorly to meet anyone.'

'I perfectly understand,' said Shireen. 'Would you like to lie down for a moment?'

'Yes, perhaps.'

Taking hold of her hand Shireen led her visitor indoors, to her own bedroom, where she helped her remove her headgear and lie down.

Mrs Burnham's veil came off to reveal a face that was beaded with moisture. The feverishness of her appearance alarmed Shireen. 'Should I fetch a doctor, Mrs Burnham?'

'Please, no!' said Mrs Burnham, stretching herself out on the bed. 'It is just a spell of the chukkers. It will pass in a minute.'

'Are you sure?'

'Yes.'

Mrs Burnham patted the bed. 'Won't you sit beside me, Mrs Moddie?'

'You must call me Shireen. Please.'

'Of course. And you must call me Cathy.'

Mrs Burnham's eyes wandered to the framed picture that stood beside the bed. 'That is your late husband, is it not, Shireen?'

'Yes.' Shireen picked up the picture and handed it to her.

Mrs Burnham studied the portrait for a few minutes, in silence. Presently she said, in a soft voice: 'He was a handsome man.'

Shireen smiled in acknowledgement but said nothing.

'I have heard,' Mrs Burnham continued, 'many stories about your husband. Mr Burnham thinks the world of him – that is why he asked me to call on you today.'

The words brought a quiver to Shireen's lips; she turned her face away and buried her head in her shoulder.

'You must have loved him very much,' Mrs Burnham whispered.

Unable to speak, Shireen smiled wanly.

Mrs Burnham continued: 'But you know, Shireen, even though you have lost him, you must count yourself very lucky – it is not given to every woman to spend her life with the man she loves.'

She seemed to choke as she was saying this. Shireen shot her a startled glance and saw that she too was wiping her eyes now.

'Cathy? Whatever is the matter?'

Mrs Burnham was struggling to compose herself now, trying to summon a smile – but instead she succeeded only in looking more and more stricken. Where her grief came from Shireen did not know and nor did it matter – even though they knew very little about one another, it was as if they understood each other perfectly.

Mrs Burnham too seemed to be moved by the intimacy of the moment. She took hold of Shireen's hand and whispered: 'We shall be good friends I think, shan't we, Shireen?'

'Yes, Cathy – I think we shall.'

'Well then, I hope you will come to the *Anahita* next week – Mr Burnham and I are holding a sunset levée, on the first day of the New Year. We would both so much like to have you with us.'

'Oh that's very kind of you, but . . .'

Suddenly Shireen was bereft of words: how could she possibly explain that for her the *Anahita* was no ordinary ship? Every time Bahram set sail from Bombay she had been present at the dock, praying that the *Anahita* would keep him safe – in vain, as it turned out, since it was from that very ship that he had fallen to his death.

Mrs Burnham gave her hand a squeeze: 'Oh please, do say you will come.'

'I would like to come, Cathy,' said Shireen. 'It's just that it's bound to be a little trying for me since I suppose I shall be reminded of my husband's accident . . .' She paused. 'But it might be a little easier if I could bring some friends of my husband's – Mr Karabedian and perhaps his godson . . . ?'

Before she could finish, Mrs Burnham broke in: 'Yes, of course. Do please bring your friends. It'll be a pleasure to have them with us.'

*

At the end of the day, when Kesri and the officers were back at the camp on Saw Chow Island, a runner came to deliver an order: Kesri was to report at once to Captain Mee's tent.

Although it was quite late, Captain Mee was still in his uniform. 'Havildar, there's a message from Commodore Bremer. He says we have to be prepared for a resumption of hostilities. A few days ago Captain Elliot sent the mandarins an ultimatum, warning them that they would face attack if they did not meet our demands immediately. The ultimatum has expired so we may have to move any day now.'

'When will we know, Kaptán-sah'b?'

'It'll probably be a while yet,' said the captain, yawning. 'I'm sure they'll carry on buck-bucking as long as they possibly can. But I thought you should know.'

Ji, Kaptán-sah'b.

For the last several hours, Kesri had been hoping for an opportunity to speak to Captain Mee in private. Sensing that he was about to be dismissed, he said: 'Kaptán-sah'b, there is one more thing.'

'What is it, havildar? Jaldee please.'

'Kaptán-sah'b – today, when I was waiting for you at the house of the Parsi merchant, in Macau . . .'

'Yes?'

'. . . a memsah'b recognized me.'

'So?' The captain raised an eyebrow. 'What of it?'

'It was Miss Cathy, Kaptán-sah'b.'

The captain's head snapped back and the colour drained slowly out of his swarthy face.

'You mean . . . ?'

'Ji, Kaptán-sah'b: it was Jarnail Bradshaw's larki.'

Picking up a paperweight the captain began to spin it on his desk, like a top. Without looking at Kesri, he said: 'Was she the lady in the veil?'

Ji, Kaptán-sah'b.

'You're sure it was Cathy?'

'Yes, Kaptán-sah'b. She saw me and we talked. She asked about you.'

'What did you tell her?'

'I said you were here, with the expedition – she did not know till then.'

A look of incomprehension appeared on the captain's face now as he raised his eyes from the desk. 'What is Cathy doing in China, havildar?'

'She is here with her husband, Kaptán-sah'b. His name is Mr Bunn-am. Something like that.'

'Burnham?'

'Yes, Kaptán-sah'b. She said her name is Mrs Burnham.'

'Oh my God!'

Rising from his chair, the captain began to pace the tent. 'I should have known . . . I just didn't think of it . . .'

'Think of what, Kaptán-sah'b?'

Captain Mee shot him a sidelong glance.

'I met her husband the other day, on the *Wellesley*. It just didn't occur to me that he was . . . that he might be . . . anyway he's invited the officers of this company to his ship on New Year's Day. He wants to make a proper tumasher out of it – presenting arms, saluting the flag and all that. I told him I'd bring along a squad of sepoys, and some fifers and drummers too.'

The captain stopped to look out at the estuary. 'I suppose Cathy will be there, won't she?'

Ji, Kaptán-sah'b. Clearing his throat, Kesri coughed hesitantly into his fist. 'Maybe, Kaptán-sah'b . . .'

'Yes, havildar?'

'Maybe you should not go.'

To Kesri's surprise the captain did not snap at him as he had half-expected. Instead he sighed, in a manner that seemed to suggest a kind of resignation in the face of a kismet that he was powerless to change. 'It's the devil's benison, havildar,' he said. 'But I can't not see her – I have to go—'

Breaking off, he turned to face Kesri. 'But I'd be glad if you were there too, havildar. I'd like you to take charge of the squad that'll be going with me.'

'That is an order, sir?'

'No,' said the captain. 'It's not – but I'd like you to do it anyway.'

The captain's air of authority had completely evaporated now; in his eyes there was a look of almost childlike confusion and vulnerability. It was as though the accumulated bitterness of the last many years had drained away and he had become once again the impetuous and open-hearted boy that he had been when Kesri was his orderly, all those years ago – except that even in those days he had never pleaded with Kesri in this way; nor had he ever revealed his emotions to this extent. It was as if the cavity in which he hoarded his anguish had grown deeper and deeper over time, even as his outward self was growing harder and more coarse: now that the pain had broken through he seemed to be helpless, completely at the mercy of his emotions.

Kesri made no further attempt to dissuade the captain from going; it was clear to him now that it was beyond his power to protect his erstwhile butcha.

'Ji, Kaptán-sah'b. I will come with the squad.'

Sixteen

The *Cambridge* was a good distance away, riding at anchor at Whampoa, when Jodu pointed her out to Neel. She was like no vessel that Neel had set eyes on, a curious amalgam of West and East. In outline she was like any full-rigged English merchantman but the adornments with which she was bedecked gave her the appearance of a war-junk in disguise: pennants with yin-yang symbols and flags with the Chinese character for 'courage' fluttered atop her masts; paper lanterns were strung up over her decks; and long banners, with Chinese lettering, were suspended from her gunwales, hanging down almost to the water, like gigantic scrolls. As with any junk, her bows sported two huge eyes. This touch made her appear at once familiar and faintly comical: in Bengal too locally made boats of all kinds, large and small, commonly had eyes painted on their bows – yet there was no denying that the design looked out of place on a Liverpool-built three-master.

On stepping aboard Neel encountered many other surprises: while the geography of the vessel's interior remained European the pattern of use was quite different. The ship's Chinese officers had chosen to occupy the fo'c'sle, which on Western vessels was always assigned to crewmen; it was the lascars who were berthed in the roundhouse, which, on an English ship, would have been the exclusive preserve of the ships' officers.

The functioning of the *Cambridge* too was unlike that of a Western ship. There was no 'captain' as such, but rather an officer whose position was like that of the *lao-dah* of a junk – more a co-ordinator than a commander in the Western fashion. This suited the crew very well since most operational matters were left to them: decisions were generally arrived at by consensus which meant that the atmosphere on board was more relaxed than on most ships.

The crewmen were a varied lot – apart from Indian lascars there were contingents of sailors from Java, Sumatra, the Moluccas, the Philippines and of course Guangdong – but they generally got on well together and there was a great deal of camaraderie on board.

But for all that, there was also something a little unreal about the atmosphere of the *Cambridge*. The vessel was always surrounded by guard-boats and the crewmen were never allowed ashore except with an armed escort: whether this was for their own protection or to prevent them from deserting was not clear. But Jodu was certainly not the only member of the crew who joked about the *Cambridge* being a floating jail.

For Neel the most discomfiting thing about being on the *Cambridge* was the lack of news: she could have been at sea for all that her crew knew of what was happening around them.

Fortunately Compton had become, by default, the go-between who conveyed the orders of the Guangzhou authorities to the crew of the *Cambridge*. He was always a fount of information so his visits were eagerly awaited, and by none more so than Neel.

After a year of working closely with Compton, Neel had become very finely attuned to his friend's moods. As the weeks went by he noticed a marked change in Compton's usually buoyant spirits: at every visit he seemed more and more despondent. Other than ferrying messages he had little work to do, he said. The new Governor-General, Qishan, had brought along a translator of his own, a man by the name of Peng Bao. The trouble was that this man was not really a translator but rather a linkister, whose knowledge of English was limited to *Yangjinbang* or pidgin English: for many years he had worked for a notorious British opium smuggler, Lancelot Dent. This Peng Bao was a *hou gau*, a low fellow, the kind of man who 'lies even while praying'. Yet, he had somehow succeeded in gaining the Governor-General's ear even as Commissioner Lin's advisors and translators were being shoved aside. The old translation bureau had been more or less disbanded and Zhong Lou-si was no longer consulted on matters of any importance.

At the start of November Compton confided something that came as an even greater surprise to Neel: he said he was in the process of moving his family away from Guangzhou. He had decided to send them back to his village, which was on the coast, not far from Chuenpee.

Neel was startled to hear this because he knew that Compton had a great love of Guangzhou, as did his family.

Why? Has something happened?

Compton's face darkened. Things were changing very fast in Guangzhou, he said. Words like 'traitor' and 'spy' were being thrown around so freely that everyone who had ever had any contact with foreigners had reason to be afraid; the place was becoming a 'crocodile pool'. If things got worse there was no telling what might happen: it was for their own safety that he had decided to move his family.

Even on the *Cambridge* the crewmen were aware that tensions were rising around them. But this did not deter the ship's Muslim lascars from continuing to make their monthly visits to the Huaisheng mosque in Guangzhou. For reasons of prudence, they no longer took the public ferries that connected Whampoa and Guangzhou but travelled instead on hired boats with armed escorts. Their usual practice was to go up on a Thursday afternoon; they would stay the night at the mosque and return to the *Cambridge* the next day, after the noon prayers.

Opportunities to escape the confinement of the *Cambridge* were rare enough that Neel took to accompanying the lascars on their monthly outings. After Jodu and his friends had gone off to the Huaisheng mosque, he would cross over to the other side of the river, to make his way to the Ocean Banner Monastery where he could always be sure of a warm welcome from Taranathji. Often Compton too would come over to meet him there.

On one such visit, in the depth of winter, the three of them – Neel, Taranathji and Compton – had a long talk. Compton said that he had it on good authority that the new Governor-General, Qishan, did not want to provoke another armed confrontation with the British; if the decision were his own to make then he would have acceded to the British demands. But the Emperor had expressly forbidden him to make any concessions. The orders from Beijing remained unchanged: the 'rebel aliens' had to be expelled from China at all costs.

Here Taranathji interjected that the best chance of achieving this end would have been to follow the advice of the Gurkhas:

to attack the British in the rear by launching a joint expedition against the East India Company's territories in Bengal. Had the British been compelled to defend themselves in India they would have had no option but to withdraw from China.

This brought a rueful smile to Compton's face: he revealed that he had heard from Zhong Lou-si that the present Gurkha king, Rajendra Bikram Shah, had recently renewed his offer of military intervention; he had urged Beijing to support him in an attack on British forces in Bengal.

On hearing this Neel sat upright, his hopes soaring. And what had come of the Gurkha offer? he asked. Was there any chance that the Chinese would join the Gurkhas in an overland attack on British India?

Compton shook his head: No, he said, it was against Beijing's policy to make alliances with other kingdoms. And in any case the Qing did not entirely trust the Gurkhas.

Something snapped in Neel's head when he heard this.

Oh you are fools, you Han-ren! he cried out. Despite all your cleverness you are fools! Don't you see, this is the only stratagem that might have worked? The Gurkhas were right all along!

Compton made a gesture of resignation. What does it matter now, Ah Neel? It's already too late.

That night Neel lay awake thinking how different things might have been, in Hindustan and China, if the Qing had acted on the advice they'd received from their Nepali tributaries. The Gurkhas might even have succeeded in creating a realm that straddled much of the Gangetic plain; a state strong enough to hold off the European powers.

But for the short-sightedness of a few men in Beijing the map of the world might have been quite different . . .

Just as Neel was drifting into sleep there was a sudden outburst of noise, across the river, in the foreign enclave. Running outside he saw that a fireworks display was under way at the threshold of the American Factory, where a number of foreign merchants were still in residence.

Evidently they were celebrating the arrival of the Western New Year: 1841 had just begun.

*

Shireen had initially planned to wear her best evening dress to the Burnhams' New Year's Day levée. But as the days went by the thought of stepping on the *Anahita* in European clothes became oddly disturbing to her: she could not rid herself of the idea that Bahram – for whom the ship had been built – would not approve. When the day came she decided to wear a sari instead – one that Bahram had given her, a mauve silk *gara* that had been embroidered in Canton.

In keeping with Shireen's choice of clothing Freddie and Zadig also decided to dispense with their usual jackets and trowsers. On the afternoon of the levée, Zadig arrived at the villa looking like a grandee of the Sublime Porte, in a burumcuk caftan and a tall, black calpac. Freddie was a step behind him, dressed in a simple but elegant Chinese robe, with a finely ornamented collar. On his freshly shaved face there was an expression that Shireen had never seen before, a look of taut, expectant alertness: it was evident that the prospect of re-visiting the *Anahita* had stirred up a ferment of emotions in him.

It had been arranged that they would meet the *Anahita*'s long-boat at a quay on the other side of the Macau promontory, on the shore that faced the Outer Harbour. Shireen was transported there in a sedan chair and much to her surprise she was recognized as soon as she stepped up to the boat. The serang came hurrying forward to greet her, with a hand cupped to his forehead: *Salaam, Bibiji. Khem chho?*

Shireen was startled to be greeted in Gujarati, and that too in a fashion that suggested that the man knew who she was. But then, looking at him more closely, she realized that he was a member of the *Anahita*'s original crew. As with many others in that contingent he had been with her family even before the ship was built, having been recruited from Kutch, as a boy, to work on her father's own batelo yacht.

Yusufji? said Shireen. Is it you?

Ji, Bibiji.

The serang was pleased to be recognized and a wide grin spread slowly across his bearded, weather-beaten face.

Are you still working on the *Anahita* then?

The serang nodded in affirmation: Mr Burnham had retained the *Anahita*'s crew in its entirety, he said. Every man on the ship had once worked for Seth Bahram; she was 'Bibiji' to all of them and the news that she was coming aboard that day had caused much excitement on the vessel.

Bibiji, said the serang, the timbers of the *Anahita* may have changed hands, but her spirit will always belong to you and your family. Ships are like horses, Bibiji; they remember the people who rear them.

The affinities of mutual recognition seemed to deepen as the pinnace moved ahead. Shireen had no difficulty in picking out the *Anahita* amidst all the other vessels that were at anchor in the channel: neither a merchantman nor a warship, she had the sleek elegance of a pleasure yacht.

The *Anahita* too seemed to stir in recognition as the pinnace drew up: many of her crewmen flocked to the bulwarks, craning their heads over the deck-rails to catch a glimpse of the returning Bibiji. Their enthusiasm embarrassed Shireen – it was almost as though she were coming back to claim an inheritance that had been seized by usurpers. She could not help wondering whether her hosts would be affronted by her reception.

But if Mrs Burnham was put out she gave no sign of it; she greeted all three of them with great cordiality but was especially warm to Shireen. Linking arms with her, she said: 'You must know this ship very well, don't you, Shireen dear?'

'Yes, so I do.' Shireen was glad to see that Mrs Burnham was completely recovered from her attack of ill-health: she was wearing a very becoming evening gown, of a primrose colour with a high, roxaline bodice and ballooning mameluke sleeves.

'Would you and your friends like to take a dekko at the after-quarters, for old times' sake?'

'That would be very nice. Yes, thank you.'

'Well come on then,' said Mrs Burnham, 'I'll show you around before everyone else arrives.'

Shireen had expected to find the interior of the *Anahita* much changed, and so indeed it was. The companion-way that led to Bahram's suite of cabins had once been decorated with paintings and carved panels, featuring Zoroastrian and Assyrian motifs. The pictures and woodwork were gone now; there were no images anywhere to be seen.

A still greater surprise awaited at the far end of the gangway where lay the 'Owner's Suite'. This was the most lavishly appointed part of the vessel and had been especially designed to serve as Bahram's personal living quarters. It was here that he had always slept, in a large, richly decorated cumra with windows that overlooked the *Anahita*'s stern.

Shireen had assumed that the Burnhams, as the new owners, would take that suite for themselves – but when the door swung open she saw to her surprise that it was being used, instead, as a baggage hold. A great jumble of furniture was piled up inside – chairs, tables, disassembled bedsteads, settees, chaises-longues, even an upright pianoforte. One of the two windows was wide open.

'I'm afraid this suite has had its troubles,' said Mrs Burnham. 'We were hit by a squall as we were approaching the China coast and the windows in this cumra flew open. The whole suite was flooded and will have to be completely refurbished, at a shipyard. Until then we've decided to use it as an attic.'

She raised a hand to point aft. 'Look at that window over there. I told a kussab to shut it just a few minutes ago but I suppose the badmash forgot.'

Freddie took a step towards the window. 'You want me to close it, lah?'

'Would you please?'

After shutting the window Freddie stepped back to look towards the reddening horizon, through the glass.

'Bahram-bhai loved those windows,' said Zadig. 'I remember so well how he would lie in his bed, gazing into the distance.'

These words, evocative as they were, conjured up for Shireen so vivid an image of her husband that it was as if he had himself appeared within the darkening shadows, to watch the sunset. At home in Bombay too she had often seen him in that attitude, gazing at the sea with a pensive, slightly melancholy air. She had sometimes wondered what was on his mind and it struck her now that he must have been thinking of Canton: of his mistress and his son, Freddie, who, at this very moment, was looking out of the window in a manner that was strangely reminiscent of his father.

Or was it just that the cabin was so saturated with Bahram's memory that it seemed to conjure up his very presence?

A shiver went through Shireen. 'Please, Cathy,' she said. 'I think I need some fresh air.'

'Why yes, of course,' said Mrs Burnham. 'It's rather musty in here, isn't it? Let's go back on deck.'

She slipped her arm through Shireen's and they stepped back into the gangway. As they were heading towards the deck they were waylaid by Baboo Nob Kissin. Captain Mee and sepoys had arrived, he said. The Burra Sahib had asked Mrs Burnham to come to the maindeck, to receive them.

'Thank you, Baboo.'

Mrs Burnham's voice sounded languid, almost indifferent – but Shireen, whose arm was still entwined in hers, felt a tremor passing through her body, followed by a distinct quickening in her breath.

'Cathy? Is something the matter?'

'Why no,' said Mrs Burnham in a slightly breathless voice. 'I'm perfectly theek.'

But even as she said this, she was tightening her grip on Shireen's arm, leaning on her, as if for support. 'You know Captain Mee already, don't you, Shireen? Won't you come with me to receive him?'

'Yes, of course,' said Shireen.

They went out on deck to find a line of fifers and drummers filing up the side-ladder. After stepping on board, the boys crossed smartly over to the far end, where the sepoys had already assembled, between the bows.

Captain Mee was the last of the officers to come up the ladder: he cut a splendid figure, in his full dress uniform, with a sword at his side and a scarlet cape slung over his shoulder. As he was stepping on deck Mrs Burnham again tightened her grip on Shireen's arm, which she had been leaning on all this while. Her agitation seemed to mount as her husband welcomed the captain on board. They stood talking for a minute and then Mr Burnham was led away by another guest – so it fell to Shireen to introduce the captain to Mrs Burnham. And as she was doing it Shireen noticed that Mrs Burnham had turned pale; then her eyes went to Captain Mee and she saw that he too had changed colour, his face growing a bright red. When he took hold of Mrs

Burnham's hand the cockade of his shako, which he was holding under his arm, began to tremble like a leaf. For a minute they both stood tongue-tied, staring at each other; then Captain Mee began to tug at his collar as though he were about to choke.

It was all very puzzling to Shireen and she looked away, wondering whether she was imagining things. But then she noticed that Havildar Kesri Singh was also observing the encounter between Captain Mee and Mrs Burnham with keen interest. When his gaze met Shireen's he seemed to take it as a signal to intervene and came hurrying over to the captain's side: 'Sir – something has come up . . .'

As Kesri was leading the captain away, Shireen said to Mrs Burnham: 'Is something the matter, Cathy?'

'No – not at all!' said Mrs Burnham – but her eyes, Shireen noticed, were still following Captain Mee and Kesri Singh.

'I saw you talking to the havildar that day,' said Shireen, 'at the Villa Nova. Do you know him?'

'Yes,' said Mrs Burnham faintly. 'Kesri Singh was in my father's regiment, I knew him many years ago.'

'Really?' Struck by a chance thought, Shireen said: 'But surely then you must know Captain Mee too? He once mentioned that he and the havildar had been in the same regiment for close to twenty years.'

Mrs Burnham's response startled Shireen; her lips began to tremble and she shut her eyes for a moment. 'Yes you are right, Shireen dear,' she whispered. 'As a matter of fact I do know Mr Mee. Some day I will tell you how we met . . .'

And just then Baboo Nob Kissin appeared again to make another announcement: 'Miss Paulette Lambert's boat has arrived.'

Shireen stood back to watch as Mrs Burnham went to greet the new arrival.

Paulette was dressed in an old-fashioned black carriage dress, with a high collar, and her head was covered with something that looked like a widow's bonnet. Her clothes sat awkwardly on her and her face too was not pretty in a conventional sense. Yet it struck Shireen that there was something about her that was arresting to the eye, a kind of luminosity.

From the other side of the maindeck Zachary too was watching and when Mrs Burnham and Paulette threw their arms around each other a strange oscillating jealousy took hold of him, ricocheting from Paulette to Mrs Burnham and back again. It was as if the two women represented the poles of his desires, one of them forthright, spontaneous and simple in her tastes; the other engimatic, sophisticated, wedded to luxury. The image of them together sparked an epiphany: he realized that different though they were, he would always be in thrall to both – but it didn't matter, for he knew also that they were both forever lost to him.

*

Paulette too had caught sight of Zachary, from the corner of her eye, and was instantly thrown into a ferment: the wounds inflicted by his letter were still so raw that she could not bear the thought of speaking to him. Had she known that he would be at the levée she would not have come – but now it was too late.

Spinning around on her heel she headed almost blindly in the other direction, towards a companion-ladder. On reaching the top, she found herself on the quarter-deck where a sizeable company had already gathered: it consisted mainly of uniformed officers, most of them young. Stewards were circulating within the throng, bearing trays laden with beverages and refreshments. Although the sun had yet to sink below the horizon, brightly coloured Chinese lanterns were already alight, hanging in rows from the ship's beams and rigging.

Almost at once Mr Doughty appeared at her side. 'Oh shahbash, Miss Lambert!' he cried out. 'I didn't know you'd be here – I am ekdum khush to see you! I'd heard that you were in these parts and have been looking out for you!'

Paulette too was glad to see a known face: 'Mr Doughty! What a grand surprise to re-encounter you here – chez the Burnhams', encore!'

This resulted in the unspooling of a chain of reminiscences, about the Burnhams' entertainments in Calcutta. 'Oh they were fine old tumashers, weren't they, those Burnham burra-khanas? Do you remember the ortolans, Miss Lambert? And the chitchkies of pollock-saug? Just to think of the Burnham table is enough to bring on a shoke for more.'

'You have reason, Mr Doughty . . .'

At this point Paulette became aware that a figure had entered the edge of her field of vision: even without looking she knew it to be Zachary. A tremor went through her, as the shadow moved from the periphery of her vision towards its centre, yet somehow, by an effort of will, she succeeded in keeping her eyes focused on Mr Doughty's face, grimly noting the details – the pores on his fleshy cheeks and the twitching hairs of his mutton-chop whiskers. Then, hearing an ominous clearing of the throat, she realized that Zachary was now attempting to enter the conversation. In an effort to pre-empt him, she began to talk at great speed, hoping to shake him off by prolonging her conversation with Mr Doughty: 'And do you remember Mrs Burnham's way of dressing a quail, all wrapped up in bacon? Like a cock in a capote, she liked to say.'

'Oh yes, who could forget those? The very thought sets my jib a-twitch.'

'And what of all the marvellous stews that were served at her table, Mr Doughty? I own that I have never had a better dumbpoke than in that house.'

Mr Doughty, who was still unaware that Zachary was looming behind him, responded enthusiastically. 'And what of the relishes and condiments, Miss Lambert? Do you remember those? Would you not agree that if ever there was a chutney to be chartered it is Mrs Burnham's?'

At this stage Paulette realized, with some relief, that her stratagem had met with unexpected success: Zachary had withdrawn a little and was hanging his head, as if in shame. His discomfiture, inexplicable though it was, heartened her and she would not have been averse to drawing it out still further – but this proved impossible for the talk of food had whetted Mr Doughty's appetite. Spotting a steward with a laden tray, he sped away with an abrupt 'Excuse me!' leaving Paulette in exactly the situation that she had most wanted to avoid: alone with Zachary.

As Zachary cleared his throat, Paulette cast a panic-stricken glance around her. But there was no rescue at hand: all she could do was to look away, hoping that it would dissuade him from addressing her.

But the result was not as she had hoped: her averted face, far from discouraging Zachary, had the effect of transporting him back to the days when quarrels were his only means of coaxing her out of the shadows and into his arms. It was as though he had reverted to an earlier avatar of himself, when his ambitions had been simpler and Paulette had been the principal object of his desire. The carefully worded apology that he had composed, at Mrs Burnham's behest, slipped his mind: all he could think of to say was: 'Miss Lambert, there is something I need to say to you.'

Zachary's all too evident discomfort gave Paulette the courage to answer with a sharp retort: 'Mr Reid, your needs are nothing to me. I do not wish to know about them.'

Zachary ran a finger around his neck, to loosen his collar. 'Please Miss Lambert—'

And at this critical juncture, when she was all but cornered, Paulette's rescue was sounded by a gong.

'Ladies! Gentlemen!'

The voice was Mr Burnham's and it gave Paulette the perfect reason to turn her back on Zachary.

*

'Ladies and gentlemen,' Mr Burnham began, 'a few words before we say a prayer for the success of the mission for which this expeditionary force has been assembled.'

Mr Burnham's stance was like that of a preacher at a pulpit, with one hand on the binnacle, and the other on the lapel of his jacket.

'As you may know,' said Mr Burnham in his booming voice, 'a fortnight ago Captain Elliot issued an ultimatum to Qishan, the new Governor-General of this province; he warned him that Canton would face attack if our demands were not met. That ultimatum has long since expired and there is little likelihood that we will ever receive an answer. It is common knowledge now that the Emperor's edict to his mandarins is to "annihilate the barbarians".'

Here Mr Burnham paused to survey his audience, which was listening in hushed silence. His voice swelled as he continued: 'Well, the Manchu tyrant shall have his opportunity soon enough! I have it on good authority that hostilities will resume very soon, possibly within the week. The outcome – which is not in the slightest doubt – will be of truly historic importance.'

Now Mr Burnham turned to Captain Mee, who was standing

beside him. Raising a hand, he placed it on the captain's epaulette.

'On shoulders such as these will fall the task of freeing a quarter of mankind from tyranny; of bestowing on the people of China the gift of liberty that the British Empire has already conferred on all those parts of the globe that it has conquered and subjugated.'

Mr Burnham paused to gesture at all the young officers who were assembled on the quarter-deck.

'It is you, gentlemen, who will give to the Chinese the gifts that Britain has granted to the countless millions who glory in the rule of our gracious monarch, secure in the knowledge that there is no greater freedom, no greater cause for pride, than to be subjects of the British Empire. This is the divine mission that the Almighty Himself has entrusted to our race and our nation. I do not doubt for a moment, gentlemen, that you shall once again prove yourselves to be worthy of it.

'Let no one say that our government has voluntarily sought this conflict. To the contrary, we have been exemplars of patience; we have suffered insults, indignities and oppression with unmoving fortitude; we have sent mission after mission to parlay with the godless tyrant who calls himself the Son of Heaven – but all our efforts at diplomacy have come to nothing. Our ambassadors – representatives of the most powerful nation on earth – have been insulted or turned away; epithets like "barbarian eye" have been hurled at them; they have been told that they must prostrate themselves before the despot who claims to enjoy a divine mandate. All our efforts at conciliation and compromise have been unavailing; the Manchu oppressor has rebuffed them all. It is he who, through his vainglorious ignorance, has brought upon himself the dreadful reckoning that shortly awaits him and his cohorts. It is he who bears the ultimate responsibility for the intolerable affronts that Commissioner Lin has inflicted on us, culminating as they did in an act of the grossest thievery – the seizure of our cargoes. But let it not be said for a moment that our present crusade is motivated by a desire for monetary restitution. This was a predestined conflict, as inevitable as the struggle between Cain and Abel. On one side stands a race that is mired in depravity, tyranny, self-conceit and evil; ranged on the other side are the truest, most virile representatives of freedom, civilization and progress that history has ever known.'

Here a burst of applause interrupted Mr Burnham; he raised a hand to acknowledge it before resuming.

'Let us not forget that at the heart of this conflict lie two precious and inviolable values, freedom and dignity. This war will be fought not only to liberate the Sons of Han from Manchu tyranny, but also to protect our own dignity, which has suffered greater outrages in this land than in any other.'

This was answered by a spontaneous chorus of 'Shame! Shame!'

Mr Burnham let the shouts die down before continuing: 'Is it conceivable that we should forever swallow the insults that are hurled at white men in this land? Shall we always permit ourselves to be vilified as "barbarians", "foreign devils", "red-haired demons" and the like?'

The gathering responded with a roar: 'No! Never!'

'Is it conceivable,' said Mr Burnham, 'that we, who stand under the proudest, most warlike flag on earth, should not seek satisfaction for repeated and heinous affronts to the representatives of our most gracious Sovereign?'

Again he paused and again the gathering answered with a roar: 'No!'

'So be it!' said Mr Burnham. 'Let the Celestials taste the retribution they have invited upon themselves and let us hope that it will make them turn towards the path of redemption – for does not the Good Book say, "If ye endure chastening, God dealeth with you as sons; for what son is he whom the father chasteneth not?" Indeed I envy the Chinese their good fortune in that the rod of their chastening will be wielded by hands like these.'

Reaching for Captain Mee's wrist, Mr Burnham held up his arm, drawing cheers from the audience.

Now, with the last rays of the setting sun shining directly on him, Mr Burnham's face reddened, as if in exaltation: 'I have not the least doubt, gentlemen, that God will bless and aid you in your endeavour, for it is His work that you will be doing. When the task is finished China will be changed beyond recognition: this will be your legacy to history. Future generations will read with wonder of the miracle that you have wrought. Truly will it be said that never in the history of the world was so great a transformation brought about by so small a company of men!'

As cheers erupted around him, Mr Burnham raised a hand: 'And now, gentlemen, let us say a prayer.'

*

Paulette was murmuring the words of the prayer, with her head lowered, when she caught another glimpse of Zachary and realized that he was still hovering nearby. She would make her escape as soon as the prayer was over, she decided – but before she could slip away she was distracted by another announcement: 'And now, ladies and gentlemen, a salute to our flag, by our fine Bengal sepoys.'

Even as Kesri was calling out the first command, Zachary was whispering in Paulette's ear: 'There is something I need to say to you . . .'

Escape being impossible now, Paulette headed aft, to the far end of the deck, where there was no danger of their being overheard. At every step she felt that she was being pushed literally to her limit; when she reached the bulwark she turned on Zachary, eyes blazing: 'No, Mr Reid!' she hissed. 'There is nothing that you need to say to me. Was your letter not enough? I know you now for what you are – a liar and betrayer. You are a person whose words are without worth or value. There is nothing you can say that would be of the least interest to me.'

These words, and the vehemence with which they were spoken, stung Zachary so deeply that his carefully composed apology wilted on his tongue. He could not think why he had indulged Mrs Burnham's hopes of a reconciliation: why should he be saddled with the task of making amends for a misunderstanding on her part? He had done more than enough for Paulette in the past and had never had anything but grief for his pains: his chief impulse now was to make Paulette eat her words, even the least of them – and at just that moment a shouted command drew his eyes to Kesri, who was standing at attention, at the far end of the maindeck, with his sword ceremonially upraised.

Suddenly Zachary knew exactly what he had to say.

'Did you mean it, Miss Lambert,' he said, 'when you said that I have nothing of interest to say to you?'

'Yes I did.'

'Very well then – I shall undertake to prove you wrong.'

Zachary turned to point to Kesri who was now shouting a command at the squad of sepoys.

'You see the havildar over there?' said Zachary. 'That tall sepoy? Well, I think it will be of great interest to you, Miss Paulette, to know who he is.'

'Why? Who is he?'

Zachary paused so that his revelation, when it was made, would have the maximum effect: 'He is the brother of your friend from the *Ibis* – Ditty.'

Paulette drew back, in shock. 'I do not believe you, Mr Reid,' she said, in a wavering voice. 'You have misled me many times before – why should I repose any trust in what you say?'

'Because it is true, Miss Lambert. The havildar and I travelled here on the same ship, the *Hind*. Somehow he found out that I had been on the *Ibis*. He came to speak to me about his sister and I told him what I knew. He asked me not to tell anyone about it, and I have respected his request, till today. But you at least should know who he is – for perhaps it will help you to remember that it was because of Ditty that you came to my cabin that night, on the *Ibis*; it was for her sake that you begged me to let her husband escape, along with the other fugitives. I did as you asked, and for that I have had to spend many months in confinement, sleeping on cold stone floors, while you' – now, as the memories of all his old grievances came flooding back, Zachary's tone sharpened – 'while you were lying on a bed of flowers and roses, having been adopted by a rich man.'

Stung into silence, Paulette could think of no retort.

'Yes, Miss Lambert,' Zachary continued, 'the *Ibis* has left us with many secrets and I have been faithful in keeping them. I may not be as much of a betrayer and liar as you think.'

Listening to him Paulette was suddenly, blindingly, aware of the import of his words: she understood that no matter how much she might want to be finished with Zachary, she would never be free of him – the bond of the *Ibis* was like a living thing, endowed with the power to reach out from the past to override the volition of those who were enmeshed in it. It was as if she were being mocked for harbouring the illusion that she was free to decide her own destiny.

Before she could think of anything more to say Zachary tipped his hat at her and bowed: 'Good day, Miss Lambert. I do not know if we shall meet again, but if we do you may be sure that it will not be by my design.'

*

A burst of applause rang out as the sepoys' salute drew to a close. When it had faded Mrs Burnham, who had been sitting beside Shireen, on the quarter-deck, rose to her feet: 'The sepoys have performed so splendidly that I feel I should thank the havildar myself.'

This proposal received an enthusiastic endorsement from her husband: 'Of course you must, dear,' he said. 'And we must make sure that they are served some refreshments.'

Down on the maindeck, by dint of habit, Kesri was tracking the flow of people on the *Anahita's* decks as though they were troops on a battlefield. For the most part his attention was centred on Captain Mee and Mrs Burnham: they were like standard-bearers, providing points of orientation in the midst of the dust and smoke of battle; he kept track of their whereabouts almost without being aware of it. He had noticed that after their initial meeting beside the side-ladder – when his own speedy intervention had saved the captain from making a fool of himself – the two of them had stayed well away from each other. Now, seeing that Mrs Burnham was coming towards him, Kesri snapped to attention, fixing his eyes on a point in the middle distance. When she said – Salaam Kesri Singh! – he snapped off a salute, without looking directly at her.

Salaam, memsah'b.

You and your men performed very well, Kesri Singh.

Aap ki meherbani hai; you are kind to say so, Cathy-memsah'b.

Then passed a moment of silence and when she spoke again it was in a completely different tone, flat and urgent. Kesri Singh, she said, we have very little time and I do not want to waste any of it.

Ji, memsah'b.

I want to ask you something, Kesri Singh. It is about Mee-sahib.

Ji, Cathy-memsah'b.

Is he married?

440

No, Cathy-memsah'b, he is not.

Oh.

She paused and her voice fell: Then maybe he has a . . . a . . . *kali-bibi*, 'a black wife'?

I cannot say, Cathy-memsah'b. He is my kaptán-sah'b. We don't speak about such things.

Even as he was saying this Kesri guessed she would not be taken in; as a military daughter she was sure to know that such matters were impossible to conceal within a battalion.

Nor was he mistaken; he could tell from her face that she had interpreted his response as a rebuff.

So you don't want to talk to me, Kesri Singh, is that it?

There is nothing to tell, Cathy-memsah'b. Mee-sah'b is not married and there is no woman in his keep.

Has he ever spoken of me?

Not to me, no, memsah'b.

Is that all then? You have nothing else to say to me?

The desperation in her voice stirred Kesri's pity.

There is one thing I can tell you, Cathy-memsah'b, said Kesri.

Yes?

Ek baar, said Kesri, one time, twelve years after that winter in Ranchi, Mee-sah'b was wounded in some fighting. I was beside him and I was the one who removed his koortee. In the pocket, near the breast – Kesri raised a hand to touch his heart – there were some papers.

She gasped: What papers?

I think it was your letter.

My letter?

Yes, Cathy-memsah'b. I think it was the letter you gave me, to give to him, all those years ago, in Ranchi.

Kesri knew, because two shimmering dots had appeared at the lower edge of his vision, that her eyes were glistening. And at the same moment he saw that Captain Mee was coming down the companion-ladder, advancing towards them. In an attempt to warn Mrs Burnham, he allowed his eyes to flicker towards her. Glancing over her shoulder she saw that the captain was heading in their direction; she turned quickly away to busy herself with her reticule.

'Ah Mrs Burnham,' said Captain Mee, in a tone of forced banter.

'I hope my havildar is not giving away all our battalion's secrets? He seems to have a lot to say to you.'

'Why Captain Mee,' said Mrs Burnham, speaking as he had, in a bantering tone. 'I trust you're not jealous of your havildar?'

Then suddenly the air seemed to go out of her lungs.

'Oh please, Neville,' she said in a soft, shaky voice. 'How long must we pretend?'

The directness of her tone caught Captain Mee off-guard, wrecking his composure. Like rings on a pond, the pain, yearning and disappointments of the last twenty years seemed to ripple across his face. When next he spoke, his tone was like that which Kesri had heard in his tent, a few days before: the voice of a hurt, bewildered eighteen-year-old.

'Cathy, I don't know what to say. I've been waiting so long – and now . . .'

From under the brim of her hat Mrs Burnham shot Kesri a glance that brimmed with gratitude. Then slowly they moved away.

*

'There you are, Reid!'

Throwing an arm over Zachary's shoulder, Mr Burnham led him aside. 'Have you been able to have a word with Captain Mee yet?'

'Not yet, sir,' said Zachary. 'It may be difficult here, with so many people about, but I'll try.'

'Best to do it now,' said Mr Burnham. 'If we don't get to him soon you may be sure that someone else will.'

With that Mr Burnham went off to talk to a guest while Zachary took a turn around the crowded quarter-deck, looking for Captain Mee. Seeing no sign of him, his eyes strayed to the maindeck and landed instead on Mrs Burnham: he saw, to his surprise, that she was deep in conversation with – of all people! – the sarjeant of the Bengal sepoys.

Zachary had watched Mrs Burnham from afar at many parties and levées: it seemed to him now that there was something odd about her bearing; her posture was not at all like that of her usual, social self. Her head was cocked in such a way as to suggest that she was hanging on the sepoy sarjeant's every word.

But what could a havildar have to say that would be of such interest to her?

442

Even as he was mulling this over, Zachary noticed that a uniformed figure was heading towards the pair. A moment later he realized that this was none other than Captain Mee.

Zachary froze. Standing riveted to the deck, he watched as Mrs Burnham and Captain Mee spoke to each other. When they moved away from Kesri, he leant forward, his knuckles whitening on the deck-rails. At that point Mrs Burnham happened to turn her head so that the glow of a paper lantern fell directly on her face. Zachary had to stifle a gasp – for the countenance she had turned to Captain Mee was not her public visage but rather the one that Zachary had himself come to recognize in her boudoir. So far as he knew there was only one other man who had ever been privy to this other aspect of Mrs Burnham – and that man was a soldier, a lieutenant, she had said, her first and only love.

Zachary noticed now that Captain Mee's red-coated shoulders were also inclined towards Mrs Burnham in a manner that suggested a more than casual acquaintance. Suddenly suspicion boiled up in him, to be followed by an onrush of jealousy so intense that he had to hold on to the rails to steady himself.

What were they talking about, looking at each other so intimately?

Zachary had to know; the curiosity that had taken possession of him was too powerful to resist. Before he was aware of it, his feet were moving, carrying him down the companion-ladder to the maindeck. Plunging into the throng of guests, he began to work his way towards the couple. But he was only a few paces away when he thought the better of it: if Mrs Burnham spotted him she might well guess what he was up to.

He came to a halt, thinking about what to do next, and just then his eyes fell on the white uniform of a fifer: a moment later he realized that it was Raju – the boy was wandering about as though he had lost his way.

'Hey there, kid-mutt!'

'Hello, sir,' said Raju in a small, scared voice.

'How are things with you?'

'All right, sir.'

'Do you like being a fifer?'

'Yes, sir. I like it. Most of the time.'

'But not now? Is that why you're wandering around like a lost puppy?'

'Sir, the drummers told me to find them some grog. They said the youngest fifer always has to do it. But I don't know where to find a bottle of grog, sir, and I'm afraid they're going to be angry with me.'

Dropping to his heels, Zachary squatted close to Raju's ear. 'Listen, kid-mutt – I'll find you a bottle of grog, I promise. But you'll have to win it from me fair and square.'

'How, sir?'

'By playing a game.'

'What game, sir?'

Zachary inclined his head towards Captain Mee and Mrs Burnham. 'Do you see those two over there?'

'Yes, sir.'

'All right, so the game's this – you have to sneak up behind them and listen to what they're saying. But they can't know that you're there. It's a secret game, right? Only you and I are playing.'

'Yes, sir.'

'You think you can do it?'

'Yes, sir.'

'Go on then.'

Leaving Raju to work his way across the deck Zachary cornered a steward and slipped him a Spanish dollar: 'Can you bring me a bottle of grog? Jaldee ekdum?'

'Yes, sir. Ekdum jaldee.'

As he waited for the steward to return Zachary saw that Raju had circled around the deck and was eavesdropping unnoticed on Captain Mee and Mrs Burnham. Then the bottle of rum arrived and Zachary beckoned to Raju to come back.

Dropping into a squat again, he said: 'Did you hear anything, kid-mutt?'

'Yes, sir. Mrs Burnham was talking about a milliner's shop, near the St Lazarus Church in Macau. She said that she often goes there.'

'Oh? And what did he say to that?'

'He said he would meet her there.'

'Anything else?'

'That's all I heard, sir.'

Zachary patted Raju on the back and handed him the bottle. 'You did good, kid-mutt; you've won the grog fair and square. But remember, it's a secret – not a word to anyone!'

'No, sir. Thank you, sir.'

*

Not for a moment after setting foot on the *Anahita*'s quarter-deck had Shireen been able to forget that Bahram's accident had happened here; that it was from this very deck that her husband had fallen to his death. Through the duration of Mr Burnham's oration and the ceremony that followed, she had wondered whether it was from the jamná side that he had fallen or the dáwa. Or had he perhaps tumbled over the stern? In thinking about these things she was seized by a strange disquiet – a feeling that only deepened when she saw Freddie leading Paulette towards her. But once introductions had been made Shireen took a liking to her new acquaintance; she invited her to sit on the bench and for a while she listened quietly as Zadig and Paulette talked about gardening.

Then at last Shireen gingerly broached the subject that had been weighing on her mind: 'Is it true, Miss Lambert, that you were on the island the day my husband died?'

'Yes, Mrs Moddie,' said Paulette. 'I was up in the nursery that day and I saw this ship, the *Anahita*, at anchor below. Although there were many ships in the bay that morning, the *Anahita* was the one that caught my eye.'

'Why?' said Shireen.

'Because there was a ladder – a rope-ladder – hanging out from an open window, at the back.'

'You mean from my husband's suite? In the stern of the ship?'

'Yes,' said Paulette. 'That was where it was.'

Taken aback, Shireen cried: 'But why would there be a ladder at his window?'

'I cannot tell you why it was there,' said Paulette. 'It seemed very strange to me too, because there was nothing below but water.'

Shireen turned to Freddie and Zadig. 'Did you know about this ladder?'

Zadig shook his head. 'This is the first I've heard of it, Bibiji.'

445

'I did not speak of it to anyone,' said Paulette. 'To be truthful, I had forgotten about it until Freddie asked me.'

'But how would Freddie know?' cried Shireen, turning towards him. 'Had someone told you about the ladder, Freddie?'

'No,' said Freddie. 'No one told me. But I see in my dreams, lah, the ladder, hanging from the window. That is why I ask Miss Paulette, ne? Then she tell me, yes, she saw in the morning, but after an hour it was gone.'

'Vico must have taken it in,' said Zadig. 'But he never uttered a word about it to me.'

All of this was completely incomprehensible to Shireen. 'But why a ladder? Do you think there was some foul play?'

'No,' said Zadig, with a shake of his head. 'If there had been foul play the ladder would not have been left hanging. And anyway there was no sign of a struggle in the cabin or on Bahram-bhai's body.'

'But what happened then?' said Shireen. 'What was the purpose of the ladder? To climb up or go down?'

Nobody said a word, so Shireen turned again to Freddie: 'You know the answer, don't you, Freddie? Tell me what the ladder was for, please.'

Freddie did not answer at once: his eyes were closed and he seemed almost to be in a trance. When he spoke again his voice was very soft.

'I think Father went down the ladder because someone call him.'

'Who?'

'My mother.'

'Your mother?' cried Shireen. 'But that's impossible. Hadn't she died some years before?'

Freddie shook his head: 'Did not die, lah, my mother,' he said. 'Was murdered, ne? By men who came looking for me. She help me get away and did not tell them where I went. So they stabbed her and threw in the river – the Pearl River. There was no funeral, nothing, so she is still in the river, still in the water, this water that we are on. I see her sometimes, she has not found rest, so she comes to me. That night, when Father come here from Canton, in this ship, I think she come to him too and call him away. He went down the ladder to go to her. I have seen it so in my dreams, lah.'

446

'No!' Shireen's head was spinning already, and it began to turn even faster now as she jerked it violently from side to side. 'No! I cannot believe it. I will not believe it.'

Then all of a sudden, everything went dark.

*

The fuss on the quarter-deck was loud enough to cause Kesri some concern. He kept a careful eye on it and when he saw a prone body being carried away he realized that there was no reason for undue alarm: a lady had swooned and was being taken inside.

Shortly afterwards he spotted a memsahib in a black dress and bonnet coming towards him. He did not make too much of it; several sahibs and memsahibs had already approached him with complimentary words about his squad of sepoys: he assumed that this missy-mem was going to do the same.

But when she came face to face with him she said nothing; she just stood there silently, staring.

Thinking that she was unsure of whether he understood English, Kesri said: 'Good evening, memsah'b.'

That was when she began to speak – and not in English but Hindustani.

It is true, isn't it, she said, that you are Deeti's brother? I can see it in your face, your eyes. She used to draw pictures of you. I saw one once, she had drawn you holding a bundook.

Now Kesri too lost his tongue for a moment. When he regained it, all he could say was: How did you know? How did you know about Deeti – that she is my sister?

Mr Reid told me, said Paulette. I was on the ship too, you know – the *Ibis*. Your sister was my friend; we talked a lot, especially in the last days, before we reached Mauritius.

You were with her? Kesri shook his head incredulously. Did Deeti tell you why she ran away from her village after her husband's death?

Yes, she told me all about it.

Kesri was seized with panic now, thinking that there might not be enough time to hear the whole story.

Tell me; tell me what Deeti said. I have been waiting so long to hear – tell me everything.

*

447

The twilight had turned to darkness now so Raju did not see Baboo Nob Kissin's saffron-clad figure until it was almost on top of him.

Here, boy! Come aside – I have to talk to you.

Leading Raju to the bulwark, Baboo Nob Kissin knelt to whisper into his ear: Raju, listen, this is very important. Among the guests at this party there are some friends of your father's. They might be able to help you find him.

Who are they? said Raju.

Did you see a memsah'b in a black dress and a bonnet? She was talking to the havildar a moment ago. Her name is Paulette Lambert – she knows your father. She was on the *Ibis* too and she has met him here in China as well. And you may have seen also a man in a Chinese robe? He too is your father's friend. If anyone can get a message to your father it is he. You should talk to him.

Raju looked around the maindeck and saw no sign of either.

Where are they?

I think they went inside, said Baboo Nob Kissin. They went to see how Mrs Moddie is doing.

The gomusta raised a finger to point to a gangway that led astern: Go and have a look over there; that's where they'll be.

Raju set off without another word. Threading his way through the guests, he circled around until he reached the gangway that led to the cabins at the rear of the vessel.

This part of the ship was empty and silent; the gangway was dimly lit, by a few, flickering lamps.

Keeping to one side, Raju made his way slowly forward. There were cabins to the right and to the left of the gangway, but the doors were all shut. Only one door was ajar and it was at the far end; above it was a sign that said 'Owner's Suite'.

Creeping up to the entrance, Raju put his eye to the crack in the doorway. There seemed to be a lot of old furniture inside; there was a draught blowing through and it pushed the door a little further ajar, as if to invite Raju in. After hesitating for a minute, Raju stepped through the doorway.

Moonlight was flowing in through the windows, one of which was wide open. Raju saw now, to his great surprise, that someone was sitting by the window, in a chair: all Raju could see of him was a turbaned head, silhouetted against the moolight.

To Raju's relief it seemed that the man had not noticed his presence. Holding his breath, he took a step backwards, thinking that he had better leave while he could.

But just as he was about to slip away the turbaned head turned to look in his direction: the silvery moonlight gave Raju a glimpse of a man with a broad, square face and a clipped beard.

'Sorry, sir,' said Raju apologetically. 'I didn't know you were here.'

To his relief, there was no torrent of abuse as he had half-expected: the man only smiled silently.

Mumbling another 'Sorry, sir,' Raju ducked out. Pulling the door shut behind him, he turned around to find that two figures, a man and a woman, had stepped out of one of the cabins that lined the gangway. The man was dressed in a Chinese gown and when he caught sight of Raju he said: 'Hello? Who are you, eh? And what you doing here?'

Suddenly Raju understood that this was the couple that Baboo Nob Kissin had told him about.

'I was looking for you, sir,' he blurted out. 'And for ma'am too.'

'You were looking for us?' said Paulette in surprise. 'But why?'

Raju stepped quickly towards them. 'You both know my father,' he said, lowering his voice. 'Baboo Nob Kissin told me so.'

'Who is your father?'

'His name is Neel.'

*

Kesri was still recovering from the shock of his meeting with Paulette when Zachary appeared in front of him.

'Good day there, Sarjeant. Could I have a word with you please?'

'Yes, Reid-sah'b?'

'Sarjeant, you remember that evening, on the *Hind*? How you came to my cabin and asked me questions about your sister?'

'Yes, Reid-sah'b.'

'Sarjeant, I need you to return the favour now. I've got some questions that I need you to answer.'

'Questions?' said Kesri in surprise. 'For me?'

449

'Yes, Sarjeant. You said you were Captain Mee's orderly seventeen years ago – isn't that right?'

'Yes, sir.'

'Were you ever with him in a place called Ranchi?'

'Yes, Reid-sah'b.'

'Was he a lieutenant then?'

'Yes.'

'And was Mrs Burnham there too?'

Kesri's face hardened and the muscles in his jaw began to twitch. 'Why you want to know, Reid-sah'b?'

'Listen, Sarjeant,' said Zachary sharply, 'when you asked me questions about your sister I answered. You told me then to come to you if I ever needed anything. Well I've come to you now with a question, a very simple one, and if you're a man of your word you'll answer it. Let me ask again: was Mrs Burnham in Ranchi at the same time as Captain Mee?'

Kesri nodded reluctantly. 'Yes, Mr Reid,' he said. 'She was there.'

'Thank you, Sarjeant. That's all I need.'

Now that he had received confirmation, Zachary felt vastly more calm than he had been when the idea was just a suspicion in his head. It was as if Mrs Burnham had given him yet another gift; it was up to him now to use her secret to his own advantage.

*

Tu kahan jaich? Kai? Where are you going? Why?

As her eyes flew open Shireen experienced a moment of pure terror: she had no idea of where she was or how she had got there.

Then she heard Zadig Bey's voice, somewhere close by: 'It's all right, Bibiji – I am here, with you.'

She sat up with a start and a cold towel flew off her forehead. 'Where am I?'

Holding up a lamp, Zadig Bey turned up the wick: 'You are in Mrs Burnham's cabin, Bibiji, on her bed. After you fainted she suggested that we bring you here. I've been sitting with you all this while. Paulette and Freddie just looked in on you; seeing that you were still unconscious they stepped out.'

Casting her eyes around the panelled cabin, Shireen fell back against the pillows. Her heart was beating wildly, erratically, and she pressed a hand against her chest, as if to slow it down.

'What's the matter, Bibiji?'

Zadig Bey took hold of her other hand and pressed her fever-ishly hot palm between his own cool fingers. 'What is it, Bibiji? Tell me.'

Shireen closed her eyes. 'I had a dream, Zadig Bey; it was very strange – like the dreams that Freddie talks about.'

'How do you mean, Bibiji?'

'I saw my husband: he was standing beside me. He had come to see me; there was something he wanted to say.'

She began to cough, choking on her words. Zadig Bey handed her a glass of water. 'Go on, Bibiji.'

'He asked my forgiveness and said that I should put the past behind me. He said I should look to the future and make the best of my remaining years. Then he took his leave, saying *jauch*, and that was all. He was gone. That was when I woke up.'

Snatching up the end of her sari, Shireen began to dab her eyes.

'Why are you crying, Bibiji?' said Zadig. 'There was nothing bad in what you heard.'

Shireen swallowed a sob. 'It's just that I don't understand – why was he asking my forgiveness, Zadig Bey? What for?'

There was no answer, so she turned to look him in the eye. 'Tell me the truth, Zadig Bey – did Bahram . . . did he die by his own hand?'

Zadig pursed his lips. 'I don't think it was as simple as that, Bibiji,' he said. 'If anything, it probably happened as Freddie says: he must have thought that he had heard Chi-mei's voice. Bahram-bhai told me once that he had had a vision of her, on this very ship, the *Anahita*.'

'A vision?' scoffed Shireen. 'Impossible! Bahram never believed in such things!'

'But he told me so himself, Bibiji: it happened on his last voyage, long after Chi-mei's death. The *Anahita* was hit by a storm, in the Bay of Bengal. Bahram-bhai's cargo of opium was knocked loose so he went down to secure the chests. That was when he heard her voice and saw her face. He said the hold was filled with the smell of raw opium – the fumes could have conjured up all kinds of things in his mind. Maybe that's how it happened on the night of his death as well. Opium probably had something to do with it.'

'I don't follow,' said Shireen. 'Are you saying that my husband was taking opium?'

Zadig shifted uncomfortably in his chair: 'I wish I didn't have to tell you this, Bibiji, but the truth is that Bahram was smoking a lot of opium in his final days. After the crisis in Canton he was in a very downcast state of mind.'

'Because of his financial losses?'

'Yes, but it wasn't just that, Bibiji. He had other things on his mind as well.'

'Tell me, Zadig Bey.'

'Bibiji, the opium crisis was a great trial for Bahram-bhai – he was torn between his two families, between Canton and Bombay, between China and Hindustan. There he was in Canton, with a huge cargo of opium; to lose it would bring ruin, not just on him but also on you and your daughters. On the other hand he knew very well what opium had done to Freddie; he was aware of what it was doing to China; he knew that it was slowly corroding families, clans, monasteries, the army; every chest that came in was creating more addicts . . .'

Zadig stopped to scratch his chin.

'Bibiji, one thing about Bahram-bhai, he was not a moralizer; he was not a man to hold forth about religion, or good and evil. His emotions, his thoughts, they followed his flesh, his blood, his heart. He was above all a family man – but it so happened that fate gave him two families, one in China and one in India. He knew that his actions in Canton, as an opium-trader, would haunt both his families, for generations, and it was more than he could bear. I think that was why he began to smoke so much: it wasn't just that he was seeking escape; it was as if he were sacrificing himself, in expiation for what he had done.'

Shireen crumpled the wet end of her sari between her hands. 'Did he talk to you about these things, Zadig Bey? Did he talk about Chi-mei? Did he say he loved her?'

'No, Bibiji!' said Zadig emphatically. 'Bahram-bhai was not a romantic man. He thought love and romance were not for practical men like himself.'

Zadig stopped to clear his throat. 'In this, Bibiji, he and I were completely different.'

'What do you mean, Zadig Bey?'

'When I first fell in love, as a young man, I knew I had no choice in the matter: I was helpless.'

He swallowed a couple of times, his Adam's apple bobbing up and down. Then, in a low, hoarse voice, he said: 'And with you too, I knew – since that day in the church.'

The words sent a shiver through Shireen. When he placed his hands on hers she did not pull them back.

*

Hearing a drum-roll in the distance Paulette pulled Raju into her arms and kissed the boy on the cheek. *Onek katha holo,* she said. 'We've been talking a long time now. Your friends in the band will be wondering where you went.'

'Yes, I'd better go,' said Raju. 'Goodbye, Miss Paulette.'

'Goodbye.'

Then Freddie's hand fell on his shoulder: 'Good thing we saw you, eh? Coming out of that suite?'

'Yes, sir, Mr Lee.'

'Why were you there, lah? What were you doing in that suite?'

'The door was open so I went in,' said Raju. 'I didn't know anyone was inside.'

'There was someone inside?'

'Yes, a gentleman.'

'Gentleman, eh?' Freddie dropped into a squat and looked him straight in the face. 'Who was he?'

'I don't know who he was,' said Raju. 'I had never seen him before.'

'What did he look like?'

'He had a beard and he was wearing a white turban.'

'Oh?'

Reaching for Raju's shoulder, Freddie pulled him to his chest and gave him a hug. 'Don't worry, lah. Everything will be all right. I will get a message to your father. It may take a little time, but he will know that you are here.'

'Thank you, sir,' said Raju. 'And goodbye.'

'Goodbye. Be careful.'

As Raju ran off, Freddie seemed to lapse into a trance. Then, without a word to Paulette, he began to walk towards the door at the end of the gangway. Following on his heels, Paulette looked over his shoulder as he put a hand on the doorknob and pushed it open.

There was a heap of furniture inside, silhouetted against a pair of moonlit windows. One of the windows was open and its shutter was flapping gently in the breeze; beside it stood an empty chair.

Freddie walked over to the window at a slow, measured pace, almost as though he were afraid of what he would find. Paulette heard a deep sigh as he looked over the sill.

'Come. See.'

Stepping up to the window she saw that a rope-ladder was hanging from the rim, flapping gently in the breeze.

'Is it this ladder you saw that day?' said Freddie. 'Was is it hanging like this, eh?'

'Maybe, I cannot say,' said Paulette. 'Anyway why is it hanging there now?'

Freddie made no reply. Leaning forward, he thrust his head out of the window and looked down into the water, at the shimmering reflection of the moon.

For a while he seemed to listen to the waves, with his eyes closed. Then she heard him say: 'I can hear them, lah – calling me, the two of them, my mother and father.'

On an impulse she put a hand on his shoulder and pulled him back. His angular cheekbones stood out in the silvery moonlight, lending a strange beauty to his gaunt, haunted face.

'You cannot go,' said Paulette. 'I will not let you.'

'Why?'

'Didn't you say yourself? That the bonds of the *Ibis* are very strong? We all need each other.'

Seventeen

Two days after the start of the English New Year, Compton came over to Whampoa unexpectedly, bearing freshly issued orders: the *Cambridge* was to move to a new position. The authorities wanted her to be taken downriver to the island of North Wantung, which lay directly opposite Humen, at the centre of the Tiger's Mouth.

The *Cambridge* weighed anchor that very day, with Compton on board: he was under instructions to accompany the crew. About the reasons for these changes he said nothing and Neel knew better than to ask.

This was the first time the *Cambridge* had undertaken a voyage of any length. Somewhat to Neel's surprise the crew performed well together and the vessel made good time.

As they sailed downriver it became apparent to both Neel and Jodu that some kind of military action – offensive or defensive – was imminent. Extensive preparations were in progress along the river: earthworks and fortifications were being strengthened; new, camouflaged gun-emplacements had been built, and flotillas of war-junks were patrolling the channel. Twice, the *Cambridge* had to stop to pick up contingents of 'water-braves': they were travelling upriver to augment the naval force that was stationed at Humen, under the command of Admiral Guan Tianpei (whom Neel and Compton had seen in action, in those very waters, fifteen months before).

On drawing abreast of Humen, they spotted a vessel with an American flag lying at anchor near the customs house. The flag was a decoy, Compton told Neel; the ship was actually carrying a cargo of tea for Lancelot Dent, the prominent British merchant. The transaction had been arranged by Dent's old compradore, Peng Bao, who was now Governor-General Qishan's translator.

That a man in as prominent a position as Peng Bao was openly colluding with an infamous opium trader like Lancelot Dent was shocking enough to Neel. But he soon learnt that this was by no means the worst of it: Compton told him that after Commissioner Lin's removal from power many of Guangdong's officials had gone back to their old ways and were busy feathering their own nests.

The *Cambridge* dropped anchor just off the tip of North Wantung Island, which was a steeply rising massif of rock, in the centre of the mile-wide channel. Here too there was a formidable fort, equipped with many heavy guns. Not far from the fort were the moorings of a new defensive barrier: a massive iron chain that ran all the way across the main shipping channel, to Humen.

Later that day Admiral Guan arrived in person to inspect the *Cambridge*.

Neel and the lascars watched from a respectful distance as the ship's Chinese officers showed the admiral around: he was a distinguished-looking man in his early sixties: plainly dressed, in a dark winter cape; on his hat was a red button. Compton explained later that this was an emblem of very high rank.

Before returning to his own junk the admiral offered a few words of encouragement to the lascars, telling them the British might attack any day and that they would earn rich rewards if they succeeded in bringing down a warship: the prize money for a seventy-four-gun frigate had now been raised to fifty thousand Spanish dollars.

Neel's impression was of a genial, capable and highly intelligent man; this assessment was shared by Jodu who said that the admiral seemed much more knowledgeable and businesslike than the other dignitaries who had visited the *Cambridge*.

The next morning Neel, Jodu, Compton and a few others took a tour of the Tiger's Mouth in a sailboat. Cruising around that wide expanse of water Neel understood how this section of the channel came by its name: narrow at both ends, the basin seemed to be bounded by powerful jaws on all sides. At one end the river flowed in as if through a gullet: here lay the area's mightiest defences – the battlements and gun-emplacements of Humen and North Wantung. At the other end, where the river debouched into the estuary, lay two more sets of fortifications: the island of Shaitok –

or Chuenpee as it was known to foreigners – was on the eastern side. Facing it across the channel was another citadel, on the headland known as Tycock.

At the end of the tour their party went ashore and walked around Chuenpee. Neel saw that there had been many changes in the fifteen months since he and Compton had last visited the island. The hamlet they had stayed in was now empty, abandoned by its inhabitants. At that time the island had been defended by two fortresses: one was on a hilltop while the other was a fortified gun-emplacement on the shore. The two had now been joined together to form a single rambling fort, enclosed by ramparts that ran all the way up the hill. These in turn were flanked by a dry moat and breastworks.

Seen from the ramparts of Chuenpee the whole of the Tiger's Mouth looked like a vast fortified stronghold with a lake at its centre: on every eminence and promontory there were battlements and batteries. On all sides of the channel were gun-ports, hundreds of them, each marked with a colourful device: the head of a tiger.

The fortifications were impressive enough to reassure even Jodu, who had earlier voiced some doubts about the effectiveness of the defences. The British would not be able to break through, he declared confidently; the Tiger's Mouth was a trap, primed to close upon their fleet.

They returned to the *Cambridge* in high good humour, convinced that the British would be courting disaster if they were foolhardy enough to thrust their heads into the jaws of this gargantuan beast.

*

Soon after the start of the English New Year the weather turned very cold and the Pearl River estuary was whipped by icy winds. On Saw Chow Island, where there was little cover, the effects were especially severe: the sepoys and camp-followers were forced into a kind of semi-hibernation; only when it was absolutely necessary did they leave their tents. Few were those who thought of anything but stuffing their stomachs and huddling under their coverings.

The sepoys were fortunate in that they had been issued greatcoats before the winter chill set in. The fifers and drummers were also lucky for they too had received woollen capes; although these were not as warm as the sepoys' coats, they had the advantage that they could be spread out at night. Nor did the banjee-boys have any reason to complain for they were well-off compared to the camp-followers, many of whom had not received any cold-weather clothes at all. The woollens were meant to be provided by the sirdars of every group, but only the honest ones, of whom there were very few, were willing to defray the costs – and even they offered no more than a blanket or two, to be used as garments during the day and coverings at night. For the most part, the sirdars were skinflinting kanjooses who thought only of their own pockets: they gave their followers nothing more than a few moth-eaten lengths of cheap cotton cloth – these men were left with no option but to spend their own meagre earnings on locally made quilted jackets.

But when icy blasts lashed the treeless island, even the best clothing offered little protection. Predictably, dozens of men fell ill and the field-hospital was soon filled to capacity.

Through much of the time that the weather was at its worst – the first days of January – Captain Mee was on leave in Macau. It was not till 6 January that he came back to Saw Chow, and within minutes of his return Kesri received a summons to report to his tent.

The captain offered no explanations for his absence and nor was it Kesri's place to ask questions: they got briskly down to business.

The expedition's high command had at last come to a decision, said the captain: an attack was to be launched on the fortifications of the Tiger's Mouth. It would be a complex, amphibious operation involving ships, soldiers, marines and small-arms' men from the warships.

Rolling out a chart, the captain pointed out the fortifications and gun-emplacements that encircled the Tiger's Mouth. Their configuration was such that an attack from the seaward side would necessarily have to commence by neutralizing the two outermost forts – Chuenpee on the right bank of the channel and Tycock on the left. The operation would therefore start with simultaneous assaults on both positions: the Bengal Volunteers were to be a part of the force that would attack Chuenpee. They would be transported to the landing-point – a beach, some two miles east of the island's gun-emplacements – by the *Enterprize* next morning.

There would be an early reveille and the sepoys were to be ready to embark by 7 a.m., said the captain. This time they would deploy in full marching order, with drummers, fifers, gun-lascars, runners, golondauzes, bhistis and, of course, medical attendants; their baggage was to be packed accordingly.

'Better get to it jaldee havildar.'

Ji, Kaptán-sah'b.

*

It took only a few minutes for the whole camp to learn that B Company was to go into action the next day, with a full complement of supporters.

In the fifers' tent the weather was quickly forgotten as the boys got down to checking their equipment and taking inventory of the contents of their knapsacks. This would be Raju's first deployment and he was careful to follow Dicky's lead in making his preparations, down to details like stuffing a few sugary sweets into his pockets: 'You'll see, men – when the fighting starts it helps to have something sweet in your mouth. Adds to the fun.'

Having experienced battle before, Dicky was full of bravado – yet Raju could sense a change in his mood. That night, huddled together under their shared blankets, Dicky was very restless, thrashing about and moaning in his sleep. He woke not just Raju but several others as well, earning himself volleys of curses, fisticuffs and kicks.

'Shut your gob, bugger, and let us sleep – there's fighting ahead tomorrow, ya. You can cry all you like then.'

The next day Kesri was up long before dawn. Accompanied by two lance-naiks he went from tent to tent, lantern in hand, carrying out random inspections to make sure that the sepoys had packed their knapsacks exactly as required by Heavy Marching Orders: with a spare uniform, including a second koortee and another pair of shoes; a durree to sleep on and a 'cumbly' blanket, the last being neatly rolled up and strapped under the brass lota that sat atop every knapsack.

The fifers and drummers also rose early and they were among the first to take up stations on the beach, to provide accompaniment for the sepoys as they paraded. It was a cold morning and a thick mist had risen off the surface of the water, dimming the glow of the sun.

459

The tide crested just before the *Enterprize* arrived. Because the water was high, the unit was spared the bother of using lighters for the embarkation: the steamer was able to nudge her bows so close to the shore that a gangplank was all that was required to go on board.

The followers went first and while they were boarding the 'bell of arms' was rung to summon the sepoys to roll-call: it turned out that so many were in hospital that the company was at three-quarters its usual strength.

After roll-call the sepoys fell in line in front of the gangplank, their tall, black topees receding into the mist. Then, with drums beating and fifes trilling, they went marching up to the steamer, their Brown Besses slung over their shoulders. After the sepoys came the banjee-boys, and then the officers, in ascending order of seniority. Captain Mee was the last to board, and the steamer's paddle-wheels began to churn even as the gangplank was being pulled in after him. With water foaming around the hull, the vessel turned her head slowly northwards.

The fifers and drummers were seated between the bows. As the steamer built up speed they were hit head-on by the wind. They huddled together, teeth chattering, and Raju buried his face between his knees; he was sleepy enough to fall into a doze. When he looked up again he found, to his surprise, that the mist had lifted and the skies had cleared. The steamer was cruising through a miles-wide wedge of water, a deep, iridescent blue in colour. Looming on either side were ranges of serene grey-green mountains.

Dead ahead lay the twin hills of Chuenpee: the larger of the two was crowned by an impressive set of ramparts and towers, with hundreds of colourful pennants and banners fluttering on the battlements: some were long strips of cloth, with ideograms imprinted on a crimson background; some were shaped like doubled flames, with green and yellow edges; some were immense streamers on which dragons undulated as if in flight.

As they came closer they saw that the battlements were bristling with guns and gun-ports. Only one part of the island lay beyond the reach of the hilltop battery: this was the section that was sheltered by the second hill. There lay the landing-point.

The waters around the landing-point were thronged with vessels of many sorts. Three steamers, *Madagascar, Queen* and *Nemesis,* had pushed close in to shore and were discharging their detachments directly on to the beach. The larger warships were at anchor in deeper water: these consisted of two frigates – the forty-four-gun *Druid* and the twenty-eight-gun *Calliope* – and four smaller warships. Their contingents were in the process of being ferried ashore in cutters and longboats.

Such was the congestion that the *Enterprize* had to hold back for a bit. As a result Raju was able to observe the debarkation as though it were an exercise staged specially for his benefit. The spectacle was mesmerizing: teams of soldiers and sailors were executing complex manoeuvres with clockwork precision, working in synchronized co-ordination with each other as one cutter after another pulled up to the beach to offload its men and munitions.

By the time B Company reached the shore the landing of troops was almost complete: there were around fourteen hundred soldiers assembled on the beach, along with a couple of hundred camp-followers and auxiliaries, almost all of whom were Indians. Of the fighting men about half were sepoys: six hundred and seven from the 37th Madras and seventy-six from B Company. Amongst the British troops the largest contingent was a five-hundred-strong battalion of Royal Marines; the rest consisted of artillerymen and a detachment of convalescents who had been evacuated from Chusan.

In command was an officer of the Royal Irish, Major Pratt. At his orders the heavy artillery led the way, with teams of gun-lascars dragging two six-pounders and one massive twenty-four-pound howitzer up the road that led to the top of the island's second hill. After them came the marines and then the Madras sepoys. The Bengal detachment brought up the rear. The fifers and drummers were grouped together at the centre of the column, flanked by sepoys on either side.

As they marched up the hill clouds of dust rose from the sepoys' stamping feet, blowing straight into the fifers' faces. Raju was flustered at first and missed several notes, but only Dicky seemed to notice. He flashed Raju a nod and a wink which did much to settle his nerves.

Soon, absorbed in the effort of keeping his fingers and feet moving in correct time, the flutters in Raju's stomach abated and he fixed his eyes on the back of the fifer in front, making sure that he was neither too far nor too close. So absorbed was he that he did not hear the sound of cannon-fire in the distance; it was Dicky who alerted him to it by jogging his elbow.

Kesri was at the head of the Bengal detachment with Captain Mee. Just as they reached the top of the ridge the guns on the opposite hill opened up. But the shells fell well short and they had no reason to seek shelter.

Kesri was able to take careful stock of the island's defences and he saw at once that its newly built fortifications were vulnerable on many counts: although the ramparts were tall and solid, they were constructed in an old-fashioned way. They ran straight, like curtain walls: there were no projections to create interlocking fields of fire; nor were there any angles or buttresses to provide additional stability. The breastworks that ran along the walls were also of an antique variety, known to sepoys as *bās-ke-zanjeer* – 'bamboo chains'. They were made of sharpened staves, nailed together to form a continuous barrier: the officers called them 'Frisian horses'.

The fire from the fort's guns and ginjalls grew steadily heavier as Kesri and Captain Mee stood on the crest of the hill, surveying the defences. But the barrage continued to be ineffective with most of the shots going awry, slamming into the hillside and throwing up geysers of dirt. The landing-party's artillerymen were able to go unhurriedly about their business as they assembled their own field-pieces and howitzers.

At a signal from Captain Mee, B Company's golondauzes and gun-lascars stepped ahead to set up their artillery pieces. Maddow was, as usual, carrying two wheels of a gun-carriage; after slinging them off his shoulders he fell in with the other loaders, each of whom was holding a projectile, ready to reload.

There was a moment of stillness as the gun-crews awaited the order to fire. Then a cry went echoing down the line and the golondauzes lowered their smoking fusils to the touch-holes of their weapons. Suddenly, with a great roar, the guns erupted and the hillside was blanketed in black smoke.

In the meantime two steamers, *Queen* and *Nemesis*, had also manoeuvred themselves into shelling distance of the battlements on the hill. Now a jet of flame spurted out of the muzzle of the *Queen*'s enormous sixty-eight-pounder; at the same time the two pivot-guns of the *Nemesis* began to rattle, shooting canister. These were powerful anti-personnel weapons – cans filled with musket-balls. When fired, the canisters would explode in the barrel, creating hailstorms of bullets.

It was as if a tempest of fire and iron were pouring up the hill; within minutes pillars of smoke began to rise out of the forts.

*

Shireen was at the breakfast table, eating a plate of akoori, when the first dull thuds of distant cannon-fire were heard in Macau. Dinyar was sitting across from her, and he glanced up with an expression of surprise.

Oh! *Seroo thie gayou* – so it's started after all! I didn't think they'd go through with it.

With what?

The offensive. I'd even taken a wager that the Plenipotty would find some excuse to dither again.

Shireen could think of nothing to say: with trembling hands she reached into the folds of her dress, to touch her kasti, for reassurance.

You should be glad, Shireen-auntie, said Dinyar cheerfully. It's good news for all of us. It'll speed up our compensation.

Fond as Shireen was of Dinyar, she could not let this pass.

But Dinyar, think of the men! And the boys too.

Oh they'll be all right, said Dinyar with a laugh. No harm will come to them – not while they have the *Nemesis* for protection.

Picking up a bell, Dinyar called for his hat and cane; now that the battle had started he would have to settle his lost wager. On his way out, he stopped at the door. Don't worry, Shireen-auntie, he said. We're perfectly safe here. Look!

Shireen saw that he was pointing to the Inner Harbour, where a British sloop-o'-war lay at anchor, bristling with guns.

With Dinyar gone the sound of cannon-fire seemed to grow even louder. Abandoning her breakfast, Shireen went to her bedroom and seated herself in front of the small altar that she had set up in one corner, with a lamp burning under a picture of Zarathustra. Opening her Khordeh Avesta prayer-book Shireen began to recite the 'Srosh Bāz' prayer: *Pa name yazdan Hormazd* . . . May the Creator, Ahura Mazda, Lord of the Universe . . .

This prayer had always been her first recourse in times of trouble. Often in the past it had helped to lighten the load of whatever was weighing on her mind – but now, with the sound of gunfire drumming in her ears, she found it hard to recite the words properly. Faces she had come to know on the *Hind* kept appearing before her: Captain Mee, the fifers, Kesri Singh.

As she was coming to the last lines of the prayer Shireen heard a squeak from the front gate. Thinking that it was Zadig Bey she put away the prayer-book and moved to her sitting room.

But when the steward opened the door it was not Zadig Bey who stepped inside but a woman in a veil.

'Mrs Burnham! Cathy! This is a surprise.'

'I hope you don't mind, Shireen . . .'

It turned out that Mrs Burnham had just moved into a house that her husband had rented, at the end of the road. But he was away on the commodore's ship so she was on her own.

'I thought it would be nice to have a little gup-shup, Shireen-dear, and couldn't think of anywhere else to go.'

'Of course. I'm glad you came.'

When Mrs Burnham's veil came off Shireen saw that she was deathly pale, as she had been on her first visit to the villa.

'Are you feeling poorly again, Cathy?'

'No, it's not that . . .' Mrs Burnham closed her eyes.

'It's the guns, isn't it?'

Mrs Burnham nodded. 'My head went into a chukker the moment the firing began.'

'It's distressing, isn't it?'

'Well, it shouldn't be for me,' said Mrs Burnham. 'I grew up with cannon-fire, you know. It was always in the background in the cantonments where my father was stationed; artillerymen were forever doing live drills, so the sound was all too familiar. But it's a different kind of tumasher, isn't it, when it's a real battle, and the men who are in harm's way are known to you?'

Shireen nodded. 'Ever since it started I've been seeing their faces – especially the havildar and Captain Mee.'

'I have too.'

Mrs Burnham folded her hands in her lap and lowered her eyes. 'Except that I keep seeing them as they were when I first met them.'

'Were they very different then?'

'Not Kesri Singh perhaps,' said Mrs Burnham. 'But Neville – Captain Mee – he certainly was.'

Shireen sensed that Mrs Burnham needed to unburden herself of something. She said gently: 'Did you know Captain Mee well then?'

'Yes.' Mrs Burnham paused and her voice fell to a whisper. 'To tell you the truth, Shireen, I knew him as well as I've ever known anyone.'

'Oh?'

'Yes, Shireen, it's true.' Mrs Burnham's words began to tumble out in a rush. 'There was a time when I knew Neville so well that I never wanted to have anything to do with any other man.'

'So what went wrong?' said Shireen.

Mrs Burnham made a tiny gesture of resignation. 'My parents . . .'

There was no need to say any more.

Shireen nodded, in sympathy. 'Did you not see him again after that?'

'No. I had lost track of him until the day I came here, to this house, to invite you to the levée. And after that, when he came to the *Anahita* on New Year's Day, it was as if kismet had handed him back to me, wiping away all those years. In my heart it was as though not a day had passed.'

She stopped to jerk her head in the direction of the estuary. 'And now he's over there – in the midst of the fighting. He was in Macau these last few days and it was the most precious time of my life. I don't think I could bear to lose him again.'

Opening her reticule, Mrs Burnham took out a handkerchief and dabbed her eyes. 'I must seem utterly depraved to you, Shireen. But please don't think too badly of me; none of this would have happened if I had been as lucky as you.'

'What on earth do you mean, Cathy?'

'I mean, if I too had been fortunate in marriage.'

'Fortunate?'

The word had burst involuntarily from Shireen's lips but once it was said she too was seized by a need to unburden herself. 'Oh Cathy – my marriage was not what you think.'

'Really?'

'After my husband died,' said Shireen softly, 'I discovered that he had a mistress and another family, here, in China.'

'No!'

'Yes, Cathy, it's true. It was a terrible shock to me. I could not believe that he, who had always seemed so devoted, so dutiful and devout, could be entangled in this way with someone from another country, someone who did not share his faith.'

Now Shireen too paused to dab her eyes. 'It's only now that I've begun to understand how life takes those turns.'

Mrs Burnham gave her a long, searching look and then came to sit beside her. 'Things have changed for you, haven't they, Shireen,' she said gently, 'ever since Mr Karabedian came into your life?'

Shireen was choking now; all she could do was nod.

'But Shireen,' Mrs Burnham whispered, 'you're very lucky you know. You are a widow; you can remarry.'

'That's impossible,' said Shireen adamantly. 'My children, my family, my community – they would never forgive me. And I have a duty to them after all.'

Mrs Burnham slipped her hand into Shireen's and gave it a squeeze.

'Have we not done enough by our duty, Shireen? Do we not also have a duty to ourselves?'

The question caught Shireen unawares, shocking her into silence. She was still trying to think of an answer when a steward stepped in to say that Karabedian-sah'b was at the front door.

*

Once the bombardment had started, the banjee-boys were allowed a brief rest: they seated themselves on the ground, in a sheltered spot. As the barrage intensified they could feel the shock-waves coursing through the earth and into their bodies. The sound was so loud that Raju had to clap his hands over his ears.

Then Dicky jogged his elbow: 'Look – over there.'

Glancing down the line Raju spotted a man coming towards them: on his back was something that looked like a dead goat.

'It's the bhisti, bringing water,' whispered Dicky. 'This is it – it's going to start now. The bhisti always comes before the charge.'

When the bhisti reached him Raju drank his fill from the spout of the mussuck before filling his water-flask. Then, following Dicky's example, he popped a sweet into his mouth.

Just as abruptly as it had begun the barrage stopped. A strange, crackling quiet followed, in which screams could be heard, echoing over from the Chinese lines. Then Captain Mee shouted, 'Fix bayonets!' and the fife-major began to call out orders in rapid succession. Suddenly the boys were all on their feet, advancing in echelon, with the sepoys flanking them on both sides.

Even though Raju had practised the manoeuvre many times he found himself struggling for breath, head spinning. In drills no one warned you about the dust, or the pall of smoke; nor did they tell you that the sepoy beside you might stumble on a cannonball's crater and lurch towards you in such a way that his bayonet would miss your face by inches. The noise too was almost overpowering, the sheer volume of it: the thudding of feet, the pounding of drums, the 'Har-har-Mahadev' battle-cry of the sepoys, and above all that, the whistle and shriek of shots passing overhead. And cutting through all that noise was the eerie, reverberating sound of bullets hitting bayonets.

Raising his eyes, Raju saw that they were now very close to the walls of the fort: he could see the heads of the defenders, topped with conical caps, desperately trying to aim their antiquated match-locks, which were fired not with a trigger but by holding a slow-burning wick over the touch-hole.

Then all of a sudden the advance stopped.

'Prepare to fire!' shouted Captain Mee and the sepoys fell to their knees to prime their muskets. On the next command the soldiers and sepoys threw up a curtain of fire, to cover the sappers who were racing ahead to plant explosives along the breastworks.

The respite came as a godsend to Raju; his throat was parched, his nose clogged with dust, his eyes smarting from the smoke. Within seconds his flask was empty and when a bhisti appeared it seemed as if a prayer had been answered; Raju clung to the spout, sluicing water over his face and into his mouth; he would have emptied the mussuck if Dicky hadn't shouldered him aside.

In the distance, at the foot of the hill, down by the water, there was another eruption of flame as the *Queen* and the *Nemesis* began a second bombardment, aimed, this time, not at the fortifications on the hill but the gun-emplacements along the shore. Then came an explosion that silenced everything else: it was the blast of the sappers' charges, going off under the breastworks on the hill. When the smoke and debris had cleared Raju caught a glimpse of Major Pratt, with his sabre drawn, racing towards a breach in the walls, followed by a company of marines.

The banjee-boys jumped to their feet, expecting that B Company would be the next to charge into the breach. But then suddenly the fife-major sprang up in front of them: their orders had changed, he said; instead of signalling a charge they were to pipe the sepoys' column into wheeling to the left, on the double.

What was happening? Were they advancing or retreating? Raju did not know or care; his only thought was of staying in step with the other banjee-boys.

They were going downhill now, so the pace accelerated steadily until the whole detachment seemed to be running headlong. One by one the fifers gave up trying to blow on their instruments; there was not enough breath in their lungs. Glimpsing blue waters ahead, Raju realized that they were almost at the bottom of the hill.

Then the road made another turn and they found themselves on an incline that led to the rear of the fort. They saw that the ramparts had crumbled under the bombardment from the two steamers; they saw also that the vessels were still abreast of the battery. The strip of water between them and the shore was filled with the bodies of defenders: some were still alive, thrashing about helplessly. The sailors on the steamers' decks were picking them off, one by one.

Kesri was in the first rank when the rear of the fort came into view. He saw that hundreds of Chinese soldiers were pouring out of the gates. He guessed that they were being driven out of the walls by the marines, who had attacked the shore-side battery after storming down from the hilltop fort. Now the remaining defenders were rushing out to meet the sepoys in a headlong charge: having endured a bombardment of terrifying intensity they seemed almost to welcome the prospect of hand-to-hand combat.

But the sepoys were prepared for the onrush; falling to their knees they met the charge with a barrage of bullets, mowing down the vanguard and causing panic in the ranks behind. And then, with the Chinese front lines already decimated, the sepoys fell upon the milling survivors at close quarters, with swords and bayonets.

When the two lines collided the shock reverberated through the column. The pace slowed so abruptly that Raju bumped up against the fifer in front of him. Brought suddenly to a halt, Raju and Dicky stood motionless, fifes hanging uselessly in their hands. All around them metal was clanging on metal, drowning out the cries of dying men.

Slowly as the carnage unfolded, Raju and Dicky were pushed ahead by the irresistible weight of those behind them. After a few paces they found themselves stepping over the heaped bodies of slaughtered defenders. Almost without exception the clothes of the Chinese soldiers were scorched or burned – this was true even of those who were still on their feet. When hit by a bullet or a bayonet their clothing would burst into flame and they would light up like torches.

Suddenly the fife-major materialized again, within the cloud of smoke; he told Raju and Dicky to get to work, slinging corpses off the road. Tucking their fifes into their belts they took hold of a pair of lifeless ankles and dragged the corpse to the side of the road, where the hillside sloped into the water, a few yards away. As the body rolled down they noticed that the narrow strip of shore between the road and the channel was filled with the corpses of defenders. They were lying in piles, two or three deep in some places. Many had rolled into the water; the channel seemed to be full of them, floating like logs. On some, the clothes were still burning.

The boys turned away abruptly and went back to the road. As they were taking hold of another corpse they heard a grunting sound close by and looked up.

A few yards ahead a fallen Chinese soldier had struggled to his feet: his clothes were scorched and his left arm was hanging uselessly at his side, almost severed at the shoulder. In his right hand was a sabre which he raised when his eyes found Raju and Dicky.

Pressing up against each other they froze in shock as the man stumbled towards them, brandishing his sword.

Then Dicky found his voice and screamed: 'Bachao!' – and miraculously a sepoy emerged from the swirling cloud of dust and bayoneted the man through the stomach. Scarcely pausing to look at the two boys, the sepoy put one foot on the corpse, wrenched out his bayonet, and plunged back into the fray.

As Raju's breath returned he realized that his trowsers were wet. He was staring at the dark patch when Dicky said: 'Don't worry about it. Happens to everyone, ya. It'll dry up soon.'

Glancing at his friend, Raju saw that Dicky's trowsers showed a similar stain.

*

Less than a hundred yards away Kesri was trying, vainly, to hold back his men.

From his position at the head of the Bengal detachment he had seen the carnage unfold, as the defenders ran straight into the sepoys' barrage of bullets. In the beginning Captain Mee and a few other officers had called on the surviving Chinese soldiers to surrender. Uncomprehending and panicked, they had responded instead by flailing about with their weapons. The officers had perforce had to cut them down, and as the lines closed, the marines and sepoys had abandoned themselves to a frenzy of blood-letting.

The sight sickened Kesri: in all his years of soldiering he had never seen a slaughter like this one. There were corpses everywhere, many of them with black scorch-marks on their tunics. On some, the clothes were still burning: looking more closely, Kesri saw that the fires were caused by a fault in the defenders' equipment. The powder for their guns was carried not in cartridges, as was the case with British troops, but in rolled-up paper tubes. These tubes were kept in a powder-pouch that was strapped across the chest. In the course of the fighting the flaps of these pouches would fly open, spilling powder over the soldiers' tunics; the powder was then set alight by the wicks and flints of their matchlocks.

Turning to one side, Kesri skirted around the road, to the shattered ramparts of the waterside battery. The Union Jack was flying everywhere now – on the ramparts of Chuenpee and across the channel, on the fort of Tycock, which had been stormed in a similar fashion by another British landing-party.

Climbing through a breach in the wall, Kesri made his way into the nearby battery. Here too there was ample evidence of a massacre: bodies lay in piles around the craters where heavy shells had exploded; along the bottom of the ramparts lay the corpses of Chinese soldiers who had been felled by crumbling masonry. Plastered against the light-coloured stone of the walls, in bright, bloody splashes, were clumps of tissue and fragments of bone. Here and there splattered brains could be seen dribbling down like smashed egg-yolks.

Almost uniformly the clothes of the dead defenders were scorched with the marks of burning gunpowder. It took no great effort to imagine the panic among the defenders as the flames leapt from tunic to tunic.

In some of the gun-emplacements British marines and artillerymen were hard at work, rendering the big guns useless by hammering spikes into their touch-holes and knocking out their trunnions. Amongst them was a marine who often visited the wrestling pit at Saw Chow.

'Damned fine set of guns they had here,' said the marine to Kesri, stroking the gleaming brass barrel of a massive eight-pounder. 'Have to hand it to Johnny Chinaman – he learns fast. Some of these guns are perfect copies of our own long-barrels. We even found some thirty-two-pounders. All newly cast – lucky for us they haven't yet learnt how to use them properly. Look here.' He kicked a block of wood that was wedged under the barrel. 'These jackblocks kept them from lowering the barrels – that's why so many of their shots went over us.'

In a corner, over a heap of corpses, hung a hastily scribbled sign, in English.

'What does it say?' Kesri asked.

The marine grinned, wiping his face with the back of his hand: 'One of our sarjeants put it up. It says: "This is the road to glory."'

Turning away, Kesri walked in the other direction. Ahead lay a sharp corner, and on rounding it he found himself in a dim, narrow passageway. As his eyes grew accustomed to the light he saw that there was a Chinese soldier at the far end of the corridor. Kesri knew from his tall, plumed hat and his high boots that he was probably an officer. He had evidently suffered an injury, for there was a cleft in the armoured plates that covered his torso; blood was dripping through the cracks.

On catching sight of Kesri the soldier raised his heavy, two-handed sword. Kesri could tell from his crouched stance that he was gathering strength for one last charge.

Lowering his own sword, Kesri rested the tip on the ground and raised a hand, palm outward.

'Surrender! Surrender!' he called out. 'No harm will come . . .'

Kesri knew, as he was saying the words, that they were useless. He could tell from the expression on the man's face that even if he'd understood he would have chosen death over surrender. Sure enough, a moment later the man came rushing at Kesri, almost as though he were begging to be cut down, as indeed he was.

When he had pulled out his dripping sword, Kesri saw that the man's eyes were still open. For the few seconds of life that remained to him, the man fixed his gaze on Kesri. His expression was one that Kesri had seen before, on campaigns in the Arakan and the hills of eastern India – he knew it to be the look that appears on men's faces when they fight for their land, their homes, their families, their customs, everything they hold dear.

Seeing that expression again now it struck Kesri that in a lifetime of soldiering he had never known what it was to fight in that way – the way his father had fought at Assaye – for something that was your own; something that tied you to your fathers and mothers and those who had gone before them, back into the dimness of time.

An unnameable grief came upon him then; falling to his knees he reached out to close the dead man's eyes.

*

On the island of Hong Kong, the sound of cannon-fire, muted though it was by distance, was still menacing enough to keep the gardeners away from the nursery. Through the morning Paulette worked alone, trying to stay busy, watering, pruning, digging – but it was impossible to ignore that distant thudding.

Over the last year Paulette had grown accustomed to hearing sporadic bursts of musketry and cannon-fire in the distance – but this was different. Not only was it more prolonged, there was a concentrated menace in it, a savagery, that made it difficult to carry on as usual. It was hard not to think of death and dying; of spilt blood and torn flesh. In the midst of all that, caring for plants seemed futile.

Towards mid-morning, when the cannon-fire died away and a pall of smoke appeared on the northern horizon, Paulette broke off to sit in the shade of a tree.

What had happened? What did the smoke portend? She could not but wonder, although in some part of herself she did not really want to know.

In a while she spotted a figure coming up the path that led to the nursery. Training her spyglass on the slope she saw that the visitor was Freddie. She breathed a sigh of relief: with Freddie at least there would be no need to pretend to be cheerful, or brave, or anything like that. He would be content to be left to himself.

And her intuition was not wrong. Freddie greeted her from a distance, with a nod, and seated himself on one of the lower terraces of the nursery, with his back against the trunk of a leafy ficus tree.

For a while he sat motionless, staring northwards with his back to her. She too looked towards the distant clouds of smoke and when her eyes strayed back to him she saw that he had taken out his pipe. Something stirred in her and she went down and seated herself beside him, watching quietly as he arranged his implements on the grass.

'You would like to smoke, eh, Miss Paulette?'

She nodded. 'I would like to try.'

'You have not smoked before?'

'No. Never.'

He turned to look at her, narrowing his eyes. 'Why not?'

'I had a fear of it,' she said.

'Fear? Why?'

'I feared becoming a slave to it.'

'Slave, eh?' He gave her one of his rare smiles. 'Opium will not make you slave, Miss Paulette. No. Opium will make you free.'

He inclined his head in the direction of the distant cloud of smoke. 'It is they who are slaves, ne? Slaves to money, profit? They don't take opium but still they are slaves to it. For them opium is just incense, lah, for their gods – money, profit. With opium they want to make whole world slaves for their gods. And they will win, because their gods are very strong, ne, strong as demons? When they win they too will see, only with opium can they escape these demons. Only smoke will hide them from their masters.'

As he was speaking, Freddie had lit a long, sulphur-tipped match with a flint. Now he began to roast a tiny pellet of opium over the flame. When the pellet was properly scorched he handed his pipe to Paulette.

'After opium catch fire I will put on dragon's eye' – he pointed to the tiny hole in the bowl of the pipe – 'and you must suck hard. Smoke is precious, eh, must not waste.'

Once again he held the pellet to the flame and when it caught fire he placed it on the pipe's bowl. 'Now!'

Paulette put her mouth to the stem and sucked in her breath, drawing the fumes into her body. The smoke poured in like a flood, and when the tide ebbed it left in its wake a startling stillness. Just as smoke drives away insects, these fumes too seemed to have expelled everything that carries a sting: fear, anxiety, grief, sadness, disappointment, desire. In their place was a serenely peaceful nullity, a pain-free void.

Paulette lay back against the slope, resting her head on the grass. In a while, when Freddie too had had his fill, he lay beside her, with his head pillowed on his arms, looking up into the dark shade of the tree.

'Tell me,' said Paulette presently, 'how did you learn to smoke?'

'A woman taught me.'

'A woman! Who was she?'

'She was like me, lah – half-Indian, half-Chinese. Very beautiful – maybe too much.'

'Why?'

'Sometimes beauty is like curse, ne? For her men would kill, do anything. She needed guards – and I was one. I would bring opium for her to smoke, lah, and one day she ask me smoke with her; show me how, show me secrets. I had smoked before, but I never saw secrets till she show me.'

None of this seemed real to Paulette: it was as if a story had taken shape in the smoke. In that dreamlike state it did not seem too intrusive to ask: 'And you – did you love her?'

A long time seemed to pass before Freddie answered. Paulette did not know whether the minutes were really going by or not: it was as if the hands of the clock in her head had come to a halt and time had changed into something else.

By the time Freddie spoke again she had almost forgotten what she had asked.

'Don't know, lah,' he said. 'Can't say if it was love or no. Maybe it was like this smoke, ne, that is inside us now? It was stronger than feelings – like madness, or death.'

'Why that? Why death?'

'Because this woman, she belong my boss, she his concubine. He very big man; he "big brother" for many little brother, like me: his name Lenny Chan. Only if mad will a man love woman who belong to big brother. He will always find out, ne?'

'Is that what happened?'

'Yes. He find out and he send his men. They kill her – throw her in the river. Try to kill me too, but I get away. My mother hide me, but they find out, so they kill her too – instead of me.'

He laughed. 'If Lenny Chan know I am here, I would not be alive for long. But he think I am dead, lah – does not know I have been reborn as Freddie Lee. Let's hope, na, that he does not find out.'

*

Jodu and Neel had climbed up the *Cambridge*'s foremast early that morning, as soon as they learnt that a convoy of British ships was approaching the Tiger's Mouth. From there they had observed the action through a spyglass.

When the Chinese batteries on Chuenpee opened up they had cheered, confident that the British attack would be foiled. But all too soon, as the British began to bombard the fortifications on both sides of the channel, their confidence had turned to dismay. They had watched in disbelief as the walls of both Chuenpee and Tycock were torn open by cannonballs; their disbelief had deepened as they watched landing-parties setting off from the British steamers, in longboats and cutters, to launch frontal assaults on the gun-emplacements. Such was their vantage point that they had been able to observe the landing-parties as they swarmed over the battlements. But not until the end did they spot the sepoys who had circled around the hill to attack the gun-emplacements from the rear. This detachment came into view only after the sepoys had come around the slope.

The slaughter that ensued was largely obscured by dust and smoke but Neel and Jodu still had a vivid sense of what was unfolding, because of the increasing number of bodies in the water. Yet the full horror of it only became clear when shoals of charred and blackened bodies began to drift into the channel.

Not one of the British ships, so far as they could see, had suffered the slightest damage.

The speed with which it happened was as astounding as the one-sidedness of the destruction. The assault started at 9 a.m. by Neel's watch; by 11 a.m. British flags were flying on both sides of the channel, atop Chuenpee as well as Tycock. The only remaining threat to the British was a squadron of war-junks commanded by Admiral Guan Tianpei.

The junks had come under withering fire early in the operation. Outmatched, the squadron had retreated to a defensive position, at the edge of the bay that separated Chuenpee from Humen. Between them and the channel lay a sandbar – an impassable obstacle for the larger British vessels but not for those with a shallower draught.

The British fleet ignored the junks while they were occupied in the twin assault on Chuenpee and Tycock. Only when the forts had been stormed did the warships turn their attention to Admiral Guan's squadron: a number of armed cutters went swarming in for the kill.

But before the cutters could close in they were nosed aside by the gleaming iron hull of the *Nemesis*. Speeding past the boats the steamer went straight into the shallows until finally her cutwater bit into the sandbar. Then, with a fearsome shrieking sound a volley of projectiles took flight from her foredeck – these, Neel realized, were the weapons that Zhong Lou-si had asked about: Congreve rockets, the prototypes of which had been invented in Bangalore. Arcing through the air, the rockets arrowed into the junks, with devastating effect. One of them hit a gunpowder magazine and a junk exploded with a deafening roar. Then it was as if a tide of fire had engulfed the creek: the entire Chinese squadron seemed to be ablaze.

Now gongs began to ring on the *Cambridge*, summoning the crew to their battle-stations. The entire outer tier of the Tiger's Mouth defences was now in British hands so it seemed inevitable that the victorious warships would proceed to attack the next set of fortifications – the batteries of Humen and North Wantung Island, where the *Cambridge* was stationed.

But then came a surprise. Instead of advancing, the British warships pulled back to Chuenpee, to evacuate the men who had gone ashore a few hours earlier.

Evidently the attack had been postponed till the next day.

*

In the evening, after making sure that the sepoys and their followers were properly settled below deck, Kesri met with Captain Mee, to review the day's action. The captain had suffered a slight wound: his upper arm had been grazed by a musket-ball and he was wearing a poultice, with his elbow in a sling and his raggy jacket hanging off his shoulder.

'Sorry about your wound, sir,' said Kesri.

'Are you?' The captain grinned. 'I'm not. It should be good for a few weeks' leave in Macau.'

The tally of casualties on the British side, said the captain, was thirty-eight wounded, with no fatalities. On the Chinese side the toll was estimated to be about six hundred killed and many more wounded. Thirty-eight heavy guns had been seized and spiked in Chuenpee; twenty-five on Tycock. Along with the guns found on the junks and elsewhere, the total number of cannon destroyed amounted to one hundred and seventy-three.

'Our men did well today, havildar – Major Pratt was full of praise for them.'

'Really, sir?'

Kesri knew that Captain Mee had long been hoping to have his name included in dispatches. 'Any mention of you, sir, by the commander-sah'b?'

The captain shook his head. 'No, havildar – not a word.'

'Maybe tomorrow, sir?' said Kesri. 'There will be another action, no?'

'I wouldn't count on it, havildar,' said Captain Mee. 'I'm told the Plenipot is under pressure to call off the offensive. I believe a letter has been dispatched to the Chinese commanders explaining the procedures for surrender. I wouldn't be surprised if we were sent back to our camps so that the higher-ups can go on with their endless buck-bucking.'

This sent a chilly pang of disappointment through Kesri. Now that a full-scale attack had been launched he had hoped that the campaign would at last be brought to a speedy conclusion.

But sure enough, the next morning, a boat with a white flag was seen heading over from Humen to the Plenipotentiary's flagship.

Shortly afterwards Kesri learnt that the offensive had been called off and the Bengal Volunteers were to return to Saw Chow.

*

Through the night the *Cambridge* was swept by news and rumours. As the magnitude of the disaster sank in, emotions rose to an extreme pitch, with the Chinese officers and crewmen alternating between rage and numb despair.

When word spread of the role that 'black aliens' had played in the carnage at Chuenpee the attitude of the Chinese sailors began to change: the camaraderie that had developed between them and the lascars abruptly evaporated and a new coldness took its place. It was as if Neel, Jodu and the others were somehow responsible for the actions of the sepoys.

The fact that nothing was said openly only made matters worse. Neel was relieved when Compton lapsed into an accusatory outburst: Why, Neel, why? Why are your countrymen killing our people when there is no enmity between us?

But Compton, said Neel, why do you associate us with the sepoys? We are not all the same. Jodu and I could not be sepoys even if we wanted. And why would we want to be sepoys? The truth is that they have killed more people in Yindu than anywhere else.

The one piece of good news that night was that Admiral Guan was still alive – he was feared to have died when the war-junks were attacked. But it turned out that he had managed to escape to Humen.

In the small hours an order was received from the admiral's command post instructing the *Cambridge* to move to a new position as soon as possible. Accordingly, when the sky began to lighten, the *Cambridge* moved away from the island of North Wantung, to the far bank of the channel, where there was another gun-emplacement. There they began to prepare for the impending attack.

At dawn, when three British frigates were seen to be moving up the channel, the crew of the *Cambridge* were sent to their posts. But then, inexplicably, the frigates turned back.

It was not till later in the day that they learnt that negotiations had been re-opened; a team of mandarins was again parleying with the British Plenipotentiary.

Soon it became evident that the British had an additional reason for calling off their attack: no sooner had the talks begun than the ship that was carrying Lancelot Dent's cargo began to move. Crossing the Tiger's Mouth, the vessel sailed off in the direction of Hong Kong.

Everyone understood then that the merchant Dent was behind the stoppage in the fighting: he was the *mohk hau haak sau* – the 'black hand behind the scene'. He had clearly paid huge cumshaws to the British commanders in order to ensure the safety of his cargo.

You see, said Compton bitterly. This is what happens when merchants and traders begin to run wars – hundreds of lives depend on bribes.

That evening Compton made a trip across the channel, to visit Humen. He came back with momentous news: Governor-General Qishan had capitulated; he had consented to many of the invaders' demands, including the handing over of a sum of six million silver dollars, as compensation for confiscated opium. He had also agreed to give the British the base they had long been clamouring for: the island of Hong Kong – known as 'Red Incense Burner Hill' in Chinese official documents.

A formal understanding to this effect was to be drawn up in a couple of weeks.

*

The effects of the battle at Chuenpee were felt almost immediately at Hong Kong. Overnight, like litter from a faraway storm, swarms of boats began to drift into the bay. These were not shop-boats, loaded with provisions, trinkets and produce, like those that came over from Kowloon every day. They were dilapidated, bedraggled sampans piled high with household goods – utensils, mats, stoves and clothing. Dogs, cats and poultry could be seen perched on their hooped bamboo roofs; on their prows sat broods of little children, many of them with wooden floats tied around their waists, to save them from drowning if they fell overboard.

It was as if a vast floating population were being carried in by the tides. Every night waves of boat-people would be swept in; in the morning Paulette would wake to find yet more sampans at anchor around the *Redruth*.

Freddie, who was now a daily visitor to the nursery, was perfectly at home amongst the floating population. 'They are my people, ne?' he said to Paulette. 'My mother also was boatwoman – I was brought up with Dan people.'

But why were they coming over in such numbers? What was bringing them to Hong Kong?

'Too much trouble for them in Guangdong now,' said Freddie. 'Land-people troubling them. They cannot stay, ne? Everyone say Hong Kong will soon be given to British. Boat-people think it will be safer here.'

Soon some of the new arrivals began to move ashore, building huts and shacks, settling where they could. The beach where Paulette's daily climb began did not long remain deserted. A shack appeared at its far edge one day and within a week a hamlet seemed to have sprouted around it. Although the inhabitants seemed peaceable enough, Paulette was glad when Freddie offered to accompany her on her daily climb to the nursery: she accepted without hesitation.

Meanwhile the British were also expanding their presence on Hong Kong. Every day cutters and longboats would ply back and forth between the island and the bay, bringing over soldiers, sailors, shipowners and sightseers from the naval and merchant vessels that were at anchor around the island. Teams of surveyors would roam over the beaches and slopes, taking measurements and putting down stakes and markers.

One day a group of surveyors even turned up at the nursery – a half-dozen officious-looking men armed with tripods and measuring tapes. They left after asking a few questions about the plot and its ownership, apparently satisfied with Paulette's explanation that it had been leased by her employer, Mr Penrose.

But after they'd gone, Freddie said: 'Why they were asking so many questions, lah? You think maybe they want take the land?'

The thought was like a blow to the stomach for Paulette. 'No!' she cried. 'They can't! Surely they can't?'

'People are saying so, ne? British will take whatever they want when they get the island.'

Freddie explained that the original islanders, of whom there were only four thousand, had become very concerned about the recent changes. For centuries Red Incense Burner Hill had been considered a place of misery and misfortune – insalubrious, racked by disease and lashed by devastating typhoons. In the past, mainland people had gone to great lengths to avoid Hong Kong; the inhabitants had been objects of pity because they were condemned to eke out an existence on a barren, ill-starred island.

Now suddenly it was as if the island had been transformed into a lodestar. The old-time islanders had begun to fear that their land, their homes, would be expropriated by the British. Some were so alarmed that they were selling their property and moving to the mainland.

'Maybe I talk to landlord, ne? Maybe he want to sell?'

A few days later Fitcher announced that the nursery's landlord had come over to the *Redruth* and offered to sell the site, along with an adjoining stretch of land – two acres in total, for a sum of thirty Spanish dollars. Fitcher had leapt at the offer, handing over an advance of five dollars.

On the day when the formalities were completed Fitcher made one of his rare trips up to the nursery, in a sedan chair. After looking around a bit, he said: 'Ee've done a fine job here, Paulette. Ee deserve to have it.'

'What do you mean, sir?'

'Didn'ee ken?' said Fitcher, with a smile. 'It's for ee that I've bought it; the land's to be eer dowry.'

*

Through the month of January the Parsi seths of Macau continued to gather at Dinyar's villa every Sunday, for prayers followed by a meal in which a tureen of dhansak always took pride of place. But from week to week the mood of the gatherings varied wildly. The first Sunday after the Battle of Chuenpee, the seths were exultant; none of them doubted that the Celestials had learnt their lesson; after such a resounding defeat surely they would cut their losses and agree to meet the British demands? Surely they would understand that they had no option other than that of bringing a yet greater calamity upon themselves?

When attacked by a band of dacoits on a lonely road a man might risk losing a finger or two in order to save his treasure – but what sane man would endanger his arm or his head? The instinct for self-preservation was no less strong in the Chinese than in any other people: surely they would accept that the war was already lost? After all, it was clear enough that the Chinese army was *bherem bhol ne mā'e pol* – all show outside but hollow within. And besides, for a realm as vast as China the loss of a small, barren island like Hong Kong was a trifling matter. Nor was an indemnity of six million Spanish dollars any great thing either – amongst the merchants of Guangzhou there were several who could afford to pay it out of their pockets.

So the talk went that Sunday, at lunch, and by the time the tureen of dhansak was removed everyone was convinced that the war was over, so much so that Dinyar even called for a demijohn of simkin to be opened, in celebration.

But the week after that there was less certainty: it appeared that the mandarins had once again succeeded in luring the Plenny-potty into their game of endless palavering. Then yet another week went by with nothing but more buck-buck, which cast everyone even deeper into the doldrums.

The Sunday after that despair turned to truculence and the seths began to talk about how they might bring some pressure to bear on Captain Elliot, to speed things up a little. On an impulse Dinyar suggested that they all go to Hong Kong on his ship, the *Mor*, to seek a meeting with the Plenipot. The proposal met with a warm welcome and it was decided that they would leave the next day.

Shireen was, as usual, a largely silent spectator at these deliberations: while the men talked she would orchestrate a steady flow of food and drink for them, from the villa's kitchen. It was only after the guests had left that she asked Dinyar if she too could go to Hong Kong on the *Mor.* Ever solicitious, he declared that she was most welcome.

They left at noon the next day, reaching Hong Kong after nightfall. It wasn't till the next morning that they discovered that they had been singularly fortunate in the timing of their visit. An event of great significance was due to take place that day: Captain Elliot was to meet with Qishan near Chuenpee. A convention was to be signed whereby the Chinese would undertake to hand over Hong Kong to the British, along with an indemnity of six million Spanish dollars!

The *Mor*'s passengers gathered on deck to watch the flagging off of an impressive squadron of steamers and warships. Not everyone was convinced that the meeting would produce results: there had been so many delays and disappointments in the recent past that it was hard to believe that the end was really in sight. But even to the most sceptical onlooker it was evident, from the fanfare and the prominent presence of Captain Elliot, that something significant was in the offing.

Only after the squad had departed did the seths notice that Hong Kong had changed in the last couple of weeks: they saw that a wave of settlers had washed up on the island's shores; they noticed also that a cluster of buildings was already under construction at the eastern end of the bay.

That so much had happened without their being aware of it was a matter of no little concern to the seths. As soon as the *Mor*'s cutter could be lowered, they went hurrying over to see what was afoot on the island. They stayed there several hours and returned seething. It appeared that the British military authorities had decided to hold on to Hong Kong a while ago, treaty or not; what was more, they had quietly allowed some leading British merchants to grab the choicest plots of land. There was a rocky protrusion at the eastern end of the bay that would serve very well as the foundation for a jetty; the promontory had been named East Point and some of the bigger British opium-trading firms were already constructing godowns and daftars in its vicinity.

None of this could have happened of course without the connivance of the expedition's commanders; it was clear enough that they had been paid off by the top British merchants. But what else had been settled between them, under the table, with no one's knowledge? Had all the best plots already been palmed off, in secret?

One of the seths said to Shireen: Bibiji, if your husband had been alive things would not have come to this. We Parsis would not have been kept in the dark, while the Angrezes pocketed the best bits of the island for themselves. As a member of the Select Committee Bahram-bhai would have found out; he would have warned us.

As the seth was speaking the now familiar sounds of muted cannon-fire came rolling in from somewhere over the horizon.

Hai! cried Shireen in alarm. Has the fighting started again?

Dinyar tilted his head, straining to listen. No, he said. It seems that they are firing minute-guns. They must be celebrating the signing of a treaty!

This added a fresh urgency to the seths' discussions: they began to argue about how best to persuade the British to open up the island to other buyers, either through direct sales or auctions. Some of them pointed out that if it came to the worst they could always refuse to provide opium to their British counterparts in Bombay. This was a trump card of sorts, for in Bombay foreign merchants were completely dependent on Indian suppliers for the procurement of Malwa opium.

But Dinyar and a few others argued that this would be a dangerous course: if pressed, the British government would surely find some pretext for seizing supplies of opium at gunpoint. That was the ace that was hidden up the sleeves of the Jardines, Mathesons and Dents of the world. Despite all their cacklings about Free Trade, the truth was that their commercial advantages had nothing to do with markets or trade or more advanced business practices – it lay in the brute firepower of the British Empire's guns and gunboats.

The argument was still raging when a steamer was seen to be hurrying towards Hong Kong from the direction of the Pearl River estuary. Training a telescope on it Dinyar announced that the vessel was none other than the *Nemesis* with Commodore Bremer on board.

Soon it became clear that the steamer was heading for the western end of Hong Kong Bay. This convinced Dinyar that something unusual was under way and he wasted no time in calling for his cutter to be readied: whatever was going on, he was determined not to be left in the dark.

You should come with us, he said to Shireen.

Why me?

You should take a look at the island at least. When you receive your compensation you'll have plenty of money. Maybe you too should put in a bid for a plot.

What are you talking about, Dinyar? Shireen retorted. Why would I buy land here? What will I do with it?

Why not, Shireen-auntie? Your grandchildren might want it. Maybe some day it will be worth a lot of money: it's not impossible. When my grandfather bought land in Bombay everyone laughed. But look at what it's worth now.

Shireen thought it over and decided to go along for the ride, not with a plot of land in mind, but because a sunset breeze was whispering over the bay and the conditions were perfect for a short sailing trip. She fetched a hat and a veil and was lowered into the cutter by the *Mor*'s swing-lift.

In the meantime a longboat had been launched from the *Nemesis*: a group of officers could be seen seated inside, heading towards the island. They reached the shore in only a few minutes.

By the time the *Mor*'s cutter pulled in a ceremony was under way on the edge of the island, not far from Sheng Wan village. A Union Jack had been planted near the water, and Commodore Bremer was standing in front of it, addressing the other officers.

'In the name of our Gracious Queen, I take possession of this island of Hong Kong on this day, the twenty-fifth of January, eighteen forty-one.'

'Hear, hear!'

Raising glasses of champagne, the officers drank a toast.

'In memory of this day,' intoned the commodore, 'let the spot on which we now stand be known forever as Possession Point.'

'Hear, hear!'

Dinyar and the other seths went hurrying ahead to listen, but Shireen hung back diffidently.

In a while she heard a cough, and a familiar voice: 'Bibiji . . . ?'

'Oh Zadig Bey! I'm glad to see you.'

'I'm glad to see you too, Bibiji. Would you like to go for a walk?'

'A walk, Zadig Bey?' said Shireen with a laugh. 'Why, are you looking to buy a plot of land, like everyone else?'

'Yes, Bibiji,' said Zadig gravely, 'I've been thinking that I would look.' He paused to clear his throat: 'But not just for myself.'

'What do you mean, Zadig Bey?'

Zadig scratched his chin. 'Bibiji, there is something I've been meaning to ask you and perhaps it's fitting that I should ask now.'

'Yes, Zadig Bey?'

A bright flush rose to his face as he turned to her.

'Bibi . . .'

Zadig stopped and started again. 'Shireen . . . will you marry me?'

Eighteen

After a medical examination, Captain Mee was given three weeks' furlough to recuperate from the wound he had received at the Battle of Chuenpee. He elected to spend that time at Macau and lost no time in setting off. Kesri assumed that he would not return to Saw Chow a minute short of the full term of his leave. To his surprise Captain Mee was back a couple of days early.

'Kaptán-sah'b is looking ekdum fit-faat!' said Kesri, with a smile.

'Am I?'

Kesri could not remember when he had last seen Captain Mee in such fine fettle.

'Ji, Kaptán-sah'b, you look very well.'

Captain Mee smiled. 'It was good to be away, havildar.'

'But why you came back early then, Kaptán-sah'b?'

'Orders, havildar – from the Plenipot himself.'

The captain explained that there was to be a ceremonial parade and trooping of colours at Hong Kong the next day. Captain Elliot and Commodore Bremer were to issue a proclamation, and the Bengal Volunteers had been asked to send a squad to the ceremony. They would be taking a field-piece and gun-crew with them, for the gun-salute.

'The big brass will be present, havildar, so you'll have to make sure that our lads are on their toes.'

Ji, Kaptán-sah'b.

Next morning their detachment was taken to Hong Kong by a steamer. Disembarking at the eastern end of Hong Kong Bay, they marched up a hill to a stretch of level ground. A tall flagstaff had been planted there with the Union Jack fluttering atop. Several other squads had already mustered on the ground and were preparing for the ceremony: Kesri spotted the regimental colours of the Royal Irish, the Cameronians, the 49th and the 37th Madras.

The Bengal Volunteers were placed next to the Madras sepoys, to the rear of the British squads. After taking his position at the head of the squad, Kesri took a look around: he saw that a large group of civilians, mainly British, had gathered on the far side of the ground. A still larger crowd, composed of local people, had collected higher up the hillside.

A half-hour passed before Captain Elliot and Commodore Bremer appeared: the Plenipotentiary was in civilian clothes and the commodore was in full dress uniform. Marching solemnly to the flagstaff, they turned to face the ground. Then Captain Elliot began to read from a sheet of paper.

'The island of Hong Kong having been ceded to the British crown under the seal of the Imperial minister and High Commissioner Keshen, it has become necessary to provide for the government thereof, pending Her Majesty's further pleasure. By virtue of the authority therefore in me vested, all Her Majesty's Rights, Royalties, Privileges of all kinds whatever, in and over the said island of Hong Kong, whether to or over lands, harbours, property or personal service, are hereby declared, proclaimed and to Her Majesty fully reserved . . .'

Through years of practice Kesri had perfected the art of letting his gaze stray while standing at attention. His eyes wandered now to the civilian spectators at the far end of the ground. He spotted several familiar faces in the crowd: Shireen and Dinyar, with Zadig towering above them; Mr Burnham, with his wife on one side and Zachary on the other.

'. . . given under my hand and seal of office,' the Plenipotentiary continued, 'on this twenty-ninth day of January, in the year one thousand eight hundred and forty-one.'

Tucking away the sheet of paper, Captain Elliot looked up at the assembled soldiers and civilians.

'God save the Queen!'

A chorus of voices returned the cry and then Commodore Bremer stepped forward to read from another sheet of paper.

'I Bremer, Commander-in-Chief, and Elliot, Plenipotentiary, by this Proclamation make known to the inhabitants of the island of

Hong Kong, that the island has now become part of the dominion of the Queen of England by clear public agreement between the high officers of the Celestial and British Courts: and all native persons residing therein must understand that they are now subjects of the Queen of England, to whom and to whose officers they must pay duty and obedience.'

Kesri's gaze strayed now to the other, less privileged, group of spectators, on the hillside above. Among them too he recognized a face: Freddie's. Standing beside him was a youth in jacket and breeches; he looked distantly familiar but Kesri could not recall where he had seen him before.

*

It was the eighth shot in the gun salute that drew Paulette's eye to the the tall, broad-shouldered gun-lascar who was standing behind the Bengal Volunteer's field-piece. After watching him for a while she took her spyglass out of her pocket.

'What you looking at, eh?'

'That man over there. Standing behind that cannon.'

'Who?'

Paulette handed Freddie the spyglass. 'Here. You have a look. See if you recognize him.'

'Who you think it is?'

'Just look.'

Freddie raised the instrument to his eye and kept it there for a good few minutes. Slowly a smile spread across his face. 'You think it could be him, eh? Kalua, from the *Ibis*?'

'Yes, could be,' said Paulette. 'I'm not sure.'

The ceremony had ended now and the parade ground was filling quickly with people. Spectators were pouring down the slope, to gawk at the soldiers and sepoys.

'Come,' said Paulette, tapping Freddie on the arm. 'Let's go closer.'

Stepping down the hillside, they mingled with the crowd. When they were about fifty yards from the gun-lascar, Paulette came to a halt. 'Yes,' she said, 'I'm sure it's him.'

Just then Maddow too happened to glance in their direction. His eyes rested first on Paulette and then passed over to Freddie and back. Suddenly his sleepy gaze brightened and a smile played over his lips. He cast a glance around him, and seeing Kesri nearby he gave them a tiny, almost imperceptible shake of his head, as if to warn them not to come any closer.

Struck by a thought, Paulette murmured: 'I wonder if Kalua knows that Havildar Kesri Singh is Deeti's brother?'

Across the fifty-yard distance, Maddow seemed to understand what was going through her mind. He answered with another tiny nod.

Paulette smiled. 'Yes,' she said. 'He knows.'

*

At the other end of the ground Mr Burnham was surveying the surging crowd with an expression of marked distaste. 'I can't say I care much for this riff-raff,' he said to his wife, 'we'd better be on our way – but I'll need to have a quick word with the commodore first.'

'Yes of course, dear,' said Mrs Burnham. 'I'll wait for you here.'

Mr Burnham turned to Zachary: 'Reid, can I trust you to make sure that my wife's reticule is not snatched by some opium-crazed la-lee-loon?'

'Yes certainly, sir.'

Mr Burnham hurried off, leaving an awkward gap between Zachary and his wife. Slowly they edged closer until they were standing almost shoulder to shoulder.

After a few minutes of silence Mrs Burnham said: 'It has been a while, Mr Reid, since I last saw you. I trust you've been well?'

'Yes I have, thank you.'

This was Zachary's first encounter with Mrs Burnham since the levée. Apart from two days in Macau, he had spent the intervening weeks at Hong Kong, assisting Mr Burnham with the construction of his new premises on the island.

'And what about you, Mrs Burnham?' said Zachary. 'How have you been?'

'Not too well I'm afraid,' she said. 'That is why I had to remain in Macau while my husband was at Hong Kong. My sawbones told me that the island's air is unhealthy and I would do well to stay away.'

Her voice was languid, her manner indifferent, in a fashion that Zachary had come to know all too well from watching her at social

490

occasions. In the past, when they had conspired to deceive the world together, he had delighted in observing her cool public demeanour. But now he knew that he too was among those whom the mask was meant to deceive and it was like having salt rubbed on an open wound.

But Zachary was careful to keep his voice level. 'It must have been pleasant to be in Macau,' he said. 'I'm told the town is filled with convalescing military men.'

She was silent for just long enough that he knew he had rattled her. Then, recovering herself she continued: 'Were there many military men about in Macau? I didn't see any, but then I hardly left the house.'

'Really?'

Zachary had been waiting for this moment and he knew exactly what he was going to say. Mimicking the silky tone that she herself often used, he said: 'As it happens I was in Macau myself for a couple of days and I could swear I saw you going into a milliner's shop one afternoon, down the street from the St Lazarus Church. As a matter of fact, I even saw you coming out after an hour or two, with Captain Mee. I'm told this milliner sometimes has a room to rent.'

'Mr Reid!' Mrs Burnham had gone white. 'What on earth are you implying?'

A bark of laughter broke from Zachary's throat. 'Oh come, Mrs Burnham, there's no need to pretend with me. You forget that I am perfectly familiar with your play-acting.'

'What on earth . . . what do you mean, Mr Reid?' she said, stumbling over her words.

Zachary saw from the corner of his eye that Mrs Burnham's face had disappeared behind her parasol. 'Captain Mee is the one, isn't he, Mrs Burnham? The lieutenant you told me about?'

This set the parasol twirling in agitation so he softened his tone. 'There's no need to hide your face, Mrs Burnham.'

Now at last she answered, in a faltering, breathless rush. 'Oh please, Mr Reid. All we did was talk – you will not speak of it to anyone, will you?'

Her capitulation softened Zachary a little. Without quite meaning to he voiced the question that had been circling in his head ever since the night of the levée.

'Why him, Mrs Burnham? What do you see in that clodhopping dingleberry?'

'I can't tell you,' she said softly. 'I don't know the answer. All I can say is that if it were in my hands I would not have chosen him.'

'And why is that?'

'Because we're different, he and I. He is utterly without calculation, without guile; he is ruled entirely by his sense of duty. It is strange to say so, but I do not think I have ever known anyone so completely selfless.'

A thin smile rose to Zachary's lips. 'You are either deluded or naive, Mrs Burnham,' he retorted. 'There is nothing selfless about these military men. They are all drowning in debt; they can be bought for fifty dollars apiece. You should ask your husband about it – he has plenty of them in his pocket.'

'Not Neville,' she said with calm certainty. 'He is not that kind of man.'

Zachary noticed now that her eyes had strayed to the other end of the parade ground, where Captain Mee could be seen, leaning against the hilt of his sword as he chatted with some other officers.

'Is that what you believe?' said Zachary. 'That Captain Mee is immune to the inducements that tempt other men?'

'Yes,' she said. 'I am sure of it.'

He permitted himself a smile. 'Well,' he said, 'we shall see.'

To grease the captain's palms would not be easy, Zachary knew, but he was certain that it could be done: it was certainly a challenge worth rising to. And the more he thought about it the more important it seemed that he should succeed in the endeavour – for would it not thwart the design of the world if one man were allowed to flout the law of cupidity, that great engine of progress that matched needs to gains, supply with demand, and thereby distributed the right rewards to those who most deserved them?

*

Compton was visiting the *Cambridge* the day the gun salute was fired at Hong Kong.

The sound was heard clearly at the Tiger's Mouth, where the *Cambridge* was still at anchor. Everybody understood that the shots had been fired by the English to celebrate their acquisition of the island; this affected the spirits of all on board but it was Compton who took it hardest, burying his face in his hands and grinding his teeth in anger and outrage.

Yet he knew very well that there was nothing to be done about it: Governor-General Qishan was in the impossible position of having to reconcile his instructions from the Emperor – to drive out the invaders at all costs – with the realities of the situation, which was that the British already had effective possession of the island; to wrest it from them was impossible without a change in the balance of firepower. If the Governor-General had not conceded their demands the British might have pushed on to Guangzhou, inflicting even greater losses. The best hope now was that the Emperor, on receiving the governor's dispatches, would perceive the wisdom of following a policy that was geared to limiting the damage.

But the Emperor was unpredictable; there was no knowing how he would respond. And until word came from Beijing, what else was there to do but prepare for another British attack? This indeed was why Compton had come to the *Cambridge*: he had brought orders for the vessel to move up to the First Bar of the Pearl River.

The First Bar was a feature that Neel knew well: it was a kind of cataract, only a few li from Whampoa. There were two such bars, or cataracts, on the Pearl River; at these points in the river's course the water ran shallow and the channel was broken up by shifting shoals and sandbars. The navigable lanes changed from week to week and deep-draughted ships had to hire specialized pilots to guide them past the obstacles.

Neel had grown familiar with the First Bar during his time at Whampoa: the terrain there was flat and green, the river being flanked on both sides by rice-fields, orchards and scattered villages. In normal times the landscape was reminiscent of the Bengal countryside, lush, bucolic and sleepy.

But when the *Cambridge* arrived at the First Bar now, Neel saw that there had been dramatic changes in its surroundings. In the last month thousands of troops and workers had set up camp on either side of the river. A mud-walled fort had risen on the east bank: extending outwards from it was a gigantic raft, built with massive timbers; it stretched from shore to shore and was so solidly built that it looked like a dam. Hundreds of acres of forest had been cut down for the construction of the raft; the cost had been borne by the merchants of the Co-Hong: they were rumoured to have spent thousands of silver taels on the timber alone.

One section of the raft was removeable, to allow traffic to go through when necessary. The *Cambridge* crossed over to the other side and anchored just abaft of the raft, across the river from the fort. The *Cambridge* was to serve as the fort's counterpart, a floating gun-emplacement: her mission was to protect the raft's moorings on the western bank of the river.

After experimenting with various angles it was decided that the *Cambridge* would be tethered with her bows pointing in the direction from which the invaders' warships were expected to come. The advantage of this was that it narrowed the ship's profile, presenting a smaller target to the attackers; the disadvantage was that it reduced the number of guns that could be brought to bear on the stretch of river that lay ahead: in the event of an attack only the guns in the *Cambridge*'s bows would be in play. To remedy this more gun-ports were created in the ship's nose, on all decks. The forward guns being of critical importance, great care was invested in their manning. A dozen of the ship's most competent sailors were chosen to be golondauzes and they were given free rein to pick their own men. Jodu was one of the first to be appointed: much to Neel's joy, Jodu picked him for his gun-crew, giving him the job of *sumbadar* or rammer-man.

For the next fortnight the gun-crews spent their time devising and practising drills. The officers could provide little guidance, being unaccustomed to Western-style ships, so the crewmen had to draw up their own protocols, from memory. A Macahnese lascar who had served on a Portuguese naval vessel took the lead: it was he who made up the drill for clearing the deck and summoning the crew to battle-stations.

Through this time Compton continued to visit the *Cambridge* regularly, bearing news. Talks were still under way, he said, between the British and Chinese; Compton himself often translated for the Governor-General's emissaries. But for now there was little to report: so far as the British were concerned there was nothing to be discussed except the ratification of the convention of Chuenpee. They would not be satisfied unless the Emperor conceded all their demands.

For his part, Compton was convinced that the Daoguang Emperor would not make any concessions. And sure enough he returned to the *Cambridge* one morning with the news that the Emperor had indeed repudiated the treaty in its entirety. Not only that, he had severely reprimanded Governor-General Qishan for making concessions to the British. His instructions to the authorities in Guangdong remained unchanged: no compromise was possible and the invader had to be repelled at all costs. But this time the Emperor had done more than issue exhortations: he had personally sanctioned funds for the rebuilding and strengthening of all the Pearl River fortifications. In addition thousands of troops from Hunan, Sichuan and Yunnan were to be sent to Guangdong to reinforce the province's defences.

Over the next few days a great number of fresh troops poured into the area around the First Bar. A fortified encampment arose beside the *Cambridge*, manned by a battalion-strength unit of tough, seasoned troops from Hunan.

It was evident from these preparations that the raft had become a key element in the safeguarding of Guangzhou: in effect it was the city's last line of defence. Past this point the river branched off into many channels; there were so many of them that it was impossible to effectively block them all. This meant that if British warships succeeded in breaking through at the First Bar then Whampoa and Guangzhou would be at their mercy.

One day, during a 'live fire' drill, Neel burst into laughter.

Why are you laughing? said Jodu.

It just occurred to me, said Neel, that the responsibility for defending Canton has fallen on a motley crew of 'black-aliens'.

*

Towards the middle of February Mr Burnham accompanied the expedition's commanders on one of their periodic expeditions to meet with Qishan. On his return, he told Zachary that the Plenipot had at last realized that the Emperor would not accept the terms that he and Qishan had agreed upon at Chuenpee. At the most recent meeting Qishan had seemed very much cast down, not at all his usual polished self; his manner had been strangely evasive as though he were concealing something. Captain Elliot had garnered the impression that the proposed treaty had already been repudiated by the Emperor; he would make no concessions without a further show of force.

As for Commodore Bremer, he and several other officers had long believed that Captain Elliot was on a fool's errand; it was clear to them that the mandarins were just playing for time in order to shore up their defences. Of late many signs of a military build-up had been observed around the Tiger's Mouth. Information had also been received that the Celestials were taking steps to block the river's navigable channels with chains, stakes and rafts.

These preparations had caused much outrage among the British leadership: they were seen as a clear sign of Chinese perfidy, offering vindication to those who believed that the victory at Chuenpee should have been consolidated with an attack on Canton. These officers were now urging swift action: if the Chinese were given more time to prepare then it would only make their own job harder in the end. Many were pressing for a renewed offensive, leading to the seizure of Canton itself.

Yielding to the pressure, Captain Elliot had agreed to issue an ultimatum to Qishan: if the ratified treaty were not received within four days then Guangzhou would face attack.

Few were those, said Mr Burnham, who entertained any hope of a peaceful resolution. Preparations for the renewal of hostilities were already under way, on both sides. The British commanders had put out word that merchant ships would be needed to serve as support vessels for the British attack force.

At this a thought leapt to Zachary's mind. 'Is there any chance, sir,' he said, 'that the *Ibis* might be used by the expedition? She is sitting idle after all and there is nothing I would like more than to support our brave soldiers and sailors.'

Mr Burnham smiled and patted Zachary on the back. 'Your enthusiasm does you credit, Reid! That thought had occurred to me too. I will try to put a word in the commodore's ear – I cannot promise anything of course. Everyone is clamouring to lend their ships to the fleet, even the Parsis, so it will not be easy.'

The next few days passed in great anxiety for Zachary. Such was his eagerness to join the expedition that he found it hard to keep his mind on the construction of Mr Burnham's godown. But there was no further news until the day that Captain Elliot's ultimatum expired. That afternoon a beaming Mr Burnham came striding up to the work site to announce that he had good news: the British attack would be launched in a day or two and the *Ibis* had been included in the list of six support vessels that were to sail with the fleet. Her job was to carry supplies of munitions and to serve as a holding-ship for the badly wounded.

Zachary was overjoyed: to witness a seaborne attack at first-hand seemed to him as great an adventure as he could ever have wished for.

'And you, sir? Will you be sailing with the fleet too?'

'So I shall,' said Mr Burnham proudly. 'I'll be on the *Wellesley* again with Commodore Bremer. He has invited me to join him on his flagship. It is a signal honour.'

'Indeed it is, sir, but it is no more than your due. And what about Mrs Burnham? Will she remain here at Hong Kong, on the *Anahita?*'

'Yes,' said Mr Burnham. 'My wife has decided that she would like to remain here. The commodore has advised the merchant fleet to move to Saw Chow but I think he is being overly cautious. I cannot imagine that there will be any danger.'

'I'm sure you're right, sir.'

Mr Burnham glanced at his fob before giving Zachary a pat on the back. 'You'd better be off now, Reid; I'm sure there's a lot to be done on the *Ibis.*'

Eager to get to work, Zachary hurried back to the schooner – but no sooner had he stepped on board than he learnt of a minor setback. The Finnish first mate was waiting for him, on the main-deck. His shirt was splattered with blood and he was holding a large poultice to his face.

The door of his cabin had slammed into him, said the mate, knocking him off his feet. He suspected that he had suffered internal injuries as well; in any case, he was in no state to sail.

Zachary had suspected for a while that the mate was looking for an excuse to abandon ship: he paid him off and told him to empty out his cabin.

It was too late to find a man to take the Finn's place, but Zachary did not allow that to dampen his enthusiasm: he was confident that he and the second mate would be able to manage well enough between them.

*

The night before the embarkation Kesri was summoned to Captain Mee's tent, for a briefing on the plan of attack. On the captain's field-desk lay a large chart of the defences of the Pearl River's lower reaches.

The fortifications that had been reconstructed or newly erected were marked in red ink, so the area around the Tiger's Mouth was a sunburst of colour: the recently demolished fortifications at Chuenpee and Tycock had all been rebuilt, said Captain Mee. Chains had once again been slung across the shipping lanes and at certain points stakes had been sunk into the river-bed, to obstruct entry.

The most heavily reinforced forts were those on the island of North Wantung, which lay right in the middle of the Tiger's Mouth, halfway between Chuenpee to the east and Tycock to the west. The island was now bristling with cannon: one set of guns faced the main shipping channel to the east; the other overlooked the lane to the west. In addition, a third battery had been built on the island's peak.

Along with a number of other officers, Captain Mee had surveyed the fortifications of North Wantung from the deck of the *Nemesis*. The forts were undoubtedly impressive, he said: the island was now encircled by some two hundred cannon: the month before there had been only a few dozen guns on the island; that such a vast project could be so quickly completed was in itself an astonishing thing.

But just to the south of heavily fortified North Wantung lay another, much smaller island: South Wantung. The batteries of North Wantung were within easy shelling distance of its southern neighbour – yet, unaccountably, the Chinese had failed to occupy and fortify this second island. From a military point of view this was an elementary error, said the captain: if taken, South Wantung might well be the lever with which to force open the Tiger's Mouth. This was the thinking behind the British plan of attack, which would commence with an assault on that island.

Once again the Bengal Volunteers were to be transported on the *Nazareth Shah*; they would be accompanied by a full complement of followers and baggage. The fighting would probably take several days if not weeks, said the captain, so the men had to be prepared for a long stay, on the ship.

'This time there're no two ways about it, havildar,' said the captain. 'We're going to push on to Canton, come what may.'

*

Next morning Hong Kong Bay was swept by a gale of excitement and anticipation. Everyone – merchants and lascars, Parsi shipowners and Chinese boat-people – knew that a critical moment was at hand. When it came time for the warships to set sail, a procession of British merchant vessels, festooned with pennants and Union Jacks, left the harbour to line the route to the estuary; their decks were crowded with passengers, some cheering, some praying; their masts and yards were aswarm with crewmen who had climbed aloft to watch the fleet go by.

Three seventy-four-gun ships-of-the line, *Melville*, *Blenheim* and *Wellesley*, led the way, and were followed by the forty-four-gun *Druid* and the twenty-four-gun *Jupiter*. They sailed out in stately fashion, with the spectators whooping and shouting hurrahs as though they were at a regatta.

The *Ibis* and the other supply and troopships were the last to weigh. They were escorted out of the bay by the *Queen* and *Madagascar*. In their wake followed the merchant vessels that were moving to the safe haven of Saw Chow. The *Anahita* was one of the few that remained at anchor at Hong Kong Bay.

The weather was perfect, cool but not cold; the sky was a clear blue and a steady breeze took the fleet briskly up to the mouth of the Pearl River. This was the first time that Zachary had ventured into the estuary: even though he had seen many fine prospects on the China coast, he was awed by the grandeur of the view – the channel was like a vast valley of lapis lazuli, set between mountains of jade.

The assembly point was a mile or so below South Wantung Island; by the time the support vessels arrived there preparations for the attack were already under way. The force's warships were anchored in a broadly triangular formation, headed by the *Wellesley* and two other seventy-four-gun frigates. Behind them were seven smaller warships and a flotilla of cutters and rocket-boats. Supporting the sailships were three heavily armed steamers.

The formation was like an arrowhead, pointed directly at the forts of North Wantung Island. The island was sphinx-like in shape, with its head facing the British fleet. Upon its crown sat a massive battery, the gun-ports of which were already open, with the muzzles pointing at the warships. The surrounding shores were ringed by an almost continuous circle of fortifications; battlements ran up and down the slopes, ranging over the promontories and peaks of the Tiger's Mouth.

From the quarter-deck of the *Ibis* Zachary had a fine view of the preparations for the attack. Of the fleet's complement of steamers, three were busy paddling around the anchored vessels. Only one steamer was stationary, the *Nemesis* – but that was only because she was to be the spearhead of the coming attack. Half a dozen longboats were clustered around her, discharging men and munitions; a string of cutters was attached to her stern, ready to be towed.

Just as the sun was going down a cloud of dense black smoke spurted from the tall funnel of the *Nemesis*. As steam built up in her boilers she seemed to quiver and shake, like a racehorse champing at the bit. Then all of a sudden she darted forward, pulling three cutters behind her, heading towards the islet of South Wantung.

South and North Wantung were separated by a narrow strip of water. South Wantung was of negligible size: had it not been topped by a couple of small hillocks it could have been mistaken for a mudflat. Like a mouse beneath a cat, it seemed to cower in front of its lofty neighbour to the north.

As the *Nemesis* moved towards South Wantung two Chinese batteries opened up simultaneously, one from the heights of North Wantung, and the other from across the water, at Humen. The first few shots went astray and before the Chinese gunners could find their range the *Nemesis* had edged close to the shore of the islet. She pulled up to a beach that was protected by a hillock.

While the batteries of North Wantung continued to pound away, ineffectively, a landing party leapt ashore. All of a sudden the dun-coloured hillocks of the islet were aswarm with the blue uniforms of artillerymen.

Zachary's spyglass was now riveted on the islet: having been trained as a shipwright he had a professional interest in the ways in which things were assembled and taken apart. He was captivated by the scene that now unfolded on South Wantung – two hundred men working together with the synchronized precision of wasps building a nest.

The gun-lascars of the Madras Artillery had brought a stack of gunny sacks with them; these they now proceeded to fill with sand from the shore. As the sacks accumulated they were passed from hand to hand, up to the saddle that separated the island's two hillocks. Here, sheltered by the slope, stood an officer of the Royal Artillery; under his direction the sandbags were stacked to form a protective breastworks.

Meanwhile squads of artillerymen had lowered an arsenal of dismantled weaponry from the *Nemesis*. A set of massive brass and iron barrels came first, each of them weighing half a ton or more; they were followed by the wheels and limbers of their carriages. The various parts were put together with astonishing speed and before the sun had gone down the makings of a small battery were already visible on the beach.

The fusillades from the Chinese batteries had been intensifying steadily all this while. The islet took many hits, but because of the intervening hillock none caused any harm to the artillerymen.

When night fell the Tiger's Mouth became a vast panorama of light and fire. On the surrounding headlands the cooking-fires of the Chinese troops flickered dimly in the darkness. And all the while the guns on North Wantung continued to shoot so that the heights of the island looked like the mouth of a smoul-dering volcano, constantly ejecting tongues of flame.

On the protected side of the islet too, lights glimmered through the night as the British and Indian artillerymen went about the business of erecting the battery. When daylight broke it was seen that they had succeeded in finishing the job – a small artillery park, sheltered by a thick wall of sandbags, had arisen in the saddle between the island's two hillocks. It consisted of three howitzers, two eight-inch field-pieces and a brass twenty-four-pounder. Behind the gun-carriages was a platform for the launching of Congreve rockets.

At about eight in the morning, with clear skies above and the whole estuary bathed in bright sunlight, the newly erected British battery opened up. The first rounds fell short, with the shells slamming into the cliff of North Wantung, gouging out clumps of rock and earth. But slowly the impacts crept up the rock-face until they began to crash into the walls of the battery, knocking out embrasures and castellations. Soon the field-pieces switched to canister and grapeshot, sending a hailstorm of musket-balls into the Chinese gun-emplacements. Then a flight of Congreve rockets, armed with explosives, took to the air. A series of blasts followed as they arced over the battlements. A powder magazine blew up and the explosion pushed a massive sixty-eight-pounder through its gun-port: it teetered on the edge for a moment and then toppled over and went spinning down the cliffs, with a great clanging of metal on rock. A plume of water shot up as it bounced off a boulder and plunged into the channel.

In the meantime the British fleet had separated into three squadrons in preparation for the coming attack. For a while the ships were held back by the retreating tide; nor was there a breath of wind to fill their sails. The pounding of North Wantung continued while they waited for a breeze; in the windless air smoke and debris rose from the island's heights in roiling clouds, as if from a belching volcano.

It was past ten when a breeze stirred the air. Hoisting sail, the largest of the three squadrons set off for Humen, to the east; it was led by two seventy-four-gun line-of-battle frigates, *Melville* and *Blenheim*. The second squadron headed westwards, towards the restored fort of Tycock on the other shore: it consisted of only two vessels, the *Wellesley* and the twenty-four-gun *Modeste*. The third squadron converged on the battered and smoking island of North Wantung. Accompanying each group of attack vessels was a complement of rocket-boats.

Till this time no British warship had fired a single shot. Now, as the squadrons drew abreast of the gun-emplacements, they dropped anchor with springs on their cables, so that they could stay beam-on to their respective targets. Then, almost simultaneously they unloosed their broadsides at all three sets of defences

– Humen, Tycock and North Wantung. The thunder of their cannon was accompanied by the shriek of Congreve rockets.

The firing was of such concentrated ferocity that it was as if a deluge of metal and flame had swept around the channel, setting fire to the water itself. As broadside followed upon broadside a dark thundercloud blossomed around the Tiger's Mouth: the fumes were so dense that the warships had to stop firing to let the air clear.

When the smoke lifted it was seen that much of the Chinese artillery had been knocked out. The fort of Tycock had fallen silent while the guns at Humen and North Wantung were firing only sporadically. At all three points the battlements and defences had been badly battered and breached.

Now, as preparations for the ground assault got under way, the warships redeployed: the *Wellesley* and *Modeste* had already succeeded in reducing the fort of Tycock to a smoking ruin. Turning away, they crossed over to join in the attack on North Wantung.

It was only now that Zachary could bring himself to lower his telescope: he had watched the entire operation with breathless excitement, focusing now on the channel's right bank, now on the left, and sometimes on the island in the middle.

Never had he seen such a spectacle, such a marvel of planning and such a miracle of precision. It seemed to him a triumph of modern civilization; a perfect example of the ways in which discipline and reason could conquer continents of darkness, just as Mrs Burnham had said: it was proof of the omnipotence of the class of men of which he too was now a part. He thought of the unlikely mentors who had helped him through the door – Serang Ali, Baboo Nob Kissin Pander and Mrs Burnham – and was filled with gratitude that destiny had afforded him a place in this magnificent machine.

*

Kesri and the Bengal sepoys had been assigned to the landing-party that was to attack the island of North Wantung. This force included troops from the Royal Irish, the Cameronians and the 37th Madras: each detachment was allotted a cutter of its own. Two were taken in tow by the steamer *Madagascar* and the others by the *Nemesis*.

As the cutters were pulling up to North Wantung, they were met by volleys of arrows and matchlock-fire. Even before the landing-parties reached the shore, the defenders came rushing out of the battered remnants of the fortifications, brandishing swords, pikes and spears.

Kesri knew then that what had happened at Chuenpee would repeat itself here: having endured a devastating bombardment, knowing themselves to be hopelessly outgunned, the defenders had decided that their only hope lay in hand-to-hand combat. This had given them a desperate courage, prompting them to abandon the shelter of the battlements. But once on exposed ground they were fatally vulnerable: before they could close with their attackers they were mowed down by musket-fire and grapeshot. As at Chuenpee a great number of defendents were set afire by their powder-scattered clothing; many had to fling themselves into the water, to douse the flames, only to be picked off as they thrashed about.

By the time the landing-parties stepped on shore the ground was already carpeted with dead and dying defenders. Some of the British officers began to call out: 'Surrender! Surrender!'; some had even learnt the Chinese word – *Too-kiang!* But their cries went unheeded; many of the defenders fought on, flinging themselves on their attackers' bayonets.

The landing-parties had brought escalade ladders with them but only a few were used. The battlements had been so badly battered that at some points it was possible to climb through the breaches.

On entering the fortifications, the landing-parties split up as the remaining defenders retreated towards the island's heights. Kesri found himself running through corridors that were empty except for dead and wounded Chinese soldiers. In many of the gun-emplacements the bodies of the gunners lay draped over the barrels, pierced all over by grapeshot. Kesri was amazed to see that instead of seeking shelter they had stayed at their posts until the end.

Near the island's summit Kesri came upon a large group of disarmed defenders, squatting in a courtyard, under the guns of a detachment of British troops. His friend Sarjeant Maggs was in charge.

'These gents had the good sense to surrender,' said the sarjeant. 'But take a dekko at that lot over there.'

He pointed to an embrasure that faced the channel. Looking down, Kesri saw that the rocks below were littered with corpses: evidently rather than surrender, dozens of Chinese soldiers had chosen to throw themselves down from the heights.

Once again Kesri was reminded of earlier campaigns, in the Arakan and against the tribes of the hills. There too the defenders had fought in this way, squandering their lives in desperation. For sepoys and other professional soldiers there was nothing more hateful than this – it seemed to imply that they were hired murderers.

Why? Why fight like this? Why not just accept defeat and live? Kesri wished he could explain to them that he, for his part, would much rather have let them survive than see them die: he was just doing his job, that was all.

Averting his eyes, Kesri looked ahead, at the fort of Humen which lay directly across the water. British flags were flying on it now, wreathed in plumes of black smoke. Suddenly there was a flash and an ear-splitting noise; as the sound faded an enormous chunk of the fort's battlements slid slowly into the channel. Kesri realized that British sappers were now systematically demolishing the fort and its walls.

So much death; so much destruction – and that too visited upon a people who had neither attacked nor harmed the men who were so intent on engulfing them in this flood of fire. What was the meaning of it? What was it for?

A tremor went through Kesri as he thought of the part that he himself had played in what was unfolding around him now: deep within, he knew that his actions would have to be answered for in many lives yet to come. To combat the dread in his heart, he reminded himself of those heroes of the Mahabharata who had fought, against their own inclination, on the side of evil, only because it was their duty: because not to fight would have brought dishonour. He reminded himself of Dronacharya battling Arjuna, the pupil he had loved more than his own son; he thought of Bhisma Pitamaha, most righteous of men, committing himself to an unjust cause; he thought of King Shalya, making war upon his own sister's sons, only because a few words, unmindfully spoken, had bound him to that fate. It was in just that way, Kesri told

505

himself, that he too had sworn an oath to the British and could not now go back on his word without dishonour.

He tried to find some comfort in these thoughts, but without success. The question kept coming back to him: So much death; so much destruction – what was it all for?

*

More than anything else it was the swiftness of the operation that dazzled Zachary: within four hours all the fortifications of the Tiger's Mouth were in British hands. No sooner was Humen captured than the chain that had been slung across the river was torn from its moorings and allowed to sink to the bottom.

Then began a spectacle that was, in its way, just as awe-inspiring as the co-ordinated assault: the destruction of captured guns and the demolition of the forts.

This too proceeded simultaneously at three locations – the channel's two banks and the island in the middle. One after another, enormous guns were pushed out of their emplacements and sent tumbling into the water. Some were blown to bits from within: sandbags were stuffed into their barrels with massive charges of powder packed inside. They exploded like ripe fruit.

But these explosions were nothing compared to the earth-shaking blasts with which the forts were taken down. Each detonation sent a tornado of smoke and rubble spiralling upwards; the debris seemed to vanish into the clouds before it came crashing down. Soon the slopes around the Tiger's Mouth turned grey under a hailstorm of dust.

Zachary was so mesmerized by the spectacle that he barely heard Baboo Nob Kissin's voice at his elbow: 'Sir, message has been received requesting for delivery of munitions to Bengal Volunteers.'

'You take care of it, Baboo,' said Zachary curtly. 'I'm too busy.'

No sooner had the Baboo departed than Zachary received a message asking him to prepare the *Ibis* to receive some wounded men: he was told to expect a complement of three officers and some twenty soldiers; they would arrive in separate groups, each accompanied by doctors, surgeons and medical attendants.

The schooner's tween-deck had already been partitioned so that sepoys and troopers could be accommodated in different spaces. But no special provision had yet been made for officers. Zachary guessed that they would not take kindly to being sent below deck.

The first mate's cabin was empty, but it was too small for three men. Zachary decided to move there himself, yielding the captain's stateroom to the wounded officers. The stateroom was by far the best appointed and most spacious cumra on the schooner; Zachary knew the officers would appreciate the gesture.

The empty cabin was only a few steps from the stateroom, across the cuddy where the mates usually dined. It took Zachary very little time to move his things over. By the time the first boatload of wounded arrived, the *Ibis* was fully prepared to receive them.

The soldiers' injuries were slight for the most part and many were able to walk to their respective berths – very few needed litters. While they were settling in, another contingent arrived, of some half-dozen men from the Madras Engineers: it turned out that they had been injured by flying debris while demolishing the forts. There was an officer among them, a Yorkshireman. He told Zachary that the engineer companies had used captured stocks of Chinese powder to blow up the forts: the walls were so solidly built that it had taken ten thousand pounds of powder to bring them down.

The intent of the demolitions was not only to flatten the defences: it was hoped also that the fearsome explosions would have a salutary effect on the Chinese, inducing shock and terror and making them mindful of the futility of continued resistance.

'A few big bangs,' observed the officer sagely, 'can save a great many lives.'

*

When the Bengal Volunteers mustered on the deck of their transport vessel it became clear that B Company had been very lucky, once again. Apart from a few scratches and cuts the sepoys had no injuries to report. The only casualty was an officer, a young ensign who had fallen while scaling the walls of North Wantung. He had suffered a spinal injury and was in great pain. It was Captain Mee who had brought him back to the transport ship, and he stayed with him while he was waiting to be moved to the holding-ship.

After roll-call Kesri went down to see the captain and found him still in his blood-spattered uniform.

'Sir, will the ensign-sah'b be evacuated?'

'Yes,' said Captain Mee. 'I'll take him over to the holding-ship myself; he'll be sent to Saw Chow or Hong Kong tomorrow.'

Kesri went back to the maindeck and joined the men who were gawping at the eruptions around the Tiger's Mouth. They watched mesmerized until their trance was broken by a sudden outcry: some lascars were shouting for help as they attempted to pull up an exceptionally heavy weight on the swing-lift.

Kesri and several other sepoys flung themselves on the winch and tugged on the lines with such a will that the swing came shooting up and was catapulted to the apex of the derrick with its load still cradled in it – and it was now discovered that the load was neither a crate nor a sack but an unusually portly visitor.

For a long moment the mechanism froze, holding the visitor aloft on the teetering swing. The sepoys and lascars stared openmouthed at the apparition that had suddenly appeared before them – it was as if some supernatural being had risen out of the sea to levitate above the ship.

The skies too seemed to conspire in casting a heavenly light on the suspended figure – for just at that moment an opening appeared in a bank of clouds, allowing a beam of sunlight to shine down upon the swing. Yet, despite the brightness of the light, it was impossible to tell whether the visitor was male or female, man or woman, so strange was the appearance of the apparition: the body, imposing in its girth, was clothed from neck to toe in a voluminous saffron robe; this was topped by an enormous head, undergirded by heavy jowls and set off by a billowing halo of hair. Complementing this extraordinary ensemble of features were two huge eyes, now so filled with alarm that they appeared to be on the brink of shooting out of their sockets, like projectiles.

Suddenly the suspended figure unloosed a thunderous invocation, in a man's voice: *Hé Radhé, hé Shyam!*

The cry resonated deeply with the sepoys and they roared back: *Hé Radhé, hé Shyam!*

The sound seemed to unhitch something within the machinery of the winch and the ropes began to turn again, gently lowering the visitor to the deck.

All this unfolded in a scant minute or two but the effect was electrifying. Kesri realized now that he had seen the visitor some-where before but he could not remember where. Before he knew it, the words *Aap hai kaun?* had burst from his lips. Who *are* you?

My name, came the answer, is Babu Nobo Krishna Panda.

The moment Kesri heard the word *panda* everything was clear: the robes of auspicious colouring; the sacred invocation – all of this made sense, for a panda was, after all, a kind of pundit. In the past, when visiting temples, pandas had often roused Kesri's ire with their incessant demands for money – but now the word 'panda' sounded like an answer to a prayer: it was as if the sea and sky had conspired to produce a figure who could answer the questions that were buzzing so insistently in his head.

Without another word, Kesri led Baboo Nob Kissin to the deck-rails and gestured at the immense columns of smoke that were rising above the surrounding forts.

Punditji, he said, what is all this for? What is the meaning of it? Do you know?

Baboo Nob Kissin nodded in affirmation. Yes of course I know, he said, as though it were the most self-evident thing in the world.

Tell me then, punditji, said Kesri humbly. I too want to know.

Zaroor beta, said Baboo Nob Kissin cheerfully. I will certainly tell you: what you are seeing is the start of the *pralaya* – the begin-ning of the world's end.

Arré ye kya baat hai? cried Kesri in disbelief. What is this you are saying?

A beaming smile now lit up Baboo Nob Kissin's face: But why are you so shocked, my son? Do you not know that we are in Kaliyuga, the epoch of apocalypse? You should rejoice that you are here today, fighting for the Angrez. It is the destiny of the English to bring about the world's end; they are but instruments of the will of the gods.

Baboo Nob Kissin raised a hand to point to the *Nemesis*, which was steaming past the burning forts, wreathed in dark fumes.

Dekho – look: inside that vessel burns the fire that will awaken the demons of greed that are hidden in all human beings. That is why the English have come to China and to Hindustan: these two lands are so populous that if their greed is aroused they can consume the whole world. Today that great devouring has begun. It will end only when all of humanity, joined together in a great frenzy of greed, has eaten up the earth, the air, the sky.

Kesri's head was spinning now. I am a simple man, punditji, he said. I don't understand. Why should I be present at the beginning of the end? Why should you be here either?

Isn't it clear? said Baboo Nob Kissin in a tone of some surprise. We are here to help the English fulfil their destiny. We may be little people but we are fortunate in that we know why we are here and they do not. We must do everything possible to help them. It is our duty, don't you see?

Kesri shook his head. No, punditji, I don't see.

Baboo Nob Kissin put a hand on his head, as if in blessing.

Don't you understand, my son? The sooner the end comes the better. You and I are fortunate in having been chosen to serve this destiny: the beings of the future will be grateful to us. For only when this world ends will a better one be born.

*

On the *Cambridge*, which was moored less than twenty miles from the Tiger's Mouth, a hush fell on the decks when several immense plumes of smoke and dust were spotted in the distance, rising slowly towards the clouds.

The size of the plumes was such that only one conclusion was possible. The forts of the Tiger's Mouth were on fire.

As reports came pouring in, it became evident that it was just a matter of time before the First Bar was attacked. The only question was when: would the English ships press on that very day or would they wait awhile?

With the passage of the hours the possibility of an immediate attack began to fade: the stretch of water between the Tiger's Mouth and the First Bar was known to be treacherous and it was unlikely that the English warships would attempt to navigate it so late in the day.

At sunset, when the distant columns of smoke were turning red in the fading daylight, a silence descended on the *Cambridge*: after many hours of fevered speculation the quiet was almost eerie. When Jodu called the vessel's Muslims to prayer, there was something serene and reassuring about the sound of the azaan, even for those who were not of the faith.

After the prayers were over, a huddle formed around Jodu who began to speak in a low, earnest voice. The intensity of his expression piqued Neel's curiosity; he could not resist eavesdropping.

It turned out that Jodu was talking about Judgement Day and how to prepare for it.

Later Neel asked Jodu if he really thought it would come to that. Jodu answered with a shrug: *Ké jané?* Who knows? But if it does, I want to be ready.

*

A little after sunset a seacunny came to tell Zachary that yet another boat had pulled up beside the *Ibis*. Leaning over the bulwark Zachary saw that the boat was carrying a single litter: lying in it was a very young subaltern, an ensign. He was accompanied by a few dooley-bearers and an officer – none other than Captain Mee.

Zachary caught his breath: this was exactly the opportunity he had been waiting for. He went to stand beside the side-ladder and when Captain Mee stepped on deck, he held out his hand: 'Good evening, Captain Mee.'

Captain Mee's uniform was stained with grime and streaks of blood: evidently he had been so preoccupied in looking after the wounded ensign that he had not had time to clean up or change. He seemed barely to recognize Zachary: 'I take it you're the skipper of this vessel?'

'Yes I am.'

The captain peered at him. 'Oh you're the . . .'

Zachary steeled himself for an insult but it never came: instead the captain gave his hand a cursory shake. 'Good day to you.'

Meanwhile the wounded ensign had been winched up from the boat: when his litter landed on the deck of the *Ibis* he gave a cry of pain.

'Hold on there, Upjohn,' shouted Captain Mee. 'We'll have you snugged down in a minute.'

The captain's voice was uncharacteristically mild, almost solicitous; evidently his concern for the young officer had softened the edge of his habitual abrasiveness. Zachary took this as a propitious sign.

'Badly hurt, is he?'

'Took a nasty tumble when we were scaling the walls at North Wantung,' said the captain gruffly. 'May have broken his back.'

'I'm sorry to hear that, sir,' said Zachary. 'If there's anything I can do for him please do let me know.'

Captain Mee seemed to thaw a bit. He gave Zachary a polite nod. 'That's kind; thank you.'

Zachary hung back while the captain followed the wounded ensign's litter into the stateroom. When he came out again, Zachary was waiting.

'May I have a quick word, Captain Mee?'

The captain hesitated. 'I don't have much time.'

'Oh it won't take long.' Zachary held open the door of the first mate's cabin. 'Would you mind stepping inside?'

The cabin was very small, illuminated by a single candle. After Zachary had shut the door they were barely an arm's length apart.

'What is it then?'

The back of Captain Mee's head was pressed against the ceiling even though he was standing with his shoulders hunched. The only place to sit was the bunk, with its grimy and tangled sheets; Zachary decided that it would be best for them to remain on their feet.

'It's a very simple matter, Captain,' said Zachary. 'I wanted to suggest a business proposition.'

'Business?' The captain spat out the word as though it were a piece of grit. 'I don't twig your meaning.'

'Captain, I happen to have at my disposal a large stock of provisions, of the kind favoured by sepoys – rice, lentils, spices and so on. My partners and I would be most grateful if you could bring this to the notice of your purchasing clerks.' Zachary paused to cough into his fist. 'And of course we would make sure that you were suitably compensated for your consideration.'

A look of bewilderment descended on the captain's face. 'What do you mean, "suitably compensated"?'

To Zachary the question seemed like an expression of interest and it sent a thrill of excitement through him. The hook was in now and all that remained was to set it.

Picking his words carefully, Zachary said: 'I am referring to a small token of our appreciation, Captain Mee. I am sure you know that we Free-Traders are very, very grateful to you and your fellow soldiers for the wonderful job that you are doing here in China. Since you've had to work hard and face many hazards it's only fair, surely, that you too should receive a share of the benefits? It seems a shame that middle-ranking officers such as yourself should be rewarded with nothing more than a few paltry allowances' – here again Zachary stopped to cough into his fist – 'especially considering that many of your seniors have already received substantial considerations.'

The expression on Captain Mee's face changed as comprehension slowly dawned on him. 'Oh, so that's the bustle, is it?' he said. 'You're offering me a backhander – a bribe.'

'You mustn't jump to conclusions, Captain Mee.' Only now did Zachary realize that he had taken the wrong approach – but no matter, he had other cards up his sleeve.

'Don't pitch me your gammon – d'you take me for a muttonhead? I know very well what your fakement is, you spigot-sucking shitheel.'

The captain's big, heavy-jawed face was contorted with rage now; his fists were knotted and twitching. Zachary took a step back, flattening himself against the bulkhead. 'Captain Mee, may I remind you that you are on my vessel? You need to get ahold of yourself.'

Captain Mee's lips curled into a sneer. 'Oh, don't you worry about that – if I didn't have a hold on myself you'd be decked already. But that's too good for a kedger like you – what I have in store for you is going to hurt a lot more.'

'And what, pray, is that?'

'I'm going to blow the dicky on you,' said the captain. 'Now that I've smoked out your game I'm going to take this all the way to the top; I'm going to make sure you never try your flummery on anyone again. Bilkers like you have been responsible for too many deaths to count – why, between you, you've killed more of our men than the Chinese have! God damn my eyes if I don't see you brought to book, you cunny-lapping cockbawd.'

The torrent of abuse fell on Zachary like a cold shower: far from intimidating him it made his mind quicker. He knew exactly what he had to do now, to bring the captain to heel.

'Well, Captain Mee,' he said, with a thin smile. 'You must do as you wish of course. But perhaps you should ask yourself which is the greater crime in the eyes of the world: bribery or adultery?'

The captain's eyes flickered, in shock: 'What the devil do you mean?'

Zachary's smile widened, in relish. 'I mean, Captain Mee, that you have far more to lose than I do.' He paused, so as to add emphasis to what he was going to say next.

'And as for Mrs Burnham, she stands to lose the most, does she not?'

The captain froze for an instant. Then suddenly a fist came flying through the air and hit Zachary in the jaw. He staggered sidewise, until the rim of the bunk dug into the back of his leg causing his knees to buckle. The next he knew he was lying flat on the bunk and his mouth was full of the metallic taste of blood. Yet strangely the pain was not unwelcome; it seemed to quicken his mind: he understood that by provoking the captain into losing control of himself he had seized the advantage. He had to make the best of it now.

Rubbing his jaw, he summoned another smile. 'Mrs Burnham must have had the devil of a time,' he said, 'slipping a capote on an ox like you.'

Again he had the satisfaction of seeing the captain reel, as though it were he who had been hit in the jaw. On his big, heavy face there was a look of almost comical disbelief.

'Oh yes,' said Zachary, with slow relish. The throbbing in his jaw added immeasurably to the pleasure of knowing that it was the captain who was now helpless in his hands. Zachary smiled again: 'Mrs Burnham sure has a way with capotes, doesn't she? I'll never forget the first time.'

Suddenly Captain Mee's long limbs began to move, at great speed. Crossing the cabin with one stride he took hold of Zachary's throat.

This only made Zachary laugh. 'Why, Captain Mee!' he said. 'You seem surprised. All these years that you were wearing your hair-shirt – did you really think she was waiting for you? That you were the only one?'

'Stubble your whids, you bastard: you're lying!'

'Oh you don't believe me then? Would it be more convincing perhaps if I were to show you the little trick she does with the capote?'

The captain leant closer. 'Have you no shame, you filthy poodle-faker?' The words were hissed between his teeth, so that a fog of spittle settled on Zachary's face.

Zachary slid the tip of his tongue slowly over his lips, as he had seen Mrs Burnham do many times in the past.

'Why Captain Mee,' he said. 'I do believe the taste of her still lingers in your mouth – I would recognize it anywhere. I am sure you would recognize it on me too, if you'd care to put your tongue where hers has been. "Chartering" she calls it, if I remember right; and never better than on the goolie-bag . . .'

'Dab your mummer!' Goaded beyond endurance the captain shook Zachary by the neck. 'You know what happens to black-mailers, don't you? They always die before their time.'

The captain's thumb was pressed against Zachary's windpipe now, blocking off the flow of air to his lungs. Zachary began to struggle, and as he was thrashing about his thumb brushed against the handle of his jack-knife. Slipping his hand into his pocket, he pulled it out, but just as he was flicking it open Captain Mee caught sight of it. Lunging at Zachary, he enveloped his fist with the fingers of one hand, knife and all. Then he flung himself over Zachary, pinning him down with his weight, pushing him into the bunk and immobilizing his limbs. In the midst of this, there was a slight slackening in the throat-hold; Zachary tried to catch a breath but his nose was crushed against the captain's collar and he found himself breathing in the acrid, sweat-and-blood-sodden odour of his uniform. He gagged and turned his head to the side: phys-ically, he was helpless now, yet the more completely he was over-powered, the more his body succumbed to the strength of the bigger man, the sharper and clearer his mind seemed to become. Snatching another breath, he hissed into the captain's ear: 'Poor Mrs Burnham! Bedding you must be like fucking a howitzer.'

The captain grunted, tightening his grip on Zachary's fist. 'You shouldn't have pulled this knife on me,' he snarled. 'You've only made it easier.'

With slow, relentless pressure he forced Zachary's arm up until the blade was resting on his throat. As its edge began to dig into his skin, a memory flashed through Zachary's head. He remembered that the knife was not his own: it had belonged to Mr Crowle, who had held it to his throat in this very cabin three years before.

The memory emboldened Zachary. 'Go on,' he said. 'Do it; kill me. And you know what'll happen? Let me tell you: Mrs Burnham's letters will be found among my effects – I've kept them all, you know. Is that what you want? To bring ruin on her?'

Zachary knew that this had made an impression because there was a slackening in the pressure against his throat. With a sudden twist of his body he squirmed loose and jumped off the bunk. Dusting himself off, he held out his hand: 'My knife please.'

The captain was now sitting on the bunk with a look of crushed bewilderment on his face. He handed over the knife without a word.

'Thank you, Captain,' said Zachary. 'And if I may say so, you would be well-advised to think carefully about my proposal.'

'Fuck you,' said the captain. 'I don't ever want to set eyes on you again.'

Zachary smiled and went to the door. 'Oh I'm afraid you won't be so easily rid of me, Captain,' he said, holding the door open. 'I am sure we shall meet again soon – but until then, I bid you a very good night.'

Nineteen

On the *Cambridge* the first hours of the morning passed in gut-churning uncertainty, without anyone being sure of what to expect. Then a runner arrived with urgent news: five British warships and two steamers, one of them the *Nemesis*, had left the Tiger's Mouth and were proceeding upriver; they would soon be crossing the First Bar.

It was a relief to have the matter resolved, to know that the battle they had so long been preparing for would soon be joined. There were some who thought that the warships might be thwarted by the shifting shoals and sandbanks of the Pearl River. But as the reports came in it became clear that no such thing would happen: the British had evidently worked out a system to deal with the obstacles of the river. The shallow-draughted *Nemesis* was proceeding ahead of the rest of the squadron, taking soundings and charting a safe course.

As the warships drew closer the reports began to come in faster: now they were twenty-five li away, now twenty.

At the start of the Hour of the Horse, in the late morning, the gun-crews took their stations and went through their usual preparatory drills; each sirdar checked his cannon over and again, readying it for the first shot, making sure that the touch-hole was primed with powder, and that the first cartridge and ball were properly loaded and plugged in place, with waddings of oakum, made from old hemp ropes.

It was a warm day and as noon approached it became scorching hot on the fo'c'sle, which was exposed to the sun. Conical hats no longer sufficed to keep the gun-crews cool so they rigged up a canvas awning over the forward gun-ports. But as the sun mounted the sweat continued to pour off their bodies; many of the lascars stripped down to their banyans, draping chequered gamchhas around their necks.

At noon the breeze died away and the air became very still. Soon word arrived that the British ships were becalmed nine li short of the First Bar; only the *Nemesis* was still moving upriver.

This set off a hopeful murmur among the gun-crews: if the 'devil-ship' could be caught in a cross-fire, between the fort and the *Cambridge*, then there was a chance that she might be taken down.

Hopes rising, the gunners kept their eyes ahead, on the river. In a while, sure enough, puffs of black smoke appeared in the distance; then they heard the thudding of the steamer's engine, growing steadily louder.

Across the river too, on the ramparts of the mud fort, there were many who were looking out for the steamer. The fort commanded a better view of the channel so its lookouts spotted the *Nemesis* first. A signal was flashed to alert the crew of the *Cambridge* and a minute later Jodu pointed ahead: There! *Okhané!* And through a stand of acacia and bamboo Neel caught sight of a towering smokestack.

The *Nemesis* cut her speed as she came around the bend. She was almost within range when the *Cambridge's* gunners got their first good look at her long black hull and her two giant paddle-wheels. Between the wheels was a broad, bridge-like platform: a row of Congreve rockets could be seen lined up on it, ready for launching.

The steamer's appearance had changed since Neel had last seen her: on her bows there were two large, freshly painted eyes, drawn in the Asian fashion. Neel had never imagined that this familiar symbol could appear so sinister, so imbued with evil intent.

Jodu too was studying the steamer intently, his scarred eyebrows knitted into a straight line. He raised a finger to point to the base of the smokestack. That's where the steam-chest is, he said. If we can hit her there, she'll be crippled.

The steamer's pivot guns had already begun to swivel; one turned towards the fort and the other to the *Cambridge*. Suddenly the stillness was shattered by the report of a gun; it wasn't clear who had fired the first shot, but within seconds the steamer and the fort were hurling volleys at each other.

On the *Cambridge* a few more minutes passed before the steamer was properly within range. When the order to fire rang out, Neel and the rest of the gun-crew threw themselves at the tackles of their gun-carriage. Heaving in unison, they pushed the carriage against the bulwark, thrusting the muzzle out of the gun-port. Now, as Jodu squinted along the barrel, taking aim, the rest of the team armed themselves with levers and crowbars so that they could adjust the barrel as directed.

When the gun was angled exactly as he wanted, Jodu punched a quoin under the muzzle, to hold it steady. Waving the others back, he lowered a smouldering fusil to the touch-hole.

Only in the instant before the blast did Neel realize that the *Nemesis* had also opened fire and that the whistling noise in his ears was the sound of grapeshot. Then the recoil of their own eight-pound shot brought the gun-carriage hurtling backwards, until it was stopped by the breech-ropes that were knotted around the base of its cascabel.

After that there was no time to think of anything but reloading: dipping his rammer into a bucket of seawater, Neel plunged the head into the smoking barrel, to extinguish any lingering sparks and embers. Then their powder-monkey – Chhotu Mian the lascar – placed a fresh packet of powder in the muzzle, followed by a handful of wadding. Another thrust of the rammer drove the cartridge to the end of the bore and into its chamber; then the ammunition-loader pushed a ball into the muzzle, to be rammed in again, with yet more wadding.

This time Jodu was slow and deliberate in his sighting. He had stripped off his banyan and was bare-bodied now; lithe, slight and deft in his movements, he snatched up a crowbar and began to make minute adjustments in the angle of the barrel, his coppery skin gleaming with sweat.

What are you aiming at? said Neel.

The steam-chest, grunted Jodu. What else?

Murmuring a prayer, Jodu lowered the fusil and stepped back.

An instant later the *Nemesis* shuddered and Neel saw that a jagged gash had appeared under the smokestack, roughly where the steam-chest lay.

A hit! shouted Jodu. *Legechhe!* We've hit it!

Amazed, almost disbelieving, the crew raised a cheer – but soon the steamer's giant paddle-wheels began to turn again, making it clear that the vessel was merely damaged, not disabled.

Yet to force the *Nemesis* to turn tail was no small thing either. The gunners on the *Cambridge* paused to catch their breath, giddy with excitement, savouring the moment.

But their elation was short-lived.

Even as the *Nemesis* was withdrawing, the masts of several other warships were seen in the distance, moving quickly towards them. The squadron hove into view with the steamer *Madagascar* in the lead; under heavy fire from the fort and the *Cambridge* the British ships began to deploy around the channel.

The warships held their fire as they manoeuvred into position; in tandem with the *Madagascar* a corvette pulled very close to the raft and turned broadside-on to the *Cambridge*. Then there was a rattling sound, as the wooden shutters of the vessels' gun-ports flipped open. Suddenly Neel found himself looking into the muzzles of dozens of British guns.

The two ships delivered their broadsides in unison, with a blast that shook the planks under Neel's feet.

Stay low! Jodu shouted over the din. They're shooting canister.

As the musket-balls whistled past, Neel looked up. He saw that the awning above the deck had been shot to shreds; a patch of canvas, smaller than a kerchief, lay at his feet, pierced in a dozen places.

Crouching low, the gun-crew pushed the carriage against the bulwark again. They were preparing to fire when Chhotu Mian toppled over with a powder-cartridge in his hands. Glancing at his body Neel saw that he had been hit by a cluster of grapeshot; his banyan was riddled with holes; blood was spreading in circles around the punctures in the fabric.

Don't stop! shouted Jodu. Load the cartridge.

Neel snatched up the packet of powder and rammed it in. After the ball had been loaded, Jodu shouted to Neel to fetch the next cartridge; he would have to take over as powder-monkey now that Chhotu Mian was dead.

Racing to the companion-ladder, Neel saw that the maindeck of the *Cambridge* was shrouded by a pall of smoke. As he stepped off the ladder his foot slipped on excrement, voided by some mortally wounded sailor. When he picked himself up again, Neel found that he was in the midst of a blood-soaked shambles: men lay sprawled everywhere, their clothes perforated with grapeshot. A cannonball had knocked down a heavy purwan and in falling on the deck it had pinned several men under it. The smoke was so thick that Neel could not see even as far as the quarter-deck, less than thirty feet away.

It turned out that the sailor responsible for distributing the powder had been grazed in the head. He was sitting on his haunches, with blood pouring down his face. The packets of powder were lying behind him; Neel took one and raced back to the fo'c'sle deck where he thrust it into the eight-pounder's muzzle.

Theirs was now one of the last gun-ports on the *Cambridge* that was still active. But the gunners of the *Nemesis* were closing in; even as their eight-pounder was recoiling from its next shot, a heavy ball struck the bulwark, knocking out one of the rings that held the gun's breech-ropes. A slab of wood fell out, yanking the gun-carriage towards the water. As it tumbled over the side, barrel and all, Neel heard the whoosh of a rocket and looked up: in the bright afternoon sunlight the projectile seemed to be heading directly towards him.

Neel froze as he watched the rocket arcing down from the sky. He would not have moved if Jodu had not pushed him: *Lafao!* Jump!

*

Shireen was walking along a beachside pathway in Hong Kong, with Freddie, when the smoke from the battle at the First Bar appeared over the horizon, spiralling slowly upwards.

It was Freddie who drew her attention to it. 'Look there – must be more fighting, lah. Very far; too far for us to hear. Maybe near Whampoa.'

The smoke was just a dark smudge in the sky, but Shireen did not doubt that Freddie was right about its cause.

'Do you think the British will press on to Canton now?' said Shireen.

'Yes, this time for sure, lah.'

On the *Mor* Shireen had overheard a long discussion of this subject that morning. Many of the seths were persuaded that this offensive would be called off like others before; they had convinced themselves that the Plenny-potty would again lose his nerve – and if not that, then the mandarins would surely succeed in bamboozling him once more.

The day's tranquil beginning had only deepened their conviction; the excitement of yesterday, when the bombardment of the forts of the Tiger's Mouth had jolted them out of their berths at sunrise, was still fresh in memory and the contrast between the din of that morning and the silence of this one seemed an ominous portent.

The mood had changed briefly when the first shots of a gun-salute were heard – but the seths' spirits had plunged again when it was learnt that the shooting did not presage a renewal of hostilities but was intended, rather, as a tribute to a Chinese admiral. Of all things! Almost to a man the seths concluded that the salute was a sure sign that the hapless Captain Elliot had once again been duped by the mandarins.

Dinyar alone had remained incorrigibly optimistic. The night before, on hearing of the storming of the Tiger's Mouth, he had predicted confidently that this time the British would not stop short of Canton itself.

The officers are all gung-ho now, he had told the other seths. The Plenipot wouldn't be able to hold them back even if he wanted to.

Shireen had listened to the discussion with only half an ear; it was Freddie who was uppermost in her mind that morning. She had thought of little else but of how she might contrive to see him without anyone learning of it.

Fortunately it happened that Dinyar had an errand to run in Hong Kong that day. Hearing him call for the *Mor*'s cutter, Shireen had made up a story about needing to visit Sheng Wan village, to buy provisions. As luck would have it she had run into Freddie within minutes of stepping off the cutter.

'Listen, Freddie,' she said to him now. 'There is a reason why I came to see you today.'

'Yes?'

'There is something I want to tell you – something important.'

Freddie nodded: 'So then tell, lah.' And when she hesitated he added with a smile: 'Do not worry – I will not say anything to anyone.'

Shireen fortified herself with a deep breath and then a string of words came tumbling out with her scarcely being aware of it: 'Freddie, you should know that Mr Karabedian has asked me to marry him.'

To her surprise Freddie took the disclosure in his stride, quite literally. Without missing a breath or a step he said: 'And what your answer was, eh?'

'I told him I wanted to talk to you first.'

'Why me, lah?'

'But of course, I had to talk to you first, Freddie,' said Shireen. 'You have known Zadig Bey all your life – he has been like a second father to you. I do not want to do anything that might hurt you.'

'Hurt me?'

Freddie glanced at her with a raised eyebrow: 'Why it will hurt me, eh, if you marry Zadig Bey? I will be happy for him – and for you too, lah. You should not worry about me – or Father also.'

A weight seemed to tumble off Shireen's shoulder. 'Thank you, Freddie.'

Acknowledging this with a grunt he shot her a sidewise glance: 'But what about all your Parsis, eh? What they will say if you marry Zadig Bey? They are very strict, ne?'

Shireen sighed. 'They will cut me off, I suppose. Even my daughters will, at least for a while. And I will probably never again be able to enter a Fire Temple: that will be the hardest part. But no one can take my faith from me, can they? And maybe, in a few years, people will forget.'

They had come to a sharp bend in the path now and as they turned the corner Shireen caught sight of Dinyar: he was walking briskly towards them.

Freddie too had come to a stop beside her. 'Oh, see there,' he said, under his breath. 'One of your Parsis.'

It had not occurred to Shireen that Freddie might be acquainted with her nephew. 'Do you know Dinyar?' she said.

'Only by sight, lah,' said Freddie. 'He know me too but will not speak.'

'Why not?'

Freddie's lips curled into a crooked smile: 'Because I am half-caste bastard, ne?' he said. 'He is afraid of me.'

'But why should Dinyar be afraid of you?'

Freddie flashed her another smile. 'Because he also have made half-caste bastard, ne? In Macau. He know I know. That is why he is afraid.'

Freddie smiled again as she stared at him, her eyes widening in shock. 'Now I must go, lah. Goodbye.'

*

The tide happened to be coming in when Neel tumbled headlong into the Pearl River: it was to this fact that he owed the preservation of his life – if the current had been flowing in the other direction then he would have been swept towards the raft, to be picked off by British sharpshooters. Instead he was carried in the other direction, towards Whampoa.

Neel had never before been out of his depth in a river; his experience of swimming consisted of paddling around *pukur*s and *jheel*s – the placid ponds of the Bengal countryside. He had never encountered anything like the surge of the Pearl River's incoming tide. For the first minutes he could think of nothing but of fighting his way to the surface to gulp in a few breaths.

As he was tumbling through the murky waters he caught a glimpse of a dark trail swirling around his limbs: one end of it seemed to be stuck to his right hip. Thinking that some floating object had attached itself to his body he twisted his head around to take a closer look. He saw then that the trailing ribbon was his own blood, flowing out of a wound. Only then did he become conscious of a sharp, stabbing pain in his flank. Flailing his arms he pushed himself to the surface and shouted for Jodu: *Tui kothay? Tui kothay re Jodu?*

Twenty feet away, a head, bobbing in the water, turned to look in his direction. A few minutes later Jodu's arms were around Neel's chest, pulling him towards the shore, into a thicket of reeds and rushes.

Leaning heavily on Jodu, Neel staggered out of the water but only to collapse on the bank. There was a long rent in his banyan, and underneath it, just above his hip, was a gaping wound where a musket-ball had entered his flesh.

The bullet had to have hit him when he was about to jump, or even perhaps as he was falling. In the tumult of the moment he had not been aware of it – but the pain seemed to have been waiting to waylay him for it assailed him now with a force that made him writhe and thrash his arms.

Lie still!

Neel gritted his teeth as Jodu examined the wound.

The ball's gone too deep, Jodu said. I won't be able to get it out, but maybe I can stop the bleeding.

Pulling off the bandhna that was tied around his forehead, Jodu tore it into strips and bound up the wound.

The barrage from the British warships had continued without interruption all this while. Jodu and Neel were not far from the fighting, for the current, strong as it was, had brought them only a few hundred yards upriver from the *Cambridge*. Now, suddenly, there was an explosion that shook the breath out of them: the *Cambridge* had erupted, throwing up a solid tower of flame. The column climbed to a height of over three hundred feet, ending in a black cloud that was shaped like the head of a mushroom. A few seconds later debris began to rain down and Neel and Jodu had to duck down, with their arms wrapped protectively around their heads. They did not look up even when the top half of a ship's mast, thirty feet in length, landed nearby, with a huge thud. It had fallen out of the sky like a javelin, burying itself in the riverbank a few yards away.

A few minutes later there was another powerful explosion, on the river this time. When the smoke cleared they saw that a section of the raft had been demolished. Within moments dead fish began to float up from below, clogging the river's surface.

Soon they spotted puffs of smoke heading in their direction. Peering through the rushes they saw that a British steamer had pushed through the shattered raft and was moving rapidly upriver, swivel-guns twitching and turning. Suddenly a fusillade slammed into an already crippled war-junk; then another stream of fire hit something on the shore.

Neel and Jodu flattened themselves on the bank as the steamer swept past, unloosing bursts of fire, apparently at random. In a few minutes a second steamer appeared and went paddling after the first. Then came a couple of corvettes.

After the vessels had passed, Jodu climbed to the top of the bank.

There are some abandoned sampans nearby, he said, after looking around. The owners must have taken fright and run away. Once it gets dark I'll get one.

Neel nodded: he knew that if they could get to the Ocean Banner Monastery they would be safe, at least for a while.

Shortly before nightfall Jodu slipped away, to return soon after, in a covered sampan. He had changed into some clothes he had found inside the boat: a tunic and loose trowsers, the usual garb of Cantonese boat-people. Of his face, almost nothing was visible: the upper part was hidden by a conical hat and the lower by a bandhna, tied like a scarf around his nose and mouth.

Jodu had found the garments below a deck-plank; after helping Neel into the boat he reached under the plank again and pulled out some more clothes, for Neel. He also came upon a jar of drinking water and some fried pancakes. The pancakes were stale but edible; Jodu devoured two of them before pushing the boat away from the shore.

Their way was lit by fires, kindled by the British gun-boats: blazing war-junks lay slumped over on their beams; the embers of shattered gun-emplacements smouldered on the river's banks; on a small island trees flamed like torches. Jodu kept to the shadows and was careful to feather the oars so the boat glided along with scarcely a sound.

At Whampoa Roads a British corvette could be seen, in the flickering light of burning houses. The vessel was riding at anchor, her looming silhouette pregnant with menace, her guns swivelling watchfully. Along the edges of the waterway hundreds of boats were slipping through, heading in the direction of Guangzhou. Such was the panic that nobody paid Jodu or the sampan any notice.

As they drew closer to Guangzhou the signs of destruction multiplied. At the approaches to the city two island fortresses were on fire. Abreast of each was a British warship. The vessels had created such fear that people were pouring out of their homes, jamming the roadways.

Approaching the Ocean Banner Monastery they found a steamer

anchored off it, abreast of the Thirteen Factories. On both shores people were milling about in large numbers; in the midst of the confusion no one noticed as Neel staggered through the monastery's gates, leaning heavily on Jodu.

*

For ten days after the Battle of the Tiger's Mouth the Bengal Volunteers remained in the vicinity of Chuenpee, on their transport vessel. Through that time they were constantly on the alert. Even though all Chinese troops had been withdrawn from the area new threats appeared every day: there were random attacks by bandits and villagers; some British units lost stragglers while patrolling ashore; there were rumours of camp-followers and lascars being kidnapped and killed.

As a result the men of B Company became impatient to return to their camp at Saw Chow. But instead the opposite happened: the troops who had proceeded up the Pearl River earlier were withdrawn and sent back to Hong Kong, and the Bengal Volunteers were ordered to move forward to Whampoa.

When it came to be learnt that B Company was to move upriver, there was much swearing and cursing. Only Raju was pleased: he knew that Whampoa was close to Canton and he imagined that if he could but get to the city his father would miraculously appear.

But on arriving at Whampoa Raju saw that nothing much could be expected of it. It was just a way-station on the river, ringed by small townships and villages: it reminded Raju of the Narrows at Hooghly Point, where ships and boats often anchored on their way to and from Calcutta. The worst part of it was that nothing could be seen of Canton – and nor was there anything of interest nearby except a few pagodas and temples.

The boys' first excursion ashore ended at one of those temples. It was like no temple that Raju had ever seen, with its hanging coils of incense and its unrecognizable images – yet there was an air of sacredness in it that was very familiar.

At a certain point Raju succeeded in giving the other fifers the slip. Stealing into a darkened shrine-room, he knelt before the figure of a gently smiling goddess and joined his hands in prayer.

'*Ya Devi sarvabhutéshu,*' he prayed, mouthing the first words of a remembered invocation: 'Devi, my father is somewhere nearby. Help me find him, Devi, help me.'

*

For Zachary, the excitement of the Battle of the Tiger's Mouth was followed by several weeks of oppressive tedium. His orders were to keep the *Ibis* at anchor near Humen, which was occupied by a small detachment of British troops. Other than ferrying provisions ashore and watching for thieves and bandits, there was little to occupy him.

With time hanging on his hands Zachary fell prey to anxiety, especially in regard to Captain Mee. The inconclusive end of their last meeting gave him much to worry about: he had no way of knowing whether the captain had reconsidered his threats or not. To wait for him to make his move would be an error, he knew, and he was impatient to bring matters to a head. But there was no chance of doing that while the captain was away at Whampoa.

It became especially galling to remain at Humen after news arrived that trade had been resumed at Canton, as a condition of continuing negotiations. After that British and American merchant ships were seen daily, proceeding upriver to acquire teas, silks, porcelain, furniture and all the other goods for which Canton was famed. To be idling while others made money was exasperating; Zachary soon began to regret the onrush of enthusiasm that had led him to offer his services to the expedition.

One evening, when Zachary was fretfully pacing the quarterdeck, a boat pulled up beside the *Ibis*. 'Holloa there, Mr Reid!' shouted a familiar voice. 'Permission to come aboard?'

'Yes of course, Mr Chan.'

It turned out that Mr Chan was on his way to Guangzhou, at the invitation of the province's new head-officials. 'You see, Mr Reid,' he said with a laugh, 'how the tide turns? The mandarins who drove me from the city are all gone now. The new prefect has decided that he needs my advice. So after an absence of two years, I am at last able to return to my native city without fear of harassment.'

'You're lucky, Mr Chan,' said Zachary enviously. 'I wish I were going with you – what I wouldn't give to see Canton!'

'Have you never been there then?' said Mr Chan.

528

Zachary shook his head. 'No – I've been stranded here for over a month and I don't think I can take it much longer.'

'Well something must be done about that!' said Mr Chan. 'Mr Burnham is in Canton, isn't he?'

'So he is.'

'I shall probably be seeing him,' said Mr Chan, 'and I'll certainly put in a word for you. I'm sure something can be arranged.'

'Oh thank you, Mr Chan! I would be ever so obliged.'

Mr Chan wagged a finger. 'But you mustn't thank me prematurely,' he said. 'You should know that my assistance hangs upon the outcome of the little errand that brings me here today.'

'Of course.'

Zachary couldn't for the life of him imagine what service he could offer to a man of such consequence; and Mr Chan's first remark, which was uttered in a casual, almost uninterested tone of voice, served only to deepen his puzzlement: 'This vessel, the *Ibis* – I gather she has an interesting history?'

Zachary could see shoals in the waters ahead and chose to answer cautiously: 'Are you referring to what happened on the *Ibis*'s late voyage to the Mauritius Islands?'

'Exactly,' said Mr Chan. 'Am I right to think there was a half-Chinese convict on board? A man called Ah Fatt?'

'That is correct.'

With a nod of acknowledgement Mr Chan continued. 'I had been led to believe that this man had died. But it has recently come to my ears that he may instead have washed up at Hong Kong. I gather he has changed his appearance and is using a different name.'

Since no specific question had been asked Zachary did not think it necessary to respond. But his silence seemed to provoke Mr Chan, who removed his hand from Zachary's shoulder and wheeled around to face him. 'I should explain,' he said, in a sharper tone of voice, 'that this man is of great interest to me, Mr Reid.'

'May I ask why?'

'Let's just say that I have some unfinished business with him, a trifling matter. It would be a great help to me if you could confirm that he is indeed in these parts.'

Such was the contrast between the blandness of Mr Chan's

words and the silky menace of his tone that Zachary knew that the nature of his unfinished business was anything but trifling. Nor could he imagine that anyone would want to trifle with Mr Chan, or with the ex-convict either: the man was a killer after all – Zachary had seen that with his own eyes, on the *Ibis*, on that night when he had settled his accounts with Mr Crowle. That he, Zachary, had thereby himself been spared injury – or perhaps even death – was the only consideration that made him hesitate to betray Freddie to Mr Chan.

'Come now,' said Mr Chan, prodding him gently. 'We are partners, are we not, Mr Reid? We must be frank with each other – and you may be sure that no one shall know but I.'

All of a sudden now, Zachary recalled the veiled threats and innuendoes that had issued from the convict's lips in Singapore. It was then that he made his decision: the man knew too much; to be rid of him would be no great loss for the world.

Zachary looked into the visitor's eyes: 'Yes, Mr Chan – I think you're right. I too have reason to believe that he has come to the China coast.'

Mr Chan continued to stare at him intently. 'And would you by any chance happen to know what name he is using?'

'He calls himself Freddie Lee.'

A smile spread slowly across Mr Chan's face.

'Thank you, Mr Reid, thank you. This makes everything much easier for me. I am glad we understand each other so well! One good turn deserves another – you will hear from Mr Burnham very soon; I will make sure of that.'

Zachary bowed. 'It's always a pleasure doing business with you, Mr Chan.'

'And with you, Mr Reid.'

Mr Chan was as good as his word. At the end of the week a letter arrived from Mr Burnham, to tell Zachary that he had been released from his official commitments. He was to proceed at once to the foreign enclave in Canton, leaving the *Ibis* at Whampoa.

*

For several weeks after the extraction of the bullet from his side Neel was incapacitated by a fever. Of the extraction itself he remembered only that it was performed by a group of Chinese and Tibetan monks, armed with fearsome-looking needles and instruments. Fortunately he lost consciousness at the start of the procedure and did not regain it until the next day.

After that he woke intermittently, to find himself lying on a mat, in a small, low-ceilinged room. In one corner lay the books and writing materials he had left behind at the Ocean Banner Monastery, with Taranathji. When he could summon the strength he would read or make notes.

Often he would hear musket- and cannon-fire in the distance; the noise would fade into his fevered dreams. From time to time familiar faces would appear – Taranathji, Compton, Baburao – and if their visits happened to coincide with a period of lucidity, they would speak of what was happening.

A truce had been declared, they told him; British warships were stationed all along the Guangzhou riverfront; steamers and gunboats were roaming the waterways, destroying batteries and gun-emplacements at will, attacking any vessel that aroused their suspicions. In the foreign enclave the Union Jack had once again been hoisted over the British Factory; many merchants had moved in and trade had been forcibly resumed. A very senior officer, General Sir Hugh Gough, had taken command of the British forces and he and Captain Elliot had issued a series of proclamations and ultimatums, demanding that the seizure of Hong Kong be formally ratified by the Emperor; that six million silver dollars be handed over immediately; that the ban on the opium trade be rescinded.

And so on.

But the Emperor was adamant: not only had he refused to make any concessions, he had recalled Qishan to Beijing in disgrace. The Governor-General had been replaced by a new set of officials, one of them a famous general; the Emperor had said to them: 'The only word I accept is annihilation.'

But on arriving in Guangzhou the Emperor's new envoys had been confronted with the same dilemma that had confounded their predecessors: the British forces were too powerful to be openly challenged – extensive preparations would be required if they were to be repulsed. So they had continued to parlay with the invaders while redoubling their efforts to strengthen their own forces.

Now thousands of fresh troops were pouring into the city, from other provinces and cities; new vessels, modelled on British gunboats, were being built at secret locations and guns were being cast in a foundry at nearby Fatshan, among them a colossal eighty-pounder.

Everybody knew that it was just a matter of time before war broke out again, this time with Guangzhou as the battlefield. This had caused great alarm, especially among those who lived outside the city walls; thousands had already fled from the suburbs and many more were planning to go. In some areas law and order had collapsed. The influx of troops from other provinces had added to the chaos; rumours were in the air that soldiers from faraway provinces had violated local women. This had led to clashes between the townsfolk and the newly arrived troops.

Turmoil such as this had not been seen in Guangzhou since the fall of the Ming dynasty, two hundred years before.

It wasn't long before Neel's friends began to leave. One day Baburao came to the monastery to tell him that he was taking his whole family to Hong Kong. Guangzhou had become too unsafe, especially for boat-people; most of their relatives had already left.

Aar ekhane amra ki korbo? said Baburao, in Bengali. What are we to do here? In today's Guangzhou there is no place for an eatery like ours.

In Hong Kong Asha-didi would be able to start over again, serving biryani, puris, samosas, kababs and all the other items for which her kitchen was famous; with so many lascar-crewed ships in the bay, there would be no shortage of Indian customers.

The move had been in preparation for a while, said Baburao. Over several weeks he and his sons had secretly transferred their household goods to his junk; they would leave in a day or two.

And the houseboat?

It will lie empty here for now, said Baburao. Maybe we'll come back to get it some day.

Then it was Compton's turn to say goodbye. He had decided to go back to his village, he said, but he probably would not stay there long. There was no work for him there; he would have to move to a place where he could earn a livelihood.

So where will you go? said Neel.

Where *can* I go? said Compton despairingly. If I am to set up a print-shop again I will have to go to a place where an English-language printer is needed.

Such as?

Macau maybe, said Compton shamefacedly. Or maybe even Hong Kong.

You? In Hong Kong?

What else can I do, Ah Neel? Everything has changed. To survive I too will have to change.

A dispirited smile appeared on Compton's face: 'Maybe from now on we speak English again, jik-haih? I will need to practise.'

When they shook hands Neel said: 'Thank you, Compton: for everything you've done for me – for all your help.'

'Don't thank me, Ah Neel,' said Compton. 'After this maybe it will be you who help me, *haih mh haih aa?*'

The one face that never appeared at Neel's bedside was Jodu's. When Neel asked about him he was told, by Taranathji, that Jodu had remained in the monastery for only a few days after their arrival: then a visitor had come looking for him, a sailor from foreign parts – a fierce-looking man with a mouth that was stained red with betel.

Jodu had left with him and had not been seen since.

*

Within half an hour of reaching Whampoa, Zachary was seated in the *Ibis's* longboat, heading towards Canton's foreign enclave. He had heard a great deal about the size and populousness of Guangzhou but when the city walls came into view he was trans-fixed nonetheless: the ramparts seemed to stretch away forever, disappearing into the sunset sky. He had once overheard Captain Hall, of the *Nemesis*, saying that the two most marvellous sights he had seen in his life were Niagara Falls and the city of Canton: now he understood why.

Zachary's amazement deepened as the *Ibis's* longboat made its way along the city's miles-long waterfront: the sprawl of habitation, the traffic on the river, and the sheer density of people was almost beyond comprehension. Grudgingly he admitted to himself that his native Baltimore would be dwarfed by this vast metropolis, even if it were three, four or five times larger than it was.

To find Mr Burnham in this vast honeycomb of a city would be a devil of a task, he assumed. But when the boat drew up to the foreign enclave he had no difficulty in deciding which way to go: a tall flagpole with a fluttering Union Jack led him directly to the British Factory where Mr Burnham had taken an apartment.

On entering the factory Zachary was handed over to a bowing, gown-clad steward who led him through a series of richly panelled hallways and carpeted corridors. Zachary's eyes widened as he took in the gilt-framed pictures, the gleaming sconces, the tall porcelain vases, the ivory doorknobs, the lavishly painted wallpapers, the thick carpets – the opulence of the place was marvellously seductive; this, Zachary decided, was how he would like to live.

Mr Burnham's apartment too was lavishly appointed, so much so that the luxuries of Bethel seemed modest by comparison. The door was opened by another pig-tailed, black-gowned servant, and Zachary was led through a wainscoted vestibule to a large study.

Mr Burnham was sitting at a desk, enthroned in a rosewood chair. 'Ah there you are, Reid!' he said, as he rose to welcome Zachary. 'You've arrived at last.'

'Yes, sir,' said Zachary. 'And I'm much obliged to you for making the arrangements.'

'Oh it was nothing. And you've come not a moment too soon.'

'Really, sir? Why?'

'There's a reception this evening in this factory.'

Mr Burnham paused, as if to add emphasis to what he was about to say.

'A large contingent of military officers will be present.'

Zachary was instantly on the alert. 'Yes, sir?'

'I believe Captain Mee is expected.'

'I see, sir.'

'I was wondering,' Mr Burnham continued, 'whether there's been any progress on that little matter that we talked about?'

'Well, sir,' said Zachary. 'I did speak to Captain Mee a while ago and I do believe I succeeded in planting a thought or two in his mind. He's had some time to consider the matter over – I should be able to get an answer from him now.'

'Good,' said Mr Burnham, glancing at his fob. 'Well we should go then – the reception will have started already.'

Zachary followed Mr Burnham down a flight of stairs to a mahogany-panelled refectory. A dozen or so merchants had already gathered there and they pounced on Mr Burnham as soon as he stepped in.

'Burnham, have you heard? The mandarins have moved four thousand more troops from Hubei to Canton.'

'And a new battery has been built on the Dutch folly!'

'There can be no doubt of it now – the Chinese are preparing another offensive!'

'And what I want to know is what in hell is the Plenny-potty doing about it?'

As others joined in the outcry Zachary retreated to the edges of the group, manoeuvering himself into a position from which he could keep an eye on the door.

It wasn't long before Captain Mee entered, with a group of red-coated officers: he was in full dress uniform, with a sword at his side. Their eyes met briefly as the officers stepped in and Zachary knew, from the way the captain flushed, that he was rattled to see him.

As he stood watching Zachary heard Mr Burnham's voice, speaking in tones of reassurance: 'I have it on good authority, gentlemen, that General Gough has already issued orders for the troops at Hong Kong to be brought forward to Whampoa. As long as he's at the helm we have nothing to fear!'

'Hear, hear!'

Zachary listened with only half an ear; his attention was now wholly focused on Captain Mee.

The captain too seemed to be aware that he was being watched and his discomfiture became steadily more evident: he kept mopping his face and fidgeting with his collar. Seeing him drain several glasses of wine in quick succession, Zachary realized that he would have to act quickly if the danger of a drunken scene were to be averted. When the captain drifted away to a window he decided to make his move: he crossed the refectory and stuck out his hand: 'A very good evening to you, Captain Mee.'

The captain turned his head slightly and an angry flush rose to his large, heavy-jawed face. A vein began to throb on his temple and, as if by instinct, his fingers began to fidget with the hilt of his sword.

This was a decisive moment, Zachary knew, and he kept his gaze fixed unflinchingly on the captain's face. Their eyes met and locked together; for a long moment it was as if two powerful currents had collided and each were trying to force back the other. Then something seemed to shift and Zachary sensed that he had only to keep his nerve in order to prevail; without dropping his eyes he repeated, 'Good evening, Captain Mee,' and again thrust his hand at him.

And now at last the captain brushed a hand across Zachary's fingertips. 'Good evening.'

Zachary smiled. 'It's always a pleasure to see you, Captain.'

The captain turned away with a grunt. 'What the devil do you want?'

'I was wondering,' said Zachary evenly, 'whether you'd given any thought to my proposal?'

The captain's chin snapped up and his eyes flashed in anger.

Zachary returned his stare with an unperturbed smile. 'We must recall, mustn't we, Captain Mee,' he said, 'exactly what is at stake, for yourself and others – especially a certain lady?'

The veiled threat hung between them for a second or two while Captain Mee struggled for words. Then, in a low, gruff voice, he mumbled: 'What do you require of me?'

At that a warm exultancy surged up in Zachary: he knew that he had won, that he had bent the captain to his will. He had suspected that the captain's truculence was an expression not of strength but of insufficiency, and this was now confirmed; Zachary understood that outside soldiering Captain Mee was at a loss to deal with the world and expected only failure and defeat. That he should capitulate to a bluff; that he should so readily abase himself to protect the woman he loved – all this seemed laughable to Zachary: how weak they were, these bumbling warriors, with their childlike notions of honour and integrity. It was all he could do not to gloat.

'We mustn't worry about the details, Captain,' he said. 'It's the principle that matters and I'm glad we find ourselves in agreement on that.'

Zachary stuck out his hand again and this time he made sure to give the captain's reluctantly proffered fingers a hearty shake. 'It will be a pleasure doing business with you, Captain.'

As he turned away, Zachary heard the captain mumble, 'Go to hell,' and was tempted to laugh.

On the other side of the room Mr Burnham was still deep in discussion with his fellow merchants. Zachary made his way over, tapped Mr Burnham on the elbow and led him aside.

'I've had a word with Captain Mee, sir.'

'And what came of it? Is he amenable?'

'I'm glad to tell you, sir,' said Zachary proudly, 'that he is.'

'Good man!' Mr Burnham beamed as he clapped Zachary on the back. 'That's all I needed to know. You can leave him to me now, I'll handle the rest. It's enough that you've brought him around – can't have been easy, I imagine.'

'No, sir,' said Zachary. 'It wasn't.'

'I won't ask how you did it,' said Mr Burnham. 'But I do think you deserve a commission.'

In any other circumstances Zachary would have been flattered by Mr Burnham's words. But the successful resolution of his encounter with Captain Mee had given him a new sense of confidence; nothing seemed beyond his reach now.

'I hope you will not mind me saying so, sir,' he said, 'but a commission is not what I want.'

'What do you want then?' said Mr Burnham, taken aback.

'What I'd really like, sir,' said Zachary, 'is to be a partner in your firm.'

Mr Burnham's face darkened as he took this in. But then his lips curved into a smile. 'Well, Reid,' he said, stroking his beard, 'I've always said that when the spirit of enterprise stirs in a young man, there's no telling where it will take him! Let's wait for this campaign to come to an end and then we'll see what can be worked out.'

Reaching for Mr Burnham's hand, Zachary gave it a hearty shake. 'Thank you, sir. Thank you.'

This second success was enough to make Zachary giddy with triumph. But as he was wandering off in search of a celebratory glass of wine, it struck him that his victory was still incomplete and would remain so until Mrs Burnham knew of it. Only when word of it had been conveyed to her would his triumph be properly concluded; there would be a sweet, subtle pleasure in stripping her of her illusions about her knight-in-armour.

The thought brought on a sharp pang of desire, making him hungry to see her again. It struck him now that if he played his cards carefully then she too might be persuaded to yield to him again. It was no more than he deserved. After all wasn't it she herself who had broken the promise she had made to him? Hadn't she said that when the time came to end their liaison they would meet one last time, for a night of delirious delight, before saying goodbye?

*

The distraught wavering of Neel's handwriting, when he learnt of Raju's arrival in China, was perhaps a better illustration of his state of mind than the disordered jumble of words that he jotted down in his notebook that night.

What happened was this: appearing unexpectedly at the Ocean Banner Monastery, Jodu told Neel that he had spent the last several weeks with Serang Ali, who had been summoned to Canton to help with the preparations for a renewed Chinese offensive.

One of Serang Ali's tasks was to gather information about British troop and ship movements. A few days earlier rumours had reached Guangzhou that a large British force was to be moved to Whampoa; Serang Ali had been sent to Hong Kong to investigate. While there he had met up with their old comrade from the *Ibis*, Ah Fatt: he had confirmed that only one company of troops and a single ship now remained at Hong Kong; every other soldier and vessel in the British force had been sent forward to Whampoa and Canton.

But there was some other news too . . .

This was when Neel learnt, to his utter shock, that Raju had travelled to China and was now at Whampoa, on a ship, with a company of sepoys.

To remove the boy from the ship would be impossible, Jodu told Neel; their best hope of spiriting him away was to wait for the sepoys to come ashore. In Serang Ali's current crew there were many local men; they would help.

But when will they come ashore?

Maybe very soon, said Jodu enigmatically. For all you know something big may happen soon; maybe even tomorrow.

The date was 19 May 1841.

*

All through the last week the hallways of the British Factory in Canton had been abuzz with rumours of an impending Chinese offensive. During this time Zachary had been busy shuttling between the foreign enclave and Whampoa, transferring Mr Burnham's goods to the *Ibis*.

Going back and forth in a longboat, Zachary had been able to observe for himself the renewed military preparations around Guangzhou: a huge encampment of soldiers had appeared at the eastern end of the city; new batteries had been built including a large one near Shamian Island, very close to the foreign enclave; and flotillas of war-junks had gathered inside the creeks that debouched into the Pearl River.

All of this was in plain view – as was the British force that had recently come to Whampoa from Hong Kong, bringing thousands of additional troops: it was led by the seventy-two-gun *Blenheim*, which towered over every other craft in the anchorage.

From all this and more it was amply clear that both sides were again preparing for war. Zachary was not in the least surprised when Mr Burnham announced, one afternoon, that the Chinese were expected to launch a surprise attack that night: Captain Elliot had issued instructions for the British Factory to be evacuated; the merchants who were resident there were to move to a vessel that was anchored opposite the foreign enclave. The *Nemesis* would be nearby, standing guard.

'I think you had better stay with us tonight, Reid,' said Mr Burnham. 'I'll have to remove all my goods from the factory and that'll take a while. And the situation being what it is, it'll be too risky to go back to Whampoa after nightfall.'

A couple of hours went by in moving the last of Mr Burnham's crates and chests to the longboat. It was almost sunset by the time the job was completed.

A brief ceremony was held in front of the British Factory as the Union Jack was taken down: it was a solemn moment, for the flag had flown atop that mast for almost three months now. Then, along with all the other merchants, Zachary and Mr Burnham were rowed over to a schooner, *Aurora*, that was anchored off the foreign enclave: this was where they were to dine and spend the night.

No sooner had they stepped on board than Manchu bannermen were seen moving along the waterfront. It was clear that the attack was now imminent.

The guests ate a hurried meal and then gathered on the foredeck. It was a dark, moonless night and the riverfront, usually so noisy, was unnaturally quiet. There were no coracles shuttling between the shores and nor were there any pleasure-boats circling around White Swan Lake. British warships and cutters had been stationed at intervals along the riverfront; their lanterns formed a thin necklace of light in the darkness.

The foreign enclave was dark too, except for the American Factory, where a few merchants had stayed on. Although the British Factory was empty and shuttered, its steeple-clock was still working. Just as it struck eleven the battery at Shamian Island opened up with a great thunderclap. Seconds later the whole waterfront erupted as bright jets of fire spurted from a string of concealed batteries and gun-emplacements.

The *Nemesis* was the first to return fire. One by one the other warships followed, unloosing broadsides at the city's batteries and gun-emplacements. Then, with a great crackling noise, sheets of flame appeared in the surrounding creeks.

'Fire-raft! Dead astern!' shouted the *Aurora*'s lookout.

Rushing aft, Zachary saw that a blazing boat was heading towards the *Aurora*. Nor was it the only one – many others quickly appeared, on the river and on White Swan Lake. It was as if a tide of fire were roiling the water.

But the use of fire-rafts had been anticipated by the British commanders: this was why cutters had been positioned along the river. They moved quickly now to intercept the blazing boats; armed with gaffs and poles, sailors pushed them aside, to burn out at a safe distance.

Even as this was going on, British gunships were intensifying their bombardment of the city. The *Nemesis* too took some hits and her engine was disabled for a while, but her guns continued to fire and the *Algerine* quickly pulled up alongside to provide support. Between them the two warships unleashed a terrific fusillade at the battery on Shamian Island. It wasn't long before its guns fell silent.

Yet, despite the pounding, the Chinese artillery continued to fire, hour after hour. Every time a gun was knocked out another would appear somewhere else.

Meanwhile fires were blazing in various parts of the city and crowds were milling about on the roadways. Through all this the foreign enclave had remained unscathed, for the British warships had been instructed to direct their fire away from it. This special treatment did not long escape the notice of the townsfolk: with the foreigners beyond their reach the foreign enclave was now the only target on which they could vent their rage.

In the small hours of the night a large crowd was seen to be advancing upon the enclave. A detachment of Royal Marines was sent over to rescue the Americans who had stayed behind; they were whisked away just as the crowd poured into the enclave.

From the safety of the *Aurora* the merchants watched as the doors of the factories were battered down. Then the crowds rushed inside, to carry away whatever they could find. After the buildings had been emptied they were set alight.

The factories were all lavishly constructed, with fine wooden panelling and parquet floors. They burned mightily, with upcurling plumes of fire shooting out of their doorways and windows.

The merchants on the *Aurora* watched in horror as the factories went up in flames. The spectacle was poignant even for Zachary whose acquaintance with the Thirteen Factories was very brief. Some of the other merchants had frequented those buildings for decades; some had accumulated vast fortunes there. Many began to weep.

By the time the sun rose the buildings had been reduced to charred skeletons.

After breakfast the senior merchants on the *Aurora* were summoned to a meeting on the *Nemesis*. On returning, Mr Burnham told Zachary that British gunships had destroyed dozens of war-junks and fire-boats during the night; as for guns, so many had been silenced that the number was yet to be computed. On the British side the toll was negligible: some injuries, a couple of dead, and a few lightly damaged ships. The *Nemesis* had been swiftly repaired and she had seen a great deal of action afterwards. In a single sortie the steamer had destroyed forty-three war-junks and thirty-two fire-rafts.

But the Chinese offensive was far from exhausted, said Mr Burnham: it was thought that they still had many fire-rafts and attack-boats in reserve. The mopping-up operations would continue for a while yet: once completed the British forces would probably launch a punitive attack on the city, to demonstrate, once and for all, that these attempts at resistance were futile and that no more prevarication would be tolerated.

While these operations were under way, the *Ibis* was to remain at Whampoa with the other merchant vessels that were anchored there. When things quietened down, a convoy would be organized to take them to the coast. Zachary was to take the *Ibis* downriver, with the convoy, to Hong Kong Bay.

'And you, sir?' said Zachary to Mr Burnham.

'I've been asked to stay on in Canton for a while,' said Mr Burnham. 'When you get to Hong Kong would you be so good as to tell my wife that I'll be back in a fortnight or so, after this bit of nonsense has been sorted out?'

'Yes of course, sir,' said Zachary. 'I'll go over to see Mrs Burnham as soon as I get there.'

*

At Hong Kong Bay it was so sultry that morning that Paulette woke up wondering whether she was in the grip of a fever. Her sheets and her nightclothes were drenched in sweat – yet inside her, at her core, there was an icy feeling of disquiet.

But when she mentioned it to Fitcher he said there was no reason to worry: it was just that the weather had taken an odd turn. The temperature had risen sharply and he had a feeling that a big storm was on the way.

During his time in southern China Fitcher had become familiar with the signs of an approaching typhoon: the sudden heat, the stifling humidity, and the stillness of the air were to him as much harbingers of a 'big blow' as a falling barometer. So certain was he of this that he went out to the western end of Hong Kong Bay, in a boat, to see whether clouds had appeared on the southern horizon. That was the direction from which typhoons usually came, sweeping up from the south to lash the coast, battering Macau, Hong Kong and Kowloon before travelling northwards to Canton and beyond.

But there was not a cloud anywhere to be seen that morning; the sky was a flat white mirror, radiating heat.

The storm would not break for a while yet, Fitcher told Paulette, and it would probably be preceded by a few showers and spells of rain. That was how it usually happened: there was no immediate reason for concern.

All of this made sense to Paulette yet her mind was not set entirely at rest. Fitcher understood then that she was fretting about something else and he urged her not to go to the nursery that day; there was no need, he said, the caretakers would be able to manage perfectly well on their own.

But Paulette decided that she would go over to the island after all – despite the heat it would be better to be at work than to fret on board.

So the *Redruth*'s gig set off, as it did every day – except that today the water, like the air, was unnaturally still: the boat's ripples carved grooves upon its glassy surface.

Paulette was sitting with her back to the bows and as they drew closer to Hong Kong one of the oarsmen told her to turn around. Glancing over her shoulder she saw that dozens of people had gathered to form a ring around something lying on the beach.

A memory stirred of another day, two years ago, when a body had been washed in by the tide. Her heart lurched and she told the oarsmen to row faster, faster. When the gig pulled up to the shore she leapt out and went running across the beach.

She had to push past a number of people to get through the ring. At the centre lay a man's body. The wet clothing was pierced all over with rents and slashes – but there was no mistaking that ragged jacket and the shapeless trowsers.

A stout, elderly man was squatting beside the body; he had covered the face with a piece of cloth but on seeing Paulette he took it off.

'Mistoh Freddie Lee.'

It turned out that the old man was Freddie's landlord in Sheng Wan village. The night before, he said, a couple of men had come to the house asking for Freddie. They had said that they were friends of his and that he was to meet them on the beach.

Freddie had responded warily when the message was conveyed: 'Who they ask for, eh?'

'Freddie Lee,' the landlord had said, and this had settled Freddie's doubts.

'Only friends call me that, ne?'

He had put on his hat and set off for the beach.

That was the last time he was seen alive.

Twenty

A round Canton the attacks and counter-attacks, the explosions and bombardments continued for three long days, to the accompaniment of a continuous and rising din – the howling of unseen mobs, the panicked cries of children, the crackling of flames.

On the British side the fighting and shooting was done entirely by the navy; the infantry battalions that had been brought upriver remained on their respective ships, at Whampoa, through this time.

The confinement was particularly trying for the Bengal Volunteers since they had been at Whampoa for many weeks already. To make things worse, on the second day of the offensive, there was a sudden change in the weather, which became increasingly torrid and sultry. Without a catspaw of wind to stir the air the stench of the bilges permeated every corner of the vessel, making it as hard to remain below deck as it was to venture out into the sun.

The conditions were particularly hard on Captain Mee, whose mood had taken a turn for the worse ever since the day of the fighting around the Tiger's Mouth. The change in him was particularly striking, or so it seemed to Kesri, because at the start of the operation he had seemed still to be riding on the high spirits in which he had returned from his sojourn at Macau. But from the time of his visit to the *Ibis*, to drop off the wounded ensign, he had fallen into a black humour: Kesri had thought at first that it was just that he was distressed to see the young ensign's career ending so sadly and suddenly. But he soon realized that something else must have happened to make the captain brood and fret to this degree; not since the days of his abrupt separation from Miss Cathy, at Ranchi, had Kesri seen him in such a dark state of mind. Now, as the troops sat stewing in their transport vessels, at Whampoa, the captain seemed at times to be almost beside himself:

Kesri had never known him to be as morose and irascible as he was during those three long days.

On the third day the turmoil around the city reached a climax, with the sound of gunfire echoing along the riverfront from sunrise onwards. That afternoon the officers' daily briefing on the *Blenheim* went on for an unusually long time. Soon after Captain Mee's return from the flagship Kesri received a summons to his cabin. On stepping in Kesri knew at once that they would soon be going into the field: for the first time in days Captain Mee seemed untroubled and at ease. He sounded almost cheerful as he said: 'It's on at last, havildar! The Plenipot has finally understood that the Longtails won't call off these attacks unless they're taught a lesson. And that's what we're going to do – we're going to storm the walled city.'

A chart was lying open on a desk: following the captain's fore-finger, Kesri saw that the citadel of Guangzhou was shaped like a dome, with its base resting on the Pearl River, to the south, and its apex lying upon a range of hills and ridges, to the north. Sitting finial-like on its crown was a five-storeyed edifice called the Sea-Calming Tower. Opposite the tower, just beyond the city walls, were some hills topped by a cluster of four small forts. Three of these were circular in shape but the largest, which faced the Sea-Calming Tower, was rectangular.

These four forts were lightly defended, said Captain Mee: the Chinese commanders had calculated, no doubt, that if the British launched an attack on the city it would come from the south so they had concentrated their forces along the banks of the Pearl River. But General Gough had prepared a surprise for them, a two-pronged assault. A small British detachment would land at the Thirteen Factories, on the Pearl River shorefront, with the aim of seizing and clearing the foreign enclave. But the main force would continue along the Pearl River to White Swan Lake at the western end of the city, before veering northwards, along another river: it would land well above Guangzhou at a village called Tsingpu. Between the landing-point and the four forts lay a few miles of farmland: this was a rural area, with only a few scattered villages so no resistance was expected. Once the hills had been scaled and the forts seized, the city would be helpless: a single battery of guns positioned on the northern heights would be enough to control all of Guangzhou.

Some 2,400 fighting men were to be deployed for the operation, accompanied by the usual contingents of auxiliaries and camp-followers. The force would be divided into four brigades: the Bengal Volunteers, with its 112 sepoys, had been assigned to the 4th Brigade which would also include 273 Cameronians and 215 men of the 37th Madras.

'Any questions, havildar?'

The only aspect of this plan that worried Kesri was the composition of the 4th Brigade: he knew, from his experience with the Cameronians, that they would be none too pleased at having to join forces with sepoy units – there was bound to be some friction.

Other than this he had no concerns: the meticulous planning, the carefully drawn chart and the precise numbers were all reassuring, presaging as they did a set-piece operation of the kind at which British commanders excelled. With any luck the battle would bring the campaign to an end and they would be able to go home soon afterwards, with some decent prize money in their pockets.

'Embarkation will be when, sir?'

'Tomorrow, 1 p.m., havildar.'

The lateness of the hour surprised Kesri; it was unusual for a big operation to start so late in the day. 'Why that time, sir?'

Captain Mee smiled. 'Have you forgotten, havildar? It's the twenty-fourth of May tomorrow – Queen Victoria's birthday. There'll be a gun salute at noon.'

Kesri had indeed forgotten about the Queen's birthday. He was glad to be reminded of it, however, for this was one of those occasions when sepoys were entitled to a special 'wet batta' of grog.

*

There being no one else to claim Freddie's body it fell to Zadig Bey and Shireen to make arrangements for his funeral.

They quickly agreed that he would be buried according to Chinese rites; that, said Zadig, was what Freddie would have wanted. As for the site, it was Shireen who suggested that he be buried next to his father.

This suggestion drew a quizzical look from Zadig. 'But what about Dinyar and the other Parsi seths?' he said. 'What will they say about Freddie being buried next to Bahram-bhai? What if they object, because he wasn't a member of the community?'

'Let's not worry about the seths,' Shireen said. 'What matters is what Bahram would have wanted. And in death at least I think he would have wanted to give Freddie the acceptance he could not give him in life. It's only right that Freddie should be buried beside him.'

Zadig did not demur: 'Yes, that is true – Bahram-bhai would have wanted it so.'

They agreed also that the funeral would be held that very day. The body had been in the water a long time already and the weather being as hot as it was it would not do to put off the interment. In any case the island would be celebrating the Queen's birthday the next day, and who knew what problems might arise?

Since neither Zadig nor Shireen had any idea of how to organize a Chinese funeral, the arrangements were left to Freddie's landlord. It was he who found a coffin and pasted yellow and white papers on it; he also hired grave-diggers, a cart and a few professional mourners.

It took a while to get all this done and it was not till late afternoon that the corpse was properly prepared and the coffin closed.

The sun was dipping towards the horizon when the procession set off from Sheng Wan. As they were leaving the village Zadig said to Paulette: 'Have you had any news from Robin Chinnery?'

Paulette nodded: 'Yes, he sent a letter recently, from India. He fell very ill in Chusan and was evacuated to Calcutta—'

She broke off to point to the bay, where a longboat could be seen heading towards Sheng Wan. 'Look, there's Mrs Burnham.'

The cart was told to go on while Paulette, Zadig and Shireen went back to the seashore to greet the visitor.

Despite the heat and humidity, Mrs Burnham was wearing gloves and a veil, as always, except that today they were black instead of white. She was mortified to find the others dressed in light-coloured clothing.

'Oh good heavens!' she said, clapping a hand over her mouth. 'I've made an ooloo of myself, haven't I? I don't suppose they wear black at Chinese funerals, do they? Should I go back and change?'

'Oh no,' said Shireen. 'I'm sure it'll make no difference. It's enough that you came.'

Mrs Burnham gave Shireen's hands a squeeze. 'Of course, Shireen dear: I'd have come earlier if I had known.'

The cart was now a long way ahead so they had to hurry after it.

The old coastal pathway that ran past Sheng Wan village had recently been widened and paved, but work on it was still continuing: the road was to be formally named the next day, in honour of the Queen. Gangs of labourers were putting in milestones and removing rubble as they passed by.

The cart was waiting for them at the top of the ridge that led to the Happy Valley. On arriving there they saw that a cloud was coming across the valley, trailing a sheet of rain.

'It's just a shower,' said Zadig Bey. 'But we'd better take shelter here while it passes.'

There were some trees beside the road and they huddled under them to wait.

From where she stood Shireen could see much of the shoreline of Hong Kong Bay. The year before, when she had gone to visit Bahram's grave for the first time, the beachfront had been empty except for a few little villages. Now there were godowns, barracks, parade grounds, marketplaces and clusters of shanties. Preparations were already being made for the first land auction: plots had been marked out along several stretches of the shore. At some points sampans and junks were anchored so closely together that it was as if the very soil of the island had expanded.

Paulette too was looking down at the shoreline and she saw that a large, official-looking boundary had been staked out right above the beach where Freddie's body had washed up earlier in the day. It was there too that he had been sitting the year before when she came down from the nursery and unexpectedly ran into him. The memory brought tears to her eyes and she raised a hand to wipe them away.

Mrs Burnham was beside her, and she slipped her hand into Paulette's.

'Do you miss him already, Paulette?'

Paulette buried her face in her hands. 'I cannot believe,' she said between sobs, 'that he too has left me.'

*

At Whampoa the next day, when the guns went off to mark the Queen's birthday at noon, the blasts seemed to congeal the heat and humidity, making it hard to breathe: Kesri was reminded of the sultry weather that preceded the coming of the monsoons, back home.

The embarkation took unusually long because the transport vessels were a disparate assortment of junks and local boats, captured only the day before. There were no fewer than thirty of them and it was 3 p.m. before the convoy began to move, with all the boats being taken under tow by the *Nemesis*. But on the way there were further delays because of attacks by fire-boats; as a result there was only an hour of daylight left when the convoy finally reached the designated landing-point, at Tsingpu village, to the north of Guangzhou.

When the boats pulled in Kesri was with Captain Mee on the highest deck of the Bengal Volunteers' transport vessel. Spyglass in hand, the captain was surveying the salient features of the landscape that lay ahead of them: the four forts he'd pointed out on the chart lay almost due south and were dimly visible through the haze.

The distance between the landing-point and the forts was not great – only three or four miles, as the captain had said – but Kesri saw at a glance that the intervening terrain would not be easy to cross. In between lay a stretch of land that was strikingly similar to the surroundings of his own village in Bihar: it was a flat patchwork of fields, covered with green shoots – the crop was rice and Kesri guessed that many of the paddies were flooded. As at home the paths that wound through the fields were very narrow, scarcely wider than a man's foot, with surfaces of slippery wet clay. Even experienced rice farmers were apt to lose their footing on such pathways; for soldiers and sepoys, balancing muskets and fifty-pound knapsacks, it would be hard going.

Nor was the area as sparsely populated as Captain Mee had led Kesri to think. Kesri guessed that several thousand people lived in the tightly packed clusters of houses that dotted the plain. It was probably in order to resist dacoits and marauders that they lived so close together – and evidently this was exactly what the people of Tsingpu had in mind now. Armed with sticks, staves and pikes they were pouring out to confront the squad of marines that had gone ashore to establish a perimeter around the campsite.

The villagers' response did not surprise Kesri – people in his own district would have reacted the same way – but the marines were caught off-guard and for a few minutes it looked as though there would be an all-out confrontation. Then an officer took matters in hand: a couple of warning shots were fired, a cordon was formed and the angry villagers were pushed back, past a small temple at the edge of the settlement.

As soon as the situation had been brought under control General Gough stepped off the *Nemesis* and marched over to the crest of a nearby elevation, to take stock of the terrain. After he had gone some of the junior officers, Captain Mee among them, went into the village temple to look around. They emerged whooping with delight, having found quantities of offerings inside the temple, among them haunches of fresh meat, which they requisitioned for their own table.

'That fat heathen joss-god can't have any use for venison, can he?' said Captain Mee, with a sardonic laugh. 'So it may as well be used to celebrate the Queen's birthday.'

The theft of these offerings further inflamed the villagers and groups of men began to collect around the campsite, brandishing scythes and throwing stones; some were even armed with match-locks. The marines had to shoot into the air to disperse them.

These incidents further delayed the disembarkation. When it finally started the Bengal Volunteers, being small in number, were the first of the 4th Brigade's units to go ashore.

Sensing an opportunity, Kesri decided to secure a good location for B Company's tents. He chose a spot on the riverbank, where they were likely to catch a breeze. The sepoys and followers would be grateful, he knew, for an opportunity to wash away the day's grime in the river – this was a comfort they prized above all others.

But just as Kesri was issuing instructions to the tent-pitchers, Colour-Sarjeant Orr of the Cameronians appeared: 'Who the hell said you coolies could settle your black arses here?' He pointed to the tents of the 37th Madras: 'You belong back there with the Ram-sammies.'

Kesri tried to hold his ground but was outranked and heavily outnumbered. When Captain Mee himself took the other side – 'I'm sorry, havildar, you'll have to move,' – he had to give in.

The Cameronians' taunts rang in Kesri's ears as he walked away.

'... let that be a lesson to you, boy ... !'

'... and you'd better be sure we don't see any of your nigger-snot back here!'

Worse still, the only remaining spot was at the back, where there was not a breath of fresh air, but mosquitoes aplenty, swarming in from the rice-fields. The perimeter site was also uncomfortably close – a group of angry villagers had gathered around a clump of trees, just beyond the nearest picket. But there was nothing to be done about any of this: they would have to spend the night here.

Kesri sighed as he looked around. He could only hope that B Company would soon be gone from this place.

*

That night, because of a shortage of camping equipment, the banjee-boys were billeted with the company's bhistis and gun-lascars, in a tent where their bodies were packed together as tightly as cartridges in a case. The trapped air reeked of unwashed clothing, stale sweat and urine, and the drone of mosquitoes was as loud as a gale. The ground too was swarming with insects so everybody had to sleep fully clothed, with sheets swathed around their bodies for additional protection – and these too were soon soaked in sweat.

Raju could not sleep, and in a while, hearing a rustling sound, he peered out from under his sheet and saw a shadow slipping out of the tent.

Beside him, Dicky too was awake. 'You know where that bugger's going?' he whispered.

'Where?'

'Bet he's going to have a dip. I heard the bhistis have found a pond nearby. Let's follow him, ya? We can also cool off a little.'

'But what if Bobbery-Bob ... ?'

Raju remembered that the fife-major had said that he'd flog anyone who was found outside the tent.

'Balls to bloody Bobbery-Bob,' hissed Dicky. 'Don't be scared, ya; the wet batta's put them all out for the night. Come on; let's go.'

With a twist of his body Dicky slipped under the tent-flap. A second later Raju followed.

A red-rimmed moon was shining dimly through a pearly haze. In the faint light they caught a glimpse of the bhisti's crouched figure darting past the nearest picket, heading towards an incline where a body of water could be seen shimmering in the darkness.

They followed slowly, staying low and keeping their eyes on the bhisti as he crept ahead to the water's edge. Having made sure that nobody was around, the man stripped off his ungah and his pyjamas, and slid quietly into the pond.

'It's safe, see?' said Dicky. 'Come on, men, let's go.'

They took a few more steps forward and were only a short distance from the water when they saw the bhisti coming out and reaching for his clothes.

Then something else caught Dicky's eye and he ducked under a bush, pulling Raju down with him.

Peering through the leaves, they saw that three shadowy figures had crept up behind the bhisti as he was pulling on his ungah. Before he could push his head through the neck-hole the shadows lunged at him; with his face still swaddled in the garment, the bhisti was pushed down on to his knees.

All this happened very quickly so that the bhisti's single cry for help – *Bachao!* – was still hanging in the air when a blade flashed in the silvery moonlight. Then the man's decapitated trunk tumbled forward and the ungah was whisked away, with the head still inside.

The bundle of white cloth seemed to float off into the darkness as the three figures melted back into the shadows.

A voice called out from the picket – *Kaun hai* – who goes there? – and then the guards went running past. Somewhere in the distance an alarm bell began to ring, causing a stir in the camp.

'Come on, ya.' Dicky gave Raju's arm a tug. 'Follow me and stay low.'

The camp was in an uproar now so nobody noticed the two boys as they slipped back into their tent.

Once they were under their sheets Raju whispered into Dicky's ear: 'We should tell someone what we saw, no?'

'Fuck off, bugger!' Dicky hissed back. 'Mad or what? Bobbery-Bob will stick a tent-pole up your chute if he hears you were out there. And mine too.'

Raju tried to close his eyes but found that he was shivering, despite the heat. Through the chattering of his teeth he caught the sound of metal tools biting into the soil – somewhere nearby a grave was being prepared for the decapitated bhisti.

In a while Dicky whispered into his ear: 'You know why they took his head, ya?'

'Why?'

'Must be for the reward, no?'

'How do you know, ya?'

'What else? Don't you wonder, how much they'd get for your head or mine?'

*

At dawn, when the reveille was sounded, the air was still hot and heavy. The men and boys of B Company were drenched in sweat even before the morning hazree – and as luck would have it they were served the item they hated most: potatoes.

As they were eating an alarm bell began to ring: Chinese soldiers had been spotted in the distance, issuing from the city's northern and western gates.

Kesri had barely drained his mug of tea when Captain Mee came striding over. He told Kesri that B Company and the 37th Madras would be the first units to move out of the camp; General Gough wanted to study the enemy's movements and they had been detailed to accompany him to a hillock, a mile or so away.

The sepoys fell in hurriedly and marched out of the camp with drums beating and fifes playing. But once they entered the rice-fields it became impossible to keep good order: just as Kesri had thought, the paddies were flooded. The men were ordered to fall out and advance in single file, along the bunds.

Soon all pretence of marching was abandoned; to keep their footing was as much as the sepoys could do. Churned up by their feet, the clay turned into a slippery slurry; the sepoys had to plant their musket-barrels in the mud to steady themselves. But even then some could not keep their balance and toppled over into the paddies. Once down, pinioned by their knapsacks and constrained by their tight, heavy uniforms, they could do nothing but flail their limbs until they were pulled out.

The officers had an even harder time of it: unlike the sepoys, who were in sandals, they were shod in heavy boots and were reduced to shuffling along sidewise, with their arms spread out for balance.

The Jangi Laat himself was only a short distance ahead of Kesri: a tall, mournful-looking man with a walrus moustache, General Gough – or Goughie, as he was spoken of by the officers – usually held himself stiffly upright. But now he was teetering along as though he were walking a tightrope, with his arms extended and his shako skewed dangerously to one side. His son, who was also his principal aide-de-camp, was right behind, trying to steady him by supporting his elbow. But he was himself wobbling precariously and it seemed almost inevitable that something untoward would occur. Sure enough, just as they were approaching the hillock, the general and his son both tumbled over into a rice-field. A halt was ordered while they were pulled out and wiped down.

The pause gave Bobbery-Bob an opportunity to berate the boys, many of whom were tittering and giggling. 'You buggers think this is a joke, eh? I'll teach you to laugh at the general-sahib! You just wait and see, ya; you'll soon be laughing out of the wrong hole.'

Raju was not among those who had found the incident amusing; nor, unlike the other boys, had he enjoyed the walk across the rice-fields. While Dicky and the others were sliding and slithering along the paths, Raju's mind was elsewhere: thoughts and images that had never visited him before now kept passing through his head. How did it feel to be speared in the neck, or the chest? What was it like to be bayoneted in the groin? What happened when a bullet hit you? If it struck a bone were there splinters?

When the column began to move again Raju was slowly over-taken by nausea. On reaching the hillock, when the boys were given permission to relieve themselves, he went aside and vomited up a slew of potatoes and bile.

Dicky fetched some water, from a bhisti, and whispered urgently in Raju's ear: 'What's the matter with you, bugger? Have you been thinking about what happened last night? I told you to forget it, no?'

'It's just the heat, ya,' said Raju quickly. 'I'll be all right now.'

*

On the other side of the hillock Kesri was surveying the ground with Captain Mee. The four hilltop fortresses were shimmering in the haze, straight ahead. The slopes below them were dotted with detachments of Chinese troops; to the rear of the fortresses lay the walls of the city, stretching away for miles, pierced at regular intervals by soaring, many-roofed gates.

The fortresses' guns had been shooting intermittently since daybreak but now the rhythm of the firing picked up, gradually intensifying into a full-scale barrage. The distance was too great for the guns to do much damage, yet the cannonade was more spirited, and better directed, than any they had faced before.

Meanwhile the general had settled on a plan of attack. First the fortresses were to be softened up by the British field-artillery, which consisted of a rocket battery, two five-and-a-half-inch mortars, two twelve-pound howitzers and two nine-pounder guns. Then, under cover of the bombardment, the four brigades would advance up the slopes that led to the forts. The 4th Brigade was to attack the largest of the four fortresses – the rectangular citadel that faced the Sea-Calming Tower. The final attack would be mounted in echelon and the fortresses would be carried by escalade: the quartermaster would issue ladders to every company.

Escalade ladders were both heavy and unwieldy: it took only a moment's thought for Kesri to realize that Maddow was the only man in B Company who would be able to shoulder the weight. Looking around, he saw that Maddow had almost reached the hillock, with two enormous wheels on his shoulders.

'Sir, we will need that gun-lascar, for our ladder,' Kesri said to Captain Mee. 'He will have to be taken off the gun-crew.'

Captain Mee nodded: 'All right; I'll tell his crew to release him.'

*

The first element of the general's plan – the initial bombardment – quickly ran into difficulties: transporting the artillery pieces through the flooded paddies presented unforeseen challenges. The crumbling bunds would not bear the weight of the massive barrels so the gun-crews were forced to flounder through knee-deep mud. Had the fortresses been closer to a waterway the guns of the *Nemesis* and the other steamers might have been brought into play – but they were too far inland and out of range.

Kesri realized that there would be a long wait before the field-artillery arrived so he led his men to a patch of shade and told them to get some rest. He himself had slept so little the night before that he fell asleep at once and did not stir until the bombardment was well under way.

It was only mid-morning now but the air was stifling. Heated by the sun, the rice-fields were giving off so much moisture that the slopes ahead seemed to be shimmering behind a veil of steam.

It had been decided that the Cameronians would lead the advance of the 4th Brigade; when the bugle blew they were the first to move. The fields immediately ahead of the hillock were almost dry; they leapt right in, pushing through the knee-high rice.

The Bengal Volunteers went next. As they came around the hillock the sound of cannon-fire, British and Chinese, suddenly grew deafeningly loud. A shell crashed into a field a hundred yards to the right, sending up a plume of mud and green stalks.

Maatha neeche! Kesri shouted over his shoulder: Heads down! And at the same time the fifers and drummers changed tempo, switching to double-quick time.

With his head lowered Kesri lengthened his pace, trying to shut out the whistling of incoming shells. His high, stiff collar was soaked and its grip tightened like a vice on his neck as he ran; on his back, his knapsack had taken on a life of its own, flinging itself from side to side, trying to throw him off balance; between his legs the sweat-caked seam of his trowsers had turned into a length of fraying rope, sawing against his groin.

Then the rice-fields ended and they were racing up a scrub-covered slope, with shells throwing up dust all around them. Kesri saw an officer go down and then a cannonball landed right on the Cameronians, felling three troopers.

In the distance Manchu bannermen were banging their shields and brandishing spears, almost as if to taunt the attackers. Then a volley of projectiles took flight from the ramparts of the nearest fortress and came arcing down the hill, towards the sepoys. Kesri caught a glimpse of them as they slammed into the scrub, amidst clouds of smoke. He realized, to his disbelief, that the Chinese were launching rockets.

All of this was new: the improved gunnery, the rockets – how had the chootiyas learnt so much so fast?

Up ahead the Cameronians had halted to catch their breath,

under the shelter of an overhang. Captain Mee brought B Company to a stop too and then went to join the Cameronians.

Shrugging off his knapsack, Kesri dropped gratefully on to the rocky soil. They were within musket range of the Chinese troops now and volleys of grapeshot were whistling through the air. Keeping his head low, Kesri reached for his flask; it was almost empty so he was careful to take only a sip. It would be a while yet before the followers caught up and they too were probably running low on water now; the company had been so thirsty at the last stop that the bhistis' mussucks had shrunk to less than half size.

When at last the bhistis arrived, Kesri signalled to them to stay low and serve the sepoys first. From here on it would be a straight run up to the rectangular citadel: only the sepoys would advance now; the fifers, drummers, runners and bhistis would remain here. Of the followers Maddow alone would accompany the fighting men, with the ladder.

Glancing back, Kesri saw that Maddow had kept up with the front line despite his unwieldy burden. Beckoning him forward, Kesri said: You'll stay beside me from now on: understood? *Samjhelu?*

Ji, havildar-sah'b.

*

Further down the slope the fifers were still scrambling after the sepoys. Now, as grapeshot began to hum and whistle around them Bobbery-Bob shouted, 'Get down, you fucking barnshoots! Do you want to get your balls shot off?' They flattened themselves on the ground.

Raju's mouth was as dry as sawdust: he was thirstier than he had ever been. Snatching at his flask he pulled at the cap with trembling fingers – but only to discover that the cork had come loose and all the water had leaked out.

A disbelieving wail burst from his throat: 'It's gone – all my water.'

Dicky, lying beside him, had already drained his own bottle. On impulse he grabbed Raju's flask and jumped to his feet: 'Wait, ya – I'll get some more from a bhisti.'

Dicky started off at a run but came to a sudden stop after a few steps. For a moment his body stayed upright, as if frozen in motion, and then he spun sidewise and fell to the ground.

'Dicky?' screamed Raju. Leaping to his friend's side, he took hold of his shoulder and gave him a shake. 'Dicky, what's the matter with you, bugger?'

Raju could not understand why Dicky would not look at him, even though his amber eyes were wide open.

'What's happened, Dicky?' Raju shook him again. 'Get up, bugger, get up! This is no time to play the fool.'

There was still no answer so Raju flung himself on the unmoving figure and wrapped his arms around him.

'Please, Dicky, get up. Please listen to me, ya. Get up!'

*

The British barrage had risen to a crescendo when Captain Mee came scrambling back to tell Kesri that he was going ahead with the Cameronians.

That the captain was impatient to be in the thick of the fighting was amply evident to Kesri; during the advance he had exposed himself to fire with a recklessness that was unusual even for him: it was almost as if he were courting a bullet.

'Be careful, Kaptán-sah'b,' said Kesri.

The captain gave him a nod and ran off, ducking and dodging as grapeshot whistled through the air.

As he lay on the gravelly slope Kesri was aware of a quickening in the rhythm of his breath; when he tried to tighten his grip on his Brown Bess the barrel slipped through his palms which were oozing sweat. In his stomach too there was a peculiar gnawing tightness, a sensation that puzzled him until he recognized that his guts were churning in fear. He shut his eyes and pressed his cheek into the ground, so that the pebbles pushed against his teeth.

His old wounds had begun to throb now; it was as if his body had become a storehouse of memory, a map of pain. Yet what he recalled most vividly was not the fiery burning that had accompanied each injury but rather the dull, crushing pain of recovery – the weeks of lying in bed, of not being able to turn over, of having to soil himself. He did not want to go through that again; he did not want to die, not now, not for nothing, which was what this was.

Somewhere nearby there was a sound of convulsive swallowing.

Opening his eyes, Kesri saw that it was coming from the sepoy who was lying next to him – a man not much younger than himself.

559

He was from the hills, Kesri remembered, and was the father of a large brood of children. Was he thinking of them now? Was he remembering the shadows of the mountains as they stretched across his valley on frosty evenings? It was plain to Kesri that the sepoy too had been seized by fear: his lips were white, his hands were shaking and his eyes were showing their whites. In a minute or two he would curl up; his whole body would be paralysed by fear. When it came time to move he would not be able to rise to his feet. It would fall to Kesri to report him to Captain Mee; there would be a court martial and the man would probably be shot for cowardice – and he, Havildar Kesri Singh, would be as much to blame as the man himself, for it was his job, his duty, his karma, to protect his men as best he could, even from themselves.

Sticking out an elbow, Kesri jabbed the sepoy in his ribs: Chal! It's almost time now.

The words stuck in his throat and he had drag them out as though he were making himself retch.

Then, abruptly, the noise of the gunfire diminished and the British barrage drew to an end.

'Fix bayonets!'

A bullet threw dust into Kesri's face as he pulled himself over the escarpment; his feet slipped on the loose gravel but he managed to stay upright and began to stride uphill, head lowered, moving with a stooped, lumbering gait, which was the only way you could run up a slope with a fifty-pound knapsack on your back and a musket in your hand. Between steps he sucked in a mouthful of air and shouted – *Har har Mahadev!* – and the battle-cry came roaring back at him, propelling him forward.

After another two hundred yards Kesri saw that the Cameronians had stopped their advance. They had come under heavy fire from a detachment of Manchu bannermen, positioned at the crest of the hill.

Looking rightward, Kesri spotted a grove of trees and held up his hand to signal to the sepoys to follow him there.

Just as Kesri had thought, the spot offered a clear line of fire to the bannermen. It took him only a few minutes to site the sepoys to his satisfaction. Then they unloosed one volley after another until the bannermen withdrew.

As soon as the firing had ceased Kesri sprinted over to the Cameronians: 'They're gone!' he shouted. 'They're gone!'

The Cameronians seemed to be unaware of the little sideshow to their rear.

One by one their faces turned blankly towards him. Then he heard Colour-Serjeant Orr's voice shouting into his ear. 'Where the fuck have you black bastards been? Were you hiding below so you wouldn't have to fight? Bloody bunch of cowards.'

Suddenly Kesri's musket began to twitch in his hands. The urge to thrust his bayonet into Colour-Sarjeant Orr's belly was almost irresistible: to skewer this maadarchod seemed far more urgent than fighting some unknown Chinese soldier.

But before he could make a move Captain Mee's voice cut in – 'Havildar?' – and habit took over. Kesri snapped off a salute: Ji, Kaptán-sah'b.

'Has our ladder been brought forward?'

Glancing down the slope Kesri saw that Maddow was squatting beside the sepoys of B Company.

'Ladder is here, sir.'

'Good. Let's get the job done then. The Cameronians will charge to the right – we'll take the left.'

At a signal from Captain Mee the ranks began to peel off, in staggered order, to advance slantwise, in echelon. The fire from the fortress died away as they charged. On reaching the ramparts B Company formed a protective cordon around Maddow as he assembled and erected the ladder.

The first man to scale the walls took a look around and announced that the fortress had been abandoned; its garrison had withdrawn towards the city. Kesri went up next and found himself on a parapet that led to an embrasured turret.

Kesri went into the turret and climbed up to the highest of the embrasures. Sprawled below lay the vast expanse of the city of Guangzhou. The streets and avenues, towers and pagodas, houses and shanties stretched away as far as the eye could see, to the east and to the south. Some of the gates of the walled city were open and long lines of people could be seen trickling out: they appeared to be fleeing in every direction.

Before Kesri could take it all in the guns on the city walls opened up with a tremendous roar. A shell crashed into the ramparts, just below the turret. Kesri ducked his head and went racing down, to take cover inside the fortress.

*

The rectangular fortress was a simple structure, with a large covered enclosure in the centre, surrounded by a few rooms and antechambers. The enclosure filled up quickly as the rest of the 4th Brigade poured in, through the rear gate.

In the meantime the other three forts had also been overrun by British troops. The barrage from the city walls continued without interruption all the while but failed to impede the operation. At noon word was sent back to General Gough that all four fortresses had been occupied. One was being prepared to serve as his headquarters; he could occupy it when he pleased.

On his way up the general had a narrow escape: a bullet flew right past his ear to hit the officer behind him.

Soon after his arrival the general called a meeting at his headquarters. Captain Mee was among those who attended. On his return Kesri learnt that the morning's fighting had taken an unexpectedly heavy toll. The British forces had suffered more battlefield casualties than on any other day. The Bengal Volunteers had been lucky not to lose any men.

Feelings were running high among the officers, said the captain. The hotheads were talking of teaching the Celestials a sanguinary lesson by sacking the city's temples, pagodas and markets: these were known to be vast storehouses of silver and gold – the booty would be beyond calculation.

It had been decided, in any event, that the walled city would be stormed the next day. The northern gates had been studied by the engineers and they had come to the conclusion that it would not be difficult to force an entry. Plans had been drawn up for the attack: it would start early, with all four brigades converging on the northern walls.

Through the afternoon followers kept straggling in, but none belonged to B Company. Their absence was both an inconvenience and a worry for Kesri; a couple of hours before nightfall, he dispatched a squad to look for them. They returned at dusk and only then did Kesri learn of the casualties: a runner, a cook and a bhisti injured; one fifer killed. That was why they had been so slow to arrive; because it had taken a long time to arrange for the injured men and the dead boy to be evacuated to the rear.

The news of Dicky's death had a powerful effect on Kesri: he remembered that he had himself chosen the boy, thinking that he might become the company's mascot. And so indeed he had: his ready smile, quick tongue and jaunty step had won the sepoys' hearts: it was cruel that B Company could not be present at his interment, to bury him with the honour he deserved.

Kesri recalled also that a close friendship had blossomed between Dicky and Raju: his eyes sought out the young lad, who was sitting crouched and red-eyed in one of the muddy, mosquito-infested recesses of the fortress. Kesri felt a pang of sympathy for the boy; he would have gone over to say something had he been able to be sure of keeping his own emotions in check. But instead, seeing Maddow nearby, he said: Keep an eye on that little fellow, will you? It must be hard for him, losing his friend.

*

On hearing that a storm was expected Dinyar decided to move the *Mor* from Hong Kong Bay to the inner harbour at Macau, which was said to be safer in bad weather. He offered to take the other seths with him but none accepted. Many of them had rented rooms in Hong Kong: a resolution to the conflict seemed so close now that they were loath to absent themselves from the island for so much as a day. It was common knowledge that a land auction would be held soon and they did not want to run the slightest risk of missing it.

The seths gave themselves much of the credit for having persuaded the island's current administrator, Mr J. Robert Morrison, to hold the auction even before Hong Kong was formally ceded to the British Crown. But Mr Morrison had dragged his feet over the auction and this had aroused their suspicions; they had convinced themselves that he would seize any possible opportunity to keep them from bidding, and being determined to prevent this, they spent their days dogging the tracks of the land surveyors and arguing over which plots they would bid on.

Shireen alone decided to return to Macau with Dinyar, on Zadig's advice. A south China typhoon was like no storm she'd ever experienced, Zadig told her; she would do well to sit it out within the sturdy walls of Villa Nova.

'And once the storm blows over,' Zadig added with a twinkle, 'maybe we can make the announcement?'

'Of what?'

'Our engagement.'

Shireen gasped. 'Oh Zadig Bey – it's too soon! I need more time. Please. Nothing can be made public until I've spoken to Dinyar – and there just hasn't been time.'

'All the more reason then,' said Zadig, 'to go to Macau with him. There will be plenty of time to talk during the storm.'

Of late Dinyar had been noticeably cool towards Shireen, as had the other seths. She'd been led to wonder whether they'd heard rumours about Zadig and herself, or whether something else was amiss. She had wanted to probe Dinyar about it, but he had been avoiding her and she hadn't been able to corner him.

But soon after the *Mor* hoisted sail Shireen was able to create the opportunity she needed. She had instructed the cook to prepare *aleti-paleti* – masala-fried chicken gizzards – one of Dinyar's favourite Parsi dishes. After it was brought to the table she sent the stewards away and served it to Dinyar with her own hands.

Majhanu che? How is it, Dinyar deekra?

He wouldn't answer and sat sullenly at the table toying with his fork.

After a while Shireen said: *Su thayu deekra* – what's the matter, son? Is everything all right?

For the first time since he'd sat down Dinyar looked directly at her. 'Shireen-auntie,' he said in English – and this was itself a departure for he usually spoke Gujarati with her – 'is it true that Mr Karabedian's godson has been buried next to Bahram-uncle's grave?'

So that was it: the placement of the graves had made the seths anxious about their own guilty secrets.

Shireen nodded calmly. 'Yes, deekra,' she said. 'It's true.'

'But Shireen-auntie!' he protested. 'Why should Mr Karabedian's godson be buried there? That's not right.'

'Not right?'

'No, Auntie – it's not right.'

Shireen folded her hands together and laid them on the table.

Looking Dinyar squarely in the eyes, she said: 'I think you know, don't you Dinyar, that Freddie wasn't just Mr Karabedian's godson? He was also my husband's natural child.'

Evidently Dinyar was completely unprepared for an open acknowledgement of an illicit relationship. He reacted as though he had been hit in the face. *Su kaoch thame?* What are you talking about, Shireen-auntie? How can you speak of such things?

Do you think, Dinyar, said Shireen, that these things will disappear if you don't speak of them? But they won't, you know – because it is impossible to bring children silently into this world. They all have voices and some day they too learn to speak.

Shireen tapped the table loudly, to lend emphasis to what she was about to say.

You should remember all this, Dinyar, she said. Especially in relation to your own children.

There was a sharp intake of breath across the table; Dinyar began to say something but then changed his mind. Staring at his food, he ran a finger around his neck, to loosen his collar.

Shireen-auntie, he said presently, in a shaky, faltering voice: You must remember one thing. Men like Bahram-uncle, like myself – the work we do takes us away from home for years at a time. It's very lonely – I think you won't be able to understand how lonely it is.

Kharekhar? Really? said Shireen. You think we don't know what loneliness is?

At that he turned his face towards her and she saw that he was wearing an expression of genuine perplexity.

How could you understand, Shireen-auntie? he said. Women like you – like my mother and my sisters – you live at home, in Bombay, in the midst of your families, surrounded by children and relatives, with every comfort in easy reach. The reason we travel overseas is so that all of you can live in luxury. How could you possibly know what we have to go through for that? How could you know what it's like for us? How alone we are?

Shireen's lips were trembling now, and she had to take a deep breath to regain control of herself. 'Well, Dinyar,' she said, 'if you really know what loneliness is then maybe you will understand what I am going to tell you.'

'Yes?'

'Dinyar – Zadig Bey has asked me to marry him. I have accepted.'

Dinyar's mouth fell open and his voice dropped to a disbelieving whisper. 'What are you saying, Shireen-auntie? You can't do that! It's impossible. You will be cut off by all of us. None of us will ever speak to you again.'

Shireen shook her head. 'No, Dinyar,' she said with a smile. 'You're wrong. You *will* accept it. And not only that, you will persuade all the others to accept it too. You will tell them that you will all be better off if I marry Zadig Bey and stay on in Hong Kong.'

Shireen paused to take a breath. 'For there's one thing you should know, Dinyar: if you and the other sethjis make a great fuss and create a scandal; if I am driven away from here and forced to go back to Bombay – then you can be sure that many Parsi families are going to find out that they have unknown relatives in China. And yours will be the first.'

*

The shelling of the four fortresses continued through the night, not as a steady barrage but in fits and starts, which was worse because it preyed on the nerves. But even without the shelling it would have been difficult to sleep in that stifling heat, with hundreds of dust-caked, sweat-soaked men crammed into a small space.

The enclosure had no windows and the stench inside was over-powering. Dysentery spread very rapidly through the ranks that night; many men were in a state where they soiled themselves before they could get to the latrines. The sour, acrid stink of their almost liquid, blood-spotted excretions hung upon the hall like a miasma.

The Cameronians were especially badly affected by the 'bloody flux' – but it was the sepoys who had to put up with volleys of abuse about 'nigger-stink' and 'darkie-dung'. Had they been in India fights would have broken out and the Madras and Bengal sepoys might even have joined forces against the Cameronians. But here, caught between the Chinese on the one hand and the British on the other, they were helpless; they had to bear the insults in silence. And men like Colour-Sarjeant Orr understood this very well, and it made the insults and curses flow still more freely from their tongues.

Around dawn Kesri and Captain Mee went up to the fortress's turret to take another look at the city. Kesri saw that the trickle of refuge-seekers had turned overnight into a flood. The roadways around the city were jammed with people, carts, sedan chairs and carriages; they were pouring out of the gates, fleeing in every direction. The roads were so crowded that people had spilt over into the rice-fields.

'I suppose they want to get out of the city before it's attacked,' said Captain Mee.

Ji, Kaptán-sah'b.

Now that all the preparations were in place Kesri was anxious for the attack to begin. No matter what the dangers, it would be better to fight than to spend another night in this hell-hole of a fortress.

But it was not to be. A white flag appeared above the city's northern gate just as the brigade was mustering.

'The devil take me!' cried Captain Mee. 'I'll be damned if it isn't talkee-time again.'

The troops were told to stand down and the officers spent the rest of the morning shuttling back and forth between the fortress and headquarters.

Later Captain Mee told Kesri that the mandarins had sued for peace and the Plenipot had agreed to an armistice on condition that an indemnity of six million silver dollars was handed over immediately and all Chinese troops were withdawn from the city.

As so often before the mandarins had agreed – but the officers were to a man convinced that nothing would come of it and the sweat and blood they had spent in seizing the fortresses would be wasted. General Gough for one was eager to press on with the attack but his hands were tied: Captain Elliot had insisted that the Chinese authorities be given time to meet the conditions of the armistice. The force would probably have to remain in the fortresses for a while yet, possibly several days.

As the hours passed the heat continued to mount and vast swarms of flies, midges and stinging gnats invaded the fortresses, drawn by the smell of rancid sweat and overfilled latrines. Soon supplies dwindled to a point where water and food had to be strictly rationed. The only spot of good news was that a few clouds had at last appeared in the sky, scudding in from the south.

In the afternoon, Captain Mee was summoned to headquarters again: he explained later that yet another meeting had been called, to address the shortages of food and water. The high command had authorized the four brigades to send out foraging parties. They were to operate under a strict set of rules: nothing was to be taken by force; they were to go from house to house asking for donations of rice, vegetables and livestock. Every household that made a contribution was to be given a placard to put over their doorway so that no further contributions would be asked of them. Under no circumstances were civilians – men, women or children – to be molested or harmed. Infractions of these rules would be severely punished.

'Do you understand, havildar?'

Ji, Kaptán-sah'b.

Captain Mee took out a chart and pointed to a road that led to a village called San Yuan Li. Kesri was to put together a foraging party and head in that direction. As for the captain, he was planning to join a group of fellow officers who were on their way to explore some of the nearby pagodas and temples.

'And listen, havildar,' said the captain, directing a stern glance at Kesri. 'I don't want anyone making any trouble. No looting and no monkeying about with the local women. Do you understand?'

Kesri snapped off a salute: Ji, Kaptán-sah'b.

*

Assembling a foraging party was no easy task: to make sepoys carry loads was difficult at the best of times for they baulked at anything that hinted of manual labour. Nor were there many camp-followers left to choose from – their numbers had now dwindled to fewer than twenty. In the end Kesri had no option but to include the fifers and drummers – they too hated to serve as porters but their protests were not hard to override.

Once all the available mussucks, chagals, sacks and other receptacles had been gathered up, the party set off with the sepoys guarding the flanks and Kesri in the lead.

The path to San Yuan Li ran down a steep slope. On reaching the plain the path joined a road that led northwards. Marching up this road they passed a good number of people who were fleeing the city. They were families for the most part and took fright easily; the mere sight of the sepoys sent them running into the fields.

The heat was so unrelenting that the party soon began to tire: Kesri was glad to spot a group of Madras sepoys at the entrance of a pagoda: they were lounging in the shade of a sweeping, red-tiled roof. Kesri decided that it was time for a rest-break; he sent the men to sit under a tree and went over to talk to the Madras sepoys. They told him that they had come to the pagoda with Captain Mee and some of their own officers. There was a graveyard at the back of the compound and the officers had gone to inspect it, leaving them on guard outside.

What are they doing in a graveyard? said Kesri.

At this the sepoys shot sidelong glances at each other. One of them inclined his head at the gate: Go in and see.

Kesri stepped inside and after making his way through a succession of courtyards and incense-scented hallways he came to a corridor that led outside. He could see the officers through a doorway; they were in the adjoining graveyard, issuing orders to a squad of sepoys. Kesri went a little closer and saw that a team of sepoys was digging up a tomb under the direction of a pink-cheeked young lieutenant. Several graves had already been broken open; the lieutenant was examining their contents and scribbling in a notepad.

In the distance a crowd of local people had gathered and were being held back at gunpoint by a line of sepoys.

Kesri caught a whiff of putrefaction: evidently some of the exhumed graves were quite new. A shiver – brought on by both disgust and fear – went through Kesri. The idea of disturbing the dead filled him with dread; his instincts told him to get away from there as quickly as possible.

With a hand over his nose Kesri spun around but only to find Captain Mee coming towards him, down the corridor. The captain's eyes went from Kesri to the graveyard and back again.

'Don't get the wrong idea, havildar,' said the captain. 'Nothing is being taken from these graves. Lieutenant Hadley over there' –

he nodded at the officer with the notepad – 'is a scholar of sorts. He's making a study of Chinese customs and practices. That's all.'

Ji, Kaptán-sah'b.

'You'd better be on your way now.' The captain dismissed him with a nod.

*

As the foraging party marched away from the pagoda Kesri spotted a bank of dark clouds moving towards them, trailing sheets of rain. This was not the long-awaited storm, he guessed, just a preliminary shower: it would pass soon.

A short way ahead lay a compound that looked as though it belonged to a family of farmers: a small dwelling and several store-houses were grouped around a paved courtyard and a well. There was no placard at the gate to indicate that the house had already been visited: it seemed as good a place to start as any.

Seeing no one around, Kesri sent the followers to the well, to fill their mussucks and chagals. The main doorway was to the left: Kesri rapped on it several times without receiving an answer, although he could see the eyes of the inhabitants glinting behind a crack in a window.

Kesri was thinking of what to do next when one of the followers came running up to tell him that two men had been found in one of the storehouses. Crossing the courtyard, Kesri went to the open door: inside were two terrified Chinese farmhands, cowering in a corner. Beside them lay several sacks of rice and baskets of freshly picked bananas, green beans and a vegetable that looked like *karela* – it was a plumper, smoother version of the bitter gourd that was so beloved of the sepoys.

The two men were dressed in threadbare tunics and pyjamas; when Kesri stepped into the storehouse they began to whimper in fear, rocking back and forth on their heels. It was clear that they were frightened half out of their minds; their faces were twisted into almost comical masks of terror.

Kesri made a half-hearted effort to signal to them that he had come in search of food. But the men wouldn't so much as glance at his clumsy attempts at mime; they kept their eyes averted as though he were an apparition too terrifying to behold.

What to do now?

Kesri spat on the ground, in exasperation.

What sense did it make to ask these men for donations? The food in this storeroom was probably not theirs to give away in any case – and even if it were, why would they willingly part with things they had laboured hard to produce? No farmer would do that, Kesri knew, not here nor in his native Nayanpur – not unless the request was tendered at the point of a gun, by a dacoit or soldier, and it was a matter of saving one's skin. Yes, that was what this was, dacoity, banditry, and why should it fall on him, a mere havildar, to pretend otherwise, just because Captain Mee had asked him to? Kesri decided that to leave quickly was the most considerate thing he could do for these people.

Kesri signalled to the camp-followers to pick up five sacks of rice and two baskets of vegetables.

Cover them with tarpaulin, he told them, in case it rains.

Returning to the courtyard Kesri was taken aback to find that a group of men, dressed in the usual clothing of Cantonese villagers – tunics, pyjamas and conical hats – had collected around the entrance to the compound. That was not surprising in itself; what was really startling was that Maddow appeared to be conversing with one of those men.

A roar burst from Kesri's throat – *Eha ka hota?* What's going on here? – and he went striding across the courtyard.

At Kesri's approach the men melted away; he would have given chase except that they had vanished by the time he reached the courtyard's entrance.

Turning on Maddow, Kesri snapped: *Wu log kaun rahlen?* Who were they? Did you know them?

There was no change in Maddow's usual sleepy expression.

They were lascars, havildar, he said. Chinese lascars. I had sailed on a ship with one of them. He was my serang. That's all.

Kesri glared at him: *Saach bolat hwa?* Are you telling the truth?

Ji, havildar-sah'b, said Maddow. It's the truth – I swear it.

Kesri sensed that there was more to this than Maddow had said but there was no time to pursue the matter: it had already begun to drizzle.

'Fall in!'

The foraging party had gone only a few hundred yards when the skies opened up and the rain came pouring down.

It was quite late now and the light was poor. Glancing over his shoulder, Kesri caught sight of a couple of conical hats, a little to the rear of the foraging party. It occurred to him to wonder whether the men who had been speaking to Maddow were following them. But when he ran his eyes over the party he saw that Maddow was nowhere near those men: he was marching close to the front, with an enormous sack slung over his shoulder; with his free hand he was helping Raju with a chagal of water.

Reassured, Kesri turned his eyes ahead again.

*

It wasn't long before Raju realized that Maddow was slowing down. The change of pace did not surprise him for Maddow's burden seemed enormously heavy.

Thak gaye ho? Raju whispered. Are you tired?

Maddow shook his head without answering – and this too did not surprise Raju for he knew that Maddow was not a man of many words. The night before, when a couple of the older boys had set upon Raju, threatening to take him down a peg or two, Maddow had appeared out of nowhere and somehow his very presence had scared them away – yet the gun-lascar had uttered hardly a word to Raju, even though he had stayed beside him all through the night. If not for that, Raju would have had a difficult time of it, he knew: in the hours after Dicky's death he had discovered very quickly that Dicky had been not just a friend but also a protector. With him gone it was as if Raju had become fair game for the louts and bullies. Even today they had picked on him whenever Maddow was out of sight – which was why he was grateful to be walking beside him now.

Raju thought nothing of it as he and Maddow slowly dropped back to the rear of the party.

It was still raining hard when Maddow bent down to talk into his ear: Listen, boy, there is someone here for you. Look behind.

Glancing through the rain, Raju glimpsed the outline of a figure in a conical hat. Who is he? he whispered fearfully.

Don't be afraid, said Maddow. He is a friend. He will take you to your father.

My father?

Even though he had dreamt of receiving a message from his father, Raju had never imagined that it would happen like this.

You must go with him, Maddow whispered. You'll be safe. Don't worry.

But who is it? said Raju. What's his name?

Serang Ali.

At this Raju's heart leapt for he knew well that name, from Baboo Nob Kissin's stories.

What do I have to do? he said to Maddow.

You only have to stop walking, that's all.

Without another word Maddow whisked the chagal out of Raju's hands and stepped away.

It was still raining and in a few minutes Maddow and the foraging party had disappeared from view. It was the man in the conical hat who was standing beside Raju now, a fierce-looking man with a wispy, drooping moustache – a man whose face would have frightened Raju if his appearance had not so exactly fitted Baboo Nob Kissin's descriptions.

The next thing he knew, a rain-cloak made of straw had been thrown over him, covering his uniform, and his topee had been replaced by a conical hat. Then Serang Ali took hold of Raju's hand and led him into an alley.

Stay beside me, said the serang, and don't say a word. If anyone speaks to you pretend you are mute.

*

The hours of waiting, on a sampan moored a few miles from San Yuan Li, were the worst that Neel had ever endured. Had he been allowed to accompany Serang Ali and his party he would at least have had the satisfaction of doing *something* – but the serang had been inflexible on this score: on no account, he had said, was Neel to leave the sampan. Emotions were at such a pitch in the countryside that if the villagers suspected that a *haak-gwai* was in their midst he would certainly be killed.

Nor could the serang's instructions be flouted for he had left Jodu behind, on the sampan, to enforce his orders. And Jodu was diligent in doing his job, making sure that Neel did not so much as stick his head out of the covered part of the boat.

573

Luckily, just before leaving the Ocean Banner Monastery, Neel had snatched up a book – the one that he and Raju had so often read together, *The Butterfly's Ball*. He had thought that it would be comforting for Raju to have something familiar at hand. But it was Neel himself who now began to find comfort in the book's familiarity; he leafed through it many times as the rain poured down on the boat.

He was flipping through the book one more time when Jodu whispered: Look – they're coming back.

Peering at the riverbank, Neel spotted a group of shadowy figures taking shape in the gloaming. His heart almost stopped – for the shadows were all of grown men. It seemed certain to him then that something had gone terribly wrong. He would have let out a cry but Jodu was ready for that too: he clapped a hand over Neel's mouth before any sound could escape his lips.

And then, as the figures came closer, another shadow, one that had been hidden by the others, detached itself from the group: it was of about the height of a boy – but Neel's mind was now so disordered with worry that he could not be sure of what he was seeing. He began to struggle against Jodu's grip.

Only when the boy had stepped into the sampan did Jodu let him go – just in time for Neel to fling wide his arms.

Raju? Raju?

All he could think of was to repeat the name, over and over, until Raju broke in to say, in a quiet, unruffled voice: *Hā Baba* – yes, it's me.

At that Neel buried his face in the boy's small shoulder and began to sob. It was Raju who had to comfort him: It's all right, Baba – it's all right.

Then Neel's fingers brushed against the book he had brought with him. He handed it to Raju: Here, look what I've got for you.

A frown appeared on Raju's face as he read the words on the spine. Then he said in a quiet but firm voice: You know, Baba, don't you, that I'm not a little boy any more?

Twenty-one

That first shower was followed by many others over the next couple of days. But to the troops in the four fortresses the rain brought little relief: in the wake of the showers the stifling heat would quickly return, as if to warn that the real storm had yet to come.

For Kesri the showers became a new source of worry, to add to those caused by the disappearance of the young fifer. Whether the boy had deserted or been kidnapped he did not know – either was plausible – but he was determined to prevent anything like that from happening again. Now, every time a patrol was caught in a shower he sought shelter immediately; when on the road he would position himself at the rear of the column to make sure there were no stragglers.

The rain also brought new torments: it added the odour of mildew to the stench of the enclosure where the men were bivouacked; swarms of fleas appeared, to join forces with all the other insects that plagued them: their bite was so vicious that even on parade it was hard to keep the men from wriggling and scratching.

There was so much moisture in the air that inspections had to be conducted twice daily to make sure that the sepoys' powder was dry. Yet Kesri knew full well that the state of their powder would be immaterial if they were attacked during a shower. It was this fear above all that now haunted him – of being caught in a situation where their Brown Besses would not fire. He could only hope that the troops would be withdrawn from the four fortresses before a major storm blew in.

But the progress of the negotiations was not encouraging: although the mandarins had fulfilled some of the conditions of the armistice – the withdrawal of troops from the city, for instance –

they continued to procrastinate over the paying of the ransom money. To raise six million dollars was not easy, they had protested; they needed a few more days at the very least. And while they were getting the funds together the British force had to remain where it was, poised above the city and ready to strike: it was the knife at the mandarins' throat.

But while they remained there they had to forage to sustain themselves – and with each passing day it became more difficult to extract supplies from the villagers. No longer were they terrified of the foreign soldiers: often they would spit and hurl stones; gangs of urchins would shout insults; people would block the roads to stop the foraging parties from entering their villages and hamlets. An even more ominous development was that groups of young men, armed with pikes and staves, had begun to confront the foraging parties; on occasion shots had to be fired to disperse them.

The soldiers too became increasingly aggressive as the days went by: although Kesri was able to restrain his own men, he saw plenty of evidence to suggest that discipline was fraying in many units. There were rumours of beatings, looting, vandalism and also of attacks on women. One day Captain Mee told Kesri that charges of rape had been brought against a havildar and some jawans of the 37th Madras: they had been accused of invading a house and molesting the women.

But when Kesri questioned the Madras sepoys he was told a wholly different story: the havildar said he had been passing through San Yuan Li, with a squad of sepoys, when he saw an angry crowd gathering around a walled compound. Thinking that a foraging party had been trapped inside he ordered the sepoys to fire into the air, to disperse the crowd, after which he had entered the compound to see what was afoot. The situation inside was not at all what he had imagined: instead of a foraging party he had stumbled upon a rag-tag gang of British swaddies. There was a smell of alcohol in the air and the sound of women's voices could be clearly heard, echoing out of the house: there was no mistaking those terror-stricken screams.

The havildar had recognized one of the men there, an English corporal. But before he could ask any questions he had been shoved out of the compound, with warnings to mind his own business and keep his gob shut. On returning to his bivouack he had decided to report what he had seen to the company commander. This had turned out to be a bad mistake; when the corporal was summoned for questioning he had blamed everything on the sepoys. It was they who were now under investigation.

Kesri didn't know what to believe but duly apprised Captain Mee of the Madras sepoys' story.

After hearing him out Captain Mee shrugged: 'Well I'm sure I don't need to tell you, havildar,' he said, 'that in situations like these it's always easier to blame sepoys.'

Ji, Kaptán-sah'b.

'And in this instance it's a Madras havildar's word against an English corporal's.'

There was no need to say any more.

*

The *Ibis* was still a long way from Hong Kong when a bank of dark cloud hove into view on the horizon. The sight came as no surprise to Zachary: in the week that he had spent at Whampoa, waiting for the convoy of merchant ships to leave, he had seen plenty of signs of bad weather ahead. And the barometer, which had fallen steadily as the *Ibis* was sailing down the estuary, had removed all doubt about what lay in store.

But Zachary guessed that it would be a while yet before the storm hit the coast – probably not till early the next day, which meant that with any luck there would be enough daylight left for him to call on Mrs Burnham, in the *Anahita*, when the *Ibis* reached Hong Kong.

But when the convoy drew abreast of the island the *Anahita* did not immediately come into view, even though the bay was unusually thin of vessels. Evidently many skippers had decided to move their ships elsewhere, in anticipation of a storm. This was for the best, of course, since it reduced the possibility of collisions – but that was small consolation for Zachary, who had been looking forward to seeing Mrs Burnham.

But it turned out that the *Anahita* had not left Hong Kong Bay after all, she was merely hidden behind the *Druid*. She was anchored at the eastern end of the bay, abreast of Mr Burnham's recently built godown, at East Point.

Zachary took the *Ibis* in the same direction and hove to within a cable's length of the *Anahita*. As soon as the schooner was properly anchored he called for the longboat to be lowered.

Within fifteen minutes Zachary was within hailing distance of the *Anahita*. Scanning the decks he spotted a familiar daub of saffron bobbing about on the maindeck. 'Is that you, Baboo?' he shouted, through cupped hands.

'Yes, Master Zikri. And how are you? Hale and hearty I hope?'

'Yes, Baboo, never better. Is Mrs Burnham aboard?'

'Correct, Master Zikri – Burra Memsah'b is here.'

'I have a message for her, from Mr Burnham. Please tell her I'm coming aboard right now.'

'Yes, Master Zikri; ekdum jaldee.'

By the time Zachary had climbed up the *Anahita*'s side-ladder Baboo Nob Kissin was back on the maindeck, waiting to greet him.

'Baboo, you know there's a storm coming, don't you?' said Zachary.

'Yes, Master Zikri – I will go ashore this evening, for safekeeping. Burra Memsah'b will also go. We will sit in Mr Burnham's godown – a room has been specially prepared for Burra Memsah'b. Only sailors will remain on *Anahita*.'

'I'm glad to hear that,' said Zachary. 'And where is Mrs Burnham now? Did you give her my message?'

'Yes, Master Zikri – Burra Memsah'b is waiting you on the quarter-deck.'

'Thank you, Baboo.'

Zachary stepped up the companion-ladder to find Mrs Burnham standing alone by the bulwark, watching the sunset: her white carriage-dress had taken on the rosy sheen of the sky and her hair was glowing in the fading light.

Zachary came to a sudden stop: her allure had never been greater and something began to ache inside him – it was like the soreness of an old scar, a reminder not just of the injury itself but also of its cause. When Mrs Burnham greeted him by saying, 'I am very happy to see you, Mr Reid,' it was as if a scab had come off. He told himself that if she was pleased to see him it was only because she was impatient for news of Captain Mee – and in the wake of this the jealousy that was seething inside him bubbled up and brimmed over, spilling salt upon old wounds.

'I am glad to see you too, Mrs Burnham,' he said stiffly, struggling to keep his composure. 'I came because your husband had asked me to convey a message to you.'

'What is it?'

'He has been detained in Canton. He will be back as soon as things are more settled there, perhaps in a fortnight or so.'

Mrs Burnham's smile died away and a look of concern descended on her face. 'I believe there has been much trouble in Canton of late,' she said. 'I was very worried – about Mr Burnham, and you . . . and all our other friends.'

Zachary could not restrain the sardonic laugh that now burst from his throat. 'Oh come, Mrs Burnham! There is no need to be coy, with me least of all; if you were worried I am sure it was not on behalf of either your husband or myself.'

'But you are wrong, Mr Reid!' she protested. 'You are never far from my thoughts, I assure you.'

'But nor am I so close, I'll wager' – his bitterness was so powerful now that he could no longer disguise it – 'as Captain Mee. Come, admit it, Mrs Burnham, it was for him that you were worried, weren't you?'

'Amongst others, yes, certainly, I will not deny it.'

'Then I am sure you will be happy to know,' said Zachary, 'that the last time I spoke to him he was in the best of health.'

'Oh?'

He had wanted to catch her unawares and was pleased to see that he had succeeded.

'I did not know,' said Mrs Burnham, 'that you were acquainted with Captain Mee.'

'I certainly am, Mrs Burnham. I made his acquaintance at your husband's suggestion.'

This too took her by surprise, exactly as Zachary had intended. 'But what,' said Mrs Burnham, 'did my husband want with Captain Mee?'

'Surely, Mrs Burnham,' said Zachary, 'that question needs no answer? I think you know as well as I do why your husband likes to keep a few soldiers in his pocket – you've told me so yourself. It is a lucrative business and your husband has been showing me the ropes. That was why he suggested that I make overtures to Captain Mee.'

579

Mrs Burnham's eyes widened. 'Are you saying you tried to offer him a dustoorie?'

'Exactly.'

'And what did he say?'

'Oh he spurned me in no uncertain terms,' said Zachary. 'He even threatened to report me to his superiors.'

She had evidently been holding her breath for she let it out now in a long sigh.

'I would have expected no less of him,' she said with quiet pride. 'He cares nothing for money or worldly advancement.'

Zachary allowed her to feast on this thought for a few seconds. Then he flashed her a smile: 'Well, Mrs Burnham, I trust you will not be too disappointed then to learn that I was able to bring Captain Mee around.'

She turned to him in shock, her knuckles whitening on the gunwale. 'What do you mean, "bring him around"?'

'Only that I succeeded in changing his mind.'

'But how?'

'I told him,' said Zachary, 'that if he carried tales about me, he would run the risk of being exposed as an adulterer.'

Mrs Burnham gasped and clapped a hand on her mouth. 'No! You did not dare!'

'You're wrong there, Mrs Burnham,' said Zachary. 'Not only did I dare, I informed him also that he was not the only one to enjoy your favours.'

'No!' she cried. 'I do not believe it!'

'Well you should,' said Zachary, 'because it is true.'

'And what was his answer?'

Zachary laughed. 'He is, as you know, an impetuous man, so you will not be surprised to hear that he was beside himself with rage – I think he might even have killed me. But once again I was able to get the better of him.'

'How on earth?'

'I told him that I had kept all your letters and in the event of my death they would be found among my effects – in other words, that you would be ruined. This had a rather touching effect – you could even say that it was a tribute to his attachment to you.'

Mrs Burnham brushed a hand across her eyes. 'Why? What happened?'

'Oh, the bluster leaked out of him like air from a puffed-up bladder. He was evidently quite stricken at the thought that you might suffer harm. I saw then that it would be easy to take him in hand. I told him that it was in order to protect you that he should accept my offer; that he should think of it as a small sacrifice on the altar of love.'

'And then?' The sunlight had faded now and her face had turned an ashen grey.

'I gave him a few weeks to think the matter over – since the brain is scarcely his swiftest organ I thought he would need the time. I will not conceal from you that I rather doubted that he would come to a sensible decision. But I must confess that he surprised me; the last time I saw him he was perfectly amenable, quite docile in fact. His words, as I remember them, were "What do you require of me?"'

'Oh no!' Mrs Burnham's hands flew to her cheeks. 'Mr Reid, I cannot believe that you would be so ruthless, so cruel.'

'Oh but it is you who deserve all the credit, Mrs Burnham,' he shot back. 'It was you who taught me cruelty – and as you know I am a quick learner.'

She put a hand on the gunwale, to steady herself, and looked at him with imploring eyes. 'Please, Mr Reid,' she said, 'you must release him from this dreadful bargain.'

'I am sorry, Mrs Burnham,' said Zachary. 'I am afraid the matter is not in my hands any more. It is your husband who is dealing with Captain Mee now. My part was only to reel him in.'

Mrs Burnham bit back a sob. 'Poor, poor Neville,' she said. 'He prizes his honour above all things. For him there could be no worse fate.'

'Oh but there could, Mrs Burnham,' said Zachary. 'I think his fate – and yours too – would be far worse if your husband were to twig on to the history of your little dalliance.' He paused to scratch his cheek. 'And all it would take, you know, is a brief chat with the captain's havildar – that is how I myself found out. I'm sure it would not be difficult to arrange for your husband to meet him too.'

'But you wouldn't!'

'Well, Mrs Burnham, that depends,' said Zachary, studying his fingernails. 'It depends on you really.'

'What do you mean?'

'I expect,' said Zachary softly, 'that you have forgotten a promise you once made to me – that when it came time for us to part, we would have one last night together. I think the time has come for you to redeem your pledge.'

'But Mr Reid' – she whispered the syllables slowly, as though his name belonged to someone she did not know – 'how can you possibly ask that of me now? After everything you have said? It is unthinkable, unimaginable. I cannot do it.'

'Oh but you can, Mrs Burnham! And you shall. If Captain Mee can make a small sacrifice on the altar of love, why shouldn't you?'

Mrs Burnham was now clutching the gunwale with both hands, as if to prevent herself from falling over. 'Oh Mr Reid,' she whispered. 'What has become of you? What have you become?'

He was not slow to retort. 'I have become what you wanted, Mrs Burnham,' he said. 'You wanted me to be a man of the times, did you not? And that is what I am now; I am a man who wants more and more and more; a man who does not know the meaning of "enough". Anyone who tries to thwart my desires is the enemy of my liberty and must expect to be treated as such.'

Mrs Burnham began to sob, quietly. 'Mr Reid – Zachary – you cannot do this. What you're asking of me is utterly inhuman. Only a monster or demon could contemplate such a thing. I cannot believe that you are those things.'

'It is yourself you must thank, Mrs Burnham,' said Zachary. 'It was all your own doing, wasn't it? It was you who decided that I needed to be re-made in a more enlightened mould. It might have been better for both of us if you had left me to languish where you found me. But you chose instead to rescue me from that dark, unnameable continent – and now it is too late.'

Zachary broke off to look up at the darkening sky; it was still cloudless but the wind had strengthened a little.

'There is a storm coming, as you probably know. I will arrange our rendezvous once it blows over. And you need not worry, Mrs Burnham; everything will be done with the utmost discretion. But until then I'd advise you to be careful – it looks as though we're in for quite a blow. I'm glad you're going ashore. A ship is no place for landlubbers during a storm: you'll be safer in the godown.'

'You need not concern yourself with my safety, Mr Reid,' she said, turning her back on him. 'As I'm sure you know, I am perfectly capable of looking after myself.'

*

That night, word was received that six million silver dollars had finally been handed over by the Chinese authorities; the money had been transferred to the *Blenheim* for safekeeping.

In the four fortresses there was great relief: for the first time in many days, Kesri fell into a deep sleep.

But all too soon someone was shouting into his ears: Havildar-sah'b, *utho*! Wake up!

It was a little after daybreak and an orderly had brought an urgent message: Kesri was wanted by Captain Mee, up in the turret of the fortress.

Kesri dressed quickly, putting on a freshly washed vest before pulling on his red koortee. But once again the weather was hot and steamy: sweat poured off him as he climbed up the turret's stairs and by the time he reached Captain Mee the vest was plastered clammily against his skin.

Captain Mee was sweating too. 'It's going to be another tea-kettle day,' he said, mopping his face – but to Kesri it seemed that there was something different about the heat of that morning. The air was so still and heavy that even the birds and insects had fallen silent. And along the southern horizon there was a broad smudge of blue-black cloud. Kesri looked at it with foreboding: 'I think today the storm will come, sir.'

'You think so?'

'Yes, sir – looks like a real tufaan.'

'Well, it couldn't have picked a worse time.'

The captain pointed to the rice-fields at the foot of the hill. 'Look over there.'

Looking down, Kesri saw that the rice-fields were once again swarming with people, but these were not the refuge-seekers of the last few days: they were armed men, and instead of fleeing northwards they were heading towards the four fortresses.

How had so many men materialized in the fields overnight?
'You think they are soldiers, sir?'
'No, havildar – they could be irregulars, but they're certainly not soldiers.'

Kesri took a closer look with the captain's spyglass: he had the impression that the crowd was composed largely of youths like those who had been gathering in the villages over the last few days – except that their numbers had suddenly swelled a hundredfold or more.

Soon afterwards Captain Mee was summoned to a meeting at headquarters. On his return Kesri learnt that the general and his aides had taken notice of the inflow of people; they had concluded that something would have to be done to disperse the crowds. As a first step Mr Thom, the translator, had been sent to the mandarins, to demand that measures be taken to break up the gatherings.

But nothing had come of it: the mandarins had protested that they had nothing to do with the uprising and were themselves thoroughly alarmed; the crowds had gathered of their own accord, they had insisted, and for all they knew they might well turn against them too.

'It's a rabble,' said Captain Mee to Kesri, 'and since the mandarins can't send them home, we shall probably have to do it for them.'

*

At daybreak the sky over Hong Kong was a dark, churning mass of cloud and there was only a faint glimmering of light to the east. Soon sheets of rain and seawater were blasting head-on into the *Ibis*, sweeping her decks, from fore to aft. At the same time, colossal waves were coming at her from the rear, swamping her stern.

The night before, Zachary had taken every possible precaution, dropping the sheet anchor, taking in the sails and yards, checking and double-checking the anchor cables, battening down the hatches. He had taken care also to make sure that there was a safe distance between the *Ibis* and every other vessel in the vicinity; the nearest of them was the *Anahita* a cable's length away – and as far as Zachary could tell she too was holding steady against the gale.

Over the next couple of hours there was no flagging in the fury of the wind. But a pale sheen of light slowly spread itself across the sky, so that it was possible, when the *Ibis* was carried aloft by a wave, to catch glimpses of what the storm had already wrought on the island. Zachary saw that dozens of junks and sampans had been driven aground and battered to pieces; most of the newly erected shacks and shanties had been blown away too and many buildings had also been damaged. But the godowns at East Point, Zachary was glad to see, were unharmed; so long as Mrs Burnham remained within those sturdy stone walls she would be safe.

Around mid-morning, when the light in the sky was still just a fractured grey glow, the *Ibis*'s bows suddenly reared up and began to thrash about in a way that left little doubt that the cable of the bow anchor had snapped.

Zachary had anticipated that something like this might happen and had already made a plan. He took a dozen crewmen off the pumps and got them to roll the heaviest of the *Ibis*'s cannon forward. On reaching the bows they attached a cable to the gun and heaved it over the side. The effect was immediate: the *Ibis*'s head stopped its wild swinging.

As he was turning to go back inside, Zachary's eyes happened to veer towards the *Anahita*. He saw now, to his shock, that the windows in her stern – which had been closed at last glance – had flown open. Even as he watched, a huge wave rose up behind the ship and went surging through the windows, swamping the Owner's Suite.

Zachary knew that unless those windows were quickly secured, the *Anahita* would founder. In all likelihood the crew were not even aware of what had happened; they were probably down in the belly of the ship, working the pumps.

How to warn them?

Signals and lights would take too long; all Zachary could think of was to fire a shot into the air. Racing down to the captain's cabin, he snatched a musket from the arms' cabinet and took it up topside. But as he was trying to prime the gun, he realized that it was a flintlock; the powder was damp and the flint wouldn't spark. He could not get it to fire.

The *Anahita*'s stern had already begun to go under; the windows of the Owner's Cabin had disappeared beneath the waves and the jib-boom was standing at a sharp angle to the water. In his heart

Zachary knew that the *Anahita* was beyond all help already but to watch and do nothing was impossible. He ran down again to fetch a pistol and came back to find that it was too late: only the forward half of the *Anahita* was still visible; her elegant bows were pointing straight upwards, at the raging sky.

For a few minutes the *Anahita* seemed to hang in the water, her head upthrust, as if to take a last look at the heavens. Through the curtain of rain Zachary saw a longboat pulling away from her, heading towards the nearby jetty: he began to pray that the oarsmen would row faster, faster, so that they would not be sucked down by the sinking ship.

Then with gathering speed, the *Anahita* began to spin as the water dragged her under. A whirlpool took shape around the stricken ship, and as she was vanishing into it, the spinning whorls seemed to race towards the longboat. But then a wave took hold of the boat and carried it away, pushing it towards East Point.

'Thank God!'

The second mate was standing beside Zachary, fingering the crucifix that hung around his neck and muttering to himself. 'At least the crew's safe.'

'Yes,' said Zachary. 'And thank God all the live-lumber had been sent ashore well in advance.'

*

At Guangzhou, eighty miles away, the skies were still clear and people were continuing to pour out into the rice-fields. Soon crowds were gathering in so many places that it looked as though the British troops encamped in the four fortresses might be at risk of encirclement.

Inside the fortresses preparations now began in earnest. At roll-call Kesri found that B Company was almost a fifth below strength because of fevers and dysentery. The followers too were much diminished in number and every available man had to be pressed into service, including the cooks and bhandaries. At the last minute Captain Mee ordered an equipment check, to make sure that every sepoy was carrying a rain-cape.

When the bugle sounded the four brigades paraded near the rectangular fortress. The First, Third and Fourth Brigades were ordered to move downhill, to a staging-point in the rice-fields. The

Second Brigade, which consisted of marines and armed sailors, was to stay behind to guard the four fortresses.

The descent took a long time because of the narrow hillside pathways; it was not till noon that all three brigades were assembled at the staging-point. Directly ahead of them, at a distance of about a mile, was a crowd of some four or five thousand men. They were armed with pikes, spears, scythes, cudgels, sabres and even an occasional matchlock. Some were carrying long staves with hooks at the end.

There was an extended wait while the officers studied the crowds. It was the hottest hour of the day and the intensity of the sun seemed to increase as storm-clouds crept in from the south. For the troops there was not a spot of shade; the metal frames of their shakoes and topees grew so hot that it was as if they were carrying ovens on their heads. Gaps began to open up in the ranks as men collapsed and were carried away by doolie-bearers.

Meanwhile General Gough and his entourage had decided to go a little way ahead, to a shaded knoll. On the way two officers were seen to reel and lurch. One was the general himself, but he recovered and was able to walk the rest of the way without assistance. But the second officer had to be held up by others; on reaching the knoll he collapsed, falling forward on his face.

It turned out that this was the Quartermaster General; within a few minutes he was dead, of apoplexy, brought on by the heat.

This led to further delays and a good while passed before General Gough finally issued his orders. The brigades were to move in different directions with the aim of engaging and dispersing the mobs. The 4th Brigade was to tackle the crowd that had gathered directly in front of the staging-point. The Cameronians were to advance on it from the left and the Madras and Bengal sepoys from the right.

The fields ahead were flooded. When Captain Mee gave the command to advance the sepoys stepped into the mud and waded forward at a slow, deliberate pace, with their muskets at the ready, the barrels resting on their hips.

The crowd began to fall back as the sepoys advanced, but even as it withdrew its numbers kept growing. On coming to a raised embankment the crowd's retreat suddenly stopped; outlined against a lowering sky, thousands of silhouettes turned to face the sepoys.

It was late in the afternoon now and the Cameronians had disappeared from view, behind a cluster of houses on the left. The three hundred sepoys were on their own now, facing an assembly of six or seven thousand men.

The long trudge through the mud had all but exhausted the sepoys so a rest was ordered. The respite lasted just long enough for the followers to catch up and for water to be distributed to the sepoys. Then suddenly the crowd began to move towards them in a mass, brandishing weapons and shooting matchlocks.

Meanwhile a contingent of artillerymen had taken up positions to the rear of the sepoys. A flight of Congreve rockets now sailed over the soldiers' heads; the shells crashed into the crowd and went ploughing through its ranks, leaving behind furrows of fallen bodies. But still the crowd kept on coming, undeterred.

Now it was the sepoys who began to retreat, but being weighed down by heavy loads, they could not move as fast as their adversaries. When the gap between them and the crowd had dwindled to a stone's throw, the sepoys were ordered to stop and take up firing positions.

The sepoys' first volley decimated the front rank of the crowd, bringing it to a halt. The sky had darkened now and a fierce wind had arisen. A sheet of lightning flashed through the clouds and then, to the accompaniment of peals of thunder, the rain came pelting down, not in drops but in long jets. It was as if the countryside were being bombarded with liquid projectiles. The sepoys were soaked before they could put on their rain-cloaks.

To fire flintlock muskets was impossible now: swords and bayonets were the sepoys' only serviceable weapons – and both were shorter in reach than the pikes and spears of their adversaries. The storm was now the sepoys' sole ally, its fury the crowd's only check.

Through the roar of the wind Kesri heard Captain Mee's voice, shouting in his ear: the CO had ordered him to make contact with the Cameronians; he was setting off in search of them with a platoon of sepoys; Kesri was to accompany him.

'We'll need to take a runner with us, havildar.'

Ji, Kaptán-sah'b.

Shielding his face against the driving rain, Kesri went to take a look at the few followers who had managed to keep up with the company. His eyes went at once to Maddow and he beckoned to him: Chal – stay close to me.

*

At Hong Kong the rain kept falling, in torrents, even after the storm had passed over the bay, sweeping northwards, in the direction of Canton. But the fury of the gale quickly abated and the mountainous waves subsided into heavy swells. As soon as it was safe, Zachary called for the *Ibis*'s longboat to be lowered. Climbing in, he ordered the crew to row over to the jetty that led to the new Burnham godown.

The building was unharmed but there was so much wreckage all around that it took a while to approach it: Zachary had to hammer on the door for several minutes before he was let in.

The godown's cavernous interior was lit by a few dimly flickering lamps: some of the *Anahita*'s crewmen were kneeling in rows, saying namaaz; some were sitting huddled in the corners, shivering as they hugged their knees.

'Master Zikri!'

Turning to his right Zachary saw that Baboo Nob Kissin was hurrying towards him.

There was now only one thought in Zachary's mind. 'Where's Mrs Burnham?' he said. 'Is she in that room you'd prepared for her?'

Baboo Nob Kissin took a few more steps and then his enormous head shook slowly from side to side. 'Master Zikri – I am sorry.'

'What do you mean you're sorry?' Zachary snapped. 'Where is she? Just answer the question.'

Again Baboo Nob Kissin shook his head: 'I am sorry . . .'

Zachary laid his hands on the gomusta's shoulders and shook him hard. 'Baboo, this is no time for your flumadiddles: just tell me where she is.'

'Yes, Master Zikri – that is what I am trying . . .'

Mrs Burnham had changed her mind at the last minute, said Baboo Nob Kissin. She had decided to ride out the storm on the *Anahita*. She had complete confidence in the crew, she had declared, and she wasn't going to allow a bit of a blow to throw her into a funk. Baboo Nob Kissin had tried to persuade her to leave but she had silenced him in her usual imperious way. It was impossible to argue with the Burra Memsah'b beyond a point; at her orders Baboo Nob Kissin and a few others had left the ship as planned, to take refuge in the godown.

The rest of it Baboo Nob Kissin had heard from the crew, when they came ashore after the sinking of the *Anahita*.

Early that morning, before the storm hit the coast, Mrs Burnham had rung for a steward and asked for a tray of tea. The steward had returned to find her sitting in the Owner's Suite, beside a window. It was already blowing hard then: she had said that she would be safe there and that she wanted to watch the storm coming in.

Once the storm broke the crew had no time to check on Mrs Burnham. It wasn't till the ship began to take in water that a serang ran down to the Owner's Suite. He had found the suite's door jammed, perhaps by a piece of furniture: he had pounded on it and on receiving no answer he had gone to fetch an axe. But by the time he returned the ship's stern was already below water and the gangway was flooded – he would have drowned if he had stepped in. There was nothing more to be done.

'But Master Zikri . . .'

Although Baboo Nob Kissin was leaning close to Zachary now, his voice seemed to reach his ear from very far away.

'Last night, Master Zikri, before I departed from *Anahita*, Burra Memsah'b gave one letter. For you. She said to ensure that you received.'

'Where is it?'

'Here – I have safely kept.'

Withdrawing into a corner, Zachary broke the seal and began to read.

*

The platoon set off with Captain Mee in the lead and Kesri bringing up the rear. As they veered leftwards Kesri handed his now useless musket to Maddow and took his sword in his hand.

The surrounding fields had already turned into a continuous expanse of water; the bunds had disappeared and the only points of orientation were a few clusters of dwellings, dimly visible through the rain. Although nightfall was still a while away the sky was so dark that it was as if the sun had already set.

Hearing a sound behind him, Kesri looked over his shoulder;

peering into the failing light he spotted the misted outlines of moving figures. It occurred to him that these might be the Cameronians and for an instant he was light-headed with relief. But then a rock came hurtling through the rain, to hit him in the shoulder. He knew then that they were being followed by the mob.

'Halt! Halt!' Kesri shouted and in a matter of seconds Captain Mee appeared beside him, sword in hand.

'They're behind us, sir,' said Kesri – and as soon as the words were out of his mouth Kesri realized that he'd spoken prematurely. The armed men weren't just behind the platoon; they were all around, their outlines enshrouded by rain. Suddenly the pointed head of a pike shot out of the curtain of falling water; it would have pierced Kesri's ribcage if Captain Mee hadn't struck it down with his sword.

Now, as rocks and stones began to fly out of the deluge, Kesri felt something tugging at his ankles and looked down. It was a large hook, attached to a staff. He slashed at it with his sword, breaking it in two. But somewhere to the rear one such staff had succeeded in hooking a sepoy; he had fallen and was being dragged through the mud.

Two sepoys caught hold of the fallen man's arms and pulled him back. When he was on his feet again, Captain Mee shouted: 'A square! Form a square!'

Sluggishly, fending off brickbats with their arms, the men fell into a square. Standing shoulder to shoulder they thrust their bayonets at every moving shape.

After a few minutes Captain Mee's voice was again in Kesri's ear: 'We're too exposed here; we have to move. I saw some houses to the left. If we can reach them we'll have a wall at our back.'

Ji, Kaptán-sah'b.

'I'll lead,' said the captain, wiping his streaming face with his sleeve. 'You bring up the rear.'

The radius of visibility was no more than a few feet now; only when flashes of lightning streaked through the clouds was Kesri able to see beyond that. When the platoon began to move he kept his eyes fixed on the darkness, moving backwards, sword at the ready.

Projectiles kept raining down on the platoon as it waded through the mud. When at last there was a slight quickening in the pace, Kesri sensed that they were out of the paddies, on level ground. Then he glanced back and saw that a gap had opened up between him and the rest of the platoon: they were already out of his circle of visibility. He would have to hurry to catch up.

Just as Kesri was about to quicken his pace, the pointed end of a spear came hurtling towards him, from the right. He brought his sword down upon the shaft and had the satisfaction of seeing the tip fly off. And then, inexplicably, without his being aware of an injury, his left leg crumpled under him, bringing him down heavily, on his back. A flash of lightning split the sky, to reveal a circle of faces, closing in, with pikes and spears pointed at him.

Kesri's sword was still in his hand and he tightened his grip on it: he knew that his time had probably come but he felt no panic; only a kind of sadness that it should happen here, at the hands of men with whom he had no quarrel; men who were not even soldiers, who were trying only to protect their villages, as he himself would have done back home.

He saw a shadow moving towards him and slashed at it with his sword. Even as his blade dug into flesh and bone he felt an impact in his own flank. He was trying to turn when a pike crashed into his wrist and the sword dropped from his hand. And then, as he lay disarmed and helpless on the ground, he heard a deep-throated voice calling his name – Kesri Singhji? – and he shouted: *Hā! Yahā!* Here, I'm here!

Moments later a bayonet swung out in an arc above him, scattering the faces that had been closing in.

Havildar-sah'b?

The voice was Maddow's.

Kesri answered with a grunt and Maddow squatted beside him, with his bayonet levelled at the darkness.

Hold on to my neck, havildar-sah'b, said Maddow, and I'll pull you on to my back.

Kesri wrapped his arms around Maddow's neck and felt himself being lifted up; then Maddow began to back away, with the Brown Bess circling watchfully in front of him, the bayonet slicing through the darkness.

As he clung to Maddow's back Kesri became aware of a searing pain in his thigh. Only now did it dawn on him that his hamstring had been severed – and once he had become conscious of the injury the pain welled up in waves, almost overwhelming him. As if through a fog, he recognized Captain Mee's voice: 'Havildar? What the devil . . . ?' – and he realized he was back with the platoon, in the enclosed centre of a square. On every side of him sepoys were fending off attacks.

'You're losing a lot of blood, havildar.'

Through gritted teeth Kesri said: 'Kaptán-sah'b, you go back to the men. Maddow here will take care of me.'

The captain nodded and his face faded away. Meanwhile Maddow had already slit open Kesri's trousers.

Bahut khoon ba, said Maddow. There's a lot of blood; I'd better tie up the cut.

Maddow peeled off his tunic, tore off a few pieces of cloth and bound them over Kesri's wound. Then he reached into a pocket and pushed something into Kesri's mouth. In a second Kesri's nostrils were filled with the grassy, sickly-sweet odour of opium.

It was like an answer to a prayer: at the very smell of the substance the pain receded and Kesri's breath returned.

In a few minutes Kesri heard Captain Mee's voice again: 'How are you, havildar?'

'Better, Kaptán-sah'b. And the men?'

'They're doing their best – but if we can't get our guns to fire I don't know how much longer we'll be able to hold off this rabble. They're everywhere.'

An odd calm had descended on Kesri now and he remembered something he had once witnessed, as a young sepoy.

'Give me some rain-capes, Kaptán-sah'b,' he said. 'Let me see what I can do.'

With Maddow's help, Kesri fashioned a tent-like covering with a couple of rain-capes. Then he snapped open his Brown Bess; digging a sodden cartridge out of the barrel he told Maddow to find him some dry cloth.

Maddow took off his turban and tore a few strips from the inside, where the cloth was still dry. Kesri took them from him, twisted them into wicks and used them to wipe dry the inside of the barrel. Then he called for Captain Mee and told him to try firing the musket under cover of a rain-cape.

A minute or two later he heard the crack of a musket-shot, followed by cries in the distance.

'That'll scatter them for a bit,' said Captain Mee, ducking under the tented cape. 'Do you think you could do that again, havildar?'

'Already done, Kaptán-sah'b.'

As Kesri was handing over the next musket a shot rang out, in the distance, and was quickly followed by another.

'Percussion guns!' said Kesri.

'Yes,' said the captain jubilantly. 'I suppose it's the Cameronians. They must have heard our shot.'

Knowing that help was near, Kesri allowed his head to sink to the ground. By the time the Cameronians arrived he had lost consciousness.

*

My dear Zachary

I write in haste . . .

I do not know if there is anything I could do or say to persuade you that I have never meant to cause you pain. If I have seemed cruel or capricious it is only because I knew that there could be no better expression of my love than to set you free, to find your own way in the world. I am, as you know, a foolish, vain, unhappy creature and I wanted to spare you the misery and dishonour that I have inflicted upon everyone I have ever loved. But in that too I was vain and foolish: I understand now that there is only one way in which I can truly set you free –

There is but one last thing I ask of you – that you take care of Paulette, whose hopes of happiness I have also destroyed. You are now well launched in your career and will no doubt achieve great success; for her, things will be much harder. If ever I meant anything to you then you will do for me what I could not do myself: make amends.

I hope also that some day you will come to forgive both

594

yourself and the woman whose unfortunate destiny it was
to be

Your

Cathy
May 29, 1841

Twenty-two

The British force regrouped quickly once the storm had passed: the units that had gone astray were tracked down and the three brigades then made a hasty retreat to the safety of the four fortresses.

But the confrontation was far from over: the hostile demonstrations continued for two more days, with as many as twenty-five thousand villagers turning out to oppose the invaders; they marched behind the banners of their villages and answered only to leaders of their own choosing.

The British commanders countered by delivering yet more ultimatums to the mandarins, warning that the city would face attack unless the crowds stood down. These threats eventually prompted official intercession and the villagers were persuaded to return to their homes. Only then did the British troops withdraw from the heights above Canton.

Kesri was not aware of these events at the time and did not learn of them until much later: the force was still marooned in the fortresses when the wound in his thigh turned gangrenous; it was there that his left leg was amputated.

Through that time Kesri was aware of very little, having been given massive doses of morphine. But once, during a brief period of lucidity, he realized that Captain Mee was standing by his cot, looking down at him.

When the captain saw that Kesri had opened his eyes, he said, in a shaky voice: 'Havildar – how are you?'

'I'm alive, Kaptán-sah'b,' Kesri whispered.

'I'm sorry, havildar . . .'

'You should not be sorry, Kaptán-sah'b. I am here today – I did not think I would be.'

'I might not have been here either,' said the captain, 'if it weren't for you. The Cameronians probably wouldn't have found us in time if you hadn't got those guns to work. Who knows what would have happened?'

'We were lucky, Kaptán-sah'b.'

'It wasn't just luck,' said the captain. 'It was what you did with those muskets that saved us. You should know the CO's recommended you for a citation, for bravery in the field.'

'Thank you, Kaptán-sah'b.'

'Tomorrow we'll be going back to our transport ship at Whampoa,' said Captain Mee. 'From there you'll be evacuated to Hong Kong. You'll be well looked after there – I've asked them to give you a room to yourself. And the gun-lascar, Maddow, will be accompanying you; he's specifically asked to go.'

'Thank you, Kaptán-sah'b. I'm grateful.'

'It's no more than you deserve.'

The captain gave Kesri a pat on the shoulder. 'I'll come to see you as soon as I get back to Hong Kong. It shouldn't be too long.'

'Yes, Kaptán-sah'b. Thank you.'

After that, for several days, Kesri was aware of very little but of Maddow's constant presence at his side, changing his clothing, cleaning his stump, clearing away his bedpans, giving him his morphine.

One day, in a moment of consciousness, Kesri said: *Batavela* – tell me, why do you look after me like this? Why did you come back for me that day, when I was cut down? It's not your job – you're not a soldier. Didn't you know you could have been killed?

Several minutes passed before Maddow answered.

Kesri Singhji, he said at last: I did it for your sister's sake. I knew that if I didn't I would never again be able to look her in the face.

My sister? Do you mean Deeti?

Yes. Deeti.

It was all clear now; as Kesri drifted out of consciousness again, Deeti's face appeared in front of his eyes and he knew that she had once again taken charge of his destiny.

*

It was thought at first that Mrs Burnham's body had been trapped inside the *Anahita* and would be unrecoverable. But two days after

597

the storm, on the very afternoon that Mr Burnham returned to Hong Kong, the corpse was found at the eastern end of the bay.

Mr Burnham being prostrate with grief, the arrangements for the funeral were made by Zachary and Mr Doughty. It was decided that she would be buried at the Protestant cemetery in Macau. A coffin was quickly bought and the body was transported the next day. The interment was in the late afternoon and a large number of people attended.

Through the ceremony Zachary kept careful watch for Paulette. But it was only at the end that he caught sight of her: she was at the back of the graveyard, sitting on a mossy tomb, with her face buried in a handkerchief. He stole up on her quietly, so that she would not have time to make an escape.

'Miss Paulette?'

Removing the handkerchief from her face she looked up at him. 'Yes?'

'May I sit down, Miss Paulette?' he said.

She shrugged indifferently and he saw that she was past caring. She buried her face in her handkerchief again, and after waiting a while he cleared his throat: 'Miss Paulette, it was Mrs Burnham's wish – she told me this herself – that you and I should be reconciled.'

'What did you say?' Whipping away the handkerchief, she shot him a puzzled glance.

'Yes, Miss Paulette,' Zachary persisted. 'She specifically said to me that I should take care of you.'

'Really, Mr Reid,' she retorted. 'But to me she said something else.'
'What?'

'She said I was your only hope and that *I* should look after *you*.'

They were quiet for a bit and then Zachary said: 'May I at least come to take a look at your garden?'

'If that is what you wish,' she said. 'I will not prevent it.'

'Thank you, Miss Paulette,' said Zachary. 'I am sure Mrs Burnham would be pleased.'

*

Kesri did not see Captain Mee again until the Bengal Volunteers were sent back to Hong Kong.

By that time Kesri had spent a week in the island's newly built military encampment. He was dozing one evening, with a candle flickering by his bed, when the door flew open. At first Kesri thought that it was Maddow coming back from an errand. But then he saw that the silhouette in the doorway was Captain Mee's: he was bare-headed, swaying slightly on his feet; in his hands was a leather satchel.

It was a hot day and Kesri had thrown off his sheet. Now, wanting to spare the captain the sight of his exposed stump, he began to grope around, trying to cover himself. The sheet eluded his grasp and in the end it was Captain Mee who found it and draped it over him.

'I'm sorry to barge in like this, havildar.'

His words were a little slurred and Kesri could smell liquor on his breath.

'It's all right, Kaptán-sah'b,' said Kesri. 'I'm glad to see you.'

Captain Mee nodded and sank into a chair beside the bed. The candle was close to him now, and when its light fell on his face Kesri saw that the captain was haggard, his eyes bloodshot and ringed with dark circles. Pushing himself a little higher, on his pillows, Kesri said: 'How are you, Kaptán-sah'b?'

To Kesri's surprise there was no answer; instead Captain Mee fell forward in his chair and buried his face in his hands, planting his elbows on his knees. After a minute or two Kesri realized that he was sobbing. He sat still and let him continue.

Presently, when the captain's shoulders had ceased to heave, Kesri said: 'Kaptán-sah'b, what is it? What has happened?'

At that Captain Mee looked up, his eyes even redder than before. 'Havildar, I don't suppose you've heard – about Cathy . . . Mrs Burnham . . .'

'What about her, sir?'

'She's dead.'

'No!' cried Kesri, recoiling in shock. 'But how did it happen?'

'During the storm – she was on a ship that went down. That's all I know.'

Fumbling for words, Kesri said: 'Kaptán-sah'b – I don't . . . I don't—'

Captain Mee cut him short with a brusque gesture. 'It's all right – there's no need to say anything.'

Turning abruptly to his side, Captain Mee picked up the satchel he had brought with him. 'I have something for you, havildar.'

'For me?'

'Yes.' He thrust the satchel into Kesri's hands. 'Open it.'

The satchel was very heavy for its size and as he was undoing the buckle, Kesri heard the scraping of metal on metal. Captain Mee held up the candle as Kesri looked in.

At first glance Kesri thought his eyes had deceived him and he looked away, in disbelief. Then he looked again and his gaze was again met by the glitter of gold ornaments and the sparkle of silver coins.

'What is this, Kaptán-sah'b?'

'Some of it is booty – my share of it. And yesterday we were given our arrears of pay and battas – that's there too. As for the rest, don't ask.'

'But Kaptán-sah'b – I cannot take this.'

'Yes you can. I owe it to you.'

'No, Kaptán-sah'b – it is much more than you owe me. More than I have ever earned. I cannot take it.'

The captain rose to his feet. 'It's yours,' he said roughly. 'I want you to have it.'

'But—'

Captain Mee cut Kesri short by clapping a hand on his shoulder. 'Goodbye, havildar.'

'Why "goodbye". . . ?' said Kesri, but the door had already closed.

Captain Mee's abrupt departure left Kesri distraught; the captain's words kept circling through his head and the more he thought about them the more he worried.

Lying helpless in bed, Kesri tried to think of some means of preventing what he thought was going to happen. He considered approaching another officer, but he doubted that anyone would believe him unless he divulged everything he knew about Captain Mee and Mrs Burnham – and this he could not bring himself to do. They would probably think he was lying anyway: why would a havildar know about such things?

When Maddow returned, Kesri said: Did you know that Burnham-memsah'b had died?

Yes, said Maddow. I heard.

Why didn't you tell me?

I thought I'd tell you later, Kesriji. How did you find out?

The kaptán-sah'b was here . . .

If not for the intensity of the pain in his leg, Kesri would have skipped his medicaments that night; his foreboding was so acute that he would have preferred to stay awake. But when the time came he could not refuse: he took his draught of morphine and soon fell into a deep, stupefied sleep. Hours later he woke to find Maddow shaking his shoulder.

Kesriji! Kesriji!

Kaa horahelba? What is it?

Listen, Kesriji – it's about Mee-sah'b.

Kesri sat up and rubbed his knuckles in his eyes, trying to clear his mind: What is it?

Kesriji – there's been an accident. The kaptán-sah'b was cleaning his gun. It went off.

What happened? Is he badly wounded?

No, Kesriji – he's dead.

Kesri took hold of Maddow's arm and tried to swing his body around: Help me get up; I want to go there; I want to see him.

Kesri had not yet learnt to use a crutch. He hooked an arm around Maddow's neck and hopped along by his side, towards the officers' lines, where guards and orderlies could be seen rushing about.

Halfway there they were stopped by a sarjeant of the Royal Irish: 'Halt!'

'Please let me pass,' said Kesri. 'Mee-sahib was my company commander.'

'Sorry – orders. No one's allowed any further.'

Kesri could see that the sarjeant would not relent. He turned away with a sigh: *Abh to woh unke hain*, he said, more to himself than to Maddow – he's theirs now; we have no claim on him.

With Maddow's help he hobbled back to his room and fell again into his bed.

But now, despite the lingering effects of his medication, Kesri could not go back to sleep: he thought of all the years he had known Captain Mee and the battles they had fought together: it was sickening that he had died in this way; he had deserved a

soldier's death. It was a waste, such a waste, of Captain Mee's life –
and his own too. And for what? A pension? A citation?

Kesri reached for the satchel that Captain Mee had given him
and ran his fingers over the coins: they were worth much more,
he knew, than the pension that was due to him.

And then another thought struck him: the other officers were
sure to know that Captain Mee had recently received his back pay
and allowances; they were bound to search for the money in his
rooms and when they failed to find it there would probably be an
inquiry.

What would happen if the officers came to learn that Kesri was
in possession of a satchel-ful of gold and silver? Would they believe
that Captain Mee had given a gift of such value to his havildar?

Or would they find a pretext to take it away?

Kesri could not stand to think of it: to throw the satchel in the
water would be better than to lose it to them.

Turning on his side, Kesri whispered to Maddow: Listen – are
you awake?

Ji, Kesriji. Do you want some medicine for the pain?

No. I want to ask you something.

Ji, Kesriji.

That day, when that boy disappeared . . .

Yes?

You helped him, didn't you? You helped him escape, with those
men you were talking to – isn't that so?

Why do you ask? said Maddow quietly.

I was just thinking, said Kesri, that if you were to speak to those
men again, then maybe we could get away too – you and I? Do
you think it could be arranged?

*

British-held Hong Kong's first auction of land was held on 14 June
1841, a fortnight after the storm.

The area on sale was smaller than expected: it consisted of only
fifty plots, each with a sea-frontage of one hundred feet, along a
stretch of shore on the seaward side of the island's only proper
thoroughfare – the Queen's Road. The authorities announced beforehand that the currency of the auction would be pounds sterling.
But since Spanish dollars were still in wide use a fixed rate of

exchange was thought necessary – it was declared to be four shillings and four pence for one silver dollar. It was ordained also that the bidding would start at ten pounds and advance in increments of ten shillings; every purchaser would be required to erect a building valued at one thousand dollars or more, within six months of the sale; as a guarantee of this undertaking, a sum of five hundred dollars would need to be deposited with the treasury as 'earnest money'.

Although few could afford to meet these terms the event still drew a great number of spectators, from the dozens of ships that were anchored at Hong Kong Bay. Passengers, supercargoes, mates, bo'suns and even cabin boys flocked to Mr Lancelot Dent's new godown at East Point, where the auction was to be held: even if they couldn't bid they could at least sniff the scent of wealth.

Presiding over the proceedings was Mr J. Robert Morrison, the Acting Secretary and Treasurer to the Superintendents of Trade. Only a few dozen chairs had been set out, for the turnout was not expected to be large. When the godown began to fill up Mr Morrison issued instructions that only bidders were to sit; spectators would have to stand at the back, in a roped-off enclosure.

Once the bidding started it proceeded briskly. Some of the merchants had already received their share of the six-million-dollar indemnity paid by the Chinese; as a result there were many bulging purses at the auction.

One of the largest lots, a parcel of 30,600 square feet, fetched £265; another even larger lot, of 35,000 square feet, went for £250, its location being less desirable. Very few lots went for less than £25; most fetched well over double that sum. Only one lot went unsold.

The Parsi seths were among the most enthusiastic bidders; between them they acquired no fewer than ten lots. The Rustomjees, a Bombay family, acquired more land than any other group of bidders, amassing no less than 57,600 square feet. Seth Hormuzjee Rustomjee alone bought six lots, a total of 36,000 square feet, for £264.

The second largest buyer was Jardine, Matheson and Co. which acquired three contiguous lots for £565, with a total area of 57,150 square feet. Mr Dent, who had been expected to make an equally big purchase, disappointed the auctioneers by spending only £144, on two lots that added up to a mere 14,800 square feet.

As a special consideration a few prospective buyers were permitted to reserve plots for future purchase. One such was Fitcher Penrose who was unable to attend the auction for reasons of ill-health. Another was Zadig Bey who was in mourning for his godson; although he attended the auction with Shireen, neither of them made a bid.

This was Zadig and Shireen's first appearance together in public and many took it as a declaration of their intention to wed. When they entered the godown there were some who held their breath, imagining that they were about to witness a famous contretemps in which Shireen would be dealt the cut direct by her co-religionists.

But they were disappointed: far from shunning Shireen, her fellow Parsis accorded her a warm welcome; soon they were observed to be chatting with each other in a fashion so cordial as to leave no doubt that the seths had reconciled themselves to her remarrying outside the community.

By this time Shireen too had received compensation for her late husband's losses from the opium crisis of two years before. Most of it she had already remitted to Bombay to pay off his debts; in addition she had sent large sums to her two daughters. But even after these disbursements the monies that remained still amounted to a sizeable fortune, amounting to tens of thousands of silver dollars.

Those in the know were well aware that Shireen was a wealthy woman and many were surprised when she did not join the bidding. Later, when she went to congratulate Seth Hormuzjee Rustomjee he even asked her why she had refrained from making a bid. Shireen's answer was that she had decided to wait until the slopes of 'Peaceful Mountain' were made available to buyers.

Why?

The air was more salubrious there, Shireen explained, and it was her intention to endow a public hospital, in the name of her late husband, Bahram Moddie.

*

At the end of the bidding it emerged that one tract of land, consisting of lot numbers 16 to 20, had been reserved by an unnamed buyer: this being one of the largest acquisitions of the day, there was much excited comment.

Afterwards, when the spectators had dispersed and Mr Dent's servants were serving champagne to the successful bidders, Mr Morrison was besieged with questions about the buyer's identity. His protests to the effect that he was not at liberty to say found little purchase with the gathering. The clamour quickly grew so loud that he threw up his hands and cried: 'This much I can certainly tell you, gentlemen, that the purchaser is amongst us now. If he should wish his name to be known then he will reveal it himself.'

At this a hush fell. It lasted until Mr Burnham, who was dressed in deep mourning, stepped forth and turned to face the gathering. 'Ladies and gentlemen,' he said. 'I am grateful to Mr Morrison for being so scrupulous in respecting my request for confidentiality. It was not in order to create a mystery that I asked him to withhold the name of the purchaser. It is because to reveal it would require another announcement, one that I had deemed unbecoming for a time of bereavement. But it strikes me now that no one would have been more gratified by this disclosure than my late, beloved wife so there is perhaps no reason to delay it any longer.'

Here Mr Burnham stopped to gesture to Zachary who went to stand beside him. Placing a hand on his shoulder Mr Burnham continued: 'Ladies, gentlemen, I am pleased to announce that the purchaser of lots 16 to 20 is a new entity, created just this week – the firm of Burnham and Reid.'

A round of applause broke out now and Mr Burnham paused until it had died away: 'It would be remiss of me,' he went on, 'if I were to omit to mention another collaboration that we have entered into just this day, an association that will, I am certain, greatly strengthen our new company.'

Now Mr Burnham again made a beckoning gesture, at which another man stepped forward to join him and Zachary. This caused something of a stir – for when this man, who was dressed in an impeccably cut suit, turned to face the assembly he was seen to be Chinese.

'Ladies and gentlemen,' said Mr Burnham, 'it gives me the greatest pride to announce that from this time on the firm of Burnham and Reid will be working closely with our good friend, Mr Leonard Chan.'

Now, taking Zachary's wrist in his right hand and Mr Chan's in his left, Mr Burnham hoisted up their arms and held them aloft in triumph.

*

One of the few spectators to remain in the godown was Baboo Nob Kissin who was looking on from a dark corner at the back. When the three men made their gesture of triumph his heart flooded over with the joy that comes from seeing a mighty endeavour brought to its intended conclusion.

Tears came into the gomusta's eyes as he recalled the day he had first beheld Zachary, on the *Ibis*: that he should have been transformed so quickly from an ingenuous, good-natured boy into a perfect embodiment of the Kali-yuga, seemed to Baboo Nob Kissin nothing less than a miracle; he marvelled to think that a creature as humble as himself should have played a part in bringing about the change. He knew of course that his role in promoting the ascendancy of the triumphant trio was but a small one – yet he was certain also that when the day of reckoning arrived, and the Kalki avatar manifested itself on earth, he would not be denied the credit for having advanced the coming of the pralaya by at least a decade or two. This was enough; he wanted no worldly reward or recognition. It sufficed that he had been the first of his compatriots to recognize that it was their assigned destiny to serve the Kalki's chosen precursors, to be their faithful gomustas in hastening the end of the earth.

It occurred to him also that it was the *Ibis*, that marvellous vehicle of transformations, that had launched him on the path of destiny and he was seized by an uncontrollable urge to clasp his eyes once again upon that vessel of blessed memory. In a swirl of saffron, he ran outside – but only to be confronted with yet another miracle: the *Ibis*, which had for the last several days been at anchor off East Point, was gone.

*

In Deeti's shrine, high up on the slopes of the Morne Brabant, at the south-western corner of Mauritius, there was a special chamber for that episode of Maddow Colver's life that came to be known

606

as 'the Escape'. This part of the 'memory-temple' was especially beloved of the Fami Colver, particularly the young ones, the chutkas and chutkis, laikas and laikis: every year, during the Gran Vakans, when the family made its annual pilgrimage to the 'memory-temple', they waited breathlessly for that moment when Deeti would point to the stylized image of a sampan, with six figures seated inside: Serang Ali, recognizable by his blood-red mouth; Jodu with his three eyebrows; Neel, with his journals; Raju, in his fifer's hat; Kesri, who, by convention, was always drawn with a bundook – and of course, the patriarch himself, Maddow Colver.

'Ekut, ekut!' Deeti would cry, and that great horde of bonoys, belsers, bowjis, salas, sakubays and other relatives would follow her finger as she traced the path of Jodu's sampan as it edged across the bay, from the Kowloon side, to draw up beside the *Ibis*, which was all but empty, with the second mate away at the land auction, and the sailors either ashore or asleep.

There vwala!

Her finger would come to rest on Serang Ali: You see him, this gran-koko with a head teeming with mulugandes? This is the great burrburiya who had once again thought up the plan for their escape.

You see now, how he vaults on deck, with Jodu and Maddow behind him? In a matter of minutes the crew are locked up in the fo'c'sle and then Kesri, Raju and Neel come aboard too.

In a trice the sails are hoisted and filling with wind, and by the time the auction ends the schooner is long out of sight . . .

Epilogue

In embarking on the task of writing a history of the *Ibis* community, the author had hoped to include an account of the materials on which his narrative is largely founded: that is to say Neel's archive, by which is meant not only his notes, jottings and 'jack-chits' but also the extensive collection of books, pictures and documents that Neel accumulated during the years in which he ran a print-shop in Shanghai, in partnership with Compton (Liang Kuei-ch'uan).

For this author no part of this history is of greater interest than that of the archive's survival: indeed, it was once his fond hope that this episode would provide the climactic *tamám-shud* to this chronicle. But to arrive at that story, in its proper temporal sequence, would require the narrative to move forward by almost a century – that is, to the years immediately preceding the Second World War, which was when Neel's great-grandsons smuggled the most important parts of the archive out of China.

The unfortunate reality however is that ten years of diligent application have so far succeeded in advancing the narrative by only four years: from 1838 to 1841. Such being the case, with nearly a century's-worth of events still to come, the author is compelled to acknowledge that it is highly unlikely that he will be able, in the years that remain to him, to provide a full account of the archive's survival. But to tell this tale hurriedly, out of its proper order in the sequence of events, would, for him, be a betrayal of the enterprise: he would prefer that it remain forever untold than be related in such a fashion.

For the purposes of the present volume suffice it to say that the war in China dragged on for another fifteen months after Neel's escape on the *Ibis*, in June 1841. Through this period Neel kept careful track of the movements of the British expeditionary force (now vastly expanded) as it advanced northwards in the direction of Beijing, successively attacking Xiamen, Zhoushan, Ningbo and Shanghai, thereby causing so much destruction and such extensive loss of life that the Daoguang Emperor was ultimately forced to authorize his representatives to capitulate to the invaders' demands.

The most important of these concessions were: the formal ceding of Hong Kong; the opening of five ports to foreign trade; and the payment of an enormous indemnity, amounting to a total of twenty-one million silver dollars. The agreement that formalized this capitulation came to be known as the Treaty of Nanking and was signed on 29 August 1842, on the HMS *Cornwallis* (of which Neel wryly notes that 'this ship, built in the Wadia shipyard in Bombay, was named after a man whose name will forever be preceded by the epithet "Butcher" – fitting that his remains lie in Ghazipur, a stone's throw from the Opium Factory').

The text of the treaty was widely circulated, in English, Chinese and other languages: an artist called Henry Cullen even produced a photographic print of it. Neel succeeded in acquiring a copy, at great expense, but it roused him to such a passion that he proceeded to deface it by scribbling comments in the margins, and by under-lining certain passages – for example the provision that abolished the old Co-Hong trading system. A clause that attracted his special ire was that which required the British and Chinese governments to henceforth deal with each other on a 'footing of equality', through direct exchanges between their appointed repre-sentatives. Neel notes sardonically that, as so often when Westerners use words like 'equality', this clause was clearly intended to mean exactly the opposite of what it said: that it would be the British who would now dictate the terms of the relationship. He notes similarly, alongside the clause that required China to compensate the British for the costs and injuries of their invasion: 'So it was the Chinese who had to pay for the catastrophe that had befallen their country!'

Curiously the clause that would later become the most famous passage in the treaty – that which formalized the handing over of Hong Kong – he deemed almost unworthy of comment, noting only: 'But they had seized it already!'

Over the next decade Neel spared neither effort nor expense in acquiring materials related to the events that culminated in the Treaty of Nanking – that is to say, the conflict that would come to be known as the First Opium War (needless to add, the Second Opium War was to lead to an enormous expansion of Neel's collection). Later Raju too would contribute significantly to the archive: a growing desire to fully comprehend the events he had lived through as a boy would eventually send him on a long search for materials on military matters – histories, manuals, dispatches, memoirs, maps and, especially, first-hand accounts of the battles that he had witnessed.

At the time of the archive's removal from China the circumstances were such that many of the bulkier volumes had to be left behind or destroyed, in order to salvage Neel's own writings. Fortunately both Neel and Raju were meticulous record-keepers: they maintained a detailed catalogue, not only of the materials that were actually in their possession, but also of those that they hoped to acquire (nor did they fail to list certain documents, like secret government reports, that were then barred from circulation).

Although this catalogue has survived, time has not been kind to it: some pages are torn, a few are missing; many entries have been obscured by patches of dampness and mildew; others have been consumed by worms, ants and weevils. However, from the fragments that remain it was possible to piece together a 'virtual library' of the sources that Neel would have used had he himself been able to write an account of these events. This compilation led the author to the following: *The Annual Register or a View of the History and Politics of the Year 1841* (London, 1842); Capt. Sir Edward Belcher, *Narrative of A Voyage Round the World Performed in Her Majesty's Ship Sulphur During the Years 1836–42 Including Details of the Naval Operations in China* (Henry Colburn, London, 1843); William Dallas Bernard and Sir William Hutcheon Hall, *The Nemesis in China: comprising a history of the late war in that country; with a complete account of the colony of Hong-Kong* (Henry Colburn, London, 1846); John Elliot Bingham, *Narrative of the Expedition to China from the Commencement of the War to its Termination in 1842*, Vols. I and II (Henry Colburn, London, 1843);

Elijah C. Bridgman, *Description of the City of Canton* (Canton, 1834); *A Catalogue of the Library Belonging to the English Factory at Canton in China* (printed at the Hon. East India Company's Press, Macao, 1819); *The Chinese Repository*, Vols. VII–X; *The Sessional Papers Printed by Order of the House of Lords, Session 1840, Vol. VIII, Correspondence Relating to China* (presented to Both Houses of Parliament by Command of Her Majesty, 1840, printed by T.R. Harrison, London, 1840); James Cuninghame, *The Tactic of the British Army Reduced to Detail, with Reflections on the Science and Principles of War* (London, 1804); Capt. Arthur Cunynghame, *The Opium War, Being Recollections of Service in China* (Philadelphia, 1845); Sir John F. Davis, *Sketches of China* (Charles Knight, London, 1836); Capt. F.B. Doveton, 'Reminiscences of the Burmese War', *Asiatic Journal and Monthly Miscellany*, Vol. XL, New series, Jan.–Apr. (W.H. Allen, London, 1843); C. Toogood Downing, *The 'Fan-qui in China' in 1836–37*, 3 vols. (Henry Coburn Publisher, London, 1838); Émile D. Forgues, *La Chine Ouverte; Aventures d'un Fan-Kouei dans le Pays de Tsin, par Old Nick, ouvrage illustré par Auguste Borget* (H. Fournier, Paris, 1845); Capt. and Adj. F.A. Griffiths, *The Artillerists Manual and Compendium* (Woolwich, 1839); A. Haussmann, 'A French Account of the War in China', *United Service Magazine*, Vol. 1, Vol. 71, (1853, pp. 50–63; 212–20; 571–80); William C. Hunter, *The Fan-Kwae at Canton Before Treaty Days, 1825–1844; Line of March of a Bengal Regiment of Infantry in Scinde (Panorama)* (Ackermann, London, 1830); Lord Jocelyn, *Six Months with the Chinese Expedition or, Leaves from a Soldier's Notebook* (John Murray, London, 1841); Sir Andrew Ljungstedt, *An Historical Sketch of the Portuguese Settlements in China; And of the Roman Catholic Mission in China* (Boston, 1836); Capt. Granville G. Loch, *The Closing Events of the Campaign in China: the Operations in the Yangtze-kiang and Treaty of Nanking* (John Murray, London, 1843); D. McPherson, *The War in China: Narrative of the Chinese Expedition* (London, 3rd edn, 1843); Alexander Murray, *Doings in China. Being the personal narrative of an Officer engaged in the late Chinese Expedition, from the recapture of Chusan in 1841, to the peace of Nankin in 1842* (London, 1843); Gideon Nye, *The Morning of My Life in China: comprising an outline of the history of foreign intercourse from the last year of the regime of honorable East India Company,*

1833 to the imprisonment of the foreign community in 1839, Canton, 1873; Peking, the Goal – the Sole Hope of Peace. Comprising an Inquiry into the Origin of the Pretension of Universal Supremacy by China and into the Causes of the First War; with incidents of the Imprisonment of the Foreign Community and of the First Campaign of Canton, 1841 (Canton, 1873); 'Official Accounts of the Late Naval and Military Operations in China', *Calcutta Gazette*, Extra, 7 Aug. 1841, reprinted in *Nautical Magazine and Naval Chronicle* (1841); Lt. John Ouchterlony, *The Chinese War: An Account of all the Operations of the British War* (1844); *Report from the Select Committee on the Trade with China* (Parliamentary papers, 1840); John Phipps, *A Practical Treatise on the China and Eastern Trade: Comprising the commerce of Great Britain and India, particularly Bengal and Singapore with China and the Eastern Islands* (W. Thacker, Calcutta, 1836); *Remarks on the Dress. Discipline &c. of the Bengal Army*, by a Bengal Officer (Calcutta, 1798); John Lee Scott, *Narrative of a Recent Imprisonment in China After the Wreck of the Kite* (London, 1842); Samuel Shaw, *The Journals of Major Samuel Shaw, the First American Consul at Canton, with a Life of the Author by Josiah Quincy* (Boston, 1847); J. Lewis Shuck, *Portfolio Chinensis: or A Collection of Authentic Chinese State Papers Illustrative of the History of the Present Position of Affairs in China* (Macao, 1840); John Slade, *Notices on the British Trade to the Port of Canton, with some Translations of Chinese Official Papers Relative to that Trade* (Smith, Elder, London, 1830); John Slade, *Narrative of the Late Proceedings and Events in China* (Canton Register Press, Macao, 1840); *Standing Orders For the Bengal Native Infantry*, 2nd edn (Calcutta, 1840); Subedar Seetaram, *From Sepoy to Subedar*, trans. James Thomas Norgate (London, 1873); *Statement of Claims of the British Subjects interested in Opium surrendered to Captain Elliot at Canton for the Public Service* (London, 1840); Thayer Thatcher, *A Sketch of the Life of D.W.C. Olyphant: Who Died at Cairo, June 10, 1851, with a Tribute to his Memory* (Edward O. Jenkins, 1852); Henry Meredith Vibart, *Military History of the Madras Engineers and Pioneers; From 1743 Up to the Present Time*, Vol. II (W.H. Allen, London, 1883); Capt. John Williams, *An Historical Account of the Rise and Progress of the Bengal Native Infantry from its First Formation in 1757 to 1796 When the Present Regulations Took Place* (John Murray, London, 1817); and William

John Wilson, *History of the Madras Army*, Vol. 2 (Govt. Press, 1882).

Neel's catalogue has served as a tutelary hand for the present author: reaching out from the past it has guided him through several libraries and research institutions, among them the National Library of India, Kolkata; the British Library and the Greenwich Maritime Museum, London; the Yale Center for British Art, New Haven, Connecticut; the Peabody Essex Museum, Salem, Massachusetts; and the library of Northwestern University, Evanston, Illinois. The author would like to record here his gratitude for the courtesy and consideration that was extended to him at each of these institutions, by virtue of which he was able to locate a number of sources that Neel knew of but was unable to acquire. He also came upon some that neither Neel nor Raju were aware of because they were not publicly available in their lifetimes. Among these are the following: Captain P. Anstruther, *Letter written by Capt. P. Anstruther, Madras Artillery, from Ship Rustomjee Cowasjee, Canton River, China to India, dated* 12 March 1841; Maj. Mark S. Bell, *China: Being a Military Report on the North-Eastern Portions of the Provinces of Chih-Li and Shan-Tung; Nanking and its Approaches; Canton and its Approaches; &c., &c., together with an account of the Chinese civil, naval and military administrations &c., &c., and a narrative of the wars between Great Britain and China*; prepared in the Intelligence Branch of the Quarter Master General's Department in India, from various sources, and notes taken during a reconnaisance of the neighbourhoods of Peking, Nanking and Canton, carried out in 1882, 2 vols.: Vol. I, Confidential; Vol. II, Secret (Government Central Branch Press, Simla, 1882); Rick Bowers, 'Notes from the Opium War: Selections from Lieutenant Charles Cameron's Diary During the Period of the Chinese War 1840–41', *Journal of the Society for Army Historical Research*, Autumn 2008, Vol. 86, 347, pp. 190–203; Colin Campbell, *Journal* (1816); Edward H. Cree, *The Cree Journals: The Voyages of Edward H. Cree, Surgeon RN as related in his private journals, 1837–1856* (Webb & Bower, Exeter, 1981); John C. Dann, *The Nagle Journal; A diary of the life of Jacob Nagle, sailor, from the year 1775 to 1841* (Weidenfeld & Nicolson, New York, 1988); Lt. Henry Dundas, *Personal diary written in retrospect of his time on the China coast on board HMS* Calliope, Cornwallis *and* Clio (Jan. 1841–Oct. 1844); M.L. Ferrar, *The Diary of Colour-Serjeant George Calladine, 19th Foot, 1793–1837* (London, 1922); *Frontier and Overseas Expeditions from India,* Vol. VI (Anon, Intelligence Branch, Army HQ, India, *c.*1913, reprinted Mittal Publications, Delhi); Thomas Gardiner, *Journal kept on 3 voyages to Bengal and China on the EIC's ships, 1829–30;* Capt. H. Giffard, *Diary of events,* HMS Volage *& Cruiser; Bengal Military Letters Received* (1840); *Bengal Military Letters Received* (1841); *Plan of Attack on the Heights and Forts near the City of Canton Under the Command of Major General Sir Hugh Gough, 25th May 1841,* Sd. Lt. W.S. Birdwood (bequeathed by Lord Broughton in 1869); *Sketch [Map] of the Operations against Canton, January to March 1841; Madras Despatches 12 Jan to 29th June 1842; Madras Despatches 4 Jan to 28th Aug 1839; Madras Despatches 1st Jan to 2nd July 1841; China Foreign Office Instructions and Correspondence, Secret Dept, 1841; India and Bengal Despatches 12th Jan to 30th March 1842; India and Bengal Despatches 13th July to 1st Sept 1841; Madras Despatches 4th Nov 1818 to 21st Apr 1819; Madras Despatches 3rd May 1826 to 21st March 1827; Board's Collections 8675 to 8750 1812–13, Vol. 359; Board's Collections 19297 to 19375, 1823–1824;* Richard Glasspoole, *A Brief Narrative of my Captivity and Treatment Amongst the Ladrones* (London, 1935); William C. Hunter, *Journal of the Occurrances at Canton, 1839* (reprinted from the *Journal of the Hong Kong Branch of the Royal Asiatic Society,* Vol. 4, 1964); Phyllis Forbes Kerr, *Letters From China: The Canton-Boston Correspondence of Robert Bennet Forbes, 1838–1840* (Mystic Seaport Museum, Mystic, CT, 1996); Daniel Irving Larkin (ed.), *Dear Will: Letters from the China Trade 1833–36* (Amherst (self-published), 1987); Pamela Masefield (ed.), *The Land of Green Tea: Letters and Adventures of Colonel C.L. Baker of the Madras Artillery 1834–50* (Unicorn Press, 1995); Ian Nish (ed.), *British Documents on Foreign Affairs: Reports and Papers from the Foreign Office Confidential Print, Part 1, Series E. Asia,* Vol. 16, *Chinese War and its Aftermath, 1839–49* (Univ. Publications of America, Frederick, Md., 1994); E.H. Parker, *A Chinese Account of the Opium War* (Shanghai, 1888 (a translation of an account by Wei Yuan)); Sylvia Parnham, *'My Dear Mother . . . sell not my old close!': Gunner John Luck's Letters from India 1839–44* (London, 1983); Sylvia Parnham and Duncan Phillips (eds.), 'The Canton Letters

1839–1841 of William Henry Low', *The Essex Institute Historical Collections*, LXXXIV (1948).

The present author has had the advantage of Neel and Raju in one important respect which is that he happens to be writing at a time of an extraordinary efflorescence of scholarship on many subjects that touch upon the experiences of the *Ibis* community. He has therefore been able to draw upon the work of a great number of scholars and experts, among them the following: Ravi Ahuja, Robert Antony, Patricia Barton, Pradeep Barua, Alan Baumler, Christopher Bayly, Jack Beeching, David Bello, N. Benjamin, Gregory Blue, Timothy Brook, B.R. Burg, Antoinette Burton, W.Y. Carman, Annping Chin, Lorenzo M. Crowell, John C. Dann, Santanu Das, Mary Des Chene, David Deterding, Frank Dikotter, Stephen Dobbs, Jacques M. Downs, Hal Empson, Peter Ward Fay, H.G. Gelber, Durba Ghosh, L. Gibbs, Jos J.L. Gommans, Nile Green, Raffi Gregorian, D.A. Griffiths, Amalendu Guha, Deyan Guo, David Harris, James Hevia, Susan Hoe, Edgar Holt, James W. Hoover, Laura Hostetler, Paul Howard, Toni Huber, Ronald Hyam, Raphael Israeli, Hunt Janin, Graham E. Johnson, John Keegan, David Killingray, B.B. Kling, Elizabeth Kolsky, P.C. Kuo, Haiyan Lee, Peter Lee, Philippa Levine, Heike Liebau, Elma Loines, D.N. Lorenzen, Julia Lovell, Joyce Madancy, Rachel P. Maines, Keith McMahon, Glenn Paul Melancon, Steven B. Miles, James H. Mills, Yong Sang Ng, David Omissi, C.J. Peers, Douglas M. Peers, Roger Perkins, Glen D. Peterson, William R. Pinch, Rajesh Rai, John L. Rawlinson, Stuart Reid, J.F. Richards, Derek Roebuck, Franziska Roy, Kaushik Roy, Geoffrey Sayer, Narayan Prasad Singh, Jonathan Spence, Peter Stanley, Heather Streets, Paul A. Van Dyke, Bob Tadashi Wakabayashi, Frederick Wakeman Jr., Erica Wald, Arthur Waley, Betty Peh-T'i Wei, Channa Wickremesekera, Lawrence Wang-chi Wong, Don J. Wyatt, Anand Yang, Tan Tai Yong and Yangwen Zheng.

The author would like to express his gratitude to all the above-named for they have each opened a window into the world of this book. He would be remiss however if he did not acknowledge the special debt that he owes to the work of the following: Seema Alavi, Joseph S. Alter, Amiya Barat, Dilip Basu, Kingsley Bolton, Hsin-Pao Chang, Tan Chung, Amar Farooqui, D.H.A.

Kolff, Thomas W. Laqueur, Lydia Liu, Matthew W. Mosca, Jean Stengers, Carl A. Trocki, Madhukar Upadhyaya and Anne van Neck.

The author has been fortunate also in being able to avail himself of the help and guidance of a number of other scholars, students and independent researchers; he would like particularly to record his gratitude to the following: Shahid Amin, Clare Anderson, Prasenjit Duara, J. Daniel Elam, Dilip Gaonkar, Shernaz Italia, Ashutosh Kumar, Rajat Mazumder, Robert McCabe, Ashim Mukherjee, Dinyar Patel, Tansen Sen, Rahul Srivastava, Mihoko Suzuki and J. Peter Thilly.

To everyone named here the author extends his pranaams and salaams, while exonerating them of any culpability for whatever is objectionable or blameworthy in this account, the responsibility for which he claims solely for himself.

As to his family, immediate and extended, to thank them is unnecessary since it is their shared history that has made possible this telling (which, needless to add, has as yet scarcely begun . . .).

FICTION
GHOSH, AMITAV
15   8/15

14

WITHDRAWN

BEDFORD HILLS FREE LIBRARY